Also by Clark Howard

The Arm
A Movement Toward Eden
The Doomsday Squad
Last Contract
Siberia 10
The Killings
Summit Kill
Mark the Sparrow
The Hunters
The Last Great Death Stunt
Six Against the Rock
The Wardens
Zebra
Traces of Mercury
American Saturday
Brothers in Blood
Dirt Rich
Quick Silver

HARD CITY

Clark Howard

DUTTON   NEW YORK

DUTTON
Published by the Penguin Group
Penguin Books USA Inc.,
375 Hudson Street, New York, New York, U.S.A. 10014
Penguin Books Ltd,
27 Wrights Lane, London W8 5TZ, England
Penguin Books Australia Ltd,
Ringwood, Victoria, Australia
Penguin Books Canada,
2801 John Street, Markham, Ontario, Canada L3R 1B4
Penguin Books (N.Z.) Ltd.,
182–190 Wairau Road, Auckland 10, New Zealand

Penguin Books Ltd, Registered Offices:
Harmondsworth, Middlesex, England

First published by Dutton,
an imprint of Penguin Books USA Inc.
Published simultaneously in Canada
by Fitzhenry & Whiteside, Limited.

First printing, April, 1990

1   3   5   7   9   10   8   6   4   2

Library of Congress Cataloging-in-Publication Data

Howard, Clark.
Hard city / Clark Howard.—1st ed.
p.   cm.
ISBN 0-525-24857-9
I. Title.
PS3558.0877H37   1990
813'.54—dc20   89-23359   CIP

Printed in the United States of America

Designed by REM Studio

Publisher's Note: This novel is a work of fiction.
Names, characters, places, and incidents either are
the product of the author's imagination or are used
fictitiously, and any resemblance to actual persons,
living or dead, events, or locales is entirely coincidental.

For the next generation

Robert Clark Howard
Scott Ryan Howard
Kyle Steven Howard

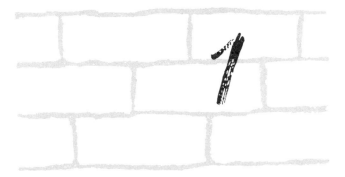

*R*ichie stared at his mother. His twelve-year-old eyes had seen a lot, but never anything like this.

His mother was on her knees, alternately clawing the wall with her fingernails and pounding the wall with her forehead. Several of her fingernails had torn and were bleeding. An ugly spot on her forehead was beginning to darken. Richie's throat constricted and he fought back tears.

"Don't," Richie pleaded. "Stop it now. Please."

From behind, Richie clutched his mother's wrists and held her back from the wall. It was not difficult; as thin and undernourished as he was, Richie was stronger than the skeleton his mother had become. Richie tried not to grip her arms too tightly; he was afraid her skin, which looked like old paper, might crack if he did. Slowly pulling her away from the wall, Richie drew the frantic woman to her feet and walked her toward the apartment's tiny bedroom. She turned an anguished face toward him.

"Richie, get me something. Please get me something . . ."

The only color in her face, Richie saw, was the almost artificial looking dark circles under her eyes; the rest of her face was that same fragile papery tone, the shade of dying skin or proud flesh. Even her lips looked that way. Under her chin some of the flesh hung down to her neck, and on each of her upper arms it draped down in little folds. Her breath was putrid from several rotten teeth that she had not yet pulled out. Patches of hair were gone from her head, and what was left had creeping streaks of gray in it. She looked much older than her thirty-four years.

In the little bedroom, Richie guided her onto a creaky, unmade bed. "Lie down and rest," he said.

"Richie, get me something, please," she begged again.

"Okay, I'll get you something," he said.

Richie hurried to the side of the other room that was the kitchenette. Turning a porcelain knob on the stove, he lit a stick match and touched the flame to one of the grease-caked burners. Removing the top from a chipped, dented percolator, he poured its old, dried coffee grounds into a little brown-stained sink and pulled back the chintz curtain of a cupboard for the coffee. Twisting the lid off the can, he saw with despair that there were only a few grains left.

"Richie . . ." his mother called agonizingly from the bedroom.

Desperately Richie turned to the sink and began to scoop the used coffee grounds back into the percolator. At least it'll be hot, he thought. The stark little apartment was like an icebox. Every few minutes he could hear the sound of some tenant pounding the radiator pipes with a skillet or hammer to get the landlord to fire up the furnace a little—all the while knowing that he would just continue to dole out coal like the miser he was, keeping his own apartment warm with an electric heater.

While Richie was filling the percolator with water, the grease around the gas burner caught fire and he quickly had to find a towel to beat out the flame. He knew better than to throw water on it; he had done that once at the age of ten, in another little apartment; the liquefied hot grease had splattered on his arms. An old woman in an adjoining apartment had put ointment on his burns and told him philosophically, "Poor people learn hard lessons."

As Richie relighted the burner, after wiping off the grease, he heard his mother again.

"Richieee . . . !"

He put the percolator on the burner and hurried to her. "I'm making you some coffee—"

"Richie, I don't need *coffee!*" Forcing her head up a few inches, she looked fiercely at him. "You get me something—*right now!*"

"I can't."

"Why not?"

"I don't have any money."

The fierce eyes turned angry. "Goddamn you, why not?" she demanded, outraged at this new particular of her torment.

"Is Miss Menefee there?" Richie asked.

A click and another ring, then: "Grace Menefee."

"This is Richie. You gotta help me."

"Richie? Richie who?" It was too sudden for her. But then she remembered. "Oh, *Richie!* My god, where are you? I looked for you and your mother for a month!"

"My mother's on dope again," he said. "Heroin this time. She's clawing the walls. We don't have nothing to eat, no money, I've got holes in my shoes . . ." He bit down on his chapped lower lip to keep from crying aloud.

"Where is your mother, Richie?" the welfare worker asked.

"I want to know first what will happen to her if I tell you," Richie hedged. His young mind was in turmoil about a long-ago pact he had made with his father. "*She's not a strong person, but we'll take care of her, won't we boy?*" his father had asked, man-to-man, and Richie had proudly said yes.

But his father was not there anymore. It wasn't *we* anymore.

"If your mother is addicted to heroin," Miss Menefee said, "she'll probably be sent to Lexington."

"What's Lexington?" Richie asked suspiciously.

"It's a federal public health hospital where they cure addicts."

Richie felt his throat constrict as he worked to hold back the tears. Strangers, he thought self-accusingly, she'll be with strangers. "What kind of place is it?" he demanded. Starting to cry again, he covered the phone's mouthpiece with one hand so Miss Menefee would not hear him.

"It's a very nice place," Miss Menefee, sensing his dilemma, assured him. "It's a hospital, not a jail; they treat people there, they don't punish them. It's down south in Kentucky."

"Down south?" Richie said, feeling a spark of relief from the terrible guilt of what he was doing. "Down where it's warm?"

"Yes, where it's warm." Miss Menefee's words hung in the air, tentatively. She wanted to project as positive an attitude as possible for the obviously troubled boy, yet she refused to lie to him. She was too fond of him to lie to him. "I'm sure it's warmer than it is here," she amended.

The telephone booth, which for a couple of minutes had seemed like a refuge from the windswept sidewalk on which it stood, was becoming a refrigerator. With a finger poking through a hole in his woolen gloves, Richie wiped tears from both cheeks and thought about Lexington. If it was even a little warmer than that lousy building where people constantly banged pipes pleading for heat, it would be better for her. And if they could cure her—

"It's 1923 Adams Street," he said quickly, before he could change his mind. "Third floor in the back."

"You took it the other day, Mother—"

"That is a dirty lie! I never did!" Paper-gray lips peeled back over the rotting teeth. "You're a dirty liar, just like your lying father! Get out of my sight! Get out!"

Richie went back into the kitchenette and stood staring at the percolator, waiting for it to bubble, thinking about his father. It was the same thought he always had: *Where are you? Where—are—you!*

From the bedroom he heard a thudding sound being repeated like a slow knock at a door. Going back there again, he saw his mother once more on her knees, clawing and pounding her forehead against the wall.

Shaking his head, Richie returned to the stove and turned off the burner. Coffee, even if it had been fresh, wasn't going to help. What his mother needed was the kind of help he could not give.

He hesitated, fearful, then made up his mind. Beginning to cry, Richie went over to his folding cot. From under it he pulled a cardboard box that held his few extra clothes. There wasn't much to take, he thought, wiping away the first tears, but he knew he'd better take what he had. Removing the thin case from his lumpy pillow, he stuffed into it the few things from the box, all of them pitifully threadbare, some even ragged. Crying harder, his nose beginning to run, he pulled out a loose baseboard and retrieved a tobacco can from which he removed a few coins, less than a dollar's worth. Pocketing the money, he quickly put on his jacket and cap; sobbing, he tried to ignore the thudding sound coming from the bedroom. But it was like a jackhammer in his head. Twisting the top of the pillowcase tight, he put it under one arm and quickly left the apartment.

As Richie hurried along Damen Avenue, the relentless Chicago wind whipped its January cold against his legs and chest and tear-streaked face. It was past mid-afternoon, the day already beginning to wane toward its early darkness. Shoulders hunched and chin to chest, Richie headed purposefully toward Jackson Boulevard. There, on the corner, he got into a freestanding glass-and-wood telephone booth and quickly closed its folding door against the wind. Immediately it was as if he had entered a tomb: quiet, still, suspended.

Unzipping his worn but greatly treasured Buck Jones billfold, Richie rummaged in its secret compartment until he found the scrap of paper with the telephone number. Lifting the receiver, he deposited a nickel and waited. Presently the operator said, "Number, please."

"State five-oh-oh-oh," Richie said.

"State five thousand. One moment, please."

After two rings, he heard, "Afternoon, County Welfare."

□□ 3 □□

"I'll get some help and be right there," Miss Menefee said. "You wait there with your mother."

"I'm not waiting nowhere," Richie told her emphatically. "I'm going to find my dad."

"Richie, for god's sake, are you starting that again?" There was an irritated impatience in her tone that she worked to control. "If your mother couldn't find him, the welfare department couldn't find him, and the federal parole authorities couldn't find him, you certainly can't. He's gone, Richie— for good." When Richie remained silent, not arguing, a sudden fear seized Grace Menefee. She had dealt with Richie before; she knew how headstrong he was. Keeping her voice as calm as she could, she said, "Anyway, we'll talk about it when I get there."

"I won't be there," Richie said. "You just take care of my mother. I'll take care of myself."

"Richie, you are *twelve* years old; you cannot survive alone in this city."

"I'll survive."

"You don't even know if your father is *in* Chicago—"

"I'll find him."

Miss Menefee's tone became authoritative; it was the only way she could keep the panic out of her voice. "The juvenile officers will catch you, Richie," she warned. "When that happens, it won't be foster homes anymore, it'll be the state reformatory."

"I'll take my chances," Richie said.

"Don't pull your John Garfield act with me, Richie."

"I'm not pulling nothing. You just make sure my mother's okay."

The welfare worker's voice lost all emotion except desperation. "Richie, *please*," she implored, "wait until I get there."

Richie was silent for a long, woeful moment. Tears veined the dry skin of his cheeks, his legs seemed to turn warmly weak, his bowels threatened. It would be so simple, but the boy could not lie to the woman any more easily than she could lie to him. At the same time, he was determined not to allow her to change his mind about what he had decided to do. *He had to find his father.* It was, he felt deep in the core of his young self, the only way he and his mother could ever escape the dreadful, harsh level of life to which they had descended. To Richie, his father was salvation. The *only* salvation.

"Richie, wait for me," Miss Menefee pleaded.

"No."

Richie hung up.

Holding the pillowcase securely under one arm again, he pulled open the telephone booth and stepped into the great cavernous concrete valley that was Chicago. It was almost dark now; streetlights and headlights had been turned on. For a moment Richie merely stood on the sidewalk, staring at nothing, in limbo, suspended by a frightening realization.

He was utterly and absolutely alone.

Walking away from the booth, he began to shiver, not from the cold but from the sobs that began again. At the first alley he came to, he turned in and began to run.

ichie looked over at the man behind the bowling alley counter. "Mister, can I get a job setting pins?"

The man was not much taller than Richie. He had silky red hair and beady eyes set close together. "You're too young," he said, giving Richie only a cursory glance. He turned to sell a customer a package of Chesterfields. "Twenty-one cents."

The customer paid him, said, "Thanks, Red," and walked away. "I'm fourteen, mister," Richie said.

The man named Red gave him a slightly longer look. "You're not fourteen. You're probably twelve."

"I'm really thirteen," Richie lied again. "Could you give me a job setting pins? Please."

A tall, stoop-shouldered man in a sagging, shapeless overcoat came up to the counter. His nose was very red and his eyes were watery. "Where you got me, Red?" he asked.

"Nine and ten," Red replied, making a notation on his pinboy list. His beady eyes seemed to move closer together as he frowned at the man. "You sure you can work?"

"I'm okay. Got a bad cold."

"You got the Seagram's flu," Red said. He pointed a threatening finger. "I don't want no drinking in the pits, Pete."

Red and Richie both watched as Pete shuffled down the walkway along the wall that led back to the pits. "I've got a full crew, kid," Red said then, capping his fountain pen and clipping it on one pocket of a beautifully laundered white shirt. Red was dapper: knit tie with a Windsor knot, cuff links, tie clip. The way my dad used to dress, Richie remembered, staring at Red. The dapper little man saw that he was still there. "You're too young to set pins," he said. "Come back in a couple of years."

Richie picked up his pillowcase and wandered around the bowling alley. It was a large place, sixteen lanes on each of two floors, with a bubbling fountain inside the entrance, a coffee shop, bar, checkroom, men's and ladies' rooms on each floor. Richie had been there before, with his mother and one of her boyfriends. Cascade Bowling Lanes, it was called. Hoping to get a job, Richie had also come there tonight because he had remembered it as big enough maybe to have someplace where he could sleep: a corner under the stairs where the light did not reach, or a broom closet or something. Richie had experience finding places to sleep; he had run away from five consecutive foster homes in which Miss Menefee had placed him. As Richie wandered around the second floor, he got a glance inside the ladies' lounge and saw that it had a divan. Maybe he could spend the night there.

By the time the six-thirty league started, Richie felt hungry and walked outside to West Madison Street. It was early 1945 and the war was still on; the busy commercial street was in its modified blackout mode: no exterior lights, no neon, no marquees. As Richie walked along the semi-dark street, the pillowcase under his arm, he suddenly felt miserable about what he had done to his mother, and before he knew it tears were streaking his chapped cheeks. Even though she caused him nothing but grief most of the time, abusing him terribly when she needed a fix, she was nevertheless all he had and he missed her already.

Seized by sudden loneliness, by an enormous fear of what lay ahead— for his mother as well as himself—he felt a sob explode in his chest again. Quickly stepping into a dark doorway, he moved to its farthest corner and hunched down on his heels. Burying his face in the pillowcase, he let himself bawl for several minutes. I had to do it, he cried to himself. I had to, I had to, I had to.

A while later, red-cheeked, his misery under control once more, Richie emerged from the doorway and continued along Madison Street. Walking to the nearest corner, where there was a large drugstore, Richie passed an unattended newsstand and in a glance counted four nickels and a dime in the open cigar box on top of the *Herald-Americans*. Peering in the drugstore window, he saw a man with a canvas change holder tied around his waist, sitting at the soda fountain with both hands on a mug of steaming coffee. Seeing no one else around, Richie hurried to the newsstand, snatched the thirty cents, and ran up the street.

In a hamburger joint, Richie sat at the end of a long counter, nearest the door, and ordered a hamburger and milk. The counterman scrutinized his shabby appearance and noted how close to the door he sat.

"Twenty cents," he said. "Pay now."

"How come?" Richie asked.

" 'Cause I don't wanna have to chase you down the street, that's how come."

Richie put twenty cents on the counter, muttering an obscenity under his breath.

"What'd you say?" the counterman asked suspiciously.

"Nothin'."

"Don't get wise with me, kid." The counterman pointed a threatening finger. Ringing up the twenty cents, he went back and gave the order to the fry cook.

The hamburger joint was deep and narrow, like a railroad car, with a counter down its middle. On the stool next to him, Richie put his pillowcase, which by now he had tied a knot in to keep his things from falling out. It angered him that the counterman had made him pay before he got his hamburger and milk. It had not been his intention to beat it without paying; he always sat near the door because he never knew when he might have to run—for any reason. Richie could accept being caught and punished for things he did, but it infuriated him to be blamed for something he did not do, or plan to do. The counterman, to his mind, was an unfair son of a bitch.

Waiting for his hamburger, listening to it sizzle on the grill in back, Richie suddenly felt scared again. The counterman had reminded him how vulnerable he was—at the mercy of every adult. Fear was by no means a new sensation for him; off and on for as long as he could remember, he had been afraid: afraid of each new school, each new neighborhood, afraid each time his mother moved that she would not take him with her. But fear brought on by the counterman was a different fear, a fear born of Richie's strange new status: a kid on his own in the city. Before, when he had run away from the foster homes, he had known that his plight would only be temporary; he had taken it for granted that in three or four days he would be caught and there would be Miss Menefee, upset with him, sure, but *there* anyway and, in her own fashion, on his side. Now there was no one on his side, and that would be the case permanently until he found his father.

I've just *got* to find him, Richie thought, simultaneously clenching both fists and his jaw. Life without his dad was always misery. Both Richie and his mother *needed* his dad; needed his quiet strength, his sureness. Just as soon as he found his dad, Richie fantasized, the two of them would go to that Lexington place and get his mother out and take care of her. His young jaw unclenched and his lips parted as he stared dreamlike into space, wondering how his mother was doing at that very moment.

The counterman gave him his hamburger and milk, either carelessly or deliberately slopping the latter down the side of the glass and making a ring on the counter. Bastard, Richie thought as he laced the burger with mustard and catsup. He wolfed the food down. It was hot and delicious, the greasy meat and fried onions and dill pickles mixing with the condiments to create a taste that no poor kid in any big city would ever be able to duplicate as an adult. Washing it down with cold, creamy milk made it even better. It was all gone in three minutes, Richie out the door before the counterman even knew it. Which, Richie realized, probably made the man think that he had been right in the first place.

Pillowcase under one arm again, Richie walked to the next corner and scrutinized the streetcar barn for a possible place to sleep. A sprawling, one-story red-brick building with streetcar tracks running through it, the barn served two functions: a place to maintain and repair cars and, between midnight and six A.M., a place to park the cars that were not needed for the overnight schedules. It was the latter cars that interested Richie. Idle, easy to get into, unoccupied, dark, they were a perfect hiding place, except for the cold. Richie filed them away in case he could not find anyplace warmer.

Across the street at the Royal Blue market he snooped around in the alley behind the store where there was a large wooden bin for flattened cardboard boxes that had to be picked up and reused because of war shortages. The bin was about half full. If worse came to worst, Richie decided, he could burrow down to the middle of the pile of boxes and spend the night there. Looking in a back window of the market, he saw what appeared to be a storeroom. Carefully and quietly, Richie tried to open the window and then the rear door, but both were locked.

Walking back toward Cascade Bowling Lanes, Richie decided that the divan in the second-floor ladies' lounge of the bowling alley still offered him the best accommodation for a warm, reasonably comfortable place to spend the night. But he had to figure out a way to stay in the bowling alley after it closed. Back inside Cascade, he was deep in thought about the problem when a voice said, "Hey, kid. Hey, you, come here—"

Head snapping around, Richie felt a spike of fear in his chest and was ready to break and run. Then he saw it was Red, the manager. Following Red's gesture, Richie went over to the counter.

"You still want to work?" Red asked.

"Sure!" Richie said eagerly.

"Okay, go back and help Pete on nine and ten for the second league. He says he's not feeling good. Work one of his alleys. You'll split thirty lines with him at six cents a line, so you'll make ninety cents." Red suddenly frowned. "You ever spot pins before?"

"Sure, lots of times," Richie lied. "Alleys nine and ten," he said, hurrying away before Red could question him further. He had never set pins in his life, but after observing what he could see of pinboys from the front of the alleys, he was certain he could do it.

Richie trotted down the walkway back to the pits and found Pete sitting against the wall with his knees drawn up in front of him. "Red says I should help you," he told the lanky man. Pete looked up with eyes that were still watery.

"Work nine," he said, bobbing his chin at the pinboy pit where alley nine terminated.

Looking up and down, Richie saw the other pin spotters sitting or lying down or eating something between leagues. They were a mixed group: older men with gray stubble on their cheeks, muscular younger men wearing tee-shirts with packs of cigarettes rolled into one sleeve, high school kids. Behind the pits was an access walk about four feet wide, and it was there that the pin spotters rested between leagues. There was little talk; between leagues rest was the important thing in the pits.

Richie found a place to put his coat and pillowcase, and swung his legs over to drop into the pit of alley nine. It was as wide as the alley, as deep as the access walk—four feet—and recessed into the floor twelve inches. When a ball came down the alley and hit the ten wooden pins standing immediately in front of the pit, both ball and pins came back into the pit, falling to a floor that was covered with a rubber mat. The pinboy would have to slide down from a partition between pits, pick up the ball and send it rolling back on the wooden return rack, pick up the pins that had been knocked down, and reach up to put them into slots in the hand-operated set-up rack. When all ten pins had been knocked down, or the bowler had rolled two balls at them without knocking them all down, the pinboy pulled down on the rack and re-spotted all ten in the traditional triangle formation.

Completing his inspection of the pit, Richie climbed out and sat on the return rack.

Pete reached up to where his shabby overcoat was hanging and pulled a pint of whiskey from one pocket. Twisting off the cap, he took a swallow, then sat holding it and studied Richie for a minute. "Don't lemme catch you telling Red about this," he said.

"No," Richie said, shaking his head, shrugging.

"Do a good job helping me and when the league's over," Pete said, "I'm gonna give you half a buck."

"Red said ninety cents."

"Red's full of shit. They're my alleys. Half a buck."

Feeling the old familiar outrage begin to stir inside him, Richie clenched his jaw and kept himself in check. Fifty cents and that divan in the ladies' lounge, he told himself. Fifteen minutes earlier he'd had neither. Diverting his eyes, not looking at Pete, he did not complain. In his peripheral vision he saw the lanky man take another swallow and return the bottle to his overcoat.

At nine sharp, a loud buzzer sounded and the pin spotters manned their pits as the first bowlers approached the alleys. A moment later began the sharp, resounding noise that is so unique to a bowling alley: the striking of ten solid maple pins by a slate ball weighing an average of fourteen pounds.

Richie's hands were small and he was not very strong. It took both hands for him to lift and return a ball. He could pick up only one pin at a time in each hand. When a bowler on his alley got a strike, knocking down all ten pins with a single ball, Richie had to bend over and straighten up six times. Before fifteen minutes had passed, he felt as if he'd been kicked in the back.

It began in the lower back, a dull ache that soon spread all the way up to his shoulder blades. Then his wrists began to burn. Looking up and down the line of pits, he saw that he—and Pete—were the only ones working single alleys; everyone else, even the old men with gray stubble on their faces, were working double alleys. Between balls on nine, Richie watched in amazement as the men seemed to glide effortlessly from one pit to the other, never, as he was doing, getting to rest while waiting for the next balls. When you worked two alleys, the next ball was always *there*.

Half an hour after the league began, Richie was miserable. His arms felt like lead, the wooden pins like lead weights, the bowling balls like cannon balls. Jaw slack with fatigue, he had to force himself to move. Pete looked over from ten. "You okay, kid? You don't look so hot."

"I'm okay—" Fifty cents and that divan, he thought.

"Don't mess up on me, kid," Pete half warned. "I can't handle both alleys right now."

Richie did not reply. By the time an hour had passed, Richie's entire undernourished young body was one solid ache. Every movement of his legs stabbed pain into his lower back, every movement of his arms sent volts of it to his elbows and neck. His temples throbbed, his dry throat burned, even his testicles hurt. He was kept going only by the recurring thought that he had no one to depend upon except himself. He did not let himself think about his mother. He had to think, act, work, and plan how to take care of himself.

For another long hour Richie gritted his teeth and compelled his angry aching limbs and torso to do what was required of them in the pit of alley nine. By five of eleven, some of the other alleys were shutting down as their bowlers finished; by ten after, only Richie, Pete, and one of the old men were still working. The old man finished up at a quarter past and, finally, at eleven-twenty, the last ball rolled down alley nine and the nightmare of labor was over. Richie could hardly believe he had made it.

"Come on out to the counter, kid, and I'll give you half a buck," Pete said, pausing for a drink of whiskey before he left the pits.

When everyone had left, Richie, with a surge of new energy now that the compulsory work was over, made a quick inspection of the area behind the alleys and found, to his surprise, a flight of stairs that led up to the pits on the second floor. Going up, he found those pits now deserted too, the upstairs leagues finished and their pinboys up at the counter checking out. Hurrying back to the first floor, Richie got his pillowcase and took it up to the pit of alley thirty-two, which was directly next to the stairs. Then he returned downstairs, got his coat, and went out front where Red was paying the first-floor spotters.

When Red handed Pete his money, the lanky man in the shabby overcoat balked. "You only gave me $2.70. I got $3.60 coming."

Red shook his head. "Forty-five lines at six cents a line is $2.70. The kid," he bobbed his chin at Richie, "spotted fifteen lines."

"I'll pay the kid," Pete said.

"No, *I'll* pay the kid," Red demurred. "I hired him, I pay him. Here, kid—" Red pushed ninety cents across the counter to Richie.

"Thanks, mister," Richie said, adding quickly. "Can I go back to the pits for a minute? I left my gloves back there."

"Sure, but hurry up; we'll be closing in a few minutes."

As Richie pocketed his ninety cents and hurried away he heard Pete resume the argument. "Those were my alleys, Red; I should be the one to pay that kid if he works one of 'em—"

Back in the pits, Richie sat up on the ball return rack of alley sixteen, next to the downstairs door, and watched through the grille above the alley as Red and Pete continued to argue. Richie could not make out their words, but there was a great deal of head shaking and finger pointing until finally Red simply waved one hand in disgust and turned his back, and Pete stalked angrily away.

As Richie watched for the next few minutes, he saw the coffee shop manager come out and say goodnight to Red, then the bartender stopped to talk to him while Red was closing out the cash register. Presently Red was all alone, doing something in the little office behind the counter. He came out, wearing an overcoat, hat, and gloves, locked the office door and started turning off lights at a master panel. Halfway through that procedure, he paused and squinted his beady eyes toward the pits.

"Kid?" he called loudly. He listened for a moment, then called again. "Hey, kid! You gone?"

Behind the grille, Richie watched silently and motionlessly.

After what seemed like a very long time, Red turned off the rest of the lights.

After he heard Red walk out to the front entrance, leave, and lock the six entrance doors behind himself, Richie slipped quietly down into the pit of alley sixteen and sat there, his knees up in front of him, for half an hour by the big, illuminated Pabst Blue Ribbon electric clock above the counter.

The interior of Cascade Bowling Lanes was dim rather than dark. There was subdued lighting from a number of sources: the clock above the counter, two large vending machines that were lighted, some indirect lighting around a mirror behind the counter, several red exit signs, and two small spotlights that shone on the bubbling fountain near the entrance, which were left on because the fountain could be seen from the sidewalk outside. The overall effect was like a haze, a soft multicolored glow, with yellow the dominant color being picked up from the shiny maple of the sixteen alleys.

Richie was not afraid—not filled-with-dread afraid—he had spent nights in basements and under stairs before, so getting through the hours between midnight and dawn in an unfamiliar place was not entirely new to him. In the emotional space where fear would have been, there was nervousness, wariness, readiness, and caution.

As he sat in the quiet vacuum of the place, Richie allowed himself to think of his mother. Was she mad at him for telling Miss Menefee? Probably, he decided. But she'd forgive him; she'd have to when he and his dad showed up to get her.

After sitting in the pit of alley sixteen for half an hour, scrutinizing the first floor for any sound or movement, Richie slowly crept up to the second floor. There, in the pit of alley thirty-two, he sat for another half hour, looking at an identical Pabst clock above the upstairs counter. This time he sat with his pillowcase under outstretched legs. During his second vigil, Richie again began to feel the heavy fatigue in his body, especially in the shoulders and elbows, where he now suffered a burning sensation that he was unable to rub away. To take his mind off the discomfort, he played an old game in his mind: imagining where his father might be. Maybe he went out west and got a job on a ranch, and was saving money to send for Richie and his mother. But that couldn't be; he would have written them if that was what he was doing. Well then, maybe he got a job on a *ship*. One that was sailing around the *world*. There was no way he could mail a letter from a ship sailing around the world.

It occasionally occurred to Richie that his father might be back in prison somewhere, but he was usually quick to dismiss that possibility. His dad was too smart to get sent back to prison. Anyway, his mother was sure to have known if he had.

Richie began to think about how he was going to search for his father. There were two people he thought might be able to help him. One was a woman named Estelle, who had once been his mother's best friend; the other was a garage mechanic named Mack, who had helped Richie's father get a job when he was released from federal prison. One of those people, Richie was certain, would be able to provide a clue of some kind.

Richie intended to start looking for Estelle and Mack the very next day, but for now he knew he badly needed rest. He had been sick a lot most of that winter, hungry a lot, and at one point had been badly beaten up, so he was not in the best condition and he knew it. Pulling himself up out of the pit, he put the pillowcase under one arm and made his way stealthily along the walkway to the front of the alleys. With the second floor eerily lighted too, his movements cast long dissolving shadows that seemed to have life independent of him. Several times the wooden walkway creaked under his step, causing him to pause and look around warily before continuing. Proceeding cautiously like that, it took him ten minutes to reach the ladies' lounge.

Richie carefully pushed open the door to the lounge and felt inside for a light switch. He flipped it up and down several times, but it did not work. Remembering how Red had turned off all the downstairs lights from a master panel, Richie went out to the second-floor counter to look for a similar box. He found it, in the same location as the one downstairs. Looking over the dozen switches, Richie found one labeled LADIES and moved it to the "On" position. Back in the ladies' lounge, there were now lights. Quickly checking for windows, Richie was relieved to find that there were none. He could leave the lights on.

Sitting on the green, two-cushion divan, Richie found that it sagged a little and squeaked a little but was generally comfortable. It was a lot better than a cold streetcar in the repair barns, or the pile of boxes behind the Royal Blue. Taking off his coat, he pulled an old shirt from the pillowcase to use with his coat for cover, then with the rest of his scant belongings he fashioned a pillow for himself. Suddenly hungry, he went back out to a candy machine he had noticed near the counter, and with a nickel bought a Milky Way. Sitting on the divan, he ate it quickly, then cupped his hands to get water at the sink to satisfy a thirst it created.

Very tired now, emotionally drained as well, Richie laid his head on the makeshift pillow. His coat he used to cover his upper body, the old shirt for his legs. He rested on his left side, for a while staring at the wall, not wanting to close his eyes. As soon as he did close them, he saw his mother's agonized face. He began to cry.

It took him a long time to cry himself to sleep.

he woman on the bar stool was heavier and not as pretty as Richie remembered. Estelle stared at Richie with her mouth open in surprise.

"My god almighty," she exclaimed finally, "look how you've grown! Come here to me . . ."

Estelle pulled Richie to her and wrapped her fleshy arms around him in a tight hug, them smeared wet lips on his cheek. She smelled of Evening in Paris perfume; the fragrance at once reminded Richie of the days before the war when Estelle and his mother and he had lived together, sharing an apartment. Estelle had married a sailor during the war and moved to California for a while. After she divorced and came back, she and his mother had not been as close. Richie had not seen her in nearly three years.

Releasing him from the suffocating hug, Estelle held him at arm's length and asked, "What in the world are you doing here, sugar?"

"I was just walking down Kedzie Avenue and looked in the window and saw you," Richie lied. He had been searching for Estelle for a week, starting at the last place he knew she had worked, a Walgreen's drugstore on Division Street, tracing her through other employees from job to job, and, after running out of jobs, from rented room to rented room. She had not been difficult to find: Estelle, like Richie's mother, was from a small town and felt more comfortable staying in the same general neighborhood. And she wasn't trying to hide from anyone.

"That kid shouldn't be in here, Estelle," the bartender said.

"It's okay, Dan, he's my nephew," Estelle lied.

"Take him over to the café side, will you? I don't want to get in no trouble."

"Sure, Dan. Come on, sugar," Estelle said to Richie. She took her glass of beer and they went to the other side of a partition to an area where food was served and customers under twenty-one were allowed. "You want a hamburger, sugar?" Estelle asked. When Richie shrugged, she smiled and said, " 'Course you do." She ordered him a hamburger and a glass of milk, then asked, "Are y'all living around here?"

Having made up a story ahead of time, Richie told her he was in a foster home while his mother was being cured at Lexington. Estelle's expression turned sad and she shook her head.

"Poor Chloe. I always had a feeling that was going to happen to her. I remember when she kept increasing those doses of paregoric she took. I told her once, 'Chloe, honey, that stuff's only going to lead you to worse things.' " Estelle patted Richie's hand across the table. "But why have they got you in a foster home, sugar? Couldn't you go back to Lamont and live with your grandmamma?"

Richie had a lie for that one too. "The Welfare lady wanted me to stay in Chicago in case they found my daddy."

"Your daddy? He never did come back?"

Richie shook his head. "Do you know where he might be?"

"I sure don't, sugar." Estelle sighed dejectedly. "Lord, it's no wonder poor Chloe got herself messed up. It was bad enough that your daddy got hisself sent to the penitentiary, but then to run off like that once he was out, well—" She shook her head again. "Poor, poor Chloe."

When Richie's food came, Estelle sipped her beer while he wolfed it down in his usual fashion. She studied his chapped cheeks and lips, the worn coat, the threadbare shirt she could see beneath.

"Don't look like they give you very good clothes in that foster home," she observed.

"These aren't my regular clothes," Richie lied again. "These are my old clothes that I deliver papers in. My regular clothes are lots nicer than these."

"Well, I'm glad to hear that." Estelle sighed quietly. "I was just wishing a little while ago that I had the money to buy myself a warmer coat, but I've been out of work for going on a month now." She forced an uneasy smile. "That's the only reason I'm in this bar so early in the day; I'm meeting a man who might have a job for me."

Now it was Richie who said, "Oh." Then he glanced away. After a moment, he suddenly asked, "Can you help me find my daddy?"

Estelle frowned. "I don't see how, sugar. I never really knew that much about your daddy. *Nobody* did. Not even when we were all back home in Lamont. He came and went pretty much as he pleased, did pretty much what he wanted to do—up until they put him in the penitentiary." Estelle tapped one finger in the center of the table. "I hate to have to say this, sugar, but a lot of what's happened to your mother is your daddy's fault. Hadn't been for him getting hisself sent to the penitentiary, why, Chloe never would have come to Chicago in the first place. You probably don't remember, sugar, you were just a little boy, but you were right there in the room with us, at your grandmamma's house, the day Chloe made up her mind to leave Lamont. And it was all because your daddy was off in the penitentiary . . ."

Richie had been three. Blond, freckle-faced, with serious blue eyes, he had an unusual reserve for his age, perhaps because he knew his daddy was a convict. He was not sure what a convict was, but he knew it was bad from the way people said it. And he knew it must have something to do with his daddy not being there.

Sitting in a corner of the back bedroom of his grandmother's house in Lamont, he quietly played with a small metal windup truck, rolling it on the linoleum floor covering while he pretended not to pay any attention to his mother and her girlfriend Estelle.

"I just can't stand it anymore, 'Stelle," his mother said tensely. She had a cardboard suitcase open on the dresser top and was nervously transferring clothes into it from the drawers. Covertly watching, Richie noticed that so far she had put only her own clothes into the suitcase. He began to worry. Lowering her voice, his mother turned to Estelle, who was sitting on the bed smoking a cigarette, legs crossed, one foot bobbing rhythmically. "It drives me crazy, the way they all look at me, the way they cock their heads and whisper," she said to Estelle. "Them and their little smirks and their stares and their clever little remarks. 'Mighty pretty dress, Miss Chloe.' Looking right at my bosom when they say it. 'You look a little flushed, Miss Chloe; are you feeling warm?' In other words, are you hot yet, girl? Your man's been a convict for two years now; are you ready for somebody else yet? I can't say six words to any man in Lamont without him getting ideas; if I say *more* than six words to one, every jealous, skinny bitch in town starts a story about it. I just can't stand it anymore."

Richie glanced up as his mother lighted a cigarette of her own. She was a tall woman, darker than most women in the little Southern town because she did not go to any lengths to avoid the sun. Her hair was dark and fashionably short, her eyes dark and large. She was pretty even at times like this when she was upset.

"Just where in the world do you think you're going, Chloe?" her girl-friend asked.

"Chicago."

"That's asking for trouble," Estelle said, wryly. She took several short puffs on her cigarette without inhaling. "What do you think Richmond will have to say about you moving up there?" she asked, lowering her own voice and glancing at Richie. He began to listen even more closely; Richmond was his father.

"I'm not going to tell him," Chloe replied. "Not at first, anyhow. I'll send my letters down here and Mamma can mail them." Chloe paused and bit her lower lip. "We haven't been writing all that much lately anyhow. He doesn't have much to write about from prison, and I . . . ."

Chloe's words trailed off and she stared into space, frowning. Estelle knew what she was thinking. The last year before Richmond had been caught and sent to prison, things had not been very good between Chloe and him. Chloe had wanted Richmond to go straight; she was constantly on him about it. Estelle couldn't remember how many times she had heard Chloe say, "If you'd go see your daddy, I just know he'd take you back and make you a partner in the farm like he did your brother." Richmond would always flash that quick, engaging smile of his and reply, aghast, "You want me to start wearing bib overalls and hightop field shoes again? Give up my Memphis suits and wingtips? Turn in my Packard for a *plow?*" He would give Chloe a kiss on the cheek or throw her a wink. "If I did that, I wouldn't be the man you fell in love with anymore," he'd remind her, and as far as he was concerned the conversation was over. Afterward, Chloe would always lament to Estelle the foreboding she felt. "Everybody in West Tennessee says his days are closing fast. The Feds call him 'Tennessee Slim' now; he's the biggest bootlegger in the state and the one they want to catch the worst. It's only a matter of time. When it happens, 'Stelle, I might not be able to wait for him. I might not be able to stand it."

"Stand what?" Estelle had once asked knowingly. "The scandal or being without a man?"

Chloe's eyes smouldered when she replied. "Both," she said frankly.

But for two years, and Estelle could bear witness, Chloe had tried. She had faced the scandal by day, the loneliness at night. Having her baby a year before Richmond was sent up had helped some, but not, Estelle felt, enough. As the weeks and months stretched out, she had seen Chloe coil tighter and tighter.

"You've made up your mind, I guess," Estelle said as she watched her best friend pack.

"Yes."

"Well, hell, I guess I'd better go pack too, then," Estelle said, crushing out her cigarette in the ashtray she held. "I can't let you run off up to Chicago by yourself—Lord knows what kind of trouble you'd get into."

As Richie watched, the two young women embraced and cried briefly and then giggled in delight before Estelle left to go to her house and pack.

After Estelle left, Chloe looked down at Richie with a dazzling smile and sparkling eyes. "We're going on a train ride, sugar. Won't that be fun?" At the dresser, she began putting Richie's clothes in the suitcase with hers.

On the floor, Richie felt a rush of relief; he would not be left behind. As he resumed playing with his windup truck, he wondered where Chicago was.

And what it would be like there.

In the bar on Kedzie Avenue, Estelle drank the last of her beer and Richie glanced at a clock over the bar. It was nearly five. He had to be at the bowling alley by six to see if he could spot pins for the early league. During the past week, Red had used him every night as a relief pinboy, filling in for any regulars who wanted a respite. And Red always paid Richie himself so Richie got the full six cents per line just like everyone else.

"Where did we live when we first came to Chicago?" Richie asked Estelle.

"In the thirty-three-hundred block of Walnut Street, sugar. I think it was thirty-three-eighteen. Why?"

"Could you tell me about it? If I can try and remember what's happened since we came to Chicago, maybe I can figure out why my daddy left. And maybe that'll help me figure out where he went to."

"I don't see how," Estelle started to argue. But then she saw the yearning in Richie's face and her expression softened. "But sure, sugar, if you want me to." Estelle looked up as a well-dressed older man entered the bar on the other side. "Only I can't right now, see, because like I said I'm meeting this gentleman who might have a job for me, and he just walked in the door. But you come see me again, hear?" Digging in her purse, she found a pencil stub and on a paper napkin wrote an address on Monroe Street. "That's where I live."

Rising, she smoothed down her dress and patted her hair, then walked around the partition into the bar.

Richie folded the napkin and put it in the secret compartment of his Buck Jones billfold, before leaving the bar and hurrying to the streetcar back to the bowling alley.

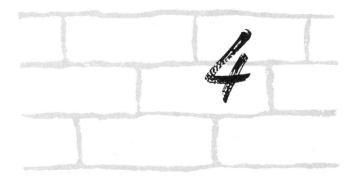

It took Richie a week to adjust to living in the bowling alley. It had not been easy.

On that first morning in Cascade, he had been awakened shortly after eight o'clock by a loud, buzzing sound that seemed to be very near him. The droning, vibrating whine had shocked him wide awake; he had sat bolt upright, scared half to death. Leaping off the divan, he had looked around in fear and confusion; for several terrifying seconds he had not known where he was. Remembering, he had rushed out of the lounge. It's a fire alarm going off, he had thought in panic; the bowling alley was on fire!

Following the sound to the top of the front stairs, Richie had stopped abruptly at the sight of a black man moving a waxing machine slowly along alley eleven. He had also seen a black woman emptying ashtrays in the spectator area.

Trembling, Richie had hurried back to the lounge. Only then had he realized how stiff and sore his whole body was from the previous night's work in the pits. He had felt like one large, moving ache. Quickly gathering his things from the lounge, he had run behind the counter to return the master light switch to "Off," then had made his way down to the first-floor pits. From there, through the screen, he had been able to see the two janitors as they went about their maintenance work. Nervous, feeling ill, he had waited until they were occupied away from the alleys, then quietly let himself out a rear fire exit.

On Madison Street, Richie had stood in a doorway, pillowcase under his arm, trying to decide what to do next. People moved past him on the sidewalk, coming, going, a purpose to their step. Everyone seemed to have someplace to go—except him. Presently, a man in a suit gave him a curious look, went on, then turned to look back. Richie had hurried from the doorway and gone in the other direction.

He spent most of that first day wandering around, looking for places to get warm: other doorways, stores, anyplace where he could go unnoticed for a few minutes. He had been frightened; never before had he been so totally alone, so *cut off* from everybody. He had found himself constantly moving in the face of approaching strangers. Ordinary businessmen in suits he was sure were juvenile officers; women with briefcases like Miss Menefee carried were welfare case workers; men whose coats and trousers did not match were truant officers. Everyone was the enemy now. Richie had kept moving.

When he stayed anywhere for a few minutes, in some doorway shifting from foot to foot, blowing on his hands, watching warily, he had tried to figure out what to do next: how to search for his father; how to get—probably steal—some decent clothes; how to find another place to sleep if he could not stay in the bowling alley again. His problems seemed enormous; the situation, now that he was *in* it, was numbing. The terrible life he had just left behind him now seemed oddly comfortable. But it was too late to turn back.

Time dragged by tediously that first day, but he had managed to survive the hours, returning to Cascade at three-thirty in the afternoon when school had let out. Red was surprised to see him.

"What are you doing here so early?" he asked.

Richie shrugged. "I came to see if I could set pins again."

"I won't be assigning league alleys for two more hours," Red had told him. He bobbed his chin at Richie's pillowcase. "What do you carry in that thing anyway?"

"My gym clothes, for school," Richie lied.

Red nodded and began opening cartons of cigarettes and restocking a bin behind the counter. "Well, hang around if you want to," he said presently, "but don't get in anybody's way."

Richie had slumped down in one of the spectator seats and for a while had watched a few people bowling open games. From noon to six Cascade had nonleague open bowling at reduced prices, using pinboys who were too slow to work the fast evening league play. Richie would have liked to set pins for the open bowling, but knew it would be unwise to show up at Cascade during school hours. One of the places truant officers regularly checked were bowling alleys.

After he had been there half an hour, Red called him over to the counter. "Here," he handed Richie a sheet of paper with a couple of dozen numbers written on it, "the guy that usually does this hasn't shown up. These are balls that some of tonight's league bowlers reserved to use. The number is engraved right above the thumb hole. Find 'em and put them in that reserved rack over there. I'll give you a penny a ball; you can make twenty or thirty cents while you wait."

"Thanks, Red!" Richie said elatedly. He had set about enthusiastically looking for the bowling balls on the list.

During the next week, Richie had gradually integrated himself into the routine of the bowling alley. Now on mornings when the waxing machine woke him, he got up unafraid; the cleaners never came upstairs before finishing the first floor, so Richie felt comfortable taking his time. He washed his face at one of the sinks and brushed his teeth with a new toothbrush he had stolen from Woolworth's and a shaker of salt he had taken from Walgreen's soda fountain. He had shoplifted a navy turtleneck from a surplus store and snatched a pair of rubber galoshes from the foyer of an apartment building. He still kept his extra belongings in the pillowcase, but instead of carrying it around all the time, he now put it in one of the small bowling ball lockers in the upstairs checkroom, securing it with a combination lock he had swiped from Neisner's Variety Store. At night when he crept upstairs after Red closed up, he would get his belongings out of the locker and, spreading paper towels on the floor of the lounge, take a sponge bath before settling down for the night. He usually got a candy bar from the vending machine to eat as he sat on the divan, back against the wall, and read. Regularly stealing several paperback books a week from wire racks in cigar stores, he often stayed awake as late as two A.M. before finally closing his eyes.

And every night he cried himself to sleep.

Richie began his search for Mack in a neighborhood on the far South Side, where he thought he remembered his father saying the mechanic had a small auto repair garage. Riding a streetcar out, Richie walked around the area inquiring at filling stations.

"Hey, mister, do you know a man named Mack who fixes cars around here somewhere?"

"What's his last name?"

"I dunno."

"What's he look like?"

"I dunno."

"All's you know is the one name? All's you know is 'Mack'?"

Richie could only shrug and say, "Yeah."

"Can't help you, kid," was the usual response.

Richie kept looking every day, expanding the perimeter of the area block by block until he was a mile in each direction from the intersection where he had started. He was constantly on the alert for authority; wherever he searched, he was always ready to bolt and run. He never relaxed. His stomach hurt a lot.

One day when he asked about Mack at an Esso station on Calumet near 87th, one of the attendants asked back, "Is he a gimp?"

Richie frowned. "Huh?"

"A gimp, a crippled guy."

A new vein of memory suddenly flowed in Richie's head. His father had called Mack a "clubfoot." Richie had not even known what it meant. But now it made sense. "Yeah," he quickly replied, "I think so."

"He had a garage a couple of blocks from here. He closed up after the war started 'cause he couldn't get no parts. I heard he went to work in Commonwealth Edison's garage down near the Loop. On Harrison Street, I think it was."

Richie found the Edison garage and talked to a repair foreman. "Yeah, I know who you're talking about. Mack Swain. Had a clubfoot, wore one of them built-up shoes. Worked for me three years. Good mechanic, fix anything that had pistons. He quit me back last summer to open a place of his own again. Down on Clinton Street near the river."

"Thanks, mister!"

Hopping a ride on the back of a coal truck, Richie rode to the area around Clinton and 20th Street, where the Chicago River made its southwest curve. He spent the rest of the day asking at filling stations, cigar stores, taxi stands, and other small businesses in the area. But no one had ever heard of Mack Swain. Finally Richie had to quit and hurry to Cascade.

The next day he was back, asking at more businesses, even stopping people on the street. Grimly determined, he went up one side of a block and down the other. He asked other kids, delivery men, housewives doing their shopping. Desperation drove him; the same desperation that had convinced him that finding his father was the only salvation for his mother and himself; the same desperation that led him to conclude that his father was somewhere in Chicago. I *know* my dad's here, he repeated time and time again in his mind as he prowled the streets. I *know* I'll find him.

It was Richie's dream; he clung to it tenaciously. He would *make* it come true.

Locating Mack Swain was the first step.

On a day when it was warmer than most, Richie went out to West End Avenue and hung around a little neighborhood candy store near Tilton Elementary, the last school he had attended before going into hiding. When school was out, he watched groups of kids coming down the street and filtering out in different directions toward their homes. A girl named Linda walked with two friends until she got to Keeler Avenue, then said goodbye and walked away alone. Richie followed her until they were well away from any other kids, then hurried to catch her.

"Hey, wait up," he said.

Linda's mouth fell open when she saw him. "The *police* are looking for you!" she said, aghast.

Richie went into his John Garfield act. "Yeah, I know. I'm on the lam."

"Stop trying to act tough," Linda said in a no-nonsense manner very advanced for her age. Richie grinned. It was good to see Linda again; he realized for the first time that he had missed her very much. A plain girl from a poor family, she and Richie had liked each other almost from the first day he transferred to Tilton. An avid reader herself, Linda had been the only one in the sixth grade to consistently earn an A on her book reports. Then Richie had come along and begun to get A-plus. Instead of being piqued, Linda had been pleased; he was a kindred spirit, the first she had ever discovered, wonder of wonders, a *boy* who liked to read. Deeply troubled when he had suddenly disappeared from school, the young girl was in no mood for his hard-guy act now. Taking him by the arm, Linda guided him to the front steps of the building where they were standing. "Tell me what happened," she ordered.

Richie told her that his mother had been sent to a hospital for a drug cure and that he had run away rather than be sent to a foster home. "I been through that foster home stuff already," he said, "before I came to Tilton."

"But where are you living?" she asked, concerned.

"Promise you won't tell anyone?"

"You know better. I won't."

"I sleep in a bowling alley where I work."

"A bowling alley?" The no-nonsense maturity dissolved; her eyes became teary. "By yourself? All alone?"

"Sure." Her tears made him uncomfortable. "It's okay," he assured her. "I get along just fine."

"You don't look like you're getting along just fine," Linda said, removing her woolen gloves and taking from one of her sleeves a handkerchief to blow her nose. "Look at yourself—the knees are about to come out of your pants, you don't have a muffler, those galoshes look ten sizes too big for you—where in the world did you get them, anyway?"

"I found them."

"You stole them." Anguish took over her expression; she gripped both his hands. "Oh, Richie, wouldn't you be better off in a foster home? Where you wouldn't have to go around stealing? And you could come back to school?"

Richie shook his head emphatically. "They watch you too close in a foster home. And I don't have time to go to school. I'm spending all my time trying to find my dad."

"You told me you didn't have a father."

"I got one. I just don't know where he's at. But I know I can find him if I look long enough."

Linda shook her head. "Richie, you can't keep on living like you are . . ."

Her tears continued. He wondered if he could get her to stop crying by making up a story that he wanted her to help him.

"I thought if you would tell me what you're reading in class, I could check the same book out of the library and read it on my own," he said. "That way I could kind of keep up; I wouldn't be so far behind when I find my dad and can start back to school."

"That's a wonderful idea!" Linda said, immediately enthusiastic. Wiping her tears, she opened her three-ring notebook and wrote in a neat, precise cursive handwriting the name of the last three books the class had been required to read and report on. Opening the rings and carefully lifting the page out, Linda handed it to him, saying, "There," very pleased.

Looking at the list, Richie nodded. "Thanks," he said. The books she listed were *The Adventures of Huckleberry Finn, Treasure Island,* and *Rebecca of Sunnybrook Farm.* Richie had read the first two when he was ten; the third one he had declined to finish after reading one chapter. Developing reading skills unimpeded by formal supervision, he was far ahead of Linda and other sixth-graders. In his locker at the bowling alley at that moment were two paperbacks he had stolen from Walgreen's: *The Bridge of San Luis Rey* by Thornton Wilder, which he had finished, though with difficulty, and *The Glass Key* by Dashiell Hammett, which he was enjoying thoroughly.

Folding the sheet of notebook paper and putting it in his pocket, Richie said, "This will help a lot."

He did not ask if he could walk Linda home; he had asked that once when he was still attending school and she had said, "I don't think you'd better. My father doesn't like me to walk with boys. He works on a route truck for the *Tribune* so he gets home before I do. He's usually watching for me out the window."

"How come?"

"He likes me to rub his shoulders when I get home," she replied, blushing. "His shoulders get sore from throwing bundles of papers. And my mom's not there to do it 'cause she doesn't get home from work until six."

They had never had more than a few moments after school, but had spent recesses and eaten lunch together. Richie had taken some bullying for that from several of the tougher boys on the schoolyard; they called him a sissy and punched him around in line and told him to go play jump-rope with the girls. Such treatment was not new to him; every time he had changed schools, which for several years was frequently, he had faced the same test: someone in the class had to find out for all the rest of them how tough the newcomer was. Richie was not tough at all; he was not strong and he did not know how to fight. After the initial encounter on the schoolyard, in which he was thoroughly humiliated, he would be relegated to the ranks of the weaklings: the ones the girls called "scaredy-cats" and the tougher boys called "chicken livers." Richie put up with the bullying until it eventually slacked off and he was left alone—most of the time, anyway. It was because Linda knew he was not tough and could not fight that she, like Grace Menefee, refused to put up with his John Garfield act. And for the same reason she worried about him.

"How will I know whether you're all right?" she asked, concerned.

"I'll come back and see you after school again," Richie said.

"Promise?"

"Sure."

As they were parting, she put her hand on his arm and said, "Promise you'll stay out of trouble too." When they were a few feet apart, Linda said, "Do you want to kiss me goodbye?"

"Can I?"

"If you want to. You don't have to."

"I want to. Do you want me to?"

"Yes, I do."

They stepped back together and kissed, briefly, sweetly, innocently.

Both blushing then, they said goodbye again and went separate ways.

That night, Red assigned Richie to alley eleven, working with one of the old men who only wanted to spot one alley. When Richie got back to the pits, Pete was already sitting behind his regular alleys, nine and ten. "You owe me forty cents, kid," he said.

"I don't owe you nothing," Richie replied disdainfully.

"Red shoulda let me pay you for working my alley that night. Forty cents of what he gave you was mine." He pointed a finger at Richie. "You pay up tonight after we check out."

"I'm not paying you nothing," Richie told him flatly.

Pete got to his feet with surprising speed and grabbed Richie by the coat with both hands. "You little cocksucker! You're gonna pay me what you owe me or I'll slap your teeth out!"

"Leave me alone!" Richie yelled, struggling to break away.

Pete manhandled Richie back against the wall and started shaking him. From alleys fifteen and sixteen, a surly looking man in an undershirt, with tattoos on both arms, came over and said quietly to Pete, "Turn him loose."

"This ain't your business," Pete snapped, spraying saliva with his words.

A tattooed arm shot up and powerful fingers closed on Pete's throat. "Turn him loose or I'll tear your fucking windpipe out."

Pete let go of Richie's shirt and the tattooed man let go of Pete's throat. Pete stumbled back, trembling. "This ain't—your—business!" he said again, livid.

"Find somebody your own size to shove around," the man said, returning to his own alleys. "If Red didn't pay you right, take it up with Red. But leave the kid alone."

Pete climbed into the pit of alley nine, muttering obscenities. Richie hung up his coat and went over to sixteen. "Thanks, mister."

"Forget it." The tattooed man shook a cigarette from a pack of Lucky Strikes and dug his thumbnail into a stick match to light it. Just then the buzzer sounded and Richie had to hurry over to eleven as the first league got underway.

Richie was slowly improving as a pin spotter. With experience, his back and shoulder muscles, his elbows and wrists, no longer made him feel like he'd been in a car wreck. With practice, he began picking up three pins at a time: one in the middle between the ones he had in each hand. The fearful ball, rolling like a runaway train down the narrow alley, its sound growing ominously louder, no longer frightened him. Nor did the even louder assault of its striking the pins and sending them slamming into the pit like dead men; he knew now that because of the design of the alley, with its recessed pit, the chance of a pin flying up and hitting a pinboy was remote.

No longer uncomfortable in the pits, Richie worked purposefully and efficiently with the old man in alley twelve. There was little talk between them; a sixty-year-old semi-derelict and a twelve-year-old runaway had many of life's low blows in common, but they didn't know it. They could easily have become friends but neither even considered it.

During the second league, the spotting went faster and more smoothly than in the first. It was an all-male league and more attention was paid to bowling; no time was spent trying to impress or instruct, there was no preoccupation with tight slacks or sweaters, no one was involved in making arrangements to try to take anyone home. It was all bowling. Richie was glad to be working the alley for both leagues; it meant he would earn $1.80 for the night. He had also been filching coins off newsstands on a regular basis, wherever he went in the city, and stealing empty quart beer bottles from bins behind taverns and taking them to other taverns for the nickel deposit, and shoplifting Zippo lighters from the counter at Woolworth's, selling them for a quarter apiece to guys who hung out at a poolroom across from the streetcar barns. With what he earned tonight, he would have enough extra money saved up to buy an army blanket at the surplus store to sleep warmer at night. Then he had to steal another combination lock for the extra bowling ball locker he would need to keep it in. He had his eye on a gumball machine he was going to grab one day soon also. Being on his own he had found required constant effort to keep his head above water.

Chicago was a big sea; drowning was very easy.

Richie kept going back to Clinton Street near the river, covering the same ground over and over again trying to locate Mack Swain. The more he searched unsuccessfully, the more frustrating and depressing it became. Each time he failed to find Mack, each time he glumly rode the streetcar back to the West Side, he could not help but remember his mother's words the last time he had mentioned looking for his father. It had been just a few days before they hit bottom, a few days before Richie had turned her in. Chloe had been coming out of one of her stupors, already dreading having to face getting her next fix. When he brought up finding his father, she looked at him as if he were crazy.

"You want to *what?* Look for your *father?* For Christ's sake, why don't you look for the pot of gold at the end of the rainbow? You'll have a whole lot better chance of finding that than you will finding him."

Richie had been burning at the time with such desire to do it, to start looking for him in earnest, that he had pestered her relentlessly until she had finally pointed a finger at him and said angrily, "Look, you might just as well get used to the idea that you don't *have* a father anymore! He's gone for good, see? Now don't bother me about him again! Just pretend he's dead, understand? Dead!"

After days of futile search, it would have been easy for Richie simply to accept that. But he refused to do it. His father was alive; he *knew* it. And he would find him even if it took a hundred years.

Doggedly he went on.

One day at a Sinclair filling station on the corner of Cermak Road, one of the attendants remembered Richie being there before, looking for someone.

"No luck finding that guy yet, huh, kid?" he asked.

"Nobody knows him," Richie said, shaking his head.

"Ain't you got no idea what the address is supposed to be?" the attendant asked, fishing a toothpick out of his shirt pocket.

"Just Clinton Street near where the river crosses," Richie shrugged, "that's all I know."

"Say, wait a minute, I just thought of something," the attendant said, pointing the toothpick at Richie. "Come on in the office with me."

Richie followed him into the station office where the man had a city map tacked to the wall.

"Look here, this is where we're at right now," he pointed to where Clinton met the south branch of the Chicago River. "But lookit here," his finger traced Clinton Street about two miles across town to a point near Illinois Street, where it intersected the *north* branch of the river. "Clinton's near the river over there too, kid. Maybe that's the neighborhood you should be looking in."

"Jeez," Richie said. He shook his head in amazement. "I never knew the river was crooked like that."

"Lots of things in this ol' world are crooked and we don't know it, kid," the attendant said philosophically, sticking the toothpick back in his mouth.

The attendant went out to service a car that had just pulled in. The driver was a man in a dark suit. From the driver's seat, he seemed to study Richie curiously. Tensing, Richie said to the attendant, "Thanks a lot, mister," and trotted out of the station. He headed toward Canal Street, where there was a crosstown streetcar line.

Less than an hour later, Richie was on Clinton Street again, near the Chicago River on the north side of the city. There, a few doors down from Clinton and Hubbard streets, he found an old garage with swing-out double doors and a sign above them that read: MACK'S AUTO REPAIRS.

Mack studied Richie's face for a moment, then smiled and scratched his head. "Yeah, I guess you're his kid, all right. How is your dad?"

"I don't know how he is," Richie said. "I don't even know *where* he is. I thought you might know."

Mack shook his head. "I ain't seen him in six or seven years. I thought he left Chicago, went back down south."

"He did," Richie said. "My mother and me rode back with him on the train. Then he disappeared. I think he might have come back up here."

"If he did," Mack said, "he didn't look me up." Mack was short, stocky, with receding kinky hair and an easy manner. His right foot was encased in a triple-soled shoe that laced up well over the ankle. When Mack walked, it was with a half lurch that caused his right shoulder to move up and down with each step. Whenever he talked, he habitually scratched his head at the edge of the receding hairline, leaving slight grease marks from his fingernails.

"Do you know anybody who might know where my dad is?" Richie asked.

"Let's see now," Mack said, sitting on an upturned wooden box and reaching down to rub his deformed ankle. He was dressed in old gray coveralls with a Commonwealth Edison patch on one of the top pockets. "You know," he said, shaking his head, "I can't think of nobody who might be able to help you. I don't think your dad had any real friends in Chicago—except me, that is. Him and me hit it off pretty good." Mack's brow wrinkled as his eyebrows went up. "I think he took to me 'cause he needed somebody to talk to, him just being out of prison and all. It had tore him up pretty bad, going back home to that little town in Tennessee and finding out that his wife wasn't there waiting for him. I guess your ma had taken you and come up here. Your dad told me about how he took off looking for you—"

"Would you tell me what he told you?" Richie asked eagerly.

Richie felt a new excitement inside. This was as close to his father as he had been in a long time. Maybe, he thought with a spark of hope, this would be *it*. Maybe what this man told him would be the link that would bring his father and him back together at last. Then his dad and he could go get his mother out of Lexington, and everything would be swell again.

Just the thought of it made Richie need to blink back tears. He did it quickly so that Mack would not see them.

*T*he young man who stood before the deputy warden's desk was tall and lean, with darkish blond hair and intense light blue eyes. The collar of a denim work shirt was buttoned tightly around his neck, as prison regulations required. The trousers of his prison-made gray discharge suit made the back of his sweating legs itch. New hightop shoes, also prison-made, the inside leather unfinished, were stiff and heavy on his feet. In one hand he held a gray wool cap that matched his suit. A uniformed guard holding a fifteen-inch nightstick stood to his left and behind him.

"James Richmond Howard," the deputy warden read from an open file on his desk, "alias Tennessee Slim Howard. Prisoner number 45660. Age twenty-nine. Convicted at Memphis, Tennessee, of violation of the Volstead Act. Received at Atlanta Federal Penitentiary on January 29, 1933. Sentenced to five years. Probationary good time: one year, five months, nine days. Time served: three years, six months, twenty-one days. Discharge date: August 19, 1936."

The young convict's eyes flicked to the top page of the deputy warden's desk calendar. Just to make sure. The deputy warden caught him looking and smiled knowingly.

"Today's the day, all right, Slim. We don't make mistakes about things like that." The deputy warden sat back in his wooden swivel chair, making its springs squeak gratingly. " 'Cording to our records, Slim, you been involved in bootlegging one way or another since you were fifteen years old. 'Side from a little farming when you was younger, that's about all you've ever done. But a funny thing happened while you was doing time, Slim. The Volstead Act got repealed. Prohibition's over."

Slim could not suppress a grin. "Yessir, I heard," he admitted. The joke was on him and he accepted that.

"Looks like you're going to have to find a new way of making a living," the deputy said.

"Already have," Slim told him. "My daddy's got a place in the Tennessee bottomland that grows the whitest, fluffiest cotton you ever saw. I'm gonna take my wife and little boy and move back to my daddy's place." Slim stuck his chin out an inch. "I'm gonna be a farmer."

The deputy's expression became thoughtful. "Slim, your wife hasn't written to you in nearly a year," he pointed out, not unkindly. "Suppose she hasn't waited for you?"

Slim's eyes seemed to shadow. "I guess I'll just take my little boy then," he replied quietly, his throat constricting slightly. It hurt him to think that Chloe might not have waited for him. But he knew Chloe. She might not have. She might not have been *able* to.

The deputy warden sighed quietly. "Well, I hope things work out for you, Slim. But I think you ought to prepare yourself for the possibility that your wife might have somebody else by now, that your daddy might not let you come back, and that even if he does, you might not be able to make it as a farmer. Not after living the way you did when you were bootlegging. Everybody knows that one of your old partners, George Kelly, stepped up from bootlegging to bank robbery and kidnapping. They call him Machine Gun Kelly now. I hope you don't end up the same way, Slim."

The deputy handed prisoner number 45660 an envelope. "This contains a one-way bus ticket to Memphis, Tennessee, your place of conviction, and five dollars in United States currency. Sign this voucher." After Slim had bent over the desk and signed his name, the deputy warden said, "Good luck, Slim." Not offering to shake hands, he nodded to the guard. "Walk him out."

From Memphis, Slim hitchhiked to Lamont, the little town fifty miles away where he had grown up on the cotton farm of his father, Solon Howard. The produce trucker who had given him a lift dropped him off north of town at a little combination grocery–filling station called Luckey's. In the window was a sign showing a pretty girl in a tight white swimsuit drinking a Coca-Cola. Slim was hot and the thought of a cold Coca-Cola was tempting, but he was so close to where he was going, and so anxious to get there, that he did not want to waste the time to stop.

Slim walked down to Moreridge Street, to a neat little white frame house with a porch running across the front of it and a swing at one end of the porch. A stoutish woman with graying hair and bifocals, an apron over a plain cotton dress, sat on the swing shelling green peas into a pan.

Slim walked across the yard and stopped at the porch steps. "Hey, Miz Clark," he said quietly, removing his cap.

The woman's lips parted in surprise. "My lord," she said. "Is that really you, Richmond?"

"Yes, ma'am, it's me. They turned me loose on a probationary release."

"What in the world is that?"

"It just means they let me out early on my good behavior. If I stay out of trouble, I stay out; if not, I get sent back."

"Well, I declare," Mrs. Clark said again. "Well, come and sit down, Richmond"—she pointed to a wooden rocking chair—"no need to just stand there."

"Thank you, ma'am." Slim sat on the rocker without rocking, his feet in the uncomfortable new hightop shoes flat on the porch and close together in front of him, cap held on his lap. "I've come for Chloe and the boy, Miz Clark," he said.

"Chloe's not here, Richmond. She's not anywhere in Lamont."

Slim looked down at his prison-calloused fingers holding the cap. He felt his chest tighten. "Where might she be then?"

"Richmond, I don't hold nothing against you for what's happened," Mrs. Clark said, "but Chloe's my girl and I promised not to tell you where she went. I can't break my promise."

"Where's my little boy?" Slim asked, looking up, fixing his eyes on her.

"He's with Chloe."

"I've got a right to know where my son is at," Slim said evenly. His intense light blue eyes, locked on the woman's face, did not blink. Mrs. Clark started to cry.

"Richmond, I'm sorry, but I can't help it. Chloe's *mine;* I have to keep my promise to her. I'm not aiming to hurt you; there's just nothing else I can do."

Slim released her from his accusing gaze; he looked off at the road for a moment, watching two barefoot black boys making puffs of dust with each step. Then he looked back at his widowed mother-in-law. "Miz Clark, I'm not looking to do no harm to Chloe. What I'd like is for us to make a fresh start. I'm not gonna be bootlegging no more; I'll be going straight from now on. I'd like to make a decent life for Chloe and the boy."

"Richmond, I'm sorry," said Mrs. Clark, "I truly to God am. But there's just no way in the world I can help you without turning on my own child. I just can't do that."

Slim nodded his head in resignation. "I reckon I understand how you feel," he said.

"I haven't ever been one to preach, Richmond," the stoutish woman said, "but you know as well as I do that you've got a lot to live down before you can get folks to accept you as decent. You've been on the wrong side of the law since you wasn't nothing but a boy. All that bootlegging of yours never done anything but hurt the folks who cared for you. Hurt lots of other people too. Why, I heard about a farmer out on the Covington Highway that got drunk on your bootleg liquor at a high school dance and got in a car wreck and killed hisself. Folks remember things like that, Richmond. Things like that take a lot of forgiving."

"Might not have been my bootleg liquor," Slim reasoned.

"Might *have* too," Mrs. Clark countered, without animosity.

Slim sighed quietly. "Well, maybe it's gonna be a longer road back than I figured." Standing, Slim put on his cap and extended a hand. "Thank you for talking to me, Miz Clark. Take care of yourself, hear?"

Wednesday might was prayer-meeting night at the First Baptist Church of Lamont, and Slim knew that Mrs. Clark had always made a practice of walking uptown with one of her lady friends to attend. Hoping she had not changed that habit since he had been in prison, he slipped into a field next to her house and crouched hidden in the brush where he could watch her front door. As he waited, he remembered that it was the same field he and Chloe used to walk through before they were married. They liked to stroll in the afternoon sun and talk about the new songs—Libby Holman singing "Body and Soul," and Ruth Etting singing "Ten Cents a Dance." They would walk along, Chloe smoking one of her Avalon cigarettes when they were far enough away from the house so that Mrs. Clark could not see her, and laugh about the Marx Brothers movies they had seen, *Animal Crackers* and *Monkey Business*. Chloe had teased Slim, saying he looked like Douglas Fairbanks, Jr., in the new suits he had bought at Goldsmith's in Memphis. Four million people were out of work in America but Slim had new suits, a new DeSoto coupe, and money in his pocket. He also had a growing reputation, but at that time neither one of them paid much attention to it. Life was all sunshine then.

At half past seven, Mrs. Clark, wearing a bonnet, came out of her house and walked across the road to get her friend Mrs. Samuels. Several minutes later, the two women started uptown. Relieved that his mother-in-law had not changed her Wednesday night routine, Slim waited a little while until it was dark, then left the field and slipped stealthily across the backyard of Mrs. Clark's house and onto her rear porch. The back door was unlocked, as was the front door and all the windows; people in Lamont did not insult their neighbors by locking their homes.

Slim went into the living room first. Feeling in the drawers of two endtables by the sofa, he found nothing of interest. In the dining room, he did the same with the drawers of the china closet, again with no results. In the front bedroom, he started with the dresser drawers; he opened and felt in three of them before he found what he was looking for: a bundle of letters held together by a rubber band. Kneeling below the windowsill, Slim struck a stick match and held its light close enough to the top envelope to read its return address: Chloe Howard, 3318 W. Walnut St., Chicago, Illinois. Slim felt a knot in his chest; it had been a long time since he had seen Chloe's handwriting. She had a simple but beautiful style that looked like samples in an instruction book. For a time after she stopped writing, Slim had regularly reread her old letters, but after a few months it had become too hard on his peace of mind and he had stopped. Reading old letters in prison was like masturbating: it only reminded you of what you didn't have.

Slim quickly memorized the return address. As he was about to put the letters away, he noticed the postmark and frowned. April 28, 1936. It was four months old, all right. Quickly he flipped through the stack; all the other postmarks were earlier.

Returning the letters to the drawer, Slim slipped out of the house as he had come in. Walking uptown in the dark, he worried about what it all meant. Chloe had not written her mother in nearly four months. What had happened to her? And why hadn't Mrs. Clark told him she hadn't heard from her daughter in that long? Had Chloe found another man, and did Mrs. Clark know about it? The deputy warden's words came back to him: *"Suppose she hasn't waited for you?"*

Slim remembered his reply: *"I guess I'll just take my little boy then."*

He decided to leave for Chicago as quickly as he could.

*S*itting in Mack's garage, hearing for the first time the story of his father's release from prison and return to Lamont, Richie found his own emotions at odds about his mother. Why hadn't she waited for his father?

"Your dad," Mack said, "got on a bus the very next morning to come up here." He picked up a rag and wiped some grease off his hands. "Well, quitting time. You want to come upstairs and eat some supper with me?"

"I can't," Richie said. "I've got to get to the bowling alley; I set pins at night. Can I come back and talk to you again? I'd like to hear how you and my dad met."

"Sure, kid. Come back anytime." Mack winked confidentially. "I'll tell you all about how your dad and me used to work for Al Capone."

Richie stared at Mack in surprise. He knew who Al Capone was; every kid in Chicago knew who Al Capone was. But this was the first Richie had ever heard that his father had worked for the notorious gangster.

A new keenness fired up inside Richie. Once again he had the feeling that he was getting closer to his father. But as he left Mack's and rode the streetcar back to the West Side, the excitement of that feeling was dampened by the new resentment he was now feeling toward his mother. Why *hadn't* she been there when his dad came home from prison? If only she'd waited, the three of them would have been together and none of the bad things in their lives would have happened.

Goddamn her, he thought sullenly.

Richie walked into the big Woolworth's at Madison and Karlov, several blocks from the bowling alley. Unbuttoning his coat, he let it hang open in front. As he approached the jewelry counter, the saleslady's eyes flicked over his shabby appearance and became suspicious. Richie smiled at her.

" 'Scuse me, ma'am. I'm saving money from my paper route to buy my mom a watch for Mother's Day. Could you please tell me how much they cost?"

The saleslady's eyes immediately became sympathetic.

"There are all prices," she said. "How much do you think you'll have saved by Mother's Day?"

"I guess about eight dollars."

"We have some very nice Elgin ladies' watches for seven ninety-five. All those on the bottom row there—" she pointed to a glass showcase behind the counter. On the counter itself, which stood between Richie and the saleslady, were recessed bins containing costume jewelry and other less expensive merchandise.

"How much is one of those?" Richie asked, leaning over the counter and pointing to a row of watches on the top shelf. The saleslady turned to look where he was pointing. Richie's right hand, in his coat pocket, came out through a split in the seam and, concealed by his coat hanging open, closed around half a dozen expandable watchbands in one of the bins. In an instant they were pulled up inside his pocket.

"Those are Benrus watches," the saleslady said. "They're twelve-fifty."

"I'll probably have to get the seven ninety-five one," Richie said, looking very serious. Glancing up and down the aisle, he checked to see if any other clerks had seen him. No one was paying any attention to the jewelry counter. "Thanks a lot, ma'am." Richie smiled at the saleslady again. "I'll come back when I have enough saved."

The saleslady smiled back. "Your mother's very lucky to have a little boy like you," she said solemnly.

"Thank you, ma'am."

Making it out of Woolworth's without incident, Richie immediately ducked around the corner of Karlov, the side street, and trotted a block to Washington Boulevard, a residential street. Only then did he slow to a normal walk, transfer the watchbands to his good pocket, and button up his coat. It was four in the afternoon, still light as the winter days now grew longer, but still bitingly cold. Richie now had a new sweatshirt, a pair of earmuffs he had stolen and—finally, thankfully—a new pair of shoes with no holes in the soles. He had bought them with money changed for nine dollars worth of pennies he got out of the gumball machine he'd snatched and later pried open.

Coming toward him on the same side of the street was a tall man in a topcoat with the collar turned up. Richie thought he recognized him from somewhere—cop, truant officer, welfare caseworker? Taking no chances, he dashed across the boulevard, dodging traffic, and watched over his shoulder as the man went on his way. Only when he was well past him did Richie realize what had made the man seem so familiar: tall, slim, light-haired, he had reminded Richie of his father. Richie paused and looked back at him again, then shook his head and continued on his way.

After two o'clock on weekday afternoons, Richie usually moved freely around the city without fear of truant officers. Schools let out between two and three, and he guessed that most "school cops" were back in their offices by then. There were still the welfare investigators and the juvenile cops, but they normally were after individuals, and looked for them in specific places they had frequented in the past. School cops were the most dangerous; they *cruised*, looking for anybody they could catch.

The time between nine A.M., when he slipped out of the bowling alley, and two P.M., when he felt free to be on the streets, were the most precarious for Richie. He had learned as a foster-home runaway to avoid places that school cops usually looked: movie houses that were open in the morning, pool halls, pinball parlors, bowling alleys. Never under any circumstances did he show up at Cascade before three or four o'clock in the afternoon. Likewise, he never tried selling shoplifted merchandise in the bowling alley. Cascade was his place of steady employment as well as his place to sleep; he felt safe there, and he was careful to do nothing to compromise that security.

The place where Richie eventually hid the most between nine and two was in the main public library downtown on Michigan Boulevard. The block-long building, which sat facing Grant Park between Randolph and Washington, was a veritable maze of rooms in which an inconspicuous boy with a notebook could go virtually unnoticed. And it was a place, Richie had learned, that school cops never checked, on the theory that truants from school would not go to a library, because it was too much like school. Richie had shoplifted a spiral notebook and an elementary-school dictionary, and carried them wherever he went during school hours on weekdays. He found that cops on the beat, streetcar conductors, and others rarely gave him a second glance when he was carrying the books. In the library, where he was always quiet and well-behaved, he even received an occasional smile from one of the librarians. Once he overheard one say quietly to another, "It's so refreshing to see a poor kid like that coming here instead of loitering in front of some pool hall."

Richie loved the library. Under the pretext of preparing a report for school, he was able to read early issues of the *Chicago Tribune*, which were kept in large, heavy binders in a special room. Richie read newspaper accounts of Civil War battles, Abraham Lincoln's assassination, the death of Billy the Kid and Jesse James, Teddy Roosevelt's charge up San Juan Hill, the beginning of World War I, the Lindbergh baby kidnapping, and many other events that galvanized his curiosity.

When not in the old newspapers section, or roaming the special exhibit rooms that featured temporary displays on a single subject—great ships, oil exploration, Eskimo life—Richie would spend hours in the reference section, poring over every imaginable kind of encyclopedia, almanac, year book, atlas, guide, and whatever else he could find. Sometimes when he got carried away on a subject, such as how a motion picture was made, he lost track of time and stayed in the library long after the streets had become safe for him.

After Richie had been on his own for a few weeks and felt reasonably secure, he went back to the neighborhood where he had previously lived. A boy who had been his best friend, Stan Klein, was sitting in front of a candy store with another kid, Bobby Casey. It was Bobby who saw Richie first. "Jesus Christ, look what crawled up out of the sewer," Bobby said.

"Hey, Richie, where the hell you been?" Stan asked with a grin, happy to see him. They had lived in the same building on Adams Street, and it had been with Stan that Richie had stolen the first time. For a while Richie and Stan had been inseparable; after Richie was sent to foster homes, Stan would sometimes hide him or give him money when he ran away.

"The cops were around twice asking about you," Stan told him.

Shrugging, Richie sat down with them. "I'm running again," he said matter-of-factly. "They put my old lady in a place to get her off drugs; I didn't want to go back to no foster homes." Normally Richie never referred to his mother as his "old lady," but since Stan and Bobby both did, he seemed naturally to use their vernacular here.

"Hope you ain't thinking of working with us again," Bobby Casey said flatly. "We ain't making enough for two, much less three." Richie had teamed up with Stan and Bobby several months earlier for a while, committing thefts of gumball machines.

Stan gave Bobby a disgusted look. "Richie can come back in with us any time he wants to," he said evenly. "When there was three of us, we made a hell of a lot more scores than we can make with just two of us. I can think of a dozen machines right now that three guys could grab that two can't." Stan turned to Richie. "You wanna come back in with us, Richie?"

Richie shrugged. "Sure, I guess." He knew that Bobby Casey did not like him, was jealous because Stan *did* like him; he also knew Bobby was tougher than he and could beat him up if he wanted to. But at the moment he could not concern himself with that. He needed money to get by, and he could steal more with Stan and Bobby than he could alone. Stan was the leader anyway; if Stan said Richie could join them again, there was nothing Bobby could do about it. And Stan would not let Bobby beat up Richie just because he didn't like him. If Bobby had a legitimate reason to challenge Richie, that would be another matter; Stan would not interfere, and Richie would have to take his whipping.

"Where are you living?" Stan asked.

"Cascade Lanes," Richie said. "I ain't told nobody else that," he added, glancing at Bobby Casey. His implication was clear to Stan.

"Don't worry," Stan assured him. "We won't tell nobody either."

"I can't go out nights," Richie informed him."I get regular work spottin' pins and I don't wanna lose it."

"We ain't been going out nights anyways," Stan said. "Bobby's old man's boozing again an' makes him stay home nights so's he'll have somebody to kick around."

Bobby Casey blushed and looked away, causing Richie to feel a pang of sympathy for him. Bobby was an unsmiling youth with tightly curled blond hair above shifty, unfriendly eyes. Somehow feeling Richie's sympathy, further embarrassed by it, he glared at Richie. "At least my old man ain't no junkie," he said spitefully.

"All right, lay off," Stan told him. "Didn't none of us pick who had us. My old lady brings home a different guy two or three times a week from the bar where she works, so what?" For a moment he stared off into space, a clean-cut boy with ordinary features made irregular by a slightly large lower lip that tended to give him a pout when he was concentrating. An easy smiler, he liked most people; although a good street fighter, he never bullied. "How 'bout Saturdays?" he asked Richie now.

"Yeah, I can go Saturdays."

"Okay, meet us by the el tracks on Crawford, Saturday at ten o'clock. I'll have some machines lined up."

"If you don't show up," Bobby Casey said, "we'll just figure you turned chicken."

Ignoring him, Richie bobbed his chin at Stan. "See you Saturday."

When Richie left, he walked past the building in which he and his mother had once lived, where Stan still lived, and was swept by a moment of melancholy. He had known some bad times in that building—but at least he had not been all alone. He and his mother had gone through those bad times together. Her being there, Richie had begun to realize, counted for something.

He wondered how she was doing in the hospital. Briefly he considered calling Miss Menefee and asking if the caseworker knew, but his instincts quickly vetoed that idea. He was afraid they might trace the call and catch him in the phone booth, like he'd seen happen in the movies. Anyway, he was pretty sure his mother was doing okay.

She usually did when she had somebody to take care of her.

One of the places Richie hung around to sell his shoplifted merchandise was the Midwest Athletic Club on Hamlin Avenue, where local boxers trained. On the second floor over a row of stores, it was a long, high-ceilinged place with three regulation-size training rings, heavy punching bags on chains, speed bags on ball-bearing swivels, corner areas with full-length mirrors on the wall for shadow-boxing and skipping rope, and complete locker and shower facilities in the rear. Across one side of the room were high windows that had to be opened with a long pole and looked out across the avenue to Garfield Park. On the other long wall was a balcony of spectator seats where for twenty-five cents one could spend all afternoon watching fighters work out.

It was worth a quarter to Richie to get into the balcony; most of the spectators, ninety percent of whom were men, were gamblers, grifters, hustlers, and others of dubious respectability. Almost without exception they were open to anything shady.

"Hey, mister, wanna buy a watchband?" Richie would ask. "Brand-new, half price."

Without a second thought, most of them said, "Lemme see 'em."

Richie would bring out his assortment of watchbands—or Zippo lighters, or Parker fountain pens, or cuff link sets, whatever he had—and the sharpies in the gym balcony would make their selection. Rarely did Richie get the half price he asked for; more often he settled for whatever they offered. "Give you two bits for this one, kid. Take it or leave it."

Once when Richie was peddling genuine leather wallets, one man, when he reached for the money to pay Richie, pulled back his coat and exposed a holstered pistol and a detective's badge on his belt. Instantly Richie felt ill. His face must have shown it because the man said, "Relax, kid," and paid him without even asking his name. After that, Richie felt totally at ease in the balcony of the Athletic Club gym. Some of the regulars even nicknamed him Marshall Field, Jr. It was a rare occasion that he was unable to dispose of whatever he had to sell there.

One afternoon when Richie was in Midwest earlier than usual, he saw down on the gym floor that one corner of the big room was being used by a slightly built older man and four boys in their mid-teens who were wearing boxing gear. The older man, who was bald from the top of his ears up and had an almost pained expression on his face, was giving the boys instructions in the proper delivery of a left jab. Richie was fascinated. He was aware that fighters had to train to stay in condition, but for some reason it had never entered his head that the training might include instruction in *how* to fight.

When Richie finished his merchandising, which that day consisted of snap-on belt buckles, he went down to the gym floor and stood off in a corner, watching. The bald man—whom Richie heard called "Myron"—finished talking to the four boys about the left jab and had them stand in front of the mirrored walls practicing it. When Myron came over to a bench to pick up a towel and pat the back of his neck with it, Richie walked up to him.

"Hey, mister, you teaching those guys to be fighters?" he asked.

"Trying my best," Myron replied wryly.

"Could you teach me, mister?"

"I think you're a little young yet, sonny. For club fights you're supposed to be fourteen."

"Club fights, what's that?"

"Amateurs," Myron said. "All the athletic clubs sponsor young amateurs. Kind of in teams. They fight at the different clubs. But like I said, you gotta be fourteen."

"I'll be fourteen in a few months," Richie lied. "Couldn't I just learn while I'm thirteen?"

"You're kinda small even for thirteen," Myron observed.

"I was sick for a while, but I'm okay now," Richie explained.

"Well, it don't matter anyways," the bald man told him. "Midwest only sponsors four kids and I already got four. Come back and see me next year. Couple of my kids'll be moving up to Golden Gloves then. Try to build yourself up, meantime."

"Sure," Richie said, disappointed. As he slouched away, a sudden thought occurred to him. "Hey, mister," he said, turning back, "what if I just watched? Over in the corner by myself?" Myron saw a pleading in the boy's eyes. "I really need to learn to fight, mister," Richie said.

"Jeez, I don't know," Myron worried. "I don't wanna be responsible for you hanging around a few days and then thinking you're a tough guy."

"It won't be like that, mister, I promise," Richie pleaded. "I'll learn, I really will."

"All right, I guess," Myron finally agreed, with the most pained expression yet. "You'll have to stay over there out of the way, though. Don't bother nobody. And don't say I told you it was okay."

"Thanks, mister! Thanks a lot!"

Taking off his coat and sweatshirt, Richie stood in his undershirt in the corner, studying how the four boys in boxing gear were practicing the left jab. Presently he began doing it himself. What he did not realize was that he was not watching the boys themselves, but rather their reflections in the mirror; consequently, he had assumed a left-handed stance and was practicing a *right* jab. Myron, watching, felt sorry for him because he was so pale and thin, while the boys Myron was training were well-nourished and ruddy. When he saw Richie using a southpaw stance, the trainer simply thought he was a natural lefthander.

Richie practiced the jab as long as the other boys did, then copied them as they did some calisthenics Myron showed them. Only when Myron finally said, "Okay, knock off. See yez tomorrow at three," did Richie put his sweatshirt and coat back on to leave. Walking out the door, he waved to Myron and the bald man nodded glumly at him.

"See you tomorrow," Richie called.

"Yeah, yeah." Myron did not really expect to see him again.

Richie felt elated as he hurried toward the bowling alley—*he was learning to fight!*—but when he got there, his buoyant spirits were rudely shattered. Bobby Casey was waiting outside.

"I wanna talk to you," Bobby said menacingly. "Come here."

Knowing what was coming, Richie went over to him. Richie could have cut and run, but he refused to do that, ever. On the schoolyard, the street, wherever it happened, he never gave any bully the satisfaction of running from him. Richie had learned long ago that if he stood and took his licking, the humiliation was less than if he ran, was caught, and then had to take it anyway.

"What do you want?" he asked Bobby Casey.

"I want you to forget about coming back in with Stan and me, that's what I want," Bobby said belligerently, poking a stiff forefinger against Richie's thin chest. "Him and me's doing just fine without you, see?"

"Stan said you'd do better with a third guy—"

Bobby grabbed the front of Richie's coat with both hands and jerked him forward. "We don't need to do better!" He shook Richie back and forth. "An' we don't need no chicken like you hangin' around!"

"I'm no chicken," Richie protested. "I'll do anything you'll do—"

"Yeah, anything but fight!" Bobby reminded him scornfully. "Just stay the fuck away, you hear me?" He let go of Richie's coat and shoved him back. "You hear me?" he insisted.

"Yeah, I hear you," Richie said, feeling his face flush, his throat constrict.

"You goddamn well better!"

Bobby stalked off. Tears welled in Richie's eyes and he hated it, but he could not control them. The bastards! he thought, infuriated. The dirty sons of bitches, all of them! Bobby Casey and every bully that had ever shoved him around on the schoolyard just to get a laugh from the other kids . . .

He'd get even someday, he swore in silent, surging rage.

*S*itting on the curb across the street from 3318 West Walnut, Richie, now a runaway for six weeks, studied the building and found that he was able to recall exactly how the apartment had looked seven years earlier when he and his mother had lived there with Estelle. As he sat there remembering, he periodically glanced down the block at a heavyset man leaning in a doorway. The man didn't seem to be paying any attention to him.

Looking back at 3318, he pictured the apartment. It had a small living room with a sofa that had three individual cushions on it; that was where he had slept, in a bed his mother made up for him every night. It had not been a comfortable bed; the cushions never stayed straight and he rolled off onto the floor at least once every night. There was a double bed in the bedroom, but Richie's mother and Estelle slept in it. The rest of the apartment consisted of a tiny kitchen, with a bathroom directly next to it.

They had lived on the first floor. Upstairs was a family with two daughters, Helen and Dorothy. Helen had been fourteen; Richie's mother often hired her to take care of him when she and Estelle went out for the evening. Chloe would give Helen money to take Richie and Helen's nine-year-old sister Dorothy to a double-feature at the Kedzie Annex. When the show was over and they returned home, Helen would send Dorothy up to bed while she remained with Richie until his mother got home. Richie had hated coming home from the movie house: although Helen pretended to like him when adults were around, she delighted in asserting her authority over him and mistreating him when they were alone. She frequently slapped his face and made fun of him because he had no father. And she warned him against complaining about the treatment. "If you tell on me, I'll sneak in some night when you're sleeping and snip your thing off with a pair of scissors," she threatened.

Sitting on the curb thinking about Helen, Richie looked back at the man in the doorway. He lighted a cigarette, glanced at Richie, then stepped out of the doorway and walked away. Richie watched him all the way to the corner, then turned his attention back to the apartment building and his memories.

Richie had always been able to tell when his mother and Estelle were going out. They would be in their housecoats, sharing a vanity bench in front of the mirror as they applied makeup. Richie made a habit of wandering in and pretending to build something with his Tinkertoys on the bed so he could eavesdrop on them. Usually he found out where they were going.

"Did Jack say where they were taking us tonight?" Estelle would ask.

"The Aragon Ballroom, I think," Chloe might reply.

"Oh, good. That one-armed trumpet player is there. You know, the one who got run over by a streetcar in New Orleans when he was a kid, and lost his right arm. Then learned to play trumpet left-handed—"

"Wingy Manone," said Chloe. "Yes, he's there."

"We going to Jack's after?" Estelle wanted to know. Chloe would throw Estelle a cautionary look, glance at Richie, and not answer. Lowering her voice, Estelle would say, "I declare, sometimes he's so quiet I forget he's around."

By then Richie would have heard enough to know how his evening would be spent: with Helen and Dorothy at the Kedzie Annex, then with Helen alone in the apartment. His mother always came home late when she went out with the man she insisted he call "Uncle" Jack. He would begin to wonder what excuse Helen would find for slapping his face tonight. He wished he could keep from crying when she did it, but he never could.

Presently, Chloe would say, "Run on into the other room, sugar. Aunt Estelle and I have to dress."

Aunt Estelle. *Uncle* Jack. Richie did not feel comfortable calling either one of them that, although he was not certain just why. His mother constantly had to remind him to do it, saying. "You want them to like you, don't you, sugar?" Richie always lied and said he did, but he did not really care.

"Pull the door closed on your way out, sugar," his mother would tell him as he took his Tinkertoys and left the bedroom.

On the living room side of the door, Richie would immediately look through the keyhole. Invariably he would see either Estelle or his mother remove her housecoat and put on step-ins and a brassiere. He liked it better when it was Estelle whom he saw; she had bigger titties and lots more hair between her legs, and for some reason that excited him more. Besides which, he was not altogether certain that he should be spying on his own mother like that. It didn't matter, he was sure, if he saw *Aunt* Estelle undressed. Whichever one it was, however, Richie was fascinated by the sight of them naked.

If only it had not meant he would have to be slapped in the face by Helen.

After looking at the building on Walnut Street and remembering the life he had there, Richie fished the piece of napkin from his Buck Jones billfold and looked at the address Estelle had given him. It was about two miles away— sixteen city blocks. He decided to see if she was home.

Walking along Kedzie Avenue, he was thinking again of Estelle's nice, big tits, when a hand reached out of a doorway and grabbed him by the arm.

"Truant officer, boy," a gruff male voice said. It was the same man Richie had seen earlier on Walnut Street. "What's your name and what school do you go to?"

"Lemme go," Richie said, resisting. "I ain't done nothing!" He struggled, but the truant officer's grip was too strong to pull out of.

"Why aren't you in school?" the man demanded.

"My mother took me to the doctor. I've got a cough." Richie coughed several times to prove it. The truant officer looked skeptical.

"You better come along with me, boy."

"Wait, there's my mother now," Richie said urgently. "Ma! Hey, Ma!"

The truant officer turned to look, relaxing his grip, and Richie wrenched free and bolted. In an instant he ran across the sidewalk, between two parked cars, and dodged traffic to cross the street.

"I'll get you, punk!" he heard the truant officer yell behind him.

When he looked back, he saw that the man was not even chasing him.

An hour later, scurrying mostly through alleys, Richie reached Estelle's address. It was a run-down three-flat converted into housekeeping rooms: bedrooms with a small sink and a hotplate to cook on, with the bathroom down the hall.

"Why, hello, sugar," Estelle said when she opened the door. She was wearing only a slip and her hair looked as if a cat had been trapped in it and fought its way out. The room itself was in total disarray; it reminded Richie of some of the places he had lived with his mother. "Come on in, sugar," Estelle said. " 'Scuse the mess; I slept late today."

Richie started to ask if she had gotten the job the man in the bar was supposed to have for her, but thought better of it. Instead he said, "I went over to the Walnut Street place. After I saw it, I remembered lots of things."

"Oh?" Estelle eyed him warily. "What sort of things?"

Richie shrugged. "Just things. Like those two sisters that lived upstairs— Helen and Dorothy. And how I used to fall off the couch at night 'cause the cushions wouldn't stay in place. You know, just different things like that."

"Oh." Estelle sat down at a card table covered with a piece of checkerboard oilcloth. Lighting a cigarette, she put the match in an already nearly full ashtray, and picked up a cup half full of black coffee. Richie sat across the little table from her. He wished she would put on a robe or something; her breasts were very distracting. The slip Estelle wore was pink, not sheer at all, but her breasts, much larger than they had been when Richie used to see them through the keyhole, were clearly outlined under the bodice of the garment. Every time Estelle moved to raise her cigarette or coffee cup, they shifted enticingly.

"What else did you remember about Walnut Street?" she asked.

"I remembered when that guy Jack started coming around; 'member, I had to call him 'Uncle' Jack? Do you think my dad went away 'cause he found out about Jack?"

"Why, no, 'course not, sugar," Estelle assured. Seeing the concern in his young face, Estelle's own expression, as it had when she talked with him in the bar, softened noticeably. "Your mother seeing Jack Smart had nothing in the world to do with your daddy going off. That's the god's truth, Richie."

"Why'd she ever start going with him in the first place?" Richie asked. "Why didn't she wait for my dad to come home from prison, like she was supposed to?" His last words had become a troubling, bitter thought, seeded by the image created by Mack: of Richie's father returning home from prison and finding his wife and little boy gone.

"Richie, honey, listen to me," Estelle said, reaching over to clutch one of his hands, "your mother *did* wait. She did. For a long time she waited. Why, even for a long time after we moved up here, she waited. Don't you remember how she'd sit at home with you night after night, reading magazines, listening to the radio, doing her fingernails over and over?

"She was thinking about your daddy all the time," Estelle insisted. "I know, because she used to spend hours on end composing letters to him, trying to explain where she was, and why she had moved away from Lamont. She showed me some of the letters and, I swear, honey, they like to broke my heart. She was suffering, Richie; she was *hurting* inside, she was so lonely. She had been without your daddy for three long years, and she couldn't help but blame him for not being with her. She had *begged* that man to get out of the bootlegging business; she had *warned* him that his luck was running thin, that the Federal agents were going to catch up with him. But your daddy was a hardhead if ever there was one. He never learned an easy lesson in his life. He didn't believe he'd *ever* get taken." Estelle let go of Richie's hand and patted it. "But he did. He got hisself sent to the penitentiary and left your mother all alone with a little baby to take care of."

Estelle sighed a weary sigh. "Your mother was resentful, sugar. She had a right to be. But she was faithful to your daddy for a long, long time. She'd sit at home night after night and write those long, heartbreaking letters to him and then she'd show them to me and I'd say, 'Why, Chloe, honey, this is a wonderful letter, you go right ahead and mail it,' and then first thing I knew I'd see it all torc up and thrown in the wastebasket. She never mailed one letter to your daddy after we came to Chicago—not a single one."

Staring sadly at the checkered table cover, Estelle blinked. Then she tamped out her cigarette in the nearly full ashtray, drank the last swallow of coffee, and got up to pour another cup. She felt the coffeepot and turned on the hotplate under it. Daylight from the room's single window made her slip diaphanous, outlining her fleshy thighs. Richie noticed but now was not preoccupied by them; his mind was still struggling with past inequities that he was trying to understand.

"But why did she start going out with Jack?" he insisted.

Estelle turned around and studied him for a long moment, her lips pursed in troubled thought. "How old are you now, sugar?" she asked.

"Going on fifteen." He lied so often about his age that the answer came out automatically before he realized that Estelle would probably know better. But to his surprise, Estelle did not challenge him; she merely frowned briefly, then nodded her head in acceptance.

"Do you remember—or did you even know—what happened to your mother just before she started seeing Jack Smart?"

Richie shrugged. "I guess I don't know."

"Well, I'm going to tell you," Estelle said, returning to the table with her empty cup. "Going on fifteen is old enough for you to know. Do you remember when your mother was working for the Grubb brothers, Ed and Lew? They were the plumbers; I used to date Ed and he came over to the apartment sometimes. Matter of fact, I was the one that got your mother the job—"

"Was that the place where she used to take me to work with her and let me play in the back room?"

"That's the one," Estelle confirmed. "That's where your mother first met Jack Smart . . ."

□

It was a little storefront office back then in 1937, on Van Buren Street, with GRUBB PLUMBING lettered on the window. In front of a partition was just enough room for two old wooden desks and a three-drawer filing cabinet. Behind the partition was a large supply room where Ed and Lew kept piles of various size pipe, elbows, catch-basins, toilet fixtures, and other accoutrements of their trade.

Chloe's job was to answer the telephone, quote the hourly rate the brothers charged, take orders for service, and take care of the billing and the daily mail. It was an easy job, the pay was fair, and the brothers had no objection to Chloe's bringing Richie to work with her and letting him play in the storeroom. The brothers came in first thing in the morning to pick up their work orders and supplies, then were gone most of the day. One of them usually came back by late in the afternoon to look over the day's messages. The rest of the time, Chloe was on her own. The only unusual part of her job was the man named Jack, who stopped in every morning around ten to either drop off or pick up an envelope.

"He's a runner for our bookie," Ed Grubb explained. "Lew and me, we play the ponies every day. We usually call our bets in when we're having lunch. If Jack drops off an envelope, it means we won the day before; if he picks one up, it means we lost. When we have to pay him, we'll leave the envelope in your top desk drawer."

Estelle, who clerked at a Walgreen's in the next block, had taken a few minutes off and walked down to see how Chloe was doing her first morning on the job. She was there when Jack Smart came in. A dapper, handsome man, he had an incongruous stutter that invariably surprised people.

"Hi, Est-st-stelle," he said, recognizing her from the drugstore. "Changing j-j-jobs?"

"No, but this is my friend Chloe," Estelle said. "She's working for Ed and Lew now."

"Pleased to m-m-meet you, Chloe," he said, holding out his hand. "I'm Jack Sm-mart." After they exchanged a few pleasantries and Chloe gave him the envelope that had been left for him, he said, "Maybe you'll l-l-let me take you out to d-d-dinner some night. We can d-d-double date with Estelle and Ed."

Chloe had politely turned him down, after which Estelle had chastised her. "For god's sake, girl, go out and have a little fun once in a while. You don't have to *sleep* with him, you know." But Chloe had declined to reconsider. Richie, listening to everything from the back room, was glad his mother was not going out with the man. He was still uneasy about this new place called Chicago, and he didn't want his mother going anywhere without him.

For Richie, the city was a strange, sometimes exciting, but more often frightening place, far different from the small Southern town where he spent his first four years. Streetcars and elevated trains were new sights for his young eyes, and made noises new to his ears. On the streets he saw black people dressed like white people, something he had never seen in Lamont. Instead of the yard of his grandmother's house, he played on the floor of the storeroom where his mother worked. The only thing that was the same was that his father still was not with them.

Playing in the storeroom of the plumbing office became, after a while, interminably boring for Richie. Chloe did what she could to keep him occupied; she bought him sets of toy soldiers, windup cars and trains, all manner of picture books, coloring books, cut-out books; she even tried to make up games that he could play by himself. But Richie could amuse himself just so long; then he wanted Chloe's attention. Sometimes he drove her to distraction, particularly when she was having a busy day. Even though it was a small, two-man business, there were invoices to prepare, account ledgers to keep up, telephone calls to answer, supplies to order. Sometimes she did not even have time to chat with Jack Smart when he made his daily stop to drop off or pick up the betting envelope. Jack continued to try and get her to go out with him, but was always polite and good-natured about it.

"How a-b-b-bout that dinner?" he would ask with his handsome smile, hurrying the words past the speech impediment that, as Chloe had discovered, was relegated to the ordinary by the rest of the man's personality and charm.

"Jack, how many times do I have to tell you no?" Chloe would reply patiently.

"T-t-two or three thousand more t-t-times ought to do it," Jack usually said, or "Not too m-m-many more. I think you're w-w-wearing down."

Sometimes he would bring her a bunch of posies that he bought on the street corner, and Chloe would put them in a glass of water, saying, "Jack, save your money." Other times it might be a bag of jelly beans for Richie, and she'd tell him wryly, "Won't work, Jack." But he always smiled, winked, and kept trying. Secretly, Chloe seemed pleased by the attention.

One afternoon, Estelle got off work early at the drugstore and stopped by the plumbers' office to take Richie off Chloe's hands for a couple of hours. "I'll take him for some ice cream and then over to Humboldt Park for a little while. There're some swings and a slickey-slide he can play on. It'll get him out of that back room for a little bit. I swear, I'll bet that child feels like he's in jail sometimes. Just like—oops, never mind."

Chloe was grateful for the break. She straightened Richie's clothes, combed his hair, admonished him to "be good for Aunt Estelle," and kissed him goodbye.

In the two free hours that she did not have Richie there, Chloe was able to accomplish as much as it usually took her a full day to do. Even when he was not bothering her directly, Chloe was always aware of her son's presence; if he was playing, she heard his little boy make-believe noises; if he was quiet, she knew he was bored and would be sitting against the wall staring at nothing, brooding, reminding her of Richmond when he had been in the Memphis jail awaiting trial. Although it was a great relief for Chloe to be away from Lamont, with its many real and imagined gossips, she nevertheless was acutely aware that in escaping she had also moved her son to a less desirable environment. Many times when she paused in her attempts to write a letter to her husband, it would be to consider ways in which she might somehow improve life for Richie. But without the money to enroll him in a private nursery, and disinclined to even consider sending him away to live with her mother, she was no more able to alter Richie's existence than she was to complete a satisfactory letter to his father.

One day Richie heard Estelle quietly broach the subject of sending Richie to live in Tennessee. "You know your mamma would take good care of him," she had said. "And, god knows, it'd make your life a lot easier."

"No, it wouldn't," Chloe disagreed. "You don't have children, so you don't know how it feels. I love Richie and I need him with me. He's *my* little boy. I wouldn't think of sending him to live with Mamma or anybody else."

Richie had felt good when he heard his mother say that.

On the day that Estelle took Richie to the park, Chloe was getting ready to close the office when Lew Grubb stopped in to look at the day's mail. Coming in the back door, noticing Richie's absence, he asked, "Where's your kid?"

"Estelle took him earlier," Chloe said. Of the two brothers, she, like most people, cared the least for Lew. Big and beefy, he often went unshaved, did not wear clean work clothes every day, and was less communicative, almost to the point of surliness, than his younger brother Ed. Today, Chloe noted as he passed her desk, was one of those days when Lew left a distinct body odor in his wake. "Here's the envelope from Jack," she said. "Do you need me for anything else before I go?"

"Uh, yeah, stick around a minute, will you?" Lew said. "I'll be right back . . ." Lew went into the storeroom. Chloe rolled her eyes toward the ceiling thinking, Keen—I have to hang around here while Gorilla Grubb relieves himself.

Turning to her desk, Chloe busied herself by restraightening everything on it. A couple of minutes later, Lew called her from the storeroom. "Chloe, come here a minute, will you? I wanna show you something."

When Chloe walked into the back, Lew stepped from behind the door, closed it, and stood against it. Grinning, he had his fly unbuttoned and was exposing an erect penis.

"What do you think of this piece of pipe?" he asked.

"Lew, for god's sake," Chloe said, more disgusted than frightened.

"Wait'll I get it in you."

"You're not going to get it in me," she assured him. Rape had not even occurred to her. "Please open the door, Lew—"

"Ed's been plumbing your girlfriend Estelle and says Southern nookie is sweet and wet. I wanna see for myself—"

"Lew, what Estelle does is her own business, but *I* am not about to—"

"Yeah, you are," Grubb said before she could finish. Grabbing Chloe's arms, he twisted them behind her and nibbled her neck.

"Goddamn you, Lew! Let me go!" Chloe tried to pull away but Grubb's big hands and powerful arms held on almost without effort. His unshaved cheek raked against her neck. She smelled whiskey on his breath. Calm down, she thought. Reason with him. Instead she said, threateningly, "Lew, you'll get in trouble over this—"

"Not if you wanna keep your job, I won't. 'Sides, you're gonna like it . . ." He pulled at the front of her dress, sending buttons flying; exposing her slip, he tore the front of it away from its shoulder straps. Chloe screamed. "Cunt," Grubb muttered. Spinning her around, he slapped her hard across the face. Chloe stumbled back but managed to scream again. "Shut up!" Grubb hissed urgently. Closing his hand into a fist, he hit her solidly on the jaw. Chloe dropped like a wet sponge.

On the cold linoleum floor, Chloe was vaguely aware that one of Richie's toy trucks was under her back, pressing painfully into her. Lew Grubb pushed her skirt up around her waist, held her hips up, and pulled down her step-ins. Kneeling beside her, he put one hand between her legs and rubbed while he moved the other hand up and down his erection.

"You got lots of hair," he praised. "That's good. I like nookie with lots of hair—"

Standing, Grubb dropped his trousers and shorts down around his boots and used both hands to force Chloe's legs apart. Getting between them, he lay heavily on her, reaching between them with one hand to work himself into her.

"God, no . . ." she said dizzily, her face throbbing with pain from the blow, Richie's toy truck beginning to cut her back.

Presently Grubb was inside her, but not thrusting as she expected him to do, not moving in and out; rather, he was violently shaking one booted foot to produce enough vibration to make his erection tremble. Closing his eyes, he groped at the breast in her brassiere with one hand and drooled into her ear as he made a humming-grunting sound, keeping with the rhythm of his foot.

Suddenly, Chloe saw a shadowy figure looming over Lew Grubb. The figure's hand, clutching a length of pipe, raised up and came down on Grubb's head with a muted thud, like the single thump of a rabbit's foot multiplied in volume many times. Groaning, Grubb dropped limply onto Chloe, his chin digging into one of her eyes.

"Get him—off of—me!" she yelled as her senses snapped back.

The length of pipe was dropped and two hands grabbed Grubb and rolled him on the floor. Then the hands were helping her up and draping a coat around her shoulders, and for the first time Chloe recognized who it was.

"Come on, let's g-g-get out of here," Jack Smart said.

"Okay," said Stan, as usual very serious and all business when it came to stealing. "First place we try is a cigar store I seen on North Avenue. There's two machines outside the front entrance, one gumball, one peanut, both on the same stand. The peanut machine is closest to the sidewalk. And listen to this," he flashed a quick grin, "from inside the store, you can't see the peanut machine because the gumball one is in the way. If we can get it, the guy in the store might not even know it's gone until somebody tells him."

They rode the streetcar to North Avenue, stopped in an A & P market to steal a large shopping bag, then walked to the store two blocks away. Across the street in a doorway, Stan said to Richie, "Me and Bobby'll take this first one. You get the guy to the back of the store. When we get it, we'll head down that alley there."

In the cigar store, Richie went to the rear and stood in front of the magazine rack. The man behind the cigar counter watched him for a minute, then yelled back, "What are ya looking for, kid?"

"My sister sent me to get a movie magazine for her. But she couldn't remember the name of it."

"How the hell ya gonna buy a magazine if ya don't know the name of it?"

"She said it's got a picture of Tyrone Power on the cover. In his Marine uniform." Richie had already scanned the row of movie magazines without seeing Tyrone Power on any of the covers.

The man at the cigar counter walked back and started helping Richie look for the magazine. Glancing past him, Richie saw Stan and Bobby move into the doorway, Stan blocking the machines from view and watching up and down the street, while Bobby, facing him, unscrewed the peanut machine from the stand.

"I don't see no cover with Tyrone Power in his uniform," the man finally said. "Why don't you take this one here, with Clark Gable in *his* uniform?"

"Could I see it?" Richie asked.

The man handed him a copy of the magazine. Richie pretended to study it thoughtfully, looking just over the top of the magazine at the store entrance. Usually, unless a vending machine was rusted on, it took less than a minute to unscrew it from the stand. This one obviously had not been rusted on; Stan was already holding the shopping bag open while Bobby carefully lowered the peanut machine into it. Then the two boys were gone.

"Well?" the man in the store asked impatiently.

"I better not," Richie said, with a feigned grimace. "My sister said Tyrone Power—"

Snatching the magazine from him and returning it to the rack, the man said, "Go on, beat it, kid. Tell your sister to come in herself." Under his breath, he muttered, "I'll give her something she'll never get from Tyrone Power."

Leaving the store, not even glancing at the two-machine stand that now only had a gumball machine on it, Richie hurried to the alley Stan had designated. Halfway down the alley, partly concealed by a wooden telephone pole, Stan had pried the bottom off the machine with a chisel and was scooping pennies into a paper bag held by Bobby. "Any trouble?" Stan asked tensely.

"No trouble," Richie said.

When the machine was out of pennies, the boys removed several bags of garbage from a big iron drum, put the machine inside, and covered it up with the bags of garbage. Then they beat it down the alley.

"The next place," Stan said as they hurried to the streetcar line, "is a dime store on Belmont. There's a Dentyne gum machine outside the front door. It can't be seen from inside by nobody but the woman at the front counter. That's the candy counter. Bobby, you go in and buy a nickel's worth of penny candy. You take your time picking it out, see? Richie and me'll act like we're waiting for somebody. Whenever there's nobody going in or coming out, we'll give the machine a couple of turns. It's one of them square machines, so it'll be easy to turn. Should be a cinch . . ."

□

On weekday afternoons, Richie put all other activity aside in order to go to Midwest A.C. and "train."

If he was short of money, which became more infrequent after he started stealing vending machines with Stan and Bobby, he took his chances on the street during school hours to filch off newsstands, steal deposit bottles, or shoplift. If he had enough money for a few days and wanted to go visit Estelle or Mack, he went in the morning and made sure he had plenty of time to get to the gym by two o'clock. The training regimen he had committed himself to was becoming almost as important to him as the search for his father. He somehow felt, without actually putting it into a conscious thought, that if he failed to find his father, what he was learning in the gym might somehow compensate.

Once, after the first couple of weeks, Richie had overheard Myron, the trainer, talking to one of the pro fighters about him. "I never seen a kid with such moxie in my life," Myron had said. "Skinny as a rail, don't look like he eats too good, and he definitely ain't the best-dressed kid I ever seen. Don't have no training equipment of any kind, nothing. But he works harder than any of the four kids on my team. Trains like a guy with a title shot."

After that, Richie worked even harder. Every afternoon, in a corner by himself, stripped down to his skinny waist, he listened, observed, and practiced, exactly as the four young club fighters did. Eventually they noticed him too. "Who's that, Myron?" they wanted to know.

"Just a kid that admires you guys," Myron said diplomatically. "He wants to be like you guys, but he's too young yet." Then a thought occurred to him. "Be nice if one of you guys let him use your jump-rope once in a while."

Finally the gym manager noticed Richie. "Who's that skinny kid in the corner every day?" he asked, around a cigar stub in the corner of his mouth.

Myron, who always tried to have an answer for every question, on the theory that it prevented further questions, replied, "He's kind of a mascot. We're kind of letting him hang around. It's good for the morale of the club kids to have somebody look up to them. But listen, if you don't want him around, I'll tell the guys you said we should get rid of him—"

"No, no," the gym manager quickly demurred, "no need to do that. No, he's okay." He removed the cigar stub from his mouth and nodded. "Mascot, huh? Good idea, Myron. Good idea."

The following day, Myron drew five towels instead of four from the locker-room attendant, and left the extra one in the corner so Richie wouldn't have to wipe the sweat off his face with his shirt. When Richie came in and found the towel, he looked over at Myron and smiled. The trainer, without smiling back, winked.

Later, when there was a heavy bag available, Myron motioned for Richie to come over. "What's your name, kid?" the trainer asked.

"Richie."

Myron handed him an old pair of training gloves. "These are a little big, but they'll do you. Pay attention and I'll show you a routine you can use to build up your arms and shoulders."

That day was the beginning for Richie and the trainer. From then on, Richie was part of the daily routine. As Myron did with each of the club kids, he selected individual exercises for Richie designed to strengthen particular weaknesses—in Richie's case just about everything, he was still so run-down. Myron even drew up a food program for Richie to follow. "Now be sure," he cautioned with his usual worried demeanor, "that your parents don't think I'm trying to tell your mother what to fix at mealtime. But if you get a chance to eat these particular foods, you should do it. They'll put some weight on you, build you up."

During the instruction periods of the training program, Myron positioned his club fighters with their backs to Richie's corner, so that Richie could get full benefit of whatever Myron was teaching that day. From long hours spent in the main library, from the necessity of constant deliberation in order to remain vigilant and survive, and from the conscientious reflection he was putting into the search for his father, Richie's ability to concentrate was honed to a keen edge. He was almost constantly on the alert, ready at split-second's notice to function at full capacity. In the gym, when Myron spoke, Richie's mind absorbed his words, thoughts, meaning, like energy from an electrical outlet.

"Today," Myron might say, "I'm gonna teach you a little bit about stance. You've already learned that the jab is the key blow of boxing, because it's delivered in both attack and defense. Stance is the basis of being able to deliver that blow, because it makes it possible to do so without losing your balance. And balance is important because it allows you, by the use of foot-work, to both move *and* punch at the same time . . ."

In the corner, Richie's mind, while absorbing and sealing in every word, was also thinking elatedly: Yeah! Sure! Because it all made *sense*. It exhilarated him to realize that the world was not forever divided into guys who could fight and others who could not. He was beginning to understand that a person could *learn* to fight.

Whenever he could, Richie would wait somewhere around Tilton Elementary and spend a few minutes with Linda. If he had on a new article of clothing, she would question him suspiciously, reminding him, "You promised me you wouldn't steal."

"I'm not!" Richie always swore, trying to muster indignation. "I don't have to, honest," he would try to convince her. "I'm working two jobs now. 'Sides spotting pins, I got a job in a gym, helping fighters train. I bring 'em towels and stuff like that. I'm making more'n enough to get by without stealing. Honest, I wouldn't lie."

With reservations, Linda believed him. Because she wanted to. "I'm glad you're all right, Richie," she said, holding his hand. "I'm always worrying about you, wondering where you are and what you're doing."

"You don't have to worry about me," he assured her. "I can take care of myself okay."

"Oh, sure. That's why you've always got scared eyes."

"What do you mean scared eyes?"

"Things show in people's eyes, Richie." She was talking beyond her years again. "Every time you got picked on in the schoolyard, I could tell how scared you were by your eyes. I bet you're a little scared all the time."

Richie shrugged self-consciously. "Nobody likes getting shoved around. Guys that know how to fight, they had to *learn* how, you know. Prob'ly their fathers taught them. If mine had been around, I'd prob'ly know how to fight too." He did not tell her that he was learning how now, from Myron. Instead, someday he'd show her, like the guy in the Charles Atlas ads who went back to the beach and knocked the shit out of the bully who kicked sand in his face.

"Are you getting any closer to tracing your father, do you think?" Linda asked.

"I might be. I'm learning a lot about him, I know that. Things I never knew before." He glanced at her. "What about your dad? He still watch out the window for you to come home?"

Linda blushed and looked away. "Yes." She quickly changed the subject, asking, "Did you finish those books yet? From the list I gave you?"

"Oh, sure." The list was still in his billfold; he had forgotten all about it. "I been reading mystery books too," he admitted. "Right now I'm reading one called *The Big Sleep*."

"Who wrote that?"

"Somebody named Raymond Chandler. It's real good."

"How do you manage to get the librarian to let you check them out? Every time I take a book from the adult section, they always catch it at the desk and take it back."

"These aren't library books. They're the little books that they sell in drugstores and dime stores, the ones that fit in your pocket. They only cost a quarter."

Stopping on the sidewalk and facing him, Linda raised one eyebrow.

"If they fit in your pocket, how would you know how much they cost?"

"I pay for them, honest I do," Richie protested. He stared at her eyebrow in fascination. "How do you do that?"

"Do what?"

"Raise just one eyebrow like that."

"I don't know, silly, I just do." They resumed walking, holding hands again. At the corner, Linda said, "You'd better stop here. Sometimes if I'm a few minutes late Pa comes out on the porch to look for me."

"Okay. I gotta get to the gym anyway."

"Come back to see me soon?"

"Sure." Richie started to leave, but Linda did not let go of his hand.

"Don't you want to kiss me goodbye again?' she asked.

"Oh, sure."

They briefly touched lips and then she let go of his hand. Parting, they went separate ways. They looked back frequently.

Later at the gym, Richie asked Myron if he had ever heard of "scared eyes."

"If you mean seeing fear in somebody's eyes, sure," the trainer said. "I never heard it called 'scared eyes' before, but I guess it's the same thing. Usually, if an opponent's frightened of you going in, you've got the fight half won. Some sportswriter in New York says it's a 'psychological advantage,' whatever that's supposed to mean. Way I figure it, all it means is that the guy that's scared is going to be thinking defense, instead of defense *and* offense. The guy he's scared of will be thinking both. That's the advantage."

"And it really shows?" Richie asked. "In a guy's eyes?"

"Absolutely. Haven't you ever seen it in the eyes of some kid that's been afraid of you?"

Richie grunted wryly. "No kid's ever been afraid of me. It's always me that's been afraid. But I never knew it *showed*."

Myron studied the boy for a moment, his own pained expression turning almost sorrowful. "Listen, I been thinking," he said. "If your parents wouldn't mind you staying out late on Saturday nights, how'd you like to come along to the club fights with me. You can help out in the locker room, maybe even work the corner with me."

"Jeez, you mean it?" Richie was thrilled. "Could I? Really?"

"Your parents have to say it's okay. I'll need a note or something."

"I'll ask 'em tonight," Richie promised excitedly. "It'll be okay with them. And I'll get a note saying so." He'd get the note after school the next day. From Linda, whose handwriting was as good as the teacher's. "I think I'll prob'ly have to be home by midnight," Richie qualified. He had to be hidden inside Cascade when it closed.

"Oh, you'll be home before twelve," Myron assured him. "The first bout is at seven. They're usually over with by ten at the latest."

After the training session that day, on his way to the bowling alley to go to work, Richie was exuberant. Myron was actually going to take him with the club boxing team; he was going to be *part* of it. It was unusual for Richie to feel good about something like that. Normally when he was included in a group—a classroom of students, half a dozen kids in a foster home, a long line of pin boys working the pits—he nevertheless remained detached as much as possible. He did not like running with a pack. It was much easier, he found, to rely only on himself and not others, to work only for himself, trust only himself.

With the boxing club, he felt different; he did not know why. Perhaps because there was no threat there, no danger, no price to pay. Myron liked him, the older boys liked him, even the gym manager had bought him a Coca-Cola one day. They accepted him for what he was: a poor kid with nothing, who wanted *something*. Their acceptance: that was new to Richie, because it was unqualified. Others extracted tribute: on the schoolyard, he had to pay with submission and humiliation; in the foster homes, it was with obedience, compliance; in the pits he paid in wariness and tension. Only in the gym did he feel at home.

As he turned the corner, Richie saw Bobby Casey waiting for him again outside Cascade. Ducking out of sight, Richie stood against the building and considered the situation. He was sure Bobby could still whip him, although it would not now be as easy as it would have been before Richie learned the proper delivery of a left jab. Bobby was after him because Richie had refused to chicken out in rejoining him and Stan on stealing forays—despite the fact that Bobby's share of the three-way split had been more than he had made on two-way splits in months. Bobby did not care about that. The reason, Richie knew, was Bobby's jealousy of Richie's friendship with Stan, which went back long before Stan and Bobby ever met.

Richie knew that sooner or later he would have to fight Bobby Casey. He wanted it to be later rather than sooner. The longer he could put it off, the more he would learn in the gym, and the better prepared he would be for it. Richie had never actually been in a fight, at least not one in which he did much more than try to protect himself. He never ran, but he never fought back either.

For now, however, he was faced with five hours of hard work in the Cascade pits, and he did not want to take a beating before he had to perform that labor. Pushing away from the building, Richie trotted back the way he had come. In the middle of the block, he crossed the boulevard into Garfield Park. Half a block into the park, he emerged on the Madison Street side and dodged traffic to get across to another section of the park. As he did, a police car cruised by and the two officers inside gave him more than casual looks. Jesus, Richie thought, hurrying on his way, looking over his shoulder to see if the car turned around. It did not. Stomach churning now, he dashed through the park, recrossed the boulevard, and entered the alley behind Cascade. At the rear of the bowling alley, he pounded with the side of his fist on one of the fire doors behind the pits. An old man who was a regular pin spotter let him in.

Observing Richie's tense expression, the old man asked, "Who's after you?"

"Who ain't?" Richie replied.

Away from the gym, there was still the rest of the world to contend with.

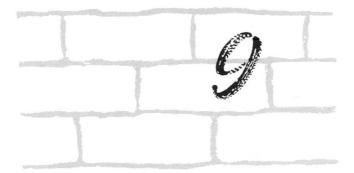

When Slim got off the Greyhound Bus in Chicago that day back in 1936 to search for his wife and son, he went to a Travelers Aid counter in the terminal and asked how to get to 3318 W. Walnut Street. The lady there wrote down instructions for him: take a Madison-Kedzie streetcar to the end of the line, transfer to a Kedzie–North Avenue car, get off at Walnut Street and follow the numbers. Apprehensive about getting around in Chicago, Slim was surprised at how easy it was. The largest place he had previously been was Memphis, which could have been set down in one small corner of this hulking, sprawling place. Chicago kept going on forever. It took Slim forty-five minutes to get to the end of the Madison-Kedzie line, another fifteen to ride the second streetcar to Walnut. Easy to get around if one followed the numbers, but it took a lot of time; the numbers, like the city, kept getting bigger.

At the apartment building at 3318, Slim learned that Chloe was no longer there. "She moved out before summer," the landlady said, studying Slim. "You a relative?"

"I'm her husband."

"I kind of thought you favored the little boy."

"Can you tell me where they moved to?" Slim asked.

"Gee, no. But I can tell you where you might find out. The other one,

Estelle, was going with a guy who tended bar in a place called the Dew Drop Inn, down on Sacramento. Know where that is?"

"No, ma'am."

The landlady gave him directions and Slim began walking. He was not surprised that Estelle was with Chloe; in retrospect he should have guessed it: they had been like sisters all during school and had maintained their best-friend relationship into adulthood. Nor did Slim object to them being together. Estelle was a little too loose in her ways to suit Slim; he knew half a dozen men back home that she had taken off her bloomers for, but by the same token, having been around a lot more than Chloe, she was, Slim guessed, probably able to handle herself a lot better. She would see to it that Chloe didn't get taken advantage of.

At the Dew Drop Inn, the barkeep on duty said, "Yeah, sure, I know Estelle. What ya looking for her for?"

"I'm looking for my wife. Name's Chloe. She's living with Estelle."

The barkeep thought about it for a moment, then said, "Well, I'll tell you, bud, Estelle ain't been in for a while. She was going with one of our bartenders here, fella named Bill, but she found out he was married. Try where she works, the Walgreen's over on Homan and Van Buren."

Getting new directions, Slim began walking again. It had been seven blocks to the Dew Drop Inn. It was eight to Walgreen's. Estelle had left her job there three months earlier. The manager thought she had gone to work for another drugstore somewhere in the area, but he wasn't sure which one or where. He asked if Slim had checked to see if they had a telephone; Slim admitted he did not know how, and the manager did it for him, but with negative results. "Nope," he said, hanging up. "Information's got no number for either one of them. Sorry."

After thanking him, Slim left and began walking up and down one street after another, inquiring about Estelle in every drugstore he came to. He walked for four hours, until he felt a blister on his heel begin to bleed from his new prison-made shoes. Finally he ended up back at the end of the Madison-Kedzie streetcar line. There he rented a sleeping room on the third floor above a used furniture store.

"No cooking allowed in the rooms," the landlord warned. "No playing the radio after ten o'clock. If the rent ain't paid the day it's due, I padlock the room."

It was a seedy little room that matched its landlord: squeaky bedsprings, cracked window shade, a single naked bulb hanging from the ceiling, a rickety dresser with a badly flecked mirror. But it was cheap. After the landlord left, Slim took off his shoes and socks, walked barefoot down the hall to the bathroom, and washed his blistered feet in cold water. Tomorrow he would buy some Dr. Scholl's heel pads before he resumed his walking search for the drugstore where Estelle worked.

When he got back to his room, Slim stripped to his underwear and lay down on the bed to look at a week-old newspaper he found in one of the dresser drawers. On the front page he read the first paragraph of a story about sit-down strikers occupying the Chevrolet plant in Flint, Michigan. That was as far as he got.

Completely done in, he closed his eyes and fell deeply asleep.

A month later, Slim sat on a bench in Garfield Park, leaning forward with his elbows on his knees, hands clasped together. Staring at the park lagoon, he pondered the predicament he found himself in. He was nearly broke, down to less than three dollars. He had not been able to find Chloe and his little boy, or locate Estelle. He could not take a chance asking for work anywhere because he had violated his probationary release from prison by leaving Tennessee, and was pretty sure that had been found out by now. And he did not want to try stealing because he was afraid he would not be any good at it and would get caught, which would mean going to jail, then back to prison, and probably never finding Chloe and the boy.

Sitting up, Slim pulled from his pocket a well-worn Chicago street map. On one side of it he had used a pencil to outline a square, block-by-block section of the West Side. Bounded by Homan Avenue on the west, Western Avenue on the east, Harrison Street on the south, and Fulton Street on the north, it was an area of approximately one-and-a-half square miles: ten blocks long and nine blocks wide. During the past month, Slim had walked some two-thirds of the area, inquiring at every drugstore he encountered whether they had heard of Estelle. He found two at which she worked for short times but had not stayed on, because either they had not liked her or she them. At the one that had not liked her, they unhesitatingly gave Slim the home address they still had in their payroll book. It was a building on Sawyer Avenue. Slim hurried to it, only to find that she was no longer there. But she *had* been there, and Chloe and the boy had been with her. At that location he learned of another bar Estelle was known to frequent, but like the Dew Drop Inn she was not coming around anymore.

Slim was certain that Estelle was both living and working somewhere within the penciled area on the street map. Every address where she had either lived or worked, and every bar where she was known was, without exception, within that area. It was only a matter of time, he was convinced, before he could track her down. And when he found Estelle, he would find Chloe and his son.

But he had to have money to carry on his search. And there were only so many ways one came by money. You could find it, beg for it, borrow it, work for it, or steal it. Slim much preferred to work for it. But he could not go to work for anyone who would ask too many questions, or want him to get one of those new Social Security cards that the government put into law a few months before his release. He had to work for someone who either didn't know anything about him and didn't care, or who knew *all* about him and didn't care.

Turning the map over, Slim studied it until he found Prairie Avenue on the South Side. With his finger, he traced the street some ten miles out from the downtown area until he reached 72nd Street. In his mind, etched there because he had seen it so many times in prison, was an address: 7244 S. Prairie Avenue. Pursing his lips in thought for a minute, Slim stared out at the lagoon, considering a plan. Abruptly, he returned the map to his pocket and took out his billfold. He had several small snapshots stuck in the corner of the currency section: one of Chloe and him sitting on a riverbank, one of Chloe and their boy when he was a baby, one of his own mother, and one of a diminutive woman with gray streaked hair, wearing an ankle-length black dress. Slim had never met the woman, but he knew much about her, and he knew that he would find her at the 7244 S. Prairie Avenue address. He had originally intended to mail the snapshot to the woman with a short note of explanation as to how he got it, but with the business of finding Chloe occupying his mind and time, he never got around to doing it. Which, as it turned out, may have been a good thing.

Returning the billfold to his hip pocket, Slim kept the snapshot and put it in his shirt pocket, buttoning the flap so he wouldn't lose it. With his mind made up then, he left the park bench and walked briskly toward the streetcar line.

The address was a formidable-looking, two-story red brick mansion. Slim guessed it had at least a dozen rooms. It was set back from the street like all the other large houses on the block, and had a wide walk laid in a series of steps leading to the front porch. There was no fence around it and no guards, as Slim had somehow imagined there would be.

Walking up to the front door, Slim rang the bell and waited. When there was no answer, he rang again. After a few moments of indecision, he left the porch and followed another walk down one side of the house to the rear. The backyard, he found, was enclosed by a brick wall that matched the house—not a high wall, perhaps five feet, with a wrought-iron gate leading to the alley. On one side of the yard, further enclosed by a low white picket fence, was what Slim recognized at once as a small vegetable garden. In it, dressed in the same kind of long, black cotton dress, was the woman in the photograph. A handbasket hanging from the crook of one arm, wearing old, soiled cotton gloves, she was methodically and selectively gathering vegetables from the dirt of the garden.

Slim stopped a few feet from the picket fence. " 'Scuse me, ma'am," he said, quietly so as not to startle her. He remembered that his own mother, when concentrating on something, had been easily startled. When the woman turned to look at him, Slim asked, "Are you Miz Teresa Capone?"

"What you want?" she asked matter-of-factly, not nearly as suspicious as Slim thought she ought to have been.

"My name's Howard, ma'am," he said. "I was a friend of your son down in, uh"—he glanced away, embarrassed, unable to speak the name of the prison—"down south," he finished lamely.

The woman squinted at him in the sunlight, then put one gloved hand up to shield her eyes. "Ina penitentiary?" she asked, her English broken. "You friend of Alphonse ina At-alanta?"

"Yes, ma'am."

"I'ma Alphonse's mamma," she acknowledged. She raised her chin an inch. "Teresa Riolia Capone."

Slim stepped forward, removing the snapshot from his pocket, and handed it to her. "Uh, this here is Al's, Miz Capone. He had to leave it behind when he went to, uh . . ." Again words failed him.

"Al-acatraz," Teresa Capone helped him again. Her voice became grave. "That'sa not very good place, you know?"

"No, ma'am, I heard it wasn't. I'm sorry Al, uh, Alphonse, got sent there."

Holding the snapshot, Teresa Capone studied the tall, fair, blue-eyed Slim. Tilting her head slightly, she asked, "Why a nice boy like you in At-alanta?"

Slim turned crimson, feeling like a little boy, feeling he was under the scrutiny of his own mother. This olive-complexioned little wisp of a woman in her long black dress, graying hair pulled together in the back, holding her handbasket of vegetables—it was as if she were looking at him with his dead mother's eyes.

"Why, huh?" Teresa Capone repeated her question. "Nice-a young man like you. Why in At-alanta pen?"

"I was bootlegging whiskey, ma'am," Slim mumbled like a schoolboy. "Back when whiskey was outlawed."

Teresa Capone sighed wearily. "Ah, me," she said, pulling off one cotton glove and putting the hand briefly on her forehead. "Whiskey, beer, wine,

bootlegging. This a funny place sometimes, America. Alphonse too, he bootleg. But they never catcha him, not for that. Ah, me." She looked curiously
at him. "Nice boy like you, where'sa you mamma?"

"She passed," Slim replied quietly. "She died while I was on the inside."
His expression darkened. "They offered to take me out for her funeral, but
they said I'd have to wear leg irons. I wouldn't do it, I wouldn't wear chains
to my own mother's funeral. So I didn't go."

Teresa Capone shook her head again. "Plenty worries ina world, that'sa
for sure." Putting the snapshot in the pocket of her dress, Teresa Capone
looked down at the basket of fresh-picked vegetables and asked, "You like
eat nice-a salad?"

Slim grinned widely. "Yes, ma'am! I grew up on a farm; I eat anything
that comes out of a garden."

"Here, you carry this," the woman said, handing him the basket. Putting
her cotton gloves between two pickets of the fence, she took Slim's arm and
led him toward the back door.

Thirty minutes later, his coat hanging on the back of the chair, shirtsleeves
rolled up, Slim was at Teresa Capone's kitchen table halfway through a large
wooden bowl of fresh carrots, cucumber, garbanzo beans, lettuce, and tomatoes, all mixed with slices of Genoa hard salami and shredded mozzarella
cheese, the whole of it laced with an oil-vinegar-herb-spice dressing as delicious as anything he had ever tasted. "This is wonderful, Miz Capone," Slim
told her with his mouth full. "Is this the salad Al used to brag on so much?"

"What'sa 'brag on,' I dunno," Teresa Capone replied. "But that'sa salad
Alphonse like-a best."

"Yes, ma'am, that's what I meant."

"Listen," she patted his arm, "You don't have to call-a me 'Miz Capone,'
You call-a me 'Mamma Teresa,' that'sa okay."

"Yes, ma'am. If you say so." Slim looked down, a little embarrassed,
and mumbled, "Mamma Teresa."

The little woman smiled and sat down at the table with Slim. Watching
him wolf down the salad, she nodded approvingly and asked, "You like-a
spaghetti?"

Before Slim could answer, there was the sound of a door slamming at
the front of the house, and a female voice called, "Mamma! We're home!"

Mamma Teresa rolled her eyes toward the ceiling. "Like I couldn't a-tell
from-a the door being slammed."

A moment later the kitchen was entered by two striking young women,
both with waist-length hair shiny as Algerian onyx, and large plum-dark

eyes. They looked like sisters, perhaps even twins. The only noticeable distinction between them was that one had a flawless olive complexion, while the other's face bore pockmarks on her left cheek.

The two stopped just inside the door, clearly surprised by Slim's presence. "Who is this, Mamma?" one of them asked.

"He's a friend of Alphonse, from At-alanta," Mamma Teresa said. Pointing at the young woman who spoke, she said to Slim, "This Alphonse's baby sister, Mafalda. And this"—she moved her finger toward the one with the scarred cheek—"is her-a cousin, Avellina Gela. She'sa called Ava for short. They were-a born on the same Day—Mafalda ina Brooklyn, Ava ina Naples."

Mafalda walked up to the table. "Who are you?" she asked Slim, her tone curt. Before Slim could reply, Mamma Teresa answered for him.

"I justa tol' you, Mafalda, he's a friend of Alphonse."

"How do we know you're Al's friend," Mafalda bluntly challenged Slim, ignoring her mother. "Anybody could walk in here and say that."

"Mafalda, you hush!" Mamma Teresa scolded. "You too suspicious, sounda like you brothers."

"Ralph isn't going to like this, Mamma," Mafalda warned.

Mamma Teresa looked at Slim. "I always worry whata Ralph don't like," she said sarcastically. At that moment, as if on cue, the front door slammed again. "Slama doors," Mamma Teresa complained. "Ever'body ina this family slama doors!"

Ralph Capone walked into the kitchen. He was swarthy and stocky, handsome in a fleshy way, immaculately dressed. Following closely behind him were two large men in suits. As the women had done, Ralph stopped short, taken aback by the sight of Slim. "What the hell?"

"You don'ta swear in this house," Mamma Teresa pointed a finger at him.

"Mamma says he says he's a friend of Al's from Atlanta," Mafalda told her brother.

"Mamma, Mamma," Ralph said, half chastising, half pleading. At the same time he made a barely perceptible motion to the two men with him and they immediately moved to each side of Slim, took him by the arms, and stood him up against the wall. Ralph came over and twisted his fist in the front of Slim's shirt. "Who are you, punk?"

"Like I told Miz Capone, a friend of Al's from Atlanta—"

"What's your name?"

"Al called me Slim."

"He never mentioned no 'Slim' to me."

"He never mentioned you to me either," Slim retorted.

"Don't get funny with me," Ralph warned, twisting the shirt tighter.

"Ralph, you stop it!" Mamma Teresa ordered. She waved the snapshot of herself in his face. "He bringa me this asa proof!"

Letting go of Slim, Ralph gave the photo a cursory look and handed it back to her. "He could've stole that, Mamma." When she started shaking her head, Ralph exhorted, "He was in a *prison*, Mamma! Prisons are full of thieves!"

"I believe-a him," Mamma Teresa declared, with heavy emphasis on the *I*. Barely reaching Ralph's shoulders, she tilted her face up defiantly. "If he no friend of Alphonse, how he know where we live, tella me that?"

Ralph's eyes rolled, as his mother's had done earlier. "Our address is no big secret, Mamma; it's been in the newspapers fifty times. Everybody in Chicago probably knows where we live!"

"Aha!" Mamma Teresa seized. "He's *no* from Chicago! That proves I'ma right!"

"Oh, Mamma!" Ralph turned back to Slim. "You claim Al told you to come here to the house?"

"I didn't say that," Slim corrected. "He just said if I ever came to Chicago, I could always have some kind of a job with his family."

"Why would he tell a hillbilly like you a thing like that?" Ralph sneered.

"I done him a favor," Slim said.

"What kind of a favor?"

"That's between him and me. You want to know, you'll have to ask him." Glancing past Ralph, Slim saw that Mafalda was frowning slightly.

"I don't believe you, hillbilly," Ralph said, putting a rigid finger in Slim's face.

"Don't believe me then!" Slim snapped back, his anger reaching the surface. "Tell these gorillas of yours to turn me loose and I'll beat it! And get your finger out of my face!"

Ralph colored and drew back a fist to hit him, but Mafalda said, "Ralph, wait!"

Ralph's head snapped around to glare at his sister. "You too? I'm supposed to be in charge around here."

"You *are*, Ralphie," the pretty young woman assured, quickly coming over to put a placating hand on his arm. "But what if Al did say we'd give him a job? He's going to be plenty sore if you break his word. You know how he is about his word."

Ralph stared at Mafalda, indecision in his eyes. Mafalda's own eyes flicked over to Slim, her glance seeming to say: *Keep quiet.*

"Listen," she said to Ralph, "why don't you play it safe? Find something for him to do, at least until Mamma and I visit Al again. Then we can ask him."

Thinking it over for a moment, Ralph finally expelled a tense breath and lowered his fist. But the finger went back in Slim's face. "I'm gonna keep you around until I hear from my brother. God help you," he warned, "if you're conning us." Nodding brusquely to the two men holding Slim's arms, he said, "Take him across the alley to the garage. Tell Mack to find something for him to do."

"The first time I met your dad," Mack told Richie eight years later, "was when Ralph's boys brought him over. The Capone garage was across the alley from the backyard of the house. All the family cars was parked there, and I kept 'em serviced and clean."

Mack was sitting on a low stool in his own garage, putting brake shoes on the wheels of an old Nash sedan. Richie sat next to him on a wooden box, eating a Baby Ruth.

"Your dad told me all about what happened in the house. Didn't surprise me none. Ralph was Al's older brother, you know, but he'd always been second to Al in running the Capone family, and I guess he always felt kind of funny about that. Actually, he wasn't even in the rackets for a long time. He had a lot of legit jobs: Western Union messenger when he was a kid, then he was a longshoreman, then a bartender. He was even in the Marines in the First World War. It was only after Prohibition come in that Al talked him into finally joining the organization. When Al got sent up, it naturally fell to Ralph to take over. He tried his best; he just wasn't the man his brother was."

"Did my dad really do Al Capone a favor in prison?" Richie asked, fascinated by the gangster lore.

"You bet," Mack verified. "Did him a *big* favor. Your dad told me all about it—in confidence, of course."

"What kind of favor?"

"Well, I'll tell you how it happened, just like I heard it. When Slim got to the Atlanta pen, he was assigned to an eight-man cell, one of the big bullpen cells, they called them; all the prisons used to have them. Already in the cell was two mail-truck robbers, a former judge serving time for graft, a con-man promoter, a mail fraud swindler, a safecracker named Red Rudensky, and Big Al Capone, king of the Chicago rackets. Al had been convicted of income tax evasion and was serving ten years.

"Well, your dad felt pretty much like an outsider in that group. All the rest of 'em were from up North, and aside from the judge, were really professional criminals. So Slim kind of became a loner and kept pretty much to himself, and the others in the cell, why, they couldn't figure him out, so they just left him alone. Big Al, he was real tight with Rudensky, used to call him 'Rusty.' Rudensky, he'd worked for Al at one time, picking locks on government warehouses so's Al's boys could steal back Canadian whiskey that the Feds had seized. So Red got to be Al's right-hand man in Atlanta.

"Anyways, like I said, your dad went his own way, minded his own business, did his own time; all's he wanted to do was finish his stretch and get back home to you and your mother. But out on the yard one day, Slim heard some young punk say he was gonna get Capone because he said Al slighted him. Al was always running into that problem; some punk would wave at him in the yard and if Al didn't wave back, the punk would get a burr up his ass—didn't make no difference whether Al even saw him or not.

"Anyhow, this particular day some punk moved in on Al with a shiv, and Slim, because he'd overheard the guy say he was gonna do it, got in his way, took the shiv away from him, and flattened him right there on the yard. The guy got up and fought Slim, and both of 'em ended up in the hole.

"Well, Rudensky, he found out what happened and told Al about it. When Slim got out of solitary and come back to the cell, Al asked him why he done it. Slim, he said it was because Al was his cellmate, said he'd have done the same thing if it'd been the judge or Rudensky or any of the others if the punk had gone after them. See, even though your dad kept to himself, he still felt a loyalty to the men in his cell. Well, Big Al Capone, you know, that was the kind of thinking he understood. In his own way, Big Al was always a very upright individual. He was proud of the fact that his word was his bond, and he never went back on it.

"As it turned out, your dad and Big Al and Red Rudensky became the best of friends." Mack paused in his work and smiled. "Your dad said they were the funniest-looking friends in the whole prison: Slim, a tall, blond hillbilly bootlegger; Al, a roly-poly dago gangster; and Rudensky, a great big, strapping red-haired Jew from New York. They stayed friends for the rest of the time they were together, which was about a year. Then Al got transferred to the Rock."

"The Rock?" Richie asked.

"Alcatraz." Mack's face turned sad. "His family had paid over a hundred thousand dollars in bribes to keep him from being sent there. It was a brand-new federal prison, converted from an old military jail. The Feds designed it for all the big-time Prohibition outlaws that was making headlines back then: Doc Barker, Machine Gun Kelly, Alvin Karpis. It was set up to be the country's hardest prison, with the toughest rules: silent system, no time off for good behavior, dark cells, only one visitor a month—that sort of thing. What hurt Al the most was that his only kid, Sonny, who was fourteen, wouldn't be allowed to visit at all. Al was crazy about his kid; Sonny was partly deaf from a mastoid infection—that's some kind of ear trouble—and Al liked to see him as often as possible. But he knew on the Rock he couldn't.

"Well, despite all the bribes and all the high-priced lawyers and all the appeals, they decided to transfer Al to the Rock. Your dad said that when the guards came to get him, they told Al he had to leave all personal belongings behind, including his family photographs. Al went berserk. You know, Al was shorter than average, and looked a little fat, but lemme tell you, he was strong as an ox. And he knew how to use his dukes too; he'd been a bouncer at one time in a real tough joint back in Brooklyn; that's how he got the scar on his face—fighting some guy who pulled a knife on him. Anyways, your dad said it took six guards to drag Big Al out of that cell and get him shackled to a seat on the Alcatraz Express. When another guard came in and started collecting Al's belongings for disposal, your dad managed to swipe the snapshot of Mamma Teresa that Al had taped to the wall."

"So everything he told Ralph Capone was the truth," Richie said.

"Right down the line," Mack confirmed.

"And Ralph let him stay? And that's how he came to work for you in the garage?"

"That's the way it happened."

"Did he still keep on looking for me and my mother while he was working for you?"

"Oh, sure. That was his whole point of getting a job with the Capone family. There was no chance of him being turned in for violating his probationary release, and he could still keep on trying to find you. He went out every night, prowling that section of the West Side that he had marked on his street map. He never quit looking, not even after he got in trouble and had to go into hiding."

"What kind of trouble?"

"With Ralph Capone. Ralph had ordered him killed. He had guys out combing the city for your dad."

"Did they catch him?" Richie asked, wide-eyed.

Mack slowly nodded his head. "Yeah. They caught him all right."

*I*n the locker room of the Legion Park Athletic Club, Richie watched as Myron got their first fighter ready for his bout. The kid's name was Frankie Broski and he weighed one-hundred-eight pounds. He had blond hair cut in a flattop, over sharp Polish features. Myron was rubbing Frankie's shoulders to loosen up the boy's trapezius muscles, which, if too stiff, would affect both the speed and power of a punch thrown with either arm.

"Gimme his jacket," Myron said, bobbing his chin at a blue-and-white zipper jacket with MIDWEST ATHLETIC CLUB lettered across the back. Richie handed Myron the jacket and Myron draped it around Frankie's shoulders.

A man stuck his head in the door and yelled, "Third bout! Hunnerd-and-eight pounds! Let's go!"

"Let's go," Myron repeated, throwing a towel over his shoulder and picking up a zippered bag containing a first-aid kit, four hard-rubber mouthpieces, a dog-earred copy of *Rules of Amateur Boxing*, and a miscellaneous selection of shoelaces, adhesive tape, extra protective cups, and jockstraps. Richie grabbed a wooden bucket containing a quart milk-bottle of water with a rubber bathtub stopper in it to prevent spills.

As the trio left the locker room, the other three Midwest A.C. fighters yelled their encouragement: "Go get him, Frankie!" "Tear him up, Frankie!" "Take him apart, Frankie!"

At the same time, from another section of the locker room, Frankie's opponent, with his trainer, was also leaving, amid shouts of support from the other Legion Park fighters. Sitting across from the Midwest fighters were several boys from the Scandinavian A. C., who were also on the night's card. They all laughed when one of them said, "Couple of creampuffs. It'll be a draw."

Myron led the way out to the ring, Frankie, already gloved, right behind him, Richie bringing up the rear. Richie had been helping Myron for a month now, and as usual was wide-eyed: he thought the clubs were the most exciting places he had ever been; each Saturday night was a more arousing experience than the previous one, each trip with Myron and the Midwest A.C. fighters an intoxicating event. He was taken by the sight and sound of the crowd, the electricity in the air, the tension of the evening. None of it looked seedy or cheap or tawdry; he saw nothing brutal in what was happening, nothing pathetic about those who watched, sensed nothing savage in the scene around him. To Richie, it was magnetic, it was magical, it was *real*.

In their corner of the ring, Myron climbed through the ropes, held them apart for Frankie, and guided the fighter onto his stool. Richie knelt just outside the ropes with the water bucket and the zippered bag. The noise of the crowd engulfed him; at club fights it never stopped, only subsiding a little as the two young battlers were being introduced, then erupting as each of their names and respective athletic club affiliations were announced: ". . . in the red trunks, at one-hundred-and-eight pounds, from the West Side, fightin' outta the Midwest At'letic Club, wit' a amatoor record of t'ree wins and one defeat, here's pop'lar Frankieee Broskiii!"

The two boys met in the center of the ring with their trainers where the referee told them to fight a clean fight and made them go through the ritual of touching gloves. When the moment was over, the boys and their trainers returned to their own corners. Myron pulled the jacket off his young warrior's shoulders and handed it to Richie. In that instant, Richie would always look closely at the fighter to see if he had scared eyes. The fighter almost always did. But as Myron had pointed out, the other fighter usually did too.

"Seconds out!" the referee called.

Richie hopped off the ring apron and Myron came down the steps to stand next to him, one hand on the stool, ready to pull it out when the fighter rose to answer the bell. Club fights were three rounds of two minutes each for preliminaries, four rounds for main events, occasionally five rounds for special matches—third fights, when each fighter held a victory over the other, which they called a "rubber" match, or bouts between undefeated fighters who had never fought each other. However long a bout was to be, as Richie would later learn, its most terrible moment for the young fighter was that great, hollow void after the trainer had left the ring and before the opening bell sounded. It was an emptiness that a fighter felt all the way into his bowels and his balls; a warm, dry, weakening feeling that at the same time tickled and started a surge of elation coursing through him, like climaxing sexually with a totally repulsive partner. The feeling could only be checked by that first bell of the bout. It was the sound of the moment of manhood. No one who ever experienced it was ever completely a boy again.

Up close, Richie watched the blood sport and loved it.

When it got warm enough, Linda would meet Richie in Garfield Park on Sunday afternoons and use her movie money to buy hot dogs and soda pop for them from vendors who could not sell in the park but pushed their carts along the perimeter sidewalks. They sat on a bench and ate, watching people float around the lagoon in rowboats rented at the park boathouse. As usual, they talked about books.

"Miss White belongs to a reading club," Linda told him. Miss White was Linda's teacher at Tilton, and Richie's former teacher. "She and the other members of the club buy all the new books and then exchange them among themselves every week. Whenever Miss White finishes a book early enough, if she thinks it's suitable for me, she loans it to me. I have one of her books at home now called *The Song of Bernadette*, by Franz Werfel. It's really a beautiful story, about a young girl in France who is visited by the Blessed Virgin."

"Sounds real good," Richie said, hoping he sounded sincere.

"What are you reading this week?" Linda asked.

"*The Maltese Falcon*, by Dashiell Hammett," he said. "You prob'ly never heard of it."

"I haven't," she shook her head. "How do you pick out what you read, anyway?"

"I picked this one out because I read another by the same guy, called *The Glass Key*, and I 'membered liking it. But most of the time I just read the first page and if it's good I take—I mean buy—the book."

"I heard you the first time, Richie, you little crook," she said, catching his slip of the tongue. With her fist, Linda punched him on the arm. Then, as was often the case, she gripped his arm with both hands and laid her head on his shoulder. "Richie, I'm so afraid you'll get caught and be sent to reform school."

"Don't worry, they're probably not even looking for me no more," he tried to reassure her. Even though he knew it to be a lie. They never stopped looking for people. Especially kids who had the guts to break their lousy rules.

Sometimes Linda made an unexpected comment about her home life.

"My mom and dad have been fighting a lot lately," she said one day. To Richie that did not sound too terrible; they had to *be* there to fight. "I think it's over me, but I'm not sure," she added.

"Why would they fight over you?" Richie asked.

"Dad says Mom's jealous because she thinks he likes me more than he does her," Linda explained.

"Does he?"

Blushing, she glanced away and replied, "I think so."

Other times, Linda seemed to forget her own life in lieu of curiosity about his. "What's it like," she asked, "*living* in a bowling alley?"

"It's not so bad," Richie shrugged. "Not as bad as it was at first. I'm kind of used to it now. I've got three bowling-ball lockers, see? The lockers are big enough for a ball, a pair of bowling shoes, talcum powder, and whatever else a bowler wants to keep there. Okay, in one locker I keep my blanket and a small pillow. In another locker I keep my extra clothes; I fold everything real nice so it stays neat. An' in the third locker I keep my other stuff—books to read, the school notebook I carry around during the day, extra stuff to eat at night—cheese, crackers, vienna sausages, pork-and-beans, Twinkies. I keep wooden Dixie Cup spoons to eat with, my toothbrush and toothpaste, a box of Rinso to wash my underwear and socks with—"

"How do you wash yourself?" Linda wanted to know.

"I spread paper towels on the floor, fill one of the sinks with hot water, and use soap from the dispenser."

"You mean you just stand there *naked?* In the *ladies'* room?"

"It's one o'clock in the morning," Richie said. "There's nobody there but me."

"Still and all, don't you feel funny?"

Richie shrugged. "Not any more." He went into his John Garfield: "After Red, the manager, locks the place up, that bowling alley is *mine*, see? I do whatever I want."

"Yeah, well you just better hope you don't ever get caught in there, Mr. Tough Guy."

"I don't get caught."

"Sure, I know." Suddenly she grinned. "Know what?" she asked, leaning over to kiss his cheek.

"What?"

"I think it's cute that you fold your clothes so nicely."

Richie turned red. "Cut it out."

As the weather became increasingly warmer, they met in the park first without coats, later without sweaters, and the first time Richie saw Linda in just a cotton blouse that spring he noticed a slight swelling in front and found himself surprised to realize that her breasts were developing. Why he was surprised, he did not know; he was certainly aware of breasts in general and some even in particular. Noticing Linda's made him think of Helen, the girl that his mother used to leave him with; the one who had slapped his face a lot; her breasts had been about the same size that Linda's now seemed to be.

"What are you looking at?" she asked once when she caught his eyes on her. Richie had blushed and turned away.

"I wasn't looking at nothing."

Linda took his arm and leaned her head on his shoulder. "It's okay, silly. I guess we must be growing up faster than we know." Squeezing his arm, she then commented, "You're not as skinny as you used to be, I don't think."

"Myron, my friend at the gym, wrote me out a diet," Richie told her. "It's got stuff on it to build me up. I try to go to Thompson's Cafeteria once a day and pick out the stuff Myron wants me to eat. I been drinking malteds with an egg in them too. Costs a nickel extra."

"When you pay the check, you mean."

Smiling, Richie said, "I always pay the check now. Mainly 'cause I always eat at the same couple of places. In the fry joint across from Cascade, the counter guy don't even make me pay ahead of time anymore. One day he just stopped asking. I guess he's seen me in there so often he must trust me now."

When it was time for them to part on Sundays, they tried to find a place in the park where no one was close by so they could hold each other and kiss. Their kisses had progressed from those first quick touchings of pursed lips into longer, flatter, twisting meshes that sometimes they broke only when they needed more breath. Because she liked to kiss, Linda never resisted overtures to do so, which he now made instead of her. All she did, when they were embracing and she felt his hand moving up under her arm, was gently push it back to her waist. Neither of them ever spoke of his attempt or her restraint; it was simply something that he had to try and she had to check.

Richie realized that Linda was right about one thing that spring: they *were* growing up faster than they realized.

One Saturday night three months after Richie started going to the gym, at the Calumet Athletic Club on the South Side, Myron hung up the receiver of a pay phone in the locker room and looked thoughtfully at Richie, who was helping three of the four Midwest fighters put away their street clothes as they got into their trunks and ring shoes.

"Richie, come here a sec," Myron said after a moment. Richie hurried over. "All this time you been watching the guys train, doing what they been doing, listening to me like they did, right? So tell me, do you think you learned anything?"

"Sure," Richie said enthusiastically. "I guarantee you I did!" Inside, Richie knew exactly what was up. Myron's next words confirmed it.

"Dutro ain't coming," the trainer said. "He's sick." Sammy Dutro was the club's one-hundred-two-pounder. Myron's eyes flicked up and down Richie. "What do you weigh now?"

"Hunnerd, hunnerd and one," Richie said. His blood was racing.

"You wanna go in as a sub for Dutro?" Myron finally asked.

"Yeah! You bet!"

"Ordinarily I wouldn't consider doing this without having you spar with somebody so's I could see how you handle yourself, but unfortunately we ain't got time for that. I'll just have to take your word that you've been learning these past weeks. I know you got the moxie for it. Main reason I'm doing it is that this kid you'd be fighting, this is only his second fight an' he lost the first one, so it ain't like I'm putting you in with no Golden Gloves champeen. So, are you game to try it?"

"I'm game," Richie emphasized. "Yeah, I'm game!"

"Okay." Myron bobbed his chin toward the gear bag. "Get out Dutro's shoes and see how they fit."

The shoes were a little too big, but not enough to bother him; Richie had been wearing stolen galoshes two sizes too large for him all winter. He was still a year under the minimum club fighting age of fourteen, but now that he had gained some weight and built himself up he could easily pass muster. Myron gave him a new jockstrap and protector cup, and Richie put on Dutro's blue boxing trunks, which were also slightly big in the waist and which Myron took in with a safety pin. They were barely ready when they heard from the door, "Okay, let's go, opening bout, hunnerd-and-two pounds!"

"I'm first?" Richie said, as much a realization as a question. He stared at Myron with wide eyes.

"Somebody's gotta be," Myron said matter-of-factly. To one of the other boys he said, "Georgie, grab the water bucket for this fight. Let's go."

"Bust him up, Richie," one of the remaining Midwest fighters encouraged. "Tear into him, Richie," the other said.

Richie nodded, smiling weakly. Across the locker room he saw his opponent from the Calumet Athletic Club being sent out with a loud team cheer of some kind. Richie swallowed drily as Georgie Miller, one of the other club fighters who was carrying the water bucket, nudged him to follow Myron.

The aisle leading to the ring was at least five miles long, and Richie was sure there were ten thousand unfriendly faces glaring at him as he walked it. Each of the three steps leading up to the ring apron was as high as a wall, and the ring itself, when he finally, miraculously, got into it, was a vast prairie of canvas with a seemingly endless expanse of space in which to run, but not a single place to hide. Richie felt the old sickness that always came when he walked into a new schoolyard.

Sitting on the stool in the corner, a towel instead of a club jacket around his shoulders, Richie heard Myron ask, "What's your last name anyways? I don't even know."

"Huh? Oh, Clark," Richie said, using his mother's maiden name. No one was looking for him under the name of Clark.

Myron walked out to give the information on his substitute fighter to the announcer who would introduce him. While the trainer was away from the corner, Georgie Miller, in language none of the boys was allowed to use around Myron, said, "Kick the shit outta this fucking punk, Richie."

"Sure, sure," Richie said, trying for John Garfield but not even coming close.

He was only vaguely aware of Myron returning to the corner and bending over him; off in the distance he heard occasional disconnected words: ". . . what you learned in the gym . . . proper stance . . . correct delivery of the jab . . ."

From the loudspeaker above the ring he heard, ". . . club fight debut . . . a hunnerd-and-two pounds . . . from the West Side . . ."

Then, with shocking suddenness, all the preliminaries, the parts Myron called the priming and the rites, were over, and with a resounding noise that sounded as if it were directly next to his ear, the bell rang. Staring out from the corner where he now stood, Richie was surprised to see that the vast canvas prairie had shrunk to the approximate size of a door mat and moving quickly across it toward him was the Calumet A.C. fighter.

Richie's instincts took over: he moved out of the corner and brought his arms up defensively, just as he always did in the schoolyard. Backing up in a tight circle, he allowed the Calumet fighter to hit him at will, keeping his head and face—ears, nose, lips—as well hidden behind his raised arms as he could. Most of the blows he took on the forearms, elbows, upper arms; there had been times, after his first day at a new school, when his arms looked like he was in the early stages of leprosy, and he could barely move them to get dressed, eat, or use a pencil. In the ring now, being hit with gloves instead of bare knuckles, Richie found that the punishment was less intense. For the full two minutes he protected himself like that without once retaliating.

Back in the corner after the round, Myron said, "That's an unusual defensive tactic, but it'll never win you any points."

The referee came over and said to Richie, "Start t'rowing some punches or I'll disqualify yez."

"He will, he will," Myron assured. To Richie he said, "Remember the jab. Everything starts with the jab. Pop, pop, pop, right in your opponent's face. Break his rhythm, get him off balance. Pop, pop, pop. I know you can do it."

The break between rounds could not, Richie thought, have lasted more than ten seconds, and then he was being pushed out of the corner again. Arms automatically going up, he went into his shell again. There was some scattered booing from the spectators. The Calumet fighter was pasting him again and the referee said, "I'm warning you, Midwest, I'm gonna disqualify yez."

Richie came out of his shell at that, went fluidly into a southpaw stance, and let go with a right jab. It snapped the Calumet fighter's head back. Richie heard Myron yell, "Good! Good!" He went back into his shell. The Calumet fighter moved in and battered him some more. After another thirty seconds the referee said, "Come on, Midwest, fight!"

Richie let loose the right jab again. It landed solidly, stopping the Calumet fighter in his tracks. While he stood there, Richie fired it again. *I can hit this guy!* he thought, exhilarated. *I can fight back!* When the Calumet fighter came forward again, Richie met him with the jab. Then he went into his shell and backed up, but this time it was not defense, it was strategy: when the Calumet fighter started after him, thinking he would pound on him as usual, Richie unfolded and shot the jab three times in rapid succession. The Calumet fighter stopped dead again; this time, instead of ducking back into his shell, Richie took one step to the right and peppered him in the face with the jab. By the time the Calumet fighter regained his composure and moved back out of range, Richie saw that his face, around the nose, had turned fiery red. As the Calumet fighter retreated, Richie, inspired, lunged in and hit him four more times. Confused by Richie's unusual style, he flailed out with several wild punches but all of them missed. Richie had begun to stick the jab in his face again when the bell rang.

"Congratulations, you just won your first round," Myron told him in the corner, "and you done it with only one hand. Next round I want you to start using the *other* hand too. Left-handed fighters have their best power in the left hand—"

"I ain't left-handed," Richie said, heaving breaths, "I'm right-handed."

"Whaaat?" Myron looked incredulously at him. "Then how come you box out of a left-handed stance?"

"That's how I learned in the gym, watching the other guys in the mirror."

"The mirror . . . ?" Myron's mouth hung open as he shook his head. "Well, I'll be a dirty name," he said, mainly to himself. Then to Richie, "Are you comfortable fighting that way?"

"I guess," Richie said, his bare shoulders raising and lowering with his answer. "I can hit the guy fighting that way," he added.

"You can do that, all right," Myron agreed. "Okay then, fight like that."

In the third round, Richie stayed out of his defensive shell more than he stayed in it. When he was in the shell, he continued to take most of the Calumet fighter's punches on his arms and shoulders; when he was out, he pop-pop-popped his right jab into his confused opponent's face with relentless regularity and precision accuracy. Only now and again was the Calumet fighter able to hit Richie in the face or stomach, and then not with any punishing power. Richie was amazed at how much easier it was to take a punch with boxing gloves than without. And also amazed at what a constant jab could do to an opponent. By the final bell, the Calumet fighter's nose was bleeding steadily.

Winning the third round by a comfortable margin, Richie was also given round two and declared a decision winner.

"I won!" he said over and over as they all walked back to the locker room. "I won, Myron!"

"You did indeed," the trainer said, with a rare, if weak, smile.

"I won, Georgie!"

"Yeah, yeah, I know."

"I won! I can't believe it—I actually won a fight!" Richie kept up the announcement all the way up the aisle as Myron shook his head resignedly and Georgie tried not to be embarrassed. Once in the locker room, Richie continued to marvel aloud at his success, even after Myron had returned to the ring with Nick Bolly, Midwest A.C.'s 120-pounder. The others in the locker room ignored him; they had all been through first wins and knew Richie would get over it easily enough. What was hard to handle was the first loss.

To Richie, however, who had lost so many times in so many ways, no such fate awaited him. He was a winner now.

Later, on the streetcar going back to the West Side, Myron handed out their "prizes": seven dollars and fifty cents for winners of the three-rounders, ten dollars for the boy who won the four-round co–main event, three bucks for the one boy who lost a three-rounder. The prizes were not official; on record, the boys were amateurs and did not get paid.

When they got back to the Midwest, the three regular fighters went their separate ways home and Richie, as usual, helped Myron carry their equipment bags up to the deserted gym. Then Myron, as usual, took Richie down the block to a café and bought him a cheeseburger and a malted, with an egg in it, while he himself had a bowl of soup and a glass of milk.

"Tell you what," the trainer said as they ate, "I'm gonna talk to the president of the club on Monday and ask him to let me put you on the regular roster—"

"Jeez! You mean it?" Richie was ecstatic.

"It'll mean showing two fighters at the same weight—you and Dutro are bot' hunnerd and two—but there won't be no problem getting matches 'cause nearly all the meets involve three clubs. I think I can get 'em to go for the extra dough, 'specially after I tell how you won tonight. You wanna 'nother cheeseburger?"

Richie shook his head. "I'm full, thanks anyhow, Myron. If they approve me, will I get a jacket and everything?"

"You bet. First-class all the way. I'll have to get some forms signed by your folks."

"Can I take them home to be signed?"

Myron glanced curiously at him. "I suppose," he said after a moment. "Say, what kinda work does your dad do, anyway?"

"Delivers beer."

"Oh. Route man, huh. Your mother work?"

"Yeah, she works in a drugstore."

"I notice you been gaining weight. Your mother using the diet I made out for you?"

"Yeah."

Myron looked at him as if contemplating further questions, but finally gave up on it. The kid apparently had an answer for everything, but was not about to volunteer any information.

When they finished eating and left the café, the somber trainer and the boy said goodnight. Myron started walking toward the streetcar line on Pulaski Road. Richie went in the opposite direction; half a block down, he ducked into a doorway and waited until Myron was out of sight, then cut back toward Cascade.

Feeling good, feeling confident, feeling for a change like something besides a running, hiding, scurrying little rodent of some kind, Richie walked with a new bounce to his step, a new balance in his legs, a new swing to his arms. He had *won* tonight! He had faced another kid and for the first time in his life had not been humiliated, pushed around, or beaten up. And now Myron was going to try to get him on the club team, to be a real fighter just like the other guys: train with them, have a jacket, a locker in the gym, everything. First-class, Myron had said. Richie could not help grinning. He *was* going to be like John Garfield!

As he approached Cascade, Richie saw Pete sitting on the curb, his gaunt frame folded like a puppet. Richie's face darkened. Pete better not mess with me tonight, he thought, squaring his shoulders. I don't care if he is a grown man; I'll let him have one right in the mouth, then run like hell. He won't expect it, he'll be off guard; maybe I can get in a right *and* a left . . .

But Pete only glanced at Richie and made no effort to move. As Richie passed him, he saw that Pete was staring forlornly into the gutter. Richie paused in the bowling alley entry to look back at him. After a moment, he walked over to him.

"Hey, Pete, you okay?"

"Beat it. Leave me alone," Pete growled. Under his breath, he added, "Little prick." Richie stood there, trying to think of something to say. Presently, Pete started rambling. "Goddamn Red won't let me work no more. Won't even let me spot goddamned open bowling in the daytime. But he lets a little shit like you work the goddamned leagues five nights a week. You got a mother an' father to give you a place to sleep, but I ain't even got four bits for a flophouse bed. Go on," he said again, "beat it!"

Instead, Richie knelt next to him and held out a dollar bill. "Here, Pete. It's the forty cents I owe you. Plus interest." Pete stared at him in disbelief. "Go on, take it," Richie said. He pushed the bill into one of Pete's hands.

Walking away, going into Cascade, Richie mentally chastised himself. Sucker, he thought scornfully.

11

*F*or several weeks after Lew Grubb tried to rape her, Chloe had refused to leave the apartment. The first ten days, she would not even get out of bed. There every day, helping Estelle take care of her, was Jack Smart. Jack came over in the morning and helped Estelle fix breakfast for Chloe and Richie, and to see how Chloe had done during the night. He could not stay long; by nine he had to be on his route, making pickups and leaving payoffs for his bookie employer. But he always returned around noon, sometimes with a bag of White Castle hamburgers, or lunchmeat and rolls from a deli. Estelle, who had given up on drugstores and gone to work for Woolworth's, could not get home for lunch, so Jack took it upon himself to see that Chloe and Richie had a good lunch.

Sometimes when Richie was in the kitchenette eating, if he listened very carefully he could make out what his mother and Jack Smart were talking about in their confidential tones in the bedroom. He did not understand what a lot of it meant, but he knew by his mother's voice that she was upset. Chloe had heard horror stories about the city; she was terrified not only that she might be pregnant but that she had caught something from Lew Grubb. Jack tried to reassure her.

"I d-d-don't think he was, you know, f-f-finished, was he? I mean, he was still g-g-going when I hit him, wasn't he?"

For the first few days, Chloe was too distraught to be pacified by the fact that Grubb had not ejaculated. But gradually Jack Smart's dependable presence and easy manner had a positive effect on her. He quietly and gently refused to let her give in to the situation; when she dwelled on it and became maudlin, he teased her out of it and cheered her up; when she became fearful of the future, he found some way to bolster her confidence, even offering to help her find a new job when she was ready. "I got l-l-lots of connections," he bragged, trying to impress.

After Chloe finally left her bed and began to sit at the table for meals, Jack Smart made a habit of joining them for supper, frequently bringing the main course with him: a chicken, a bucket of chili, hot dogs, beans. Obviously taken with Chloe, Jack tried to impress both her and Estelle by enhancing himself.

"I'm not just a s-s-sharpie," he emphasized. "I don't just l-l-live from day to day like a lot of people d-d-do. Not me. I've got p-plans. I'm a g-good card player; I p-play nearly every night after I leave here, and I s-save what I win. Soon's I have enough dough p-put away, I'm going back to Gary, Indiana, where I c-came from, and I'm going to open myself a b-bowling alley. Indoor recreation, that's the c-coming thing." He jerked a thumb at his chest. "I'm going to get in on the g-ground floor."

Chloe could not help being drawn to Jack Smart. Not only had he saved her from that animal Lew Grubb, but she realized that he was the first man she had ever met who had a real purpose in life. "I know this sounds funny," she defended her position to Estelle, "but you just think about it for a minute. Did you ever know Richmond to make a plan in his life—unless it had something to do with brewing, transporting, or selling hooch? And think about all the boys we knew back home. Remember the things they were going to do when they got out of school? One was going to become a flyer, one wanted to get into pictures, one wanted to hitchhike around the world. Far-fetched! Jack might be a gambler, but at least he's working *toward* something."

"Sounds to me like you're trying to talk yourself *into* something," Estelle observed.

"I'm not doing anything of the kind," Chloe demurred. "But you know as well as I do that as soon as Richmond gets out of prison, he'll go right back to bootlegging. He can still bootleg in Tennessee; half the counties stayed dry. I don't want that anymore, 'Stelle. I don't want it for me and I don't want it for Richie."

It pleased Chloe as she recuperated to see Jack trying to win Richie's approval while he tried to win her affection. Jack brought the boy Baby Ruth candy bars, Richie's favorite, and picture books and building blocks and toy cars. He always found a few minutes to sit and play with Richie, and never failed to give him a nickel for the Good Humor man the next day. Richie accepted the gifts, and enjoyed them, but nevertheless had reservations about this new man in their lives.

It was when his mother began going out on dates with Jack Smart that Richie was left in the care of Helen.

Being left with her was an even more cogent reason for Richie to dislike Jack Smart. But as he wished harder and harder for his daddy to come home and run Jack Smart off, he could see his mother and the handsome, stuttering man becoming closer and closer. And he heard his mother become angry at Estelle because she took exception to the relationship.

"I can't believe my ears!" Chloe proclaimed. "Aren't you the one who kept telling me to get out of the apartment and have some fun?"

"I didn't mean for you to go this far," Estelle countered. "I surely didn't mean for you to be unfair to Richmond."

"What about him being unfair to me?" Chloe demanded. "Leaving me all alone with a little boy to raise! He knew I couldn't get along by myself . . ."

Chloe burst out crying, and Estelle, as she had always done, embraced and comforted her. "Don't cry, honey," Estelle said. "I'm not trying to be mean to you. I just can't help thinking that with Jack you're jumping out of the skillet into the fire."

"But he *cares* for me, 'Stelle," Chloe tearfully pleaded. "He wants to do something for the two of us, together. He's not such a loner like Richmond. I *need* somebody, 'Stelle."

"I know you do, honey," Estelle said, patting her head. "God knows, I know you do."

Jack took Chloe and Richie to Cascade Lanes one Saturday afternoon to show Chloe how a bowling alley operation worked. "There's n-not much to it, really," he said. "Once you g-get a location, the bowling alley supplies firm will put in the alleys on a t-time p-payment plan, in exchange for which we agree to b-buy all of our bowling balls, pins, score pads, and stuff like that from them. 'Course, th-they have a lien on the place until it's p-paid off. That usually takes about t-ten years. It could be done faster, if the m-money comes in right. Way to start making a profit right off is to sign up a lot of leagues; that's t-team bowling, sponsored by companies and c-clubs and things. That's why I want to g-go back to Gary; league bowling is very b-big with the steelworkers there."

While Jack taught Chloe to bowl that day, and was giving her a rudimentary introduction to how the business operated, Richie was allowed to wander around and look at things, as long as he remained in sight. It was his first exposure to a bowling alley and he was fascinated by the lights, the noise, the pinball machines, the perpetual motion.

As they rode the streetcar home, Richie, sitting in the seat in front of them pretending to concentrate on looking out the window, heard his mother ask Jack, "How long will it be until you have enough money to get a location, hon?"

"I need to win b-big in just a few more poker games," he told her. "I already g-got my eye on a spot in Gary."

"It all sounds so exciting, hon! Gee, I hope you don't lose any of the money you've got so far."

"I'm a very c-c-conservative player," Jack said. "I don't l-lose often, and when I do, I don't l-lose much."

Listening, Richie was not sure what poker was, but he did have a child's understanding of winning and losing. He hoped fervently that Uncle Jack would lose.

Chloe started trying to condition Richie for the change she anticipated in their lives. She had noticed how fascinated he had been at Cascade. "Wouldn't it be nice, sugar?" she ployed. "Our very own bowling alley! Just imagine!" Eventually she drew him onto her lap and said, "Listen, how would you like for Uncle Jack to be your new daddy?"

"I don't know," Richie replied vaguely, directing his attention to one of his shoelaces. Chloe put a knuckle under his chin and turned his face back to her.

"Pay attention to me, please. You like Uncle Jack, don't you?"

"Yes." He knew that was the answer his mother expected. It often re-sulted in a toy or a candy bar or a nickel.

"I like him too," Chloe said. "When I'm with Uncle Jack, I don't feel so scared."

"What are you scared of?" Richie wanted to know.

"Life, sugar," his mother told him in a moment of searing honesty. "Life all alone. Life without a man."

"I can be your man," Richie said. Chloe squeezed his face between her palms.

"You are my man. My little man. But I need a big man too."

"Isn't Daddy your big man?"

"He used to be." She bit her lower lip, then forced a painful smile. "But he's been gone too long now, sugar. Besides, he wouldn't get us a bowling alley like Uncle Jack will. We want that bowling alley, don't we?"

Richie did not answer, and she did not make him. When Jack was around, Chloe dismissed the boy's reticence as natural. Of his stubborn refusal to call Jack "Daddy," she said, "He's just bashful, hon. He really does like you a lot."

"S-sure," Jack agreed. "He'll c-come around." Jack playfully mussed

Richie's hair, and Richie hated it. In his mind Richie kept thinking: I hope you lose.

Richie knew from the beginning when his mother and Jack Smart became intimate. The first time it happened in the apartment, he was lying on the floor on his stomach, using crayons to carefully and methodically fill in the figures in a Buck Jones Big-Little Book. "Sugar, Uncle Jack and I are going to take a little nap," his mother said. "You go on coloring like a good boy, hear?"

Richie nodded and went on coloring, seeming to pay no attention to the adults. He had learned very early that the more he pretended to show no interest in what grownups were saying or doing, the more they were likely to say or do with him around, and the more he got to hear and see. When his mother and Jack went into the bedroom and closed the door behind them, Richie unhurriedly finished coloring Buck Jones's gunbelt, then got to his feet and went quietly to the bedroom door. Looking through the keyhole, he saw Jack remove his trousers and undershorts, and his mother, skirt pulled high, step-ins off, hose rolled and gartered around each thigh, lie back on the side of the bed and raise her bent legs up, widely apart, to let Jack lie over her—his feet still on the floor, arms braced—and begin bouncing up and down on her like some funny man in a comedy short subject. Richie was aware of two things: they weren't taking a nap, and he wasn't supposed to see what they were doing. He watched until Jack stopped bouncing, then quietly returned to his coloring.

A couple of times Estelle had brought a boyfriend home, paid Helen and sent her upstairs, and, thinking Richie was sound asleep on the couch, taken her boyfriend into the bedroom. Richie, who frequently only pretended to go to sleep but rarely did until everyone else was sleeping, always watched Estelle and her boyfriend through the keyhole. He liked watching Estelle take all of her clothes off, liked watching her suck on her boyfriend's thing with her mouth. It made him feel very funny.

It was not long after Chloe started dating Jack Smart that she and Estelle moved from Walnut Street to a place on Kedzie Avenue, above a butcher shop. It was the same size apartment, one bedroom, but they had to pay less rent because Estelle knew one of the butchers and went out with him. Richie liked the new place better; Kedzie was a commercial street, with a streetcar line on it, and always seemed to be busy and interesting. He never tired of watching all the different people who passed by—local merchants and their customers, streetcar drivers and conductors who plied the tracks endlessly in both directions, children going to and from nearby Biedler Elementary school, patrolmen on the beat, newsboys delivering their papers, delivery trucks, stray dogs and cats—always someone or something moving, starting, stopping, going, coming, returning: a street of perpetual ebb and flow, that was Kedzie Avenue.

One Saturday afternoon, sitting on the windowsill with his knees drawn up, Richie was playing a game he made up, picking out people who looked like they might be crooks on the "Gangbusters" radio program, or outlaws on "The Lone Ranger." He tried to match their faces to the voices he had heard: the unshaved, burly ice delivery man fit a growling, rough-talking character, while a slight little man with thick eyeglasses could easily go with the soft-spoken master criminal who usually led the gang. Sometimes Richie would switch them around, imagining the meek voice in the burly man, the gruff voice in the little guy; that was amusing and made him laugh quietly to himself. He was laughing at just such a combination when suddenly he saw on the street a tall, lean man with darkish blond hair, standing idly in front of a barber shop. Richie's eyes grew wide and he stared incredulously at the man.

The face of the man was familiar to Richie from a framed photograph that, for as long as Richie could remember, his mother had kept displayed wherever they lived. Only since Chloe had become serious about Jack Smart had she relegated the picture to a drawer of an end table next to the couch. Sliding off the windowsill, Richie went quickly to the drawer and got out the photograph. Hurrying back, he held it up, flicking his eyes from the face in the frame to the face of the man in front of the barber shop. His eyes grew wide again.

It was his father.

Head snapping around, Richie bit his lip as he looked at the closed bedroom door. They were in there, his mother and Jack Smart. But maybe they hadn't started yet . . .

Hurrying to the door, Richie looked through the keyhole. They *had* started; two naked bodies were locked together on the bed, and good old Uncle Jack was bouncing away. Richie ran back to the window. He had been warned not to open any windows because his mother was afraid he would fall out and kill himself. But he didn't care, he was going to open this one. Putting the photograph aside, he climbed back on the sill. In front of the barber shop, his father—Richie was certain it was him—put his hands in the pockets of his trousers and walked slowly toward the corner, looking around. Bracing himself in the windowframe with one hand, Richie tried to open the turn-lock in the center of the window. The lock would not move; someone had painted over it and it was sealed shut.

Getting down from the window, Richie's expression changed from urgency to panic. Back at the bedroom door, he saw that Jack was still bouncing and had his head bent, sucking one of Chloe's titties. *Hurry up!* Richie thought frantically. If Jack would just hurry and finish, Richie knew his mother would presently come out and go into the bathroom. Then he could stop her and tell her about his father. Rushing back to the window, he saw his father loiter momentarily on the corner, take a toothpick from his shirt pocket and put it between his lips, and continue looking around.

Impulsively deciding to break another rule of Chloe's, that he never leave the apartment alone, Richie started for the door to go down the long flight of stairs next to the butcher shop and, once on the busy street, call out to his father. As he hurried toward the door, he heard from the bedroom a low, ecstatic moan from Jack, followed by a hissing shush from his mother. Pausing indecisively, Richie's worried eyes darted from front door to bedroom door, back and forth, as he tried to make up his mind what to do. The low moan meant that Jack had finished bouncing; his mother would come out in a minute or two, spreading that funny smell wherever she went. She would, Richie instinctively knew, have a better chance of reaching his father than he would. Going to the bedroom door again, he looked through the keyhole and saw Jack lying half on the bed, breathing heavily, holding a Kleenex on his thing, while Chloe was getting into a housecoat for her trip to the bathroom.

Relieved, Richie returned to the window—and there his relief instantly faded. His father was no longer on the corner. Or, as far as Richie could see, anywhere up and down the block. Awash with dread, Richie pressed each cheek to the windowpane in order to look as far as he could each way down the busy street. A streetcar was on its way; Richie wondered if his father had got on it. And there was a tavern where men came and went nearly all day on Saturday; might he have gone in there? Maybe he had simply walked around the corner. Whatever, wherever, he was gone. One cheek still pressed to the pane, Richie felt his tears run down and fall on the glass.

Hearing the bedroom door open, then close again, he knew his mother had come out. Straightening, he kept his back to the room so she would not see that he was crying. At that moment he hated her for making him lose his father again, and he hated Jack Smart for taking so long at what he had been doing. Both fists clenched on the windowsill, Richie stared straight ahead until he heard the bathroom door close and knew he was alone again, for the moment anyway. He used the backs of his hands to wipe away his tears. His mother would come out of the bathroom in several minutes, smelling of toilet water to cover the odor she brought from the bedroom. She would speak to him then, saying something like, "Sugar, are you having fun looking out the window?" She never spoke to him on her trip into the bathroom because, he knew, she did not want him paying any attention to her smell and her sweat and the the funny look she always had on her face after Jack had bounced on her.

Tears wiped dry, Richie waited patiently for the bathroom door to open. When it did, he heard his mother's light step across the room, followed by her cheerful voice, a voice he could remember loving but would love no more, asking, "See anything funny out the window today, sugar? Any fat ladies or midgets?"

Turning to her, face emotionless, Richie replied, "I saw Daddy."

Chloe frowned. "What?"

"I saw Daddy. He was standing down on the corner with his hands in his pockets and a toothpick in his mouth, looking around." Pointing to the photograph on the floor, he added, "I got out the picture to make sure. It was Daddy, I know it was."

Picking up the photograph, Chloe stepped up behind her son at the window and searched the street with her eyes. Her face had turned marble white, and her lower lip quivered. Richie heard her whisper a barely audible question to herself.

"My god. Is he out?"

From the very beginning, Mack and Slim got along like old friends. They were truthful, direct, and totally unpretentious with each other. Slim never treated Mack like a cripple, and Mack appreciated that. Mack believed Slim's story about helping Al Capone in prison, and Slim appreciated that. When Ralph Capone's men brought Slim out to the garage with orders from Ralph for Mack to find something for him to do, Mack's first inclination was to use him just to wash and polish the cars and sweep out the place when it needed it. But when they took to each other so quickly and naturally, Mack started teaching Slim some of the rudiments of automobile mechanics.

When Mack was not teaching him engine work, Slim still had to do the washing and polishing. Pulling one of the cars into the alley between the garage and the mansion's backyard, he hooked up a hose, took off his shirt, and went to work. Frequently observing him over the brick fence were Mafalda and Ava. Standing on a bench in the yard, they ate homemade spumoni out of cups and teasingly discussed Slim as if he were not there.

"He doesn't look bad without a shirt on," Ava said. Her English was only slightly accented, a much softer version of the way Mamma Teresa spoke.

"Kind of pale," Mafalda pointed out.

"Probably been staying indoors a lot."

"Most convicts do, Ava."

"Are his eyes blue or green?" Ava asked innocently.

"Blue," Mafalda said.

"You know what they say about boys with blue eyes," Ava reminded. Both girls laughed uproariously.

Slim ignored them when he could, letting them have their fun. Sometimes his lack of reaction piqued them and one of them, usually Ava, unmarried and less reserved, would address him directly.

"Boy, you missed a spot there on the fender."

"I'm not a boy," Slim said quietly, wiping the sweat off his bare chest. His eyes locked with Ava's. "And I never miss anything," he added pointedly.

Ava blushed furiously and was trying desperately to think of a suitable retort when Mamma Teresa scolded both young women from the garden. "You girlsa leave that nice-a young man alone! Letta him work! Come ina the house right now, I finda something for you to do." As she left, Ava stuck her tongue out at Slim. Shaking his head, he laughed softly. It was the first time he had laughed in a long time.

Slim lived in a sleeping room on Wabash Avenue, a few blocks from the garage. Ralph Capone never mentioned anything to Mack about paying Slim, so Mack, who had a bank account to run the garage, decided what he thought was a fair wage and began paying Slim in cash on Saturday night. Slim bought a few clothes and some decent shoes, finally throwing away the prison brogans, and started saving as much as he could against the day when he found Chloe and the boy and could take them back down south.

Slim's search for his wife and son was continued with quiet relentlessness. He had been hoofing it in a plotted zigzag pattern all over the central West Side for so many weeks now that he no longer even had to refer to the street map on which he'd outlined the area in pencil. Having long since inquired about Estelle in every drugstore within the boundary he had adopted, and not uncovering any fresh leads at all, Slim now turned to the small taverns and clubs of the type he had been referred to by the Walnut Street landlady when he first arrived in the city. It made for a more tedious search since most of the bartenders, unlike the one at the Dew Drop Inn, were close-mouthed and not inclined to give out information, even when they had it. Occasionally Slim caught a hint of recognition in someone's eyes at the mention of Estelle's name, but when he finally did coax them into talking about her it usually resulted in old information that Slim had already checked. Nights were long and frustrating as Slim walked Madison Street, Kedzie Avenue, Sacramento Boulevard, Lake Street, Van Buren, Albany, Wilcox, Congress, a score of others—checking every bar in every block of every street until some nights he felt like a zombie: a walking dead man released from the grave of prison and set loose to wander forever the netherworld that was Chicago.

He let nothing deter him. "Maybe they ain't even in Chicago no more," Mack suggested once, after observing him search futilely every night for a month.

"They're still here," Slim replied grimly. "I can feel it."

He kept searching.

One night it paid off.

In the Shuffle Club on California Avenue, a friendlier than usual bartender answered his query by saying, "No, I haven't seen Estelle for quite a while. I see that friend of hers, Chloe, once in a while. She comes in with her boyfriend, guy named Jack Smart. You know them?"

"Know her," Slim said, his stomach knotting, "don't know him."

"He's a small-time card player, usually in a game in some back room."

"He play here a lot?" Slim asked.

"Once in a while. We don't have that many games here. Why?"

"I was thinking," Slim lied, "if I could catch him he might be able to tell me where Estelle's living. If I give you a telephone number, could you call me when you know he's going to play cards here again?"

"Could, I guess." The bartender shrugged. "What's it worth to you?"

Slim gave him five dollars and the telephone number at the garage. "Five more if you find him," he said.

The next night, he started a new search, for a card player named Jack Smart.

During the day as he worked around the garage, Slim had difficulty concentrating on what he was doing. He knew nothing about Jack Smart except his name and the fact that he was a small-time card player, but Slim could not get the man out of his mind. It was a faceless image: a suit and hat, a pair of hands dealing cards. Chloe would always be in the background of the scene, watching. Chloe, the wife he loved, the woman he had never been certain would wait for him . . . and who apparently had not. His little boy was never in the scene with Chloe and the faceless man, and that more than anything caused dark thoughts to spawn in Slim's turmoiled mind. Where was the boy? Who was looking after him? Slim had always known Chloe was vulnerable, dependent, needed someone to lean on and be there for her; he was not shocked that she had taken up with Jack Smart. What troubled him was that she might have grown so weak that she put her own needs before the needs of their little boy. That he could not condone, would not forgive. When he found them, if Chloe wanted to stay in Chicago with her card-playing boyfriend, that would be all right with Slim. He would cause her no trouble. Providing the boy had been properly cared for, and providing Chloe let Slim have him with no fuss. If not, if he found out the boy had been neglected, or if Chloe tried to prevent him from taking the boy back to Tennessee, there would, Slim vowed, be trouble the likes of which neither Chloe nor Jack Smart could imagine.

His head filled with so much consternation, Slim's expression was somber, his attitude brooding, as he went about his chores at the Capone garage. Mamma Teresa noticed it and tried to cheer him up. Calling him into the house on the pretext of having him move a cupboard or a table for her, she would fix him a big bowl of salad as she had done the first day, and tell him, "You gotta relax. Stopa looking so grim. Thingsa get better for you, wait anda see." Mafalda and Ava, who had grown to womanhood around men of serious moods, recognized the tension in Slim and for a while refrained from teasing him. They still watched him over the back wall, and talked about him when he was not around. Or when they thought he was not around. One day when Slim was taking five minutes off, sitting against the wall and drinking a bottle of Nu-Grape from Mack's icebox, he overheard Mafalda and Ava talking softly on the other side.

"I think you're getting a little too interested in him, Ava," Mafalda said frankly.

"Maybe," Ava admitted. "I think it's that blond hair and those blue eyes."

"That blond hair and those blue eyes mean just one thing around here— he's not Italian. You better hope Ralph doesn't find out how you feel."

"I don't answer to Ralph," Ava declared indignantly. "Mamma Teresa brought me over here; I answer to her."

"*Al* brought you over here," Mafalda pointed out. "You answer to Al, through Ralph, just like we all do. If you want to have a little fun with this guy, go ahead. Just don't let Ralph find out—and don't get serious about him."

The following day, when Slim was waxing the Cord, Ava, in the backyard alone, leaned over the wall with her cup of spumoni. "Hello there, blue eyes," she said.

"Hello there yourself," Slim said. He paused in his work. Ava spooned some spumoni out of the cup.

"Want a bite?"

"What is it?"

"Italian ice cream. It's got candied fruit and nuts in it. Mamma Teresa makes it."

"I'll eat anything Mamma Teresa makes," Slim said, walking over.

Ava fed him the spumoni, then took a bite herself, licking the spoon clean. Their eyes held.

"I think I kind of like you," Ava said quietly.

"I think I kind of like you too," Slim replied, feeling an attraction that he knew would have surfaced earlier had it not been for the other matters occupying his mind.

"Do you ever come back to the garage at night?" she asked.

It was not in Slim to deceive her. "Ava, I have a wife," he said. "And a little boy."

As Ava stared at him in surprise, Slim told her briefly about Chloe and the boy, and how he had been searching for them since his release from prison. He explained how he had begun bribing a couple of bartenders a week to look for Jack Smart for him.

When Slim finished, Ava shook her head in amazement and muttered something to herself in Italian, then said in English, "I sure know how to pick them." She spooned some more spumoni, held it out for him to eat, and added, "Funny thing of it is, I still kind of like you." Cocking her head curiously, she asked, "How do you feel about this card player she's running around with?"

"Not good. But if things are that way, I can take it. Long's I get my little boy back."

Ava went into the house and Slim resumed waxing the Cord. A few minutes later, she returned and, making sure Mamma Teresa was not around to see, handed him some currency through the gate. "This will help you get a few more bartenders on your side," she said. Slim looked at the money: fifty dollars.

"Why are you doing this?" he asked.

"The quicker you find your wife, the better for both of us. If she's coming back to you, I'd like to know it. And if she's not, I'd like to know it. Now, what do you do on Sundays?"

"Same thing I do at night—walk, look, ask questions."

"This Sunday I want you to spend with me," Ava said. "I want you to take me to Riverview Park. I'll pay for all the rides and the hot dogs and stuff. But I want to go out somewhere with you, blue eyes. Someplace where we can hold hands and be together. I want to see how strong this thing is. I'll tell Mamma Teresa I'm going to visit Mafalda for the day. We can meet at the streetcar line near her house after the driver drops me off. Okay?"

"Okay," Slim said, not smiling. "I intend to pay this back to you," he added gravely, putting the money in his pocket.

"Doesn't matter to me whether you do or not," she shrugged. "That's part of the money my brothers gave me before I left Naples. I've never spent any of it; Mamma Teresa won't let me. It's just lying in a drawer of my steamer trunk." Ava started back for the house, then suddenly turned around again. "Oh, I almost forgot. Mamma Teresa and Mafalda are taking the train out to San Francisco next week to visit Al in Alcatraz. When they get back, maybe Ralph will give you a better job. If you've been telling the truth about doing Al a favor, that is."

"I have," Slim assured her.

"I'm glad," Ava said. "I'd hate to think of what Ralph would do if you were lying."

After Ava left and Slim returned to his work, a slight frown settled on his face. Before Slim's release from Atlanta, rumors had reached that prison that Al Capone was going crazy—literally losing his mind—in the hellhole of Alcatraz. Slim and Red Rudensky had talked about the stories. Neither believed them. Big Al was far too tough to let anyplace break him. Even Alcatraz.

Shaking his head, Slim put the apprehension out of his mind. Al would vouch for him. Slim was sure of it.

ichie climbed into the ring at the Laramie Park Athletic Club,
Myron holding the ropes apart, then coming in behind him. Before he sat
down in the corner, Richie glanced around the club. It was one of the nicest
he had been in: everything painted and polished, mopped and scrubbed,
swept and neat. Even the folding chairs set up for the Saturday night club
fights were upholstered instead of just metal. Riding out on the streetcar with
Myron and the other boys to the far Northwest Side, Richie had stared in
fascination at the neighborhood they entered: well-kept, single-family homes
with lawns and driveways and sidewalks that didn't have cracks in them.

"Nice out here," Richie said.

"Yeah," Myron agreed. "Especially for you."

"What do you mean?"

"These kids out here, they ain't tough," Myron explained. "They think
this here is a sport. This Laramie Park club, it trains boxers, not fighters. Kids
out here grow up and get sent to college. They don't have to fight their way
out of nothin'. They don't understand that getting into the ring might be all
some kids has got. They never been hungry—for nothing."

Looking across the ring, Richie saw his opponent in a red and gold satin
robe with a tasseled belt. The trainer wore a matching shirt. Even the ring
post in their corner was decorated in red and gold. Richie studied them only
a moment, then turned away disdainfully. He would not have traded his

Midwest A.C. jacket, now draped around his shoulders, for a dozen satin robes. And the plain old gray sweatshirt that Myron wore suited Richie just fine; Myron looked like the kind of trainer you'd expect to find in John Garfield's corner.

"Sit down," he heard Myron say. "Quit sightseeing."

Richie sat on the stool, keeping his back straight as Myron had taught him. If he slouched, Myron said, or leaned back against the ring post, his lungs would compress and his breathing would alter; when the bell rang, it would take at least thirty seconds for the lungs to adjust back to an upright motion of the body. In thirty seconds a guy who was just a tad slow could get hit with some good shots.

As Myron began to massage Richie's upper arms, he said, "You got three wins now—two decisions and that knockout last week. Next Saturday we fight at Midwest—our own club, our own crowd, our own sponsors. I'd like to see you go in next week with two decisions and two kayos on record. So I want you to knock this kid out, understand? Forget about boxing him; go out and street-fight him."

"Sure," Richie said.

That was all Myron said until after the fighters had been introduced, the referee's instructions given, and Richie returned to the plain canvas corner while the Laramie Park kid went back to his red and gold corner. Then Myron squeezed the back of Richie's neck and said, "Beat him up quick, Richie."

The bell rang and Richie moved to ring center with both gloves up protecting his face, both forearms in close to deflect body punches, the same schoolyard defensive posture he had used for as long as he could remember. Only now it was not exclusively for defense; it was a cover from which his right jab, right cross, and right hook could shoot out on attack, and from which his less precise and more imperfect left hand could move, usually in a feint, to distract for the split-second needed for one of the right-hand punches to connect. Richie was, as Myron had now evaluated him, a one-handed fighter with an extraordinary defensive style and the ability to think quicker in the ring than most any kid he had ever seen. "I ain't going to try altering your style to make you more orthodox," the glum trainer said. "Not so long as it's working."

It worked tonight. In the center of the ring, while the Laramie Park fighter was concentrating on the one-two-three of his textbook boxing, Richie came out of his shell and hit him four solid right hands to the face. The kid danced and jabbed; Richie crouched, came out again, and ripped both hands to the kid's ribs. He heard the kid groan. Several light snaps landed on Richie's forearms, and a right thumped him on the temple. Taking a step back as if beginning a retreat, he stopped suddenly and caught his opponent coming after him, drilling him with three thudding rights to the face. A stream of blood ran out of the kid's left nostril. Startled by the blood, he resumed his initial upright, classic-boxing stance and pawed at Richie with his left. Richie clubbed him in the left ribcage to make him lower the left, then methodically pounded the left side of his face, driving him across the ring onto the ropes, beating him on the eye, cheekbone, nose, lips, ear. Blood gushed from the kid's nose and from a suddenly split lip, and when the kid turned sideways and covered his head to escape the shots, Richie felt himself being pulled away and pushed toward his corner by the referee. Myron came out to meet him.

"Bell ring?" Richie gasped as Myron took his mouthpiece from him.

"No, it was stopped. You got it on a TKO."

"I won again," Richie grinned happily. "I won again!"

"You won again," Myron confirmed. Winking at Richie, he almost smiled.

Later, riding the streetcar back to the West Side, Richie thought about the boy he had fought. "I wonder how he feels right now?"

"Like a piano fell on him," Myron guessed.

"Bet he'll have scared eyes next time he fights," Richie said.

"Probably," Myron agreed. "He won't have a lot of confidence, I don't imagine, not after a licking like that. Maybe he'll only fight one or two more times. When the confidence starts to go, you might as well quit. You ain't dependable anymore."

Richie became quiet after Myron said that. He thought about it all the way back to the West Side.

At seven o'clock on Sunday morning, Richie awoke and sat up on the side of the davenport in the ladies' lounge. The red linoleum tile was cool on the bottoms of his feet. Untangling one leg from his army surplus blanket, he rose and went into the nearest stall to urinate. He was careful always to put the toilet seat back down, lest the cleaning woman become suspicious. At one of the sinks he washed his face and wet-combed his hair. From a cigar box he got out toothbrush and paste and brushed his teeth. He put back on the clothes he had worn after showering at the Laramie Park A.C. the previous night.

Dressed, Richie used paper towels to wipe down the sink so the cleaning woman wouldn't find it wet. Picking up the wrappers from two Butterfinger bars, he tossed them into a tall metal receptacle with a hinged opening. He folded his blanket into a precise square block and put his pillow inside the top fold. A paperback copy of *The Great Gatsby* went into the cigar box.

With everything under one arm, Richie turned off the fluorescent light and opened the door a crack. Listening carefully, he heard no sound in the great empty bowling alley. The cleaning people did not come as early on Sundays because Cascade did not open until noon. Richie always checked for sound and presence anyway; despite his bragging to Linda about the bowling alley being "his," he never completely got over the fear of being in there all alone. Only in the ladies' lounge, with the tall metal wastebasket braced against the door, did he ever completely relax.

Moving quietly into the corridor, Richie went up two doors to the locker room. The lockers were fifteen inches square, stacked five high, ten across, covering three walls of the room, with a center island of back-to-back units in the middle, a total of two hundred and ten small lockers. Although Richie had once kept padlocks on three of them, now he kept only two: one for his blanket and pillow, the other for his personal items. His clothes he now kept on hangers in a full-size locker at the gym. Working the combinations to his padlocks, he stowed his things and left the locker room. A few moments later he was downstairs letting himself into the alley through a fire door.

An hour later, he had finished breakfast at the corner drugstore and was getting on a Pulaski Road streetcar to meet Stan and Bobby.

In four hours that Sunday, the three boys stole, in broad daylight, three gumball machines, two peanut machines, one Beeman's gum machine, one Arcade Movie Stars machine which disbursed cardboard photographs of cowboy stars, and one Chiclets gum machine. From them they secured forty-three dollars worth of pennies, which they rolled in fifty-cent tubes after each theft and cashed in at stores in the next neighborhood before stealing machines there. As usual, the jimmied machines were left in garbage cans in the alley where they were pried open. The boys never bothered with the remaining contents of any of them, not even the red-and-yellow striped gumballs which were "winners" and could be exchanged in stores for nickel candy bars. The only exception was the Arcade machine, which Richie smashed the back of in order to go through the cards for photos of Buck Jones. Enduring scathingly derisive remarks from Bobby Casey, he found and pocketed six of them.

When they were through for the day, having made fourteen dollars each, they used the extra dollar to buy hot dogs and soda pop from a street vendor and sat on the curb to eat. That was when Richie told them he was quitting.

"You yellow punk!" Bobby Casey said at once, incensed.

"Shut up," said Stan. Studying Richie for a moment, he asked, "Why? What's the matter?"

"Nothing's the matter," Richie said. "It's just that I'm making enough at the bowling alley and the gym to get along okay, so I figure why take chances if I don't have to?"

Bobby Casey was seething. "I always knew you was a chicken-shit prick!"

Richie turned on him. "What the fuck's eating you, man? You never wanted me to come in with you in the first place!"

Dropping his hot dog, Bobby stood up. "Who the fuck do you think you're talking to, you little bastard?"

"Shut up!" Stan ordered. "Sit down!" he snapped to Bobby. To Richie he said, with an edge, "You mean you're quitting on us because *you* got enough to get along on? What about us?" Stan stared coldly at him. "We ain't got jobs, Richie. My old lady sleeps around and don't come home every night; me and my sister have to buy groceries and sometimes even pay the fucking rent on Saturdays. Bobby's old man blows his paycheck on booze and leaves his mother up the creek and Bobby has to come through with some help or his mother and little brothers and sisters go hungry and maybe even get evicted. You know, in a way you're lucky you don't have to worry about nobody but yourself. Which," he accused, "it looks like is all you *are* worrying about."

"It's not just that I'm getting along okay," Richie tried to explain. "It's that I'm scared of getting caught," he admitted. "My mother's probably gonna be getting out of the hospital pretty soon—I don't know how long they keep them in there; I guess until they don't want dope no more—anyway, I want to be here to help her when they turn her loose. I don't want to be in the juvenile home or someplace—"

"You saying we're gonna get caught, asshole?" Bobby demanded.

"I'm saying we *could* get caught," Richie answered, to Stan, not Bobby. That infuriated Bobby even more and he jumped to his feet again.

"Get up!" he ordered. "I'm gonna whip your ass!"

Richie remained sitting, looking up at Bobby. He was certain he could do to Bobby Casey just what he had done to the Laramie Park fighter in the ring the previous night. He had seen Bobby fight; he was a grunting, swearing, wild-swinging street fighter whom, from a crouch, Richie knew he could uppercut to a pulp. Which, if he did it in front of Stan, would totally humiliate Bobby. Getting his ass kicked by the kid he had bullied since the day they met would be more than Bobby could take. He would lose his confidence completely. Myron's words of the previous night came back to Richie: *"When the confidence starts to go . . . you ain't dependable anymore."* Bobby would not be dependable anymore—and Stan would be left with him.

For a long time, when Richie was training on his own in the corner of the gym, he had fantasized about Bobby Casey being the first kid against whom he would fight back. That had all changed when Myron had put him on the club team; a kid he had never seen before, who had never done anything to him, had been the first one against whom he fought back. Since then there had been three others, two of whom had ended up bleeding and helpless in the face of Richie's attack. The thought of doing the same thing to Bobby Casey was almost too delicious to pass up. But he had to.

"I ain't fighting you, Bobby," he said.

"You gutless motherfucker," Bobby said, and kicked him in the ankle. Grabbing his ankle, Richie turned angry red. Stan grabbed Bobby by the sleeve and pulled him back to the curb.

"Leave him alone," Stan said. He had been sticking up for Richie so long that it was the natural thing to do. When Bobby tried to get back up, Stan drew back a fist. That was all he had to do. Stan rarely had to fight, mostly he only had to threaten.

"Pansy cocksucker," Bobby snarled. "Go on, beat it! We don't need you!"

"Okay," Stan said quietly to Richie. "You're out." He looked at the gutter between his shoes. "Maybe we'll see you around."

"Sure," Richie said. "See you."

Taking his hot dog and soda pop with him, Richie rose and walked away, gritting his teeth to keep from limping on the ankle Bobby Casey had kicked.

Richie had learned enough from Myron to go straight to the gym to take care of his ankle. Although open seven days a week, Sunday was the gym's slowest day; when Richie got there, he saw only three young novice fighters, fresh from the recent Golden Gloves tournament, working out to get ready for their respective professional debuts. Someday that'll be me, he thought, as he limped past the training rings to the locker room.

Removing his shoes, socks, and trousers, he took a clean towel from the shelf and, at the icebox, rolled enough crushed ice into it to make a compress. Sitting on a bench in his undershorts, he folded the compress around his ankle and held it in place. Benny Stein, one of the novices, came in to shower, and asked, "Hey, Richie, wha' happened to your foot?"

"Bowling pin nicked me while I was setting pins this morning," Richie said. "Don't say nothing to Myron if you see him, okay."

"Check." When he had stripped off his sweaty training clothes, Benny walked over naked and asked, "Want me to tape it for you after?"

Richie shook his head. "It ain't that bad. Thanks, Ben."

Richie kept the compress on for two minutes, off for a minute, then back on, and after half an hour the swelling had almost completely disappeared. Tossing out the ice and putting the wet towel in a hamper, Richie took off the rest of his clothes, hung them in his locker, and got another clean towel from the shelf. In one of the stalls he took a long, warm shower and washed his hair. After he finished and dried off, he examined a slight abrasion over the peak of his ankle, swathed it with iodine, and covered it with a gauze pad and a strip of adhesive.

Back at his locker, he dressed in a pair of inexpensive cotton trousers and a short-sleeve shirt he had bought in Goldblatt's Bargain Basement. He had two pairs of shoes now, one for "good" wear when he went to meet Linda, and two new pair of argyle socks that he alternated, washing one pair each night.

Leaving the gym, wearing his Midwest A.C. jacket, Richie walked west on Madison to the same drugstore at which he had eaten breakfast that morning. Loitering next to the entrance, he watched down Pulaski Road until he saw Linda come around the corner from Washington. Feeling a warm surge at the sight of her, he dodged traffic in the middle of the block to go meet her.

"You're going to get hit by a car someday," she nagged at once, as they slipped their arms around each other's waist.

"The car that's fast enough to hit me ain't been made yet," Richie bragged.

"Oh, sure. Faster than a speeding bullet. Can you leap tall buildings in a single bound too?" Before he could reply, she quickly got in, "And stop saying 'ain't.' "

"I ain't gonna say it again," he promised. Linda pinched his arm for punishment.

"Did you win last night?" she asked.

"I always win. Four straight now."

It had originally been Richie's intent not to tell Linda that he had been made a member of the Midwest team; he simply planned to show her that he could fight the next time someone tried pushing him around. But after his second win he had not been able to contain the secret. "Guess what!" he told her in a burst of exuberance when they met in the park the next day. "Myron's letting me fight with the other guys! I mean, really fight! I've got my own trunks and ring shoes, and he's got a jacket ordered for me and everything! He even took me to a dentist and got me a mouthpiece!"

"Aren't you afraid you'll get hurt, Richie?" she asked, young-girl concern in her eyes. "You don't know *how* to fight."

"I do!" he exclaimed. "I've been learning for weeks, practicing and training in the gym. I know how to jab and hook and uppercut, I know stance, I know—"

"What's a mouthpiece?" she interrupted.

"Oh. It's a piece of hard rubber that's made to fit over your teeth. Keeps them from getting broken."

He had spent most of their time together that day telling her all about everything that had happened from the night he subbed for Sammy Dutro, the special training Myron had given him the following week, how the other guys on the team, even Dutro, who was the same weight as Richie, had made him feel welcome, made him feel like one of them, and how he had subsequently won his second fight the following week. Linda was impressed but skeptical.

"How can you be sure you're not going to get hurt?" she worried. Richie shrugged.

"I'm not sure. A guy's bound to get hurt sooner or later. But you can still win, even if you do get hurt. That's the main thing—winning." His expression hardened a little. "And not being afraid to fight back."

"It never bothered me that you didn't fight back," Linda told him quietly.

"It bothered me," Richie said, staring off away from her. "You don't know how it feels to have everybody think you're a sissy. Even girls."

"Not this girl." She had put her arms around his neck and kissed him lovingly on the lips, a long, arousing kiss that made both of them wish they had a lot more privacy than the park provided. That was when they decided to start going to movies on Sunday afternoon, which was where Linda was supposed to be anyway.

They would sit in the back row of the balcony so that no one would be behind them and they could kiss and neck when they felt like it, which was frequently. Richie loved the taste of Linda's lips and mouth, the smell of her breath; there was a sense of warm milk about kissing her. He liked tasting too the light sweat that exuded just under her ears when she became warm. Now and then, perhaps once during the feature and once during the short subject, she would allow his hand to move over and cover her left breast, leaving it there until they both felt her nipple hardening under the cotton bras she had lately begun wearing. Then she would gently take his hand away and put it somewhere less compromising. She was always acutely aware of his feelings for her, how important she was in his strange young existence. She regularly gave him reassurances of her own feelings for him—with her kisses, the weekly "feels," and expressions of her worry, which was sincere and genuine. What reassurances she got from him, she had to subtly extract.

"Do you think she's pretty?" she would ask of Elizabeth Taylor when they saw *National Velvet*.

"Sure, she's pretty," Richie replied guilelessly. "She's a movie star; she's supposed to be pretty."

After an appropriate moment of silence, Linda would sigh and say, "I wish I was pretty like that," and Richie would realize what was expected of him.

"I think you're a lot prettier than she is."

"Oh, I am not. I'm plain and I know it."

"You're not either. You're just as pretty as that girl on the screen is."

"It's sweet of you to say so, but you don't mean it."

"I do so mean it. I think you're prettier than any girl I've ever seen."

"Really?"

"Honest to God."

There was more kissing then, with the lips parted a little, and maybe an extra feel for good measure.

After the movie, Richie would walk Linda back to her neighborhood near Tilton Elementary. They started out walking with their arms around each other again, but as they progressed closer to where Linda lived and was known, they abandoned that in favor of holding hands, then yielded even that simply to walk side by side. Her father still did not permit her to go out with boys.

"See you next Sunday?" she always asked.

"Sure."

"Be careful next week. Stay out of trouble."

"Sure."

"Good luck next Saturday. Hope you win."

"Thanks," Richie said. "I'll win."

They kept talking as they parted, getting farther away from each other. Finally they would blow kisses and go their separate ways.

Everything, it now seemed, was becoming more exciting in Richie's life. Kissing and feeling-up Linda. Winning fights. And learning more all the time about his father. Tomorrow Mack had promised to tell him everything he knew about Ralph Capone ordering Slim killed, and about a woman named Avellina Gela who had known Slim.

Richie was certain the knowledge would bring him closer to his long lost father.

*T*heir Sunday afternoon at Riverview Amusement Park was, for Slim and Ava, like showering their minds and hearts with rays of sunshine, cleansing them of their troubles and warming them to life again. They had fun—something neither had experienced for a long time.

Ava already knew of Slim's problems; now, on the long streetcar ride out Western Avenue, she shared hers with him.

"I'm like a prisoner in that house," she said. "Mamma Teresa won't let me date because she says the American boys will take advantage of me. And she doesn't approve of the Italians that Ralph and Mafalda bring home from time to time for me to meet; she says she doesn't want me getting involved with men in the rackets, she wants me to wait for a respectable man to come along. How she ever expects me to meet anybody respectable, I'll never know."

Ava put a hand on Slim's arm. "Please don't misunderstand what I'm saying. I love Mamma Teresa more than anybody in the world since my own mother died. But sometimes she doesn't understand anyone's position but her own. I'm like a daughter to her; she wants to protect me from marrying anyone associated with Al, like Mafalda did, and like Rose, her older daughter, did. She's done so much for me all my life—sent money to Naples for me to attend a private school and learn to speak English, paid for me to be treated in a hospital in Rome when I got smallpox, bought two of everything for

Mafalda so she could send me clothes. She was doing these things *years* ago, when her own family was growing up, back in Brooklyn, when she had to manage on what my late uncle, Gabriel, earned as a barber, and what she could make as a seamstress working at home. I owe her more than I'll ever be able to repay. But sometimes it's very hard to have someone so totally in control of your life.''

"I know.'' Slim understood. "It was that way for me in the pen. Al, too. Everybody, I guess.''

They rode in silence for a while, her hand still on his arm, shoulders touching, each still with somber thoughts, not yet in the shower of sunshine that would warm them. Then Ava broke the spell by squeezing his arm, saying, "Oh, look, we're there!''

As they joined a stream of people into the big park, Ava pressed twenty dollars into Slim's hands. Slim turned red. "I don't much like this arrangement,'' he said.

Hands on hips, Ava warned, "Don't give me any trouble, okay? I've been planning this for a long time and I mean to have fun.'' She bobbed her chin at one of the park's three rollercoasters, the Silver Streak. "I'll bet you're afraid to go on that.''

"I'm not afraid of nothing,'' Slim said. Half under his breath, he added, "That's why I'm in trouble so much.''

They went on the Silver Streak, sitting close together in a little enclosed cage on wheels, gripping a safety bar that locked back over their knees, while the train rose and fell and curved and sped along it narrow-gauge track as if racing toward doom. Slim clenched his jaw as his knuckles turned white; Ava, ripe-plum eyes wide, screamed from first turn to last. Staggering off, they headed for the nearest bench.

"That was fun,'' Ava said defiantly.

"Sure was,'' Slim forced himself to agree. "What's next?''

They looked around. There were two more rollercoasters, the Greyhound and a monster called the Bobs, which had the steepest drop, two hundred feet, of any ride in America. Nearby was another ride called the Caterpillar, which went up and down low hills in a circle. There was a line of children waiting to go on it. Ava and Slim looked at each other and laughed—then went and got in line with the children.

For a while that day they were two people all alone in the world, knowing no one, no one knowing them, like two children turned loose in a wonderland. They went on every ride they came to except the other two rollercoasters; they ate hot dogs and cotton candy; they tried for prizes in a shooting gallery, where Ava outshot Slim, who failed to hit the target once. "Some big-time crook you are,'' she chided afterwards.

Sometime during the afternoon, they began to hold hands, to touch, to hug when they were happy. At a penny arcade, they posed for separate metal-framed photos from a machine, which they exchanged. Ava turned her face slightly to the left to conceal her pocked cheek, blushing as she did so. On a ride called Mill on the Floss, which was a long leisurely boat trip through a series of dark tunnels, they kissed for the first time.

"I don't care if you are married," Ava whispered breathlessly. "I've never felt like this before."

"Neither have I," Slim admitted.

From the start, their kisses were passionate. Lips parted, Ava tried to devour him; body alive again after so long, Slim tried to devour her back. Turned awkwardly toward each other in the flat-bottomed boat, they pressed their upper bodies together; Slim put a hand under her blouse and cupped her breast; Ava moaned softly into his open mouth and squeezed the inside of his thigh. The ride ended much too soon.

It was dusk when they left the park. In a shadowy doorway on their way back to the streetcar stop, they paused a few minutes to kiss over and over, pressing their whole bodies together now, squirming against each other with a mutual fever that was consuming them. Slim tried to pull her skirt up to take her right there.

"No, not like this," Ava said. "Later, tonight. Come to the back gate at midnight."

"I feel like I'm about to explode," Slim said.

"Explode tonight," Ava told him. "In me."

Chloe at first could not believe Richie when he said he had seen his daddy out the window on Kedzie Avenue. The boy had such a wild imagination. And lately, since Jack had come into her life, there was no length to which he would not go to get her attention. So she thought he was making it up.

But the possibility nagged her nevertheless. Finally, she got two dollars worth of change and telephoned her mother from a sit-down booth in the candy store.

"Hello, Mamma," she said when the phone in Lamont was answered.

"Lord Almighty, girl, I have been worried sick about you," Mrs. Clark complained at once. "Do you know how long it's been since I've had a letter from you?"

"Mamma, is Richmond out of the penitentiary?" Chloe asked without further preliminary.

"Yes, he is," Mrs. Clark verified. "I wrote you that he was, but the letter came back saying you'd moved. I'm your mother, Chloe, I think the least you could do is let me know you're still alive now and then."

"All right, Mamma. All right. I'm sorry and I'll do better. Do you know where Richmond is?"

"I know he's not around here. The law's already been here looking for him; he was supposed to stay in the county until his probationary release was done."

"You didn't tell him where I was, did you?"

"You know better. I don't treat you like you treat me."

"Oh, *Mamma*. Don't start in on me. I've got problems."

"Well, why didn't you say so? That's different. I've never had problems myself."

Chloe placated her mother for as long as she could until the operator said her three minutes were up. Hanging up, she went out on the street and stood, wary eyes scanning the block. It did not really matter, she thought, whether her mother told Richmond where she was or not. Richmond was like a bloodhound; he would have—he *had*—found out somehow. Nervously lighting a cigarette, hurrying back to the apartment, she thought grimly of what she had to do now: stay ahead of him. Too far committed to Jack to back out, she must *not*, at all costs, allow Richmond to catch up with her.

In the bedroom of the apartment she paced, chain smoking, talking to herself, scolding Richie and sending him away when he came to the bedroom door. As soon as Jack arrived, she barely let him pause to give Richie his nightly Baby Ruth before urging him into the bedroom and closing the door. Richie went immediately to the keyhole to listen.

"I've got to get out of Chicago," he heard his mother say tensely. "How soon will you be ready to move to Gary?"

"W-what's the m-matter?" Jack asked.

"My husband is out of prison. He's looking for me. I think he may be close to finding me."

"J-Jesus." Through the keyhole, Richie saw Jack Smart begin to pace. "There's a b-big game coming up n-next Saturday night. At Ritter's T-tavern on Fulton Street. If I c-could win big in it, I th-think we could get out of town r-right away." Jack adjusted his knit tie and stretched his neck an inch. "Only th-thing is," he said worried, "it's a t-time game. You gotta agree to p-play till midnight unless you g-go broke. You can't quit w-winners. But maybe we can figure a w-way around that."

"Oh, Jack, I hope so," Chloe said nervously, putting her arms around his neck. "I'm scared, hon. I'm really scared."

Jack patted the back of her head. "D-don't worry, kid. I won't l-let nobody hurt you. I don't give a g-goddamn if he *is* your husband."

Listening and watching through the keyhole, Richie now knew for sure that his mother believed him about seeing his daddy from the window. When he first told her, he had done it to hurt her, but had secretly hoped she would restore his faith in her by going out and trying to find his daddy. When she did not, he began to wonder if she even believed him. Now he knew. She believed him, all right, but she was not going to try to *find* his daddy, she was going to *run away* from him.

With Uncle Jack.

Mack answered the garage phone and turned to hand it to Slim. "For you."

Slim's heart accelerated. There was only one reason he would be getting a telephone call. "Hello—"

"This is Jerry Green, the bartender at Ritter's. You know, on Fulton Street. I got a tip for you about your friend Jack Smart. You did say there was another five in it, didn't you?"

"I'll come by and pay you tonight," Slim said.

"I'll be here till eleven."

When Slim hung up, Mack asked, "Find him?"

"I'll know tonight."

Later that day, when Slim was washing a car in the alley, Ava came through the gate and leaned back against the wall to smoke a cigarette and visit with him.

"Mamma Teresa and Mafalda get back from San Francisco tonight," she said. "I'm going downtown with Ralph to meet them at the depot. We'll be back about nine. I'll still meet you in the backyard at midnight."

"Okay." Slim told her about the telephone call from the bartender. "I'll be going down there right after work."

"God, I hope you find them," Ava said. "The quicker we get this thing settled, the better I'll like it." She looked down at the ground, avoiding his eyes. "Have you decided yet what you're going to do?"

Slim shook his head. "I know what I want to do." Pausing in his work, he stared at her across the hood of the car. "I want to be with you. But I want my little boy too. And I don't really know if I've got reason to take him away from Chloe. I ain't heard her side of the story yet. All these bits and pieces that I've picked up, they could all be wrong. This feller Jack Smart might be Estelle's boyfriend, not Chloe's. Could turn out that she's been true to me all this time. If she has, why, then I owe her something. You see that, don't you?"

"I see it," Ava acknowledged. "I don't like it, but I see it."

"You wouldn't want me to be less than a man about it, would you?"

When he got off work, Slim went back to his room and cleaned up, then made the long streetcar trip to the West Side. It was just getting dark when he walked into Ritter's Tavern on Fulton Street. Behind the bar was a stocky man wearing a shirt with *Jerry* stitched above the pocket. Slim sat at the end of the bar and put down a five-dollar bill. Jerry came over and asked, "What'll you have?"

"You called me," Slim said, tapping the bill with one finger.

"Oh, yeah. I wasn't sure if it was you or not." Jerry drew a glass of draft beer and put it on a cardboard coaster in front of Slim. "On the house." Leaning closer on one elbow, he said in a confidential tone, "On Saturday night there's a big game set for our back room. Smart's one of the players that's bought a chair. Game starts at seven and the play is for five hours, until midnight, except if a guy goes broke." Jerry's eyebrows went up. "Okay?"

"Okay," Slim said and pushed the bill to him.

Sipping his beer, Slim thought: It's been a long road home. But he would have made it if he got his little boy back. And if Chloe had waited for him, and he had to give up Ava, well, that was just how it would have to be. The main thing was to get the hell out of Chicago, get back down south where he belonged. There was the question now of his violation of probationary release to face, but if his daddy took him back on the farm, and if he explained how he *had* to go up to Chicago to find his wife and son, maybe they would go easy on him and give him another chance.

He was going straight and he wasn't running—that ought to count for something.

At ten minutes before midnight, Slim crept up to the backyard gate of the Capone mansion, prepared to wait there in the dark shadows until Ava came out. To his surprise, the gate opened at once and Ava's hand reached out to draw him into the yard. Slim tensed; she had never been early before. "What's the matter?"

"You're in trouble," Ava whispered as they moved a few feet along the inside of the wall and crouched down. "Ralph has got his men out looking for you. Three of them are waiting in your room."

"What's he looking for me for?" Slim asked, puzzled.

"Mamma Teresa and Mafalda got back from their visit to see Al," Ava said. "He doesn't remember you."

"Doesn't remember me? That's crazy. I kept him from getting a knife stuck in his belly."

"Listen to me," Ava urged. "Al is sick. They haven't told Mamma Teresa what's the matter with him, but Mafalda knows. He's sick with syphilis. The doctors think he's had it for years without knowing it. They say it's damaging his central nervous system. He has trouble concentrating on things." Ava paused to stifle a sob that came from her breast. In the moonlight, Slim could see that her large lovely eyes were wet. "Mafalda said that when she and

Mamma Teresa were talking to him, Al would look away and start humming to himself as if they weren't even there."

"Jesus . . ." Slim said, staring at her. It was beyond his capacity to imagine Big Al Capone in such condition. But he did not have time to dwell on it; he had to think about himself. "Don't Ralph realize that's *why* he didn't remember me?" he asked. Ava shook her head emphatically.

"Ralph says no matter how sick Al was, he'd remember giving his word to someone who did him a favor. Ralph is convinced you lied to him just to get a job. He even thinks you might be a plant from one of the Irish mobs on the West Side—"

"Hell, that's crazy. I've got to talk to him—"

Slim started to rise, but Ava seized his arm. "No! You can't! He won't listen to you, Slim! He's ranting and raving that you made a fool of him; he says he's going to kill you."

"That's crazy," Slim said again. "Crazy."

"You've got to get out of town," Ava said.

"I can't," Slim said. He told her what he had heard from the bartender. "I'll have to find a place to lay low until that game Saturday night."

Ava took his hands. "Come with me."

"Where?"

"Come on . . ."

Ava led him across the dark backyard and down some steps into the basement of the Capone mansion.

"Nobody would ever think to look for you down here," she whispered. "You can stay here until Saturday night, until that poker game. Maybe after that, you'll be leaving town anyway."

Slim felt for her and took her in his arms. "Maybe we'll both be leaving town," he said.

They clung to each other in the blackness.

The night of the big poker game at Ritter's, Jack Smart took Chloe and Richie to eat supper at Thompson's Cafeteria, several blocks from the tavern. While they ate, Jack explained again to Chloe his plan for getting out of the game early if he was winning.

"Nine o'clock is when I want you to c-come into the c-card room. There's a ladies' entrance on the side; the c-card room is to the left at the end of the b-bar. There'll be people standing around watching the g-game; you and the kid stay b-back with them, but make sure I c-can see you, okay?"

"Yes, okay," Chloe said. Nervous, she wished Jack did not need her help. Earlier, Richie had heard her say to Estelle, "Doing this kind of thing scares the hell out of me. But Richmond finding me scares me even more."

In the cafeteria, Richie sat by the window, eating the food his mother had cut up for him and pretending, as usual, not to pay any attention to the adult conversation.

"If I'm losing when you c-come in," Jack continued, "I won't pay no attention to you; I'll just keep playing. But if I'm winning, if I'm ahead enough to want to get out of the game, I'll ask you what you w-want, understand? That's when you say you have to t-talk to me for a minute. You say you're s-sorry, but it's an emergency. I'll pick up my money and take a t-time out; that's allowed, for p-players to take a leak or g-get a drink. We'll g-go sit by the ladies' entrance and w-when nobody's paying any attention, we'll sk-skip out.''

Chloe lit a cigarette, her hand unsteady. "I wish it was over," she said. "What if somebody comes after us?"

"Nobody will," Jack assured her. "I'm a r-regular player; they'll never suspect what I'm d-doing."

"Do I have to bring Richie with me?"

"It'll look more legit that w-way, less like a s-set-up."

Chloe crushed out the cigarette after one drag. "God, I hope it goes all right. I don't like things like this."

"Everything will be f-fine," Jack assured her.

Down the side street from Ritter's corner entrance, Chloe found a door marked LADIES ONLY. Churning up her courage to go in, she cautioned Richie, "Now, you hold my hand, don't pull away, stay right next to me, and don't say a word while we're in there, you hear me? We're going to help Uncle Jack get us our bowling alley, but we have to be very careful how we do it. I'm depending on you to be good and do exactly as I say." With a fixed, almost sick-looking half smile, she pushed open the door and they went inside.

Leading Richie by the hand, Chloe went through the tavern to the open door of a private room and edged inside among a dozen or so spectators already watching the card game. Maneuvering around the wall to the right of the door, she reached a spot where she could see Jack's face at the table, and when he looked up he could see her. Richie, who could see nothing, tugged at her hand. At first she paid no attention, but he persisted. Bending, she warned, "I told you to be good."

"I can't see anything."

Chloe sighed tensely. There was a chair nearby, against the wall; she pushed him over to it. "Stand on that. And don't fall."

On the chair, Richie could see over the shoulders of people in front of him, see the round, felt-covered table at which Uncle Jack and four other men sat, all of them with stacks of currency in front of them. There was little talk in the room; what there was, muted, came from the men at the table: "Raise twenty-five . . . Call . . . Two cards . . . Fold . . . Up to you . . . Pot's right . . ."

Of the people watching, all were men except for Chloe and a large Slavic-looking woman with no makeup who was drinking Blatz from a bottle. Chloe and five others were in front of Richie on the same side of the room, while the rest of the spectators were in a half-circle facing him from the other side. A door leading into the alley was propped open a foot by a case of beer to let some air in and some smoke out. Because of the smoke, and the fact that the only light in the room was from a low-hanging, green-shaded fixture directly over the table, the standing people were in shadow from mid-chest up. Richie could make out their faces, but not too clearly. Nor was he trying to; he was more interested in watching the men playing cards. But as he watched, he had the eerie feeling that someone was about to touch him. But no one was near him. Looking across the table at those people facing him, he became aware of a pair of eyes fixed unblinkingly on him. Richie stared back, frowning.

The staring eyes belonged to a man who was standing back from the others, in the shadows of the opposite wall. Only part of his face showed: a clean line of jaw, one ear, darkish blond hair.

Richie's eyes grew wide as he realized suddenly who it was. The man he had seen out the window. His father. Lips parting, Richie was about to speak to his mother, when the man in the shadows shook his head no. Then a hand came up out of the shadows and one finger beckoned Richie to come to him. Richie was about to get down off the chair when he heard Jack Smart's voice. "Hi, honey. What are you d-doing here?"

And he heard his mother reply, "Jack, honey, I'm sorry to interrupt your game, but I've got an emergency. Can I speak to you for a couple of minutes?"

"Okay. Just one more h-hand," Jack said. "And let's have a fresh deck for it," he added, tossing the cards into a nearby wastebasket and taking a new, unopened deck from a carton on a chair next to the table.

As Jack was removing the cellophane from the deck, a new voice said quietly, "Just a minute." The speaker was a swarthy man with a drooping moustache, heavy-lidded as if sleepy, but his eyes beneath the half-closed lids were alert and penetrating. "I'd like to take a look at that old deck."

"What the hell for?" Jack demanded. Richie stared at him; it was the first time he had ever heard Uncle Jack speak a complete sentence without stuttering.

"I don't have to give you a reason," the swarthy man said evenly. Without taking his eyes off Jack, he backed his chair up until he could reach the wastebasket. Reaching into it, he pulled out a dozen cards. Still without taking his eyes from Jack, he moved his fingertips lightly over the back of each card. When he finished, he pushed them aside.

"S-satisfied?" Jack asked with a smirk.

"Not yet." The swarthy man reached down and got a dozen more cards.

"I d-don't have to take this," Jack announced, putting his hands flat on the table to get up.

"It's his right to look at the cards," another player said. "Stay put."

Once again the swarthy man was lightly running his fingertips over the backs of the cards. After several cards he stopped and smiled coldly. Tossing one of the cards into the middle of the table, he said, "Crimped." Then, in a sudden, unexpected move, he reached across the table and grabbed Jack's left hand, turning it over to reveal the underside of a signet ring. On the back of the ring was a tiny needle point with which Jack had pricked a barely discernible nick—a "crimp"—that his fingertips could detect in certain key cards as he dealt.

"You son of a bitch!" one of the other players snarled.

Jerking his hand away, Jack leaped up, knocking his chair back, and reached for a small pistol stuck in his waistband under his vest. He managed to pull it clear but was not quick enough to level it and aim; the swarthy man, also on his feet now, already had his own gun ready; he shot Jack twice in the stomach.

"Jack!" Chloe screamed, and began pushing through to the table. Jack, after slamming back against the wall, pitched foward over the table clutching his stomach with both hands. Grabbing what money they could off the table, the card players scattered. The spectators began rushing into the tavern and out to the alley. The chair on which Richie stood was next to the door connecting to the tavern. Wide-eyed, he looked at the door, then across the commotion at his father.

"The alley, boy!" his father yelled. He pointed to Richie and the tavern door, then to himself and the alley door. "The alley!" he yelled again.

Richie's face lighted up as he understood. He was to go through the tavern door and meet his father around in the alley. Nodding yes, he leaped off the chair and threw himself into the press of people hurrying into the tavern. Behind him, he heard his mother still screaming, "Jack! Jack!" Glancing back once, he looked briefly at her, thrown over the bent form of Jack Smart, who was oozing red onto the green felt of the table. Then Richie's eyes shifted and located his father; he was in the other press of spectators who were struggling through the alley door.

Dropping to his knees, Richie plunged forward into the tavern. As he scurried, someone's heel kicked back and struck the point of his chin. Moaning, he scrambled on, getting past the doorjamb, then bounded to his feet and dashed toward the LADIES ONLY door. Most of the patrons in the tavern were fighting to get out the front door, the access they used and were familiar with; only a few people even thought of the ladies' entrance. Richie got to it in an instant and burst headlong onto the sidewalk.

Outside, people had heard the shots and were looking out windows and coming out on front porches to stare. Fifty feet away from the mouth of the alley, those who had been fighting to get out the back door now ran to the street and hurried off in various directions. Richie darted to the alley and skidded to a halt under a streetlight that threw its yellow glow barely past the tavern's rear door. There he froze, shocked by what he saw.

His father was pushed back against a black sedan, a burly man's hand on his throat, a pistol pointed at his face. Another man was searching him, while a third man, at the wheel of the car, kept revving the engine and saying "Come on! Come on!"

"He ain't packing," announced the man doing the searching.

"Okay, hick, get the fuck in the car," said the man with the pistol, jerking Slim forward and shoving him into the back seat.

Car doors slammed; headlights came on, blinding Richie; there was a screech of tires. The sedan shot forward, oblivious of anyone in its path.

"Jesus, kid, look out!" someone shouted, and a rough hand grabbed Richie by the upper arm and jerked him from the mouth of the alley, snapping his head and neck viciously, getting him out of the way of the car by inches.

Richie watched helplessly as the sedan sped away with his father.

"They was Ralph Capone's boys, sure," Mack told Richie the summer Richie turned thirteen. "And I found out later that the same bartender that tipped Slim that Jack Smart was going to be there, also tipped one of Ralph's men that Slim was going to be there. See, the Capone family had guys on its payroll in every precinct in the city. Ralph put out the word on your dad, and those guys spread it around. It wasn't hard for that bartender to put two and two together and come up with Slim. He saw a chance to get paid twice and he done it."

"Dirty bastard," Richie said.

Mack shrugged indifferently. "Everybody gets along as best they can," he said. They were in Mack's little kitchen above his garage. He was at an old, chipped porcelain stove stirring a pot of steaming Mulligan stew with the handle of a screwdriver. When it was mixed to suit him, he lifted the pot with two pieces of rubber sliced from an old tire and poured two bowlsful. With a bottle of beer for himself and a glass of milk for Richie, they sat down to eat.

"What did they do with him?" Richie asked.

"Brought him to the garage in back of the mansion," Mack said. "Ralph and a half a dozen of his boys was waiting there. Ralph was mad as a castrated bull. Walked up to Slim and punched him right in the mouth. 'You lying son of a bitch!' he yelled. 'My brother never heard of you!' Slim tried to hit Ralph back, but two of the boys grabbed him and pinned his arms. Blood was coming out of Slim's mouth and he spit it on the front of Ralph's suit. 'Al don't remember me because he's sick!' Slim yelled. Ralph punched him in the face again. 'I don't give a fuck if he is sick!' he yelled back at Slim. 'He'd remember giving his word to somebody! My brother's word is sacred to him! He'd never forget it!' And with that, he slugged Slim a couple times in the gut." Telling about it, Mack was a little embarrassed. "I was there, you know, but there wasn't nothing I could do for him. Even if I'd've tried, why, a crippled garage mechanic ain't no match for professional gorillas like them. I thought about going over to the mansion and telling Ava what was happening, thinking maybe she could get Mamma Teresa to step in, but I realized all I'd be doing was getting Ava in a lot of trouble, and I knew Slim wouldn't want that."

As he talked, Mack shoveled stew into his mouth and washed it down with beer.

"Ralph wanted to do your old man in," he said. "A couple of his men advised against it, saying there was no need for nothing that drastic. But Ralph, he couldn't be reasoned with. 'I want the son of a bitch iced! Give him some cement shoes and drop him in the fucking lake!' He was like a madman. I remember thinking, it'll take a miracle to save Slim." Mack paused to point his spoon at Richie. "And that's what happened too—a miracle."

"Go on, get him the fuck out of here!" Ralph ordered. "Run him over to the Michigan side of the lake and dump him there." With a silk handkerchief from his breast pocket, Ralph wiped away some of the blood Slim had spat on him.

Two of Ralph's men dragged Slim back to the sedan. Before they put him in the back seat, one of the big overhang doors opened at the front of the garage and a gray Buick drove in. Its driver, one of Ralph's lieutenants, got out, grinning, and said, "Hey, Ralphie, look who they finally turned loose!"

From the passenger seat stepped a muscular, smiling man with carrot-colored hair. Ralph Capone's angry expression was replaced by a wide smile.

"Rusty! I'll be goddamned!" Red Rudensky came forward and the two men embraced warmly. "Rusty!" Ralph said again. "How the hell are you?"

"In the pink, Ralphie," said Rudensky. Looking past Capone, he saw the bloody-faced Slim. "Hey, Slim! What the hell are you doing here?"

"You know this farmer?" Ralph asked.

"Hell, yeah, I know him," Red replied. "Him and Al and me were all cell partners in Atlanta. He kept Al from getting a shank in his gut one day on the yard."

Ralph turned chalk white. "Sweet Jesus," he said quietly to himself.

"What's going on?" Red wanted to know.

"Come on in the office and I'll tell you," Ralph said. Going over to the sedan, he said to his men, "Clean him up. Fix his face. Then bring him to the office. Mack, get us some coffee, will you?"

In the private office at the rear of the garage, Ralph told Red Rudensky about the day Slim showed up at the mansion with Mamma Teresa's photograph, and what had happened since. He was just finishing the story when Mack limped in and put two mugs of coffee on the desk. Ralph reached for his but could not pick it up, his hands were trembling so. "I almost had him taken for a ride," he said thickly, "and the guy didn't do nothing. Jesus. Al never would've made a mistake like that."

"Take it easy," Red soothed. "Ain't any of us in Al's league when it comes to smarts. Main thing is, the mistake was caught in time."

Mack got out a bottle of brandy and laced their coffee, just as Ralph's men brought Slim in. Slim's bottom lip was swelling and there was a bruise spreading on the surface of one cheek. Standing in front of the desk where Ralph sat, Slim glared at him with cold, unmoving eyes. Ralph spread his hands helplessly.

"I was wrong," he said.

"I kept trying to tell you that." Slim's lips barely moved. His hands closed into fists and Ralph saw it.

"Okay," Ralph said. "Okay." He stood up. "I don't want it to leave this room. I got enough on my mind without having to worry about a hardhead like you carrying a grudge. So go ahead. Get even right now. I won't swing back."

Slim's fist moved a little as his arms tensed with the invitation. Ralph's face was there, just across the desk, and Slim's own face throbbed from the punches he had taken just minutes ago. But Slim would not hit a man who would not fight back. Slim knew what it was to be wrong. He opened his hands and relaxed his arms. "All right," he said quietly, "let it lay."

Rudensky came over and put an arm around Slim's shoulders. "Good man, Slim," he said.

Slim grinned at him with his puffing lip. "They must be letting just anybody out these days."

"You want a job, Red?" asked Ralph Capone. Rudensky shook his head.

"Already got one. I just stopped by to say hello. I'm on my way to St. Paul to work for a company named Brown and Bigelow. They make calendars.

And they hire ex-cons." Red's big chin jutted out in an extra inch of determination. "I'm going straight."

Ralph and Slim stared at him for a moment, then Slim nodded in somber understanding.

"I am too, Red."

Behind the desk, Ralph Capone shoook his head in disgust. "You two better beat it." He told them wryly, "you're gonna give my garage a bad reputation." Taking a roll of bills from his pocket, he gave each four fifty-dollar bills. "Good luck, " he said.

The big red headed Jewish safecracker from New York and the lanky blond bootlegger from Tennessee left the garage and walked down the alley together.

It was Estelle who put the final piece of the puzzle in place for Richie.

"Your daddy watched the obituary columns for the next few days until he seen where Jack's funeral was going to be held. He figured your mother would be there, and he was right. She was scared as hell to go, because she knew from you that your daddy had been in the card room at Ritter's; she knew Richmond had traced Jack that far, so she knew he was smart enough to find out where the funeral was at. I told her she ought to just take you and run away if she was that scared of Richmond, but she wouldn't do it. 'Jack *cared* for me, 'Stelle,' she said. 'He was probably cheating at cards just to help me get out of Chicago. I couldn't let him go to his grave without being there. It wouldn't be decent.' " Estelle sighed sadly and reached for a cigarette. "You remember the day of Jack's funeral, don't you, sugar?"

"Yeah," Richie nodded. "That girl Helen, where we used to live, stayed home from school and came over to take care of me."

"Your mother didn't want you going to the funeral," Estelle explained. "It was an open casket and she didn't want you seeing a dead person; she said it might give you nightmares. It wasn't much of a funeral, really. Wasn't even in a church, just the chapel of the funeral parlor. Jack's two sisters, they came from Indiana; that was all the family he had. Your mother and I were both pretty nervous all during the service, expecting Richmond to walk in any minute. But it wasn't until the service was over, when we were walking up the aisle, that we seen your daddy at the back of the chapel with his cap in his hands, waiting for your mother. And we could tell by the look on his face that he wasn't aiming to cause no trouble for nobody. If ever I've seen a man who'd had enough trouble for a lifetime, it was your daddy that day. Your mother seen it too. 'He understands, 'Stelle,' she said, 'I can tell.' So we just walked right on up the aisle to where he stood . . .'"

□

"Hello, honey," Slim said.

"Hello, Richmond."

The two women stared frankly at the marks left on his face by Ralph Capone. Slim grinned sheepishly. "Little misunderstanding. It's all straightened out now." His eyes settled on Chloe. "The boy all right?"

"Yes. He's fine."

"I've been looking for the two of you for a spell. Figured to take you back home. That was before I knew about this feller Smart."

Chloe's eyes shifted away from his and she said nothing.

"Listen," Estelle said. "I'll wait over there." She walked away and sat in one of the pews. The chapel was now deserted; she could still hear what the two of them said.

"I done a lot of thinking in the pen," Slim said. "A lot of figuring. I made up my mind to make a new start when I got out. I was hoping you would wait for me—but I guess I knew you wouldn't. Or couldn't."

"Richmond, I don't know why things happen like they do," Chloe said, her voice quavering. Estelle saw her dab at her eyes with the handkerchief she had held throughout the funeral. "But I know one thing—I'm not a strong enough woman for you. I don't have what it takes to be part of the kind of life you live."

"The kind of life I live is going to be different from what it was before," Slim said. "I'm going straight. I don't want no more of the penitentiary. I made up my mind to ask my daddy if he'd let me come back and work the place with him."

Chloe looked at him incredulously. Never since she had known him, never even as a boy, certainly never as a man, had she heard him speak like this. Looking closely at him now, she saw that even his presence had changed. He no longer held his head arrogantly, no longer carried his shoulders and arms with the old cockiness. He had been the only man she had ever seen who could strut standing still. Now the brashness was gone.

"The only thing I ever wanted," she told him quietly, "was a decent, safe life . . . for me and for Richie. The reason I didn't wait for you was because I never believed you'd ever give us that. I never believed your own life would be anything but back roads and bootleg booze. You told me yourself you'd never change."

Grunting softly, Slim said, "In the pen I learned never to say never." On a sudden urge, he took both her hands, "Listen, honey. Neither one of us don't belong up here in this hard city. We've both learned some mean lessons up here. But there's still a chance for us to get out before this place traps us for good. Let's take the boy and do it. There's a train south every day at six o'clock. Let's get on the one that leaves today."

Bursting into sobs that she could no longer contain, Chloe plunged into his arms, his strong embrace, his protection, and let her anguish discharge against his chest as he stroked her hair and said, "There, there, honey. There, there, now," as a parent might comfort a hurt child.

In the nearby pew, Estelle cried along with her friend.

"Hello, boy," Slim said quietly to Richie. "You know who I am?"

"My daddy," Richie said, looking down. His shyness now was not the act it often was; so overwhelmed was Richie by this man that he could not look him in the face. When he felt strong hands picking him up, strong arms holding him, he could only bury his face in Slim's shoulder and bask in the consuming security he felt.

But there was one thing he had to know, to make it right, to make it real.

"Are you going to live with us now?"

"You bet," Slim assured him. He mussed Richie's hair a little and Richie loved it. "Listen, how would you like to live on a great big farm where you can run and play outdoors and where there's chickens and cows and horses? You think you could stand that?"

"You bet," Richie replied, copying his father.

"What about you, honey?" Slim asked his wife. "You think you can stand being a farmer's wife?"

"I can stand being anything," Chloe replied starkly, "when I know I'm safe. When I know somebody's looking out for me."

"Richie and I'll do that, won't we, boy?" Slim asked.

"You bet!" Richie said again. Slim laughed. Richie's face glowed. At last, he had his father back.

Slim left for a while and then came back with his things in a shopping bag, and Chloe packed them in the suitcase with her things and Richie's. There was a tearful goodbye scene between Chloe and Estelle, and Estelle slobbered on Richie a little and tried to kiss him on the lips, but he turned his face aside and took the kiss on the cheek: he did not want Estelle kissing him on the mouth after watching her suck on men's things so often through the keyhole. Finally it was over, and the three of them were on a Roosevelt Road streetcar riding downtown to the big Illinois Central depot.

The train ride was memorable. When they got hungry, Slim bought sandwiches and soda pop and cellophane-wrapped slices of apple pie from a black man in a white coat and cap who pushed a cart up the aisle. The coach was not crowded, so they were able to shift a seat back so that Slim and Chloe could sit on the aisle facing each other, and Richie could alternate between the two window seats watching the southern Illinois countryside go by. It pleased Richie to see his mother and father touch often and exchange brief kisses and smile at each other; not to be left out, he wiggled between them when he could to share some of the affection. His proudest moment was when he had to go to the bathroom and it was his father, not his mother, who took him. It had always embarrassed him to be taken by his mother into the women's restrooms when he had to go; now he felt like a real boy when his father held his hand and walked down the aisle with him. His father even taught him to shake his thing when he finished peeing to get the last few drops out; something his mother had not known to show him.

When darkness came, Chloe rented a pillow from the porter and had Richie lie down on one of the seats with his father's coat over him for a cover. The window shades were drawn and the coach's dim night lights came on. "Go to sleep now, sugar," his mother told him. With his head on the pillow, Richie kept his eyes open and watched his parents snuggling up across from him. Presently his mother saw him looking and said, "Close your eyes, sugar, and go to sleep."

To Richie's delight, his father interceded. "Let him be," Slim said. "It's all new to him, seeing us together. He'll fall asleep soon enough."

"I just wanted us to be able to talk," Chloe said in a quieter voice.

"There'll be time."

Richie smiled to himself. His daddy was the boss!

Later on, Richie decided to pretend to go to sleep so he could listen to what they talked about. Closing his eyes, he lay very still; after a few minutes his mother, as she always did, straightened his cover a little and pushed the hair back out of his eyes. He was careful not to move, knowing that was her way of checking to see if he was asleep. When she thought he was, she said the same thing every time: "Well, I think he's in dreamland at last."

As Richie listened that night he heard his father talk about the long frustrating search he had conducted for them, all the while working for a man named Mack Swain of whom Slim obviously thought a great deal. "He's a clubfoot, poor feller," Richie heard Slim say, "but I swear, he knows more about car engines than anybody I ever seen. He wants to open a place of his own someday. Got his eye on a spot around 76th and Cottage Grove, you know where that's at?"

"No," Chloe said, "I never got out to the South Side."

Slim talked about Mack for a while longer, then Chloe talked about Estelle. "I feel guilty leaving her behind. But I don't think she ever wants to come back to Lamont. 'Stelle likes Chicago; she says she can do all the things she enjoys without being afraid she'll be the main topic of discussion on the town square the next day. She'll probably spend the rest of her life right there around Kedzie Avenue."

After a while, Slim had to ask about Jack Smart. "A man's got to know how a woman felt with another man," he said quietly. "If he don't know, it'll drive him crazy."

Chloe said the only thing she could say. "It wasn't anything like it was with you, honey."

When the coach was very quiet, Slim whispered, "Do you suppose the boy'd be all right if we left him here for a few minutes?"

"I don't see why not," Chloe whispered back. "Where can we go?"

"The restroom. There's a little sink in there that you can sit up on. I can put it in you standing up."

"All right."

Richie knew exactly what they were going to do. After they were gone, he smiled to himself in the darkness. Then he relaxed and let the click-clack of the rails and the motion of the coach lull him to real sleep.

The train they rode was a local and they did not get off in Lamont until early the next morning. Slim carried Richie and Chloe carried the suitcase, and they walked up the hill that was Depot Street until they came to Moreridge. By then Richie was awake and on his feet, holding his daddy's hand.

"You go on down to your mamma's house," Slim told Chloe. "Wait for me there. I don't have no time to waste 'cause I'm sure the law is after me for leaving the state. I'll get on out to Daddy's place and make everything right with him. Then me and him'll get one of the lawyers uptown to see about me turning myself in. Since I ain't been in no trouble, and since I had a good reason for going up north, I think they'll go easy on me. If they know I'm back to stay on my daddy's land, I think they'll give me another chance."

"Oh, god, Richmond, I hope so," Chloe said nervously. Richie saw the old familiar worry-fear in his mother's face again.

"Ever'thing's going to turn out all right, honey," Slim assured her. He mussed Richie's hair. "We're going to *make* it all right, ain't we, boy?"

"You bet!" Richie piped.

Slim kissed them both goodbye. "Go on now. I'll be back soon."

The suitcase in one hand, holding Richie's hand with the other, Chloe walked down the gravel road toward Mrs. Clark's house. Now and then both she and Richie looked back at Slim's lean figure striding determinedly in the other direction, toward the main highway. They would have waved, but Slim did not look back. Soon he was out of sight.

Chloe waited ten days.

Slim never came back.

The first thing Chloe thought was that he had been picked up for violation of his probationary release and was back in jail. She asked a neighbor to drive her out to Solon Howard's farm and talked to Slim's father. He had not seen his son and made it clear that he did not care to. But he did agree to let Chloe know if he heard from Slim.

Chloe made some discreet inquiries around town, but no one had seen him. After several worried days and miserable, sleepless nights, Chloe finally checked with the sheriff. He also had no knowledge of Slim. While Chloe waited, the sheriff telephoned Federal authorities in Memphis and learned that the U.S. Marshal's office had an outstanding warrant on Tennessee Slim but did not know his whereabouts.

Slim had simply disappeared.

Finally exploding in anger and anguish, Chloe began throwing her clothes back into the suitcase. Mrs. Clark tried to reason with her.

"Hadn't you ought to give him a little longer, Chloe?" she asked.

"Longer! What for?" Chloe shrieked. "He's not coming back, Mamma! For god's sake, isn't it obvious?"

The older woman wrung her hands. "Well, even if he don't, is that any reason to run off back up north again?"

"What would you have me do instead, Mamma?" Chloe demanded. "Stay here in Lamont—for everybody to talk about *again?* I've had enough, Mamma! I don't know what's happened or where he is this time; I just know he's not with me and Richie, where he belongs. I'm through with him, Mamma, so you might as well save your breath. I'm leaving—and that's final!"

Playing on the front porch, listening as always, Richie knew that his daddy had gone off somewhere again. Confused and disappointed, Richie did not understand why. His daddy had said he was going to live with them from now on; he said they were going to live on a farm where Richie could play outdoors. Richie wondered why his daddy kept going away. If Richie ever got to be a daddy, he promised himself, he would never tell his little boy he was going to stay and then not do it. He wondered if his daddy realized how much it hurt him.

As Richie was thinking unkind thoughts about his father, his grandmother said something that greatly disturbed him. "At least leave the boy with me," Mrs. Clark said. "There's no need to drag him back up north, is there?"

Peering in between the curtains, Richie saw his mother pause in her packing. Pursing her pretty lips, she seemed to think about it for a very long time—long enough to make Richie start feeling sick inside. He hardly knew his grandmother; he hardly knew *anyone* except his mother. Suddenly he loved his mother very much; suddenly no one else in the world mattered—whoever or wherever they were.

To his great relief his mother finally shook her head. "I can't leave him behind, Mamma. He's all I've got and I love him. Whatever happens, I'll never give up my little boy."

Richie relaxed as he watched his mother start packing his clothes with hers.

He immediately began to think: when he got back to Chicago, maybe he could find his daddy again. He'd done it before.

At the Irving Park Athletic Club, the bell sounded for the fourth round and Richie moved out of the corner and dropped into his awkward, converted-southpaw stance. Circling to the right, his mind told him by rote: *jab, jab, jab*.

His opponent was a Greek kid named Tony Vetos. "He's shorter than you," Myron had briefed him, "thicker in the middle, and slower. He's also prob'ly a lot stronger, but that ain't gonna matter; his arms is short, so you should be able to paste him with right jabs wherever you want to."

Myron was right. Hitting Tony Vetos was only slightly more difficult than hitting the speed bag. Richie made the kid's face as red as a shiny apple.

Twelve wins, Richie was thinking. This fight would give him twelve wins. He had six knockouts and five decisions. On the way over on the streetcar earlier, he had hoped he could stop his opponent tonight for a lucky seventh kayo, but after the second round he knew that goal was hopeless; Vetos was so strong, Richie would have needed a crowbar even to knock him down. So he had to settle down and go for the decision.

This was his fourth four-rounder; the first eight fights had been three-rounders. Sometimes Richie felt he could fight ten rounds, or fifteen. "Some-times," he had told Linda the previous week, "I think I could stay in the ring all night, just circling and jabbing and going in and out of my shell. I don't get tired, I don't even breathe heavy a lot of the time. And sometimes, it's funny, but it's like I'm *outside* the ring too, like I'm watching *me*, like it's a movie or something."

"John Garfield watching John Garfield," she had kidded.

Jab—jab—jab! He felt his right glove impact on the Greek kid's face as Vetos plodded forward like some wind-up toy. At last the final bell rang and he and Tony Vetos stopped fighting and put their arms around each other.

"Clean win," Myron said back in the corner. "Every round was yours."

"I wish I could've got my seventh kayo," Richie said. The remark carried no dejection.

"I'm just as glad you di'nt," Myron replied. "I'll tell you why after."

Even though he was a legitimate member of the boxing team now, Richie still acted as Myron's helper, assisting as he had always done in taking care of the equipment each Saturday night. Following the Irving Park Athletic Club card, after they had put everything away at Midwest and gone out to eat, Myron told Richie what he had meant earlier.

"I'm gonna put yez in a five-round semi-main next week," he said, with customary glumness. "With a colored kid out at the Stony Island Athletic Club. His name is Willie Wakefield and he's got an iden'ical record to what you've got—undefeated, an even dozen wins, exac'ly half of 'em by kayo or TKO. It's a dream match."

"Five rounds!" Richie beamed. "That's swell, Myron!"

"This kid is very good, Richie. He's tall, skinny as a soda straw, and fast, very fast. His punches come in from a lot of different angles and that tends to split the skin; five of his six kayos were stops on cuts."

"I'll beat him," Richie said around a mouthful of cheeseburger.

"I think you can beat him, sure," Myron said, "else I wouldn't put you in with him. But"—he pointed a finger at Richie—"you're gonna have to work extra hard in the gym next week to do it. I wanna learn you next week how to fight when *you're* the slowest one in the ring. That's gonna be something new for you."

"Sure, Myron. I'll do whatever you say."

"Good. Come on in the gym tomorrow about one; instead of taking Sunday off, we'll get in an extra day."

Richie thought at once of Linda, whom he met every Sunday at one. "Can I come in at one-thirty?" he asked.

"I guess so. What, do you go to church or something?"

"Yeah," Richie seized on the excuse, "church."

"That's good," Myron commended. "It's good for a young man to get some religion." Staring down at the remainder of his vegetable soup, Myron's expression changed from its habitual gloom to a mournfulness that had more definition. "I used to be religious," he said. "My wife and son too."

"I didn't know you had a son," Richie said, surprised.

"I don't no more," Myron told him. "He died of scarlet fever a long time ago. My wife kind of wasted away after that; the doctors said she had something called 'involutional depression,' brought on by the death of our boy. They promised she'd come out of it in time. She didn't. She died of a broken heart, is what happened." A trace of a cynical smile showed briefly. "The doctors say such a thing ain't possible, but take my word, it is. If a person loves deeply enough, it is."

They finished eating in silence and went out on Madison Street to, as usual, go their separate ways.

"I'm sorry about your son, Myron," Richie said, a little self-consciously.

"Thanks." The trainer patted Richie on the back of the neck. "In a way I'm lucky, though," he said philosophically. "I know a few other men who've lost their families and are all alone. Know what they do, mostly? Sit and stare. They sit in the parlor of the boarding house, or on the front porch, or on a park bench. Just sit and stare, remembering. Every once in a while one of 'em just closes his eyes and dies. Me, now—I got you and the other boys to look after. Yez is a big responsibility. I ain't got time to sit and stare." He bobbed his chin at Richie. "See you tomorrow, one-thirty."

"Yeah," said Richie, and watched Myron go, feeling a little sad.

At the garage the next morning, Richie showed up with half a dozen eggs in a bag and two inch-thick slabs of ham wrapped in butcher paper.

"I guess you won last night," Mack observed, limping in from the bedroom to find Richie fixing breakfast in the kitchen. Mack had been teaching him how to cook.

"Sure, I won," Richie said matter-of-factly. "Nobody beats me."

Sitting down at the table, Mack began laboriously working his grotesquely clubbed foot into the specially made hightop shoe he wore. He had done this several times in front of Richie, who always tried to avoid looking at the pathetic foot.

Filling the percolator with water and ground coffee, Richie asked, "Mack, can you help me find Ava?"

"You think she might know where your old man is?"

"It's worth a try," Richie said. He added quietly, "He might have gone back to her when he disappeared in Tennessee." In his mind he could not help thinking: the son of a bitch.

"Jeez, I dunno if I can help you or not," Mack said. "I ain't seen or heard of none of the Capones for a long time now. I know they ain't got the mansion on Prairie Avenue no more; it was in the paper when they sold it. Mamma Teresa and Al's wife and Sonny moved to Florida, and when they finally let Al out of prison, he went there to live. Still lives there, far as I know. There's a lot of rumors that he's nutty as a fruitcake, but nobody knows for sure; they live in a big walled place on the ocean, and Al ain't been seen in years. As for Ava, who knows? Maybe she's down there with them, maybe she went back to Italy. I guess it's possible your dad might be with her. I know he was crazy about her. He came around the day he was fixing to take you and your mother back to Tennessee. He'd come over to pick up the things in his room and he stopped in to say goodbye. Gave me fifty dollars to give back to Ava, part of the dough Ralph had given him a few nights earlier." Mack stared off into space for a moment. "I knew he'd been meeting Ava behind the mansion every night. Wasn't none of my business; I just told him he'd better be careful—'cause of Ralph, you know. When I first heard that Ralph had put his boys to looking for Slim, I thought it was because he found out about him and Ava."

Richie put breakfast on the table and they ate as Mack tried to think of a way to help him locate Ava.

"One of Al's younger brothers, John—everybody calls him Mimi—I heard was hanging out at the Hi Ho Club up in Cicero. He used to live in the mansion, so he'd remember me. I think he'd help me get in touch with Ralph. He might even know what happened to Ava." Mack winked at his young friend. "I'll see what I can do."

"Thanks, Mack." Richie's expression softened. "Y'know, you and my trainer Myron are the two best guys in the world." An idea suddenly struck him. "Hey, how about coming to see me fight next week? It's my first five-rounder. You and Myron can meet each other."

"I don't know," Mack said, looking away. "I ain't much for meeting new people. They usually look too long at my foot."

"Not Myron," Richie assured. "He prob'ly won't pay no attention at all to it. Myron looks people in the eye," he added almost proudly.

"Well, maybe," was all Mack would say.

On his way back to the West Side, Richie was more excited about Mack and Myron meeting than he was about the possibility of finding Ava.

Riding the streetcar to meet Linda, Richie reflected on the search for his father. With so many other things in his life now—Linda, training, boxing, Myron— the search for Slim was no longer the most important consideration. He was no longer convinced that his father was the *only* answer to his and his mother's problems. Being on his own over the past months, learning that he could not only survive but, to some degree, even *succeed*, solely on his own, against the odds, in spite of the obstacles, had instilled in him a growing knowledge that he *could* get by—without Slim. And he could help his mother too.

When he reached Pulaski Road, Richie chose a parked car and sat on the fender and waited for Linda. As soon as she got there, he explained that he had to go to the gym and train instead of taking her to a movie.

"The fight next week is a special one. Myron says I need extra workouts to get ready for it."

"Gee, okay," Linda said. Worry set in at once. "Is it going to be a harder fight? Do you think you might get hurt?"

"I ain't gonna get hurt," he assured her. With an arm around her waist, Richie guided her into a doorway between two stores. "The guy's just got a different style that I'm not used to, and Myron wants to show me how to handle it."

"I hope you don't get hurt." Linda put her arms around his neck and they kissed, bodies pressed close, both of them feeling her firming nipples, his erection. "God, I wish we were old enough to run away," she said when their lips parted.

"I *am* old enough."

"That's not the kind of running away I mean, wiseguy." She pinched his arm for emphasis. "I mean the kind where a boy and girl run off together. Like to get married." Linda laid her cheek on his chest. "Wouldn't it be swell if we were old enough to do that, Richie?"

"We will be someday."

"We'll probably never do it," she said cheerlessly. "You've got other things to do. Look for your father. Take care of your mother someday. Fight for your friend Myron. Things that are important to you."

"You're important to me," he stressed. Taking her by the shoulders, he held her away from him so that he could look at her. "I don't know what I'd do without being able to see you every Sunday. You're the most important person in my life."

"Really, Richie?" Her cheeks glowed. "Do you mean it?"

"Sure I mean it. You're the only one in the world I trusted enough to tell where I was living." That was a lie; he had told Stan Klein and Bobby Casey. But it was a harmless lie, he decided, if it made her feel good.

"Richie, I love you so much."

"I love you too, honey." Over her shoulder he looked at a clock in a jewelry store window across the street. It was ten past one. "I gotta get going. I'll see you next Sunday, okay? I'll tell you all about the big fight."

Leaving her, feeling rotten because he would not have his time with her today, would not be able to hold her and kiss her as much as he wanted to, Richie walked briskly down Madison Street toward the gym. He would feel better, he knew, as soon as he got his workout clothes on and started doing what Myron told him to do; as soon as he started learning what Myron wanted to teach him. Intense concentration, Richie knew by now, served two purposes: it helped him to learn a thing really well—and it helped him to forget his problems, for a while anyway. Learning was exciting to him, as books and boxing and being free and on his own were exciting. When he learned a new thing, when something fell into place in his ever roiling mind, it was almost sexual it felt so fine.

Passing on the opposite side of the street from Cascade, Richie heard a sharp whistle that he recognized at once. Pausing, his eyes swept the street until he located the source: Stan Klein, lounging next to the bowling alley's entrance, smoking a cigarette. Richie immediately crossed the street to him. As he approached, Stan glanced at the Midwest A. C. jacket he wore, but said nothing.

"Where you headed?" Stan asked.

"The gym, to work out." Richie bobbed his chin down the street at the athletic club. Stan still did not know Richie was boxing. Looking around, Richie asked, "Where's Casey?"

"In the fucking Cook County Hospital with his jaw wired," Stan replied tightly. "His old man came home drunk the other night and kicked him in the face. Without a word, the cocksucker just came in, walked over to where Bobby was sitting, and kicked him right in the face."

"Jesus," Richie said quietly. What the fuck was wrong with fathers anyway? "Is he gonna be okay?"

"His jaw's gonna mend, if that's what you mean," Stan said. The eyes of the two boys met as each realized the deeper meaning of the answer.

Then a sudden suspicion rose in Richie. Was Stan there to enlist Richie as a replacement for Bobby Casey, to help Stan steal? A slight wave of nausea rushed through him. If Stan asked, what would he say? He dreaded the prospect of turning Stan down; Stan was the best, often the *only,* friend of his own age that Richie had. Yet Richie could not, would not, jeopardize everything he had accomplished for himself by becoming a street thief again. Bracing himself to refuse if Stan asked him, Richie learned with shocking incredulity that he would not have to.

"I di'nt come here to tell you about Bobby," Stan said. "I came to tell you your old lady's back."

"*What?*"

"I seen her down at Madison and Kedzie last night. I went down there to a movie and when I was walking home, I seen her come out of a building and go down the street. I di'nt know if you knew or not."

Richie mutely shook his head. He stared into space, shocked by the news. He had known his mother would be returning from the federal narcotics hospital someday, known he would have to contact Miss Menefee, or someone, to find out when. But he had relegated that obligation to some time in the vague future when he did not have so many other things on his mind. It was a task that nagged his thoughts now and then, usually when he was trying to go to sleep at night, but since it was not urgent, not demanding of his time *then*—like looking for Slim, seeing Linda, training, boxing—he always deferred thinking about it. Now he suddenly had to face it.

"The number she come out of was thirty-three-forty," Stan told him. "Up near the Homan Avenue end of the block, where the park starts."

"Yeah," Richie said, in barely a whisper, thickly, "I know where it's at."

After a moment of silence between them, unintruded upon by the street sounds around them, Stan shrugged and said, "I gotta take off." Lips tensing a little, he added, "Gotta see if I can find some machines I can get by myself. See you."

Richie watched him go without saying goodbye. For several minutes he remained standing on the sidewalk, mesmerized by his own rushing, confused thoughts. Finally, becoming aware that passersby were looking curiously at him, he walked slowly away.

Without consciously deciding, he walked down to the corner and waited for a streetcar that would take him to the address Stan had given him.

ichie stood across the street from 3340 West Madison and scrutinized the building. There was a dry cleaner's at street level, with a stairway directly next to it leading up to three floors above. Over the doorway to the stairs was a faded sign that read: HOUSEKEEPING ROOMS. Staring up at the windows above the dry cleaners, Richie wondered if his mother was behind any of them, looking out. He backed under an awning to keep from being seen, should she be.

He would go in to see her in five minutes, he told himself. There was a clock in a pawn shop window by which he could time himself. That decision made, he turned his thoughts to what he would say to his mother. She would know, of course, that it had been he who turned her in. But there was no reason for her to be sore about that . . . was there? She had probably been very angry about it at first, but in time wouldn't she have realized that it had been the best thing to do? Lexington had not been easy for her, he was sure of that, but it had been *right*—and she would know that.

And what of the future? He had it all scaled out in his mind how the two of them could get along, make it in life, by working together. But would she listen to him; would she follow *his* plan? Always she had been the one to chart the course of their lives, she had done the leading, merely taking him along as she did her suitcase and purse. She had led—and the path she had chosen had eventually always taken them from good to bad, bad to worse. Would she realize that—and if she did, would she admit it?

With a minute to go on the pawn shop clock, Richie began steeling himself to cross the street and walk into 3340—when out of 3340 he saw Chloe emerge. Tensing, Richie moved almost fearfully farther into the shadow of the awning. He did not want her to see him; it was important that he go to her, not that she run into him. Remaining on the opposite side of the street, she walked purposefully down Madison toward Kedzie. Richie followed her on his own side, a few yards behind.

As they walked, Richie studied his mother. He had expected her to look heavier, healthier, than when he last saw her. From a distance she appeared very thin; her stride, her movements, seemed nervous, jerky. As she walked, her hands never stopped moving: she touched her hair, straightened her collar, smoothed an eyebrow, brushed one of her sleeves, put a finger to her lips. Behind her, Richie could not see exactly what each of the restive movements were, but he did not have to; he had lived with his mother long enough to recognize the condition she was displaying. Jittery. Unstrung. Like a doper who needed a fix.

Could that be possible? he asked himself. The mere thought of it made him feel ill. Had they failed to cure her? Did they turn people back on the streets who were still addicts? Richie could not believe it.

At Kedzie, Chloe turned north and walked toward Lake Street. Richie crossed to the opposite side just as a streetcar was starting to leave. Hurrying, he swung onto the rear platform. Giving the conductor a nickel, he remained on the platform as the streetcar passed his mother. He rode one block and got off, the conductor looking curiously at him. On the same side of the street on which Chloe was walking, Richie went into a grocery store and stood a little back from the front window. Presently, his mother came by and he got his first close look at her.

Chloe did not look as bad as when Richie had last seen her, but she certainly did not look good either. She *was* as thin and gaunt as she had appeared from across the street; she was also very pale and hollow-eyed; the circles under those eyes, while not as dark as he had seen them in the past, were nevertheless present. She walked directly ahead in a determined, single-minded manner, and Richie knew exactly where she was going.

Down Lake Street. To the colored section. To make a buy.

Chloe was still a doper.

Leaving the grocery, he followed her; he had to prove it to himself, even if there was no doubt in his mind. He had to see it.

At Lake Street, Chloe turned and walked east. Staying half a block back, Richie walked behind her on the same side of the street. They were both in the cool shadow of the el tracks now. Richie did not even stay on the inside of the sidewalk, where he could duck into a doorway if Chloe should turn around. He knew that she would not; what she wanted was in front of her, not behind. Dopers needing a fix never looked back.

Down Lake Street the nervous woman walked, traversing blocks that gradually changed their citizens from white, to white and black, to just black. Years earlier when Chloe had sent *him* to pick up her dope, he had been terrified of Lake Street and its dark, unsmiling faces. Colored boys had chased him trying to get the money that was wrapped up in the notes from his mother. Now Richie simply ignored the hostile looks; he no longer ran from anyone.

Chloe finally entered one of the tenement buildings. Richie crossed the street and leaned in a doorway to wait; he did not even bother to sit on the curb, knowing she would not be inside long. Dope transactions, he knew from experience, were quick and uncomplicated.

His mother was back outside in five minutes. Chloe was a different person now. Just *having* the little packet of dope was enough to calm the fidgety hands, the restiveness. Now she walked with elbows close to her sides, left arm bent up around her purse, right hand covering the purse from above. No fullback ever protected a football like Chloe protected that purse, no young mother ever held her infant with more care. The same fixed resolve was on her face, the same constancy of purpose in her eyes, but now, on the return trip, there was a slight anticipatory smile on her lips, a hint of cunning shrewdness, *knowing*. She *had* something. Something that would let her transcend ordinary life. It was heaven and hell—but it was heaven first.

Richie followed his mother all the way back to 3340 West Madison and watched her go into the building she had come out of less than an hour earlier.

Richie walked up to Homan Avenue where the park began. Finding a park bench no one else was sitting on, he slumped down and rested his head against the wooden back, looking up at the sky. He should be on his way to the gym to start getting ready for the Willie Wakefield fight; Myron was probably still there waiting for him, even though he was more than an hour late. But Richie had no heart for it. His enthusiasm was suddenly gone, his zeal wasted by the sight of his mother in the same doper condition in which he had last seen her. Inside, a new and terrible realization spread.

Nothing had changed.

Everything was the same as it had been a year ago, two years ago, three, four . . .

It was the old nightmare all over again. Richie had seen that nightmare begin once before, back when his father had abandoned them, back when Chloe had returned with him to Chicago, back when she started taking "medicine" in the form of paregoric, to calm her nerves.

He had seen the nightmare begin, he thought now, but he would never see it end. Daylight never came in nightmares of dope. Richie knew. He had lived in the darkness of such a nightmare when he was eleven years old.

And ten.

And nine.

And eight . . .

When Richie was eight years old, if he was even five minutes late getting home from school, Chloe would be upset.

"I told you to come *straight* home! You'd better start listening to me, young man, if you know what's good for you! Now hurry up and change into your play clothes. I've got some places for you to go."

Richie knew what the "places" were, and he knew *where* they were. It was the same every afternoon; daily he faced it with dread.

In the bedroom, Richie pulled open the bottom drawer of a dresser and got out an old pair of knickers and an old shirt. From under the dresser, he pulled a pair of old scuffed shoes, their heels worn up to the soles on opposite sides. Standing next to the bed, Richie changed clothes. It was not his bed; he slept on the couch, as usual. But the bottom drawer of the dresser was his; he kept his school clothes on one side of it, his play clothes on the other. The furnished apartment they lived in was on Carroll Street just off Kedzie, in the same neighborhood in which they had once lived with Estelle.

"Richie, will you hurry *up!*" Chloe yelled from the living room.

Folding his school clothes, he put them in the drawer and put his school shoes under the dresser. Then he went into the living room. His mother was waiting impatiently, one foot tapping nervously. She had the notes all ready.

"Take this first note to the white drugstore down on Francisco. Get a fifteen-cent bottle with the quarter wrapped in the note and don't forget to get a dime change. Then go down to the nigger drugstore on Lake Street and use *this* note to get a twenty-five-cent bottle. Then take the dime change and put it with the nickel in *this* note, and go to the other white drugstore on Talman by the railroad tracks and get another fifteen-cent bottle. And don't you *dare* play on those railroad tracks, you hear me? As a matter of fact, don't you play *anywhere*; you just hurry up and bring my medicine back here because I have a splitting headache that is about to drive me *crazy*." Chloe paused for a moment, thinking, then added, "I'm pretending to be Mrs. Johnson today, so if anybody asks you, you tell them your name is Richie Johnson. Let me hear you say it."

"Richie Johnson," he mumbled, barely audible.

"All right, go on now," Chloe said, urging him toward the front door. "And remember to carry each bottle in a different pocket so they don't bump together and break."

Knowing she would be watching out the window, Richie hurried down the street until he rounded the corner on Kedzie. Out of sight he slowed down and lagged along at a spiritless pace that matched his mood. As he walked, he fingered the notes in his pocket. He knew what the notes said, at least in general. Chloe's "medicine" was something called paregoric. Sometimes one of the white-coated men to whom he handed the note would open it and read it aloud. *"Please send me a 25¢ bottle of paregoric to take for a toothache,"* it would say—or a headache, or female cramps, or arthritis, or something else. His mother, Richie thought, had many things wrong with her. At first he had been troubled by that; he hadn't minded going to get her medicine. But when the number of drugstores he had to visit continued to increase—there were now more than two dozen of them, some so far away he had to ride the streetcar—and when his mother never went to the doctor, and never complained about anything but "splitting headaches" and her "nerves," Richie began to resent the daily chore to which he was subjected.

Richie hated going into the drugstores. His mother had a daily routine planned for him that only required him to visit each drugstore once a week. Even so, he still got suspicious looks and at times was even questioned. "Weren't you just in here for paregoric a few days ago?" Richie always said no, as his mother had coached him to do; he lied and said they had just moved to the neighborhood, and if necessary gave his pretend name.

Mustering up as much mettle as he could, Richie entered the first drug-store of the day. The counter where they sold paregoric was in the rear; always in the rear, those suspicious white-coated men. At the pharmacy counter, the man in the white coat said, "Yes?" Richie handed him the note with the quarter wrapped in it. The man read it, glanced at him, grunted softly, and stepped behind a frosted glass partition. Momentarily he returned with a three-ounce bottle of whiskey-colored liquid, which he put in a small brown bag, twisting the top closed. Punching a key on the cash register, he cranked a handle on the side that rang a bell and opened the cash drawer. Tossing in the quarter, he handed Richie the bag and a dime change. Richie walked out, feeling the man's eyes on him all the way.

Outside, Richie began to dawdle even more; the next stop was the colored drugstore on Lake Street. It was one of half a dozen colored drugstores that Chloe sent him to; he dreaded and feared them all—not the *places*, but getting to them. Young colored boys who lived and played around the drugstores did not like pale little white boys walking *their* streets; Richie invariably was harangued, challenged, even chased. It was a lucky day that he made a trip to any of the colored drugstores without incident.

No matter how slowly and reluctantly he moved, eventually Richie reached Lake Street. Once there, he immediately began to walk faster to get in and out of the neighborhood as quickly as possible. His eyes moved in constant scrutiny checking doorways, corners, empty lots, any place where the black kids might congregate. When a black adult passed him, Richie glanced away, never meeting his eyes. He kept to the outside of the sidewalk, where he could break and run.

At the black drugstore he made the long walk to the rear and handed the second note to the black pharmacist. The man glanced at it, clamped a cigar between his teeth, and without looking reached under the counter and got a five-ounce bottle of paregoric. He wrapped it in white paper and sealed it with a strip of brown tape. Richie took the bottle and left the store without a word being spoken.

Three black boys were waiting for him when he got back outside.

"Say, boy, what you got there?" one of them asked, pointing at the wrapped bottle. He was no taller than Richie, but had muscles that Richie had never developed.

"Medicine for my mother," Richie said. He started walking. They walked along with him.

"Wha's the matter wif' yo' mamma?" the same boy asked.

"I don't know," Richie shrugged. "She's just sick and has to take medicine."

"She got the V.D.?"

"What's that?" Richie asked.

"Wha's that!" another of them exclaimed. "Shit, boy, don't you know nuffin'? Tha's the ven'ral disease."

"Womens gets that from too much fucking, " the third boy said.

Richie felt his face turn hot. "That ain't what my mother's got."

One of them grabbed his arm and stopped him. "How you know?" he demanded. "If she ain't got the V.D., what has she got?"

"She's got headaches," Richie said. Twisting his arm loose, he resumed walking.

"Say, lemme have a dime," the muscular boy said, still walking next to him. "I pay you back nes' time you come to get yo' mamma's medicine."

"I ain't got a dime," Richie said. "Maybe I'll have one when I come back." One hand was in his pocket, closed tightly around fifteen cents and the third note.

" 'Lonzo, I think he's lying!" another boy said. "I think he gots a dime!"

Alonzo grabbed Richie's arm and stopped him again. "If you lying to me, I gon' whip yo' ass."

"Okay," Richie said with a pained expression on his face, "lemme see if I've got one." Alonzo let go of his arm and Richie began to feel around inside his knickers pockets. Under the elevated tracks, traffic moved in both directions. On their side of the street, a large, canvas-covered produce truck cruised toward them. "Oh yeah, I think I got one," Richie said. Alonzo and his two friends smiled. Richie smiled too. "Can I ask that policeman if I have to give it to you?" he said, pointing behind them. All three of their heads snapped around.

Richie broke and ran. Darting between two parked cars, he bolted in front of the produce truck, hearing its tires screech, its horn sound sharply and angrily. Dodging an oncoming car from the other direction, he heard a second horn but no screech of tires. Reaching the opposite sidewalk, he glanced back to see a glowering Alonzo and his friends run around the back of the produce truck after him.

Richie tore down the sidewalk and around the next corner. He was not as afraid now as he had been when they were close to him. He was a fast runner and he knew it; all he needed was a headstart and he could get away nearly every time. Picking up medicine for his mother, he had been chased before; only twice had he been caught and the money he was carrying taken away. When he arrived back home, frightened and crying, Chloe had paddled him with a shoe and then gone out herself to get her medicine. Later, when she returned and had taken it, she had made up to him with money for a Dixie Cup from the ice cream truck.

The secret in getting away on the streets, Richie had learned, was turning corners. At the first alley he came to, he changed direction and entered it; several doors down, he turned into the gangway between two buildings and cut out to the street. Rushing down the street half a block, he crossed, went through another gangway, turned into another alley, and kept going. After two or three quick turns, he could not see Alonzo and his pursuers behind him. He kept going for several blocks anyway, just in case.

When he was back in the comparative safety of a white neighborhood, Richie slowed down and headed toward Talman Street, glad that it was his last stop of the day.

It had been Estelle who introduced Chloe to paregoric, during their first stay in Chicago before Richmond showed up. Estelle had learned of the opiate in one of the drugstores she worked in.

"This stuff," she praised to Chloe, "must be God's way of trying to make up for menstrual cramps. I'm telling you, honey, a teaspoon full of paregoric and you won't *care* what time of month it is. Be sure to mix a little sugar with it, though; it is the *awfulest* tasting stuff in the world. There's a price to pay for everything, I guess."

At first Chloe only used paregoric like Estelle did: two or three days a month during her period. After the attack by Lew Grubb, she had begun using it daily to help her relax and get through the emotional anguish the rape had caused. Jack Smart had gently warned her about it. "You w-w-want to be careful of that st-stuff, honey. It can g-get to be a habit." Gradually, as Jack ingratiated himself into her life, Chloe was able to cut back on the doses, not yet having used enough to become addicted. For a while she resumed taking it only for her period; Jack was the substitute that calmed her nerves.

Then Chloe learned that Richmond was out. Out and looking for her. And apparently in Chicago. Unknown to Jack, as she urged him to get on with the plan to move to Gary and start a bowling alley, she again began to use the drug daily to steady her nerves. During her brief interlude with Richmond, which began at Jack Smart's funeral and ended the following morning when they got off the train in Lamont and parted company, and during the subsequent ten days that she spent there, Chloe had no paregoric at all; it was not sold over the counter in Tennessee. Without it, and burdened by the growing realization that Richmond was not coming back, she became a fingernail-biting, lip-chewing, chain-smoking example of living jitters. From restless and apprehensive, she went to fearful and fidgety, and ended up, again, just plain scared and on the verge of hysteria. That was when she had packed up, taken Richie, and returned to Chicago.

From the very beginning of her second tenure in the city, Chloe was determined to stick to more stable ground. She promised herself *not* to get involved with anyone like Jack Smart again, not, as a matter of fact, to even get involved with Estelle again, because, as much as she had always cared for Estelle, there was something about her that instinctively attracted the wrong kind of men. Married men, hustlers, drinkers, gamblers—Chloe wanted nothing to do with any of them. So determined was she to avoid future occasions of such involvement, that she found a furnished apartment for herself and Richie, moved in, and lived there a week before even contacting Estelle to let her know they were back. Estelle was hurt.

"I just can't believe it," she lamented when she came to visit. "It's almost like I'm being punished for *doing* something. Like I was being disowned."

"It's not anything of the sort, 'Stelle," Chloe defended. "It's just that I have to think of Richie now. He's getting too big to be around the things that go on when you and I share a place—"

"Things *I* do, you mean," Estelle challenged. "Go on and say it."

"Things we both do. I was just as bad as you; only difference was I was just doing the things with Jack, and you had a whole string of men—"

"I don't have to put up with this," Estelle simmered, rising from the kitchen table, taking her purse. "You are as much as calling me a slut, Chloe."

"I am not!" Chloe disclaimed.

"I love that boy of yours like he was my very own and you know it. And you sit there and practically tell me that I'm not fit to be around him!"

"Estelle, I didn't say anything of the kind!"

Richie heard it all from the living room where he was tracing a figure of Charles Altas from a magazine ad and drawing Buck Jones Western garb on it. Arguments between Chloe and Estelle usually did not last long, but this one, Richie eventually found out, did. Chloe's decision not to live in the same apartment with Estelle any longer apparently cut her friend far more deeply than Chloe had expected it would. Chloe had expected Estelle to be peeved; in fact, Estelle was emotionally mangled. She fled the apartment in tears and it was months before she and Chloe spoke again.

Chloe resumed taking daily doses of paregoric as soon as she got back to Chicago. She told herself that she was only taking it to calm her nerves and give her a steady approach to the responsibilities she had to face. She had no one on whom to depend now but herself, but she was firmly resolved that she would be smart enough and strong enough—for her *and* Richie. No one had ever thought she could do anything on her own, not her mother, not Richmond, not Jack, not even Estelle. Well, she would show them. She would show them all. She didn't need anything or anybody.

Except the paregoric.

When Richie got back home with the three bottles, Chloe patted him on the head and gave him a nickel. "Did you have any trouble?" she asked.

"No." Telling her about Alonzo and the other colored kids chasing him would have done no good. The one time he did tell her, his mother had said, "Well, sugar, you're just going to have to learn to take care of yourself, that's all there is to it. Sometimes it's a cruel world." Now she nudged him toward the door. "You run on down to the candy store now and spend your nickel. I have to take my medicine now and lie down for a while. This headache is about to drive me crazy."

Richie left the apartment and went down to Kedzie Avenue again. The candy store was on the corner across from Biedler Elementary, where he attended second grade. He had gone to the first grade at Charleston Elementary, then Drake. Whenever his mother moved them to a new apartment, he usually had to transfer to a different school. He hated it. A new school meant a new schoolyard and new kids to test first his courage, then push him around for a week or so until they got tired of the sport, after which they would leave him alone most of the time except for daily ridicule and an occasional shove.

In fact, next to going for his mother's medicine, the thing Richie hated most was moving, which they did every couple of months. It would be after his mother had fallen behind in the rent and the landlord had come around with a final warning. When that happened, they usually moved out that night.

At the candy store, Richie bought a pack of Cowboy Heroes gum. Inside the waxy wrapper was a round, flat piece of pink chewing gum stamped with an outline of a mounted cowboy. Under the gum was a pasteboard card, also round, which was the real reason for the purchase. On the face of the card, in color, was a cowboy movie hero; on the back a partial list of movies and serials in which he had starred, as well as other essential information, such as the name of his horse. The cards were notched so that by the use of rubber bands they could be strung together into a belt of sorts, or a bandolier to wear across the chest. Half the boys of Richie's age in the neighborhood were wearing them.

As soon as he got out of the candy store, Richie tore off the wrapper to look at his new card. It was a smiling, white-hatted Tom Tyler. "Goddamn son of a bitch," Richie said to himself, using the swear words he was most familiar with. It was his third Tom Tyler in a row. Turning his head, he glared through the window at the candy store owner. "Goddamn dirty son of a bitch," he swore at him, certain it was somehow the man's fault. He wondered if the packs were sorted and stacked in some special way so that a kid would get a lot of the same ones and have to keep buying and buying. There were twelve different cowboy heroes in a set; so far, Richie had got only five of them: Tom Tyler, Bob Steele, George O'Brien, Charles Starrett, and Johnny

Mack Brown. He had bought at least twenty, and got only *five* cowboy heroes. All the others had been duplicates. The one he wanted, of course, was Buck Jones. He would have traded every card he had for one Buck Jones.

Stuffing the gum into his mouth, the card into his pocket, and throwing the wrapper into the gutter, Richie walked slowly back home. When he got there, his mother, as he knew she would be after taking her medicine, was feeling very good: smiling, soft-spoken, solicitous. "Sugar, would you like a nice hamburger for supper tonight? And some fried potatoes? And a nice bowl of tomato soup? I'm going to fix your supper now and let you eat while you're listening to your radio shows. Then I've got a surprise for you. Guess who's coming over to see us tonight? Helen's little sister. Dorothy—remember her? From when we lived on Walnut Street. When Helen used to take care of you sometimes, she'd take you and Dorothy to the Kedzie Annex. Well, Dorothy's as old now as Helen was then, and she's coming over to stay with you tonight while I go out."

"Go out where?" Richie wanted to know.

"Oh, just for some Chinese food maybe, and to a picture show."

"Who with?"

"A real nice fellow I met. His name's John and he's from Tennessee, just like us. I met him at the diner." Chloe worked from seven to three as a waitress at Denny's Diner, about eight blocks from where they lived. "He works the early shift at a tool-and-die plant across the street and stops in for pie and coffee every day at two when he gets off. We've been talking for a couple of weeks, ever since it came up that we're both from Tennessee. 'Course, he's from *east* Tennessee and we're from *west* Tennessee, but it's still a coincidence. Anyway, he asked me out tonight for Chinese. That's why I'm feeding you supper early." She kissed him on the cheek. "Go on now and listen to your shows. When supper's ready, we can move the radio in here."

Sullenly, Richie turned on the radio and stretched out on the floor with his head under the table. But he did not listen to the radio; he lay there staring up at the underside of the table, wondering if Dorothy was going to be as mean to him as Helen had been.

Wondering if she would slap him in the face.

And threaten to cut off his thing.

Dorothy, like her sister, had always taunted him about not having a father. She was probably going to be very glad to find out that he still did not have one.

Goddamn him, Richie thought of his father. Goddamn the dirty son of a bitch.

Goddamn him for not being there.

When Richie met John Eaton, his mother's new boyfriend, he found, to his chagrin, that he immediately liked the burly, easygoing Southerner.

Chloe invited John over for supper one night and when he came in, she said, "Johnny, this is my little boy, Richie." To Richie, who was lying on the floor looking at the latest *Action* comic book, she said, "Sugar, this is Johnny, I told you about him, remember?" She nudged Richie with her shoe. He looked up at the fixed smile on her face. "Get off the floor, sugar, and meet Johnny."

Richie rose to stand before a big, muscular man with a round, somewhat bland face and curly black hair that was already well receded. Looking down at him, Johnny stuck out a beefy hand and said, "Shake, partner."

It was the kind of thing Buck Jones would have said.

Smiling shyly, Richie put his own small hand into the big one and felt his arm being firmly pumped. Then Johnny reached down and picked up the comic book.

"This here's that new feller they call 'Superman,' ain't it?" he said, looking at the cover.

"Yeah."

"Sugar, don't say 'yeah,' say 'yes, sir,' " Chloe told Richie. And more quietly, "Johnny, I think you meant 'isn't' instead of 'ain't.' "

The man and the boy sat down on the couch, neither paying any attention to her corrections.

"You think this feller can really fly?" Johnny asked.

"Sure," Richie said.

"Right up in the air like a bird?"

"Sure."

"You think bullets really bounce off his chest?"

"Sure."

"I don't know," Johnny said skeptically, winking at Chloe.

"It shows it right here," Richie asserted, fingering through the pages to a panel showing the Man of Steel with bullets indeed bouncing off his chest. "There it is right there."

"Okay, I guess you're right," Johnny conceded. "Say, who's your favorite cowboy?"

"Buck Jones." Richie's eyes narrowed suspiciously. "You know who he is?"

" 'Course I do. Who don't?"

Chloe interjected, "You mean, 'who doesn't,' Johnny."

Ignoring her again, Johnny asked Richie, "Did you see *The Overland Express*?"

"Yeah! It was all about the Pony Express riders!"

"How'd you like the way them riders changed horses? They just jumped off one, jumped on another'n and off they went. That was something."

"Sure was!" Richie leaped off the couch. "You wanna see my Buck Jones Big-Little Books? I got three of 'em!"

"Okay," Johnny said, winking. Richie ran out of the room and the big Tennessean smiled up at Chloe and asked, "What's for supper?"

"I've, uh, got pork chops frying."

"Biscuits and gravy?"

"Yes."

"That's my favorite."

"I know," Chloe said, "you told me."

"Ain't nothing better than fried pork chops," Johnny declared, winking again.

Walking toward the kitchen, Chloe muttered to herself, "No, I guess there ain't."

After their first meeting, Richie always looked forward to Johnny's visits. Unlike Jack Smart, Johnny never brought him anything—no candy or toys—and never gave him nickels or dimes to spend, but Johnny did do something that no one else in Richie's life did: he *talked* to Richie. Talked to him on subjects about which Richie could talk back, like comic book characters and movie cowboys. Sometimes when he came over, Johnny brought an afternoon *Herald-American* and let Richie sit next to him as he read it, sharing the contents with him.

"That there's the new Hudson." He pointed to an ad. "See there where they've changed the fenders; they was rounder on last year's model."

And: "See this feller here? That there's Gabby Hartnett, the best catcher in baseball. They just made him the manager of the Cubs, but he's still gonna be their catcher."

And, tapping a photograph on the front page: "This here's a picture of Adolf Hitler. He's the kind of feller if we had him back home we'd turn the dogs loose on him."

"Is he a bad guy?" Richie asked, already certain that he was: only a bad guy would have such a dumb moustache.

"He's worse than bad," Johnny confirmed. "Ever' once in a a while some feller gets borned that never should have got borned. As the saying goes, this feller's mamma should have drowned him in the nearest creek and sold her milk."

"What milk?"

"Never mind."

"If he's so bad," Richie said, "maybe Buck Jones could get after him."

Johnny smiled. "Now that's something I'd like to see. Buck Jones in a showdown with Adolf Hitler. I reckon it would save the world a lot of trouble."

Johnny ate supper with them a couple of nights a week, and a couple of nights a week he took Chloe out to eat and see a movie. On those nights, Dorothy came over to stay with Richie. She was thirteen now and like her sister Helen, put on an act while Chloe was still there: "Hi, Richie, how you doing? Want to play Go Fish tonight? Or would you like me to read to you?" All this while bending over and smiling in his face.

Fifteen minutes after Chloe left, when Dorothy was sure she was gone, the smile vanished and the act ended.

"Take off your clothes. I'm going to give you a bath."

"You're not supposed to give me no bath," Richie protested.

Dorothy caught his cheek between her thumb and forefinger. "Do you want me to pinch a plug out of your face?"

"No!"

"Then take off your goddamned clothes!"

Richie swore back, silently: goddamn dirty son of a bitch.

In the tub, which was oval and stood on four legs, Dorothy scrubbed him with a wash rag. "Remember how I used to tease you about not having a father?" she asked. "Well, you'll notice I'm not doing that anymore. Know why?"

"Why?" Richie mumbled.

" 'Cause you're *lucky* not to have a father, that's why. Fathers do bad things to kids when they get older. Especially to girls."

She took delight in scrubbing him until his skin was red. "You're a very dirty little boy. I—have—to—get—all—the—dirt—off—of—you!" she enunciated as she rubbed vigorously with the soapy cloth. When she got to his scrotum, she scrubbed extra hard and Richie twisted back in the tub, seized with pain.

"That hurts!" He blinked back tears. Dorothy only smiled coldly.

"You don't want it hurt, do you? Someday you'll grow up and be a father, and you want to keep it good in case you have little girls, don't you!"

"No! Quit it! I'll tell!"

She threw the cloth in his face. "Finish washing yourself." At the bathroom door she looked back with the same cold smile. "You won't tell," she said confidently.

Every time Dorothy came over, it was the same treatment. Richie did not tell his mother because he was afraid. He was afraid she would not believe him, that Dorothy would find out, and that she would be even meaner to him. So the same way he steeled himself to face a new schoolyard every time his mother moved them, he steeled himself to endure Dorothy's maltreatment. It was, he found, usually brief. Almost as if it were some ritual she had to complete before silently, moodily, leaving him alone for the rest of the night. She would scrub him ferociously in the tub, hurt him in the balls once, just as she had done the first night, and then it would be over. She would do her homework then, or listen to something on the radio or sit out on the front stoop if it were warm, and then at nine o'clock she would make his bed on the couch and have him get in it. She rarely even spoke to him after the evening's initial, vehement condemnation of him as "dirty" and planning to grow up to hurt little girls. The only girl Richie ever even thought of harming was *her*. Twice a week he wished he could kill her.

At one point, things got so bad for him that Richie decided he *had* to tell his mother. It was after a night when Dorothy's washing seemed to vacillate between pain and arousal, when the roughness of the rubbing cloth hurt and then stimulated, and the two sensations somehow overlapped and Richie got an erection.

"There, see!" Dorothy exclaimed almost gleefully. "See what a dirty little boy you are! Look at it!" Becoming angrier than ever, she had hit his erect little penis with her fist, driving pain into his testicles, anus, and up his spine. He had hurt for the rest of the night.

The next day he had tried to tell his mother, but it had come off very poorly. Chloe was busy writing her drugstore notes.

"What do you mean, Dorothy hurts you?" she asked absently. "Hurts you how?"

"In the bathtub. She washes me too hard."

"Try not to get so dirty," Chloe advised.

Richie wanted to tell her about the punch to his erection, but he did not know how; the fact of the erection somehow embarrassed him. They were not new to him; he had been aware of them many times when watching through the keyhole as his mother and Estelle dressed to go out, or when they were doing things with men. But being aware of an erection and talking about an erection were two different things. Richie could not find the right words; his complaint about Dorothy sounded like whining.

More than what Richie was saying about Dorothy, Chloe was interested in what Richie might be saying to Johnny. "Sugar, have you ever mentioned to Uncle Johnny about the medicine you get for me?"

"No," Richie replied, shaking his head.

"Are you sure?"

"Yeah."

" 'Yes,' not 'yeah.' Well, I don't want you ever to mention it, you hear? To him or anybody else." Turning in the chair, Chloe had taken him into her arms. "Listen, sugar, I know you don't like going to all these drugstores for me every day. I know you'd like to go running and playing with the other children on the block; I know that because of me you spend a lot of time alone. But it's not going to be forever, hear? Life is going to get better for both of us, I promise. Listen, you like Uncle Johnny, don't you?"

"Yeah."

"Yes," she corrected.

"Yes."

"You always have a good time with him, don't you?"

"Yes."

"Well, how would you like him to be your new daddy?"

"What about my real daddy?"

"What about him?"

"What if he comes back again?"

"Sugar," Chloe said, holding his face between her palms, "your real daddy won't *be* coming back. He's gone for good. If he cared anything at all about either one of us, he'd have been back long before now. We're just going to have to get along without him." She smiled brightly but artificially. "Best thing to do now is find us somebody new. New husband for me, new daddy for you. That's why I asked how you'd like for Uncle Johnny to be your new daddy; I think Uncle Johnny and I will be getting married soon. I've already turned in some papers to get a divorce from your daddy for deserting us. Soon's I get that divorce, why, we'll probably get us a new place to live with Uncle Johnny."

A new school, Richie thought. A new schoolyard. New kids to pick on him. Sighing wearily, his eyes grew wet. Seeing such tribulation in his little-boy face, knowing she had put it there, Chloe's own eyes became teary.

"Listen," she said, hugging him close, "soon's Uncle Johnny and I get married, I'm going to see a doctor and have him help me so I won't have to take my medicine anymore. Then you won't have to go to the drugstores anymore. You can run and play after school just like all the other children. Won't that be swell?"

"You promise?" Richie asked, crying.

"Yes, sugar, I promise. I swear to God, I do."

Richie stood behind a parked delivery truck and peered around it down Lake Street. The cool, shadowy street, perpetually shaded by the el tracks, looked quiet and ordinary. People, all of them colored, came and went on the sidewalks, moving in and out of the stores. Street traffic was sparse; driving was tricky because of the steel-and-concrete supports under the elevated tracks, and the fact that the street itself was cobblestone, not paved, so it was easy to skid into a support. More than once Richie had seen a car or a truck nick one of the supports and come away with a dented fender. People generally drove on Lake Street only when they had business on Lake Street. As Richie watched from behind the delivery truck, a black-and-white squad car, from the Warren Boulevard precinct station, came by with two white policemen in it. Bolstered by their presence, Richie crossed to the opposite sidewalk and started for the drugstore.

He had been back to Lake Street four times without seeing Alonzo and his friends. Common sense told him that his luck was bound to run out soon. Today he had saved the black drugstore for last. Earlier, walking to the white drugstores, he had fantasized that Alonzo and his friends were no longer there: they had moved away, or had all been put in jail for the crime of chasing white kids. Deep in his gut, though, he knew they were still around.

Reaching the drugstore without incident, Richie hurried inside and edged around two black women at the cigarette counter to make his way back to the pharmacy. A light-brown man with thick eyeglasses asked, "What you want, boy?"

"I got a note," Richie said, handing him the piece of paper with a quarter wrapped in it.

The man read the note, studied Richie for a moment, and seemed to weigh the quarter in his open hand; then he went behind a glass partition and returned a moment later to hand Richie a paper bag twisted at the top.

"Tell your mamma not to send you in here anymore, boy," he said in a not unkind tone. "Understand?"

"Okay," Richie mumbled. Good! he thought. *Goddamn good!* He realized that it would not really change anything for him; it was only one black drugstore out of six or seven along Lake Street that his mother sent him to, but somehow it seemed like a victory anyway. Richie relished the prospect of going home and telling her. In the back of his mind he was already wondering if he could get away with lying to her that the *others* were telling him the same thing.

Outside, walking briskly toward the corner, Richie heard the sound he always dreaded. "Hey, boy!"

Glancing back, he saw Alonzo and another black boy advancing on him from the street. Breaking into a run, Richie made for the corner, hearing hard-running footsteps behind. He was nearly there when two other black kids came around the corner, and he heard Alonzo's voice again.

"Albie, catch that boy!"

The two in front of him moved apart to block Richie's path, bobbing their fists up and down threateningly. The fear that had seized Richie and started him running, now, when he had to suddenly stop, turned his heart into a throbbing wild thing that seemed about to burst out of his chest. A sound of some sort passed his lips: part groan, part whimper, part plea. In desperation, he ran back a few feet and scurried up the stairs to the elevated platform. Halfway up, he realized his mistake.

"Go up them other steps, Albie!" he heard Alonzo yell with glee. "He ain't goin' nowhere now!"

On the el platform, Richie found himself trapped between the two stairways. It was not a crossover station so he could not get to the opposite platform—unless he wanted to try crossing the tracks. That he was afraid to do; he had heard stories of kids who had tried it and been electrocuted by the deadly third rail that provided the power to move the el trains. Better to take the whipping from Alonzo than fry on the third rail.

In the middle of the platform he waited helplessly, watching a smiling Alonzo and his friend come into sight from one flight of stairs, the boy named

Albie and his friend from the other. At least, Richie thought, he only had a dime left for Alonzo to take. But he also had the three bottles of paregoric, in separate pockets; he had to try to keep them from getting broken while he was taking the beating.

"You think you a smart fucker, don't you?" Alonzo said, walking up to him. Alonzo's right fist snapped out and hit Richie on the lips. Stumbling back, Richie tried to get his arms up to ward off a second blow, but Alonzo was too fast; the left fist hit him on the other side of his mouth, and he felt a tooth puncture his bottom lip.

" 'Lonzo!" a voice suddenly called. "What the fuck you think you doing?"

Richie and the four black boys all turned to the sound. In a corner of the platform, sitting up against a billboard, smoking a cigarette, was a black girl. Getting to her feet, she walked toward them in a kind of indifferent strut, one hand on her hip, the other holding her cigarette like Bette Davis. To Richie, pressing the back of one wrist to his bleeding lip, she looked about the same age as Dorothy, thirteen, but a little taller and heavier. She was also taller and heavier than Alonzo and his friends.

"I axed you what the fuck you think you doing," she said when she got up close to Alonzo's face.

"I'm whipping this white boy's ass," Alonzo said. "What it *look* like I'm doing?"

"What he do to you?" she asked.

"What you care, girl?" one of the other boys demanded, scowling at her.

"I ain't axin' you, nigger!" she snapped, pointing a finger at him. "Don't talk to me 'less *I* talks to you, 'less you want me to th'ow your black ass on them tracks there!" She looked at Richie. "What you do to 'Lonzo, boy?"

"Nothing," Richie said.

"What you doing in this neighborhood?"

"Getting medicine for my mother from the drugstore."

"This ain't none of yo' business, Vernie!" Alonzo protested.

"Shut your mouf', boy," she snapped. Alonzo shut his mouth. Vernie turned to Richie again. "Lemme see the medicine."

Richie worked a bag out of one of his pockets and handed it to her. Opening it, Vernie looked at the bottle of paregoric. Grunting softly, she closed the bag and returned it to Richie.

"Come on, boy," Vernie said to Richie, "I walk wit' you out this neighborhood."

Richie quickly fell in next to her as she started toward the stairs.

"I gon' *get* you for this, Vernie!" Alonzo threatened.

Vernie walked back to him. From the pocket of her dress, she pulled a closed straight-razor. "Onliest thing you gon' *get* if you fucks with me, 'Lonzo," she said quietly, tapping the razor against his chin, "is you face cut. This boy's mamma takes the same kind of medicine that *my* mamma takes. If *his* mamma needs it bad as *my* mamma needs it, then I gon' help him get it for her. You and your friends leave his ass alone 'less you want me to slice you." She smiled the slightest of smiles. "You knows I'll do it too, don't you? I done cut two bad niggers already; I'm past ready to cut me another one."

"Come on, 'Lonzo," one of the others said to save face, "she crazy. They bof' crazy. Leave 'em be."

"Yeah, 'Lonzo, they ain't worf our time," another said.

Alonzo smiled widely. "I gon' do you a favor this time, Vernie," he said. "But don't you never try to cut me, girl," he warned. "You do, I mess you up good."

"Sure, 'Lonzo." Vernie smiled too: a knowing smile, shrewd, prudent. A smile that told them both that without losing stature they had managed to avoid blood in a neighborhood where blood was cheap.

Alonzo and his three friends went jiving and shucking down one flight of stairs, while Vernie and Richie went down the other. "Thanks," Richie said as they walked along the street. Vernie shrugged it off.

"Never have liked 'Lonzo no how," she said, more to herself than to Richie.

At the next corner, there was an ice cream vendor. "Wanna Dixie Cup?" Richie asked. "I got a dime."

"Yo' dime, not your mamma's?" Vernie asked.

"My dime," Richie verified.

"Okay," Vernie shrugged again.

Richie bought two Dixie Cups and they immediately pulled off the round lids and licked away the ice cream to see which movie star's picture was on them.

"Who you get?" Vernie asked.

"Robert Taylor," Richie replied glumly.

"Shit," Vernie said. "I got Claudette Colbert."

"Shit," Richie parroted.

They both threw the cards in the gutter and began eating the ice cream with wooden spoons as they walked.

"Does your mother have to take her medicine every day?" Richie asked.

Glancing curiously at him, Vernie said, "Yeah. Your mamma too?"

Richie nodded. "Yeah." Half a block farther on he asked, "Have you really cut two guys with that razor?"

"Bet yo' ass I have," Vernie asserted. "One thing I done learned: ain't nobody gon' take care of Vernie but *Vernie*. When I be 'leven years old, some niggers just like 'Lonzo and them boys got me down in a basement one day. They tied me to a ol' cot and put dirty ol' socks in my mouf' so I couldn't yell. They kept me there all day; even went and got they brothers an' they friends. When they gots tired of me, they jus' lef' me there. The building manager found me. He turned me loose—but not until he got done wif' me too. I hardly could even walk. When I finally gots home, my mamma had just took her medicine, so she weren't no help; you know how *that* be. The lady 'cross the hall help me clean up. She give me the razor too. I ain't lef' the house wif'out it since."

"Jeez," Richie said quietly. As they walked, he kept glancing at Vernie in awe.

Vernie stayed with him until the neighborhood started turning white, then said, "I be go on back now."

"Thanks," Richie said again.

Vernie shrugged and walked away, her hips rolling loosely under the cotton dress, shoulders back defiantly. Like Richie, like most street kids, she kept to the outside of the sidewalk, where it was easier to break and run.

Richie thought about Vernie all the way home. Somehow, thinking about her, his own plight seemed less terrible.

One day when Richie got home from school, his mother was wearing a new dress pinned with a corsage, and Johnny was there in a suit and necktie. Estelle had come too, she and Chloe having finally resolved their spat; with her was her latest boyfriend, Duke, a sausage stuffer for Armour who had huge hands.

When Richie walked in, his mother gave him a big hug. "Guess what, sugar?" she said with a big smile. "Uncle Johnny and I got married today!"

Richie became very grave, frowning deeply, piqued because he had not been told, annoyed because it would have been a perfectly legitimate reason for him to stay home from school; he was fully prepared to pout and put a damper on the whole affair. But Johnny came over and kidded with him and made him shake hands, and before long Richie was grinning and being given a bottle of root beer and Estelle was teaching him how to drink a toast, which the others were drinking with real beer. When no one was looking, Johnny slipped him half a dollar.

In the bedroom when Richie was changing into his play clothes, Chloe came in and told him they would be moving over the weekend. Richie's shoulders slumped immediately. "Now, I know you don't like to change schools," Chloe said, anticipating his complaint, "'but this will be the last time." Sitting on the side of the bed, she drew him to her. "And listen, remember I promised that after Johnny and I got married, I'd stop sending you for my medicine? Well, I haven't forgotten that. Just as soon as we get moved, I'm going to work it for you to just go every other day for a while, then every third day, and pretty soon not at all. After school you'll be able to run and play just like all the other kids. Won't that be nice?" Before she left the bedroom, Chloe gave him some more bad news. "Listen, Dorothy's coming over to take care of you tonight. We're all going downtown to the Blackhawk Restaurant for a wedding supper. I'd take you with us, but it's one of those fancy grownup places that you probably wouldn't like anyway. Afterwards we're going to the Oriental Theater to see a movie and stage show. But I'll tell you what, I'll give Dorothy money for the two of you to go to a show too, would you like that?"

Without waiting to find out if he'd like it or not, Chloe went back to the living room, leaving Richie to stand half-dressed staring after her. "Shit," he muttered, having now substituted Vernie's vernacular for his previous oath of "goddamn dirty son of a bitch." Not even the fifty cents in his pocket allayed the fear and the depression of thinking about transferring to still another school, a dread that was further compounded by the immediate prospect of a miserable evening of maltreatment by Dorothy. But at least he was relieved of going to the drugstores that day; he now realized why his mother had been getting so many quarter bottles and so few fifteen-cent bottles: she was stocking up.

When Dorothy came over, Johnny gave her an extra dollar and said, "You and the boy go over to White Castle for supper before the show."

"Gee, thanks!" Dorothy said with her usual smiling exuberance. It almost made Richie ill. If only, he thought, they knew Dorothy like *he* knew Dorothy. Someday he wished he could lure Dorothy over to Lake Street and have Vernie there waiting for her. Have Vernie pull a razor on Dorothy and scare the shit out of her. Yeah! That would be something! But secretly he knew he could not do it; Dorothy was too smart to be tricked into going into a colored neighborhood. There were stories about young white girls who ventured down Lake Street and were never heard from again.

After everyone left that evening, Richie and Dorothy walked up to Madison Street to White Castle and sat on backless stools eating the thin but incredibly tasty ten-cent hamburgers and drinking Kayo chocolate soda pop. Dorothy was unusually quiet, not forever snapping at and scolding Richie as she normally did. To his surprise, she hardly spoke to him at all except to say, "Come on," or "Let's go," or to give him some other minor command. When they reached the corner where the three movie houses were, however, he found out that she was still her same old hateful self.

"Hey, look," Richie said excitedly, *"Drums Along the Mohawk* is at the Kedzie Annex! I saw the previews of that and it looked swell!"

"We're going to the Senate," Dorothy replied peremptorily, "to see *Dark Victory*. It's about a rich girl who goes blind."

"Shit," Richie said, rolling his eyes toward the sky.

"What did you say?" Dorothy asked, aghast.

"Nothing."

"You did so!" She slapped his lips with her fingers. "You wait until I get you home! I'm going to wash your dirty little mouth out with soap!"

If she tries it, I'll kill her, Richie silently swore. He pictured himself running into the kitchen, grabbing a butcher knife, and plunging it into Dorothy. Then he watched her stagger, clutching at the knife handle, through the living room, out the door, down the front steps, and into the middle of Carroll Street where she fell dead for all to see.

"Why are you staring into space like that?" Dorothy demanded, jerking him by the arm. "Come on!"

She led him across the street to the Senate, a big ornate Balaban-and-Katz chain theater where the ushers wore high-collar uniforms and carried flashlights, and people were required to hold on to their ticket stubs until they left the premises. The candy counter was a brightly lit island in the middle of a big, plushly carpeted lobby. Dorothy, somewhat reluctantly, let him pick out a candy bar. Knowing her pattern of authority by now, Richie said, "Licorice twist."

"You can't have that. Pick something else."

"Baby Ruth," Richie said, selecting his favorite.

In the auditorium, Dorothy led him to seats in the center of a middle row, which further irritated Richie. He liked to sit in the front row on the aisle so that he could slump far down in the seat and have the screen loom up over him, as if he were sitting on the floor of the scene. Not that it would make much difference this night. As he feared, *Dark Victory* turned out to be the worst movie he had seen since the night his mother made him sit through *Harmony Lane*. Richie would have been hard put to decide which was more boring: a rich girl going blind from a brain tumor, or a man named Stephen Foster who wore ruffled shirts and wrote songs about the Swanee River. The only redeeming value of *Dark Victory* was that it made Dorothy cry.

On the way home, Richie renewed his silent plan to stab Dorothy to death, but when they got back to the apartment not only had she apparently forgotten that she intended to wash his mouth out with soap, she did not even seem interested in giving him the raw-rubbing bath. "Go on and get in the tub," she said absently. "Wash your own self tonight."

Richie was in and out of the tub in record time lest she change her mind. When he came into the living room, his bed was all made up on the couch.

"Go on to bed," Dorothy told him.

Richie lay in the darkness and watched as Dorothy collected several of his mother's magazines and went into the kitchen. Through the open door, he saw her sit at the table with a bottle of Coca-Cola and idly turn pages without much interest. Once in a while she would sigh quietly and sip at the Coke. It puzzled Richie.

He was practiced at pretending to be asleep and when Dorothy got up from the table, quietly came in, and stood looking down at him, he lay completely still, kept his eyes closed, and breathed very evenly. After several moments, he heard her walk away. Presently, the bathroom light clicked on.

Getting out of bed, Richie crept into the hall to the bathroom. Dorothy had left the door open an inch; Richie could not see her, but he could see, in the wood-framed mirror on the medicine cabinet, her reflection. She had removed her blouse and dropped the top of her slip from both shoulders. In the mirror she was carefully examining an angry red welt at the edge of her left nipple. Because her breasts were immature, barely beginning to develop, there was no slack to hold up to the mirror; Dorothy had to turn sideways and push the young aureola out in order to better examine the wound. As she gently touched it, her eyes became teary. Turning on the cold water, she reached for a washcloth. In the movement, she noticed Richie at the crack in the door.

"You!"

Dorothy whirled, expression changing, anger replacing distress. Snatching open the door, she grabbed him by the undershirt as he tried to bolt away. Dragging him into the bathroom, she slammed and locked the door.

"You want to see what he did?" she hissed. Holding him by the undershirt, she pulled his face up close to her breasts. "Take a good look! Those are teeth marks!"

Her young features seemed to Richie to twist into a vile mask. "Wanna see the rest?" she demanded, almost as a threat. "I'll show you the rest, goddamn you!" Quickly she stepped out of her skirt and slipped her panties over her feet. She stood naked except for Oxfords and anklets. Gripping Richie's shoulders, she forced him to his knees on the cold linoleum floor and held his face very close to the light, downy hair of her pubes. When she raised one foot and rested it on the toilet, Richie saw on the inside of her thigh, up very close to the hair, another ugly, this time purplish bitemark. "He does this to me all the time!" Dorothy protested, taking her hands off Richie's shoulders and pounding her own temples with them. "First it was Helen, now it's me! Every time my old lady goes anywhere—to the movies with my aunt, to Bingo at the church, any goddamn where!—he comes into our bedroom and makes me undress. Helen won't help me; she just leaves the room, she's so goddamned glad he ain't bothering her no more!" Dorothy grabbed Richie's shoulders again and began shaking him. "I hate him! I hate the son of a bitch! I'd like to kill him!"

Suddenly she stopped shaking him, as quickly as she had started, and stared down at him still kneeling before her. A frown settled across her brow, as if she had just then realized who he was, and was surprised by it. She put a hand on his cheek, then moved it up to brush back his hair.

"I'm sorry, Richie," she said. "I'm sorry I'm so mean to you. It ain't your fault."

"That's okay," Richie replied, shrugging. He did not know anything else to say. "You can slap me if you want," he offered.

Shaking her head, tears coming again, Dorothy said, "No."

"I don't care, honest," Richie assured her. "If it makes you feel better. Helen always used to."

But Dorothy just kept shaking her head, and finally buried her face in both hands and sobbed. Still undressed, she sat down next to where Richie knelt and he self-consciously put an arm around her.

After that night, Dorothy never mistreated him again.

That weekend, they moved to a third-floor apartment at 2242 West Warren Boulevard. There was a front bedroom off a living room, a back bedroom off the kitchen, and a bathroom off a hall that connected everything. Unfurnished, it was completely empty except for a stove and a wooden icebox in the kitchen.

Johnny borrowed a pickup truck from his brother-in-law who lived nearby, and while he and Chloe went off to a secondhand furniture store to buy beds, Richie made friends with a boy named Louis who lived in the building next door. Louis, who was the same age and in the same grade as Richie, told him about Grant Elementary, the school to which Richie would have to transfer.

"It's real tough," Louis said. "Some niggers go there who'll make you give 'em your milk money 'less you got somebody to take up for you. Or 'less you can fight good. Can you fight good?"

Richie shook his head.

"I can't neither. But I got this kid named Ham to take up for me if anybody starts in on me."

"Ham. That's a funny name," Richie grinned.

"He gets called that 'cause he's thick like a ham, and he's got fists like hams. I give him a nickel a week and steal him one cigarette a day from my ma's pack, and he takes up for me. Your ma smoke?"

"Yeah."

"What brand?"

"Avalons."

"What about your pa?"

Richie thought about Johnny Eaton. "He rolls his own."

Louis grimaced. "You might have to give Ham more'n a nickel, then. He on'y likes Camels and Chesterfields."

"What's your dad smoke?" Richie asked.

Louis shrugged. "He don't live with us."

Another one, Richie thought. He was glad he now had Johnny Eaton to pass off as his father.

"You ever sell *Liberty?*" Louis asked.

Richie shrugged. "What's that?"

"It's a magazine for grownups. I sell *Liberty* every Thursday after school. *Collier's* and the *Saturday Evening Post* too. This guy comes around in a car with a trunkful of 'em. He gives you a sack that you sling across your chest, an' six copies of each magazine. Every one you sell, you get two cents."

"Who do you sell 'em to?"

"Everybody. You can go door-to-door, or sell 'em on the street corner, or go in the stores. I go door-to-door. The block we live on is mine," he emphasized, "'but you can take the next block if you want, if nobody's got it already. When you sell out, you can come back to the car for more. I made eighty-two cents last week."

"Jeez," said Richie. That was serious money for an afternoon's work. His life, he decided, had taken a definite turn for the better.

Chloe still sent him to the drugstores for a while, but true to her promise, she began to cut down on his trips as she cut back on her consumption of paregoric. Now that Richie had Vernie for a friend, he no longer dreaded going over to Lake Street; Vernie was nearly always around, loitering on the corner with some girlfriends, sitting alone in a doorway if she was moody, pushing someone's infant in a baby carriage to earn a nickel. Whatever she was doing, she always took time to see that Richie got in and out of the colored neighborhood safely. Richie took to filching his mother's Avalon cigarettes for her, and bringing her movie magazines that Chloe threw out.

"I wish yo' mamma take to smoking something 'sides these Avalons," Vernie complained. "Dey tastes like shit." But she lit up anyway. Once when Richie brought a cigarette for himself, she slapped it out of his lips. "Don't you lemme catch you smoking, boy," she threatened. "You 'way too young, hear me?"

With his other, and newer, protector, the brutish boy called Ham, it was, as Louis had predicted, a strictly cash arrangement. " 'Less you can get me Camels or Chesterfields, it'll be two cents a day for me to stick up for you. Dime a week, same as you pay for milk in the lunchroom. Way I look at it, it's a fair deal, me and milk costing the same. We bot' keep you healthy."

Richie paid, and gladly, to keep the colored kids at Grant Elementary from bothering him. Ham made it clear to them the first day that he was on Richie's side, just by walking around the schoolyard with him for everyone to see. Richie endured some snickering from kids who were tough enough to take care of themselves, but he did not care. Nearly anything was better than being beaten up after school day in and day out. The confidence of being able to go to school without fear of being bullied greatly improved Richie's outlook on life. Even Chloe noticed it.

"You sure must like your new school, sugar," she said. "Since we moved over here you've practically stopped moping around. On Carroll Street you were getting to be a regular Weeping Willie. Do you like living here?"

"Yeah."

"Say 'yes,' not 'yeah.' I told you things were going to be swell after Johnny and I got married, didn't I?"

"Yeah. Yes."

"And guess what?" she surprised him one day by saying. "You don't have to go to any more drugstores for me. I've stopped taking that medicine for good."

"Really?" Richie stared at her with his mouth open. He could hardly believe his ears.

"Really," Chloe assured with one of her glowing smiles. She tapped him on the nose with one finger. "Don't you think I deserve a big hug and kiss for that bit of news?"

Richie put his chin on his chest and tried to turn away, but Chloe got her arms around him before he could escape and pressed a warm kiss on his lips, then hugged him fervently. "Oh, Richie," she said. "For the first time in years I feel like I don't have to be scared of life. I know that probably doesn't make sense to you; you're too young to know what it's like to be scared of life. But, believe me, it's very important *not* to be. The quieter and more peaceful life is, the better. I've been along enough bumpy roads to last the rest of my life."

There were certainly no bumps in her life now. Johnny Eaton had turned out to be exactly what he had represented himself to be—not a whit more or less. When he and Chloe had been going together, he had frequently summed up his goals in life by saying, "I don't need nothin' fancy, not me. A good, steady job, decent little wife, couple quarts of beer on Saturday night, listening to the ballgame of a Sunday afternoon—that's the life for me." Because early in their relationship he had taken her out to movies and for Chinese food and for strolls in the park, Chloe had not taken what he said literally. But after they married and settled down, she realized she should have. Those two quarts of beer on Saturday night were it for him. After supper during the week, he sat and smoked and read the *Herald-American*. When he finished the paper, he sat out in front of the building in the summertime and talked to his brother-in-law, who lived a few doors down. In the wintertime he might listen to a radio program or two. That, Chloe learned, was all the recreation Johnny needed. Along with his three or four minutes of intercourse at bedtime, that is. Chloe had sought an uneventful life; she had found it.

When the staleness of her existence began to show, Estelle detected it at once. "Tell me, Mrs. Eaton," she tried to keep it light, "does your husband know you're unhappy?"

"I am *not* unhappy," Chloe demurred.

"No, and I'm not six pounds too heavy," Estelle, who was getting fleshy, said sarcastically. "Why don't you say something to him, for god's sake," she urged. "Let him know that your main purpose in life is not to see how many nights straight you can sit out front talking to Hannah."

Hannah was Johnny's sister. It had been with her and her husband, Skeet, that Johnny had roomed prior to marrying Chloe. It was no secret that Hannah had tried to talk her brother out of the marriage. She felt that Johnny should try to find someone who had not already been through one husband and already had a child to raise. She was cordial to Chloe, in a reserved way, but had never retreated from her belief that her brother could have done much better.

"I don't want to say anything to him, 'Stelle," the bored woman replied. "I got just what I bargained for, and I'm not going to complain about it. I'm sure," she added without conviction, "that in time I'll get used to it."

She would too, Chloe promised herself. She *had* to—for Richie as well as for herself. All she had to do was work at it. Day by day. Work at being *ordinary*. Take care of the apartment. See to the meals. Give Richie some extra care and attention to make up for past burdens she had placed on him. She had to face each day—and night—with a smile. When she sent Johnny off to work in the morning, smile; Richie off to school, smile; greet Richie with a smile when he came home, greet Johnny with a smile when *he* came home; smile at supper, smile at bedtime, smile at Hannah, smile *all—the—goddamn—time*.

Diligently Chloe applied herself. Johnny took to calling her "Sunshine," and said she'd have to be put under a washtub or they'd never get any rain. Richie found her behavior curious, even a little suspicious, but welcome nevertheless. It was nice to come home from school to a smile instead of someone with a "splitting headache" who had to have "medicine" from Lake Street right away. Richie enjoyed the uneventful life they now led. As usual, he was no more attuned to Chloe's needs than she was to his. The fact that there might be desolation behind his mother's smile never occurred to him; *his* life had improved, dramatically, so he guessed hers had also. She must be enjoying life—she was smiling all the time. As far as Richie was concerned, things could go on forever exactly as they were right then. It would suit him just fine. Everything had gotten a lot better; because he was so young, Richie assumed it would *stay* that way. The measure of it, he subconsciously gauged, was his mother's smile. As long as she kept smiling, life would be okay.

But one Sunday afternoon, the smile disappeared.

Richie had been at the 4-Star Theater with Louis, where they had seen the matinee showing of a lavish new Technicolor movie, *Billy the Kid*, with Robert Taylor in the starring role. All the way home, Richie cursed and lamented the fact that the first day he had bought ice cream for Vernie and himself, he had thrown away a Dixie Cup lid with Robert Taylor's picture on it.

"How in the goddamn hell was I s'posed to know he'd turn into a good cowboy star?" Richie asked plaintively. "All's he's ever been before was a goddamned sissy in love with some stupid girl like in the *Waterloo Bridge* picture. There oughta be a rule that sissy movie stars can't change to cowboys!"

"Never throw nothin' away," Louis advised gravely.

Trudging disconsolately up the stairs when he got to his building, Richie wondered if there was any chance at all that the Dixie Cup lid would still be in the Lake Street gutter where he tossed it, safely lying there with Vernie's discarded Claudette Colbert. At least, goddamn it, he thought, *she* would never become a cowboy.

Entering the living room, Richie stopped dead still. His mother was on the sofa, face in her hands, sobbing. Sitting beside her, Johnny was patting her head, awkwardly trying to console her. After staring a moment, Richie went over to them.

"What's the matter?" he asked in a trembling voice.

"Looks like we're in a war, boy," Johnny said solemnly. "The Japs bombed our navy base at Pearl Harbor this morning. News come on the radio a little while ago. It's a war for sure."

"Why is she crying?" Richie asked, lowering his voice as if to prevent his mother from hearing.

" 'Cause I'll be one of the first ones to go," Johnny said. "I'm 1-A in the draft and I already had my six-months basic training last year. They'll call me up right quick."

Turning away, Richie stared into space. A slow dread began to spread inside of him. If Johnny left, it would be just him and his mother again. That had never worked. Whenever his mother had to fend for herself and for him, without a man to take care of her, things usually went bad. She knew it too; that was why she was crying.

"When I go," Johnny said to him, "I'm gonna depend on you to take care of your mother for me, hear?"

"Yeah," Richie replied without spirit. His father's face appeared in his mind. *We'll take care of her, won't we, boy?*

Why was it that the people who made bargains with him always left *him* behind to keep them?

Take care of his mother? Sure, he'd take care of her. He'd start going for her "medicine" again—because that was exactly what was going to happen.

A shroud of depression was falling over Richie when he saw his mother sit up, wipe her eyes, and force a smile.

" 'Course he will, Johnny, he'll always take care of his mother, won't you, sugar?" Reaching, she gathered him into her arms, pressing her cheek to his. Richie felt the warm wetness of her tears. "We'll make it just fine, won't we, sugar? When Johnny has to leave, he's not to worry a single minute about us. Everything will be exactly the same when he comes home. Isn't that right, sugar?"

"Yeah."

"I mean it, Richie," she said, fixing her eyes to his. "We'll be all right, sugar."

Richie nodded slowly.

Maybe, he thought, he was wrong.

Maybe, they *would* be all right this time.

To Richie, the interior of the Chicago Stadium looked like the biggest place in the world. From the vast arena floor, what looked like a hundred million seats could be seen spreading and rising in sweeping rows up to an intriguing conglomeration, just under a great, sprawling ceiling, of catwalks, pulleys, derricks, ropes, huge spotlights, projection booths, and a vast array of other equipment, unidentifiable to Richie.

It was during the war, with Johnny Eaton away in the Pacific. Richie had heard from a kid at school that the stadium needed boys to sell peanuts and popcorn during sporting and other events. Richie had hurried there after school and been hired for that very night.

"I'm gonna try you out on peanuts, kid," a short, swarthy man said, hanging a vendor tray around Richie's neck and resting it against his stomach. On Richie's head he put a white cap with a large red 15¢ on its front. The man's name was Rondo; he was the vending manager.

"Can I work way up there?" Richie asked, pointing to the top balcony. Rondo shook his head.

"That's nigger heaven, kid. The cheapest seats. We send black kids to sell up there, otherwise them spades won't pay for what they get. An' if a white kid takes me up to show me who cheated him, he can't never pick the guy out 'cause they all look alike. You're gonna work Mezzanine, Section D, right over there." He pointed. "You go up and down the aisles yelling, 'Hot roasted peanuts!' Lemme hear you yell it."

"Hot roasted peanuts!" Richie yelled.

"Louder."

"Hot roasted peanuts!!"

"Come on, you can do better than that. Yell it out!"

"*Hot roasted peanuts!!!*" Richie screamed.

"Good," said Rondo. "Go to it."

In Section D of the mezzanine, Richie cruised the aisles, up and down, down and up, from one aisle to the next, yelling as loudly as he could. There were other boys doing the same thing, and men, most of them frail or handicapped in some way, 4-F in the draft. Some of them carried the same kind of vending tray that Richie carried; some had coolers, for ice cream; some had heaters, for hot dogs. Their yells overlapped each other's and blended into a cacophony of sound.

Richie saw as he worked that the arena floor had now been uncovered, a dozen interlaced tarpaulins having been rolled back and dragged aside. Exposed was a shiny white rectangle of ice that two men driving small tractors were spraying with a thin stream of water and smoothing. Other men were hurrying about doing other things at the edge of the ice, and above, in the fascinating array just under the ceiling, still other men were moving about, it seemed to Richie, very precariously. Every minute or so, he glanced up from his hawking to see if one was falling. When he reached the end of his section and started back to sell to the later arrivals, Richie noticed that at the end of the arena floor, musicians in fancy red coats were filing onto a bandstand with their instruments. Their coats reminded Richie of *King of the Royal Mounted*, a new serial with Allan Lane that had just started at the Imperial.

A lot of Richie's buyers in the mezzanine were boys and girls his own age, there with their parents. They were dressed in clothes that were nicer than his best school clothes, and their parents seemed to buy them whatever they wanted; they all had souvenir programs, balloons, felt banners, and anything they wanted to eat. Sometimes when he was waiting to be paid by a parent, one of the kids would look at him in a way that rankled Richie. He could not explain what *kind* of look it was; he just knew he did not like it. Usually it would be a girl and Richie always knew he was blushing when he walked away.

It irritated him to see so many kids there with their fathers. Johnny Eaton had been one of the first called up, leaving Richie without even a surrogate father. He knew from the war lectures given in school that most of the men on what they called the "home front" were involved in jobs in war plants or as policemen or some other essential occupation that prevented them from going off to fight the war. Even so, Richie could not help feeling discriminated against again; he had done without a father for so long, it somehow did not seem fair that he had to lose Johnny so quickly.

When he sold out his tray, Richie returned to the vendor room and Rondo filled it up again. Referring to a chart he had taped to the wall, he said, "Okay, kid, move over to Mezzanine, Section H. How's your throat?"

"Getting sore," Richie said huskily.

"It'll be like that the first few nights you work. Here"—Rondo handed him several foil-wrapped lozenges—"suck on these here; they'll help."

As he was working Section H, the arena lights dimmed, the bandstand lighted up, and the red-coated band members began playing a vibrant marching tune. It played two numbers, was applauded after each, and then, after a loud drumroll, a voice announced through a loudspeaker, "Ladieees and gentlemen! Boys and girls! The Chicago Stadium proudly presents . . . the Sonja Henie Ice Show!"

To thousands of hands clapping in the darkness, large double doors opened at one end of the ice and two lines of brightly dressed skaters flowed out onto the ice and began the opening number. At that point, Richie moved back up the aisle and stood on the mezzanine floor behind the last row of seats, in case anyone wanted to come back there and buy peanuts; hawkers were not allowed to cruise during the performance. From where he stood, Richie had a splendid view of the show, and he watched it with awe. It was unlike anything he had ever seen, even in the movies. The closeness of it, the color, the extra dimension, all served to excite and thrill him, make his eyes grow wide, his mouth hang open, and an occasional "Jeez!" slip past his lips. When Sonja Henie herself skated out, a tiny blond fluff of a woman from Norway, whose country was then occupied by the German army, the audience rose and cheered as she waved a small United States flag in one hand, a Norwegian flag in the other. It brought a lump to Richie's throat.

Again at intermission Richie plied the aisles until he sold his last bag of peanuts. By that time they were not hot anymore, and Richie was not yelling very loudly because his throat felt as if the lining had been stripped out of it. But he had sold forty bags of peanuts, for which, at two cents a bag, he received eighty cents.

"Come back Tuesday night," Rondo told him. "Hockey game. Blackhawks play the Rangers. Be here at six-thirty."

Walking the six blocks home, Richie stayed on partly lit Madison Street which, as usual, had a lot of pedestrian traffic. It would not do to walk down the darker side streets, where gangs of kids, both white and black, prowled at night to see who they could catch, and with what. Only when he got to Oakley Boulevard did Richie cut over to Warren and hurry to his building.

He went directly home; it was a condition imposed by his mother when she consented to his taking the job at the stadium. His mother did not particularly like him working at night, but realistically she knew it was advantageous, with Johnny gone and a government allotment inadequately replacing his wages. Chloe herself had even taken a job, as a clerk in a nearby bakery. Allowing Richie to earn his own spending money relieved her of having to give him an allowance. Every little bit helped.

"I made eighty cents!" Richie exclaimed when he got home.

"Why, that's wonderful, sugar!" his mother praised, giving him her usual smile. She was curled up on the couch with a cup of coffee, writing Johnny a letter on a small lined tablet. "You'd better get ready for bed now," she said with the same fixed smile. "It's late."

"Sure."

Richie went down the hall toward the bathroom. Before he got there, he paused and from the darkness looked back into the living room at his mother.

As it always did lately, the smile faded from her face.

One evening when Richie was not working, his mother said, "I'm going out with 'Stelle for a while tonight. To a movie or something. If I don't get out of this house for an evening now and then, I'll go crazy. Dorothy's coming over to stay with you."

"I don't need her to stay with me," Richie said. If he was old enough to hawk at the stadium, he was old enough to stay home alone.

"I'll feel better knowing she's here with you," Chloe said.

It had been a while since Richie had seen Dorothy. After the wedding, Johnny and his mother had not gone out much, and since Johnny's return to the army, Chloe had stayed home every night.

When Dorothy arrived, she looked exactly the same to Richie, but Chloe said, "My, you're getting tall, hon." She didn't seem taller to Richie because Richie himself was taller. Secretly, he was glad to see her again. "We won't be late, hon," his mother told Dorothy. "We're just going downtown to the Garrick to see *Mrs. Miniver*." Glad I'm missing *that*, Richie thought. "And maybe for a sandwich after," Chloe added.

When Chloe left, Dorothy got a Coke out of the icebox, poured half of it in a glass for Richie, and together they listened to the new radio show, "Stage Door Canteen." On the program that night were Ronald Colman, Veronica Lake, and Teresa Wright. "Why don't they never have nobody good?" Richie complained. "Like Buck Jones or Charles Starrett or Bob Steele?"

"Maybe," Dorothy replied drily, "there's not room in the radio studio for their horses."

"They could leave 'em outside—" Richie began, but broke off when he realized that Dorothy had been ribbing him. As he grinned at being fooled, Dorothy mussed his hair and gave him a quick hug. They listened to "Duffy's Tavern" and "People Are Funny," and then Dorothy told him it was time to get ready for bed. "Go get undressed," she said. "I'll run your tub."

Several minutes later, when Richie came into the bathroom, he found Dorothy as naked as he was. "I haven't had my bath yet either. Okay if I get in too?"

"Sure," Richie said, shrugging, knowing he was blushing.

They got into the tub together, facing each other, but then Dorothy turned him around and pulled him back close to her so that she could wash him. She was very gentle with him now; she had been since the night she showed him the bite marks. Tonight, getting into the tub, he had glanced at her breasts and seen one recent mark and two older ones, so he guessed Dorothy's father was still doing things to her. He noticed too that her breasts were getting larger; no longer just swollen mounds under the nipples, they now had body and movement. When she turned him back around, he could not help looking at them.

"Do you think they're pretty?" Dorothy asked, catching him looking.

"Yeah," Richie admitted, turning his face away. Dorothy put a knuckle under his chin and turned his face back.

"It's okay, you can look." Knowing he was blushing again, Richie looked anyway. "You've never told anyone about the teeth marks, have you?" she asked sternly, reminding him of the old Dorothy.

"No," he replied quickly. "I never would."

"Okay, don't ever," she cautioned, her voice becoming gentle again. Without talking, Dorothy washed herself as Richie watched, getting on her knees to do part of it. When she was rinsing, she asked, "Richie, would you ever bite a girl's titties?"

"No!" he swore. "I wouldn't bite a girl nowhere!"

"What if she asked you to? Would you do it then?"

"I don't know," he hedged.

"I mean if she liked it and wanted you to?"

"Well, maybe then," he allowed.

On her knees, Dorothy moved very close to him. Under the water, she covered his erection with the warm, soapy wash cloth.

"I like it, Richie," she said. "I like it a lot."

She pulled his mouth to her breasts.

□

Louis had taken Richie to see the man in the car who came with the magazines on Thursdays. His name was Mr. Baker and he gave Richie a job like Louis had, peddling weekly magazines from a canvas sack slung across his chest. After taking down Richie's name and address, Mr. Baker gave him a sack with the *Liberty* logo on it, and ten copies each of that magazine plus the *Saturday Evening Post* and *Collier's*.

" 'Member," Louis cautioned, "the twenty-two-hundred block of Warren is mine. I got some reg'lar customers on that block."

"Sure," Richie agreed.

Mr. Baker told him the procedure. "I'll be parked right here at six o'clock to take the money you collect, pay you for what you've sold, and give you a supply of magazines to sell tomorrow afternoon. Then I'll be parked right here at six o'clock tomorrow to settle up for tomorrow. Got it?"

"Got it," Richie said.

While Louis started on the block where they lived, Richie went over to Madison and tried selling in front of a Walgreen's. Quickly noticing that a number of people who emerged from there already had magazines from the drugstore rack, he moved down the block. Trying a barber shop, he was told they had subscriptions. He sold a few to people on the street, then found a good spot outside a grocery store, catching women as they came out with their groceries. By the time he had to start back to meet Mr. Baker at the car, he had sold half of the magazines and made thirty cents.

That night at home, sitting cross-legged on his bed before it was time to turn out the light, Richie idly thumbed through a copy of the *Saturday Evening Post*. On one page he discovered a colorful illustration of a stagecoach being chased by marauding Indians. Richie's mouth dropped open. Previously exposed only to Chloe's movie magazines, which rarely contained photos of cowboy stars, and to *True Romances* and similar publications, which he found totally stupid, he was amazed now to discover a *Western* story in the *Saturday Evening Post*. It was entitled "Stage to Lordsburg" and had been written by someone named Ernest Haycox. Pulse quickening, Richie began to read.

He was still reading, enthralled by the story, half an hour later when his mother said, "Time to turn out the light and go to sleep, sugar." Seeing what he was doing, she added, "You shouldn't be reading the *Post*, Richie. It's way too old for you."

Richie was learning never to argue; it usually amounted to a waste of time. Putting the magazine aside, he turned off his light and got into bed. Five minutes later, he got up, crept into the hall to make sure Chloe was back in the living room listening to the radio, then returned to his bedroom, quietly closed the door, turned the light on, and resumed reading the story.

It was wonderful, exciting, thrilling—better than a comic book or a Big-Little Book, better even than a radio program, *almost* as good as a movie serial. Eagerly, he searched the issue for more stories; he found some, but no other Westerns. One war story looked promising, but it quickly turned into a gushy love story. Finally, eyes heavy, Richie turned the light out again and went to sleep. He dreamed about the Ringo Kid, hero of "Stage to Lordsburg."

Immediately after school the next day, Richie hurried home to get his magazines and get out on the street with them. He found the apartment door unlocked and a note from his mother on the table. "I went to see Estelle," the note read. "Back in time for supper." Richie frowned. Chloe worked from six to two at the bakery; usually she was lying down resting when he got home. But in the interest of hurrying to sell his magazines, he shrugged it off, changed clothes, and rushed out again.

This time he hung around an A & P market on Western Avenue, where he again sold about half of what he had. The load in the canvas sack was heavy when he first started out, the weight pulling against his neck as he walked, but at the market it gradually got lighter with each copy he sold. When business slacked off at the market, he moved down to a cigar store on the corner, selling only a few copies there before the wizened little stoop-shouldered proprietor came out and chased him away. "Beat it!" he yelled. "Don't bodder my customers. Make your pennies someplace else!" Silently calling the man filthy names, Richie moved up to another grocery on Oakley Boulevard, and stayed there until it was time to meet Mr. Baker. He sold eighteen magazines that second day, earning thirty-six cents.

When Richie got home, his mother was back, lying on the couch smoking a cigarette, listening to music on the radio.

"Sugar, I don't feel like eating supper tonight," she said sleepily. "There's two hamburgers for you in the oven. Pour yourself some milk to go with them, all right?"

"Sure," Richie said. His mother's eyelids were heavy and she had dropped cigarette ashes on the rug. Richie ground the ashes into the rug with his shoe and went into the kitchen to eat.

Sitting alone at the table, eating one of the hamburgers and drinking milk, he kept glancing over at a small covered garbage can under the sink. He wanted to look in it, yet he *didn't* want to look in it. From the living room he could hear Chloe humming softly to herself. Finally, when he finished the first hamburger, he got up and went over to the sink. Opening the garbage can, he moved an empty Wheaties box and some crumpled butcher paper and saw under them exactly what he had both known and dreaded that he would find.

An empty paregoric bottle.

*A*t the stadium on Saturday night, Richie was hawking popcorn in Mezzanine C between bouts of a fight card being put on for Navy Relief. The main event was to be a three-round exhibition match featuring Sergeant Joe Louis of the U. S. Army, who was the heavyweight champion of the world. It was a big night for Chicago boxing fans; the stadium was standing room only.

Richie had sold out his tray of bagged popcorn and was on his way back to the vendor room for Rondo to fill him up again. As he passed the top of an aisle, his glance fell on a tall, blond-haired man standing up at one of the aisle seats a dozen rows behind ringside. Next to him was a woman with long black hair. They were half turned away from Richie so that he could not see their faces. Recognition suddenly dawned and Richie's head snapped around, his eyes riveting on the tall, blond man. Moving quickly down the aisle to the mezzanine railing, Richie tried to get a better look, but as he did, the man sat down in his seat and he could only see the back of his head.

Could it possibly be . . . ?

Hurrying back up the aisle, Richie made his way to the concrete stairs that led down to the main level. On the way he was joined by another kid, a boy named Larry who had been hawking peanuts in Mezzanine F.

"Richie, wait up!" Larry said. "Hey, did you know that Buck Jones was coming to the Senate two days from now?"

"What?" Richie said, slowing a step, tearing his mind away from the urgency of the moment. "You mean a Buck Jones movie?"

"No! The *real* Buck Jones! In person!"

Stopping, Richie faced him. "Who says?"

"Russ, the beer vendor, says he seen it ina paper. Buck Jones is on a war bond tour an' he's gonna be at some fancy shindig in the Loop. but the paper says that in every city he goes to selling bonds, he always picks out a show somewheres so kids can come see him too. This time, he picked the Senate. He wants all the kids in the city to come see him. All's you gotta do to get in is buy a quarter savings stamp to help the war effort."

"Russ says it was in the paper?"

"Yeah! Ask him if you don't believe me."

"I will," Richie said, blood rushing faster now, temples pounding, excitement doubling at the possibility of his father being in the arena, and now the prospect of actually seeing—*seeing in person*—his longtime idol, Buck Jones.

Leaving Larry, Richie continued on to the main floor of the big arena and cut back to the aisle on which he had seen the blond-haired man. The middleweight exhibition had just begun. When Richie started down the aisle, an usher stopped him. "Not during the bout, kid," he said, pointing a warning finger.

"I was just gonna take a look at somebody," Richie explained. The usher shook his head.

"Not during the bout," he repeated emphatically. "You know the rules. I let you down there, I could lose my job for it."

Just then somebody yelled, "Hey, Richie! Rondo says get over here!"

Richie hurried to the vendor room. "Where the hell you been?" Rondo asked him. "When that tray's empty, you get right down here and fill up, understand? Don't hang around talking to nobody."

"Yeah, okay," Richie said. He saw Russ filling a cooler with bottles of beer. Russ was seventeen, with extremely thick eyeglasses and the mentality of a twelve year old. "Hey, Russ, what'd you see ina paper about Buck Jones?" Richie asked.

"He'll be at the Senate on Monday night at six o'clock."

"You sure?"

"Sure I'm sure. If it was ina paper, it's gotta be so, ain't it?"

"What paper?" Richie asked suspiciously.

"*Times.*"

As his tray was being filled with bagged popcorn, Richie considered the information. If it was in the *Times*, it was probably true. The *Times* and the *Herald-American* were always dependable; it was the *Tribune* that couldn't be trusted. Once the *Tribune* advertised a movie at the American Theater, down on Ashland Avenue, and after Richie went all the way down there, there was a different picture playing. The ticket girl told him the *Tribune* got the ads mixed up and ran the wrong one. Richie never trusted the *Tribune* again.

When his tray was full, he went back up to Mezzanine C and stood behind the back row of seats, watching the back of the blond man's head on the main floor. There was no way Richie could get a better look at the blond man until the boxing card ended and everyone was leaving; no way, that is, without getting in trouble and maybe losing his job. If he had been just a little more certain that it *was* his father, nothing could have kept him from charging down that aisle to where he sat. But if he did that and then found out it was only someone who *looked* like his father, and it cost him his job, that would be really dumb. A couple dozen kids showed up at the stadium every time there was an event, trying to get a job hawking; Richie was not about to lose his unless he was absolutely sure there was a good reason to lose it. So for now he watched, and waited.

The final, and feature, bout of the evening was the heavyweight match, three rounds, with the champion Joe Louis boxing one round each with sparring partners from his Special Services unit. After that bout began, the hawkers all lined up in the vendor room to check out for the evening. Richie got there as quickly as he could so that he would be finished and could station himself at the head of the aisle where the blond man had to come out. Usually the check-out went quickly; Rondo kept accurate tabs on all of his hawkers. But tonight there was a problem; one of the hot dog hawkers started an argument about the count. "I di'nt come back for four extra dogs," Richie heard him say, "on'y four extra *buns*. Some asshole spilt beer on four of my buns and I hadda t'row 'em away."

"I show here four extra hot dogs," Rondo said, tapping the guy's supply card with a pencil.

"I never got no dogs, on'y buns," the hawker insisted.

"Hey, Myrt!" Rondo called to the woman who cooked and distributed the hot dogs. "C'mere a minute, will you?"

While Richie waited impatiently in line, Russ, who was behind him, said "You going up there Monday night, to the Senate?"

"You bet," Richie said. "I wouldn't miss it for nothing."

"Me neither," Russ told him solemnly. Although older and bigger than most of the other kids, because he was slow Russ liked the same things they did and usually took part in the same activities. All of the kids accepted him and were protective of him. "Maybe I'll see you there," Russ said.

"I'm getting there early," Richie said. "I'll save you a seat."

Russ beamed. "T'anks, Richie!"

Edgy, shifting from foot to foot, Richie knew the last bout was almost over. He stuck his head out and yelled, "Hey, why ain't the line moving?"

"You shut up!" Rondo yelled back. "We got a problem up here!"

The hawkers continued to wait. From back in the arena, they heard a loud cheer and wild applause. "Main event's over," one of the hawkers farther back in the line said.

Richie bit his lip. Suppose it *was* his father? Suppose this was the only chance he would ever have in his whole life to find him again? Suppose—

"Listen," Richie said to Russ, "save my place, will you?"

"Okay."

Richie stepped out of line and headed toward the door.

"Hey!" Rondo yelled. "Where the hell you think you're going?"

"I gotta see somebody," Richie said. "I'll be right back—"

"Stay here," Rondo ordered. "The ushers don't like youse guys getting in the way when the crowd's leaving."

"I just wanna take a look at a guy I think I know. I'll be right back."

"Did you hear what I said?" Rondo demanded. "I said stay here!"

Out the door, Richie could see lines of spectators, four and five abreast, filing from the aisles into the exit lanes. The people in the main floor seats, where the blond man and the dark-haired woman had sat, were always the first ones out.

"Come on, Rondo," Richie pleaded. "Just lemme go out for one minute—"

"No! Get your goddamn ass back in that line!"

Richie stared at Rondo. All the hawkers in line had turned to look at Richie. In the space between Richie and where Rondo stood, an image of the back of the blond man's head suddenly appeared. And the tormenting words returned.

Suppose it was him . . . ?

"Get back in line!" Rondo ordered again.

"Go fuck yourself!" Richie suddenly yelled. Quickly taking the canvas strap from around his neck, he raised the empty wooden vendor tray over his head and hurled it against the wall. Then he bolted from the room and into the exiting crowd.

Working his way across the flowing stream of people, Richie edged along the wall against the crowd and got into the arena. He zigzagged through several emptying rows in several sections to get to the aisle where the blond man had been sitting. The man's seat was empty, as was the one next to it where the woman had sat. Richie's eyes searched the backs of the people moving up that aisle. Suddenly he saw the blond man, his arm around the shoulders of the woman, as they inched their way forward. They were nearly at the top of the aisle, about to move into the exit lane.

Panic rising in his chest, Richie jumped several rows of seats toward the next aisle over. Some of the spectators looked at him curiously as he reached the aisle and began trying to push his way through the people.

"Hey, look out, kid!" someone yelled. "What's the matter with you?"

"Watch it, punk, don't push," a burly man snapped.

"I'm sick!" Richie yelled. "Look out, I'm gonna throw up!"

Immediately the crowd opened up and gave him room. Holding his mouth and making regurgitating noises, Richie rushed forward to the exit lane and disappeared into a different part of the crowd.

By the time Richie got to the section of the exit lane off the aisle where he had seen him, the blond man was nowhere in sight. Richie moved back and forth in the exit lane to make certain he had not missed him. When he was sure, he hurried forward, scurrying among the dispersing spectators, until he passed through the glass exit doors and reached the street.

People were thick on the sidewalk, and traffic in the street was barely creeping. Richie hopped up on the front fender of a parked car and scanned the moving heads. There was a sea of faces—but no one who looked like his father. A policeman on a shiny brown horse came up next to him.

"Get down off there before you get hurt," he said. He fixed Richie with an unblinking stare until Richie got down.

After that, Richie just wandered up and down the edge of the sidewalk, looking at everybody who passed, everybody who got into a parked car or a taxi, everybody who went into one of the many nearby bars, everybody who piled into one of the new streamlined Madison streetcars. Minute by minute his excitement subsided and an old dull depression came over him, a depression he had felt so often when reminded that he did not have a father.

Glumly, he finally gave up as the stadium crowd thinned almost to nothing. Hands jammed into his knickers pockets, head down, thoughts as dark as the doorways of the street, he walked through the city night toward home.

On the way, he wondered if he would find another paregoric bottle in the garbage can.

On Sunday, Richie confirmed that Buck Jones was indeed going to make an appearance at the Senate Theater on Monday. The *Daily News*, another of the newspapers that could be trusted, had an item on the entertainment page reporting that the popular Western actor, who was touring the country selling

War Bonds, was scheduled to attend a black-tie affair with some other movie stars at some big hotel downtown, but that as he usually did, would be arriving in the city early enough to make an unscheduled appearance at a neighborhood movie house so that his young fans would have a chance to see him also. Balaban-and-Katz had made the Senate available to Buck because it was one of their larger, more centrally located houses.

Richie began making plans. Walking the twelve blocks up to the Senate on Sunday afternoon, he found out from the ticket taker that for Buck's appearance the following day, the doors would open at five P.M. Price of admission was the purchase of a twenty-five-cent War Savings Stamp, which when pasted in a book with seventy-four others amounted to $18.75 and could be turned in for a $25 War Bond. Buck would arrive at six and go on stage to give a short talk and answer questions from the audience, after which he would sign autographs and personally shake hands with each and every kid. After Buck's appearance, through the generosity of Balaban-and-Katz, there would be a free showing of the newest Bing Crosby movie, *Holiday Inn*.

Richie stared incredulously at the uniformed ticket taker. *Holiday Inn? Bing Crosby?* Marveling at the gross stupidity of grownups, he walked away shaking his head. It did not bother him long, however; the important thing was that Buck was coming, live and in person; the fact that the movie house owners were too ignorant to choose an appropriate picture for the occasion was insignificant.

Walking with Louis to school the next morning, Richie said, "I'm ditching at lunchtime. I wanna be one of the first ones in line at the Senate. You wanna come with?"

"Naw," Louis mumbled, looking away.

"Why not? On'y way you'll get a seat up front is to get there early."

"I ain't going," Louis said. Richie's mouth fell open. Not *going*? To see Buck Jones *in person*? "My old lady made me give her my magazine money for groceries," Louis said. "My old man didn't send no support dough last week and she was broke. So I ain't going."

Richie worried about Louis's plight in class all morning. He himself had more than a dollar: a dollar-fifteen, to be exact. But his prospects for future earnings had, he was sure, taken a turn for the worse after the stunt he pulled at the stadium on Saturday night. It would be a miracle if Rondo ever let him work again, so Richie's income would be reduced to what he earned selling magazines on Thursdays and Fridays. Thinking about that, he remembered that it had been Louis who helped him get that job.

At morning recess, Richie gave Ham a dime for his week's protection, reducing his capital to a dollar five cents. Louis, who paid by the day, had not been able to steal any cigarettes from his mother's pack, so had to give Ham his two-cents milk money instead. Obviously distraught at the prospect of missing Buck Jones, Louis asked, "You t'ink I could sneak in?"

"I dunno," Richie replied skeptically. "The Senate's tough. If it was the Imperial or the 4-Star, maybe. But the Senate, jeez, I dunno."

Throughout reading class, which bored Richie almost to tears because of the stupid, sissy, baby bullshit they had to read—shit like a kid visiting his grandpa and grandma on a goddamn farm and meeting all the goddamned animals—Richie continued to fret about Louis. By lunchtime, he had made up his mind. In the basement cafeteria, he moved through the line and got a frankfurter, a gob of mashed potatoes and gravy, a square of Jell-o, and a two-cent half-pint bottle of milk. Turning to Louis, he handed him two cents to buy milk for himself, and said, "I'll pay your way in the Senate. We'll ditch right after lunch."

Mouth agape, Louis followed Richie to a table. "No lie?" he asked, as Richie began to wolf down his food. "You're gonna pay my way?"

"If you'll promise to pay me back," Richie modified the offer.

"What if I just give you the Savings Stamp?" Louis wanted to know.

"I don't want the goddamn Savings Stamp," Richie said emphatically. One of the cafeteria monitors, an eighth-grade girl, heard him.

"What did you say?" she demanded.

"Me? Nothing," Richie denied.

"You did so. You said a swear word," she accused. She was fourteen, filling out under her sweater, on which was pinned a black-and-white MON-ITOR badge. "I'm reporting you for using a swear word. What's your name and room number?" she asked, pencil poised above a spiral notebook.

"James Warner," said Richie. The previous Thursday night he had read a *Saturday Evening Post* story about Fort Apache by a writer named James Warner Bellah. "I'm in Room Two-oh-eight." When the monitor walked away he muttered, "Goddamn bitch."

"My old man says all girls are cunts," Louis told him.

"Okay," Richie said, getting back to the important matter, "I'll pay your way in, you keep the stamp, and I'll give you a nickel for the candy counter, then you pay me back a dime a week for three weeks, okay?"

"Okay, yeah," Louis agreed.

"Hurry up and eat," Richie said around a mouthful of frankfurter, "so we can get outta here."

After they ate, Richie and Louis went out to the schoolyard and loitered around a place along the green metal fence where one of the pickets was broken at the bottom and could be pulled aside far enough to get through. Kneeling and pretending to be shooting marbles in the dirt, they watched until the teacher on duty in the yard turned her attention elsewhere, then both scurried through the opening and ran, crouching, down the block until they were out of sight.

It was one-thirty when they got to the Senate, and there were at least two dozen other kids already there. "Jeez," Richie said, "I'm glad we weren't no later." There were eight seats in each middle row; already they were back to the fourth row, unless they wanted to sit in one of the four-seat rows on either side of the aisle, which they didn't.

"Fourth row ain't so bad," Louis placated. He was glad to be in *any* row.

By two o'clock, there were fifty kids waiting, a few standing but most of them sitting on the sidewalk with their backs up against the building. It was November, but the sun was shining and there was no wind. Among the boys, a lot of the talk was about how soon the truant officers would arrive. "When do you t'ink they'll be here?" Louis asked.

Richie shrugged. "They gotta get here before three or they might's well not come at all. They can't do nothing to you after three 'cause school's out then."

The truant officers came at two-thirty. There was a woman and two men; they went along the line of boys, writing down information: name, school, grade, teacher's name.

"What'll I say?" Louis asked, frightened. They were standing by a poster advertising *Holiday Inn*. Richie's eyes searched the names on it, skipping the obvious ones like Crosby, Astaire, and Irving Berlin. Near the bottom of the credits, under "Makeup Supervision," he found a name that seemed to fit Louis.

"Tell 'em your name's Wally Westmore," he said. "And give 'em the same school and everything I do."

When one of the truant officers got to him, Richie used the same name, James Warner, that he had given the lunchroom monitor earlier, and said he was in the fifth grade at his old school, Biedler Elementary, and that his teacher's name was Mrs. York. The latter was the name of a cavalry officer in the *Post* story he had read.

After the truant officers collected their information, they left. There was really nothing else they could do; by then there were well over a hundred kids, from all over the city, and to have taken them back to their respective schools would have been impossible.

"Lot of kids are gonna be in for it tomorrow," Louis predicted solemnly.

"They shoulda lied," Richie said, shrugging.

At five o'clock, when the Senate opened its box office, there were, Richie guessed, a thousand kids waiting to get in. Most of them had arrived after school let out at three o'clock. The hundred or so who had ditched knew that the others would see Buck Jones just like they themselves would, but were smug in their knowledge that those who hadn't ditched wouldn't see him as *close* up as they would. Having guts enough to ditch school definitely had its rewards.

Each kid paid his quarter at the box office and was given the Savings Stamp and a theater ticket. Some of the kids had stamp books into which they promptly and properly pasted the stamp. Richie and Louis put theirs in their knickers pockets and immediately forgot them. Once inside, they ran, as did all the kids, past ushers who were yelling, "No running! No running!" and into the auditorium to claim the choice seats. Ditching paid off; Richie and Louis got seats on the aisle in row three, and Richie saved an extra one for Russ, his friend from the stadium. Louis held the seats while Richie returned to the candy counter. After buying candy bars, Richie looked around for Russ. A head taller than most of the other kids, Russ was not hard to find. At the sight of Richie, he smiled widely; then his expression quickly turned sad.

"Rondo ain't gonna let you work no more," he said. "He tol' us all to tell you to stay away if we seen you."

"I figured," Richie said.

"I'm sure sorry, Richie."

"Forget it." Richie knew in retrospect that what he had done was stupid. But at the time, it had seemed necessary.

After Russ bought three candy bars for himself, Richie led him to their seats. A couple of kids were giving Louis a hard time about the two extra seats he was saving, but at the sight of Russ they immediately retreated. While the lights were still on, the three boys looked around. "The joint's packed," Russ said.

"Sure it is," Richie shrugged. "This is Buck Jones that's coming. He's the greatest cowboy in the world."

"Bet there's thousands of kids outside that couldn't even get in," Louis guessed.

They ate their candy and talked and fidgeted and kicked their feet and squirmed as the interminable hour between five and six dragged by with maddening slowness. But at last the moment came. The Senate manager walked out on the stage to a standing microphone. "Who did you all come here to see tonight?" he asked loudly.

"BUCK JONES!" a roar resounded in the theater.

"Well, here he is!" the manager announced, and as he said it the house lights went off, a spotlight hit the stage, and Buck Jones—live, real, in person—walked out of the wings.

He was like a god. Tall, straight, square; there was not a curve to be seen, every facet of him made from ninety-degree angles. His narrowed eyes glinted; his black hair, combed straight back in the sensible style of a real man, shone like onyx; his lantern jaw was set in such a way that told the whole world that this man would brook no nonsense of any sort. His shoulders could have carried wagon wheels, his table-flat stomach could have taken any blow, his mighty arms could have protected any innocent from every evil. He did not need guns or knives or bullwhips; he had stature. He had *presence*. When Buck Jones was around, everybody, by god, knew it.

The cheer when Buck strode onto the stage was explosive; above the audience, the Senate's crystal chandelier actually vibrated. Every kid in the theater was standing, waving, cheering, whistling. Richie hated it that he could not whistle very well; he wished he could whistle so loudly and shrilly that it would break glass. But with his hawker-conditioned voice, he made up for it with yells that caused Louis to look at him in awe.

Buck removed his spotless white, wide-brimmed Stetson and raised it above his head. The fringe of his buckskin coat rippled like water. Without a smile, barely moving his thin, razor-sharp lips, he said, "Hello, pardners."

Another roar went up. Buck's voice was like the rest of him: deep, clear, precise, and direct. He listened to the cheers for a moment, then raised a hand for quiet. He got it—immediately. Silence before a god.

"I want to thank you all for coming out to see me tonight. I know this is a school night, so I promise not to keep you long."

The audience exploded in laughter. That Buck was something. A real kidder.

"The reason I've come to visit with you tonight," Buck continued, "is to ask you to help me to help all our brave fighting men overseas by buying War Bonds and Savings Stamps to help America's war effort. Our boys that are fighting this war deserve all of the support we can give them. I know what they're going through, believe me; I served in the army, fought in the Philippines, and was wounded in the leg by a sniper. It's a terrible thing to be far away from home, far away from your loved ones, facing death every day fighting America's enemies. But we can help all our brave soldiers, sailors, and Marines, by investing our dimes and quarters in Savings Stamps, and turning those stamps in for War Bonds. Uncle Sam will use that money to see that our fighting men have enough food and ammunition and bandages to carry on the fight until we've given the dirty Japs and the dirty Nazis the licking they deserve!"

The audience went wild again, cheering, whistling, shouting, applauding. Buck's narrowed eyes swept the house as he let the kids of the city show their patriotism. Without smiling, he nodded solemnly to show that he agreed with them. Then he held up a hand again.

"You know, pardners, America is a grand, big land. It doesn't matter whether we live in the east or the west, the north or the south. Wherever we live, we're all Americans and we owe it to our country to be good citizens. That means a heap, being a good citizen. And I know that you know what I mean by that. Be a straight shooter and a square dealer. Treat folks fair and honestly. Respect your parents and your teachers. Study hard. Always remember that America is the land of opportunity. There's nothing you can't achieve in this great country of ours if you try hard enough . . . and don't ever let *anybody* discourage you from working toward what you want out of life. Aim high, pardners." Nodding, Buck threw a wink into the audience that every boy there was certain had been meant for him alone. "Now then, anybody have any questions they'd like to ask me?"

"Where's Silver at?" somebody yelled. Silver was Buck's famous white stallion.

Buck smiled, for the first time. "Well, I'll tell you," he drawled, "Silver's back at my ranch in the San Fernando Valley in California. I'll tell you something else—there are *three* Silvers." A gasp of surprise rippled through the audience. "That's right," Buck assured. "As all you boys and girls know, a horse ages faster than a human does, so they get old lots quicker. The original Silver is twenty-seven years old now. Silver number two, his son, is almost twenty. The horse you all see in the pictures I'm making today is Silver number three, the grandson. He's fifteen."

"You got any kids, Buck?" a boy called out.

"I've got a little girl named Maxine. Actually she's not so little anymore; she's all growed up now—but she'll always be my little girl just the same."

"What's your next pitcher?"

"I've got a real good one coming out next month just in time for Christmas. It's from Monogram Studios and it's called *Dawn on the Great Divide*. My pal Raymond Hatton is in it, and I think you'll like it."

There weren't many more questions; after the obvious ones, a city kid really could not think of anything to ask a cowboy god. Most of the kids in the audience would have been content just to sit and listen to Buck talk. But as soon as he detected a lull, Buck moved into the next segment of his appearance.

"Tell you what let's do now," he said. "I want to shake hands with every one of you that bought a Savings Stamp tonight. And if you have autograph books, why, I'd be proud to sign them for you. I want one row at a time to come up here on the stage in single file. Don't run and don't push, be careful on the steps there . . . "

It took an hour, but Buck Jones shook the hand of every kid. He didn't bother with names; every boy was "Pardner," every girl was "Little Lady."

With his own gold fountain pen he signed every autograph book presented to him, while an usher stood by with a bottle of Carter's ink for Buck to refill his pen when it ran dry.

On the way up to the stage, Richie silently practiced what he had made up his mind to say: "Hi, Buck! You're my favorite cowboy and the best there is!" He pictured Buck being impressed, asking his name, talking to him about coming out to Hollywood and learning to be a cowboy movie star. It intrigued Richie that Buck had no son, only a daughter. God, wouldn't it be wonderful to have Buck Jones for a dad!

While Richie was thinking about it, the line kept moving and before he knew it he was *there*—standing in front of Buck, who looked like a mountain. Richie meekly put his hand out, felt it enveloped by Buck's huge hand, heard that marvelously deep voice say, "How are you, pardner?" At once Richie became an imbecile; without even looking up, staring at Buck's great silver belt buckle under the open coat, he found the intelligence only to mutter, "Hi," and then he was walking off the stage, and it was all over.

For a moment, Richie was mortified. But it passed quickly. He had met Buck Jones, and that was what counted. He had shaken hands with the second greatest man in the world—every kid in America knew that President Roosevelt was the greatest—and had actually been personally spoken to by Buck. *How are you, pardner?* What a wonderful thing to say! The words, Richie was sure, would remain with him forever. Buck Jones had asked him how he was! Sure, it would have been swell if Richie had been able to look Buck right in the eye and say, "I'm fine, Buck! How are you?" But that had not happened—and Richie realized that it did not matter. What Buck said was what mattered. *How are you, pardner?* Shaking Buck's hand was what mattered. It had been a magic moment that would shine forever.

Richie and Louis and Russ sat and watched as the seemingly endless line of kids snaked its way down the aisle, up the stairs, across the stage. They watched Buck's lips barely move as he greeted each one of them, and Richie was positive that at no time did Buck say to any other kid the exact words he had said to Richie. *How are you, pardner?* Richie smiled at the fresh memory of the words. Fine, Buck, he thought. Just fine. Basking in the glow of the great man, Richie began making silent promises to himself. He was going to stop swearing. And telling lies. He was going to buy Savings Stamps instead of comic books. He was going to be a square shooter and a good citizen.

When the last kid had finally shaken his hand, Buck turned back to the microphone and said, "Well, little friends, it's about time for me to hit the trail. I've got to go downtown to some fancy grown-up party. Tell the truth, I'd rather stay right here with all of you and spin a few cowboy yarns, but I promised I'd go down there and I always keep my word, just like I know you do. So I'll say so long for now. Remember to buy those Savings Stamps, and encourage your folks to buy War Bonds. Let's all work to get this awful war over with." Once again the white Stetson was raised high. "*Adios*, pardners!" Buck shouted.

The following Sunday morning, Richie awoke to the sound of Louis calling his name from the alley behind his building.

"Yo, Richie!" he yelled. "Yo-oh, Rich-ie!" Over and over. Before Richie got to the window, he heard an adult's voice shout, "Shut up down there, for Christ's sake! It's Sunday!"

Raising the window, Richie stuck his head out. Before he could say anything, Louis waved a newspaper and yelled, "Buck Jones got burned in a fire!"

Richie's eyes widened and his mouth dropped open. *It was a mistake!* His mind immediately seized on a defense. "What paper's that?" he called down suspiciously. Probably the stinking *Tribune*.

"*Times*," Louis said.

"Be right down," Richie told him.

Breaking all previous records for dressing, Richie was in the alley in three minutes. The story was on the front page, with a photograph of a building in flames. The headlines read: BLAZE SWEEPS BOSTON NIGHTCLUB. Below that: 300 FEARED DEAD.

"Here's where it says about Buck," Louis pointed to a place in the story and Richie read: "Among the scores of victims taken to Massachusetts General Hospital was Charles 'Buck' Jones, popular cowboy motion picture star. Jones was attending a party in his honor at the end of a successful ten-city personal appearance tour on behalf of the current War Bond drive."

Richie read the story all the way through, then reread twice the part about Buck.

"T'ink he's gonna die?" Louis asked solemnly. Richie shook his head emphatically.

"No." Handing the paper back to Louis, he said, "I gotta go eat breakfast. See you later."

Back upstairs, he went directly to the radio and turned it on. As he waited impatiently for it to warm up, he tuned it to the Mutual Broadcasting network, on which his mother listened to the war news each evening. There was religious music playing when it came on, so Richie stretched out on the floor with his head under the table and waited. At nine o'clock the news came on.

"In Boston," the commentator said, "police and fire department officials have determined that the Cocoanut Grove nightclub fire that has claimed at least 350 lives was accidentally started by a sixteen-year-old bus boy attempting to replace a light bulb which had been removed by a partying patron in the club's basement room known as the Melody Lounge. Standing on a chair, the boy struck a match to see where to screw the bulb in, and accidentally ignited an artificial palm tree nearby. The burning palm set fire to decorative silk loops festooning the ceiling, and the blaze spread quickly across the lounge. There were an estimated one-hundred-thirty patrons in the downstairs lounge, while above them some seven hundred more were dining and dancing in the nightclub's huge main room.

"The fire, which started about ten o'clock last night, swept into the main room in what has been described as a 'flash' or 'burst' of flame. Leather-covered walls of the nightclub had been treated with a fire-resistant compound which kept them from igniting in flames but which caused them to give off dense clouds of thick smoke. It was this thick smoke which caused panic among the patrons and caused hundreds of them to rush blindly for exits already jammed shut by crushed human bodies.

"Army and navy officers and enlisted men dining and dancing at the nightclub were credited with acts of bravery in attempting to control the panic-stricken crowd, and Western movie star Buck Jones, who was a patron in the main room, is reported to have at least twice reentered the blazing building after successfully escaping, to help others get out. Jones is reported to be badly burned and in serious condition at Massachusetts General Hospital . . ."

Under the table, tears came out of the sides of Richie's eyes and ran down into his ears.

Twelve hours later, the news had only become worse.

"Mutual Broadcasting has learned that the death toll from the Cocoanut Grove nightclub fire in Boston has now reached four hundred and fifty. Firemen, national guardsmen, and military and civilian volunteers continue to remove burned, crushed, and asphyxiated bodies from the ruins. Since noon today they have been working in a cold winter rain which has made their terrible job even more difficult. Taxicabs, delivery vans, and newspaper trucks have been pressed into service to transfer the bodies to mortuaries throughout the city. Earlier, ambulances from twenty-two hospitals worked through the night and early morning transporting the burned and injured to medical facilities. The city's doctors and nurses have been on duty for more than twenty hours. Some five hundred Red Cross volunteers are assisting them.

"As the hours pass, stories of individual heroism have begun to emerge. One movie hero who has become a real-life hero is Charles 'Buck' Jones, cowboy idol of millions of American youngsters. Jones, attending a party at the end of a ten-city War Bond tour, apparently was one of the fortunate patrons who escaped the doomed premises. But he is reported to have gone back into the holocaust at least twice, and perhaps as many as four times, to help rescue others. Jones apparently reentered the burning building the first time to help his personal manager and longtime friend, Scott R. Dunlap, who had been in attendance at the party given for Jones by area motion picture distributors. After successfully aiding Dunlap, the veteran Western actor returned up to three more times to assist others before finally collapsing and being rushed to the hospital. At Massachusetts General, physicians reported that Jones was suffering burned lungs from extensive smoke inhalation, as well as third and second degree burns on his face and neck. Although still tenaciously clinging to life at this hour, doctors state that his condition is critical and he is given only a slight chance of survival . . ."

Sitting on the floor in a corner of the living room, Richie's face was buried in arms crossed over upraised knees. His stomach growled in emptiness; he had not eaten all day. Periodically throughout the morning and afternoon, he had heard Louis calling him again from the alley, but he had not responded. His mother had gotten out of bed around noon, had several cups of coffee and smoked several cigarettes, then dressed and gone out, admonishing him not to leave the block. He had paid no attention to her because his mind was so caught up in the tragedy of Buck; nevertheless, he was still sitting where she had left him when she returned four hours later. He knew where she had been, knew what she was doing when she locked herself in the bathroom with a cup and a spoon and the sugar bowl and her purse, in which Richie knew she had several small bottles wrapped in drugstore paper. He did not even have to look in the garbage can for empty bottles anymore; his mother's two moods—preoccupation and lethargy—told him all he needed to know.

"I can't fix supper tonight, Richie," she told him later. "I'm just too tired." She gave him a quarter. "Go get a hamburger, okay?"

He did not move and she did not care; her responsibility had been taken care of.

Still later, Chloe glided back into the room and abruptly moved the radio dial. "For god's sake, isn't there anything on besides all this talk, talk, talk? Can't we have some music, for god's sake?"

Richie got up, got his coat and cap, and walked out.

It was after dark now and the block was quieting down. Mrs. Chaney's, the little basement store on the corner, was closed, so Richie walked over there and sat in the dark on the steps that led down to it from the sidewalk. Occasionally someone walked by, but nobody noticed him there; the night was getting cold and people hurried. With his collar turned up and the flaps of his cap pulled down over his ears, he sat on the cold steps as he had sat on the living room floor: knees up, arms folded, head down. Soon he was very cold, cold all over, cold inside and out, cold in his stomach and in his heart, cold even in his mind and thoughts.

Only the tears streaking his cheeks were warm.

The next morning, before he went to school, Richie could get nothing on the radio about Buck. Because he felt ill and weak from not eating, he fixed a bowl of Wheaties and managed to get it down. Chloe, as usual, was already gone; she started at the bakery at six. Before she left, she always reset the alarm for him. Every morning Richie got up, got ready for school by himself, fixed his own breakfast, and left when he heard Louis call him. This morning, because there was no news on the radio, he was going to leave early and go buy a paper. Before he left, he opened a John Ruskin cigar box that Johnny Eaton had given him, and got out his three Buck Jones badges. Two of them were round, made of tin: one white with black lettering reading FAMOUS COWBOY SERIES, with a black line drawing of Buck; the other with black lettering that read FOR U.S. MARSHAL—BUCK JONES, with an actual photo of Buck against a red background. The third was brass, shaped like a horseshoe, BUCK JONES CLUB lettered around the curve, and a drawing of Buck in the middle. Thinking maybe that wearing the badges might somehow bring Buck good luck, Richie pinned them to the inside of his coat.

There was a newsstand outside Mrs. Chaney's. Richie bought a *Times* and sat on the steps of the store to read it. The front page was all war news: the Russian army, driving the Germans back from Moscow, had killed 15,000 and captured 66,000; on the other side of the world, two Japanese destroyers had been sunk off New Guinea. Johnny Eaton was fighting on New Guinea, and ordinarily Richie would have read the item thoroughly, but today was different. Quickly turning to page two, he was, in spite of everything, unprepared for what he found there. Tears welled in his eyes as he read the ominous headline: BUCK JONES DEAD OF FIRE INJURIES.

The story followed. "Charles (Buck) Jones, cowboy motion picture star, died late Sunday night of burns suffered in the Cocoanut Grove fire. A long-time favorite of American boy movie fans, he became the 481st fatality of the disaster—"

Richie could not read the rest of it. Tearing the column out and putting it in his pocket, he left the rest of the paper on the steps and walked away.

He did not go to school. For the rest of the day, he wandered. He walked up and down the streets, up and down alleys. He rode streetcars to the end of the line and back. For hours he kept moving, like a zombie, expression slack, eyes dull, shoulders slumped. Twice someone stopped on the street to ask if he was all right, but Richie ignored them and kept going. By one o'clock, after five hours, he made his way back home, exhausted. To his surprise, he found his mother there, packing dishes in a cardboard box.

"We're moving," Chloe said. "To a cheaper place. I couldn't take that bakery one more day, so I quit. There's a man coming to buy the furniture. I've got us a little furnished flat down on Adams Street where we can get along just on Johnny's allotment check." Pausing, she saw his desolate expression. "Now, don't look at me like that, Richie. I know you don't like to change schools but this can't be helped. You have no idea what working in that bakery has been like. My nerves are absolutely shot. There's a box on your bed; you just pack all your clothes and things in it, and don't give me any trouble, you hear me? Go on now . . ."

In the bedroom, Richie put his Buck Jones badges back in the cigar box and packed that first. He felt all hollow inside, vacant, useless, like an empty popcorn bag. Everything was systematically being taken away from him: Johnny Eaton, the stadium job, Buck Jones, the first school where he had someone to protect him, everything. Everything of value was going from his life, Popsicle sticks floating in the gutter, heading for the sewer.

"Hurry up with your packing, Richie," he heard his mother say. "Before we leave, I want you to go to a couple places for me."

Floating in the gutter, heading for the sewer.

Just like him.

ichie walked out of the tenement building on Adams Street and sat on the front stoop. Pushing down one long sock and pulling up the leg of his knickers, he examined several small red bumps on his leg. They were on his other leg also, and all over the rest of him, even on his face. They itched fiercely.

As he sat there, another boy came out of the building and saw him looking at the sores. Sitting down beside Richie, he asked, "Di'nt you have no candle?"

Richie frowned. "What?"

"Candle. Ain't you got a candle? Them's bedbug bites, ain't they?"

Richie shrugged again. The other boy looked closely at Richie's face.

"Them's bedbug bites," he declared. "C'mon, I'll show you what to do about 'em."

"I gotta go to school," Richie said.

"You transferrin' to Brown?"

"Yeah."

"Fuck it. Go tomorrow. Tell 'em you couldn't find it today. C'mon."

Richie followed him back into the building and up the creaky wooden stairs past the second floor, where Chloe, Richie knew, was still sleeping, to the third floor, where the boy gestured for Richie to be quiet and wait. "My old lady's asleep," he explained. "She works nights." Richie watched as he carefully opened a door next to a hall garbage can and slipped into one of the flats.

"Stan, what are you doing back?" a female voice asked. Through the open door, Richie saw a girl about fifteen, in a tight sweater, drinking coffee and smoking a cigarette at a cluttered kitchen table.

"Forgot something," the boy answered.

"You'd better get to school on time," the girl warned. "If you get expelled one more time, Ma's gonna kill you."

When Stan came back into the hall, he had a thick white candle about four inches long, and a book of matches. "Okay, show me where you sleep," he said.

Richie took him down a flight and opened the door to his and Chloe's flat as quietly as Stan had done. "My old lady's asleep too," he whispered, using Stan's vernacular. He led Stan to an alcove on one side of the kitchen, where there was a cot with a thin, blue-striped mattress on it, covered by a rumpled sheet and a brown blanket. Stan folded everything back, mattress and all, exposing bluish metal springs.

"Watch," he said. Down on his knees, he lighted the candle wick and held its flame under one of the sections of bedsprings. Within seconds, Richie began hearing a series of soft pops. "Them's the bedbugs," Stan said. "They live in the coils an' on'y come out when it's dark to suck your blood. The fire from the candle explodes 'em; that's what makes the popping sound."

While Richie watched in fascination, Stan systematically moved the flame from coil to coil, remaining at each until the popping stopped before moving on. After a while, he gave the candle to Richie. "G'on, you try it."

Itching madly all over his body, Richie burned the bedbugs with relish. When they had done the entire bedspring, Stan said, "G'on, keep the candle. I'll get anudder."

When they got back outside, Stan said, "Some of them bedbugs go down into the mattress too. We'll swipe a bottle of alcohol today an' I'll show you what to do about them little bastards." Shoving his hands in his pockets, Stan looked up and down the street as if evaluating it. He was a confident-looking boy with curly, shiny black hair and thick black eyebrows that all but grew together at the top of his nose. A slightly enlarged lower lip gave him a pouty look when his mouth was closed, a rather stupid look when it was open, but Stan was neither. The same age as Richie, he was not as skinny. As he surveyed the block of Adams Street just below Damen Avenue, the expression on his face clearly indicated that the street was *his*; he had no fear of it. "Wanna go rat-killing?" he asked almost nonchalantly.

Richie shrugged. "I don't know how."

"C'mon, I'll show you."

Stan took Richie to a grocery on Ashland Avenue that had a dozen fruit and vegetable bins lining the sidewalk outside. Stopping two doors away, he said, "Okay, when I say 'go,' we both run like hell past the store. You grab a couple of them apples for us. I'll snatch the potatoes."

"The potatoes?"

"Yeah, the potatoes. For the rat killing. Okay, all set?"

"Yeah—"

"Go!" Stan ordered without warning.

Stan broke into a run, Richie half a step behind him. They came to the potato bin first, where, without breaking stride, Stan grabbed an Irish potato with each hand and kept going. The apples were on the other side of the doorway, through which, as he passed, Richie could see a man in a white apron already hurrying out. Two bushel baskets of apples were set next to the door, and from them Richie grabbed an apple with each hand. Fumbling the one in his left hand, he dropped it and saw it bounce into the gutter as he pumped his legs to catch up with Stan.

"You little sons of bitches!" a voice behind them yelled, but Richie heard no running footsteps coming after them. Stan beat it around the corner, with Richie right behind him. They ran another block, then slowed, panting, to a walk. Richie handed Stan the apple.

"How's come you just got one?"

"I didn't want one," Richie said. "I ate a big breakfast." It was a lie. He had eaten four slices of dry toast and washed it down with water. His mother had not bought any groceries since they had moved three days earlier; the bread he had toasted, which they had brought with them, was nearly a week old.

Eating the apple, Stan led Richie to the alley behind their block, to a building near the other corner. Near the foundation of a garage that faced the alley, Stan showed Richie several dark holes leading into the ground under the garage. "Rat holes," he said. With a pocketknife, Stan peeled the raw potatoes, tossed the potatoes themselves into a garbage can, and spread the peels on the ground a foot or so from the rat holes. "Okay, c'mon." He hit Richie on the arm and hurried to a row of ashcans near the coal chute of an adjoining tenement. From behind one can he pulled out half a dozen red bricks, giving three to Richie. "Follow me," he said. "Hurry up."

They went up the outside rear stairs of the building to a second-floor back porch. "Everybody in this building works," Stan said, "so nobody's around to bother us. The guys in the neighborhood use this porch for every-thing—to smoke, read comic books we swipe, anything we wanna do. Right here's where we kill rats."

Standing at the rail, they looked down at a forty-five-degree angle at the garage foundation and the potato peelings. Following Stan's example, Richie put two bricks on the floor and the third on top of the railing.

"I'll go first," Stan said, "to show you how it's done."

They waited quietly and patiently, bricks in hand. In less than five minutes the first rat stuck its head out of the hole and looked around. Stan's fingers tightened on his brick, but he otherwise made no move at all that might frighten the rodent. Several seconds went by, then the rat came halfway out of the hole and looked around. Glancing at Richie, Stan nodded and winked. A few more seconds and the rat was all the way out, scurrying over to the pungent-smelling potato peels, sinking its ferret teeth into the still moist skin.

Stan's brick flew through the air with uncanny accuracy. Just as the rat was turning to take its food back to the hole, the brick smashed it against the alley pavement, spreading it into a blotch of gore and dirty hair.

Richie winced. Stan grinned.

"That's rat-killing. Fun, huh? I'll go down and get rid of the mess, an' you can try your luck with the next one."

"Will another one come out?" Richie asked in amazement.

"Before you know it," Stan assured him. "Rats are the dumbest god-damned things in the world. You'll see."

As Richie watched, Stan used a garbage can lid to scrape away the mess of his victim. Then he hurried back up to the porch. "Keep your brick ready," he advised, "an don't t'row until the rat gets all the way out to the peel and gets it in his mouth. Then aim for a spot halfway between the peel and the hole. T'row fast and t'row hard."

"Right," Richie said, wetting his lips. Hefting the brick as he had seen Stan do, he then fell into a near-motionless stance, only his chest moving slightly with each breath, his eyes blinking occasionally. He hoped to god he hit the rat so he wouldn't look dumb to Stan.

It took only about three minutes for another rat face to appear in the same hole. Seconds later, it was scurrying over to the peelings, its dark, hairy body dirty and disgusting, its long, thin tail slimy and slick with the filth of its black, putrid world. Richie could see the repugnant mouth open, the ugly yellow teeth sink into the irresistible potato peel. Around the brick, he felt his fingers and palm become moist. Jaw set, lips tight, he let fly the brick.

It smashed the rat to pulp.

"Bullseye!" said Stan.

He and Richie looked at each other and grinned.

In that moment they became buddies.

Stanley Klein was a restless kid. The only time he stayed anywhere longer than an hour was in school or at a movie. "In this city it don't pay to get caught sitting still," he philosophized. "It's safer when you keep moving. 'Member that, Richie."

Richie studied his new friend like a lesson in survival, which in a way he was. At Brown Elementary, where they were both in fifth grade, Stan had developed a way of avoiding fights—simply by letting it be known that he *would* fight—anybody, anyplace. When he first came to Brown, he had four fights in three days: all-out, blood-letting, punching and kicking, no-quarter-given fights. Two with white kids, two with colored kids. One fight had actually been in a classroom, which the two combatants half wrecked. Stan lost three of the four fights and was expelled for the fourth, the classroom brawl, but in each encounter he inflicted more than moderate damage on his opponent, all the while yelling, "Come on, beat my ass! Whip me good! But you're gonna take some licks too, cocksucker! Come on!"

When Stan was allowed to return to school after his expulsion, nobody—no matter how big or how tough—bothered him anymore. The black kids referred to him as a "crazy motherfucker, ain't got sense enough to take a licking." White kids simply warned, "Don't fuck with him, he's nuts; he'll jump your ass in the fucking classroom and get you t'rowed outta school."

For Richie, being friends with Stan at Brown Elementary was the same as having Ham as a protector at Grant, except that he did not have to pay Stan. Being Stan's buddy and constant companion was enough; where Stan went and what Stan did, Richie went and did also, and for the first time in his life he enjoyed immunity from bullying *and* ridicule. Nobody fucked with him as long as he was with Stan. Richie vowed to himself that if Stan ever did have to fight anyone, for whatever reason, Richie would fight right along beside him. He was very grateful, however, that such an occasion never materialized. Stan's reputation always precluded it.

Stan, like Richie, had no father; he lived with his mother and fifteen-year-old sister. His mother worked nights as a bar maid in a tavern on Racine Avenue.

Richie was amazed at the things Stan could do. He had ways of getting in without paying at half the movie houses on the West Side, and even some of the big vaudeville theaters in the Loop. He thought nothing of taking a streetcar downtown and sneaking into the majestic, ornate Oriental, or the stately State-Lake, or the rich, velvety Woods. Stan took Richie to see stage shows with performances by Danny Kaye, Olsen and Johnson, Carmen Miranda, Harry James and his Orchestra, and numerous others who played the big stage show houses. The boys also saw all the new first-run war movies: *A Yank on the Burma Road, Remember Pearl Harbor, Wake Island, Manila Calling, Commandos Strike at Dawn,* and *Stand By for Action.* In the latter, Richie watched former sissy star Robert Taylor in still another manly role as a naval officer who rescues a boatload of mothers and babies from a torpedoed ship. Richie still mourned that Dixie Cup lid!

The only thing Richie did without Stan in the early days of their friendship was to go off by himself one afternoon and ride a streetcar out to the Kedzie Annex theater to see *Dawn on the Great Divide*, the last picture Buck Jones made. Sitting through it the first time, Richie had watery eyes; he sat through it a second time after he had composed himself. It was a fine movie, he thought, one of Buck's best, with the final shootout between Buck and an actor named Roy Barcroft, probably the best bad guy in the movies. Richie was glad that Buck's last movie gunfight had been against Barcroft and that, as always, Buck had given the bad guy an edge by letting him draw first.

After the second show, when he left the Kedzie Annex, Richie stood for several moments on the corner, looking over at the Senate Theater on the opposite corner, where he had seen Buck in person that memorable night three months earlier. Tears again came to his eyes as he raised his hand in a kid's salute, said, "So long, Buck," to himself, and started walking home because he had no streetcar fare.

Everything else Richie did, he did with Stan. Besides movies and stage shows, and rat-killing, Stan introduced him to other forms of entertainment. In a maze of alleys in and around the Cook County Hospital complex on lower Harrison Street, Stan showed him a ground-level window, hidden behind a large iron garbage dumpster, through which they could look down into a locker room and watch nurses showering and changing in and out of their starched white uniforms. The first time they looked through the window together, there was a blonde woman with enormous breasts who took a long, leisurely shower in the open shower room and then sat on a bench and slowly rubbed lotion all over her body. While they were watching, Richie noticed Stan, in a shadowy crouch, making an odd movement.

"What are you doing?" he asked.

"Jacking off." Stan paused and looked at Richie. "Ain't you never done it?"

Richie shrugged, embarrassed. "No."

"Your dick's hard, ain't it?"

Swallowing, Richie said, "Yeah."

"Take it out," Stan instructed. Unbuttoning his fly, Richie released his erection. "Okay, now go like this with your hand," Stan said, showing him how.

Looking at the blonde from behind the garbage dumpster, Richie masturbated for the first time.

□

When Chloe sent him back to the black drugstores on Lake Street, Richie saw Vernie again. She did not appear surprised to see him.

"Hey, Richie," she greeted him nonchalantly. "You mamma hooked again, I guess."

"Huh?" said Richie, not understanding.

Getting off a car fender where she had been sitting talking to another girl, Vernie said, "Come on, I walk wit'cha."

Filled out even more now, at fifteen Vernie walked with a smooth strut that was no longer practiced but now natural and confident. Her skirt was the new wartime length, three inches above the knees; she wore no stockings, and her sandals were flat-heeled, making her legs look round and strong. A black brassiere was outlined under her white blouse. In her waistband, Richie saw the handle of her straight razor.

"Is Alonzo still around?" Richie asked as they walked.

"No, 'Lonzo's fam'ly moved to the South Side someplace," Vernie said. "But they be somebody jus' like him around. They *always* be somebody think they a badass."

"We moved too," Richie told her. "Down on Adams near Damen."

"Shit, we prac'tly neighbors, Richie," she said. As they walked, Vernie glanced several times at Richie, studying him. Finally she asked, "You know any white boys might wanna come over here to Lake Street for a good time?"

"What do you mean?" Richie had a pretty good idea what she meant, but he wanted to make sure.

"A good time like boys and girls has together," Vernie elaborated. "Like when they go in the dark doorways together. You know."

"Oh, yeah. Sure."

"If you knows any, you send 'em around, hear? Tell 'em come to the corner of Lake and Hoyne after it get dark."

"How old do they have to be?" Richie inquired. He was wondering how Vernie would look with her clothes off.

"Older than you, tha's for sure," she squelched his fantasy. "Fo'teen, at least. And they gots to have fifty cents. Understand?"

"Yeah."

"Ever' one you send 'round, I give you a nickel. And I'll keep these niggers around here off your ass when you come to get dope for yo' mamma."

Richie had never heard his mother's medicine referred to as "dope" before. When he saw Stan that night he asked what "'dope" meant.

"It just means dope," Stan replied, shrugging. "It's like whiskey, I t'ink, only harder to get."

"Is it like medicine?"

"I guess," Stan allowed, shrugging again. "It makes people feel good, is why they take it. That's kinda like medicine, ain't it?"

"Sure," Richie replied. He spoke the word quietly, reflectively, as a shroud of understanding slowly slipped over his young mind. Dope. The word itself had an ominous ring to it, like "death." It sounded evil. Vernie had mentioned his mother being "hooked." That too prompted ugly images. If it was medicine she was sending him after, why did he have to go to so many places to get it; why couldn't he get it all at one place?

One afternoon, as Chloe was preparing to send him on his errands, Richie asked her about it. "Why do they call the stuff you take dope?"

"Who calls it dope?" Chloe asked.

"A girl over on Lake Street called it dope."

"A girl? What girl?" His mother's voice grew impatient.

"A girl that walks with me sometimes."

"A nigger girl?" Chloe asked contemptuously.

"Yeah."

Chloe pointed a threatening finger at him. "You keep away from these city nigger girls, young man, you hear me? You can catch bad things just by standing close to city nigger girls and breathing the same air. Now for your information, my medicine is *not* dope. If it was dope, you couldn't buy it in the drugstore. So you tell this girl, whoever she is, that your mother says she doesn't know what she's talking about. Then you stay away from her. I mean it."

Richie felt like telling his mother that had it not been for Vernie, half the time he would not even get to the Lake Street drugstores with her money. Alonzo, now gone, had been replaced by half a dozen other young colored thugs even worse than him, and the colored ghetto, shoulder to shoulder with Richie's white slum, was becoming more dangerous with each day that passed, especially for whites who ventured into it. Many companies were hiring colored delivery men now because white men would not drive a ghetto route. But Richie knew that it would do no good to tell Chloe those things; in the afternoons when she was becoming desperate for her paregoric, she would have sent him into a snake pit to get it.

Stan was always waiting when Richie got home from his drugstore errands. He would not go with Richie because he had other things to do, profitable activities in which he engaged every day: stealing soda pop bottles from the rear of stores and returning them to other stores for the two-cent deposit; filching coins from unattended newsstands; shoplifting dime store merchandise that he could peddle on the street. Stan had a repertoire of ways to acquire money; when Richie finished his errands early and was able to find him along Madison Street, Stan introduced Richie to the various methods he employed. Within a month of moving to Adams Street, Richie had become a skilled street thief.

One night Richie came home from prowling the streets with Stan and then sneaking into the Elmo Theater to see a movie. When he let himself into the dingy flat, he found his mother sitting on the sofa with a dark, handsome man wearing an Air Corps uniform.

"Hi, sugar," his mother said with forced brightness, immediately nervous. "This is George, a new friend of mine. He's in the Air Corps, isn't that exciting? George, this is my little boy, Richie."

"Hello, Richie," the dark man said with a dazzling smile. He had curly black hair, a thin black moustache, and the most perfect white teeth Richie had ever seen. His skin was the color of wet sand.

"Well, come shake hands like a big boy, sugar," his mother prompted. Richie sulked over and reluctantly offered his hand. "Hi," he said, barely audible.

"Now go on and take your bath, sugar, it's way past your bedtime. What have I told you about staying out so late on school nights? I swear, George, the older they get, the harder it is to make them mind. Go on and take your bath now."

When he came back into the room after his bath, George was gone. "Who's he?" Richie asked.

"I told you, he's a new friend. Just a friend, that's all. So don't go pulling one of your pouts on me."

"Is he a nigger?" Richie asked bluntly.

"He most certainly is not!" Chloe replied indignantly. "Say, where do you get off asking a thing like that? I ought to slap your fresh mouth, young man."

"He's a funny color," Richie defended.

"George happens to be a Spaniard," Chloe said loftily.

"What's *that?*"

"Well, it's—it's like Mexican, only much better. It's what people are called when they're from Spain."

"Is he from Spain?"

"Well, no," Chloe admitted. "Actually, he's from Texas. But he's Spanish, all the same."

"Is he going to be coming around a lot?" Richie wanted to know.

"Well, he might!" Chloe replied, her tone becoming indignant again. "Anyway, what if he does? There's nothing wrong with that, is there? I told you, he's just a friend. Somebody to talk to, maybe go to a tavern and listen to a jukebox with once in a while."

"What about Johnny?"

"Well, what about him?" she demanded. "Is it going to hurt him if I go sit and listen to some music with somebody? I swear, Richie, you're worse than a little old woman sometimes!" Seeing that Richie was upset at meeting George, Chloe abruptly dropped her indignation defense and pulled him over to the sofa next to her. "Listen, sugar, everything's all right," she assured, putting an arm around him. "I'm not going to do anything to mess things up with Johnny. George is just somebody to talk to, to keep me from getting so lonesome. It's all right, honest." She cupped his chin in her palm. "You're not going to be mad at me, are you, sugar?"

"I don't know," Richie said, shrugging.

"Come on now," she urged, squeezing his cheeks. "Say you're not mad at me."

"'All right."

"All right, what?"

"All right, I'm not mad at you."

Chloe's face, for just a second, turned sad. "Thanks, sugar," she said quietly. Then she gave him one of her dazzling smiles. "Listen, I've got an idea! Why don't we open a couple of Coca-Colas and listen to Lux Radio Theater together? They've got 'Stagecoach' on tonight with John Wayne. Want to?"

"Yeah, swell!" Richie beamed.

While the radio warmed up, Chloe got the soda pop, then they sat leaning their shoulders together and listened to Cecil B. DeMille's grandfatherly voice say, "Good evening, ladies and gentlemen. Welcome to the Lux Radio Theater . . ."

For a little while that evening, it was almost as if they were normal people.

Except that Richie could not stop thinking about George, who had been sitting with Chloe in that same place just a little while earlier.

George, the "Spaniard."

Richie knew instinctively that George would bring them trouble.

Chloe had met George through Nell, a woman with whom she had worked at the bakery. She had run into Nell one afternoon on Damen Avenue on her way to the grocery.

"This must be fate," Nell said. "My boyfriend's coming up from Chanute Field this weekend and he's bringing a pal of his. How'd you like to double-date with us?"

"For god's sake, Nell, I'm a married woman," Chloe demurred.

"Hell, so am I," Nell revealed for the first time. "My Walter is in the navy on duty in the Atlantic. I don't imagine for one minute that he's keeping his bell bottoms buttoned up when he's in port in England. Anyway, this is just for fun, Chlo."

After some urging, Chloe had hesitantly agreed. It would, she promised herself, be fun but innocent. She intended to make it clear that she was married, and she intended to establish certain rules: there would be no kissing, of course, no hand holding, no touching of any kind. She would have only one glass of beer, then switch to ginger ale, and she would excuse herself promptly at ten o'clock and go home alone. She saw nothing wrong with having an innocent evening out; god knows it had been a long time since the last one. Estelle had been gone for six months: married to a sailor and living in California. Chloe wondered if maybe she and Nell could become best friends now.

Nell was a little embarrassed when her friend's friend turned out not to be white. "I swear to god, Chloe, I had no idea!" she pleaded in the ladies' room of the tavern on Homan Avenue where they all met.

"What in the world is he?" Chloe wanted to know.

"He says he's Spanish. God knows, he's handsome, ain't he? Did you ever see teeth that perfect except in the movies?"

"I'm not sure I should stay, Nell," Chloe said apprehensively. "What in the world do you say to someone who's Spanish?"

"Hell, honey, the same things you'd say to a white man. Mainly no!" Nell laughed raucously at her own wit, but Chloe only managed to smile weakly.

In the end, Chloe had stayed, and the evening had turned out very well. George Zangara was a perfect gentleman; he held Chloe's chair for her, lighted her cigarettes, did not try to get her to drink anything except ginger ale, and at no time put his hands on her in any way. They all sat at a back table and the men, both in Air Corps browns with sergeant stripes, bought a roll of nickels with which to keep playing a large, brightly lit Wurlitzer jukebox. They talked about the things the rest of wartime America was talking about.

"Did you hear," Nell exclaimed, "that 'Amos 'n' Andy' is going off the radio after fifteen years because of the war! Campbell's soup can't get tin to make cans to sell soup in, so it can't afford to sponsor the program anymore."

"The Krauts are gonna pay for that," her boyfriend Randy said ominously.

"I read where Leslie Howard was in a plane shot down over the English Channel," Chloe said. "He was so good in *Gone With the Wind*. I certainly hope nothing happens to Clark Gable. He didn't have to go, you know; he's past forty. But he enlisted anyway."

"Did you read about that town in New York that's forming a women's fire department 'cause there's no men left? Ain't that something?"

"I heard," Nell said sadly, "'that there won't be any Christmas cards this year because of the paper shortage."

"The Krauts will pay for that too," said Randy.

"Has anybody seen that new silver penny they've put out?" Nell asked. "I'm dying to see one."

"Starting next week, we aren't supposed to eat meat on Tuesdays. They're calling it 'Meatless Tuesday.' "

"The Krauts are gonna pay for that," Randy reintoned. Nell poked his arm with a stiff finger.

"You keep saying the Krauts are going to pay, what about the Japs, don't they count?"

"Not as much, not to me," Randy said. "I'm half Jewish. My grandparents still have relatives in Europe. We used to hear what the Krauts were doing, before their letters stopped coming. The Krauts have led the way in the war. Without that agreement with the Krauts, the Nips never would've started anything in the Pacific. It's the Krauts that'll have to pay, all right." He took hold of the finger Nell had poked him with. "Come on, let's dance."

Alone in the booth with George, Chloe said, "You don't talk much, do you?"

"Sure, sometimes," George replied with a pearly smile. "And sometimes I just listen."

"How do you like the Air Corps?"

"It's wonderful, I really love it," he answered with a straight face. "I hope and pray they'll let me stay in after the war."

Chloe saw a twinkle of mischief in his eyes and knew she was being teased. "Okay," she laughed. "Sorry I asked."

"Nell says your husband's in the army."

"Yes. Fortieth Division. Last I heard they were on New Guinea. Now that the Japs have retreated from there, I'm not sure where he is."

"Those guys in the infantry, they're the real heroes in this war," George allowed. "You read a lot about fighter pilots and submariners and commandos, but if we didn't have the infantry, we'd've lost the war already. I tried to get in the infantry when I was drafted, but they wouldn't take me. My left ankle's been broke and didn't mend just right. I don't limp or nothing like that, but it's not as strong as it should be. So they put me in the Air Corps. I refuel supply planes. I guess that's important too."

"Of course it is," Chloe stressed. "My goodness, without supply planes, why, the boys overseas wouldn't have any food or ammunition or anything. What you do is *very* important, George."

"It's nice of you to say so." He gave her another brilliant smile.

Chloe almost reached out and patted his hand to reassure him that he was doing his part in the war effort, but she checked the impulse. It was, after all, *her* rule that there was to be no touching.

Chloe started seeing George three out of every four weekends; the fourth weekend he had duty and was restricted to the field. On the Saturday nights that she went out, Chloe told Richie that she was meeting Estelle to go to a show. Richie suspected nothing and was not bothered about her spending Saturday evenings out; she had finally conceded to his demands that she stop having Dorothy come over to stay with him when Chloe was out late. "You can stay home alone, but I want you to promise me that you will not leave this apartment. I will not have you running the streets at night with some of the kids I see in this neighborhood. Promise?"

"I promise," Richie said solemnly. "Can I stay up and listen to the radio?"

"I guess so."

It was never Richie's intent to listen to the radio; he only asked the question to reinforce his promise to stay in. As soon as Chloe was gone five minutes, Richie was out meeting Stan Klein.

Chloe was enjoying her evenings out so much that it never occurred to her to worry about Richie. She had never known him to disobey her, not seriously, and that was reassuring. So many kids were getting in trouble lately, with the war on and all; she decided she was very lucky that Richie was such a good boy. The only thing that was really troubling her about Richie was that she was soon going to have to start sending him to four drugstores a day instead of three. The amount of paregoric she was taking no longer seemed to calm her nerves the way it used to; she was going to have to increase her dose, which meant an additional bottle a day. Richie, she knew, was going to have a fit.

But it had to be done. The calm on the amount she was now taking, which used to last the rest of the night, was wearing off around nine o'clock. George noticed it one Saturday night at the tavern.

"You seem nervous," he said. "Anything the matter?"

"No," she said, shaking her head. She looked away, avoiding his dark, direct eyes. George was a sensuous, very attractive man. Usually the paregoric kept her composed and helped her deal with his appeal and the magnetism he exuded. Without the paregoric, conflicts arose within her.

"I'd like to help, if there's anything I can do," George said quietly. "I am your friend, you know."

"I know," she forced a brief smile. "But I'm not nervous, really I'm not."

"Yes, you are," he contradicted. Chloe's face flushed irritation.

"If I say I'm not, what in the world makes you think you know better?"

"I can just tell," George said, his voice easy and soothing, as if he were talking to an upset child. "I can tell by the way your fingers move around so much, the way your pretty eyes shift all over the place."

Chloe stared at him. On the jukebox, "Serenade in Blue" was playing, and Randy and Nell were slow-dancing to it.

"Do you really think my eyes are pretty?" Chloe asked. She had always thought they were herself, but no one, not Richmond or Jack or anyone, had ever told her so before.

"Prettiest brown eyes I ever saw," George said. "Too pretty to be nervous." After a quick glance at Nell and Randy, he leaned close to her ear. "I've got something you can smoke that will calm you down and make you feel like a million. Want to give it a try?"

Chloe felt her lower lip tremble; immediately she curled it under her upper teeth for a moment to stop it. Her nerve ends seemed like they were about to puncture through her skin. Releasing her lip, she said, "All right, why not?" She knew what he was talking about: the stuff they called "weed." Estelle had tried it once and said it wasn't as much fun as drinking whiskey. Chloe saw no harm in just seeing what it was like.

"Only thing is," George said after she accepted his offer, "we can't smoke it here. It's got a peculiar smell to it, you know. We have to have someplace private to smoke."

Chloe bit her lip again. "My little boy will probably still be up, listening to the radio. Could we sit on the steps in the hall? Will that be private enough?"

"Is there a window we can blow the smoke out?"

She nodded. "There's a window on the landing between floors."

They told Nell and Randy they were going for a walk and George leaned over to say something private to Randy. Then George walked Chloe home, without holding her hand or taking her arm, which reassured Chloe and made her think what she was doing was still altogether innocent. Although by now that aspect of it was rapidly diminishing in importance; mushrooming larger and larger in her mind was the demand of her whole being that she *give* it something. So compelling was her need that when they got to her building and she went inside to get George a bottle of beer and found that Richie was not there, it relieved instead of disturbed her.

"We can go inside," she told George. "I guess my little boy went to a show or something."

While George sat on the sofa and rolled marijuana cigarettes, Chloe went into the bathroom, reached far up under the old tub, and retrieved a John Ruskin cigar box, the same kind in which Richie kept his treasures. From it she removed her extra twenty-five-cent bottle of paregoric, the bottle she kept for dire emergencies such as Richie being kept after school and delaying her daily supply an hour or two. Drinking half the bottle, straight, without any sugar or even water, she then replaced the remainder in its hiding place.

George drank beer while smoking his weed and showing Chloe how to smoke hers. He tried to get her to drink a little beer also. "It'll make the weed work on you better," he said. But Chloe declined. She was already concerned about how much her paregoric would increase and intensify what she was smoking; she did not need Blatz beer on top of it.

The marijuana began to work first, the tide of its euphoria slapping gently at the shore of her nerves. Then the slower-acting paregoric followed with larger waves and rushes from an ocean of feeling that grew deeper, darker. Soon the two combined into a tidal wave that moved in without opposition, attacked in force, and spread itself all over the beach that was her being, flooding every crevice of her, reaching places from which she was sure she had never before experienced feeling. Delight became joy, joy became rapture, and Chloe was transported to a high, soft place where all was blissful, all was glorious, all, unlike the place from which she came, was well.

George was amazed. Even though he was getting high himself, and knew her reaction was being exaggerated in his mind, he nevertheless realized that Chloe was experiencing rare and unusual sensations. As his own well-being rapidly increased, he shook his head in wonder and said, "Jesus, I never saw nobody go up like that before. Honey, this stuff was made for you." Later, when the weed's effects had worn off, but Chloe was still in her paregoric fog, George asked, "Did you feel as good as it looked like you felt?"

"Better," Chloe replied, smiling lazily. George showed his perfect teeth.

"Want me to bring some more next weekend?"

"God, yes."

"Gee, I wish I could," George said, his dark, handsome features turning sad. "But I promised to take some to another lady I know. I like you better than her, but she, well, kind of does things for me. I mean a guy gets lonely when he's away from home, you know? This other lady, well she kind of relieves my loneliness." He moved closer to Chloe on the sofa. "Do you know what I'm talking about?" he asked.

"I know what you're talking about," she nodded sleepily. Reaching over, she felt the erection in his trousers. "You're talking about that," she said.

"Hey, that's right!" he praised.

"Is it lonely too? Like you?"

"Worse than me." He unbuttoned his fly, worked a couple of fingers around inside his trousers, and got it out. It was large, veined, and much darker than the rest of George. It was, Chloe thought, almost black. In fact, it *was* black. But George wasn't, she assured herself. George was Spanish; that was not black. It was more like brown, certainly not black. If George were black, why she would not touch his—him—no matter what it got her.

But he was not black.

Only *it* was black.

Not him.

"Be nice to it, honey," George said.

Chloe leaned over, closing her eyes. If she kept her eyes closed, she would not be able to see that it was black.

Richie hated George Zangara. Hated him with a cold consuming passion.

"What's the best way to kill a guy?" he asked Stan. His friend's eyebrows went up.

"What guy?"

"Any guy." Richie's voice was fierce.

Stan nodded knowingly. "You mean the Air Corps guy that comes to see your old lady on weekends?" He waved a hand in dismissal. "Forget it. He ain't worth killing. You oughta see some of the bums *my* old lady drags home!"

They were sitting on the curb, Richie staring straight ahead, his young face tight with resentment. Stan, recognizing the bitterness in his friend's tone, fell quiet for a moment, then took another tack.

"Listen," he reasoned, "it don't make sense to ask for that kind of trouble. S'pose you was to stick a knife in the guy's neck some night when he's coming down the stairs in the dark? What good would it do? There'd prob'ly be another guy to take his place in a week. Mothers ain't very smart when it comes to guys." Now Stan's tone became philosophical. "Way I look at it there's on'y one good reason to kill anybody. That's for money. Any other reason just ain't smart."

Although sensing that Stan was right—Stan was nearly always right, about everything—Richie's mind nevertheless continued to be consumed by thoughts of murder. And instead of trying to control or discourage them, he nourished them. He was able—by hanging far over the railing of a back stairs landing—to watch them in bed, after raising the windowshade an inch before going out. If he sneaked back into the apartment, he could listen to the sounds of their sex through the bedroom door. Once, in a moment of insane but irresistible impulse, he hid under the bed and listened and felt what they were doing just inches above his face. His mother had begged for something.

"Let's do the other first, hon," she said. "Come on, roll us a couple."

"No, no, no," George replied with a lilt to his smooth voice. "First you got to show your Georgie how much you love him."

"We can do that after, hon, please . . ."

"No, no, no. Loving first, baby—you know how I am. I'll roll us a couple of real good ones when we're through, but first I want you to show me if you remember what I taught you last week. You know, with your tongue and two fingers . . ."

Richie had no idea what it was his mother wanted George to "roll," but suspected it was probably something like paregoric, something his mother thought she could not do without. He was now going to four drugstores for her "medicine" every afternoon and on Saturday and Sunday mornings. Her reversion to paregoric, and the association she had begun with George, had the potential, Richie realized, for wrecking the orderly life he expected them to resume when Johnny Eaton returned from the war. It was a life Richie fondly remembered, a life in which he had only to concern himself with boyish things—cowboy movies, marbles, comic books, kick-the-can, radio serials; a life with a father who came home every day, a mother who *stayed* home every day, a regular, steady life, everything neat, no surprises, a life without paregoric and people like George Zangara, with his slick charm and white teeth, who had somehow managed to get control of his mother and was doing all those lousy things to her . . .

A knife in the neck as he came down the dark stairs, Stan had said. Maybe it would be worth it, just for the moment, just for the brief feel of the blade tip puncturing that smooth brown skin. But instead, Richie rebelled against his mother; it was easier, and she was to blame anyway. He punished her the only way he knew how: by making her wait for her medicine.

When he got back an hour later than she thought he should from his drugstore route, Chloe would be livid. "Where have you *been*?" she would screech, already grabbing at his pockets for the bottles. He always had an excuse.

"The stores were crowded and I couldn't get waited on," or, "Some nigger kids chased me and I had to hide," or, "I lost my streetcar fare and had to walk back."

His tardiness was premeditated and methodical. On Lake Street he lingered to talk to Vernie, who was nearly always around. On other days, Richie dawdled in the white neighborhoods, looking in secondhand stores, junk shops, variety stores along lower Madison Street, prowling amongst the carts and makeshift counters of street vendors on Maxwell Street, wandering along derelict-ridden Halsted Street, roaming at will, meandering, knowing his mother was chewing her nails waiting for him.

One day in his roving, Richie came across a double storefront building with lettering on the window which read: CHICAGO PUBLIC LIBRARY—DAMEN AVE. BRANCH. Venturing in, he was stopped as he walked past a desk.

"You're not allowed in there," said a woman at the desk. "That's the adult section. The juvenile section"—she pointed with a date-stamper—"is over there."

"Yes, ma'am," Richie muttered, turning in the proper direction.

In the juvenile section, he walked up and down the aisles of the stacks, looking at but not touching the books. There was a peculiar smell about the place; it reminded Richie of a schoolroom smell: chalk dust, people, pencil shavings. It was also, somehow, a reassuring place, as if the bulk of all the books could protect one from harm.

At the end of one stack, the lady from the desk was standing there. "Are you looking for a special book?" she asked. She was a short, round lady with beautiful, perfectly formed lips that moved precisely with each word. "I'll help you find it if you are," she said.

"Are there books with stories in them?" Richie asked.

"Stories? You mean short stories?"

"I guess." Except, he thought, the ones he had read in *Collier's* and the *Saturday Evening Post* hadn't been all that short.

The librarian led him to another stack and with one finger touched in turn three shelves. "These are collections of short stories for twelve-to-fifteen year olds," she said. "Do you have a library card?"

"No, ma'am."

"Well, you can't take books home without a library card. I'll give you a form to have one of your parents sign and then we can issue you a card."

"Can I read books here until I get a card?" he asked.

"Of course."

After the librarian walked away, Richie carefully, logically, took the first book at the beginning of the first of the three shelves, and took it to a table where he saw other children reading. Opening the book, he started with the first story, which was about a circus visiting a small town. After reading only a little of it, Richie went on to the next one. It was the story of a young boy being taken on his first fishing trip by his father. After two pages, Richie turned to the third story, about a family who adopted a lost dog, and how each member wanted to give it a different name. None of the stories—or any of the nine that followed—were able to hold Richie's interest. He did not finish even one of them, finally returning the book to the shelf, being extremely careful to put it back in exactly the same place, and then took another. And another after that. He could not bring himself to finish any of the stories in any of the books, finding them either too simple or too silly.

When he stopped at the desk for his library-card application, he asked the lady with the pretty lips, "Are there any books with stories by Ben Ames Williams?"

"*Ben Ames Williams?*" She looked at him in astonishment. "Where on earth did you get that name?"

"I read his stories in magazines. Him and Walter Noble Burns and Zane Grey and Borden Chase and—"

"Those authors," the librarian said firmly, "are in the adult section. You are only allowed in the juvenile section. Here," she handed him a printed form, "have one of your parents fill this out and sign it. Then I'll give you a library card. For the *juvenile* section."

"Yes, ma'am," Richie mumbled, taking the application.

When he got home, Chloe was seething. "For god's sake, you've never taken this long! Where in the hell have you been?"

"It just took longer today," Richie shrugged, "I don't know why." Working the wrapped bottles out of his pocket, he handed them to her one by one, and she clutched them to her body.

"Will you fill this out and sign it for me?" he asked, showing her the application. "I got it at school," he lied, because he could not tell her he had stopped at the library.

"Richie, I don't have *time* for that!" Chloe snapped. "If I don't take my medicine, I'm going to have a fit. Go on out and play!"

Richie stared at his mother, suddenly realizing that she knew absolutely nothing about the life he led. Go out and *play?* He did not know what it was to play anymore—unless smashing rats with bricks could be called playing. He had not actually *played* since they'd moved from Warren Boulevard. What he mostly did now with Stan was *prowl*: the streets, the alleys, the shadowed places of the city, places where they could steal or spy, look, listen, learn: young animals observing the pack.

Without a word, Richie left the apartment and walked all the way back to Lake Street. It was getting dark now; he found Vernie with several other girls and three black teenage boys. One of the boys saw Richie coming. "What the fuck you doing on this street, ofay?" he challenged menacingly.

"Lea' him alone, Roger Lee," Vernie intervened, "he be a friend of mine." She turned scathingly to Richie. "What the hell you doing over here at night, Richie? I swear, I don't think you got good sense sometimes! What you want?"

Drawing her aside, Richie showed her, in the glow of a streetlight, his application for a library card. "Will you fill it out and sign my mother's name to it?"

Vernie sighed impatiently, irritably. "You ain't been nuf'in but trouble since the day I found you, boy. Come on in here." She dragged him by one arm into a steamy little rib joint a few doors down and sat him at the counter. A dozen dark faces stared at him; Richie fixed his eyes on an open bottle with dried catsup crusted around its top and kept them there.

"Naomi, borrow me a pencil for a minute," Vernie said to a waitress. When she got it, she sat down next to him and began to fill out the card. Moving his eyes to look, Richie saw with surprise that Vernie wrote with a fine, neat script every bit as nice as his mother's.

"I never knew you could write that good," he said. Vernie threw him a cutting glance.

"I ain't iggernant, Richie, just po'," she said. In five minutes she had the application form completed and signed and gave it back to him, slightly grease-spotted from the counter. "Come on," she said, purposely enunciating, "I'll escort you back to your *decent* neighborhood."

"Shit, Vernie, my neighborhood ain't no better than yours," Richie defended. "We got the same rats and roaches and bedbugs and stinking garbage in the alleys that you got. We're no different from you."

Vernie, having recovered her patience, looked tolerantly at him and said, "Richie, Richie, Richie. You be got a lot to learn, boy."

Richie went to the Damen Avenue branch library every afternoon. He came to know the librarian, Miss Cashman, by name, and she him. "Hello, Richie," she greeted him each time he returned a thin volume of short stories from the juvenile section. "Did you enjoy these?" she asked.

"Yes, ma'am, Miss Cashman," he lied, with the most innocent expression he could register. He never read any of the stories in any of the books from the juvenile section; his only purpose in checking them out was to accustom Miss Cashman to seeing him on a regular basis, to have her familiar with his presence in the library, comfortable with him being around. That way it was easier for him to take books that he was not supposed to take.

It had required only three visits to the library to convince Richie that the material in the juvenile section was not for him. The *Saturday Evening Post*, he was certain, would never have any of it between its covers. By now Richie was a devoted reader of the *Post*; although not selling it on the street anymore, he nevertheless continued to read the magazine any time he could steal one from a drugstore rack. He had now progressed from considering only the Westerns to reading all of the war stories, many of the mysteries, and even an occasional romance if he suspected it might have any sexually suggestive passages. But even with the *Post's* weekly offerings, he was, with an ever intensifying desire to read, always longing for more. He was certain he could find it in the forbidden area of the library: the adult section.

Richie discovered it was easy enough to get over there; he only had to wait until Miss Cashman and her student aide were occupied, then move unobtrusively behind their backs from one area to the other. In the adult section, he found that the grown-ups paid no attention to him; they all seemed to be deeply engrossed in their own business—even the browsers seldom gave him a second glance. The problem that annoyed Richie was finding the *books* he wanted there, which were chiefly collections of the short stories he had come to love. Knowing nothing of the library's card catalogue system or how it related to locating specific books in the network of stacks, he began to find his way around in the library exactly as he had in the city—by ranging and exploring.

The first books Richie found that suited him were a series of annuals containing a selection of dramatic plays for consecutive years. Discovering them, Richie was impressed at once by their length, which resembled that of short stories, and intrigued by both the set-in dialogue and the stage directions. It would be, he concluded after very quick scrutiny, like *reading* a movie. As was his inclination, he put back the book he had inspected and moved over several volumes to the earliest one the branch had in the series—the best plays of the year 1935. Slipping it under his coat, and holding in front of him a book from the juvenile section to conceal the bulge, Richie made his way to the counter near the door, where Miss Cashman's high school aide was checking out books. Standing up close to the counter, again to conceal the bulge, he handed over the juvenile book and his new library card. When the book was properly checked out and handed back to him, Richie again held it in front of himself and headed for the door. As he left, Miss Cashman smiled at him from her desk, and waved. Richie smiled and waved back.

At home that night, while his mother lay in her usual twilight stupor, Richie devoured the book of plays. He found them surprisingly easy to read, and quicker to get through because, he figured out, they omitted all the description that a short story included. After an initial explanation of what the stage looked like, and introductions to each character, it was all voices and movement.

The first one he read, ironically, was a play called *Dead End*, by Sidney Kingsley, about, among other things, a group of young boys living in a big city tenement. The camaraderie among the boys reminded Richie of his own friendship with Stan Klein; the tenement neighborhood described in the stage setting was not unlike Chicago's lower West Side; and most of the characters in the story, with the exception of a rich young woman, were people with whom Richie could identify—people who might have lived right on his own block. He was amazed that anyone would have written about such a place and such people. This was clearly not the stuff of *Saturday Evening Post* short stories; they dealt with the Old West, with the war, and with Great Mysteries. *Dead End* was just about poor people in the city. Yet there was a magic to it that was somehow different from the enchantment he found in short stories. It was a troubling magic, much realer than that which took him to far-off places and helped him escape what and where he was.

Before finally falling asleep that night, Richie read *Winterset* by Maxwell Anderson, *Waiting for Lefty* by Clifford Odets, *Night Must Fall* by Emlyn Williams, and *Bright Star* by Phillip Barry. The rest of the plays he read the next day in school, managing to avoid the entire day's assignments in his class.

Richie hid the book of plays along with the juvenile short stories in the hallway, so his mother would not take them away from him. She had previously made him leave his marbles, cowboy trading cards, comics, and other amusement paraphernalia at home when he went to pick up her medicine, on the theory that if he had nothing of that sort to distract him and with which to amuse himself, he would get to the drugstores and back without wasting time. Since moving to Adams Street and meeting Stan, Richie had all but abandoned such things as marbles and trading cards, but he was wary of letting Chloe see the books for fear she would make him leave them at home.

At home, he no longer had to change from school clothes to play clothes; he now had only one class of clothes—old and threadbare. All he did after school now was come home to get the notes, money, and instructions as to which drugstores to visit. Chloe never kept a list or file of the drugstores; on that subject she had a memory that permitted her to review at times up to thirty drugstores, recall exactly when Richie had been there last, and whether he had purchased a fifteen-cent or twenty-five-cent bottle of paregoric. She no longer patted down Richie's pockets before he left to see if he had marbles or other playthings on his person; somehow the realization must have seeped into her mind that her son no longer possessed those boyish things which at one time had meant so much to him. If his abandonment of them gave her cause for concern or even curiosity, she never showed it. To her, Richie was now simply a net that she daily cast out into an unfriendly sea. The waiting every day for Richie to return was almost as bad for her as waiting all week for George to come on Saturdays with her other, equally demanding emotional nourishment.

After Richie discovered the library, he began hurrying on his daily errands in order to get to the library sooner. Although he had found a selection of books to steal—or, at least, borrow illegally—he still liked to prowl the adult section just to look. He had already figured out that books seemed to be kept in place by use of alphabetical letters and a numbering system; he just did not know yet exactly how it worked. But one thing he did know: he would learn.

At the library, Richie returned the book of the plays of 1935 the same way he had taken it: under his coat. And, continuing his logical approach, next took the volume containing plays of 1936. When he got it outside, he immediately checked the table of contents to see if there were another play by Sidney Kingsley. Disappointed, Richie guessed that maybe these people didn't write a play every year. Looking back on younger days, he reflected that it would be like having your favorite cowboy star appear in every serial. But even without Sidney Kingsley, Richie carried tightly under his arm his latest illegally obtained prize—along, of course, with some dreadful volume from the goddamned juvenile section. Jesus!

You'd think, he mused in annoyance on his way home, that in America the Land of the Free and the Home of the Brave, a person could read what they *wanted* to read. Life, as Stan Klein often said, wasn't even close to being fair.

After deciding not to stick a knife in George Zangara's neck some night as he came down the dark stairs, Richie did make up his mind to avoid him as much as possible. George always arrived now early on Saturday afternoon, and he and Chloe stayed in the shabby little apartment for several hours. Richie was sure he knew what they were doing, but tried not to think about it. His drugstore errands on Saturdays and Sundays were always done in the mornings, so it was easy for him to be gone before George got there. Chloe and George always left the apartment between six and seven, at which time, if he was not doing anything with Stan, Richie went home and fixed himself something to eat. If he went prowling later with Stan—to steal money off newsstands or spy on the nurses at County Hospital—he sometimes returned to the apartment around ten or eleven, to eat again, or maybe just to lie on the frayed couch and listen to the radio. He always left just before midnight, because the bars, under wartime regulations, had to close at midnight, and his mother and her boyfriend would be home a little while later. George usually stayed until sometime between two and three A.M., then went up to the Graymere Hotel on Homan Avenue where he and his friend Randy had a room. There was an understanding that Randy and Nell would use the hotel room; Nell had three kids and could not take Randy home. If Chloe had such reservations, her addiction annulled them.

When Richie had the money, he went over to West Madison Street to the all-night Haymarket Theater and stayed from midnight until around four, when he was sure George would be gone. When Stan learned Richie was doing that, he gave him his pocketknife. "Sit in a seat up against the wall," he advised, "and keep this out wit' the blade open. Anybody messes wit' you, stick 'em in the arm wit' it. Lots of queers hang out in the Haymarket."

"What's a queer?" Richie asked.

"A guy that likes to feel-up boys instead of girls. You know, a fairy."

"Oh, yeah, a fairy," Richie said, to cover his ignorance.

For the next few times he went to the Haymarket, Richie sat with the open knife as Stan had recommended. But he was never bothered by anyone, not once. It seemed to him that the only thing the adult patrons did at that hour was swig wine and snore.

It was at the Haymarket that Richie first saw John Garfield. The movie was called *They Made Me a Criminal*. In it, in addition to Garfield, were the Dead End Kids, the same group that had been gathered on the stage for Richie's favorite play, and had subsequently gone on to act in movies. It both awed and excited Richie to actually see the youths who had been in *Dead End* on the stage. They, *and* Garfield, fit perfectly the image of youthful misfits in an uncaring world. Richie recognized something in all of them that fit Stan

Klein, Louis, Ham, himself, and a dozen others. It struck him that perhaps Sidney Kingsley had written the movie, but later when he read the poster outside the theater, he saw that Kingsley had not. Nevertheless, when Richie trudged home through the dark city streets at four o'clock that morning, he had the seed of a new hero inside him. Buck Jones was dead; long live John Garfield.

For months Richie patronized the Haymarket during post-midnight hours on the three of every four Saturday nights when George had weekend leave. If Richie had no money, and Stan had none to lend him, Richie went up on the building roof, in summertime, and stretched out to look up at the stars; or, in the wintertime, hid down in the furnace room, a water pistol filled with bleach to keep the rats away from him; or sometimes, when he could not sit still, just walked the streets, block after desolate block, hands deep in his pockets, like a zombie unable to return to its grave until an intruder left. On those black walks, Richie imagined terrible, gruesome deaths for George Zangara.

So obsessed was Richie with vengeful notions about George, that the other two men in his thoughts thinned out to the fringes of his mind. Richmond, his father, had begun fading in memory when Richie settled into his new family structure with Johnny Eaton; he had diminished almost entirely until the night Richie thought he saw him at the stadium. Richmond's surrogate, Johnny, had gone away to war and with his absence occupied less of Richie's thoughts. Now, as Jack Smart had once been a threat to Richmond's return, George was putting in jeopardy a future normal life with Johnny Eaton. Richie walked the streets silently lamenting and deploring the fact that there was nothing he could do about it.

Then, suddenly, there *was* something he could do, something he never thought he *would* do: openly challenge his mother. He did it one Saturday when he expected George and was getting ready to leave the apartment after returning with his mother's paregoric.

"You don't have to go off and stay all day if you don't want to," Chloe said. "George isn't coming. Where do you go all the time anyhow, at two and three o'clock in the morning?"

"I sit in all-night movies," Richie said. "I didn't think you even knew I wasn't here."

"I know a lot more about what you do than you think I know, young man," she said, her tone more confident than usual. It was if that were the *one* thing she was sure of.

"Why ain't he coming?" Richie asked.

"Isn't coming," she corrected. Lighting a cigarette, she exhaled toward the ceiling and said, "He's been transferred to an Air Corps base in Austin,

Texas. He's going to send us some money so we can go down there to live. You'll like Texas, sugar; lots of cowboys down there. George says—" She paused to stare at him; he was shaking his head vigorously. "What are you shaking your head for?"

"Not me," Richie said.

"Not you what?"

"I'm not going to Texas and live with no nigger."

Chloe swung to slap him, but Richie pulled back and she missed. Instead she pointed a threatening finger.

"You'll do what I *tell* you to do, young man, and I'd advise you to watch your mouth. I *am* your mother."

"I don't care. I'm not going. I'll run away."

"Let me know when you get ready; I'll pack your things."

"He's nothing but a nigger and you know it!" It seemed the only way to hurt her.

Chloe swung again, and this time she did not miss. Her palm cracked Richie solidly on the cheek and turned it red instantly. "Stop saying that!" she ordered.

"Nigger, nigger, nigger!" he yelled, backing toward the door, throwing up his arms to block her blows. "Dirty goddamn son of a bitch of a nigger!"

Managing to get out the door, Richie fled the apartment.

Chloe and Richie hardly spoke for the next few days. When they did it was to make cutting remarks to the other.

"You didn't get very far, I see," Chloe said spitefully when Richie returned to the apartment after threatening to run away. Ignoring her, Richie retrieved two dollars he had hidden in his drawer, and left again. He did not come back to the apartment until late that night, when he knew his mother would be in her paregoric daze. She was, sprawled across her bed still dressed. Richie covered her up so she wouldn't catch cold.

The next morning, Richie woke up on his cot to the smell of bacon frying. Looking over at the little alcove kitchen, he saw his mother, in an old chenille bathrobe, cigarette between her lips, making breakfast, something she had seldom done since Johnny Eaton went off to the war.

"Go wash your face and hands, sugar," she said pleasantly. "I'm fixing us bacon and eggs this morning. Doesn't that sound good?"

"I'm not hungry," Richie replied, determined to be sullen.

"Oh, come on," Chloe coaxed, "you'll enjoy it."

"I said I'm not hungry."

Turning, Chloe stared at him for a moment. A deep wrinkle appeared between her eyebrows; the eyes themselves lost their gleam and became dull. "Then I guess I'm not hungry either," she said. Chloe scraped the eggs into the pan with the bacon and emptied it, grease and all, into a garbage can under the sink. Richie's mouth dropped open in shock; he had expected to be cajoled into eating. Youthful indignation rising, he stalked into the bathroom, fuming, and got dressed.

"I won't be back all day!" he yelled a few minutes later and stormed out of the apartment. That would throw a scare into her, he thought; she would have to do her own trip to the goddamned drugstores.

But Chloe was not intimidated. "Stay out all night too if you want to!" she yelled down the hall as he left.

Muttering every obscenity he knew, Richie went looking for some place to steal breakfast.

That afternoon, instead of going directly home after school, Richie sat in a doorway across the street where he could watch the entrance to their building. The scenario that had developed in his mind, and that he had nurtured all day, was that when he did not show up by three-thirty, or four at the latest, his mother would come outside and look nervously up and down the street for him. Maybe even call out for him: "Richie! Riii-chie! Please come home! Please, Richie! I need you!" When he did not respond—which he would not, no matter how much she begged—then she would have to go out and go to the goddamn drugstores herself.

So he waited, secure in his youthful confidence that he had the advantage. He knew when three-thirty came because the street had cleared of school kids and Stan had left the building to go stealing for the rest of the afternoon. His mother would be out any minute, Richie thought. Waiting edgily, time seemed to languish. He knew when it was around four because kids were out on the street playing.

When he was certain that it was at least five o'clock, Richie asked a postman on his afternoon delivery what time it was and was told four-twenty. Richie doubted it, but decided to go home anyway. Running across the street and bounding up the stairs, a new and alarming thought occurred. *What if she had gone away without him?*

As soon as he opened the apartment door, he knew she had already gone to the drugstores herself; there were two empty white paper bags on the kitchen table. From the bedroom, he heard soft, pleasant humming. For a moment, he paused and listened. His mother's voice when she hummed was as pretty and pleasing to the ear as her lovely handwriting was to the eye. Moving quietly to the bedroom door, he found Chloe with a towel spread over the dressertop, using it for a makeshift ironing board on which she was pressing a blouse.

"What are you doing?" he asked.

"Baking a pie, Richie," she replied wryly. "Can't you see?"

Annoyed, he stalked away and went to the wooden icebox. There was half a bottle of Borden's milk, but when he pulled the stopper he smelled that it was sour. Feeling the top compartment, he found it warm; his mother had not put the ice sign in the window that day. Pouring the milk out, he opened the cupboard, frightening two roaches away, and got out a box of saltines. Making sure it was still tightly closed so that the roaches couldn't have been at them, he took a handful and began munching. He closed the box as securely as he had found it; you had to be careful about roaches, because they laid their tiny, almost invisible eggs everywhere; Vernie had told him about a black girl on the South Side who had eaten roach eggs on something and given birth to a baby with a roach head. She had sold it to a freak show for a million dollars.

Going back to the bedroom door, eating crackers, Richie saw that his mother now had her battered old suitcase out and was carefully folding the freshly pressed blouse into it. "What are you doing now?" he asked. "Setting the pie out to cool?"

Chloe smiled, briefly amused by this son of hers who lately seemed to be catching on to things so very quickly. But she gave him a straight answer. "I'm getting my clothes ready so that when I get the money from George, I'll be able to leave for Austin right away."

"Well, I'm not going," Richie said evenly.

"You already told me that."

"You can't make me go either."

Chloe very deliberately walked over and put a stiff forefinger on his chin. "Now you listen to me, big shot. Maybe I don't want to make you go. Maybe I've decided not to even *try* to make you go. We can talk about it when the money gets here. In the meantime," she poked the finger against his chin, not hard, but not all that softly either, "if you think you're going to wise-off to me whenever you feel like it, you're badly mistaken. I'm still your mother; you talk to me like I'm not and I'll slap you silly." She gave him a semi-hard smack on the cheek as a sample. "Now here," she said, handing him a quarter from some change on the dresser, "go down to the corner and get a quart of milk for supper. I forgot to get ice today, so the milk we have is probably sour."

Richie lagged down to the store, sulking all the way, bemoaning the fact that it looked like his mother really *was* going off to live with that slimy Spanish nigger son of a bitch. Furthermore, there did not seem to be a damn thing he could do about it. His open defiance and threats to run away seeemed not to be bothering her a whit. The only thing that really got under her skin was when he called George a nigger. Why, why, why, Richie lamented, hadn't he disregarded Stan's advice and stuck a knife in the greasy bastard's neck some night when he was walking down the dark stairs.

Returning with the bottle of milk to the apartment, he found his mother sitting at the table, smoking, putting polish on her nails. "Put the milk away and come here and sit down," she said. "I want to talk to you."

I won't go, Richie thought as he put the milk in the icebox. She's not gonna talk me into it. Sitting across from Chloe, he stared down at the tabletop.

"Why don't you want to go to Texas with me?" she asked, immediately warning: "And don't you dare say it's because George is a nigger, because he *isn't*. He's Spanish-American."

Dirty brown-skinned nigger, Richie thought.

"Well," Chloe repeated, "'why don't you want to go?"

" 'Cause I wanna stay here and wait for Johnny to come home," Richie said. "We promised him we would."

Chloe bit her lip. Her eyes misted and she had to swallow a couple of times to get control of her voice. "People can't always keep their promises," she said quietly, "'even when they want to."

"Do you like George better than Johnny?" he asked. Surely she could not.

"Yes, I do."

Now Richie's eyes misted. This he could not understand. "But why?" It was not merely a question; it was a plea, a pitiful appeal.

"Because he's *here*, Richie," his mother declared, her own voice no less beseeching than his. "Because I need him. And because," she threw her head back and looked up at the ceiling, "I'm going to have a baby."

Richie stared at her, mouth agape, incredulity unrestrained in his expression as well as his mind. A *baby*? How could that be possible? He was aware that his mother and George *did* things together—he had watched them through the window, and his experience hiding under the bed had enlightened him about the intensity of what they did—but she had done the same things, at least he *thought* they were the same things, with Jack Smart, and she had not had a baby then. Why was she having one now? What was so different?

"How do you know you're going to have a baby?" he asked. Chloe smiled a trace.

"I just know, sugar."

"Does *he* know?"

"Yes, of course he knows. He wants us to get married after the war, when I can get a divorce. We were already making lots of plans, and then he got transferred to Texas. There was nothing he could do about it. But he wants me to move down there and stay while I'm waiting for the baby."

"Then what?" Richie wanted to know.

Chloe smiled now. "Why, we'll all stay together, sugar—George and I, and the baby, and you."

□□ 224 □□

Richie thought: The last to be mentioned is *you.*

"What about Johnny?" Richie asked.

Chloe shrugged, much as Richie frequently did: a gesture not of being uninformed, but of resignation. "I'll have to try and make him understand, that's all." She took Richie's hand across the table. "It's not Johnny I'm worried about right now, sugar, it's you. We've been through a lot together, you and me. You've always been my little man, the person I could always count on. I don't want this thing about George and the baby to come between us . . ."

As she was speaking, Richie drew his hand from hers and rose from the table. He walked toward the door, surprising Chloe.

"Sugar, where are you going?"

"I want to be by myself for a while," he said, and before she could react, left. He did not know how to tell her that he felt safer alone on the streets of the city than he did in the apartment with her.

Out on the sidewalk, Richie moved down the block with his hands deep in his pockets, cap pulled down to his eyebrows, eyes straight ahead. As he walked, he shook his head in loathing.

A baby.

A half-brown nigger baby.

Turning his head, Richie spat in the gutter.

The moods of Richie and Chloe reversed themselves. When Johnny Eaton went off to war, Richie had been the optimistic one, beginning each day with confidence and eagerness, assured of *his* place in *his* world, certain of where he was, glad to be there. While Chloe, after finding that she was stagnating in exactly the kind of secure marriage she had sought, discovered that a boring life *without* Johnny Eaton was even worse than one with him, and began to grow gloomy and moody, wondering if she would *ever* be happy. Working in the bakery to supplement Johnny's allotment check had been wretched for her: the heat from the ovens in back caused her to sweat constantly; the customers at the counter in front were brusque and indifferent because, after all, *they* were the customers, she a mere clerk; and, worst embarrassment of all, she found that she could not make accurate change— the cash register and all those little wells full of coins bewildered and flustered her. The register was short every day. Short more and more every day, until finally the owner, convinced she was stealing, fired her. Telling Richie she had quit, she began taking paregoric again to calm her nerves. And to save money, moved them to the poorer neighborhood of lower Adams Street, where they could afford to live, barely, without her having to work. There, her moods grew more dismal, her days bleaker.

Now, with the advent of George Zangara, Chloe's attitude toward life had turned around completely. The marijuana that George brought on weekends combined with her paregoric to make her feel more euphoric, more exhilarated, more *enhanced* than ever before. The things George did to her in bed, and had her do to him, which at first seemed perverted and disgusting to her, soon became deliciously desirable; she began to look forward to *him* as much as she did the "reefers" he rolled for them. When she learned she was pregnant, and that George, instead of walking out on her, wanted not only to help her but to *keep* her—her and their baby—she felt as if she had become a new person: a person of value now, worth something.

It was Richie whose enthusiasm for life diminished. He saw himself depreciate in his mother's regard—first in favor of George, then in priority to the baby. It was intensely deflating to realize that he was of less importance than someone who wasn't even born yet. Even his friendship with Stan, who was the closest friend he'd ever had, could not compensate for what he felt was Chloe's unjust, belittling attitude toward him. Always before, with Jack Smart, with Johnny Eaton, it had at least been, "Sugar, you like him, don't you?" As if what he thought meant something to her. With this goddamn "Spaniard," it was as if she did not even care.

With their now reversed outlooks, mother and son awaited word from George about the move to Austin, Texas. Chloe, serene and genial, did and redid her scant wardrobe while methodically, and surprisingly without a great deal of difficulty, reducing her daily intake of paregoric—one teaspoon at a time. George had left her some marijuana on his last visit, but after smoking only two cigarettes that she awkwardly rolled herself, she put the rest of it away to take to him. Paregoric and marijuana were not good for her baby, and she committed herself to overcoming the need for both.

"Richie, I won't make you go to the drugstores for me anymore if you don't want to," she told him one day soon after his open rebellion toward the move to Austin. She had already started going herself since the scene. "I just want you to know that I'm cutting down on my medicine; I'm giving it up again, like I did when Johnny and I got married, remember? I should be almost through with it by the time George saves enough money to send for us."

Richie did not know whether "us" meant his mother and him, or her and the baby. Not that he cared, he told himself; he still wasn't going.

"Anyhow," Chloe continued, "because of your hard feelings toward me, I'm not going to fight and argue and try to *make* you go get my medicine for me. I'll do it myself. It's not good for me to do all that walking and I'll probably get varicose veins in my legs and they'll hurt all the time, but at least it'll keep us from fussing at each other like we've been doing."

"I'll go," Richie said reluctantly. He did not know what varicose veins were, but on top of everything else in his chaotic young life, he did not want to bear the responsibility of causing his mother's legs to hurt. Plus which, he dreaded the very thought of her going over to Lake Street and being looked at, perhaps even spoken to, by black men—*real* black men, not just brown-skinned "Spaniards" like George. The possibility of Chloe being harassed on Lake Street had distressed him since he stopped running the errands.

"You don't have to, sugar," Chloe emphasized. "I know you're upset with me, and I'm not going to make you do anything for me—"

"I said I'd go," Richie told her again, already annoyed with himself for giving in so easily. He wanted to help her, yet he *didn't* want to help her. It was a disagreeable feeling.

Richie's regression to his old responsibility as Chloe's net to the drugstores brought about an informal truce between mother and son as they waited for Chloe to hear from George Zangara. Both were determined in their plans for the future: Chloe waited patiently, content in her expectation of finding, at last, total happiness with a man; Richie grimly planned—and dreaded—life alone on the streets to wait for Johnny Eaton's return.

Neither had accurate forecasts of their future.

Richie answered the door when the telegram was delivered. As he closed the door and turned back into the room, Chloe put a hand to her throat and moved unsteadily to a chair.

"It's Johnny," she said, "he's dead. I can feel it."

Richie shook his head. "Can't be. There's no star on the envelope. Dead and wounded telegrams have stars on the outside to warn people so's they won't have heart attacks."

Frowning, Chloe said, "Bring it here."

Richie handed her the telegram and she slid one finger under the flap. Unfolding the single sheet, she read its brief message. Richie watched her eyes as she read it a second time. Presently she nodded her head slowly, almost submissively, and laid the telegram on the table. Rising, she walked into the kitchen where she had left her cigarettes. Richie picked up the telegram and read: GEORGE KILLED IN TRANSPORT PLANE CRASH. BODY NOT RE-COVERED. It was signed: PAUL ZANGARA, HIS BROTHER.

Richie turned to look at his mother. Leaning against the sink, arms folded in front of her, Chloe inhaled smoke from the cigarette and blew it in quick, impatient puffs straight out in front of her. Her right foot tapped pistonlike in perfect, even cadence.

"Jeez," Richie said in awe, "a plane crash—"

"It's a lie," Chloe declared. "It—is—a—dirty—goddamned—lie!"

"But," Richie protested innocently, "if the telegram says—"

"It's his family," she said. "He told me he would have trouble with his mother and his brothers because I was white. And because I'd been married before and had a kid already." Chloe walked back to the table and read the telegram a third time, then nodded her head again. "He let them talk him out of it," she said with cold certainty. "He let his mother and brothers persuade him that the best way to deal with his white woman and her halfbreed unborn kid was to make me think he was dead. They know that because I'm married to somebody else, there's not a goddamned thing I can do about it!"

"Does this mean we don't have to move to Texas?" Richie asked.

His mother glared at him. "Yes, goddamn it, that's what it means!" Her expression became spiteful. "What the hell do you care? You weren't going anyway, remember?"

"Does this mean we'll wait for Johnny to come home, like before?"

Chloe started to snap at him again, but suddenly checked herself and considered his question. Yes, in fact, that's exactly what it *did* mean. Johnny was all she had left now. As soon as she got rid of the baby in her belly, everything would be just the same as before George showed up. Like he had never come into her life. Like he never existed. Like he *was* dead.

Taking Richie's hands, Chloe led him to the old sofa and sat him down beside her. "Listen, sugar," she said, continuing to hold his hands in hers, "if you'll help me out a little, I think we can get through this thing and go back to our old life with Johnny just like nothing ever happened. But you'd have to promise never—I mean *never*, ever—to mention a word about the baby."

"I wouldn't," Richie swore.

"Men are funny about their wives having other men's babies; you'll understand it someday, when you're older. But if Johnny doesn't find out about it, why, it'll be like it never happened. I'll just give the baby up for adoption when it's born, and that will be that. But I'll need you to help me as much as you can before it gets here. I'll have to pay for my own doctor, and the hospital bill . . ."

"I could get a paper route," Richie said optimistically. "I could get *two* paper routes!"

"That's my little man," Chloe praised. "I knew I could count on you, sugar."

She hugged Richie to her, clinging to him as if he might be all she had left.

Kenny, the newspaper circulation supervisor, was a grossly overweight man in his early twenties, who always seemed to have a partially eaten candy bar in one hand and several others, still wrapped, in his shirt pocket. He was fat by choice and intent, his obesity having earned him a 4-F draft deferral, allowing him to stay home from the war. When Richie asked him for two paper routes, Kenny shook his head, an act which caused a roll of fat around his neck to shiver.

"I'll give you one route," he said. "Mornings, delivering the *Trib*, the *Times*, the *Wall Street Journal*, and the *Jewish Daily Forward*. It's the Madison-Ashland route, hunnerd-an'-twelve papers, half a cent a paper. You make fifty-six cents every morning before school."

"I need a route after school too," Richie said. Kenny shook his head again.

"Nope," he said around a mouthful of Butterfinger bar. "First you gotta prove you could do one, then maybe I'll think about giving you anudder."

Richie took the morning route. It was better than nothing.

"Be here six o'clock sharp to fold," Kenny said.

The papers were dropped off before dawn at a storefront delivery office where, beginning at six A.M., a couple of dozen boys aged twelve to sixteen sat along the walls under route numbers chalked above them and folded the papers for their respective routes. Kenny instructed Richie in the art of folding.

"You take this here side of the paper and you stick it inside this here other side, see. Then you fold this here part that's left an' you stick *it* in the same place, see. Then you take and twist the bottom here to make the fold nice and tight. There, see that there? When they're folded tight like that, you can t'row 'em onto porches an' into doorways wit' no trouble at all. But if they's *loose*, if you don't get a tight fold, then they'll open up and the pages will fly all over an' you'll have to go chasing 'em. A tight fold"—he emphasized as he unwrapped a Milky Way—"is the secret to success in this business. Like a whore with a tight cunt."

Richie folded his papers as tightly as he could, but fully half of them came back open again the first morning when he took them out of the two-wheel pushcart to throw. Only a few came open in the air, however, because he was careful not to throw them if they felt the slightest bit loose. The addresses to which he delivered, and which paper to toss, were on heavy, dog-eared route cards strung on a metal ring that hooked to the handle of the pushcart. On the Madison-Ashland route, Richie delivered to stores and offices, none of them open at that hour, as well as apartment buildings and rooming houses. The route took him an hour and a half to cover, after half an hour of folding; he was usually back home by eight-fifteen to fix himself something to eat, some cereal or toast or oatmeal, being very quiet so as not to wake his mother, who needed extra rest as her stomach began to swell. By twenty of nine he was back outside to meet Stan and trudge off to school. Richie did not tell Stan about the paper route; Stan was contemptuous of work that adults hired kids to do for them. "They pay the kids pennies and *they* take home the quarters. Not me, pal. I'd rather take my chances stealing than be a patsy for some jackoff grownup."

Stan's cynicism aside, Richie was proud of himself for stepping in and being Chloe's "little man" to help her financially. He was even more pleased with himself when, after a month, Kenny told him he could have an afternoon route also, if he still wanted it.

"It's the Leavitt-Jackson route," the corpulent supervisor said as he ate an Oh Henry bar. "A hunnerd-twenny-six papers, mostly *Herald-American* an' *Daily News*. A nice fast route, take you maybe an hour an' a quarter, hour an' a half. Pays sixty-three cents a day. You want it?"

Richie wanted it. Chloe had by then cut her consumption of paregoric to the point where Richie needed only to hurry to one drugstore a day before he was free to do his route. Now bringing home a dollar and nineteen cents a day, his mother let him keep the change for himself, only taking the dollar. "It helps a lot, sugar," she praised. "Why, it pays for my cigarettes, that's fifteen cents a day; it buys you a bottle of milk, that's another fifteen cents; it could buy us a pound of butter for fifty cents if we could *find* any butter; it'll help pay our rent every Saturday; it really does help a lot, sugar. When Johnny comes home, I'm just going to *brag* about how you helped out while he was gone; not *why* you helped out, of course, that's always going to be our little secret. Johnny's going to be proud of you too, you wait and see."

Getting so much acclaim and commendation from his mother made Richie feel a little ashamed about continuing to go out with Stan after supper to steal coins from newsstands or empty bottles from grocery racks, or to shoplift in the dime stores. Unlike Stan, Richie did not scorn work; Richie *liked* to earn money honestly; it gave him a feeling of personal satisfaction; sometimes he even forgot that John Garfield was his new hero and secretly thought how Buck Jones would have been proud of what Richie was doing to help his mother. He knew, of course, that his dead cowboy idol would not have liked knowing Richie was out stealing at night, but Richie did not allow himself to dwell on that unpleasant thought. Stan was Richie's friend, the only friend Richie had, and Richie could not betray that friend by refusing to accompany him on his almost nightly forays of theft. Stan needed a lookout for some of his thievery; he *depended* on Richie, just as Chloe was depending on him. Some things, Richie had learned, you just had to do—like them or not.

When he grew up, he thought, it would probably be different.

Chloe was in her fifth month of pregnancy when Richie got home from school one afternoon and heard her sobbing through the apartment door. Quickly getting his key in the lock, he let himself in and found her on the sofa, her legs curled up under her, holding a wet washcloth to one side of her face. Before he could ask what was wrong, he also saw a khaki duffel bag standing in a corner. Richie's mouth dropped open as Johnny Eaton came out of the bathroom, drying his hands on a towel.

"Johnny!" Richie exclaimed, momentarily forgetting his mother's crying.

Johnny looked at him but said nothing. The big Southerner, wearing a sergeant's uniform, had an unhealthy pallor which, accentuated by a cruel curl to his lips, made his face look to Richie like an ugly caricature of itself.

"Are you okay, Johnny?" Richie asked naïvely, his young mind too inexperienced, too immature, to grasp and evaluate the situation into which he had just stepped.

"Yeah, I'm fine, boy," Johnny Eaton replied in a voice at once strained and severe. "I been fighting a war in the fucking South Pacific jungles for two years, just got out of the hospital after being sick with malaria and dysentery, and come home to find my wife knocked up with somebody else's kid. Yeah, I'm fine, just fine!" Rolling the towel into a ball, he hurled it at the nearest wall with a frantic grunt, then stretched one arm out with an accusing finger pointed at Chloe. "Do you know who done it?" he demanded of Richie.

"No," Richie lied at once, his street instincts taking over. He glanced at his mother just as she removed the washcloth from her face. One cheek was swelling and beginning to darken. Richie's head snapped back around, putting angry eyes on Johnny. "What the hell'd you hit her for?"

Johnny's grotesque face turned incredulous. "What'd I hit her for? For fucking another man, that's what for!" Now he brought the accusing finger around to Richie. "You was supposed to watch out for things while I was gone, 'member the promise you made? Where the fuck was you while she was getting knocked up? I ought to beat the shit out of both of you, 'stead of just her—"

Johnny took a tentative step toward Chloe. Frightened, Richie rushed past him to the little kitchen and from the sink counter snatched a butcher knife. "You let her alone!" he yelled.

Johnny Eaton looked at Richie again with the same incredulity that he had when Richie asked him why he hit Chloe. "Just what in the hell do you think you're gonna do with that knife, boy?" he asked.

"I'll stick it in your heart!" Richie threatened.

"You ain't gonna stick nothing in *my* heart!" Johnny declared. Crouching slightly, he moved slowly toward Richie, his pale features, his entire expression, turning into a visible snarl.

"Johnny!" Chloe screamed from the sofa, tensing, throwing her feet to the floor. "Don't hurt him!"

"Pull a knife on me, will you—" Johnny growled.

"Johnny!" Chloe screamed again. "Listen to me! The baby's not white, Johnny!"

The angry, anguished soldier stopped and stared at his wife in shock. "What?"

"This baby," Chloe said, putting one palm on her swollen belly, "isn't white."

Johnny Eaton straightened to full height, drawing his head back several inches, as if trying to increase the space between him and this woman. "Not . . . white!" He whispered the words, testing them for believability. Resentment made him square his shoulders, indignation raised his chin and jutted it forward. He became a casualty for the second time.

Turning from both of them, Johnny Eaton put on his overseas cap, retrieved his duffel bag from the corner, and went to the door. Opening it, he paused to look back at Richie.

"Know what it means when somebody gets called a son of a bitch, boy? If anybody ever calls you that, don't get mad at 'em, hear? 'Cause in your case it'll be true."

Johnny walked out the door and, Richie knew, out of their lives.

At school one morning two months later, Richie was summoned to the principal's office.

"This is Miss Menefee." The principal introduced a woman of perhaps thirty, tall, not quite pretty, but not plain either, wearing little makeup. Sensible looking. "Miss Menefee's from the welfare department. She'd like to talk to you."

The principal left and Miss Menefee, indicating the chair next to her, said, "Sit down, Richie."

His mind was racing. What was wrong? What was a 'welfare department'? What was happening to his life now?

"Richie," Miss Menefee said, "our department is going to try and help you and your mother—"

"We don't need no help," Richie interrupted.

Miss Menefee smiled slightly. "Your mother seems to think you do, Richie. She came to our office and applied for help."

Richie stared at her for a moment, then looked down at his knees. His heart felt as if it were trying to blow a hole in his chest.

"As you know," Miss Menefee continued, her voice gentle and firm at the same time, "your stepfather is divorcing your mother and has stopped the army allotment check she was receiving. As you also know, your mother is expecting a baby and is unable to work. The two of you have no income on which to live—"

"I've got two paper routes," Richie interrupted again.

"Yes, I know. Your mother told us how hard you work to help her; she's very proud of you, and we were very impressed. But I'm afraid it just isn't enough to pay rent and buy groceries and—"

"What are you gonna do to us?" Richie asked bluntly. Might as well find out and get it over with. He wished he was someplace where he could throw up.

"We aren't going to do anything 'to' you, Richie," Miss Menefee replied kindly. "We're going to try to do something *for* you. We've made some arrangements with your mother that she's waiting to tell you about. I'm afraid it'll mean you going to a different school, which is why I'm here—to get your transfer. Then we'll go see your mother and she'll explain everything to you. Do you have anything in your desk you need to get?"

Richie shook his head.

"Well, then," Miss Menefee said, "let's get your transfer and I'll drive you home."

At the apartment, Miss Menefee left Chloe and Richie alone while she went down to the corner to make a telephone call. Fear seized Richie's throat as he saw his mother putting his few extra clothes in a shopping bag.

"Sugar," she said in a strained but resigned voice, "you're going to have to stay with some people for a while."

"What people?" he asked from a suddenly arid mouth.

"Some nice people. I don't know who they are."

"Why do I have to?"

"Well, see, I have to go to this place until the baby comes—"

"What place? Why can't I go with you?"

"Because only women expecting babies can go there, that's why." Chloe's resignation gave way to impatience. "Now listen, don't give me any trouble about this, Richie. I am at the end of my rope over this baby. This is the very best I can do. This case worker, Miss Menefee, has found you some very nice people to stay with and you're going to stay with them. Now don't let's talk about it anymore!"

Richie stared at her. His anxiety over this sudden new crimp in his life slowly gave way to a spreading resentment, that quickly became a cold, bitter anger. This was not *fair!* This was not what they had planned, not what he and his mother had agreed to. She was betraying him. Without even talking to him about it, she had gone and made arrangements with other people—

made arrangements to get rid of him, to send him away, so she could go off and have the *baby* by herself.

Suddenly he hated his mother. Even so, he still did not want to leave her. Maybe, he thought, biting his lip, there was still some other way . . .

But Miss Menefee came back and said she was ready, and Chloe, trying hard not to cry, handed her the shopping bag of clothes. Forcing a smile, she took Richie's hands.

"Miss Menefee says if you'll write to me, she'll give me the letters. And I can write back to you. Won't that be nice? Sugar? Won't it?"

"Yeah." Richie was trying not to cry too.

"Now, listen," she said with as much maternal firmness as she could muster, "I expect you to be a big boy and stay out of trouble and study hard in school—"

Miss Menefee touched her arm and said, "I've found that the quicker we do these things, the better."

Stiffening, Chloe moved her arm from Miss Menefee's hand. "All right." Releasing Richie's hands, she bent and kissed him on the cheek. " 'Bye, Richie."

When Richie, eyes downcast, did not respond, Miss Menefee said, "Tell your mother goodbye, please."

Obeying, he did not look at his mother as Miss Menefee put a hand on his shoulder and guided him out the door.

In Miss Menefee's car, with the shopping bag on his lap, Richie threw off his hurt and anger and fear, and locked his mind in place to memorize the direction and distance the social worker was taking him. He had already made up his mind that he was not going to stay; he would run away at the earliest opportunity—tonight, if possible—and come back to his mother. All he needed was a few minutes to talk to her without this Miss Menefee around; he *knew* he could talk her into doing this some other way. If it was just a question of money, why, he could probably get a *third* paper route; he could start peddling magazines again; beg Rondo to take him back at the Stadium; start stealing more with Stan . . .

He would do *anything*—just as long as he did not have to leave his mother.

Concentrating, he began counting the blocks, fastening into his mind the corners at which they turned, the names of streets, numbers. Miss Menefee glanced knowingly at him. After she had driven awhile, she said conversationally, "It won't do you any good, you know."

"Huh?"

"Even if you do figure out how to get back across the city, it won't do you any good. As soon as I drop you off at your new home, I'm going back and take your mother to hers. Even if you got back to your old apartment, there wouldn't be anyone there." Reaching over, she patted his knee. "You'll be a lot better off if you'll just do what we want you to. It's for your own good, you know."

Clenching his jaw, Richie did not respond. He sat staring at the glove compartment, unsure now exactly what he should be planning. It was difficult to chart a course when there was no destination.

After an hour, Miss Menefee parked in front of a red brick three-flat building in an unfamiliar neighborhood, nicer than his old one. When they got out of the car, Miss Menefee had Richie stand still while she took a comb from her purse and pulled it through the tangles in his hair. "You've got hair like mine," she said off-handedly. "I fight a running battle with it every morning and never win. Do you have a comb in your things?"

"No."

"Here, you can have this one." She closed a button on his sleeve, tucked his shirt in neater, and patted his shoulder. "This can work out just fine for you, Richie," she said. She waited a moment; he did not respond, merely waited too. "All right," she sighed quietly, "come on."

In an immaculately clean and neat living room of the first-floor flat, Miss Menefee introduced him to Mr. and Mrs. Hubbard. Mr. Hubbard was an unimpressive figure of a man, with scant shoulders that looked like sloping extensions of his neck. He kept both hands in his pockets. Mrs. Hubbard, slightly taller, with very large, protuberant eyes, was one of those women who smiled without parting her lips, and barely moved her lips when she spoke, so that Richie could not tell whether she had teeth or not. She had broader shoulders than her husband.

"I'm sure he'll fit right in with the other boys," Mrs. Hubbard said to Miss Menefee, with a closed-lips smile. Mr. Hubbard said nothing, just stood there with his hands in his pockets, rocking back and forth slightly on his heels and toes. "Say goodbye to Miss Menefee now," Mrs. Hubbard told Richie, "and go down the hall there to the kitchen and sit at the table and wait. We'll be back when we finish talking with Miss Menefee." Without speaking, Richie started to walk away, and Mrs. Hubbard stopped him. "Say goodbye to Miss Menefee," she instructed again.

"Bye," Richie mumbled, looking at the floor.

"And when I tell you to do something," she further directed, in a firm but not harsh voice, "I would like you to acknowledge it by saying, 'Yes, ma'am.' Do you think you can do that?"

"Yes, ma'am," Richie mumbled again.

"All right, run along now."

" 'Bye, Richie," Miss Menefee said as he left the room.

□□ 237 □□

The kitchen, Richie found, was as immaculate as the living room. It looked like a display in a store window. The sink, which he had always thought was a place to stack dirty dishes, was empty and shining. Nothing was lying about on the counters, unlike in any kitchen of his mother's, because she left everything exactly where she used it, never putting anything away. Mouth open in awe, Richie put down his bag of clothes and pulled a chair out at the end of the table. He sat down, as he had been told. Maybe, he began to think, this place wouldn't be so bad, after all.

It seemed to Richie that he had been sitting there a long time when he suddenly had the feeling that he was being watched. Looking around, he saw at once that he was right: just inside the door stood a boy a couple of years younger than Richie, a boy who had the same bulging eyes of Mrs. Hubbard, the same round shoulders of Mr. Hubbard, and a funny little bullet-shaped head all his own. Richie suppressed an urge to laugh at him, but knew he had not concealed his amusement altogether, because the younger boy turned red and his lips compressed at the look on Richie's face.

"I'm telling on you for being in that chair," he said.

"I ain't doing nothing wrong," Richie told him.

"You're not supposed to be in that chair," the boy said threateningly, pointing a finger. Just then, Mrs. Hubbard strode into the room, her husband following, hands still in his pockets.

"Junior's correct," Mrs. Hubbard said, taking charge. "I see you've met our son, fine. Get out of that chair, please. That's Mr. Hubbard's chair; the one at the other end of the table is mine. Never sit in either of them. You'll find that if you listen to Junior's advice, you'll do much better here. Bring your things and I'll assign you a drawer in the dresser that the other wards use."

As Richie followed Mrs. Hubbard out of the kitchen, he wondered: What in the hell is a "ward"?

Richie found out that afternoon, when he was helping three other wards carry garbage from the building's back porches down to the alley.

"We're all wards," he was told by Lloyd, the oldest and biggest of the trio. "That means the county owns us. Means there ain't nobody who wants us, so the county has to take care of us. A ward is kinda like an orphan."

"I'm not no orphan," Richie declared. "I got a mother."

Another boy, named Gerry, looked at him solemnly. "No kidding? Jesus, you better go in and tell the Hubbards that right now! I think there's been a terrible mistake made here."

Richie turned red and Lloyd said, "Cut the shit, Ger. He's in the same boat we are."

"I got a mother too," said the third boy, Maxie, "but she's doing time in women's prison. They got her for fencin' stolen merchandise Christmas before last."

"What about your dad?" Richie asked.

"Who knows?" Maxie said, shrugging.

Because the Hubbards owned the building and were responsible for garbage removal, it fell to the wards to carry out the heavy back-porch cans every day and empty them into the big iron drums in the alley. "An' that ain't all we gotta do," Lloyd alerted Richie. "We also have the pleasure of sweeping the back porches and stairs, scrubbing down the inside stairs and landings, shoveling coal from the bin to the furnace, doing laundry in the basement and hanging it out to dry, carrying groceries home—not just for the Hubbards but for the other two tenants in the building, bringing in everybody's milk and newspaper delivery, washing windows, raking the backyard—shit, there's a thousand things. Don't count on much free time."

"We get paid for any of it?" Richie asked naïvely.

"Yeah, we each get thirty-five a week," Gerry piped up. "Be sure and tell old lady Hubbard weh'der you want yours in small bills or what."

"Lay off, will ya?" Lloyd told Gerry. Then to Richie: "We get nothing. Don't pay no attention to him."

"Yeah," said Maxie, "he thinks he's Lou Costello."

"One other thing," Lloyd told Richie as they carried an empty garbage pail back upstairs, "is don't never trust Junior. He's a rotten little prick an' he'll get you in Dutch every chance he gets."

"What kind of Dutch?" Richie asked.

"You'll see tonight at supper," Lloyd replied ominously.

The Hubbard supper table accommodated eight: three on each side, one at each end. The wards sat two on each side on the end toward Mr. Hubbard. The two places nearest Mrs. Hubbard were vacant. Junior sat at the end, next to his mother, and she fed him off her plate. Richie could hardly believe his eyes; the kid was at least ten years old, and his mother was actually spooning food into his mouth. But when Richie looked at the other wards they didn't seem to pay any attention to it, so he shrugged and ignored it also, concentrating instead on Mr. Hubbard's hands. The supper table was the first time Richie had seen them out of his pockets; they were slim, like his shoulders, and very white with nails that looked pinker than usual.

On the plate that had been set in front of Richie was half a pork chop and some mashed potatoes and cauliflower. Richie noticed that Mr. Hubbard had two pork chops, and Mrs. Hubbard and Junior one each, while he and the other three wards had a half each. As soon as Richie finished his meat and potatoes, he asked, "Can I have some more, please?"

Mr. Hubbard looked at him with an amused expression, while Mrs. Hubbard's lips tensed and her face clouded. Junior grinned like an imbecile.

"There are no second helpings. And wards are not permitted to talk at the table unless spoken to by Mr. Hubbard or myself."

"He didn't eat his cauliflower, mother," interjected Junior.

"Please eat your cauliflower."

"I don't like cauliflower," Richie said.

Mrs. Hubbard's face grew darker and her eyes seemed to bulge farther out of their sockets. "I said," she enunciated carefully, "that wards are *not* permitted to talk at the table. Please do not utter another word."

"Should I not even say 'yes, ma'am' like you—"

"I said not another word!" the woman screamed, pounding a fist on each side of her plate so that it bounced an inch off the table. "Are you deaf?"

"No, ma'am, I'm not deaf, but—"

"Stop! Stop it! Stop talking!" she yelled. "Right now! Not another word!"

"Yes, ma'am . . ."

Suddenly Mr. Hubbard was out of his chair, grabbing Richie by the back of his collar, and half dragging, half pushing him over to a corner of the room. "Stand there," he ordered without raising his voice. "Do not move and do not speak. If you do either, I will take a paddle to you."

Richie froze, jaw clenched, staring at the corner. He was aware when Mr. Hubbard moved out of his peripheral vision, aware of the sound of the chair moving as the man sat back down, and surprised to hear Mrs. Hubbard, screeching but a moment ago, say serenely, "Thank you, dear. Such impertinence. Where in the world do they find this kind of boys. Since it's his first night, naturally we'll suspend punishment this time; I have a feeling, however, that this one is going to get more than his share of the paddle. Now then, on another matter, I have a complaint from Mrs. Neeley on the third floor. She claims that someone is opening and reading her morning *Tribune* before she gets it. Does anyone know anything about it? Raise your hand if you do."

Richie assumed that none of the wards raised their hand because there was silence in the room until he heard Junior say, "I know who did it, mother."

"Tell us," Mrs. Hubbard said.

"It was Lloyd. He brought in the papers and the milk this morning. I saw him sit at the top of the stairs and open Mrs. Neeley's paper and read it."

"Thank you, Junior. Is that true, Lloyd?"

"I on'y took a quick look at the ball scores," Richie heard Lloyd explain.

"*Is—it—true?*" Mrs. Hubbard demanded icily.

"Yes, ma'am."

"I will not tolerate a sneak in this house." Mrs. Hubbard ruled. "Three licks with the paddle."

Richie heard Junior giggle.

Punishment with the paddle, which was a standard Ping-Pong paddle, was administered at bedtime, after the beds were ready. Each ward had a folding cot, which was wheeled out of a closet and opened up at a specific location within the apartment. Lloyd slept in the kitchen, Gerry in the dining room, Maxie in the hall outside Junior's bedroom, and Richie in a bay-window alcove in the living room hall, next to a radiator. When the wards had made up their cots and were in their underwear ready for bed, they had to line up and watch whoever of them was being punished that night. The offending boy, for whatever he had done, would have to drop his underwear and bend over the arm of Mr. Hubbard's big easy chair. With his peers, and Mrs. Hubbard and Junior, witnessing, the paddle would be applied to his bare buttocks by Mr. Hubbard.

His first night there, Richie watched as Lloyd got his three licks. It was like some kind of obscene dream. Round-shouldered, bland-faced little Mr. Hubbard, with one pasty white hand wrapped around the handle of the paddle, the other holding firmly to Lloyd's naked thigh; Mrs. Hubbard sitting stiffly nearby, lips compressed to a thin line, bulging eyes fixed on Lloyd's naked buttocks; despicable little Junior, his grin almost an evil leer as he squirmed impatiently, waiting for the paddle to fall; and the wards, three boys in their underwear, stripped of dignity along with clothing, without identity, without family or ties, three pieces of scrap in society's junk pile, being taught that they had no value, no worth. And the transgressor, Lloyd, bent over with shorts down, exposed, humiliated, tears running even before the blows.

"Come on now," Mr. Hubbard said cheerfully, "take it like a man. What are you crying for already; I haven't even started yet!"

"Let's get on with it, dear," Mrs. Hubbard said. "It's almost time for Charlie McCarthy."

"Say, we don't want to miss that! All right, young man, here we go!"

Grimacing, Richie closed his eyes as Mr. Hubbard's arm swung the first time. He heard the paddle strike flesh with a resounding SMACK! It sounded as if a huge piece of very dry wood had been snapped. Lloyd yelped like a kicked puppy. While Richie's eyes were still closed, there was a second loud crack and the boy being punished cried out again, not a yelp this time but a bellow of pain. Unable to hide in the darkness behind his eyelids any longer, somehow feeling that if he watched he might share some of Lloyd's punishment, relieve some of his suffering, Richie opened his eyes in time to see the paddle fall the third time, striking now a vivid red circle already there, a target provided by the first two blows. This time the sound of the blow was muted by another cry of anguish that Lloyd emitted even before the lick came. As soon as it struck, the boy became a tangle of flailing arms and legs as he struggled to get off Mr. Hubbard's lap, to get his balance, to get his underwear pulled up to cover his nakedness.

"All right, boys, off to your beds now," Mrs. Hubbard said, clapping her hands. "Junior, turn the radio on so it can be warming up for Charlie McCarthy."

As Lloyd went running crying to his cot in the kitchen, the other boys spread out to the various locations where they slept. Richie got into his cot in the alcove. Lying on his back, he was staring up at the ceiling when Mrs. Hubbard came by to turn out the light. Pausing, she looked down at him with her odd globular eyes.

"There is no getting up in the middle of the night," she advised. "We cannot have boys wandering the house at night; so if you have to go to the bathroom, you'll just have to hold it. And you are required to sleep with both hands outside the covers; this is a decent house and we won't tolerate anything nasty. Do you understand?"

"Yes ma'am," Richie replied, taking his hands out from under the covers.

The last thing he saw as the lights went out were those marble-like eyeballs of hers, looking for all the world as if they were going to pop out and fall to the floor. If they ever did, he swore, he would not even *try* to catch them.

Richie did not know what time it was. He only knew that it was still dark when his cot began to rise. There was a slight hissing sound somewhere near; he was on his back, as he had gone to sleep, and the cot left the floor and rose slowly toward the ceiling. But when it got there, there was no ceiling; it had opened up like the top of a cereal box and the cot floated up into the night sky. Somewhere on the edge of Richie's mind was the perception that this was not possible; that if the ceiling did open, his cot would rise into the second-floor apartment, not the sky. But as he was trying to rationalize that impression, his cot continued to rise higher and higher into the night sky, the strange, quiet hissing sound staying with it, actually seeming to propel it along. Being left far, far below was the night city, its lights looking from above much like the starry sky looked from below.

Richie knew he was going to fall. He did not have to think about it, weigh it in his mind, consider it from any perspective; he *knew* it. The certainty of it laced him with fear and he began to whimper and tremble. Frantically he looked around for some avenue of escape, but clearly there was none;

there was only the great black void of sky around him, and the earth far, far below. And that quiet, relentless hissing that sent him up farther and farther and farther . . .

Suddenly the cot turned completely over, like a playing card being flipped, and dropped Richie out. He fell through the blackness, screaming . . .

"Wake up! Stop that yelling! What's the matter with you?"

Shaken awake, feeling fingers pressing hard into his shoulders, Richie opened his eyes to see Mrs. Hubbard bending over him. Richie sat bolt upright. "I was . . . falling . . ." he gasped. "From the sky . . ."

"Lovely. They've given us a kid who has nightmares," Mr. Hubbard said. He was standing behind his wife, looking over her shoulder.

"Does this happen to you every night?" Mrs. Hubbard demanded, giving Richie an extra shake for alertness.

"No," Richie said, "it was that hissing. It made my bed go up—"

"Hissing? What hissing?"

"I don't know—just hissing . . ."

Mrs. Hubbard pushed him back down on the cot. "Go back to sleep," she said sternly, pointing a finger in his face. "No more out of you, understand?"

"Can I go to the bathroom?"

"Go—back—to—sleep!"

The light was turned off and the Hubbards returned to their bedroom. Richie did not know whether he had awakened any of the other boys, or Junior, or not; he had not seen any of them in the hall. Lying very still, eyes wide, staring up at the dark ceiling, he relived the dream several times, remembering the terror of it. His breath was still coming abnormally fast, his heart pumping hard in his chest. After several minutes, he got tired of thinking about the dream and his mind moved to other matters. He wondered where his mother was, wondered if Stan had discovered yet that he was gone, wondered if he was going to be able to hold going to the bathroom until morning. Gradually his heartbeat and breathing slowed and his eyelids began to get heavy and lower. He felt himself drifting into a warm, cozy sleep.

Then the hissing began again.

He had the same dream a second time.

Mrs. Hubbard became so angry at being awakened again that she sat him up in bed and shook him sporadically for five minutes. "What—is—the—matter—with—you?" she demanded.

"That hissing—" Richie managed to say, tongue thick, throat constricted, head bobbing as the irate woman jarred him back and forth.

"What hissing?" she shrieked. "I don't hear any hissing! It's part of your dream!"

□□ 243 □□

"No, it makes the dream . . . start . . ."

She shook him until her arms ached, all the while her husband, pasty hands in his bathrobe pockets, glared at him from behind her. When at last she threw him back down and turned off the light again, Richie lay there trembling like an exhausted runner. It was the hissing, his mind repeated over and over. It was the hissing . . .

It started again an hour later. The dream repeated itself.

This time Mrs. Hubbard was infuriated. Grabbing Richie by the hair and undershirt, she dragged him out of bed and walked him up and down the hall like a drunk man. "You—cannot—keep—waking—us—up—like—this—!" she bellowed.

"Put him in a tub of cold water," Mr. Hubbard suggested.

"No! I'm going to get him so tired he won't have the strength to dream!"

She pushed him, dragged him, pulled him, jerked him, back and forth, up and down, side to side, until it felt as if his brain were spinning like a top. He began to feel dizzy, then queasy, then downright nauseated. A dread fear rose in him: *What if he puked on her?* She would kill him, he knew. Grimly he tried to staunch the spreading sickness, but there was no way he could do it.

"All right! All right!" he finally promised in desperation. "I won't do it no more! I promise! I won't!"

Mrs. Hubbard let go of him and he catapulted onto the cot. Bending over him, chest heaving, a line of sweat across her upper lip, she glowered like some villainous fiend in one of the Saturday serials. "You had *better* not do it again!" she threatened. "Or else!"

His entire being jarred and unsettled, Richie worked his way back under the covers and lay on his back, with his arms outside the covers, and closed his eyes. He remained perfectly still until he heard the click of the light switch and the sound of the Hubbards' voices retreating once more to their bedroom. Then, when it was again dark and quiet in the hall, he sat up. Pulling the blanket up over him like a tent, leaving just his face exposed, he drew up his knees and rested his chin on them, determined not to go to sleep again.

He sat like that for the rest of the night.

The hissing occurred every night. The nightmare occurred every night. Richie fell through the black sky and woke up screaming—every night.

Mrs. Hubbard dedicated herself tenaciously to stopping the dreams. The second night Richie woke up the household, she had her husband get out the Ping-Pong paddle and punish him on the spot, without benefit of ceremony or witnesses. One lick the first time, two the second, three the third—

until finally Richie, his buttocks burning with pain, forced himself to sit up and stay awake again.

The third night, Mrs. Hubbard tried a preventive solution. "It's his digestion," she declared. "His system can't take decent meals. I'm going to try a little experiment."

The little experiment was to give Richie only two slices of bread and a glass of milk for supper. He went to bed hungry, but it did not work. The hissing and the nightmare happened twice. The second time, after a severe paddling, Richie was made to stand in a corner, a blanket around his shoulders, for the rest of the night.

It was while he was in the corner that he discovered where the hissing sound originated. He heard it begin as he stood there. It seemed to be coming from the radiator at the foot of his cot in the alcove. Grimly, Richie left the corner and followed the sound. Turning on the light in the alcove, not caring if the Hubbards woke up, he peered down along the concealed side of the radiator. There was a safety valve there that permitted small amounts of steam to escape periodically. A thin, barely visible line of steam was streaming out at that moment—hissing quietly.

Goddamn dirty son of a bitch, Richie thought. At the other end of the radiator, Richie quietly twisted the control knob all the way down and turned off the radiator entirely.

The next morning, Mr. Hubbard discovered what he had done and gave him a sustained jerking about, tugging back and forth on one of Richie's arms with both his pasty little hands. "Are you a crazy boy or what?" he inquired. "Do you expect the rest of us to sleep in a cold house simply because you cannot control your screaming in the middle of the night?"

"I can't help it if I dream!" Richie pleaded.

"It's not the dreaming that wakes everyone up; it's the screaming. Now you expect us to freeze in order to keep you quiet? That's ridiculous. You get the paddle tonight. And I forbid you to touch that radiator control again!"

Junior complained constantly about Richie. "I'm so tired, Mother. I couldn't get back to sleep again last night. When are you going to make that new boy behave?"

"Very soon, my little love," his mother promised, stroking his bullethead. "In the meantime, to make up for you being unhappy, Mother will give you an extra dime to spend in the show on Saturday."

Junior had other ways of causing trouble too, seeming to delight in thinking up new and more creative methods of getting the wards into difficulty with his parents. He would forget to wipe his shoes on the doormat and track dirt into the house, or leave a mess at the kitchen sink after washing his hands, then simply deny his own responsibility, therefore imputing blame to someone else. Other times it was premeditated, such as when he stole a cookie from the carefully monitored jar, secure in the knowledge that his mother would not even *ask* whether he had done it; or when he became angry with one of the wards over some real or imagined slight and falsely accused the boy of hitting him. Junior could, it seemed, cry at will, and was a more accomplished liar than even Richie himself.

Richie did not understand Junior. He had met more than his share of schoolyard bullies who pushed other kids around for the admiration and praise that it brought them. And he had, in various schools, known the occasional tattletale or squealer who could not be trusted with grave secrets, such as who threw the eraser at the clock. But never before had Richie encountered a person who seemed to take such diabolic pleasure in causing severe punishment to others.

"How come you get us in Dutch all the time like you do?" Richie finally asked him one day, not resentfully but curiously, confused by the maliciousness of the younger boy.

"This is *my* house," Junior replied defensively. "I didn't ask you to come live here."

"None of *us* asked to come live here either," Richie countered. "We didn't have no say in it."

"I don't like having you here," Junior informed him coldly. "I don't like always having other kids around. I want to be the only one."

"Tell your old man and your old lady that," Richie naïvely advised.

Junior did. He told his parents that Richie had referred to them as "old man" and "old lady." Richie got extra licks that night.

Life became totally cheerless. Along with the other wards, he attended King Elementary School, the four of them going there each morning after first walking five blocks out of their way to escort Junior to the private Catholic school where he was enrolled. King, like all the rest, was a place of torment for Richie; he faced new bullies who singled him out for daily abuse and humiliation. The other wards did not "take up for him," as Stan had once done in friendship, and Ham had done for pay; they had their own battles to fight. Richie either avoided the new bullies who sought him out, or he endured their mistreatment; he was afraid to try any other course, such as fighting back. Sometimes he wished he were dead. There was, it seemed, no reason to live. The future offered him nothing except more of the same: the dreaded schoolyard, the oppressive household, the terrifying nights.

As it got colder, the radiator in the alcove where he slept was turned up higher. The intensity of his nightmares increased as the hissing became louder.

Richie begged to be allowed to sleep elsewhere, to trade places with another ward, to sleep on the floor somewhere.

"No, no, no," Mrs. Hubbard would reply automatically, and then offer some absurd excuse for the denial. "We have everything set up in an orderly fashion here and we simply cannot go about making changes to suit one individual. Suppose Lloyd didn't want to sleep in the kitchen because he didn't like the stove? Or Gerry in the front hall for some other silly reason? Can you see the problems it would cause? You sleep in the alcove, that's that."

Richie's buttocks began to carry permanent bruises. His punishment was nightly; there was no way he could avoid it—he could not stop dreaming. He stayed awake as much as he could during the night, but eventually he had to drift off. Sometimes he was able to stifle all or part of the scream that the dream generated, but not often enough; at least once a night he went through the misery of being shaken, slapped, and shoved about the alcove for having awakened the Hubbards and Junior.

After a month, Richie decided he could endure it no longer. Early one morning, just as gray daylight was seeping into the apartment, he got up and crept to the end of the hall to the bureau used by the wards for their clothes. Quietly opening his drawer, he took out a pair of corduroy trousers, his warmest shirt, and a set of underwear and socks. He would hide them under the thin mattress of his cot; then, after Mrs. Hubbard had distributed their clothes to them to get dressed, as she did every morning, he would put on two sets. When he left that day, he would not come back. He just hoped that Mrs. Hubbard would not notice that clothes were missing from his drawer.

As he slipped back toward his cot with the clothes, Richie heard the toilet flush in the hall bathroom. Heart pounding, he flattened himself against the wall and held his breath. Junior came out of the bathroom and walked sleepily back into his bedroom. Unlike the wards, Junior was allowed to relieve himself during the night. He never wet the bed, a fact which Mrs. Hubbard proudly pointed out to them. "He is at least two years younger than all of you, and look what a good boy he is. Not like you, Maxie, who still wets your bed at least once a week." To Mrs. Hubbard it was entirely irrelevant that Junior was allowed to get out of bed and go to the bathroom during the night and Maxie was not. When Maxie protested as much to her, she scoffed at him. "No, no, no, that means nothing. Junior is simply a better boy than you, Maxie. More disciplined, more controlled. You should try to be more like him, even if he is younger." When Maxie wet his bed, as punishment he had to strip the sheets off and wash them, hang them and his mattress on the back porch to dry, be sent to school without breakfast, and be paddled at bedtime.

Richie had seen Maxie punished five times for wetting his bed, and Gerry once. Remembering that now, he stood silently in the hall and listened to Junior get back into bed. Junior seemed to fall asleep again almost at once. Richie moved over to the open door and listened. All was quiet; the whole apartment was still. Carefully putting down the clothes, Richie tiptoed into the room and stood next to Junior's bed. It was a real bed, with box springs and a real mattress, not like the folding cots with sagging bedsprings and thin blue-striped, lumpy pads that served as their mattresses. Those thin pads and the springs that could be felt through them were all the worse after a boy had been blistered by Mr. Hubbard's paddle. Richie thought of how many times he had taken it, how many Maxie had taken it, and the others. And how many of those times had been caused by Junior.

Carefully, Richie lifted back the blanket and sheet under which Junior lay. He was curled up in a ball, in warm flannel pajamas, while Richie and the wards slept in their underwear. Leaning forward, Richie took out his penis and, as slowly as he could, urinated all over Junior's groin area. Junior did not even move while Richie was doing it. Directing his stream back and forth, Richie wet his legs down to the knees, his pajama top all over the stomach.

When he finished, he covered Junior back up and hurried from the room, smiling for the first time since he had come to live with the Hubbards.

The household that morning was oddly quiet. The wards could hear Junior sniffling in his bedroom, and his mother whispering urgently to him. When Mrs. Hubbard emerged and handed out the clothes each boy was to wear, her expression was cross, her manner more brusque than usual. To Richie's relief, she gave him his clothes in cursory fashion, paying no attention to what was left in the drawer. Her hasty attitude made Richie wish he had taken another shirt, but it was too late then; the wards were sent off to their respective sleeping areas to get dressed and make their cots for folding and rolling away. Mrs. Hubbard went back into Junior's room where the grave whispering immediately began again.

"Jeez, wonder what's going on?" Maxie asked quietly as they filed down the hall.

"Maybe the little prick died in his sleep," Gerry said hopefully.

As the four boys walked Junior to school that morning, he was as uncommonly quiet as the household had been. Usually his mouth never rested; he taunted and badgered and baited the wards about anything that he thought would annoy them, anything that would remind them of the grim, sour existence they led compared to his much more privileged life. But on this morning, Junior was glumly silent.

□□ 248 □□

"What's the matter, Junior?" asked Gerry. "You break your Shirley Temple doll or something?"

"I don't have a Shirley Temple doll!" Junior said angrily. "I don't play with dolls!"

"Yeah, I forget," said Gerry, "you only play with yourself."

"That's a lie and I'm telling!" Junior threatened.

"Why don't you shut up," Lloyd said to Gerry. "You're only gonna get you ass whacked."

"I know what's wrong with him," Richie said.

"You do not!" Junior flared, turning red.

"Oh, yeah? What?" asked Gerry.

"You don't know nothing!" Junior yelled. His eyes began to water. Richie grinned at him.

"He pissed the bed last night," Richie told them. "Pissed it from top to bottom."

Gerry and Maxie burst out laughing; even dour Lloyd had to smile. Junior, overcome with humiliation, began to bawl and scream and run away from them, all at the same time. "You wait!" he yelled, hurrying ahead of them toward the nuns standing outside his school. "Just wait! I'm telling on all of you! I'm gonna say you all hit me on the way to school!"

The four wards stopped and watched him run up to one of the nuns. Turning back, they started toward their own school.

"We'll get it tonight," Lloyd predicted. "All of us."

All but one, Richie thought, trudging along in his two sets of clothes.

*S*eeing Richie huddled in the basement doorway, Stan first stared incredulously, then asked indignantly, "Where the hell you been?"

Richie told him the whole story: about George Zangara, the baby his mother was going to have, the welfare woman coming to get him at school, being taken to the Hubbard home.

"Jeez," said Stan. "I wondered why they come and took you to the principal's office that day. Where's your old lady?"

"I don't know," Richie said, shrugging. "Someplace where women wait to have babies, she told me."

"What you gonna do now?" Stan asked, and immediately suggested, "You could sleep in the basement here."

"Think so?"

"Hell, yeah, why not. My old lady's got a extra blanket under her bed; I'll cop it for you."

"Can you get me something to eat too? I ain't had nothing since supper last night."

"Jeez. Didn't they give you no breakfast in that place?"

Richie shook his head. "Not me. I didn't get breakfast 'cause I had bad dreams and woke everybody up. I'm really hungry, Stan."

"Wait here," Stan said, punching him lightly on the arm. He hurried away from the basement door and up the front steps.

It was past three in the afternoon now; the Hubbards would have found out from the other wards that Richie had not been in school since morning recess. Before long they would report to Miss Menefee that he was missing. Soon people would be looking for him. Shivering, he huddled a little farther into the doorway.

In several minutes, Stan was back with some saltines and a hunk of cheese. "This is all I could get that wouldn't be missed," he said. "Soon's you eat it, we'll go hit some newsstands and get some dough for hamburgers. Right now, you sneak back into the furnace room and meet me there. I'm gonna go swipe that blanket and bring it down the back stairs."

The blanket was actually an old quilt, worn and tattered, but it was better than nothing. They hid it behind some stacks of newspapers that the landlord saved to sell two or three times a year to the salvage wagon. Then they headed for Madison Street to go stealing. They managed to steal change from half a dozen stands as they made their way up the busy street to the main intersection at Western. With the coins they had filched, they went to White Castle and had hamburgers and milk. Stan ordered three for himself, then gave two to Richie, saying, "My sister'll fix me supper later."

It was dark when they got back to the building on Adams Street, and they sneaked into the basement from the alley just in case anyone was around looking for Richie. To make a place to hide, he and Stan fashioned a cubbyhole behind the landlord's bundles of old newspapers. By shifting some of the bundles around, not altering the pile enough to be noticeable, they made a crawl space long enough and wide enough for Richie to get into, stretch out, even sit up if he kept his head bent forward slightly.

"You can lay on one half of the blanket and cover wit' the other," Stan said. "Wit' all the bundles of paper stacked around you, and the furnace right over there, you'll probably be the warmest one in the whole building."

"What about the rats?" Richie worried.

"I don't think they can get to you," Stan appraised the situation, "not if you pull a bundle in and close the opening behind you."

Taking the quilt, Richie wiggled into his confining little hideout. Working part of the quilt under him, he bunched the rest up as a cover. "How'll I know when it's morning?" he asked.

"When I leave for school, I'll stick my head in the door and yell, 'Hey, Ma, I'm leaving now!' Like maybe I thought my old lady was down here using a laundry tub. After you hear that, wait a little while and then work your way out real quiet like. You should be able to hear if there's anybody down here. Okay?"

"Yeah, okay," Richie said, swallowing drily. This was going to be different from sitting up half the night in the Haymarket movie house while George was visiting his mother. The Haymarket was all right in that situation; if a cop had grabbed him, he would have just been taken home to Chloe. If one caught him now, he'd probably have to go back to live with the Hubbards.

"Meet me down at the corner of the alley after school tomorrow," Stan said.

"Yeah, okay."

"So long."

"So long," Richie said nervously as Stan pushed the bundle of papers in place to close him in.

He had never been in a place so dark in his life. Or so confining. Except when his arms were straight down at his sides, it was impossible to stretch them out all the way. The smell of the old newspapers began to overcome him. After several minutes, he started breathing very heavily. A sense of panic rising within him, he shimmied down and with his feet pushed the bundle out to make the opening again. Quickly he got out of the enclosure and sat up.

Sitting with his back against the coal chute next to the pile of newspapers, Richie sucked in several deep breaths and felt himself begin to relax. The basement was still and dark, quiet except for an occasional flutter of leaping flame in the belly of the furnace. Maybe, Richie thought, he could just sleep right there, sitting up. Then he remembered the rats. How many rats, he wondered, had he killed with flying bricks since the day Stan taught him how? He wondered if rats had relatives, like brothers and uncles, who might remember him and . . .

Jesus Christ, rats could be getting into his cubbyhole while he was sitting there!

In a new panic, Richie crawled back into his hideout, flapping the blanket and slapping the stacks of paper to scare out any rats that might have sneaked in. Taking off one shoe, he ran it along the floor and both sides, quietly but urgently saying, "Out, out, out!" When he was sure there was nothing alive in the space except him, he hooked his toes under the twine of the paper bundle and pulled it in place to close off the opening.

Later, when he felt more at ease in the little burrow, Richie became too warm and remembered that he was still wearing two sets of clothes. Scrunching and twisting around in the limited space, he wiggled out of his coat, sweater, top shirt, outer corduroys, and the other shoe. Rolling some of the extra clothes together, he made a pillow for himself, and used his coat to cover his feet. Soon he found that he not only was fairly comfortable but also felt safe and protected—even from the hordes of rats that might be out there waiting to take revenge on him. Sighing quietly, he let his heavy eyelids close as a soft, gentle peacefulness washed over him.

Without the radiator and its hated hissing, Richie fell into a deep, much-needed sleep.

He did not hear Stan yell into the basement the next morning. The first sound that reached him was the landlord shoveling cinders out of the furnace into a wheelbarrow. Richie lay quietly until he heard the furnace door slam shut and the sound of the wheelbarrow being rolled up two planks on the back basement stairs and pushed out to the alley. When he heard no other noise, he moved aside the stack of papers and once again slid out, pulling his shoes and coat with him, putting them on when he was out. Pushing the stack back in place to conceal his little shelter, he went over to a laundry tub and quickly washed his face and hands, drying on a towel the landlord had hung there. The landlord was rolling the wheelbarrow back toward the alley door when Richie hurried out the front.

From the basement doorway, Richie scrutinized the street. Nothing looked out of the ordinary; there were no official-looking cars parked anywhere, no men in suits or women with briefcases; everyone in sight looked liked they *belonged*. Leaving the doorway, Richie walked briskly down to Winchester Street and cut over the three blocks to Madison. He came out on Madison directly across from the Stadium. Staring at the big arena, he wondered if there was even the slightest chance that Rondo would take him back as a hawker. Thinking about that possibility, he bought two doughnuts and a bottle of chocolate milk at a market across from the Stadium's employee entrance, and sat on the curb to eat. Several people went into the arena while he was sitting there, but no one he recognized. When he finished eating, he jacked up his nerve and went over to the door.

"I'm here to see Rondo about a job," he told the security guard.

"He expecting you?"

"Yeah," Richie lied.

"Okay, go on back," the guard said. "That way."

Richie made his way around the cavernous, almost eerie empty arena to the vendor room and found Rondo shelving boxes of frankfurters in a wall-size refrigerator with glass doors. When Rondo saw him, he paused in his work long enough to ask, "What the hell are *you* doing here?"

"I came to say I was sorry," Richie told him. "An' to ask if I could have my job back."

Rondo studied him for a moment, taking a blue bandanna from his hip pocket and wiping sweat from his face. Presently he smiled slightly and said, "Wanna gimme a hand wit' these boxes?"

"Sure, Rondo!" Richie beamed as he stood at the other end of a dolly, unloading the boxes of franks and stacking them in another section of the big refrigerator. It took ten minutes to finish that load, and fifteen minutes to do a second dolly that Rondo wheeled in from the hall. When they finished, Rondo wiped his face again and asked innocently, "Now what was it you wanted?"

"My job back," Richie said, shrugging.

"No chance," Rondo told him flatly.

Richie stared incredulously at him. "But I thought . . ."

"You thought what?"

"You had me help you unload all that," Richie pointed to the refrigerator.

"I didn't *have* you help me do nothing," Rondo said. "I asked if you wanted to give me a hand and you said sure. That don't mean I'm giving you no job back. G'on, beat it."

"What about the dough I got coming from that last night then?" Richie challenged. "You never paid me for that!"

Rondo made a show of rubbing his chin thoughtfully. "Oh, that. I used that money to buy a new vending tray. The one you threw against the wall was all smashed up. So you got no dough coming. Now g'on, beat it!"

Turning, fists clenched, Richie stalked out. Wending his way back around the vast echo-filled stadium, his mind seethed with indignation and rage. His anger was awash with obscenities: Dirty rotten goddamn fucking son of a bitch bastard prick . . .

At the employee door, the security guard asked, "Get the job, kid?"

"I wouldn't work for that guy," Richie announced. "He said I could only have a job if I sucked his dick."

"Rondo said that?" the security guard asked, surprised.

"Sure did," Richie assured. "He said all the kids that work for him have to suck his dick."

The security guard's mouth hung open in astonishment. "Rondo?"

"You just never know about people," Richie declared. "I'm gonna go home and tell my old man. I don't know whether he'll call the cops or just come down here and whip Rondo's ass. He's gonna be plenty mad, that's for sure!"

Leaving the amazed security guard staring after him, Richie left the arena and crossed the sprawling, empty parking lot to Warren Boulevard. He walked the four blocks up to the 2200-block and sat on the curb across from the building where he and his mother had first moved with Johnny Eaton. How very long ago it all seemed. He wondered if Louis still lived in the building next door, and remembered that Louis still owed him thirty cents from the day they ditched school to go see Buck Jones. Thirty-*two* cents, actually, because Richie had also paid for Louis's milk at lunchtime that day. It crossed his mind to wait there and catch Louis when he came home from school, to see if Louis had any money to pay him back, but he decided not to. Louis, he knew, had a hard enough life without having to worry about old debts.

As Richie was sitting there, a squad car from the nearby Warren Avenue precinct station cruised by and the cop in the passenger seat gave him a curious glance. Richie watched as it slowed at the next corner and turned. *Going around the block!* his mind alerted. Waiting for a break in the one-way traffic, Richie dashed across the street, cut through a once-familiar gangway, and headed up the alley.

Better keep moving during school hours, he told himself.

That night, prowling with Stan, Richie worried about how to evade the authorities during the day. "I can't stay buried in that pile of newspapers until three o'clock every day," he complained. "But I can't hang around parks or movies or stay on the street either, or I'm sure to get caught—by somebody."

"Go downtown to the main library," Stan advised. They were walking the alley behind Madison Street, checking the backs of stores for something to steal.

"What main library?" Richie asked.

"The *main* main library," Stan said. "The only main library there is. That one you was pinching books out of is just a branch. The one downtown is a great big building. You could get lost in it. It's on Michigan Avenue, 'cross from the park."

On rare occasions it annoyed Richie that Stan always had an answer. "How the hell do you know so much about a library?" he asked with a trace of irritation. "You don't even read books."

"I don't fuck elephants either," Stan said blandly, "but I know where the zoo is." He touched Richie's arm and urged him into the shadows. "Look," he said in a quieter voice.

Richie looked where Stan indicated. Across the rear loading dock of a Royal Blue market, the receiving door was open an inch. An outside light above the door was on, but there were no employees in sight.

"Come on," Stan said.

The two boys crept up the loading dock steps and crossed to the door. With the tips of his fingers, Stan eased the already ajar door open an additional inch. Peering into a lighted rear storeroom, they saw a desk, a large floor safe, a scale for weighing sides of meat, and numerous cartons of canned goods stacked in rows six feet high. But no employees. Pursing his ill-matched lips, Stan opened the door wide enough to enter. Making immediately for the safe, he tried its handle and found it locked. Silently then, he opened each desk drawer but found nothing of value. Turning to Richie, who was half in, half out of the door, tensely watching both the alley and the swinging doors to the front of the market, Stan pointed to some cartons nearest the loading dock. Richie quickly lifted one and carried it outside. Stan grabbed the one under it and followed him. Seconds later, they were galloping down the alley, boxes held in front of them, looking like two pregnant midgets in a footrace.

The cartons each contained two dozen cans of Campbell's soup, one vegetable, one chicken noodle. They hid them in an alcove off Richie's hideout, made by shifting two more stacks of newspapers. The next afternoon they lugged them over to Maxwell Street and sold them to a street vendor for a nickel a can, making a dollar-twenty each.

"Jeez, what luck," Richie said, referring to the open door.

"Luck didn't have nothing to do with it," Stan corrected. "We was *looking* for something an' we found it." Gazing off wistfully, he added, "Someday I'll go back for that safe."

Richie stared curiously at his friend. Sometimes it seemed that Stan was growing up much faster than other kids. Richie considered himself very lucky to have a buddy like Stan Klein.

The fourth day after he had run away from the Hubbard household, Richie emerged from his basement hiding place and immediately felt a strong hand grab him from the side of the doorway. The hand held him firmly by the shirt collar. "Just take it easy, kid," a man's voice advised.

"Hello, Richie," a female voice said.

Richie's head snapped around and he saw Miss Menefee standing on the other side of the doorway. She nodded and the man led Richie out to a welfare department car at the curb and got into the back seat with him. Miss Menefee got behind the wheel and they drove away.

"You're very lucky, Richie, that it was us who found you and not the juvenile officers," Miss Menefee said, glancing at him in the rearview mirror. "You could be on your way to the juvenile home right now instead of to my office."

When they got downtown to the welfare department, Miss Menefee said, "Thanks for the help, Arnold," and took Richie into her tiny office and sat him down. From behind her desk, she asked unsmilingly, "Why did you run away?"

"I didn't like those people," Richie replied.

"Well, for your information, young man," Miss Menefee told him crisply, "they weren't exactly crazy about you either. They said you refused to sleep and disrupted the entire household by making noise in the middle of the night."

Richie started to blame it on the radiator, but for some reason that story now seemed a little silly and embarrassing to him. "Mr. Hubbard beat me and Mrs. Hubbard made me go without eating," he accused, sulking.

"Oh, come now," the caseworker ridiculed. " 'Beat' you? Mr. Hubbard *paddled* you. As for going without eating, as you put it, that is perfectly normal punishment. I got sent to bed without supper a few times myself when I was your age." She leaned forward, folding her hands on the desk in schoolteacher fashion. "Now listen to me, Richie. You are just one of many, many wards of this department. In fact, there are more wards than there are homes to put them in sometimes. The state doesn't pay all that much to board you; most of these foster parents are making a personal sacrifice when they take you in. No place is going to be perfect, Richie. *Life* is not perfect." Pulling a card file in front of her, she started flipping through it.

"Where's my mother?" Richie asked.

"You know perfectly well where she is. She's living at a home for unwed mothers, waiting to have her baby."

"I want to go see her."

"I'm sorry, but that's impossible. No one under sixteen is allowed to visit there. If you want to write your mother a letter, I'll see that she gets it."

Glowering, Richie looked down at the worn knees of his corduroys. Lousy fucking rules, he thought. He was beginning to think like Stan, beginning to examine and evaluate in his young mind all the adult guidelines that had been set down to control the conduct of the young. Can't see my own mother 'cause I'm not old enough, he brooded resentfully. Ain't supposed to have no feelings until I'm sixteen.

"I'm taking you to a new foster home and I expect you to behave yourself at this one," Miss Menefee said firmly. "I picked up your things from the Hubbards; they're over there." Richie looked and saw a shopping bag in the corner. "Pick it up and let's go," the caseworker said.

That night in a run-down frame house on the South Side, a haggard-looking woman in a soiled dress led Richie to a room that had two double beds in it and no other furniture. "There's cardboard boxes under the bed to put your things in," she said. "There's three other boys live in here too. I lock the door at nine o'clock every night and unlock it at six every morning. The oldest boy, Dave, is in charge of the room. Do like he says and you'll get along fine."

The other three boys came in a little while later. Two of them were about

Richie's age; Dave was a year or so older, and accordingly bigger. "You'll sleep wit' me in this bed," he decided. "The old bat turns out the light from outside when she locks the door at night, but we got candles stashed so's we can have our own light. We have lots of fun after we're locked in."

Glancing at the other two boys, Richie noticed that one of them was grinning idiotically, while the other looked distinctly glum and woeful. Richie found out why shortly after the lights went out. Lying on his side of the bed, in his underwear, he felt one of Dave's hands exploring.

"What the hell are you doing?" Richie demanded. "Cut it out!"

Dave took Richie's hand and pulled it over to his own genitals. He had an erection. "Come on, we're just gonna have a little fun—"

"No! Cut it out!" Richie said again, jerking his hand back.

The bedsprings creaked as Dave got up. A moment later there was a glow of light from a candle. "What's the matter wit' you?" Dave tried to reason. "We just wanna have some fun." Behind him, one of the other boys was grinning like a fool again. The glum one was cowering on the other bed.

"Play with yourself," Richie said. "You ain't playing with me."

Dave scowled. "What are you, a tough guy or something?" He handed the candle to the boy who was grinning. "Take off them shorts," he ordered Richie.

"I ain't gonna."

Without warning, Dave's fist shot out and hit Richie flush on the mouth. He had been on his knees on the bed, and when the blow struck, it sent him flailing backwards on the floor. As Dave came around the bed after him, Richie grabbed one of his shoes and scrambled to his feet.

"I'll bash you!" he yelled, brandishing the shoe. Dave glared at him for a moment, then opened his fists and smiled. "Suit yourself, punk. But don't get back in bed 'less you decide to play, understand? Sleep on the floor and see how you like it." He turned to the boy cowering on the other bed. "All right, you, get over here," he ordered.

"Do I have to?" the kid whimpered.

"Yeah, you have to," Dave mimicked. "Hurry up!"

Sniveling, the boy went to him. Still holding the shoe, Richie backed into a corner and sat down. In the flickering light of the candle, he watched what Dave and the grinning boy did to the other one.

At six the next morning, as soon as the door was unlocked, Richie bolted from the room, raced down the hall, and burst out the front door. Bottom lip swollen from Dave's punch, body stiff and aching from sleeping on the floor in the corner, he ran away from the place as fast as he could. He ran for five city blocks, until his chest was heaving so badly that he could barely breathe; then he hid in a gangway and rested for several minutes. When he was able, he started running again.

It took Richie all morning to make his way far across the city, back to the West Side. After the first hour, he stopped running and started looking for ways to get rides. During the morning rush of people going to work, he was able to get aboard the crowded rear platform of streetcars and stay on for a couple or three blocks until the conductor neared him collecting fares; then he hopped off and waited for the next one. That worked for an hour, until the crowds thinned out. After that, he walked until he saw a chance to hop on the back of a truck without being seen. Then he would ride until the truck stopped or changed direction.

Around mid-morning, famished, he went into a bakery and asked for a loaf of rye, sliced. When the baker turned around to run the bread through the slicer, Richie grabbed a sweet roll in each hand and ran like hell out of the place. Running down the street, hearing the baker yell, "Hey, you little bastard!" after him, he turned into the first alley he came to, cut over to the next street, and beat it into a nearby park. Sitting under a tree, he ate all of the two rolls except for some crumbs, which he threw to a nearby sparrow on the ground. Afterward, he filled up with water at a public drinking fountain and resumed his trek.

Arriving back in the Adams Street neighborhood just after noon, Richie headed directly for his old building. He had his extra clothes still stashed in the newspaper pile hideaway, along with a box of vanilla wafers, two bottles of grapeade, and a bottle opener. If no one was in the basement doing laundry or anything, he could crawl into his little refuge, eat some cookies, drink some pop, and take a nap until Stan got home from school.

Richie walked boldly down the street. He felt there was no need to exercise caution; he had only run away a few hours ago and no one would be after him for a couple of days, at least—

Up ahead, coming toward him on the sidewalk, was a man in a suit. Frowning, Richie stepped off the sidewalk and crossed the street. The man in the suit did the same thing. Fuck, Richie thought. Turning, he reversed direction. Coming toward him from that way was a second man in a suit. Tensing, Richie poised to run, eyes searching for the best route of escape. Just then a car pulled up in the street next to him, Miss Menefee behind the wheel. Rolling down her window, she scowled irately at Richie.

"Don't you *dare* make us chase you, young man," she warned. "Come over here and get in this car—at once!"

Richie glanced back and forth at the two men, who were walking briskly, closing on him fast. There was a gangway nearby, but he wasn't sure he could make it.

"Ri-*chie*," Miss Menefee said. "I'm warning you . . ."

Shoulders slumping, he relented and hurried to the car as the two men converged on him.

Richie rode in the front seat with Miss Menefee, the two male caseworkers taking the back seat. They chided her about Richie.

"Why don't you let us kick his ass, Gracie?" one of them said.

"Yeah," the other agreed, "let us impress on the little Dead End Kid that we have better things to do than set ambushes for him. Don't forget, we've got caseloads too."

"I'll do some of your paperwork to pay you back," Miss Menefee said. She glanced at Richie, an expression of gravity on her plain-pretty face as she looked at his swollen lip. "And I don't think he needs to be kicked in the pants either. Not yet anyhow." She nudged Richie's leg. "Who hit you in the mouth?"

"One of the other kids," he mumbled.

"How come?"

Richie shrugged. "He just did." Looking down, he turned very red, embarrassed at the prospect of having to explain it. Miss Menefee, seeing him blush, did not press the issue.

Downtown, when she got him alone in her office, Miss Menefee's demeanor changed.

"Who do you think you are?" she demanded hotly. She gave him a half-hearted shove. "Sit down in that chair. Do you think all I've got to do with my time is worry about you? If you don't get smart, young man"—she wagged a finger at him—"you're going to find yourself in the state reformatory. How would you like that?"

"I'd like it better than the places you've been putting me," Richie said brazenly. Grace Menefee's mouth dropped open in astonishment.

"Oh, you would! And just what makes you think so, wiseguy?"

"I seen a movie with John Garfield, called *Dust Be My Destiny*, where he got sent to a reform school, an' it didn't look all that bad to me."

"Oh, I see! A *movie*. With John Garfield. And because of that you think you know it all!" In irritation, she drummed her fingernails on the desk. "You haven't by chance seen any movies about how a caseworker deals with a stubborn, unruly little recalcitrant, have you?"

"I don't know what that is," Richie mumbled, looking down at the edge of her desk.

After a few moments, Grace Menefee sighed a careworn sigh and reached for her card file. "All right, problem child, let's start all over again."

The next foster home Grace Menefee put him in, he sat at a round kitchen table the first morning and watched as he and four other boys were served oatmeal the color of vomit. Richie liked oatmeal, but he liked it with milk and sugar. The other boys began eating it as it was served, with nothing on it.

"Don't we get no milk or sugar?" Richie asked a teenage girl who had dished it out. She grimaced and gestured for him to shut up. But it was too late.

"What?" asked a lanky, unshaved man who was doing the cooking. Removing a dangling cigarette from his lips, he turned to the table. "What was that?"

"Nothing, Pa," the girl said nervously.

"Shut up. Who asked about milk and sugar?"

"I did," Richie said.

"Do you *see* any milk and sugar?" the lanky foster parent inquired with mock innocence.

"No, I don't see none," Richie replied.

"Well, what does that tell you, boy?"

"It tells me I ain't gonna eat here," Richie said, pushing his chair back. The other boys looked up apprehensively as their foster parent's expression became incensed.

"Sit down before I knock you down," he said angrily, shaking a long wooden spoon at Richie.

"Look out!" Richie yelled, pointing at the stove. "It's on fire!"

The lanky man whirled back around to the stove. Richie kicked his chair away and darted out the kitchen door. He was down the rear stairs and vaulting the back fence by the time the lanky man got out on the porch.

"You'll be sorry, you little shit!" Richie heard him yell down the alley.

At four o'clock that afternoon, while Richie was unabashedly sitting on the curb in his old block, a squad car pulled up to him. An indifferent cop beckoned him over and asked his name. Richie told him. The cop jerked his thumb toward the back seat. "Get in."

As he rode downtown, Richie heard the cop say on his radio, "Call that welfare dame and tell her we're on our way with the kid she's looking for."

The squad car dropped Richie off in front of the welfare department, where Miss Menefee was waiting.

"You've gone too far this time, young man," she said resolutely. "Now you're going to Mrs. Raley's."

*T*he place where Miss Menefee took him was a shabby little frame house on Loomis Street, set far at the back of a yard that consisted solely of hard brown dirt, with not a blade of grass in sight. As they walked from the car to the front porch, the wood of which had faded gray with age and was rotting from neglect, Miss Menefee said firmly, "You've brought this on yourself, Richie, just remember that."

When Miss Menefee knocked, the door was opened by a stout woman in a soiled apron. She had cheeks that hung down to her neck and traces of lip hair at each corner of her mouth. Her left arm was missing a few inches below her elbow. "Another problem, huh?" she said by way of greeting.

"Richie, this is Mrs. Raley," Miss Menefee said. "It's the last foster home I'm putting you in. If you run away from here, when you're caught you'll be brought right back here again for Mrs. Raley to deal with you. And *every* time you run away, you'll be brought back here again. So you see, there is absolutely *no* point in running away; it isn't going to change a thing. I hope for your sake that you adjust."

Richie barely heard a word she said; he was staring in fascination at the stump of Mrs. Raley's arm.

Smiling a narrow smile that could not seem to penetrate her pendulous cheeks, Mrs. Raley said, "Don't you worry, dearie, I'll straighten him out. Did you bring the first week's check?"

Miss Menefee handed Mrs. Raley a welfare department draft, gave Richie a brief, cheerless pat on the head, and left. Mrs. Raley took Richie's collar between thumb and forefinger and pulled him into the house. In a seedy, musty little living room, the heavyset woman and the skinny twelve year old faced each other. Unable to help himself, Richie continued to stare at the stub of her arm. It was round and wrinkled, the folds of the skin seemed to have been tucked together like one would close a paper bag. Richie wondered what they did with the part they cut off . . .

Mrs. Raley suddenly seized him by the front of his jacket and pushed the stump in his face. "Take a good, close look, kiddo!" she snarled. "Ugly, ain't it?" Dragging him into the hall, keeping the stump in his face all the way, she snatched open a closet door and from a nail in the wall took down a razor strap of thick harness leather. "See this here?" she asked, taking her arm out of his face and holding the strap in its place. "I ever catch you looking at my arm again, kiddo, I'll lay this on your little ass until you won't be able to sit down for a week!" Hanging the strap back on the nail, she shoved him roughly into the closet, closing and locking the door. "I don't wanna hear a sound out of you!" she warned.

It was dark but Richie was not afraid. He had seen when she had the door open that the closet was almost completely empty; there was nothing in it but the leather strap hanging on the nail, and a frayed throw rug on the floor. Richie was not claustrophobic or squeamish, not after several nights of sleeping in the cubbyhole in the newspaper bundles. In fact, the dark, quiet closet seemed almost a refuge to him, a desirable haven away from the perplexities and hazards of life on the street. The old stump-armed woman couldn't keep him in there forever, Richie knew; she had to let him out some time.

He was right. Several hours later, Mrs. Raley unlocked the door and, with a grip on his collar, led him through a dining room toward a kitchen. At a rickety wooden table in the dining room, five other boys were eating, talking, and laughing; they fell silent as Mrs. Raley took Richie through, then began talking in quieter tones when he had passed. In the kitchen, Mrs. Raley had him stand at a counter where she had put a bowl of stew, crackers, and milk. "You got five minutes to eat that, kiddo," she said, looking at a large, man's watch on her flabby wrist.

She stood next to him while he ate. The stew, Richie was surprised to find, was delicious; he wolfed it down, crushing as many crackers into it as he could during the time limit, and drank the milk in two swallows.

"Let's go," Mrs. Raley said as soon as he took the last bite. She guided him back to the hall and stopped at a bathroom. "If you have to go, go," she told him. Richie went into the bathroom and Mrs. Raley stuck one foot in the door so he could not close it all the way. With his back to the door, he took a leak. When he came out of the bathroom, she put him back in the closet.

Sitting with his ear to the closet door, Richie was able to hear some of the sounds of the household. There obviously was no silence rule as there had been in the Hubbard home; the boys at the table had been talking freely, and now Richie could hear them engaging in more conversation as they moved about the squalid little house after supper. Also unlike the Hubbard household, in which either Mr. Hubbard or Mrs. Hubbard *always* seemed to be issuing orders, he did not constantly hear the voice of this foster parent; only now and again did Mrs. Raley say anything to any of the boys.

When he got tired of listening at the door, Richie stretched out on the frayed rug with his hands under his head and eventually dozed off. He was awakened at some point by Mrs. Raley and told to go to the bathroom again, which he did. When he returned to the closet that time, she tossed a pillow and blanket in with him, saying, "Sweet dreams, kiddo." Then she locked him in for the night.

Early the next morning, Richie was awakened by sounds of the other boys, apparently having breakfast and getting ready to go to school. He had to take a leak real bad, and wondered if he dared do it in a back corner of the closet. As he was considering it, the door was unlocked again and Mrs. Raley took him across the hall to the bathroom. When he was finished, she motioned him into the kitchen where there was a bowl of corn flakes and two pieces of toast waiting for him on the counter. As he started eating, she put a table knife and a jar of grape jelly in front of him for his toast. "There ain't no butter right now," she said. Then, as if an explanation was required, "We only had enough ration stamps left for butter or cheese, so we got cheese."

As Richie ate, he surreptitiously noted the distance to the back door; through a kitchen window he tried to gauge whether he would be able to vault the back fence. But he was not as crafty in his reconnaissance as he thought he was, because presently Mrs. Raley nudged him with her stumpy arm and said, "Don't even think about it, kiddo." Richie turned red and finished his breakfast staring at the counter.

When he finished eating, Mrs. Raley led him out of the kitchen. He assumed he was going back into the closet. Instead, she pointed at the rickety table. "Sit down, kiddo." After he sat, she asked, "Do you like the closet?"

"No, ma'am," Richie said without looking up. He decided to be polite, just to see where it got him. It got him nowhere.

"You don't have to use that 'ma'am' crap with me, kiddo," the stocky woman told him flatly. "I ain't no lady and you ain't here for me to make a gentleman out of you. A plain old 'yeah' will suit me just fine." As she talked, she kept her good arm on the table and the other one out of sight. "I'm gonna refresh your mind about what that caseworker dame told you. Every time you run away from Mrs. Raley's, you're gonna get brought *back* to Mrs. Raley's. And you're gonna go back in the closet. First time, it'll be for two days, next time for four. I double it every time a boy runs away. I'll keep you in there until you go blind and forget how to walk, if that's what it takes. This here," she poked a finger against the table top, "is the last stop, kiddo. Don't say you wasn't warned."

She stood up and Richie did also, not knowing what else to do. For a moment they studied each other, two mismatched adversaries in a strange social conflict in which neither, had they stopped to consider it, would ever be able to claim complete victory. Each was leery of the other because of what the other *was*—a misfit; each was guarded against showing the *other* misfit any weakness; each calculated what might be gained from the other misfit. They were like animals in the same forest—but a different part of the forest.

Finally Mrs. Raley said, "All right, I've got things to do around here. Tomorrow you'll go to school with the rest of the kids. For the rest of the day, just try to keep out of my way. Go on out and look around the neighborhood if you want to. There's some leftover stew for lunch—if you decide to come back."

The hefty woman went into the kitchen. Amazed, Richie stared after her. Then he ground his mind into gear and made for the front door. The old bat was practically inviting him to cut out. And cut out he would!

Hurrying across the dirt front yard, he glanced back several times to convince himself that she was not coming after him. Reaching the sidewalk, he shook his head in astonishment. This was too good to be true! Well, the joke's on her, he thought elatedly as he walked briskly down Loomis Street. She'd never see *him* again!

Before noon he was back. Hungry, he had remembered how good the stew was. And he had reflected on other things too: the five boys talking at the table, the apparent absence of the kind of precise regimen such as that imposed by the Hubbards, and the fact that Mrs. Raley had given him the freedom to leave the house that morning. Going back for the stew, Richie rationalized that he was not actually conceding his freedom because, the way it looked like the Raley house was run, he could take off any time he wanted. His decision to come back was justified by the first bite of the leftover stew; it was even better than it had been the night before—and he was moved to say so. Mrs. Raley accepted the compliment with a grunt, replying sullenly, almost to herself, "Stew's always better the next day. That's 'cause the flavor's had time to settle."

After Richie ate, Mrs. Raley took him to a rear bedroom crowded with three double-decker bunk beds. "That one right there's yours." She indicated one of the bottom bunks with the stump of her arm. Richie began to feel buoyant; this place might be all right. There were even a few comic books lying about.

After school, he met the other five boys. Artie, the oldest and biggest, was naturally the unofficial leader. The youngest and smallest was called Midge, short for midget. Between them were three boys of varying size named Harold, Ray, and Donny. When they had all arrived home, Artie closed the bedroom door and explained how life was at Mrs. Raley's.

"The food ain't fancy, but it's good and there's plenty of it. We gotta do our own laundry and we take turns doing the heavy chores around the place, like lugging the garbage can out an' shoveling the sidewalk when it snows— shit like that. She won't put up with a lot of real loud noise around the house, no horseplay or nothing, but she lets us listen to the radio when she does; we just ain't allowed to turn it on ourselves. She won't put up with getting in no trouble in the neighborhood or at school; she don't like teachers and she don't like the neighbors, so don't never do nothing that makes nobody come to the door to complain. And the *main* thing"—Artie judo-chopped the air with both hands for emphasis—"is don't run away. 'Least, don't get *caught* if you do. That closet is worse than you think it is; I done eight days in it, so I know."

"I done four myself," piped up Midge, the smallest.

"We *all* been problems," said Harold. "Tha's why we're here. Ray used to set fires. Donny was always pulling up girls' dresses; he has to go talk to a doctor once a week about it."

"Besides the closet for runaways," Artie went on, "the only punishment she dishes out is with her razor strap. There's no going to bed without supper, or standing in the corner, or sissy shit like that; all's she does is whip the hell out of you with that strap."

"And don't *never*, whatever you do," Midge stressed gravely, "*ever* get caught looking at her stump." There was a chorus of affirmations from the others about that.

For the rest of the day, Richie accrued more bits and pieces of information both by observation and inquiry. At supper that night, he and the other wards were given large hamburger steaks made from ground beef, while Mrs. Raley contentedly munched away at a *real* steak, tenderloin and rare. She also sipped occasionally from a water glass enclosed in a knitted glass-holder that concealed its contents.

"It's whiskey," Artie whispered to Richie after the meal. "An' she's able to have steak for herself 'cause she gets ration books for all of us."

Back in their room that night, Richie asked about the comic books he had seen earlier. "We chip in for 'em," he was told. "See, we each get a dime a week for milk in the school lunchroom, only we don't use it for that, we spend it on other things. Mrs. Raley don't care, an' we get plenty of milk at breakfast and supper. So sometimes we all put in two cents and buy a comic book." Artie paused to scratch his head. "Now that you're here, I don't know how we'll work it. Six don't go into ten."

Oldest and biggest, Richie thought, but not the smartest.

He began mulling over improving his lot in life—*without* running away again.

The wards at Mrs. Raley's attended Jackson Elementary, a tough lower-class neighborhood school no different from any of the other eight schools Richie had gone to in the past five years. Sixty percent white, thirty percent black, the rest anything from Egyptian to Filipino, it comprised the usual strata of an elementary school community. A handful of bullies ruled the schoolyard, usually with an entourage of semi-toughs and sycophants. They intimidated and terrorized at will, but—as Richie had learned was typical—they avoided challenging anyone who might have group support of some kind. For this reason, kids with several brothers in the school were let alone; the Jewish kids, who had to go for religious lessons after school, and who would stick together and fight, were let alone; and Mrs. Raley's wards were let alone. Artie and Harold were both adequate fighters and with the assurance of assistance from four others, even of inferior skills—eight arms and feet, even untrained, are *bound* to do some damage—they were able to bluff a status for the wards that was, in Richie's estimation, the most desirable on the schoolyard: neutrality.

It was easy for everyone in the school to differentiate wards of the county, whether Mrs. Raley's or anyone else's. As Richie had learned while in the Hubbard household, the welfare department periodically distributed to each ward a box of clothing of a particular size: small, medium, or large. Each box contained identical items: same knickers, same shirt, same sweater, same everything; it was the welfare department "uniform" and it marked its wearer as a charity case. Most of the clothes were drab and colorless grays, browns, or mixed blends made from surplus material that had been spun together without concern for the appearance of its final product. Richie hated the welfare clothes; he felt that wearing them was like wearing a sign. Even on the Jackson Elementary schoolyard, when the "uniform" afforded him the protective umbrella of the ward group, he still resented the infringement on his individuality.

Going to Jackson Elementary, and living on Loomis Avenue, had put Richie back within reasonable walking distance of the Damen Avenue branch library, and in the absence of any severe restrictions on his time by Mrs. Raley, he resumed using his library card. Miss Cashman, still there, seemed genuinely pleased to see him again. "Well, Richie, hello!" she said, smiling with her beautiful lips. "Where have you been for so long?"

"My dad got a job in a defense plant on the South Side," Richie said. "We've been living over there."

"Have you changed the address on your library card?" she asked.

"No, ma'am, but I don't have to now," he quickly lied. "We're back living at the same place as before, when I first got my card." Richie did not enjoy lying to the librarian, but trying to explain where he was living, and why, was too complicated. The library, like most everyplace else, had too many rules; it was easier to break them than to obey them.

Resorting again to the ploy of patronizing the contemptible juvenile section, Richie once more began to avail himself of books reserved for grownups. Ranging for the first time beyond the theater arts collection, he discovered a rich new vein of reading: adult fiction. As it happened, he came upon this treasure in the stack marked "Dos-Ell." The first book on the top shelf was *The 42nd Parallel* by John Dos Passos. Thumbing through its pages, Richie was certain he had found a volume of short stories. Segments of writing seemed to be separated from each other by large letters printed like newspaper headlines; here and there, it even seemed to read like a play. Without further consideration, Richie slipped it under his sweater, thankful that the welfare "Small" was *too* small for him, and the "Medium," which he had on, big enough to be roomy, so that the book, the thickest he had ever taken, could be concealed. From the juvenile section, he then took a book at random, something about Jimmy's first train trip or some such bullshit, and checked it out at the counter as he smiled and waved at Miss Cashman.

After supper at Mrs. Raley's, the wards cleared off the table, washed the dishes, and cleaned up the kitchen; Mrs. Raley poured herself another drink and settled into an ancient club chair in her dingy little living room to listen to the radio. One night after Richie had definitely decided not to run away, he went to where she was sitting.

"Can I get a paper route?" he asked. The old woman shook her head.

"Welfare department don't allow foster parents to put wards to work outside the home."

"But what if I want to work?" Richie asked. Mrs. Raley looked balefully at him.

"Are you deaf? I said the welfare department don't allow it. And," she added as an afterthought, turning back to her drink, "they ain't interested in what you *want*."

Richie sighed the best wistful sigh he could generate. "I sure would like to make some spending money. When I lived with my mother, I was making over a dollar a day delivering papers. I gave her half of it."

Mrs. Raley looked back at him. Each time she moved her head, her cheeks slapped like water on the side of a tub. She studied Richie speculatively. "Half of it, huh?"

"Yeah. Half of it. 'Bout fifty cents a day." That was three and a half dollars a week, which, Richie imagined, would buy at least one bottle of whatever Mrs. Raley was sipping.

"Tell me about it," she said.

"I need to get up at five o'clock so I can be at the carrier place to fold papers by five-thirty," he said. "Then I work my route. I'd get back here in time for breakfast."

"How do you know you can get the job?"

"I already asked. There's a morning route open down on Aberdeen Street." He had tried to get an afternoon route, which he would have been able to work without Mrs. Raley knowing about it, but none were available. It nettled him to have to share his earnings with Mrs. Raley; after all, she was not his mother. But half of something was better than all of nothing.

"It wouldn't look good for me if that welfare dame was to find out," Mrs. Raley said pointedly, sipping.

"No way she can find out," Richie assured. "Nobody'll know but you and me. I can stop at the bakery on the way home every morning and pick up the bread for you, an' you can just tell the others that you're getting me up early every morning to do that." A sudden thought occurred to him. "You could even let me off cleaning up the kitchen at night because I do a morning errand."

A perceptive little smile played briefly on Mrs. Raley's lips. "Pretty clever, ain't you, kiddo," she said; it was a statement of fact, not a question, as she assessed him and his proposition with the same leery eye with which she reviewed mankind in general and those within earshot in particular. She finally consented—but with a warning. "You ever blab to the welfare dame and I'll fix you for it, kiddo." Her eyes took on a hateful glint. "There's worse things than the strap and the closet. Lots worse. Remember that, kiddo."

"I will," Richie promised. The menacing look she gave him made his mouth go dry and his stomach churn. But as he left the room he also felt exhilaration stirring in him. He had pulled it off! In one shot at the old woman, he had put himself in position to earn five times as much a *day* as the other wards received in a week—and managed to duck out of the kitchen clean-up to boot.

Things, for a change, seemed to be looking up.

It felt good to get back on a paper route again. Richie liked going out in the quiet, still, early-morning city; somehow it seemed safer as a new day began, as if all the corrupt people who made the city so loathsome at times were not yet awake to practice their misdeeds. It was a fresher, cleaner place too, at that hour before daylight, when the waste of the tenements had not yet begun to reek.

Part of his route, two blocks of it, took him along the edge of Skinner Park, into a well-kept middle-class neighborhood that had not yet relinquished itself to the creeping slums. The greystone buildings facing the park were twelve-flats, with an entry foyer in front and small, individual back porches in the rear. It was on the back porches that Richie tossed the papers. That early—half of his route was worked before daylight—most of the apartments were still dark; only an occasional window was lighted, giving Richie a glimpse now and then of people getting out of bed, moving sleepily about, fumbling around in a kitchen; people in their pajamas or underwear, scratching themselves, stretching, getting *ready:* ready for breakfast, ready for work, ready for the day, ready for life walking upright with their eyes open and their identities in place. This part of it, Richie thought, the part he saw through the windows, was the *secret* part of their lives, the guarded part.

Once, just at first light, when he had paused to watch curiously through a bedroom window as a woman of at least sixty took off her nightgown and began to put on a pair of long bloomers, Richie was startled by someone speaking to him from the adjoining porch. "She's a little old for you, isn't she?" an amused voice asked.

Richie whirled around, feeling his face turn red, and seized the first lie that came to his surprised mind. "I thought the lady said something to me through the window."

He was talking to a woman of about, he thought, his mother's age, not as pretty as his mother but healthier looking. Wearing a chenille robe and felt house slippers, she had very square but not broad shoulders, and high, angular cheekbones under a head of darkish-light hair that was usually called "dishwater" blonde. Richie knew at once that she was not angry or offended; her eyes were as amused as her voice had been.

"Doesn't sound to me like she's saying anything through the window," the woman observed, tilting her head an inch. Richie had the mortifying notion that she was going to laugh at him. But she only stooped to pick up her own paper and get a bottle of milk off the window ledge.

"Guess I was wrong," Richie muttered, and hurried on his way.

Back around front, out of curiosity, he checked his route cards for the woman's name. It was Rozinski. The first name on the card was Walter.

As he pushed his cart away from the building, he shook his head in irritation at himself. Dumb goddamn fuckhead, he silently called himself. Getting caught spying on some old dame older than Mrs. Raley. Real smart, asshole.

It was full daylight when he got to the end of the block. For some reason, just before he turned the corner, he looked back at the building where the Rozinski woman lived.

She was watching him from a second-floor window.

iss Menefee found Richie sitting in a corner of the back porch, knees up, an open book in front of him.

"Hi, Richie," she said, setting her briefcase down. "What are you reading?"

"Library book," he replied. As casually as he could, he closed the book, stood, and put it under his arm, hoping she would not ask to see it and discover that it was from the adult section.

"I didn't know you liked to read," the caseworker said.

"I read all the time," Richie told her, as he might have said he ate, slept, and spoke. Reading had become second nature to him, a natural thing.

"I've got something special for you to read," Miss Menefee said, taking an envelope from her purse and handing it to him.

"Thanks." It was a letter from his mother—more accurately, a note. One page from a dime store lined tablet. *Dear Richie: How are you? I am fine. How is school? I hope you are getting good grades. Be a good boy and write to me when you have time. Love, Mother.*

The letters he wrote back to her were pretty much the same. It was awkward: mother and son in the same city, probably only a few miles apart, but not allowed to see each other or even talk on the telephone, only allowed to exchange hand-carried letters.

"Here," Miss Menefee said, handing him a stick of Juicy Fruit gum when he had finished reading the note and put it into a pocket. Grace Menefee was always giving him something: chewing gum, a dime, a new handkerchief: "A man should always carry a clean handkerchief," she told him once. It was obvious that she had a special feeling for Richie; she was forever touching him: brushing back his usually uncombed hair, wiping a spot of dirt from his face, straightening his collar, tucking the end of his belt back through a loop. Delighted that he had settled in at Mrs. Raley's, she constantly praised him for making her proud of him by not running away again.

"I want to come and get you Saturday afternoon and take you someplace special," she told him. "I think you'll like it."

"Okay," he said, shrugging as if it were fine with him. Actually, his devious mind was racing; there was an afternoon paper route opening up and it had been promised to him. If he got it before Saturday, he probably would not be home when Miss Menefee came for him. He would have to tell her he forgot, or something; he could not miss the chance for an afternoon route: it would mean sixty cents more a day—and he *didn't* have to cut Mrs. Raley in for half, because she wouldn't know about it.

When Grace Menefee left that day, Mrs. Raley came out on the porch and eyed Richie suspiciously. "What was all the talk between you and that welfare dame?"

"She was just telling me about my mother."

"Your old lady's the one who's knocked up, ain't she?"

"Yeah." Richie sat back down, opening his book again.

"Just you be careful what you say to that welfare dame," Mrs. Raley warned. "She ain't to be trusted."

"Okay."

You either, he thought, as he scanned the page of the book to find where he had left off.

Or anybody else, his street-trained mind added without consideration.

On Saturday Miss Menefee took him to a two-story institutional looking building on Jackson Boulevard near Western. A sign on the front read: OFF-THE-STREET CLUB.

"What's this?" he asked.

"It's a club for boys. Some very generous gentlemen support it so that boys like yourself can have a place to go in your spare time."

"I don't have no spare time," Richie said.

"Oh, you do so," Grace Menefee chided, mussing the head of hair she normally combed. "You have time to read; that's spare time. Here in the club, you can do other things too. They have a room for building model planes and boats, a music room if you want to learn to play an instrument, a game room where you can play checkers and dominoes and put together jigsaw puzzles—"

"I need all my spare time to read," Richie protested, lagging back. Grace Menefee tugged him onward.

"There's even a library," she revealed.

"There is?" Richie's interest swelled.

"Yes. Small but very nice. The lady in charge of it is a friend of mine. I'll introduce you to her."

"Does it have a juvenile section?" Richie asked distrustfully.

"Not exactly juvenile, I don't think," Grace Menefee said. "More adolescent, I'd say."

"What's 'adolescent'?"

"Youthful but not childish. I'm sure there'll be something to interest you."

She led him along a hall past several of the rooms she had described, to a one-room library at the very rear of the first floor. There were no island stacks, just open bookshelves along all four walls, and a librarian's desk in the center of the room.

"Richie, this is Miss Hovey, my friend," Grace Menefee introduced. "Paula, this is Richie, also my friend . . . I think." She punched Richie lightly on the arm and he threw her an annoyed look. Sometimes Miss Menefee carried the palsy-walsy stuff too far; it could be embarrassing if other kids were around, like being a teacher's favorite kid in class, which was next to death. "Paula, you'll be pleased to know that Richie's a bona fide, confirmed reader."

"Swell," Paula Hovey said.

To Richie, the librarian, who had burnt-blonde hair, bore a striking resemblance to the actress Dorothy McGuire, whom he had recently seen in the movie *A Tree Grows in Brooklyn.*

"Maybe Richie would like to take part in our book report contest," the actress lookalike suggested. "Have you ever written a book report, Richie?"

"No," Richie said, shrugging and shaking his head, "I just read books; I don't do nothing else."

"Do you know what a book report is?"

"No, ma'am."

"What grade are you in?"

"Six-A."

In an aside to Grace Menefee that Richie managed to catch, Paula Hovey said, "Christ, some educational system we've got." Then, back to Richie: "A book report, Richie, is where you sit down after you've finished reading a book, and you write out what the book was about, what you learned from it, and whether you liked it or not, and why. Do you think you might enjoy doing that?"

"I don't think so," Richie demurred. He put on his most ingratiating smile for Miss Menefee, so as not to get her upset with him. "I guess I'll keep on just reading."

"First prize for the best book report every month," Paula Hovey said pointedly, "is a trip downtown to a bookstore to pick out any book you want. Under ten dollars, that is."

The smile vanished from Richie's face. "Pick out to *keep?*"

"To keep," she confirmed. "The only requirement is that the book you report on has to come from our own library. If you want to pick one out, I'll be happy to give you an O.T.S.C. library card."

"Okay," Richie said, excitement generated, "I'll do it." A book to *keep!* What a swell prize! As he turned toward the shelves, Grace Menefee touched his arm.

"Richie, let me pick a book for you," she appealed, "please. I want you to read a book that was my very favorite when I was your age, or a little older maybe. Paula, do you have *Ivanhoe?*"

"Of course." She walked toward the shelves.

Richie frowned. He would have preferred to select his own, but did not protest. Miss Menefee, after all, had been pretty good to him, and was also helping his mother. He decided, without being able to put it into words, to indulge the devoted caseworker.

He just hoped the book about some guy named Ivan would be good.

Richie got the afternoon paper route, which was the same route he delivered in the morning, except there were only about half as many papers. On the first afternoon that he worked the new route, one of his *Herald-American* deliveries was to the Rozinskis, who got two papers a day. When he got to their back porch, Mrs. Rozinski was sitting in a wicker rocker, smoking a cigarette and thumbing through a *True Story* magazine.

"Everybody pull your shades down," she said wryly as Richie came up the stairs.

"I told you," he instantly defended himself, "I thought the lady said something to me through the window."

Mrs. Rozinski looked at him with that same amused expression that he remembered from their initial encounter. Since that incident, he had virtually crept up to her porch for the morning delivery, then hurried away, thankful at not having run into her again. Each time he left the block, however, he made a point of looking back to see if she was again watching him from her front window. Twice, to his surprise, she had been.

"How come you look at me out your window in the mornings?" he challenged, deciding to go on the offensive. He was far enough away to be able to get down the stairs if she should come out of the chair after him. But some intuitive feeling told him she would not. "How come, huh?" he demanded, seeing a smile play at her lips.

"Maybe I think you're cute," she said.

"I ain't 'cute,' " Richie rebutted. "Girls are cute."

"Oh, my. In that case, what do they call a boy who's nice looking? You're not old enough to be called handsome. How old are you, anyway?"

"Fourteen."

"I'll bet."

"I am!"

"If you're fourteen, my name's Cleopatra."

"Is it?"

"No." She paused a beat, as if deciding some minor point. "It's Frances."

"Frances, huh?" He tried to suppress a grin but could not. "That's better than Cleopatra."

They fell silent for a moment, woman and boy, she looking up from her chair, the same way, he realized, that Mrs. Raley had done while considering his proposition regarding the paper route. A little ill-at-ease under her scrutiny, Richie looked off at the adjoining porch, and suddenly remembered that it was where he had been caught peeking at the old woman, and quickly shifted his glance elsewhere. "I gotta get going now," he finally mumbled, moving toward the stairs.

"Hey, what's your name?" Frances asked as he started down. Pausing, he told her. "Well, Richie," she said in playful reproach, "don't you think you should leave my paper?"

Knowing his face was fiery red, Richie trudged back up to the porch and handed her the paper.

At first irate and indignant over Grace Menefee's choice of a book for him, Richie nevertheless quickly cleared the chasm between John Dos Passos and Sir Walter Scott, and almost at once began to enjoy *Ivanhoe*. Vastly different from anything he had ever read before, the colorful, exciting story of Ivanhoe's quest for Rowena, Richard the Lion-Hearted's struggle to regain his rightful throne, and the heroic, suspenseful rescue of Rebecca as she was about to be burned at the stake, plus the added surprise appearance of Robin Hood, whom Richie was familiar with in the form of Errol Flynn on the screen, served to introduce him to romantic historical fiction. It was not as easy to read as Dos Passos, Kingsley, and the *Saturday Evening Post* authors; the writing was very formal, almost artificially so in places, but the *story* was there, and that was what always either impressed or disappointed Richie.

The minute he finished the novel, Richie got out notebook and pencil to begin his first book report. Knowing nothing of format or style, he guided himself by Paula Hovey's advice: tell what the book was about, what he learned from it, whether he liked it or not, and why. Deciding to approach those elements in reverse order, because it seemed more logical that way, he began: "I liked the book Ivanhoe. I liked it because it was a good story about a nice guy who helped his friends when they needed help and who proved to everybody that he was good enough to marry the girl he wanted to marry. The way the story went was like this. Ivanhoe had went off to war with King Richard because he couldn't have Rowena for his wife. One day he came back, wearing a disguise so nobody knew it was him . . ."

He wrote five pages describing the highpoints of the story. At the end of that narrative, he added: "The things I learned from Ivanhoe are a lot. I learned about the way knights of old fought on horses with lances. I learned that in those days if you were a lot smarter than other people, sometimes they said you were a witch. I learned that it don't matter if you are a king because there are good kings and bad kings. I learned that Robin Hood is not only in the movies but in a book too. I learned that people talked funny a long time ago. That is what I learned."

The judges of the book report contest were the Off-the-Street-Club librarian Paula Hovey, and two others: the man who served as director of the club, and a lady who taught high school English and worked at the club as a volunteer two nights a week. They were unanimous in their choice of Richie's report on *Ivanhoe* as the best of some two dozen turned in that month. On the Saturday morning following their decision, Paula Hovey took Richie downtown on the Jackson Boulevard bus to a bookstore to select his prize. Grace Menefee, who said at least a dozen times that she was "tickled to death" that Richie had won, accompanied them.

"You know, Richie," she suggested ebulliently, "if you wanted to, you could get a copy of *Ivanhoe* for your prize. My favorite book and the very one that you wrote your report on. What do you think of that idea?"

"I'd rather pick out a book I haven't read yet," Richie replied logically.

"Let him make his own choice, Grace," Paula Hovey urged. "What kind of books do you like best, Richie?"

"Cowboy books."

"You mean the old West, like that? All right, let's see what we can find."

In the American History–Western Frontier section, Richie scrutinized a shelf of books until he found a familiar name: Walter Noble Burns. The title of the book was *Tombstone: The Town Too Tough To Die.*

"I'll take this one," Richie said.

After glancing at the price, Paula Hovey said, "It's yours."

"What in the world is *that* about?" Grace Menefee asked, with a hint of contempt.

" 'Bout a town in Arizona where Wyatt Earp and Doc Holliday shot it out with a bunch of outlaws at the O.K. Corral. I seen a movie about it, called *Frontier Marshal*."

"A movie," Grace Menefee said. "I might have known. I suppose John Garfield was in it?"

Richie almost laughed. "John Garfield don't play cowboys! Randolph Scott was in it."

After Paula Hovey paid for the book, she handed the bag to Richie and he walked proudly out of the store with it under his arm. It was a very special moment for him.

His own book.

Richie figured it out. One book per month, twelve a year. By the time he was grown, he would have about a hundred books. And all he had to do was write the best book report every month. Which not only seemed easy, but fun also. The only drawback was that the report had to be on a book from the Off-the-Street Club library, and that selection, for Richie, was extremely limited.

"Would you like me to help you pick something, Richie?" Paula Hovey asked when she saw him scanning the shelves. "I promise," she added at once, "it won't be another *Ivanhoe*. Although you *did* say you liked it. But I think I know one you'll enjoy even better."

"What is it?" Richie asked, a little warily.

Paula Hovey handed him a book and Richie read the title. *Life on the Mississippi*. The author's name was Mark Twain.

"I think you'll like this gentleman's writing better than Sir Walter Scott," Paula Hovey said.

Richie did. He found Mark Twain's collection of reminiscences about the mighty Mississippi River and its steamboat traffic one of the most vivid and interesting books he had yet read; not from the standpoint of *story*—it had none of the thought-provoking powers, nothing to make him stare contemplatively at a page to digest its meaning, that the works of Dos Passos and Kingsley contained—but for sheer pleasure, utter entertainment, pure *fun* reading, it was like nothing he had seen. When he returned it to Paula Hovey, after finishing it and writing the book report on it, he did so with a grin on his face.

"Liked it, huh?" she said smugly.

When his book report on *Life on the Mississippi* won first place the second month, Paula again took him to the Loop bookstore, this time without Grace Menefee, who was working that Saturday. Richie went directly to the same section of the store and chose a book called *The Saga of Billy the Kid*, by the same author, Walter Noble Burns, who wrote his previous prize book and whom he admired so much. Paula Hovey smiled understandingly at his choice. "You really like your cowboys, don't you, Richie," she said. On the way back to the West Side on the bus, the librarian told him, "Let me know when you're ready for another book to read for a report; I have a very good one in mind for you. Have you ever heard of a writer named Jack London?"

The book Paula Hovey checked out to him a week later was *The Call of the Wild*. As soon as Richie started reading it, he knew he was going to like Jack London better than Mark Twain. London's story of the great sled dog, Buck, and the dog's adventures, hardships, suffering, and triumphs in frontier Alaska of 1897 stirred in Richie for the first time a feeling of kinship to animals. The big St. Bernard—coincidentally having the same name as Richie's dead movie hero—lived a life not markedly unlike Richie's own existence: a loner animal passed from owner to owner, taken advantage of by some, befriended by others, but always, when it got down to fundamentals, having to do for himself or do without. It amazed Richie how closely parallel were human and animal problems at times, and he was fascinated by London's treatment not only of the actions and physical feelings of Buck, but the dog's thoughts as well.

The Call of the Wild was another glorious reading experience for Richie, and following it he produced what Paula Hovey said was his best book report yet. For the third month in succession he won first prize and was taken downtown to the bookstore.

"Can I get any kind of book I want?" he asked.

"Sure, as long as it's under ten dollars," Paula Hovey said. "What kind of book do you want?"

"One of those kinds that has maps in it," Richie told her.

"You mean an atlas?" She took him to the geography section and showed him one. "Like this?" As she handed it to him, she noticed that the price was twelve dollars and fifty cents.

"Yeah," Richie said in wonder, examining its colorful pages. "Yeah, this is what I want."

Paula Hovey watched him with delight, and even a little affection. "Why do you want an atlas, Richie?" she asked curiously.

"I want to be able to find where all the places are that I read about," he said. "Tombstone, Arizona, and Skagway, Alaska, and St. Louis, Missouri, and England, and all the other places. I can't go to all those places, but if I read about them and then put my finger on a map where they are, it'll be *kind* of like going there. Sort of."

"It sure will, Richie," Paula Hovey agreed. "Sort of." She bought the atlas for him, using two-fifty of her own money to make up the difference in price.

"I'll save up and pay you back," Richie promised.

"You don't have to," Paula told him.

"I really will," Richie swore. "I want to, honest."

Walking back to the bus stop, Paula instinctively gave him a hug.

A week later, Richie came into the Off-the-Street Club library one evening and asked Paula Hovey, "What do you think I ought to read for my next book report?"

"Well, let's see," Paula mused. "Have you ever read any books by Zane Grey?"

"Nope," Richie replied confidently. He knew the name of *every* author of *every* book he had ever read.

Paula got a book for him. "This is *Riders of the Purple Sage*," she said.

"That was the name of a movie," Richie told her, "with George O'Brien. Is this a book about the movie?"

Paula shook her head. "It was a book *before* it was a movie, Richie. They made the movie *from* the book."

"Jeez, I didn't know they did that!" he exclaimed. "I thought they only made movies from real stories, like about Wyatt Earp and Billy the Kid. Real people like that."

"No," Paula kept shaking her head, "many, many movies are made from novels. Fiction. Made-up stories."

"Jeez," Richie said again. He mulled over this new knowledge all the way home, wondering if Zane Grey's book was going to be exactly like George O'Brien's movie. He recalled that it had been a pretty good picture. O'Brien played a wandering cowboy named Lassiter who came into town, fell in love, exposed a crooked judge, wiped out the outlaws who were in charge, and took his girlfriend off to live happily ever after. When Richie read the story as written in the book, he found it to be faithful in almost every way—in fact, more so in places because there were many more details brought out that had not been included in the movie. This was Richie's first experience of seeing a movie first, then reading the book; he later questioned whether it was good or not, doing it that way. For one thing, he wondered how he would have pictured the characters if he had not seen the movie. Certainly he would not have imagined George O'Brien in the role of Lassiter; probably he would have visualized him more as Zane Grey described him. Now Richie would never know; Lassiter would forever in his mind be George O'Brien.

When he wrote his report on the book, in the section of whether he liked the story or not, Richie dealt with that aspect of it; he concluded that he *had* liked it, but wondered if he might have liked it *more* without seeing the movie first. Paula Hovey, when she read the report, was amazed at the depth with which her amazing young reader had considered that curious perspective. The report, she said, was as good or better than most high school students could have written. Richie, pleased as could be, smiled and told her he was going to select a Zane Grey book as his next prize.

"I'm afraid there won't be any more prize books for you, Richie," Paula told him quietly, briefly biting her lips as if hating the words.

"Huh?" Richie was not certain he had heard right.

"The director of the club suggested that we limit each reader to winning three times. The high school teacher who is the other judge agreed with him. So you won't be able to win again."

Richie stared at her in disbelief. "Not even if my report is the best?" He could not believe it.

"You see, Richie, the whole purpose of the program is to encourage young people to use the library, to read," Paula Hovey said. "If the same person keeps winning every month, it won't be long until the others lose interest . . ."

"So I can't win even if my report is the best?" Richie pressed.

"Winning isn't the purpose of the contest," Paula tried to explain. "It's only the incentive; it's what we use to get kids interested. The real purpose is to get kids interested in reading, and to help them learn to understand and remember what they read—"

"It ain't right to change the rules like that," Richie said, tight-lipped.

"It's right for the other kids," Paula defended, a little lamely.

"Do you think anybody's gonna write a better book report than me?" he challenged flatly.

Paula shifted her eyes to the floor, unable to look at him when she answered. "No."

"Then I should win," he said. Paula shook her head.

"No. For the good of *all* the kids, you shouldn't."

Glaring at her, Richie held out a hand. "I want my report back," he said.

"Richie, you can still turn in reports," Paula told him almost pleadingly. "It's what *you* get out of it that's important—"

"I want it back," he reiterated, eyes fixed on her unblinkingly, hand steady.

Rather than suffer his indicting stare a moment longer, Paula got the report from her desk and handed it to him. Slowly and carefully, Richie tore the pages in half, then into quarters, and dropped them into the librarian's wire wastebasket.

Then he walked out.

Miss Menefee was waiting for him when he got back to Mrs. Raley's. She was sitting in the dingy little living room, talking with Mrs. Raley. So incensed and infuriated was he, that he walked past them without noticing they were there. The dirty fucking cheaters, his mind seethed. He had planned to win enough books to have his own personal library. Lousy bastards, changing the goddamn rules—

"Hey, Richie," Miss Menefee said as he stormed down the hall, "how about a hello?"

Stalking into the living room, Richie said, "I didn't see you."

"What's the matter?" Miss Menefee asked, seeing his angry, set young face.

"Nothing."

"Yes, there is. I can tell. What is it?"

"Nothing," Richie insisted.

It was his John Garfield voice; the caseworker knew better than to press him. "Suit yourself," she said. "Come here."

He went over and stood in front of her. Mrs. Raley was observing him suspiciously. Richie kept his eyes down, looking at neither of them.

"I've got some good news for you," Miss Menefee said cheerfully. "You're going to go back and live with your mother."

"Hi there, sugar!"

His mother hugged him to her and planted several dry kisses on his cheeks and forehead, while Richie grinned shyly and tried not to act too dippy in front of Miss Menefee, who he was convinced thought he was tough. "You look so *good*, sugar!" Chloe exclaimed. "And how you've *grown! My good-ness!*"

The apartment Miss Menefee had found was in the Parkside Residential Hotel on Hamlin Avenue, just across from Garfield Park. It was the usual two rooms: living room–dining room–Pullman kitchen combination with a tiny bedroom, and a bathroom down the hall shared with three other apartments. The place was bare, sparsely furnished, but not shabby like Mrs. Raley's. Glancing in a corner, Richie saw a folding cot and knew that he was back to sleeping in the kitchen again.

"It's so nice being together!" Chloe gushed, continuing to hug him when-ever he stopped looking around the place long enough for her to grab him.

When Miss Menefee finally got ready to leave, she said, "Richie, you'll start at Tilton Elementary tomorrow; here's your transfer. And Chloe, don't forget, you start work at Walgreen's lunch counter Thursday morning at seven-thirty—and *don't* be late. I'll be around next week to see how you're getting along."

After the caseworker left, Chloe said, "How about a Coca-Cola, sugar?"

She got two bottles from a little countertop refrigerator and opened them. "Coca-Colas are on the list of things I wasn't supposed to buy with our welfare check," she confessed, "but I thought we deserved to celebrate. Anyway, you ought to *see* the things on that list—lipstick, cigarettes, magazines—I tell you!" When they sat down with their soft drinks, Chloe asked, "Well, how do you think I look, sugar?"

"Nice," Richie said, shrugging.

"A lot slimmer than the last time we were together, huh?" Chloe sighed wistfully. "Well, Richie, I had the baby. A little girl. Pretty little thing." Chloe's eyes began to blink rapidly. "They said they'd find her a real nice home." She cleared her throat and sniffed once, then said, "Anyway, it's just you and me again, sugar. I think we can get along all right, don't you?"

"Sure," Richie said, but it was not his usual confident, cocky "Sure." It was uncertain, feeble, but he knew it was what his mother wanted to hear.

Inside, Richie felt wary. He was glad to see his mother again, glad she was finished with the baby thing, glad that she seemed to be all right after her ordeal. But on consideration, he was not at all certain he was glad to be back with her. With the exception of the dirty bastards who changed the rules at the Off-the-Street Club, he'd had the rest of his life pretty much in order: his understanding with Mrs. Raley that allowed him to work and earn money; his affiliation with the other wards at Jackson Elementary that protected him on the schoolyard, his own bed at Mrs. Raley's, along with decent food and a comparatively unrestricted routine that allowed him to go to the library. It had not been a bad life.

Now he didn't know.

Looking at his mother across the table, he could not help remembering how many times she had fucked up their lives. In his mind she had done it by being with Jack Smart when his dad came home from prison; by having George Zangara's kid in her when Johnny Eaton came back from the war; and by always spending their money on her "medicine" instead of other things they needed. Stan Klein had once said to Richie, "You can't never depend on your parents; they'll let you down every time." At first Richie thought Stan was talking about fathers: the ones who always seemed to walk away and leave their kids to be raised by women. But later Richie came to learn that Stan meant both parents. Now, starting a new life with his mother, Richie for the first time understood Stan's negative philosophy.

Sharing their illicitly purchased Coca-Colas together, Richie realized, also for the first time, that he did not trust his mother.

His new school, Tilton Elementary, was not as bad as others Richie had attended. Living at the Parkside Residential Hotel, he was just inside the boundary line of a West Side neighborhood that became progressively better as it extended away from Garfield Park. Had they lived one block farther east, he would have been back in one of the tough, racially mixed schools on the Lower West Side, below Kedzie Avenue. Tilton was almost entirely white—which did not mean it was without bullies.

At recess the first day, a husky, well-built kid named Danny Provo came up to him on the schoolyard, accompanied by the usual entourage of admirers, or at least prudent followers.

"Hey, you want to fight?" Danny Provo asked.

Richie, sitting alone against the building, shrugged. "What for?"

"To see who's toughest," Danny Provo said.

"You're toughest," Richie conceded, hoping against hope that would be the end of it.

"You got to prove it," the other boy said, nudging Richie's leg with his foot. "Come on, get up. Let's fight."

"I don't want to fight."

"You chicken?" Danny Provo sneered.

"I'm not chicken," Richie said. "I just don't know how to fight good."

"Let's see, then," Danny said. He nudged Richie's leg a little harder. "Get up."

"I don't want to fight," Richie said firmly. Nearby he heard several girls giggle. Glancing over, he saw five of them standing in a group, watching. One of them, Richie noticed, was not laughing with the others.

"Get up or I'll kick your teeth out," Danny Provo threatened.

Across the schoolyard was a recess monitor, one of the kids from eighth grade, wearing a white belt with a lanyard over one shoulder. Richie knew he could make a break for it, attracting the monitor's attention by yelling. That would save him from taking a licking, but it would also label him a chicken throughout the school, fair game for everyone. Richie did not feel that he was a coward; he thought he had guts. But he knew he could not fight, knew he was skinnier and weaker than most kids his age, and was resigned to that. On rare occasions when he had access to a weapon—the knife he threatened Johnny Eaton with, the shoe he was ready to use on Dave to deter his sexual advances—Richie would face a confrontation ready to fight. But here on the schoolyard, he had only his fists.

"I said get up!" Danny Provo ordered, kicking him in the thigh.

Richie leaped to his feet, actually startling Provo enough to make him jump back a step. But when he saw the uncertainty, the fear, in Richie's eyes, he immediately resumed his bully scowl, moved back in, and hit Richie in the jaw. Richie tried to cover up, protect his face with his forearms, but Danny

Provo hit him with a left in the stomach that caused him to drop his arms, then drove a fist to his eye.

"C'mon, fight!" Danny Provo snarled.

Richie stood his ground. He did not run and he did not cry, but he would not fight back either. Based on his past experience in similar situations, he knew there was little chance of getting hit more than two or three times.

"Why don't you leave him alone, Danny!" a girl's voice yelled from the sidelines. Glancing over, Richie saw that it was the girl who had not been laughing at his predicament.

"Yeah, lay off him, Danny," one of the bully's followers said. "The guy can't fight."

Danny Provo made a big show of wanting to punch Richie again, but allowed two of his friends to hold him back. Finally he just gave Richie a shove and swaggered away, taking nearly everyone with him.

Richie sat back on the ground, up against the building. Staring down at nothing, he waited for the school bell to ring that would end recess. Outwardly, he was stoic. Inside, he was crying in humiliation.

Goddamn his father for not staying around to teach him how to fight!

Richie kept the two paper routes he'd had at Mrs. Raley's, even though it meant he had to get up earlier and ride a streetcar four times a day in order to work both routes. It cost him twenty cents a day for carfare, but he still came out ahead financially because now he did not have to pay half a dollar to Mrs. Raley, and his mother was not taking any of his income.

On the day of his encounter with Danny Provo, by the time Richie was working his afternoon route, his left eye was puffy and discoloring. Frances Rozinski was again on her back porch when he delivered her paper.

"Get caught looking in a window?" she cracked. Turning red Richie put her paper on the doorstep and turned to stalk away. Frances grabbed his sleeve. "Wait a minute," she said in a completely different voice. "Look, I'm sorry. I don't know what's wrong with me. I shouldn't be needling a kid like you. Here, let me take a look at your eye—"

"It's okay," Richie said, trying to pull away.

"No, it's not, it's got a little cut on it. Have you washed it?"

"No, I came right from school to my route."

"Come on in the kitchen," Frances Rozinski said, "let's just dab a wet rag on it."

Richie allowed her to lead him by the sleeve into her kitchen, which he saw at once was as neat and clean as he remembered the Hubbard kitchen being. At the sink, Frances ran cold water over one end of a hand towel and gently touched it to his swollen eye. As she ministered to him, with her hand at his face, he saw a starkly white, ropy scar running horizontally across the underside of her wrist. From somewhere—some movie he had seen, some book or story he had read—the words, "She slit her wrists," surfaced in his mind.

"How did it happen?" Frances asked, causing Richie to raise his eyes to meet hers, which were the blackest, deepest eyes he had ever seen; they made him think of bulletholes in a whitewashed fence.

"I got in a fight at school," Richie mumbled.

"I'd hate to see what the other guy looks like," Frances said by way of compliment. "Bet you're pretty tough, huh?"

Grunting softly, Richie looked away. Frances stopped dabbing and studied him for a moment, her expression becoming cheerless, almost sad. She put a knuckle under his chin and drew his face back toward her. "Will you let me put some iodine on the cut? To keep it from getting infected?" Richie shrugged his indifference and Frances got a small red bottle with a skull-and-crossbones on it from the bathroom. "It'll sting," she warned. He shrugged again. When she touched his cut with the glass applicator, he did not flinch. "See, I knew you were tough," she praised.

Frances gave Richie a drink of water and they exchanged smiles on her back porch as he picked up her paper and handed it to her.

"Thanks, Mrs. Rozinski," he said as he started to leave. She gave him a severe look.

"Frances," she said. "You call me Frances."

At the corner he turned back and saw her in the front window. Smiling, he waved and she waved back.

When he had two dollars and fifty cents saved up, Richie swiped an envelope from Woolworth's and sealed the money inside. He went down to the Off-the-Street Club and hung around the model-building room, from which he could see the library door, until Paula Hovey stepped out to the girls' bathroom. While she was gone, he put the envelope on her desk. As he left the club, he thought: Now I don't owe this fucking place nothing.

Several days later, when Miss Menefee dropped by to see how Richie and Chloe were doing, she asked Richie why he had stopped going to the Off-the-Street Club. Because Miss Menefee and Paula Hovey were friends, Richie was certain Miss Menefee already knew the reason. When she asked him, he remembered Stan Klein's advice on adult fair play. "It don't never do no good to tell a grownup that something ain't fair. Grownups is always *positive* that they're fair; nothing a kid can say or do is gonna change their mind.''

So Richie did not even try. He merely shrugged and said, "I'm working two paper routes, morning and afternoon. I don't have time for the club no more."

"Anymore," his mother, sitting with them, corrected. Then she changed the subject by saying, "Listen, Miss Menefee, is it all right with you if I change jobs? I just can't stand that lunch counter another day. There's a ladies' shoe store up on Pulaski where I can get a job as a salesclerk. It's just waiting on customers, I wouldn't have to work the cash register or make change at all; the manager does that. You said I wasn't supposed to change jobs without asking. So is it all right?"

Richie did not hear Miss Menefee's answer because he took the opportunity to slip unobtrusively away.

Richie soon found a new outlet for his literary bent: school. His seventh-grade teacher at Tilton, Miss White, put more emphasis on reading and English composition than any other subjects, believing that those skills provided the foundation of all other learning. So ardently did she support that theory that she gave extra credit for book reports toward the overall class grade. A student could earn a D in arithmetic, geography, history, and science, but still receive an A class grade by turning in book reports. Which is what Richie began to do. Not that he failed any other subject; he liked geography very much and usually did A work in that subject; history and science he tolerated, getting a C in each; arithmetic he found dull and tedious, rarely raising his grade above a D. But because of his extra-credit book reports, his final grade in lower seventh was an A, and in upper seventh he was well on his way to a similar grade.

Richie's only competitor was Linda, the girl who had not laughed at his humiliation by Danny Provo. Linda was plain-but-somehow-pretty, much, Richie thought, like Grace Menefee. Not one of the better off students in their class, she lived toward the poor edge of the district, not far from Richie. While obviously not as poor as Richie or on welfare, Linda nevertheless was invariably the poorest *looking* of any group of girls she was in.

"I liked your report on *Last of the Mohicans*," she said to him one day as they were walking out at three o'clock. It was Miss White's practice to read aloud to the class several times a week those reports which she considered of particular merit. This was done with the purpose of interesting others in her class in books she hoped they might then read. Although she never announced which student's report she was reading, more often than not it was either Richie's or Linda's, as each could tell by the other's expression. Before long, they were able to recognize each other's reports merely by listening.

"I liked yours the other day too," Richie replied to her compliment. "That one about the Sunny-something Farm."

"*Rebecca of Sunnybrook Farm*," Linda said. She gave him a wry look. "Since you didn't bother to remember the title, I don't guess you plan to read it."

Richie shrugged. "Prob'ly not. I'm reading *Moby Dick* right now."

"What's *that?*" she asked, recoiling slightly as if it might not be wholly acceptable. Seeing her reaction, Richie shrugged again.

"It's about sailors," he said vaguely, deciding against trying to explain Captain Ahab to her.

Gradually, although their reading tastes differed widely, they seemed to sense that they were kindred spirits because they *liked* to read—and in that sense, in their classroom anyway, they were unique.

"Has Miss White ever talked to you about *why* you like to read?" Linda asked him one afternoon. Richie shook his head. "She has to me," Linda continued. "She says she thinks it's because I have a creative mind. She says I should think about becoming a writer myself." Turning a penetrating gaze on him, she asked solemnly, "Have you ever thought about becoming a writer?"

"I got enough to do thinking about my paper routes," Richie replied. "Anyway, I don't read for no reason like that."

"Then why do you read?"

"To get away," Richie said quietly.

"What do you mean? To get away from what?"

"From me," Richie told her, looking away, feeling embarrassed. "To get away from what I am, who I am, mostly where I am. When I'm reading, I forget those things for a little while." They stopped at the corner where they customarily separated. Habitually, self-consciously, he shrugged. "Kind of a dumb reason, huh?"

"It is *not*," Linda assured him passionately. She put a hand on his arm. "Know something?"

"What?"

"I really like you, Richie." Quickly kissing him on the cheek, Linda hurried on her way.

Blushing deeply, Richie hustled off in the other direction, hoping nobody had seen *that*.

□

Chloe tried at the shoe store just as earnestly as she had tried at the lunch counter, but she did not find herself suited to clerking any more than she had found herself suited to waitressing. She tried other occupations as well, failing at all of them. Her reasons were many: customers didn't treat her right; the work was too hard on her feet; co-workers didn't treat her right; the work was too hard on her back; *managers* didn't treat her right; the work was too hard on *something*. In lieu of any specific reason, she utilized her old standby: "I can't stand this job another day; it is driving me *crazy!*"

For a time she did fairly well as a hotel maid, but after several instances of small items reported missing by guests—earrings, a change purse left in a drawer, a pre-war silk scarf—she was let go. Coming home in a paroxysm of indignation, she vehemently denied to Miss Menefee that she had committed the thefts.

"The nerve!" she ranted. "I mean, the *nerve!* Why, that housekeeping manager didn't even question the Negro maids. *They're* the ones who probably did it! Of course, why should I expect him to question *them;* he's nothing but a Filipino himself. Birds of a feather, you know how that is."

"Chloe," Miss Menefee finally told her unequivocally, "you are going to have to settle down and keep a job. The department has a limit as to how long it will continue to supplement your income. This business of working a week or two, then spending the next week or two looking for a new job does not look good in your file. If you were unable to work, it would be different—"

"Did I tell you I hurt my back?" Chloe seized on the possibility. "It was at the hotel—"

"Chloe, please," Miss Menefee shook her head emphatically, "I haven't the time for this. "You can work—and we both know it."

Before Miss Menefee could locate another job for her, Chloe found one on her own. "I am now an outside saleslady," she announced loftily to Richie one night.

"Selling what?" he asked.

"Greeting cards. Boxed and assorted."

"Door to door?"

"Yes, certainly. I'm not going to stand on the street corner to sell them. There should be a good market for greeting cards now that the war restrictions on the paper have been lifted and they can be made again."

Richie doubted it, but he said nothing. He was not surprised that the job lasted only a week. Chloe's idea of it was that at each house or apartment she visited, she would be asked inside, invited to sit down, allowed to show her samples, and be given an order. The reality of it was that she was rarely asked to come in, that a vast proportion of the job was walking, walking, walking, knocking on endless doors, ringing endless doorbells, constantly being refused and rejected, most times rudely turned away before she could even complete the introductory presentation she had been taught when she was hired.

"God, people are lowdown mean sometimes," she lamented to Richie after she quit.

Richie only grunted softly. I could tell *her* a few things about lowdown mean, he thought.

When she was between jobs, Chloe waxed melancholy about the infant she had given up. "You should have seen her, Richie. She was the prettiest little thing—great big eyes and a mop of black hair. I named her Betty, did I tell you that? Oh, yes, I had a right to name her, even if I was giving her up." Biting her lip, Chloe often had to hold back tears. "Gee, Richie, it would have been nice if we could have kept her. You would have been crazy about your little sister . . ."

Sure, Richie thought, that's just what I need: a little halfbreed kid to have to worry about. He had learned the word "halfbreed" from reading Zane Grey and other Western writers. Whenever Miss Menefee visited and Chloe asked about the baby, Richie was always enormously relieved to hear the caseworker say, "Now, you know I can't discuss the baby with you, Chloe. She has a good home, that's all I can say." Even with that continuous reassurance, Richie nevertheless lived with the nagging suspicion that somehow the baby would come back, replace him, and he would have to go back to foster homes.

It was a long time before he stopped worrying about it.

Richie began to pay attention to his mother's physical appearance. In the past he had noticed not so much how she looked but how she acted. Depending on whether she was using paregoric or not, she had been either alert and active, or lazy and lethargic; depending on whether there was a man in her life, she had been content and cheerful, outwardly at least, or anxious and afraid. But her personal appearance, insofar as Richie saw, seemed always the same. Now, with Frances Rozinski, the woman on his paper route, as a comparison, Richie became aware that his mother had changed.

From the beginning, Richie had thought Frances and his mother were approximately the same age. For some reason they *seemed* the same age. His mother, he knew, was several years past thirty; he vaguely recalled a birthday some time earlier when Estelle had made a crack about something being "all downhill" after thirty. Frances, he was sure, was probably also past thirty.

And while Frances was not as pretty as his mother had been, she was prettier now simply because she seemed so healthy and fresh, while his mother seemed to be . . . withering.

Richie did not attempt to figure out why his mother's looks were fading. His mind was too immature to reconcile two long periods of addiction, the emotional stress of her relationships with Richmond, Jack Smart, Johnny, and George, and the more recent trauma of having to give up her baby, with the fact that she was becoming gaunt and old looking beyond her years. More significantly, it did not occur to Richie that there might be a new reason for her deterioration—or at least a new aspect to an old reason. Richie was not around Chloe a great deal of the time; on school days he was up and gone very early to work his morning route, did not return for breakfast because of the time-consuming streetcar rides, after school went directly to his afternoon route, then usually to the library, where he sometimes met Linda. He came home for supper but did not stay long, returning to the streets as quickly as possible. So it took him a while to realize that something was again wrong with his mother. When he began to suspect something, he rummaged around the apartment for paregoric bottles, drugstore bags, marijuana shreds, cigarette paper, and sniffed the air for traces of either smell, for paregoric was almost as detectable as the other, though for not as long. But Richie found no evidence with which he was familiar. There was something amiss, something awry. He could feel it, yet he could not define either what it was, or his reason for believing it.

Chloe finally ended the mystery late one Saturday afternoon when he returned home from his paper route.

"I want you to go someplace for me, Richie," she said. Richie saw that her exprssion was grim, her dark, once-pretty eyes hard and fixed. Her hand shook slightly as she wrote out an address on Lake Street and handed it to him with some money. "The man there will give you something for me."

"What is it?"

"Just something I need, Richie, for my headaches," she replied. "Go on now, get it for me."

"This address is in the colored neighborhood—"

"I know where it is!" Chloe snapped impatiently. "Will you just *go!*"

"It's getting dark out—"

"I don't care! Go! Right now!"

"Okay!" He stormed out of the apartment, muttering curses.

"You hurry back too!" she shouted after him, her words a threat.

□

When Richie emerged from the closed stairway of the building on Lake Street, which stood between a liquor store and a commercial laundry, he heard somebody say, "Where you been so long, you little shit?"

Head snapping around, he saw Vernie standing in a nearby doorway with three other black girls. Sixteen now, she was voluptuous and earthy-looking in a skintight, revealing dress. As Richie grinned widely at the sight of her, she came over to him in the superb, superior strut she had long since developed and mastered.

"Hey, Vernie," Richie said, delighted.

"What you doing in that building, boy?" she asked without preliminaries.

"My mother sent me there," Richie replied, glancing down.

Nodding knowingly, Vernie fished two fingers into his shirt pocket and pulled out a small cellophane envelope that had BC HEADACHE POWDER printed on it. Sighing quietly, she said, "Well, I see yo' mamma done changed her prescription."

"I guess it's not BC Headache Powder," Richie said, his voice almost timid.

Vernie shook her head. "They buys BC Headache Powders just to get the envelopes. This here be heroin, Richie. It's bad shit."

Turning his head, Richie stared off at the deepening shadows under the el track. In the yellow of the streetlight, Vernie could see his eyes become misty. She put an arm around his shoulders.

"It be okay, Richie," she assured. "Don' nothing last forever." Giving him a squeeze and a little shake, she added, "One good thing—you don't have to worry 'bout being chased on Lake Street no more. Long as you going to *that* address, ain't nobody gonna mess wif' you. Them mens in there don't allow no interference wif' their trade. Look like you don' need Vernie to take care of you no more."

From the nearby doorway, one of the other girls yelled, "Vernie, you better get back over here, girl. You know you up next."

"Who are they?" Richie asked.

"Jus' some girls," Vernie replied. After a beat, she added softly, "Girls trying to get by, like me." Giving him another squeeze, she said, "I gots to go. I be seeing you, hon."

"Sure."

Richie watched her strut back to the doorway, flaunting every part of her femaleness with each exaggerated step.

Walking to the corner, Richie crossed the street. Instead of leaving the block, on a sudden urge he stepped into the shadow of a storefront and stood there, concealed, watching Vernie and the other girls. The four of them laughed and cut up among themselves for several minutes, smoking cigarettes, patting their hair, smoothing their skirts. Only when a car approached and slowed down did they quickly become quiet. Richie saw Vernie go over to the curb and lean down to speak to the driver, a white man, through the passenger door window. Presently, she got into the car and it slowly pulled up to a point between two streetlights where the shadows of the el tracks were darkest. Parking there, its headlights went off.

On the last week of their welfare entitlement, Miss Menefee came to see them with their final check.

"I wish there was some way we could continue to help you, Chloe," she apologized, "but the department has to have established limits of aid or some people would stay on the charity rolls forever."

"You've been very good to us," Chloe replied. "I'm sure Richie and I can get along just fine now."

Richie said nothing. He knew that as soon as Miss Menefee left, he and his mother would be moving. She had already rented a cheaper place, back on the old Adams Street block, and just that morning had applied for welfare at a different field office under the name of Chloe Clark. Miss Menefee knew her only as Chloe Eaton.

When Miss Menefee finished talking to Chloe, she said, "Come on out to the car with me, Richie; I have something for you."

Richie went outside with her and Miss Menefee unlocked her car and handed him a bag off the front seat. In it was a book: *Nevada* by Zane Grey.

"Paula Hovey told me that you were going to pick a Zane Grey book as your next prize. I hope you haven't read this one."

"No," Richie said, blushing. "Thank you." It was a lie; he had already made a book report on it in Miss White's class.

"Listen, Richie," Grace Menefee said, combing his hair a little with her fingers, "I want you to promise me something. I want you to promise me that if things start to get bad for you again, you'll call me. I've written my telephone number on this piece of paper and I want you to keep it somewhere safe in case you ever need it. Will you do that for me?"

"Sure," Richie said. Was it his imagination or did Miss Menefee look like she was going to cry? He glanced around, hoping nobody he knew was watching.

When the caseworker finally drove off, Richie breathed a sigh of relief and hurried back upstairs.

"What's that?" Chloe asked, seeing the bag.

"She gave me a book."

"A book?" Chloe made a sour face. "See if the sales slip is still in the bag; maybe we can take it back and get the money."

"I already looked," Richie lied. "It ain't there."

"Isn't there," Chloe corrected.

At first Richie had resisted moving again. "You know how many schools I been to since first grade?" he complained. "Eleven. *Eleven* schools!"

"Changing schools never killed anyone," Chloe scoffed as she went about packing their things. "Making new friends is good for you. Besides, living on Adams Street will make it that much closer for you to go get my headache powder when I need it."

Richie stared irritably at his mother. "I know that stuff's not headache powder."

"You don't know what you know," Chloe said peremptorily. Whenever possible lately, she avoided confrontations with him. "Here"—she handed him a cardboard box—"carry this over to the Hamlin streetcar stop and wait for me there. If Mr. Niemera sees you and asks what you're doing, tell him you're taking things to the dry cleaners." Mr. Niemera was the landlord; Chloe was skipping out on their rent again. She would, Richie thought, probably sneak out the rear with her suitcase.

Walking toward the streetcar stop, Richie reflected on how it might not be too bad moving back to Adams Street, after all. He would be able to pal around with Stan Klein again, and it would be a shorter streetcar ride twice a day to and from his paper route. He knew he would miss Tilton Elementary, but at least being back at Brown with Stan would relieve him of the periodic bullying he was still subject to at Tilton. But the main thing he was going to miss, he realized, was Linda. She was the one spot of brightness in his life that he could depend upon not to fade.

Maybe, Richie thought tentatively, he could still meet Linda at the Pulaski

Road branch library. He would have to take a streetcar there also, he realized; the goddamned streetcar fares were going to break him.

When Richie and his mother got back to Adams Street that day, Richie found that the two-and-a-half room apartment was not markedly different from the one they used to live in when George Zangara was coming to visit. As soon as he got his things unpacked into a box under his rollaway bed, he asked Chloe for a dime to go buy a candle for killing bedbugs. She gave him half that much, saying, "Candles are only a nickel." As he went out the door, she added, "You'll probably swipe it anyhow."

"I don't swipe things," Richie said over his shoulder. Hearing his mother laugh softly, he could not suppress a half smile.

Down the block, Richie climbed the stairs of his old building and knocked at the Klein door. Stan's sister Janet opened it. She was wearing a tight, low-scooped sweater and it looked to Richie like her breasts had tripled in size. "Is Stan home?" Richie asked.

"Stanley ain't living with us right now," Janet said. "He was getting in a lot of trouble, so Ma sent him to Ohio to live with the old man for a while. She wants the old man to straighten him out."

A sinking feeling came over Richie. "Oh," was all he could manage to say. Without even a parting glance at her breasts, he shuffled listlessly down to the street.

There were some days, he decided, when nothing in the whole god-damned world went right. As he sat on the curb brooding, he felt a cool wind whip down the dreary little street. Richie grunted resignedly.

On top of everything else, winter was coming.

Chloe eventually found a job that suited her: folding circulars and stuffing them into envelopes. She liked it so well because it was "home work" that she could do in the apartment, and the only person she ever had to deal with was a tough-looking woman with orangish hair who delivered the work to be done and picked it up when it was finished. It was also piece work, for which Chloe earned only insubstantial wages. But with the new welfare stipend she was receiving in the name of Chloe Clark, and with Richie's earnings on his two paper routes, they got along adequately if not comfortably. But only for a time.

Richie's errands to Lake Street were only twice a week in the beginning, and he was able to work them in following his afternoon route and before hurrying off to the library, where he still met Linda. After his discovery that Stan Klein was gone, Richie had opted to stay at Tilton Elementary, taking a streetcar to school every day. It was not allowed—living in one district and going to school in another—but as long as none of the teachers saw him getting off a streetcar, he would be able to do it. And if he did get caught, he planned to say he was coming back from working his paper route, which was half true anyway.

Although Richie tried not to think about it, he knew somewhere deep in his mind that the semi-weekly trips to Lake Street would eventually increase, and that when they did there would be a corresponding drop in their standard of living, which was already meager. For that reason, he helped his mother with her envelope stuffing and other piece work so that she could earn more money, in the belief that the more she made the longer it would be until they encountered money problems. To his dismay, it did not work that way at all. The more money Chloe made, the more her addiction increased, because she was able to buy more of the drug that she loved so irresistibly. Richie had no idea how she had started on this new "medicine" or even how she used it. He assumed she swallowed it, as she had the paregoric.

Winter stalked in with a vengeance. Bone-chilling cold numbed Richie on his morning paper route, and icy winds whipped him mercilessly in the afternoons. Nearly every afternoon, Frances Rozinski opened her back door and pulled him into her kitchen for hot chocolate or a bowl of steaming soup. One day she touched her fingertips lightly to his cheeks and said, "God, Richie, you're chapped almost raw. Don't your mother have no lotion at home?" She got out a large bottle of Jergens and rubbed it gently into his reddened face. It burned like fire for several minutes, but soon felt much better. Frances put some lotion in a small empty witch-hazel bottle she had and gave it to him. "Use this at night and in the morning," she instructed. "Put it on your hands too. Let me know when it's used up and I'll give you some more."

Richie still saw Frances watching him from her window sometimes when he worked his dark morning route, but she never opened the door or spoke to him in the mornings. Probably, Richie thought sagely, because her husband was at home. Richie never saw him, but occasionally he would hear Walter Rozinski's voice behind the drawn kitchen shades when he left their *Tribune* on the back porch.

At night, back in the run-down little apartment on Adams Street, the place cluttered with boxes of Chloe's work, when a very tired and cold Richie crawled under his threadbare blanket, he frequently took the little bottle of Jergens from beneath his pillow, opened it, smelled its sweet fragrance a few times, and went to sleep with thoughts of Frances Rozinski in his head.

□

As he had known they would, Richie's trips to Lake Street gradually increased to three times a week, four, then five. Just as the heroin began to tell on Chloe—she lost weight, gray began to show in her hair, her breath became putrid—so too did the strain of his expanding schedule start wearing on Richie. It seemed that he was constantly on the move: up before dawn to ride the streetcar to his morning route; riding a streetcar to school; a streetcar back to do his afternoon route; a streetcar home and then the walk over to Lake Street and back; a streetcar up to Pulaski Road to spend a few minutes with Linda in the library; a streetcar home.

"Can't you go over to Lake Street yourself some of the time?" he challenged Chloe. "I'm working two paper routes out in the cold and you stay inside all the time where it's warm."

"Warm!" Chloe belittled his complaint. "You call this place *warm*? Sometimes my hands are so cold, I have to hold them in the oven before I can stuff my first envelope."

"You're breaking my heart," Richie scorned. Chloe took a swing at him but missed when he ducked.

"Goddamn it, don't you talk to me like that!" Taking off a shoe, she flung it at him, but he was out the door and gone before it landed.

Usually he ate on the go. There was no such thing as a meal at home anymore; Chloe's own appetite became negligible, and she conveniently assumed that Richie would find some way to feed himself. He did. A lot of what he ate, he stole: milk from delivery trucks, doughnuts from bakery trucks; he got hot cereal in a greasy spoon if he had money; at noon he left school as if he were one of the kids who went home for lunch, but instead he would go to one of the larger grocery stores, an A & P or a Royal Blue, and walk through the place eating whatever he could get: apples, oranges, uncooked frankfurters, a big dill pickle from a barrel, anything. Occasionally a store manager would catch him, slap him around a little, and throw him out on the sidewalk or into the alley, but most of the time he got away with it. He bought, stole if he could, a lot of candy bars, which kept his energy level up but provided him little nourishment. At night he usually had White Castle hamburgers or chili before he went home to sleep; he always tried to save enough money each day to do that.

Eventually, Richie and Chloe were hardly talking to each other. An unspoken agreement evolved between them that Chloe would, with her paltry earnings and the welfare checks—she was managing to receive several, under various modifications of her name—pay the rent and buy her dope, and Richie would see to his own needs: food, clothes, haircuts when they became imperative. As the winter became daily more bitterly cold, the welfare clothes from the previous year proved too small for him, so he began to steal others from secondhand stores run by the Salvation Army, where the volunteer clerks smiled and trusted everyone in the name of the Lord. Richie learned to wait outside and walk in with other people so that it looked like he was with them; then he stole what he could put on while crouching under a table or behind a rack. Shoes were the biggest problem; with wartime restrictions still in effect, there were no secondhand shoes, and new ones were too expensive to buy and impossible to steal, and Chloe had long since sold their ration books. Richie cut cardboard inserts to cover the holes in his soles, and wore three pairs of socks, which *could* be stolen. Nevertheless, his feet were always cold, frequently wet.

As winter deepened, Richie's paper routes became brutal trials of endurance. The shorter, darker days were somehow more threatening. When the constant wind drove snow and sleet along the ice-covered sidewalks in a curtain of frigid cold, Richie moved along with his head bent, rarely looking up, working his deliveries from memory. The dark mornings were the worst, when his pushcart with its iron wheels on the ice required several times as much energy just to control, much less push. Afternoons were better because there was usually a break to look forward to when he reached the Skinner Park area where Frances more often than not pulled him into her kitchen to give him something hot to drink or eat, and sometimes do other things for him.

"My god, Richie, you've got holes in your gloves. Your fingers will freeze like that. Wait a sec." She hurried from the room, hurried back, and made him try on, over his own worn gloves, an old pair of men's gloves. "They're Walter's from last year. I had them in a bag for the Goodwill. Are they okay?"

"They're swell," Richie said. "Thanks a lot."

Sometimes she fed him thick, meaty stew she had been cooking all day for that night's supper. "I made extra so you could have some." Other times it was a quick grilled cheese sandwich or a can of soup. While she fixed something for him, she made him put his shoes on the radiator to dry, and brought him a bottle of Jergens Lotion to use. "Your mother should take better care of you," she criticized.

"She's sick," Richie excused. "It's all she can do to take care of herself."

Before he left one day, Frances put a new woolen muffler around his neck. "I saved up out of my grocery money and bought it for you," she said proudly, her dark, dark eyes dancing with delight. As she bent to adjust it around his neck, her face was very close to his.

"How come you're so nice to me?" Richie asked. It was a question he could not resist, something that had begun to bother him.

"Because I like you," Frances replied. She gave him a brief, dry kiss on the lips. "That's all right, isn't it? For me to like you?"

"Sure," Richie said, with his usual shrug.

Frances led him into her hall and stood him in front of a mirror on the wall. "See how nice it looks," she said, adjusting the muffler still more. "If Walter found out I bought it for you, he'd beat me up."

"Maybe you should take it back," Richie offered.

"No, he won't find out." She stepped over to stand behind him so they could both see themselves in the mirror. "Look how tall you are," she said. "You've grown a couple of inches since the morning I caught you looking in the old woman's window next door. That's what you were doing, wasn't it?"

"Yeah," Richie admitted for the first time. He turned a little red. Smiling, Frances put her arms around him from behind and gave him a little hug.

"Will you do something for me?" she asked, fixing her eyes on his.

"Sure, what?"

"Change your route around tomorrow so that you deliver my afternoon paper last. Can you do that?"

"Sure. But why?"

"You'll see. It's a surprise."

Richie smiled. "Okay."

For the rest of that afternoon, trudging the remainder of his route in a heavy snowfall, Richie tried not to imagine why Frances had made the request.

It was easy enough to alter his delivery sequence; he simply skipped the block where Frances lived and made the rest of his deliveries in a circle back to it. When he got to her door with the last *Herald-American*, leaving his empty cart parked in the alley below, Frances was waiting for him and quickly let him in. She was wearing a chenille bathrobe and had a towel tied around her dishwater hair. The kitchen was close with heat, its windows steamily opaque. Smiling, Frances led him into a warm, misty bathroom.

"Would you like to take a nice hot bubble bath?" she asked, helping him out of his coat and cap. "Of course you would," she answered for him. "Take off the rest of your clothes while I get you some hot chocolate."

When Frances left the bathroom, Richie stood there in uncertainty for a moment. One part of him was queasily fearful about what was happening, while another instinct lured him tantalizingly onward. He had been so cold for so long; even his baths in the bathroom down the hall where he lived were taken in an unheated room, in an old, chipped tub, sometimes with water that was barely warm, often rusty. This bathtub was glistening white, filled to the rim with foamy, sweet-smelling bubbles floating on water he knew was hot and clean.

Hearing the rattle of cup and saucer from the kitchen, Richie quickly began undressing. He hurried so that he could get out of his threadbare underwear to keep Frances from seeing that the knees and elbows were worn all the way through. By the time she returned, he was in the tub, hugging his knees, letting the hot water turn his flesh red.

"There, isn't that nice?" Frances said. "Here, drink some cocoa to warm up inside."

As he rested and sipped the hot, sweet chocolate, Frances soaped a thick cloth and gently washed him. Watching her, he concluded again that she was probably the same age as his mother. Maybe, he thought, she was pretending that she *was* his mother, giving her little boy a bath when he came home from his long, cold paper route. Except that, after turning up the sleeves of her robe, Frances had put her hands under the water and was washing him the way Dorothy had once done, on those nights when she had him bite her nipples.

"Well, what have we here?" Frances asked when her slippery hands came upon his erection. Richie felt himself turn red. "Don't be ashamed," she said in a softer voice. "It's really a compliment to a woman when you get like that."

When she finished washing him, Frances rinsed him off and stood him on a fluffy rug as she knelt and dried him with a soft towel. He had never felt so clean in his life; it was such a marvelous feeling, that he was able to ignore his stubborn erection. When he was dry, Frances led him into the living room to a large easy chair. "This is Walter's chair, but we can use it anyway. He'll never know." Sitting far down in the cushion, she drew Richie to his knees in front of her and opened her robe partway. Her breasts fell apart from each other, their large, dark nipples pointing off in opposite directions. Richie stared at them in turn, fascinated.

"Would you like to touch them?" Frances asked. Taking one of his hands, she guided his fingertips first to one nipple, then the other. "Would you like to kiss them?" Gently she drew his head forward. "Would you like to suck on them? Suck on them, Richie."

As he drew her nipples into his mouth, each in turn, wetting them with his tongue, licking, trying to suckle something out of them, Frances poured Jergens Lotion on her hands from a bottle on the end table and began to rub it over his genitals, careful not to bring him to a climax when she felt his young erection begin to throb at her touch.

When she had enough of what he was doing, Frances gently moved his head back and opened her robe the rest of the way. From the pocket she took a small brush and, saying "Let me show you something,"slowly stroked and parted the growth of dark pubic hair she had exposed. When she had it combed just the way she wanted it, parted neatly and brushed to each side, she said, "Would you like to kiss me there, Richie? I want you to kiss me there. Please, do it for me . . ." She drew his face down. "There, right there where my finger is, kiss it there . . . aaah . . . yes, yes, yes—"

A shudder seized her and she threw her head back, Richie stopped, looking up, not knowing whether to continue or not. She was holding both his hands flat against her fleshy, widespread thighs.

"Did you like that?" she asked after a moment. Without waiting for him to answer, asked, "Would you like to lick me there, Richie? Yes, you would, I know you would. Lick me, my darling, lick me there . . . yes, right there . . . oh, Christ in heaven—"

After another shuddering seizure, during which her naked body quivered all over the chair, Frances finally dropped back to a slack position, breathing heavily, her expression rapt, lips parted with a trace of saliva in their corners. Richie remained kneeling before her, looking at her spread legs, parted breasts, dark, hard, lumpy nipples. Remembering the window of Cook County Hospital that looked into the nurses' locker room, he curled his fingers around his lotioned erection and began to masturbate. Frances smiled lazily at him.

"Oh, so my little boy already knows a few things, I see," she said in mock surprise. "Well, come here, my darling, let Frances do it for you . . ."

Drawing him up until he was straddling her, one knee on each side as she remained lying back in the chair, she pushed her breasts together with her upper arms and with one hand cupped his scrotum, with the other began to masturbate him.

"You are going to be mine, Richie," she purred softly, "the only gentle thing in my life, the only tenderness I will have, the only thing that is not rough and brutal. You and me, Richie, we will have romance . . ."

Listening to her hushed voice, feeling her lotioned, slippery hand sliding up and down, Richie closed his eyes and let her take him euphorically to his climax.

Not once did he think about Chloe, waiting in the shabby apartment to send him to Lake Street, or that he would have to face her later.

But when he opened his eyes when it was over, he looked at Frances and saw his mother.

When Richie finally got home, much later than usual, as soon as he walked in the door Chloe, who was waiting against the wall, hit him in the side of the face with a shoe.

"Where the hell have you been?" she shrieked. Before he could answer or recover from the first blow, she landed another which sent him reeling back, off-balance.

"Cut it out, goddamn it!" he yelled. When she moved forward to batter him further, he grabbed her frail wrist and twisted the shoe away from her. Seizing his coat so that he could not get away she sniffed him, frowning.

"Why do you smell so funny? Where the hell have you been?"

"A wheel came off my pushcart," he lied. "A lady let me come in her house to use her phone. The place smelled real funny, flowery like."

Chloe began to shake him. "You knew I was waiting for you! You knew I needed you to go someplace for me!" She pointed a finger in his face. "I want you to quit that paper route, you hear me? Quit it and come right home after school—"

"Oh sure!" Richie snapped back. "Then who's gonna feed me? You sure as hell won't!"

Face up close to his, Chloe's expression slowly changed from rage to wretchedness. Her entire face seemed to sag, becoming pendulously pitiful: the circles under her eyes seemed to sag; her cheeks, what little pliancy they had left, sagged; her mouth drooped miserably. Sinking to her knees, she began to sob woefully.

"You know I need you, Richie," she choked out words. "You know you're all I've got. There's no one else to help me, no one else to go get my headache powders for me. I'm all alone without you, Richie. If you don't help me, I'll die, that's all there is to it, I'll just die!"

Looking down at her, Richie's own face reflected guilt and anguish and a wild rampage of doubts. He was still cushy and cozy somewhere deep inside himself from his experience with Frances, and on the way home he had once again instinctively thought of his mother not as she was now, not haggard and sick, but vibrant, pretty, alive, the way Frances was. It was as if Frances calling him "her little boy, her little Richie," and doing to him the glorious, delightful things she did, made Richie wish that Chloe had felt that way about him, that when Chloe was pretty and healthy like Frances was, she would have done those things with *him* instead of doing them with Jack Smart and George Zangara. All the way home Richie had pictured a voluptuous naked woman who had the body of Frances and the face of Chloe as she once was.

Now he stood before the trembling, bony, whining thing that was the Chloe of today, and he felt ashamed for putting his mother's face over the face of Frances Rozinski, and for not helping his mother when she needed him.

"Come on," he said, helping her to her feet, "quit crying and come lie down on the bed. I'll go get your . . . your headache powders . . . right now, and I'll run all the way there and all the way back. Where's the money?"

"I haven't got any money!" she wailed, sweeping an arm out to indicate stacks of boxes of envelopes, piles of twine-bound circulars, and only one small box, half full, of completed work. "They won't pay me until it's finished. They said they won't pay me for partials anymore because I take too long to finish the job—"

"How much does your stuff cost?" he asked. He could not force himself to call it "headache powder" again.

"Five dollars. They raised the price; there was a note with the last envelope."

Richie's mouth dropped open. *Five dollars!* "Jesus Christ," he said, suddenly fondly remembering the fifteen-cent and twenty-five-cent bottles of paregoric.

"But here," Chloe said urgently, hurrying into her tiny bedroom and returning with three cartons of Lucky Strike cigarettes. "These cost a dollar fifty each and the man on Lake Street will allow us a dollar each for them, so that's three dollars. Have you got two dollars?"

"Maybe," Richie said, fishing from his trousers pockets a crumpled dollar bill and some change. "Yeah, I got two bucks," he said. "But where'd you get the cigarettes?"

"Oh, Richie, I just *got* them," she replied impatiently, reverting to being in charge again. "Will you *go* now? And remember, you promised to run all the way . . ."

He did run both ways, as he said he would. The black man on Lake Street grinned as he took the cigarettes and said, "That Chloe, she getting this cigarette boosting down to a fine art, look like." After getting the envelope, trotting back home through the snow, Richie recalled over and over again with astonishment the man's words and what they meant. *His mother was shoplifting cigarettes.* Had he known how much she was paying for her dope, he would have realized that the welfare checks and her skimpy earnings were not covering it. But he had no idea, because she always sent the money in a sealed envelope, that her habit was up to five dollars a *day.* At that moment, he understood for the first time that he knew as little about his mother's life as she knew about his.

When he got back, Chloe was waiting at the door again, without a shoe this time, and seized the little envelope as soon as he produced it. Without a word to him, she hurried into the bedroom and locked herself in. Richie stood there, cold and hungry, staring at the closed door for a long, sorrowful moment. Then he simply shrugged helplessly and went back out into the winter night to steal something to eat.

The long dreary winter continued, and somehow, day by day, with meager earnings, welfare fraud, and petty theft, Chloe and Richie got by. For Richie, it was a perpetual cycle of misery relieved only by his private time with Frances, which turned out to be a single two-hour visit once each week: on the day, Richie learned, when Walter Rozinski bowled after work. Other days, Frances had him in only for a few minutes in the middle of his route to let him warm up and have something hot to eat or drink. He was always gone before Walter, who worked in the stockyards as a meat handler, got home.

For herself and Richie, Frances created something once a week that was private, intimate, enthralling, and theirs alone. In their encounters, she did things with him and to him that were truly extraordinary experiences. And she helped him understand things that otherwise might have been frightening experiences to him.

Such as the first time he ejaculated. He had masturbated a few times with Stan Klein while looking in the window of the nurses' locker room, and a few times in private, once looking in a window in the morning on his paper route and watching a woman suck off a man, and once after moving back to Adams Street and seeing Stan's sister Janet bending over, her big tits almost falling out, to pick up a coin she dropped at the corner grocery; and he had climaxed, felt the incredible thrill of the sensation, but never actually produced any semen in the process. Then one day with Frances he did, and thought there was something terribly wrong with him. But she calmed him, comforted him, explained what his body had done, then masturbated him to let him see how naturally and exhilaratingly it happened. After that, Frances began to suck it out of him, luxuriating in what she called his "virginal semen, all mine, no one else has ever seen it or touched it or tasted it. I love it, love it, love it!" Sometimes in their two hours together she would make him come four or five times, in her mouth, on her nipples, on the little knob of soft flesh just inside her vagina that she liked for him to kiss and lick. Times when she fellated him, because he was yet so small and she had an unusually wide mouth, Frances was able to get his erect penis *and* his scrotum in her mouth at the same time, and the climaxes that it generated in both of them were momentous.

Except for his time with Frances Rozinski, the rest of Richie's life was a terrible reality. The cheerless little place in which he and Chloe lived was in a constant state of slovenliness. Chloe's periods of somnolence increased in duration as her addiction, and the cost of it, grew. Richie's treks to Lake Street for the heroin generated more and more resentment in him, especially on days when he did not get enough to eat; there were a few times when all he had eaten in a single day was what Frances gave him. He knew he could have asked her for money, but could not bring himself to; too often he had heard her say that if Walter found out this or found out that, he would beat her up. To think that Frances might be physically abused because she helped him in some way was completely repugnant; he would rather go hungry permanently. Many nights, on his way home, Richie would stop in one of the markets and steal several potatoes; the potato bin was seldom watched. When he got home, he would peel and fry them in round slices and make a meal of them.

The only person who knew the dark, shameful secret of his mother's addiction was Vernie. Even though she was no longer his protector when he was on Lake Street, and he did not eagerly look for her as he once had done, they still ran into each other occasionally. Vernie would usually be sitting in the rib joint next to its steamy plate-glass window, drinking coffee and smoking a cigarette, and would motion for him to come in, asking, "How you be, Richie?" She could see how he was, of course; it was obvious from his appearance that his situation was worsening. "Po' little white boy," she said, brushing back his hair the way Miss Menefee used to do. If she happened to be eating, she would share her food with him, and twice she opened a little cloth change purse she carried in her waistband and gave him a quarter. "I'd give you more if I could," she said, "but I got it hard over here too. Nights be so damn cold, I ain't making shit mos' of the time. I swear, I don't know how I'm gon' make it through this winter."

Richie did not worry about making it through the winter. His concern was making it through the day.

He did not know when he again started to think about his father; one day he simply found himself thinking about him, and he was aware that it was not the first time Slim had reentered his mind. And just as it had always been when Richie was younger, he thought of Slim as savior, liberator, rescuer— one who had the strength, the ability, the means to lift his mother and himself from the black abyss of their lives and carry them off to a place where there was warm sunshine, lots to eat, many books to read, and no Lake Street dope, no schoolyard bullies, no people who changed the rules on you when you weren't looking.

Where the hell could his father be? he wondered as he rode the interminable streetcars every day, pushed his newspaper cart along the street, hurried along Lake Street to the dope seller, or finally, at the end of another grueling day, haggard, expended, crawling onto his cot and drawing the threadbare blanket over him for the rest he by then imperatively needed.

Where in the hell was he?

It began to haunt him again, this figure who had evolved into their only salvation. He even tried to talk to Chloe about it. She looked at him as if he were a lunatic.

"Your *what*?" she asked incredulously. "Your *father*? For Christ's sake, Richie, I'm not sure you ever *had* a father."

Chloe was in one of her blurred eclipses; when she was half hazy like that, Richie frequently did not know whether she was on her way out of reality after having just used her dope, or on her way back in as it wore off. But it was the only time he could talk to her. In her other two states— completely under from just having done herself, or sick from needing to do herself—she was neither rational nor responsible. He had to catch her halfway in or halfway out—or not communicate with her at all.

"Come on, you know I've got a father," he prompted, keeping his tone light. "Where do you think he could be? You must have some idea."

"Oh, I don't know, Richie." Shaking her head, she laughed and her foul breath reached him. "Maybe he's back in some penitentiary." Chloe waved a hand disdainfully. "He could be anywhere. Your father," she accused, "was very light on his feet." Then she smiled. "Kind of like you are, Richie."

"Whatever happened to Estelle?" Richie asked. "If she's around, maybe she's seen him."

"Oh, 'Stelle's around, all right," Chloe replied with a grunt. "I see her sometimes, here and there. When that sailor divorced her, she moved back from California. But I wouldn't count on her for any help. 'Stelle drinks, you know."

"Do you remember," Richie probed, "on that train ride we took, when you and Dad were talking and I was sleeping on the other seat?"

"You mean *pretending* to sleep, don't you?" Chloe winked at him. "Oh, yes. A lot more than you think I know. Oh, yes."

Richie shook his head incredulously. "Okay, pretending to sleep," he conceded. "Anyway, do you remember him telling you about a garage keeper, a mechanic, that he was working for?"

"I remember. Mack something. I made a couple telephone calls when we first came back, trying to find him, to see if he knew where Richmond was. But I was never able to talk to him. I think he was working for some gangsters or something."

"He wanted to open a garage of his own," Richie recalled his father saying. "I wonder if he ever did?"

"I doubt it," Chloe said cynically. "People never do what they think they're going to do. Plans never work out, Richie. Remember that. I've got to lie down now; I'm getting a splitting headache."

As winter deepened and darkened, as his existence daily became more arduous, his efforts more fruitless, future bleaker, the turmoil in Richie's desperate young mind fixated more and more on the only single, shining solution he could envision: finding his father.

He finally told Frances that his mother was a junkie. There was no other way to explain his deteriorating condition. She was outraged.

"No wonder you look so terrible. For god's sake, why didn't you tell me sooner?" She took his face in her hands. "My poor baby, we've got to do something to help you."

"What?" Richie asked. "What can we do? I don't want my mother put in jail."

"I don't know," Frances reasoned, "but look at you, for god's sake. You're skinnier than ever, some of your clothes are practically rags; Richie, it tears me up to see you like this." Expression anguished, she helped him undress and get into the tub. In the hot water, he lay limply, all over. Frances did nothing to arouse him. "You're the only gentle thing in my life, Richie," she told him quietly. "I been thinking that when you got a little older, maybe you and me could go away together somewheres—you know, and not come back."

"I can't leave my mother. She don't have nobody but me."

"Well, then, maybe we could take her with us. If she's sick, we could take care of her, or help her get cured. I could say I was her sister, your aunt; nobody'd know any different. I could work, you know, Richie. I been to beauty college, I can get a job at any beauty parlor in the city. If we did that, you and me, we could have all the time together we wanted." While he mulled over what she had said, Frances lathered his tangled hair with shampoo, muttering to herself, "You need a haircut bad."

"Are there doctors who can cure people on dope?" he asked.

"Sure, there must be; there's doctors for everything." Her eyes shifted away. "Most everything, anyhow." As she rinsed him, she asked as casually as she could, "Richie, do you think there's something wrong with me?"

"What do you mean?"

"You know, because of . . . what we do. Me being a grownup and you just a kid and all."

"Most of the time I don't feel like no kid."

"I know, but do you think there's something wrong with me?'

Richie shook his head. "No." Leaning forward, he kissed her on the lips and tongued her mouth the way she had taught him.

"Thanks, baby," she said with quiet, touching gratitude. Toweling him off, she rubbed his thin body all over with Jergens Lotion, saying, "We're not going to do anything today, you and me, except fix you a good meal, and you're going to eat every bite of it. And every day when you come at the regular time, I'm going to have a regular supper ready for you, I don't care if it is the middle of the afternoon; I'm going to get some weight on you. Plus which, first thing tomorrow morning, I'm going to go see my parish priest and ask his advice about your mother. We're going to see this thing through, Richie, you and me; we're going to fix everything just right."

Frances prepared a big meal for him, a breakfast actually: fried ham, scrambled eggs, sliced tomatoes, toast with jelly, and hot chocolate. Richie wolfed it down, even though he did not have to be in a hurry; on the one day a week he went to the Rozinski apartment last to spend time with Frances, he now used his school lunch hour to ride the streetcar down to Lake Street, get his mother's dope and take it to her, and then hurry back to school for the afternoon session, usually just making it before the final bell. He did not want a repetition of the scene where Chloe hit him in the head with a shoe for being late. Most of the time he didn't have money for lunch anyway.

When he had eaten as much as he could without making himself sick, Frances bundled him up in his worn coat and cap with earmuffs and the muffler she had bought for him, and at the back door kissed him passionately on the lips. "See you tomorrow, baby."

"Sure, see you tomorrow."

As Richie crossed the Rozinski back porch, he saw looking out her kitchen door on the adjoining porch the old woman he had been spying on the first time he met Frances. Clutching her sweater close around her neck, the old lady had the door open about six inches and was looking out, leering at him, her thin shoulders shaking from what Richie at first thought was the cold, but then, when he heard it, discovered was a quiet, obnoxious cackling. What the hell's her goddamn trouble? he wondered.

Carefully negotiating the slippery back stairs, which still had ice on them, he was hoping that the wheels of his pushcart had not frozen again. Then abruptly he stopped and stared at the bottom step. Setting on it was a black leather bowling ball bag. Frowning, Richie went on down, his eyes beginning to dart about. As his foot hit the backyard sidewalk, a strong, beefy hand reached from under the stairs and took hold of his coat, stopping him.

"Hey, lay off!" Richie said, twisting around to face a square-headed man with eyes set close together and a thin line of a mouth, the lips of which were parted incredulously.

"Jesus Christ, you ain't nothing but a goddamned kid," he said in disbelief.

"Lemme alone," Richie protested, trying to pull away, "I ain't done nothing!"

The square-headed man nodded thoughtfully. "Oh, yeah? Well, we'll see."

Richie opened his mouth to yell, but the man immediately clamped a huge hand over his mouth and dragged him down four steps into the basement laundry room. He shoved Richie against a wall.

"Drop your pants and drawers," he ordered.

Mind racing desperately, Richie intentionally let his shoulders sag in submission. "Sure, mister, okay, take it easy. I'll do like you say." Opening his coat, Richie pretended to fumble with his belt, then suddenly bolted for the door. When he was almost there, something hard hit him on the side of the temple and he dropped to the cement floor, stunned. Kneeling next to him, the man undid Richie's belt and fly and pulled down his trousers and long underwear. Bending his face close, he sniffed at Richie's genitals.

"Jergens Lotion," he said quietly. "So you ain't done nothing, huh?"

Closing his hand into a fist, he drove it against Richie's mouth, splitting his bottom lip, letting blood spurt. With his other fist, he hit him in the eye; then in the nose, the jaw, the other eye, on the chin. When Richie's head flopped slackly to one side, the man dragged him to his feet, held him up and pounded his ribcage and stomach with short powerful body blows.

Richie was not unconscious, but he was close to it; his eyes had rolled up and he could not focus or keep his head erect. With his hands he tried to tug at his underwear and trousers, which were down around his knees. As he did that, he was aware of being walked roughly outside and half dragged, half pushed back up the four steps and along the backyard sidewalk to the alley.

"Lemme get . . . my . . . pants up . . ." he pleaded thickly, feeling the thin, bitter air on his exposed buttocks.

"You should'a kept 'em up, you little bastard," the man growled. He drove a final, brutal blow into Richie's genitals, then with a shove sent him sprawling and sliding across the icy alley. "Ever come around here again, I'll kill you," he said before he walked away.

Groping, clutching, stumbling, feeling ice against his flesh, Richie managed to get his underwear and trousers pulled up and some of the buttons on his coat closed. His cap and earmuffs were gone; he looked around but could not find them. Blood was flowing from his nose and mouth, and before he realized it he was vomiting up some of the food he had eaten a little while earlier. He could only see out of one eye and it frightened him so that he started to cry. Cocking his head to one side, he felt his way along the alley to where he had left his pushcart. When he got to it, the wheels were frozen.

"Can't do it," he mumbled to himself. "Just can't do it."

Head still cocked, squinting out of his one good eye, he left the cart and walked toward the streetcar line. He did not look back to see if Frances was watching.

*T*he next morning, his mother shook him awake, asking urgently, "What's the matter with you? What are you doing home? Richie, wake *up!*" When he rolled over and she saw his face, Chloe drew back in revulsion. "Good god, what *happened* to you?"

"Got beat up," Richie said thickly, through lips that felt as big as automobile tires. "Some guys jumped me . . . on my route . . . took all my money . . ."

Chloe had not been home when he got there the previous night; with the stores open late she did some of her shoplifting then. Richie had been in such abject pain that he did not even try to clean himself up; all he did was crawl onto his cot, pull the blanket over his head, cup both hands over his swelling scrotum, and go to sleep.

As he sat up on the cot now, Chloe staring at him in repugnance, Richie felt as if he had been rolled down the stairs of the Wrigley Building; there was no part of him that did not hurt; even his toes, for some reason, hurt. But, he realized gratefully, he could see out of both eyes. Looking up at his mother, he said, "Could I . . . have . . . some water?"

"You mean you can't get up?" Chloe asked, appalled. "You can't walk? Richie, how are you going to get my medicine? Will you be all right by this afternoon?"

"I don't know," he said, feeling very rocky, holding on to the side of the cot to keep some kind of balance. "Will you . . . get me a drink . . . ?"

"All right. All right," she said placatingly. "Just sit still. I'll get it. You'll be all right in a couple of hours, I know you will."

She brought him the water and he managed a few swallows of it. Then he forced himself to get up and walk a few excruciating steps down the hall to the bathroom, and was thankful no one was using it when he got there. Unable to stand steadily, he sat down to urinate. When he finished, while his trousers and underwear were still down, he looked at his scrotum. It had ballooned up alarmingly; the sight of it made him feel sick, and he almost threw up as he had done in the alley. Holding on to the sink to balance himself, he waited until the nausea passed, then got his trousers up again. Strength ebbing fast, he nevertheless paused long enough to look at himself in the mirror. He saw, at once why his mother had stared at him with such revulsion. Both eyes were swollen, both nostrils nearly closed with coagulated blood; the automobile-tire lips stuck out grotesquely, and were coated with more dried blood; the tip of his chin was badly lacerated as if scraped, and already covered by scabbing.

Haltingly, Richie managed to get back up the hall to the apartment. As he made his way over to the cot, Chloe, sitting drumming her fingers on the table, watched him appraisingly.

"Do you feel better?" she asked brusquely.

"No," he told her, "I gotta . . . get back in bed."

Chloe's lips compressed. "All right. Get in bed. Go to sleep. After you rest, you'll be all right. I'll wake you up when it's time to go get my medicine."

Lying back down, Richie felt very thirsty again, as well as hungry, exhausted, nauseated, dizzy, and in fierce, unrelenting pain. In spite of it all, as soon as he got the blanket pulled over his head to shut out the light, he fell again into a deep sleep.

When Chloe awakened him the next time, it was with a gentler touch and a softer voice.

"Richie, honey, it's time to wake up. You have to get up now, sugar, and run your errand for me."

Richie lifted his throbbing head an inch. "I can't . . . I'm hurt. I'm sick—"

"Richie, it is *not* far over there," his mother said firmly. "I'll give you streetcar fare if you don't want to walk. Come on now, get up."

"I can't, I tell you . . . I can't." Each word he spoke hurt his face.

Chloe became incensed. "*Oh—yes—you—can!*" Jerking the blanket off of him, she grabbed his arm with both hands and dragged him half off the cot until his head and shoulders were on the linoleum floor, his legs still up on the cot.

"Cut it . . . out!" Richie yelled, as loudly as he could, feeling his bottom lip split with the effort and start to bleed. "Lea' me alone . . . !"

"*You—are—going!*" She pulled his legs off the cot, took him by the shoulders, and tried to pull him upright. A sitting position was the best she could do. "Come on Richie!" she snarled threateningly.

"I can't . . . I can't . . . I can't . . . " Richie tried shaking his head for emphasis, but it immediately made him feel sick, so he stopped. His mother kept tugging at him, trying to get him to stand up, but she was far too weak to budge him, and finally she gave up and, stepping back, began shaking both fists impotently at him.

"How can you do this to me, Richie?" she shrieked. "You know how much I depend on you! What am I going to do now, just answer me that! If I go over there myself, I'm liable to get robbed! Raped! Killed! I'm a *white* woman, for god's sake!"

Squinting up at her through slitted eyes, Richie said, "Can't you . . . get it where you got it when . . . you first started using it?"

"No, I can't! Don't you think I would if I could? I used to get it from one of the other maids when I was working at the hotel. But she got fired for stealing too." Chloe's tone became adamant. "Richie, you have *got* to do this for me!"

"I can't. I can hardly walk. Look . . ." He showed her his distended scrotum.

"How could you let that happen to you?" she accused. Pounding her temples with the heels of both hands, she began to pace, moaning beseechingly, "Oh, god! Oh, god! Oh, god!" After several minutes of that, she stalked into the bedroom, put on her worn coat, got her dilapidated purse, and stormed out of the apartment.

When he was sure she was not coming right back, Richie pulled himself back on the cot and drew the blanket over his head again.

It was dark when he awoke next. Rising painfully, he turned on a light and saw that it was nearly four A.M. Chloe, he noticed at the bedroom door, was not there. His body, in addition to the pain of the beating, was now wracked by hunger and thirst. At the kitchen sink, he had a few swallows of water, immediately regurgitated it, then drank some more that stayed down. In the cupboard above the sink he rummaged for something to eat. There were several cans of soup. Finding a can opener, Richie managed to open a can of vegetable soup. Sitting on the floor, he sipped a little at a time, cold, from the can. Finishing it, he dragged himself back up, urinated in the sink, and returned to his cot.

The next time he awoke, it was mid-morning. Chloe still was not home.

Richie opened another can of soup, this time sitting at the table to drink it. Between swallows, he tested various parts of his body for flexibility. Woodenly stiff, every muscle tightly defensive, he nevertheless seemed to be capable of moving everything: wrists, knees, ankles, elbows. His head felt huge and top-heavy, as if it might tumble off if he were not careful.

With a compelling curiosity to look at himself again, when he finished his soup this time Richie made his way into Chloe's tiny bedroom where there was a small mirror hanging above a dilapidated bureau. When he saw his reflection, Richie could only stare incredulously. It did not even look like him. His normally thin face was round and puffy, lumpy, ugly-colored, like a rotting cauliflower.

"Jesus Christ," he muttered.

As he was about to turn away, Richie noticed that the top drawer of the bureau was not quite closed; something odd-looking was sticking out of one corner. Pulling the drawer open a little, he examined what turned out to be a length of brown rubber tubing. Lying next to the rest of it in the drawer were a hypodermic needle, three blackened spoons, and a cheap Zippo cigarette lighter. Picking up the hypodermic needle with thumb and forefinger, Richie stared at it in horror as he realized what it was for. Like tiny metal shavings being attracted by a magnet, there converged in his mind bits of previously unrelated knowledge: the word "hype" that the black drug dealer sometimes used; the phrase "shooting up" that he had heard, somewhere; the fact that he had never really known for sure exactly *how* his mother used the heroin she sent him for.

Feeling nauseated at the sight of the needle and the thought of his mother puncturing her arm with it, Richie put it back and closed the drawer. After resting his head on the bureau for several minutes to compose himself, he once again maneuvered back to the cot and covered up entirely with the blanket. He slept, but he dreamed of his mother with a million tiny holes all over her body.

Chloe came back late that afternoon. The sound of the door slamming woke Richie up. He saw his mother sweep nervously across the room, stopping abruptly when she noticed the open cans on the counter and the table. Snatching up the one on the table, she hurled it across the room at him.

"Goddamn you, who said you could have this soup!" she shrieked. "That was *my* soup!"

The can bounced harmlessly off the wall and Chloe stormed on into the bedroom, slamming that door also. Richie put one of his shoes under the blanket, keeping it handy in case she came out and started beating on him.

A little while later, Chloe emerged from the bedroom and, glaring at him, opened one of the two remaining cans of soup and heated it in a pan. It was chicken noodle and the aroma of it wafted across the room to Richie, causing his innards to gurgle. He watched from the cot as his mother broke crackers into the soup and ate it from the pan. Occasionally she would glance over at him, but she did not speak. Richie wanted desperately to ask her for some of the warm soup, but he did not because he was afraid she would say no, or, worse, get angrier and throw it at him.

When she finished eating, Chloe set the pan in the sink without rinsing it and returned to the bedroom. Although the bedroom door was left open and she could see him, Richie got up anyway and went over to the kitchen alcove. With one finger he wiped the soup remains from the inside of the pan and licked it into his mouth. There wasn't much left and it was barely warm any longer, but it tasted extremely good nevertheless. As he was standing there, Chloe came back out of the bedroom, wearing her coat and carrying her purse. Seeing what he was doing, she came over to the kitchen, glowering disagreeably, and took the one remaining can of soup from the cupboard. Without a word, she put it in her purse and left the apartment.

Richie ate a few crackers, drank as much water as he could, and went back to his cot.

In the week that followed, Chloe was home for only a few hours at a time; Richie had no idea where she was. When she was home, she ignored Richie entirely, either staying in the bedroom with the door closed or heating soup she got from her purse. Richie guessed she was either buying or stealing one can at a time. She did not offer him any; once when he finally mustered up enough heart to ask her for some, she stared flatly at him and said, "You don't help me, I don't help you." She did not speak to him again.

On the third day after his beating, Richie took an old towel down the hall to the bathroom and cleaned up his face as best he could. Though still very puffy, his features looked markedly better with the crusted, scabbed blood washed off. His scrotum was only about half as swollen as it had been, making it easier for him to walk. Returning to the apartment, he took off the clothes he had been in since the beating, and washed the rest of himself as best he could at the kitchen sink. He ate the rest of the crackers, leaving the cupboard completely bare.

Pulling on some other clothes, Richie sat on the cot and contemplated his situation. He had to have food, yet there was virtually no way to get it. After leaving the pushcart in the alley and not showing up for three days, he knew he had lost his paper routes; he was in no condition to work them anyway. He could not filch coins off newsstands or steal food from markets either, because both endeavors required great speed of foot, and it was all he could do merely to walk. He knew that with his face in the condition it was, he could go nowhere unnoticed, which precluded any serious stealing. Since his mother would not voluntarily help him, there seemed just one thing left to do.

Leaving in plain sight for her to see the clothes he had taken off, Richie folded up his coat and put it under Chloe's bed, so that she would think he had gone out. With a library book, *Of Mice and Men* by John Steinbeck, he lay down on her bed, which had not been made in weeks, and started to read. Chloe had not been home all night, so he expected her sometime during the day. When he got tired of reading, he allowed himself to doze a little, but always with the book in his hands; he knew he would not fall completely asleep as long as he held the book.

When a key sounded in the apartment door, Richie knew his mother was home. Getting quickly off the bed, he shimmied under it with his book, rested his head on his jacket, and lay very still. Chloe rummaged around in the other room and the kitchen alcove, muttering to herself, but he could not make sense of anything she said. Eventually she came into the bedroom, locked the door, and hung her coat on the bedpost, its hem hanging to the floor where Richie could see it. He heard a bureau drawer being pulled open, the metallic sound of one of the spoons, some other, indistinguishable, sounds, and then Chloe sat down on the side of the bed; he could see her feet: her shoes were off and there was a run in each stocking. After she was on the bed for a few moments, Richie heard the unmistakable sound of a Zippo being sparked up. There was some more movement, a very soft sigh from his mother, then she went back to the bureau for a moment and put some things back in the drawer before closing it and returning to lie down on the bed. For the next few minutes, she moaned quietly a few times, then became very still.

Richie waited until there had been no sound or movement for a while, then slowly edged out from under the bed and peered up over its side. His mother was lying facing him, her mouth open, a line of spittle running down her chin—but her eyes, thankfully, were closed, and she was breathing evenly. Coat and book in one hand, Richie got to his feet, quietly unlocked the door, picked up Chloe's purse, and tiptoed out of the room.

In the other room, coat now on, he quickly searched her purse for money. Besides a little change, she had fourteen dollars in currency—two fives and four ones—and a welfare department check for twenty-two-fifty. Richie took half the money, seven dollars, and put the purse back on the bureau. There was no way to lock the door from the outside, so he just quietly closed it. Grabbing his library book, Richie hurried across the room and out of the apartment. He wasn't sure whether his mother would figure out what happened or just think she had spent the money somewhere and forgotten to lock the bedroom door, but Richie knew better than to take any chances.

He decided to stay away for a few days.

At the White Castle, the counterman looked curiously at Richie's face and asked, "What the heck happened to you, kid?" The other customers at the counter all turned to look.

"My dad and me was in a car wreck," Richie said. "A streetcar crashed into the side of us. It was in all the papers."

"Jeez, I must've missed it," the counterman said.

"I t'ink I seen it," one of the customers said.

"Yeah, my dad was killed," Richie continued. "He'd only been back from the war a month, too. And he had the Purple Heart."

"Jeez," the counterman said self-consciously. He glanced at the other customers, but they all turned back to their food. "Well," he asked, "what'll you have?"

Richie ate six dime hamburgers and drank two glasses of milk. When he went to pay, the counterman gave him a wink and only charged him for two burgers and one milk—twenty-five cents. "Thanks a lot, mister," Richie said, wondering as he left if he could parlay the story into discount meals elsewhere.

Back on Adams Street, Richie slipped into the basement of the building where he and Stan used to live, and was pleased to see that the superintendent's huge stack of bundled newspapers was still there. Squeezing back between the papers and the coal chute, he moved several bundles and found the concealed crawl space that had been his cubbyhole. Still *was*, as a matter of fact, for there, just as he had left them months earlier, were the extra corduroy trousers and shirt he had worn the morning he fled the Hubbard household. It delighted Richie to find them; the clothes were like old friends. The quilt Stan had given him was there too. And the basement was warm from the roaring furnace.

Now that he knew where he was going to spend the night, Richie left the basement and trudged through the snow over to Madison Street to the Haymarket Theater, where he sat through a double feature and all the short subjects, then dozed in his seat an extra hour before leaving. For supper he had more hamburgers, at a different White Castle, but it was almost deserted and no one paid any attention to his face this time. At a grocery he bought two packages of Twinkies and a bottle of Kayo chocolate drink to take back to the basement with him. He also stopped in a Neiser's variety store and bought a twenty-nine-cent penlight with battery to check for rats when he got back.

□□ 319 □□

There were no rats, and in a little while Richie was safely, warmly ensconced in his cubbyhole, extra clothes for a pillow, quilt for a cover, Twinkies to snack on, and *Of Mice and Men* to read by penlight. It amazed him that he had not thought of a penlight or flashlight the last time he slept there. He supposed it was because he had been younger. As Stan often said, "The older you get, the more you learn." Richie wondered if there was *anybody* smarter than Stan. He doubted it.

When he got sleepy enough to turn off the thin beam from his penlight, Richie put the book down by his side and tried not to think about where his mother was, or what she was doing. Tried not to think, either, about Frances and what might have happened to her. To keep those two out of his mind, he turned to another familiar thought: his father. For perhaps the thousandth time he reviewed everything he had overheard his father say during the train trip south. There had to be, Richie was certain, clues to his father's whereabouts *somewhere*. He had to find them.

He had to.

Richie went home after four days. When he entered the apartment, he found Chloe sitting at the table, drinking coffee and smoking a cigarette.

"Hi, sugar," she said hoarsely, her words slurred. "You're home early. Your route go fast?"

"Yeah, pretty fast," he said. She doesn't even know I've been gone, he thought at once, with relief. And she's not mad about the money. Glancing over at his cot, he saw that it was exactly as he had left it. The cupboard door partly open, he saw some cans of soup on the shelf.

"You want to run over to Lake Street for me a little early, sugar?" Chloe asked.

"Sure."

She got her purse from the bedroom and came back to the table. Richie sat down and studied her while she put together five dollars in currency and change. Deep, dark circles hung under her eyes now, and her skin was turning waxy and ill-looking. Her hair was streaking very gray, her teeth turning very dark, and her hands looked like witch's hands, like claw-hands.

"Hurry back now," she said automatically as she put the money in a wrinkled envelope and handed it to him. Squinting slightly, she tilted her head. "What happened to your eye, sugar?"

"Slipped on the ice," he said.

"Try to be more careful," Chloe advised.

As Richie trudged over to the dope dealer, he tried to formulate some plan for the future. Being incapacitated by the beating had effectively collapsed his economic and educational routines. He had lost his paper routes. And by being absent from school more than a week, a truant officer would by now have learned that Richie had long ago moved out of the Tilton Elementary school district. If he went back to Tilton now, they would transfer him to Brown, where he had gone once before—and this time he would not have Stan to stick up for him there.

Fuck it, Richie decided, he would not go back to school at all. With his mother in the shape she was in, she was not going to be any help paying rent and buying food until after her dope needs had been satisfied; even then, her solution to back rent was to move, and the only food she seemed to know how to buy was soup. He was not going to have time for school; just getting through the winter with enough to eat was going to be a full-time job.

When he got to Lake Street, Richie looked in the lighted windows of the rib joints and in tavern doorways for Vernie, but he did not see her. In the middle of one block, two black youths stopped him, asking, "Where the fuck you going, ofay?" When Richie told them the name of the dope dealer he was going to see, they let him alone. Richie went on to the black man's apartment, got his mother's "headache powder," and began his trek back home.

On the way, he felt an icy wetness seeping up into one sock and realized with weary resignation that it was time to change the cardboard in his shoes.

Chloe began staying out two and three days at a time. Richie had no idea where she was or what she was doing, and tried not to think about it. At least when she was gone, he reasoned, it was not necessary for him to make the trip to Lake Street, and for that he supposed he should be grateful. He did not mind staying in the apartment alone, except for the times when the landlady knocked on the door for the rent.

"My mother's at work right now," Richie lied when that happened, without much success. The landlady, a tough Slavic woman, grunted derisively.

"Your mother don't know what work is, kid. Tell her to get that rent paid or I'll padlock your apartment, got that? Work, *that's* a good one!"

Between what he was stealing on the street, using all the ways he had learned from Stan, and the little money he could get Chloe to pay, or filch from her purse, Richie managed to keep the landlady appeased enough to prevent their eviction.

When his mother was not there, and when he was simply too taxed by his daily burden of just getting along, too weary to try for anything better, Richie continued to steal potatoes to eat. It was easy enough to slip three or four of them inside his shirt under his coat. They would be all he would eat, sometimes, warmed up, meal after meal, until they were gone. If he had enough for a couple of days, and if the rent was reasonably current, Richie could allow himself the luxury of staying in out of the cold, reading for hours on end, writing book reports that he now had no place to turn in, nevertheless saving them in his school notebook as if they were assignments. Occasionally he wondered how Linda was, what she was reading for her extra-credit work for Miss White; sometimes he thought about Stan and wondered how he liked living with his father in Ohio. But mostly, when Richie's mind was not on a book or on an urgent personal need such as rent or food, it reverted to thoughts of his own father: where he was, how he could be found, and why he had left his only son, his only child, to suffer such an adverse, oppressive life. More and more Richie became convinced that finding his father was the only way life would ever be anything but trouble and hard knocks. Yet with the cruel winter dragging on so interminably, he could not find the energy or the ambition to actually begin a search either for Estelle or the garageman Mack.

One thing he did do, however, was find a way to see Frances again. He dared not go back to the building where she lived, or even to that block, for the thought of being caught again by Walter Rozinski generated in him a sick dread. But Richie knew where Frances did her grocery shopping, an A & P on Ashland Avenue. One morning he stood in the doorway of a furniture store across from the market and watched as she came down the street and went inside. Crossing, he entered the store and looked down the aisles until he found her. Waiting until she was in an aisle by herself, he walked up to her. Before she noticed him, he saw that one of her eyelids was half down, as if it had no muscle in it, and a corner of her bottom lip was misshapen, mashed out of synchronization with the rest of her face.

"Frances," he said quietly. Looking at him, her expression became frightened.

"Oh, my god," she whispered. "He told me he killed you."

"He came close to it," Richie said. "What's wrong with your eye?"

"God did that," Frances replied anxiously. "God killed the nerve in my eyelid to punish me for sinning with you."

"You mean Walter beat you up, like he did me?"

"God," she corrected. "God acted through Walter. We had to be punished, Richie. What we were doing was a dishonor to my husband and the Church and God. I had to confess everything to our priest, after I got well enough to go out. Walter, he didn't have to confess nothing, not even beating me up, because the priest said he was acting for God." Frances tried to smile, but it only made her lips look more incongruous. "I'm glad he didn't kill you, Richie. You're a good kid. I'd like to pray for you, but our priest said you was a devil in the form of a lamb." She looked nervously around. "I've got to go now. Walter and the priest have people spying on me."

Richie watched her hurry up the aisle. The way she flitted away, like a nervous animal in fear of capture, reminded him of his mother when she needed a fix.

Shaking his head sadly, Richie left the market and returned to his bleak, dismal world.

When Richie thought that he and his mother had reached the bottom of life, that things could not become any worse for them, he learned that hardship had only a horizon, never a terminus, and that from then on, the decline into greater adversity, greater misfortune, and greater suffering, was swifter and more indelible on them than ever before. When the meanest of times came, they came like bacteria, and Richie's astuteness and shrewdness and cunning, even his keen instincts, at that low tier of his existence, were not strong enough medicine to stop their spread. He could take care of himself, scurrying and scavenging around the freezing city like one of the rats he had once smashed with bricks, but he could not take care of his mother and her drug habit too.

As Chloe's need for heroin increased, her ability to help pay for it dwindled. She ran out of branch welfare offices to swindle; her nerves flagged to the point where she lost the poise and presence necessary to steal; her physical appearance withered until she no longer had anything desirable with which to barter. She became a dreg, and with an invisible umbilical cord she fed her hopelessness to Richie and made him one also. He became as thin and haggard and haunted-looking as she was, and his desperation as dire to him as Chloe's was to her. They were in the depths now; the rim of their pit could no longer even be seen; there was no tomorrow, no expectations, no optimism; they lived not even from day to day, but from hour to hour.

When the end came, it was with a sickening thud: the sound, and then the sight, of Chloe beating her head against the wall to punish the devils in her drug polluted body. When Richie forced her to stop it, she pleaded with him, "Get me something, Richie, get me something," with no grasp at all that she was begging a hungry, half-sick twelve year old with holes in both shoes, who had run out of newsstands and markets from which to steal coins and food because he had done it too often, was now recognizable, was too ragged to go unnoticed, too weak to get away if chased. Forcing Chloe to stop beating her head against the wall, Richie made her lie on the bed and tried to calm her with coffee from some old grounds that were still in the percolator. But Chloe cursed him and threatened him and resumed the thud, thud, thud against another wall.

That was when Richie gave up and telephoned Miss Menefee.

When Richie found out his mother was back, it was too late because she was hooked again, going over to Lake Street again, on her way back to hell again.

After following Chloe to Lake Street, Richie was so drained that he could not find the energy to do more than go sit in the park and stare, like Myron said the other old men at his rooming house did.

Nothing had changed.

*S*itting on the bench in Garfield Park, slumped down with his chin on his chest, Richie stared at the asphalt walk and the plain of new grass that stretched beyond it. He felt numb, and his eyes, his hands, his demeanor reflected it: he sat very still, his breathing barely discernible. A block away down Madison Street in a cheap rented room, his mother, whom he had seen today for the first time in nearly a year, was lying, he knew, in a heroin haze from the dope he had watched her buy two hours earlier. Because of that, because of *her*, it was as if all he had been able to accomplish on his own—avoiding the authorities, living at Cascade, working, reading, learning to box—all of his efforts, all of his struggles, everything he had been through, had been for nothing because he was right back where he started: he was a kid on the dodge with a junkie mother to worry about. The fact that he had survived and was a year older, could now fight, and was earning money at it, and through Mack might have a viable lead to locating his father, carried no weight at all in his stunned young mind. Only one thing seemed important: his mother was back—and she was still a junkie.

Raising his chin from his chest, Richie sighed heavily and thought of Myron, waiting for him—or probably *not* waiting for him now—at the gym where Richie was supposed to have begun training for his fight the following Saturday night with some black kid named Willie Wakefield. Tall and skinny, Myron had said he was. Very fast. Unbeaten, like Richie himself; half of his wins by knockout, also like Richie. Myron was going to give him some special training starting today on how to fight a Willie Wakefield type of boxer, but Richie had not shown up. Instead of training, he sat alone on a park bench.

Another sigh, and his thoughts shifted to Linda. She was sitting alone too, in the movie theater they were supposed to be in together. Linda had understood when Richie met her and broke their date so that he could train. If he had not done that, he realized, he would not have run into Stan Klein on his way to the gym, and would not have learned that his mother was back. But it would have made no permanent difference, he would have found out eventually, and it would have confused and confounded him just as much.

Fighting inertia, Richie rose and walked back out of the park. He thought perhaps walking, movement, some kind of purpose, would bring him out of the doldrums in which he found himself, but he was wrong. Without conscious thought, he walked back the way he had come, and in scant minutes was again on Madison Street, across the street from the stairway leading up to the three floors of housekeeping rooms, one of which Chloe occupied. Being that close to where he knew she was, and being aware that she was again, or *still*, a junkie, was like having a nail driven into his skull. Goddamn her, he thought. Goddamn her to fucking hell!

Angry, empty, having a desire to *stop* everything—thinking, moving, wondering, hating; just stop it all—Richie shoved his hands into his pockets and walked languorously down Madison until he came to the Senate Theater. He went up to the box office for a ticket. Inside, he walked past the sparkling candy counter without a glance, something he had never done in his life, and went directly into the darkened auditorium. Moving into the last row, which was empty, he went all the way over to the seat next to the wall, just as he had done in the Haymarket Theater all those nights he stayed out until George Zangara left his mother's bed. Slumping down, he propped both knees on the seatback in front of him, folded his arms across his chest, and closed his eyes.

He must have been very tired, emotionally drained, everything that made sense in an upheaval, unable to cope with the jolt of his mother's return, because the next thing Richie knew, an usher was shaking him roughly, saying, "Hey, you, come on, wake up, the show's over, we're closing up."

"Okay, okay," Richie said, coming awake, pushing the usher's hand away.

Outside, the Madison-Kedzie intersection was quiet, only a few people about. Richie looked at a clock in a window of a bank and saw that it was eleven-thirty. He ran to catch a streetcar stopped at the corner, so he could get to the bowling alley and his bedroom in the ladies' lounge before Cascade closed for the night.

As the streetcar passed the block where Chloe had a room, Richie forced himself not to look out the window. He did not want to know if his mother was out and about.

The next morning, Richie got Grace Menefee's telephone number out of the secret compartment of his now almost worn-out Buck Jones billfold, and called her from a drugstore booth. When she answered the telephone and discovered it was him calling, her voice grew cool.

"Yes, Richie. What can I do for you?"

"My mother's back and she's still a junkie!" he accused, anger and disappointment being generated anew. "I thought you was gonna have her cured!"

"She *was* cured, Richie," the caseworker replied calmly, though not any friendlier. "Your mother was off drugs for three of the five months she's been back. But she wasn't—"

"She's been back *five* months?" he interrupted incredulously.

"Yes. She tried to find you; we both did. In fact," Miss Menefee inserted drily, "there have been quite a few people looking for you. Needless to say, no one has caught up with you yet."

"Nobody's going to either," Richie told her bluntly.

"That's what you think, tough guy. No one gets away forever. In the meantime, while you've been hiding, your mother came home from Lexington cured of her drug habit and I arranged for a place for her to live and a job for her. She did all right for a few months, but then, well . . ." Grace Menefee's voice lost its edge and became softly sad. "I couldn't be with her day and night, Richie. I gave her as much time and encouragement as I could; I've got other cases, other people. Anyway, I guess it wasn't enough." The caseworker paused and Richie heard her sigh the same kind of hollow, weary sigh that had swept over him several times on the park bench the previous day. Then she asked, "Where is your mother now, Richie?"

"You don't know where she's living?"

"No, a couple of months ago she moved out without paying her rent and I haven't heard from her since. I was afraid she'd gone back on drugs. One thing I do know: she's not receiving a welfare check. We've flagged all the names she previously used to get assistance, and a description of her has been posted in all of our branches. Now I want you to tell me where she's living, please."

Richie's wariness locked in gear. "What'll happen if I do?"

"I don't know what will be done with her this time," Grace Menefee said frankly. "But she's a drug addict and she can't be allowed to roam the streets—"

Richie hung up. Fuck you, he thought. Fuck you and your whole fucking welfare department. There had to be a better way. There had to. He would just have to figure out what it was.

To give his mind a rest from the turmoil, Richie boarded a streetcar and rode over to Mack's garage to see if he had been able to find out anything about Ava. Mack was washing a carburetor in a pan of gasoline when Richie came in.

"I know what you're gonna ask me," he said before Richie could speak, "and the answer is no. I dropped out to the club in Cicero but none of the Capone family was around, so I didn't try to find out nothing. This ain't the kind of question I can ask just anybody. And I have to be careful *how* I ask it too. I mean, I can't go up to one of the Capones and say, 'Where's Avellina Gela?' It's gotta come up in conversation, real natural like. These ain't ordinary people we're dealing with. You just have to be patient, Richie. I'm going out there again Wednesday night; I might catch one of the family then." Taking the carburetor out of the pan of gasoline, Mack put it in a sink and ran water over and through it. "I been thinking about your invite to come see you fight Saturday night. Maybe I'll take you up on it. Where's it at again?"

Richie told him the location of the South Side athletic club to which his opponent, Willie Wakefield, belonged, and at which the match between the two undefeated fighters would be held. "I'll leave a pass for you at the door," Richie said.

"You don't have to do that. I don't mind paying," Mack said.

"No, I want to," Richie insisted. All the club fighters got two passes for their parents to use. Richie had always given his away, explaining to Myron that his mother and father were too nervous to stand the excitement of attending the fights. This would be the first time Richie had used a pass. It made him feel good to tell Mack a pass would be waiting for him, feel good that someone would be coming just for *him*, just to see *him* fight.

Richie left the garage to go back to the West Side feeling good. Only after he had been riding the streetcar a few minutes did he see an old drunk woman staggering along the sidewalk, and remember his mother. His mood immediately turned black again.

The first thing Myron said to him when Richie got to the gym that afternoon was, "What happened yesterday? You was supposed to be here for some extra training."

The other club fighters changing in the locker room all looked at them. Embarrassed, Richie said, "I'm sorry, Myron. My mother got sick and I had to stay with her while my dad went to get some medicine for her."

"What, you don't know how to use the telephone?" Myron asked, raising his hands in mock amazement. There were a few laughs. "I wasted two hours here," Myron asserted, "when I coulda been listening to the Cubs game. I hope you ain't getting to be some kind of prima donna just because you ain't been beat yet."

"We don't have a phone," Richie told him, blushing, "and I couldn't get out to a booth." What the hell was Myron chewing him out in front of the others for, he wondered resentfully. It was the first time, *ever*, that he had missed a workout.

"Go on, get changed," the sad-faced trainer ordered brusquely. "We'll try to make up the lost time."

When Richie got on his training gear and went out to the corner of the gym reserved for club fighters, Myron was showing Georgie Miller, the hundred-fourteen pounder, how to rotate his right cross for more effective impact on an opponent. Richie started shadow boxing in front of one of the full-length training mirrors. He was just working up a good sweat a few minutes later when Myron came over to him.

"All right, do you remember anything I told you about this Wakefield kid, or is that asking too much?" the trainer inquired glumly.

"Yeah, I remember," Richie said. "Tall, skinny, fast. Look, Myron, I'm really sorry about yesterday. I just couldn't get here and I couldn't call." Richie did not have the fiber at the moment to try to explain the real situation to Myron. Maybe at a later time. "I won't do it again," he promised.

"Okay, okay," Myron absolved, "forget it. I shouldn't have got upset about it. It's just that I brung a couple of my friends from the rooming house over to show you off to them yesterday. I been telling 'em about you, you know, how you'd come in here and train by yourself over in the corner, an' how the club kinda took you on as a mascot, sort of, an' then how now yez is going into a undefeated main event." Myron shrugged. "It just made me look foolish when you din' show yesterday."

Richie felt wretched. "Jeez, Myron, I really am sorry. I don't know what to say." Then an idea struck him. "Listen, why don't you invite your friends to the fight Saturday night? They can see me beat Wakefield. That'll be even better than watching me train. You can even give them one of my passes."

"One of them?" Myron's eyebrows went up. "You mean you're actually gonna be using a pass yourself?"

"Yeah. A friend of my dad's is coming to see me. Guy named Mack. He owns a garage. I'll innerduce you." Richie made a mental note to tell Mack not to mention to Myron that Richie did not live with his father. Mack, in fact, did not even know that Richie did not live with his *mother*; Richie had never told him that he was a runaway sleeping in a bowling alley and living out of lockers.

"Okay, let's get going," Myron said. "You're gonna be punching up in this bout, instead of punching straight over or down, so I wanna change your stance just a little . . ."

Richie tried to concentrate, he tried to rivet his mind on the instructions Myron gave, but his usual intensity of attention was not there, and Myron noticed it. Richie knew that Myron was aware that something was missing, even though the trainer said nothing about it following the Monday afternoon workout. All he said was, "Get here as early as you can tomorrow, Richie."

At Cascade that night, working his usual double alley, Richie lingered in one of the pits too long, the next bowler delivered, and Richie barely got up on the partition before eight of the ten pins came flying into the pit.

"Ain't no place to be daydreaming," a pinboy next to him said. "You ain't careful you'll get your legs broke."

It was not daydreaming that caused him almost to be hit; it was torment. Richie could not get his mother off his mind. His concern for her, for the fact that her stay in the drug hospital at Lexington had not left her permanently cured, fermented into distress, then anguish, then a chaos of mental turmoil so compelling that it took charge of his mind completely. And Grace Menefee's words haunted him: *I couldn't be with her day and night, Richie.* Would she, he had to wonder, have stayed cured if *he* had been there to be with her, to help her? Chloe had quit taking her "medicine" twice before, he remembered. But that, he mentally qualified, had been paregoric; this was heroin. "Bad shit," Vernie called it. A hundred times worse than paregoric or the weed that George Zangara introduced into his mother's life. Could Richie, only thirteen years old, have made any kind of difference for her, if he had been around? Could he have helped her at all? The question hounded his mind, intruded on his thoughts, plagued every effort he made to focus on other, more immediate matters—such as preparing for the Wakefield fight and staying out of range of flying bowling pins.

On Tuesday, when his training exhibited the same absence of sharpness that Richie had shown the previous day, Myron said something about it. "Your timing's way off, Richie. What's the matter?"

"I don't know," Richie lied. "I just can't seem to get the rhythm."

Wednesday, when Richie was sparring with Nick Bolly, the club's 120-pounder, who was two inches taller than him, Myron kept calling out from the ring apron, "You're lagging your punches, Richie! Put some snap into them!"

On Thursday, beside himself with frustration, Myron lambasted Richie as he had never done—never *had* to do—previously. "Come on, come on, come on! Pick it up, Richie!" When the session ended, Myron came into the locker room where Richie was changing and demanded, "What's the matter with you? You stunk in your workout today!"

"I'm doing the best I can," Richie snapped. And before he could check himself, added, "This ain't the most important thing in the world, you know!"

"You might change your mind about that when you're in the ring Saturday night!" Myron instantly retorted.

They fell silent then, looking at each other, Richie knowing that Myron did not, *could* not, understand what the problem was, because Richie had not told him, and Myron suddenly becoming aware that what was happening was not merely lackadaisical training but actually rooted in something much more acute, much graver. His sad face seeming to have an even more forlorn look than usual, Myron asked, "Can you tell me what's the matter?"

Looking down, Richie could only shake his head.

"Well, then," Myron said, patting Richie's shoulder, "you'll do the best you can, like you just said. Listen, I'll see you tomorrow."

Richie, feeling a catch in his chest, watched Myron walk dejectedly out of the locker room. He was letting Myron down, he thought. Just like he let his mother down. Just like he let Miss Menefee down. Just like he let Stan down.

Maybe, he told himself, he should just take off. Run away. Get out of Chicago for good. If he did not have to worry about his mother and her habit, worry about dodging the authorities, worry about finding his father, training to fight, stealing books to read, sleeping in a bowling alley, feeling responsible for this, guilty about that, scared of something else—maybe he could find some way to lead a *normal* life.

After Saturday night, that's what he would do. He would get away from all of it.

Get away from this hard fucking city.

For good.

*I*n the dressing room of the Stony Island Athletic Club that Saturday night, Richie had just finished having his hands taped by Myron, when he glanced over at the door and saw Mack standing there grinning at him.

"Hey, Mack!" Richie yelled exuberantly, hopping off the rubdown table he was sitting on, working his way through the other club fighters milling about. Several of them looked over at Mack and it made Richie feel good for them to know that someone had come to see him fight.

"Hiya, kid," Mack said sheepishly when Richie got to him. "Say, you look pretty good in them fighter's duds. Listen, thanks for the pass."

"Come on in," Richie said, "I'll innerduce you to Myron, my trainer."

"No, I'd rather not," Mack held back. Leaning close to Richie, he whispered, "I don't wanna limp across a room full of strangers. Maybe after the fight if there ain't as many people around." Smiling, he felt Richie's muscle. "You gonna win tonight?"

"I always win."

"You looked just like your dad when you said that," Mack told him, nodding, smiling. Then his expression became serious. "Listen, speaking of that, I found out something about Ava for you. It ain't gonna be much help, I'm afraid. She went back to Italy before the war. Nobody's heard from her or any of the family over there since the war started. Now that Italy's whipped, Mamma Teresa, who's living down in Florida like I told you, is trying to locate relatives through the Red Cross, but she ain't had no luck yet. It don't sound to me like there's much chance Ava and your dad got together."

"No," Richie quietly agreed. "Probably not."

"You know, kid," Mack said candidly, "you may never find him."

"Maybe I won't," Richie said resignedly.

Mack gave him a friendly punch for luck and went on into the gym to find a seat, and Richie returned to the corner of the locker room where the Midwest fighters were getting ready.

An hour and a half later, Richie was in the ring, Midwest A. C. jacket draped around his shoulders, listening to Willie Wakefield's introduction. Richie himself had already been introduced; he had taken a few steps out of the corner and raised one gloved hand to acknowledge the smattering of applause from the Midwest fans who had crossed the city to a black neighborhood to watch their fighters. Myron always held their jackets when they took their bows, then, as he had just done with Richie, put them back on their shoulders until the bell rang. When Willie Wakefield's introduction was complete, Richie heard a resounding roar from the partisan crowd, about eighty percent of which formed a sea of dark faces.

"Relax, relax," Myron purred, his hand at the back of Richie's neck, feeling him become tense.

They were called to the center of the ring for final instructions from the referee. Richie's mouth became very dry when he got close to Willie Wakefield for the first time. Although the same weight, Willie loomed over him like an adult over a child. He was a full head taller, his narrow, bony shoulders even with Richie's forehead. His gloved hands, held together at his waist, as Richie's were, made his elbows lower than Richie's. Holy Christ, who put this guy together? Richie wondered, paying no attention to the referee's words. When they touched gloves, Willie Wakefield smiled at him. Richie felt sick.

Back in the corner, Myron said, "Try to remember as much as you can from last week: get inside, punch up, dig to the body, clinch. Main thing is dig to the body. You rip to the body enough, you can break this boy in half." The bell sounded. Myron snatched the jacket away and slapped him on the shoulder. "Go on, tear him up!"

It seemed to Richie that Willie Wakefield hit him the instant he took a step out of the corner. His customary stance, which usually protected his face from too many blows, was penetrated at once, from several different angles, and he felt the leather of Willie's gloves slapping against his cheeks, chin, and nose. They were light punches, smarting rather than hurting, but Richie knew they scored points for the fighter throwing them. To counter them,

Richie began moving his own gloves away from his face, trying to pick off Willie's jabs several inches before they could land. It was a good defensive tactic; Willie Wakefield smiled at Richie for being able to modify his style so early. "Not bad, baby," Richie heard him say around his mouthpiece. Toward the end of the round, Richie was finding ways to move inside the long arms, and was getting in some shots of his own to the body. When the round was over, he thought maybe it had been even.

In the second, Willie Wakefield began to move faster, forcing Richie to increase his own speed to follow him around the ring. For the first time, Richie experienced what it was to be the slower fighter, to have to step up the pace and perform faster than was natural and normal. Before, it had been Richie who made the opponent do that, Richie who worked to tire out the other kid in the ring; now it was the other way around. Halfway through the two-minute round, he realized that in addition to increasing fatigue, it also disrupted his timing. On his toes, moving in a wide circle, snapping his long jab into Richie's face with apparent ease, Willie Wakefield was a clear winner of the second round.

"You gotta find a way to get in there, to get to him," Myron urged between rounds. "Otherwise he'll jab you raw."

"Everytime I try, he peppers me," Richie said, "and I lose my timing. When I get it back, he's gone."

"Keep trying," Myron encouraged.

In Round Three, Willie Wakefield danced around Richie like a matador teasing a bull, except that Willie was not teasing: his jabs were like cracks of a long whip, splitting the air and licking at Richie's face, sharply and stingingly, black-gloved giant mosquitos landing and leaving angry red swellings in their wake. Richie began to hurt; his eyes were puffing up, his cheeks numbing, his temples throbbing from the blows he tried to duck but was not quick enough to. It was the same pain, he realized, that he had inflicted on the twelve kids he himself had beaten, and Willie Wakefield was delivering it to him with the same precision and purpose with which Richie had administered it to others. No matter what Richie did, which tactic he tried, which maneuver, which ploy he used, which strategy, Willie Wakefield refashioned his style to suit it, aligned himself to deal with it, instantly reestablished the finesse necessary to keep from relinquishing control of the fight.

Richie returned to his corner after the third round perplexed and bewildered. "I can't seem to do anything," he said in frustration. "I'm losing, ain't I?"

"Every round," Myron confirmed, "except maybe the first—that one was close. You wanna win it, you better knock him out, or at least knock him down a couple times. I notice he's starting to show off a little, playing to the crowd; his balance ain't so perfect when he's doing that fancy stuff. You tag him when he's off-balance, he'll go down. I guarantee it."

"I can't get close enough to tag him," Richie said.

"That's 'cause you stop when he lays his jab on you three or four times."

"What the hell am I supposed to do?" Richie demanded. "Keep moving in and let him use his right?"

"That's exactly what you'll have to do," Myron declared. "You're gonna have to take three or four in order to get in one of your own. There's no other way; he's just too fast for anything else to work."

Before Richie could respond, the bell sounded for Round Four and he was up and moving instinctively. Myron's words reverberated in his head: *Take three or four . . . to get in one of your own.* His face already felt like heavy equipment had been driven over it; even his teeth and gums were hurting, despite the hard-rubber mouthpiece. His shoulders and neck muscles were pulled to the point of burning from all the punches he had thrown and missed. He started forward, determined not to stop no matter how many shots Willie got in. The jab came—once, twice, three times, like a triphammer. Richie kept going. A right cross came out of nowhere, thudding against his temple. It wobbled him one step to the side. Afraid of another, he backed into his crouch and let Willie dance away. The crowd cheered Willie's right cross and Richie's wobble.

Richie decided to try again. *Take three or four . . .* Moving grimly forward, he felt Willie's pop-pop-pop in his face again, but he refused to let it deter him. Knowing the right would be coming, he kept his left high to try to take it on the glove, feinting with the right jab to try at the same time to neutralize Willie's tattooing left. When Willie threw the right, Richie moved in close enough to take it on the upper arm. Willie's jab came immediately after it, curving and twisting past Richie's defense, popping his face as if it were a speed bag. But Richie *was* in close, and that was what he had been trying for. He dug blow after blow to Willie's body, and was still pounding him when the bell sounded, ending the fourth round.

"You hurt him," Myron said when Richie dropped onto the stool, chest heaving.

"I—know—" Richie panted as soon as Myron got his mouthpiece out. "I—heard him—groan once—"

"If you can catch him like that again, you might be able to put him down. That's what you need to shoot for."

"Can I still win?" Richie asked. Myron gave him some water; Richie rinsed his mouth and spat it into the bucket.

"Not on points. He's too far ahead. If you drop him, they might give you a draw so the two of yez can fight again."

"I'll knock him out," Richie said determinedly. "I'll get him—back on the ropes—and I'll flatten him."

From the side of the ring, the timekeeper yelled, "Ten seconds!" Myron put Richie's mouthpiece back in and patted his cheek. "Okay, go get him, Richie!"

The bell rang. Richie and Willie Wakefield met in the center of the ring and touched gloves over the referee's outstretched arm. Then the referee stepped back and Richie moved at once toward Willie, to get a headstart on the chase that he hoped would again end with Willie pinned on the ropes. He found out at once, to his complete surprise, that it was not going to be like that.

Willie Wakefield did not back up.

"Come on, boy, le's fight," Willie said around his mouthpiece.

With Willie standing his ground, Richie attacked his body with both hands while Willie pasted Richie's face and head with stinging blows that were not orthodox hooks or crosses or jabs, but were simply *punches*, such as might be thrown in a wild streetfight.

Richie worked Willie's body, ripped the uppercut, which connected solidly, snapping the fighter's chin up, and then threw the right cross. Willie pulled his head back an inch, the punch missed him, and he countered inside with a left uppercut of his own. Richie's head snapped this time, but he was not hurt; he moved back to Willie's body, digging punches, as Willie resumed snapping punches to Richie's face.

Richie tried the uppercut-right cross combination several more times, but the right never connected; Willie Wakefield was simply too alert, too resourceful, too quick. Halfway through the round, Richie felt a burning sensation at the inside corner of his right eyebrow, and seconds later there was blood running into the eye itself. He kept fighting, kept punishing Willie's body and occasionally getting in a solid punch to the chin or cheek, but he was not hurting Willie Wakefield and they both knew it. Willie, meanwhile, seemed to be seeing how many angles he could hit Richie's face from, as he snapped left-right combinations in abounding numbers, making Richie's face feel as if it were swollen so tight that it would burst at any moment. For the first time since he had begun fighting, Richie was glad to hear the final bell sound. This was one time he did not want to fight all night.

In the corner, Myron swabbed out the half-inch cut next to Richie's eyebrow and with his thumb pressed in a dab of styptic powder to occlude the cut and stop the bleeding.

"I lost, didn't I?" Richie asked dejectedly.

"Probably," Myron replied candidly. "If you did, it ain't the end of the world."

"End of my undefeated streak," Richie said, blinking back tears, both from the astringent Myron had used on his cut and from the disappointment lacing his emotions. "I should've trained harder last week," he muttered. "I shouldn't have worried about *her*. She sure as hell never worried about me."

"Who are you talking about, your mother?" Myron asked sharply. "That ain't no way to talk. She couldn't help getting sick."

"She ain't sick, Myron," Richie blurted out. "She's a junkie."

Myron stared solemnly at him, their sad faces close together. "Oh. I see." He nodded slowly. "Well, that ain't the end of the world either—"

In the center of the ring, Willie Wakefield was being announced the winner and was coming over to congratulate Richie on a good fight. Richie stood up to meet him and they clasped their gloved hands together.

On the way back to the locker room, Richie got more pats on the back than usual, even when he won, and many of them were from the black fans there to support their club, not his.

It should have made Richie feel better, but it did not.

Back at Midwest A. C. later that night, helping Myron put their equipment away, Richie felt as lowdown as he ever had in his life—or so it seemed to him at the moment. His unbeaten record was gone. Life, he was sure, would never be the same. Myron, however, was not concerned about that as much as he was about Richie's earlier revelation that his mother was a drug addict.

"I always thought there was something funny about your family situation," the trainer admitted. "What about your father, is he an addict too?"

"He don't live with us," Richie replied. His thoughts were in such disorder at the moment, he was not certain how much and what to confide in Myron. "I don't even know where he is," he added, hoping that would eliminate his father as a subject of conversation.

"Has your mother tried to get help for her illness?" Myron asked.

"Illness?" Richie grunted disparagingly.

"That's what I said," Myron declared. "That's what it is—a sickness. Your mother needs medical treatment, just like for any other ailment."

"She was in a hospital and got cured once," Richie told him, "but she went back on the stuff a few months later." *I gave her as much encouragement as I could*, Grace Menefee had said. *I couldn't be with her day and night.*

"Why did she go back on it?" Myron wanted to know. Shrugging, Richie looked away. "There must have been a reason," Myron pressed.

"A caseworker from welfare seemed to think it was because she was alone and didn't have nobody to help her," Richie told him, continuing to look away.

"By 'help', you mean encourage, give moral support, that sort of thing?" Myron asked.

"I guess so," Richie said, shrugging again.

"Well, that means a lot sometimes," Myron allowed. "But other people can do just so much for a person; after that, it's up to the person. You sound like maybe you're blaming yourself, are you?"

"I keep wondering if maybe it was my fault," Richie admitted, "on account of not being around to encourage her."

Myron shook his head. "I don't think you ought to be too hard on yourself, Richie. A person's gotta *want* to stay off dope. Best thing anybody can do is help somebody *get* off the stuff; then it's up to them. Beyond a certain point, you can't blame yourself."

When the equipment was put away, Myron as always took Richie to get something to eat. Richie was quieter than usual, not particularly over his loss now, but about what Myron had said. He had not ever really tried to help his mother get off drugs. And he wasn't even planning to help her now; all he was planning to do was run away. It troubled him that he had never really talked to her about her addiction, never told her he would help, never told her he *cared*. All he had done was bitch about going to the drugstores, bitch about the money it cost, bitch about his own involvement—and then turn her in when he could not cope with the situation any longer.

Maybe, he thought now, if he did things differently, if he offered to *help* her, if he let her know he *could* help her, let her know he wasn't just a kid anymore, that he'd made it on his own for nearly a year, that he'd learned to box and won twelve straight fights before losing one, let her know that if she was willing to try, they could make it, the two of them, *without* finding his father, *without* having a Jack Smart or a Johnny Eaton or a George Zangara in their lives—make it together, just themselves—maybe that would work. He could go back to school and get a part-time job and she could get a job, and they could find a decent place to live, not fancy but not crawling with roaches and bedbugs either, and they could both help keep the place clean, and at night they could drink Coca-Colas and listen to the radio, and he would get good grades in school and bring his report card home to be signed instead of having Vernie sign it, and they could live like regular people. Just like—

"You're awful quiet," Myron remarked.

"Trying to figure some things out," Richie said.

"Think you'll be able to?" Myron said. "Figure the things out?"

Richie thought about it for a moment, then nodded. "Yeah, I think I will."

"Think you'll be able to keep fighting?"

"I dunno," Richie said. "I hope so." He grinned slightly. "I'd like to fight Willie Wakefield again. But there's some other things I gotta do first. If I can do both, I will. But I dunno."

When they finished eating and walked out onto Madison Street, Myron said, "Listen, if there's anything I can do to help you, you know I will. I'd hate to see you quit fighting. I don't know what I could do, but if you think of anything, let me know. Okay?"

"Sure, Myron. Thanks a lot."

Myron offered his hand and Richie shook it.

"I'll see you, Richie."

"Sure. See you, Myron."

The trainer shuffled off toward his streetcar stop and Richie went in the opposite direction, toward the bowling alley.

Tomorrow, he had made up his mind, he would go see his mother.

When Richie woke up in the ladies' lounge the next morning and looked at himself in the mirror, he was reminded of what his face had looked like after Walter Rozinski had beaten him up—except it wasn't quite as bad. There was no crusted blood in his nostrils or caked on his lips; just one small scab on the half-inch cut at the edge of his eyebrow. But his eyes and cheeks were puffy and slightly discolored, making his face look like an old inner tube that had a couple pounds too much air in it.

For the next hour, Richie ran cold water over a towel, squeezed it out, and spread it over his face to reduce the swelling a little. Ice would have been better, but he had none; since it was Sunday, the gym would not be open until noon for him to use the locker room. But the cold, wet towels helped considerably; by the time Richie heard the janitors start to work downstairs, his face looked much better. Cleaning up, he unfolded a complete set of clean clothes that he kept in one of his bowling ball lockers, and dressed.

It was going to be good, he thought, to see his mother again, to talk to her and work things out for the future. He would catch her before she shot up, early enough for her to understand what he was telling her, to understand that his way was the best way, the *only* way, they could ever make it together. To show her his sincerity, later when she started needing her fix for the day, he would even go over to Lake Street and get the shit for her. Maybe, if there was room and he could get a cot somewhere, he would even move in with her while they figured out exactly how to go about getting her cured again.

Dressed, hair combed neatly, clean handkerchief in his pocket as Miss Menefee had taught him, Richie gathered up his blanket, pillow, other clothes, and a paperback edition of *Butterfield 8* by John O'Hara, whom Richie found easier to read than almost any previous author, and with everything bundled under his arm, went quickly and quietly to the locker room and stashed it in the two small lockers he still had. Going down the back stairs to the first-floor pits, he ignored the cleaning man pushing the polishing machine around on the alley, knowing that the man could not see him through the screens above the pits. At the farthest fire door, Richie eased down the locking bar and slipped out into the alley.

Richie was hungry this morning, but he was afraid to stop for breakfast in case his mother left before he got there. He had no idea how she was living, but if she was shoplifting full-time she probably had to get started pretty early in the day, especially on Sunday, when there was a smaller selection of stores open. Instead of going for his usual full, hot breakfast at one of the drugstore counters, he trotted up to the Royal Blue market on the corner of Springfield, bought a dime peach pie and a pint bottle of milk, and sat on the curb eating while he waited for a streetcar.

Everything was going to be all right, he told himself confidently. Things were going to work out now, he was sure of it.

And he wasn't going to have to find his goddamned father to make it happen, either.

Getting off the streetcar at Homan Avenue, at the east end of the park in which he had sat brooding a week earlier, Richie walked down Madison toward the building where his mother was living. When he was halfway there, on impulse he turned and went back to a small drugstore on the corner. He asked a clerk if they had *Evening in Paris* perfume, and when she showed him a selection, he bought the smallest bottle for two dollars and fifty cents.

"Girlfriend's birthday?" the lady asked with a smile.

"It's for my mother," Richie said. "She's just home from the hospital."

"How thoughtful," the lady said, putting his purchase in a bag. "I hope she'll be all right."

"Thanks," Richie smiled back.

Walking down the street again, he was very pleased with himself for having bought his mother a gift. He could remember Jack Smart bringing Chloe bottles of *Evening in Paris* and how it always seemed to please her so much. Richie hoped that doing the same thing would impress her with the fact that he wasn't just a little tagalong kid anymore; he could earn money and take care of himself just like a man. Even buy presents for people just like a man did.

At the building he had seen his mother come out of, Richie stepped into the narrow entry and checked the names on the wall at the bottom of the stairs. He found "C. Clark" next to number 3-G. Climbing two long flights of wooden stairs, he walked down a seedy hallway with worn linoleum on the floor and an uncovered garbage can at one end. There was an odor of putridness about the place: empty wine bottles, dried urine, abided decay; Richie took no deep breaths as he followed the letters on the paint-peeling doors.

At 3-G he stood close to the door and knocked softly. Swallowing, mouth suddenly dry, he waited; sweat surfaced under his arms. There was no answer and he knocked again, a little louder. After a moment, he called quietly, "Mother—" Still getting no response, he called, "Chloe—it's me—Richie." Putting an ear to the door, he heard nothing from the other side. He turned the knob, but the door was locked. It was such an old door that the doorframe was loose; he could see part of the bolt, see that it was unsturdily set and not all the way in its latch. Gripping the knob with one hand, Richie put a shoulder to the door where it met the frame, and applied gradual pressure. It came open easily.

The first thing that hit him inside the door was a stench much worse than in the hall; it was pervading and foul, like a backed-up toilet in a public restroom. He saw his mother at once, lying on her back on the bed, dressed in a slip, a sheet covering her to the waist. Eyes widening in fright, disbelief, nausea, he went slowly over and stood by the bed. With two fingers, he tentatively touched his mother's arm. It was rigid and cold. Her eyes were open, fixed sightlessly; lips, without color, were parted soundlessly.

Steeling himself against the fear of the unknown, the incredulity of the moment, the repugnance of the scene, Richie forced himself to stand very still and shift his eyes away from Chloe. Looking around, he saw a typical cheap little housekeeping room: two-burner hotplate with dried food stains on it, discolored wall sink, small table with mismatched chairs, an old couch with its stuffing coming out of both arms, and the metal bed with sagging springs and a bare, grossly stained mattress on which his mother lay dead.

With the same two fingers, Richie touched her arm again, quickly as before, as if to substantiate the stiffness and the absence of warmth found in his first contact. On the arm that he touched, below the inside of her elbow, was a spot of dried blood. Next to the bed, inches from his feet, he saw the rubber tubing, burnt spoon, book of matches, and needle. Shaking his head sorrowfully, Richie asked aloud, "Why'd this have to go and happen?" He took a step toward the foot of the bed. "I was gonna help you," he said. "I had things all figured out. I wasn't even gonna look for *him* anymore." Moving around the corner of the bed, he stood at the foot. "We might could've made it, just the two of us. We might could've had a pretty good life together." Around the other corner of the bed he moved, like a doctor talking to a patient, striving to be calm, rational, sensible, in the face of dreadful facts. When he was directly opposite where he had first stood, he asked one last time, "Why'd this have to go and happen?"

The tears finally came, not in sobs but in steady, silent streams. Now he would never be able to help her. Never be able to make up for not being there when she came home from Lexington, never be able to show her that he had learned to take care of himself and was ready to start helping take care of her. Never be able to show her that he could *get* something out of life for them, *be* somebody. With one plunge of the goddamned needle, one puncture of the fragile flesh, his mother had removed all the praiseworthy plans and purpose from his life, effectively reducing him in his own mind to a guilty failure who had given his mother too little, too late.

For which his punishment was to be left a nobody, with nothing.

The grimness of the thought made him shiver. That's what he had and that's what he *was*.

Nobody.

Nothing.

The awful smell in the room was beginning to make him sick; Richie had the urge to hurry away and quickly run the block up to the park where he could breathe deeply without fear of throwing up. Then he remembered the bag in his hand. Opening it and the box in it, he pulled out the bottle and removed the miniature cork. "Look what I brought for you," he said with a tearful smile. "It's the kind you always liked, remember? Now you won't have to smell so bad." Carefully he put a drop of perfume here, a drop there, being sure to get the places he recalled Chloe herself dabbing—wrists, throat, earlobes—when he had spied on her and Estelle as they got ready to go out. Sprinkling the liquid liberally until he could detect its fragrance penetrating the terrible stench, he then recorked the little bottle and placed it in one of her hands, saying simply, "Here . . ."

After that, Richie was shaken by a great, hollow sigh from somewhere deep in the pit of himself and, suddenly feeling very weak, sat down on the floor and leaned back against the bed. The tears were still flowing and he began to sob a little now, quietly, with an occasional shudder.

Drawing his knees up, he folded his arms over them and lowered his face into the opening they created. He continued to cry, and was still crying a little while later when two policemen came into the room.

ichie had been in the juvenile detention home for a week when one of the custody officers came into the big dayroom and shouted across the room at him, "Lady downstairs to see you! Get a pass at the visiting desk."

Sliding down off a window ledge where he had been sitting looking through the grille at Roosevelt Road, Richie started for the door. As he passed a table where four kids were playing Chinese Checkers, one of them named Jerry stuck a foot out and tripped him. Richie stumbled but did not fall. Stopping, he glared at the boy, who was about his own age and size. Jerry had just come in the previous day and had been looking for someone to pick a fight with since he got there.

"Kinda clumsy, ain't you?" he asked Richie with a grin.

How many times, Richie wondered, had he faced a Jerry with a different face and name on schoolyards all over the goddamned city? How many times had he been forced to stand and take abuse to satisfy some cocky, loud-bragging, attention-seeking bully who somehow sensed that he could not fight? How many insults had he endured, how many times had he been ridiculed and humiliated, laughed at? How many pushes had he taken, how many punches, kicks, knuckles to the back of the head? Eyes fixed coldly on Jerry, he wondered: How many times had he been tripped?

"Not mad at me, are you?" Jerry asked in mock chagrin, pretending to feel bad. Then he stood up, his expression turning mean. " 'Cause if you are, you know what you can do about it."

"I sure as hell do," Richie said softly to himself. He feinted with his left, caught Jerry off-guard, and drove his right fist into the kid's mouth. Jerry went sprawling back over the table, sending Chinese Checkers marbles in all directions. Struggling to regain his balance, Jerry did not even get his fists up before Richie hit him two more times, sending him stumbling backwards. Jerry's nose started to bleed and a look of fear replaced the tough expression he had shown a moment earlier. Richie moved in on him as he had moved in on Willie Wakefield a week earlier, only this kid was no flashy, polished, trained boxer like Wakefield was; he was just another schoolyard bully. Jerry managed to get his fists up defensively, and when he did Richie ripped two body blows to his ribcage and brought them back down. As soon as Jerry's face was unprotected, Richie threw three consecutive brutal right hands to the bleeding nose and Jerry went down, groggy, smeared with blood.

Standing over him, Richie yelled, "Watch where you put your fuckin' feet from now on!"

At that moment, strong adult hands grabbed Richie from behind and took him forcefully out of the dayroom. Five minutes later, he was sitting alone on the floor of a room known in juvenile hall as the Blackstone room: small, dark, with no furniture, it was a twenty-four-hour punishment lockup—with no meals. When the door was closed leaving him in the dark alone, Richie laughed out loud.

It reminded him of Mrs. Raley's.

The next day, he was let out and allowed to see his visitor. It was Grace Menefee.

"What did you do yesterday?" she asked without preliminary. "They were all set to let me see you, then they said I'd have to come back today because you were in isolation."

"I beat up some wiseguy who tripped me," Richie said with a hint of pride, showing her his bruised knuckles. Then he folded his hands on the table that separated them. "What did they do with my mother?" he asked bluntly. Grace Menefee's eyes got watery.

"The county coroner has her, Richie. They have to wait thirty days in case someone wants to claim her. I don't suppose you found your father?"

Richie shook his head.

"Is there anyone else?" Grace Menefee asked.

"My grandmother. But I don't even know if she's still alive."

"Where does she live?"

"Some little town in Tennessee," he said, shaking his head again.

Grace Menefee had Richie tell her all he knew about his grandmother, writing down everything he said in a spiral notebook. "Maybe we can trace her in time," the caseworker said. "If not, the county will see that your mother is buried." Turning to a clean page in the notebook, she gave him one of her determined looks and said, "What we have to worry about right now is you, Richie. I have petitioned the juvenile court to allow our department to put you back in a foster home instead of sending you to the state training school—"

"The what?"

"The reformatory. They call it the Illinois State Training School for Boys. Anyhow, I think there's a good chance that the court will look favorably on our request if we can give them a reasonable explanation of where you've been and what you've been doing for the past ten months." She poised her pencil to write. "Who have you been living with?"

"Nobody. I been living by myself."

Grace Menefee's expression became skeptical. "Where have you been living?"

Richie shrugged. "Different places," he lied.

"Richie," she said, drumming her fingers impatiently, "the juvenile court judge is not a fool. He will know, just as well as I know, that you could not have survived in this city for nearly a year without adult help. You are going to *have* to be honest and truthful with us if you expect us to help you."

"I don't," Richie told her.

"You don't what?"

"I don't expect you to help me." There was no rancor or hostility in his voice. He was simply stating fact. "I'm not asking for no help."

"If you're putting on your John Garfield act, Richie, this is not the time to do it. Today is Monday. Your hearing is Thursday."

"I'm not putting on no act," he claimed. "Sure, there were some people who helped me while I was on the street, but I'm not gonna say who they were. I'm not gonna get them in trouble after they was good to me."

"Look, young man," Grace Menefee said firmly, "the law is very clear regarding juvenile runaways. Anyone who knew or had reason to suspect that you were a runaway, was obligated to report you. If you had been gone a few weeks, the court probably wouldn't even concern itself with your whereabouts. But you violated the county's jurisdiction over you for too long for the court to simply overlook it. You're going to have to wise up, Richie"—she pointed a finger at him for emphasis—"or you're going to be *locked* up."

Looking down at the table, Richie thought of Red, at the bowling alley, who had given him work and treated him fairly when he was a skinny, scraggly, ragged urchin carrying around everything he owned in a pillowcase.

Red was not dumb; he must have half figured that Richie was a runaway. Several times Richie suspected that Red even *knew* that Richie was sleeping somewhere in the bowling alley, and said or did nothing about it.

Richie thought of Linda. She had never actually helped him in any way, but she had known that the police came to school looking for him, and she had known what he was doing and where he was sleeping. And Stan: he too had known.

And Myron. The trainer had even admitted that he had always thought there was something "funny" about Richie's family situation, so he too could probably be accused of helping a runaway. Even Estelle must have had her suspicions. And Mack.

Richie could not, would not, sell out the people who had helped him get through one of the hardest times of his life. Fuck the juvenile court judge. Looking back up at Grace Menefee, he slowly shook his head.

"No."

"You little ingrate," Grace Menefee accused. "How dare you sit there and tell me no, after all I've done for you?" Richie looked back down at the table. "Do you want me to walk out that door and just *leave* you here? Just let them do whatever they want to with you? Is that what you want?"

"I'm not trying to make you mad," Richie started to explain.

"Well, you *are* making me mad!"

"Then I can't help it. I'm not gonna get nobody in trouble just because they was good to me."

"Do you want to go it on your own, young man?" she asked curtly. Her words were clearly a threat.

Looking back down, Richie shrugged. "That's what I been doing," he mumbled, half to himself.

"Fine," Grace Menefee snapped. "If that's the way you want it, that's the way you'll get it."

Flipping her notebook closed, the caseworker rose and walked out of the visitors' room without another word.

On Thursday, Richie and half a dozen other boys were taken in a police van to juvenile court. There they were locked in a holding room furnished with wooden benches to wait for their respective cases to be called, at which time they were taken individually into the courtroom. Richie's was the third case on the docket. When the custody officer took him in, he felt like John Garfield in *Castle on the Hudson*. The courtroom looked exactly as it did in the movies.

To Richie's surprise, Grace Menefee was there; the custody officer led him to a chair directly next to her. Apparently still upset, she did not even look at him as he sat down. Richie looked at the judge and was surprised to find that he was not an elderly, white-haired man as Richie expected him to be; he was a very businesslike younger man dressed in an ordinary business suit. He looked to Richie like a goddamned truant officer.

"All right, Miss Menefee, state your case for the Welfare Department," the incongruous judge said.

Grace Menefee rose. Richie could tell by her voice that she was nervous. "Sir," she began, and at once had to clear her throat and start over. "Sir, I have been the caseworker for this boy and his recently deceased mother for more than two years. There is a great deal more to him than appears on the written record. He has a very high intelligence for his age, is an advanced reader who has won library competitions at the Off-the-Street Club and has always, as long as I have known him, been an exceptionally hard worker, even to the point of handling two paper routes during the cold winter months. He has had a very difficult time in life because of his late mother's long drug addiction and the fact that his father had been absent from the home for a number of years. In spite of it, he has never faltered in his schoolwork, always receiving better than average grades; he has a library card and has made frequent use of the city library system; I have letters here from a Miss White, a public school teacher, and a Miss Cashman, a city librarian, substantiating these facts . . ."

As Grace Menefee dug into her briefcase for the letters, Richie stared at her in surprise. He had always considered Miss White and Miss Cashman to be separate and distinct elements in his life, and it seemed odd now to think of them as somehow connected, with Miss Menefee as the link. For several moments, he let the two women occupy his mind as he wondered what they thought and said when Miss Menefee went to see them. He wondered if Miss White, who he knew was aware of his friendship with Linda, had told her about Miss Menefee's visit, and about what had happened to him. Linda, he supposed, was very worried about him now that he had missed meeting her two Sundays in a row.

Grace Menefee's voice moved back into Richie's mind. ". . . just feel," she was saying to the judge, "that to put him into the punishment sector of our system might repress and eventually suffocate the natural development of an above-average mind. We therefore ask the court to permit him to remain in our care and return to the foster home system, which we feel will provide more individual direction for him. Thank you." Grace Menefee sat down and reached over to hold Richie's hand, acknowledging his presence for the first time. Richie blushed.

"Thank you, Miss Menefee," the judge said. "The court appreciates your interest and commends the effort your department has put forth toward the welfare of the minor involved. For the record, the court would like to state that it does not agree with your reference to juvenile incarceration as 'punishment.' Rather, it is the court's belief that such confinement is rehabilitative in nature."

Glancing over, Richie saw Grace Menefee turn as red as he himself had a moment earlier. He felt her squeeze his hand, as if fortifying him for something.

"The minor in this matter," the judge continued, "has a long history of runaway problems—a history substantiated by your own department records. In the most recent incident, he was out of supervision for nearly a full year. His refusal to advise both your department and this court of his whereabouts and activities during that long period, indicates an attitude of defiance and total lack of respect for authority. Such an attitude, this court feels, is best dealt with in our juvenile custody system. Despite the positive attributes which you pointed out, it appears from the minor's refusal to cooperate with either your department or our court that he must be classified at this time as an incorrigible. That being the court's ruling, he is therefore remanded to state custody until age eighteen, at which time his case will be reviewed. Matter closed."

Grace Menefee only had time to give Richie's hand one more brief squeeze before the custody officer took him back to the detention room.

When she came to visit him the next day, Grace Menefee made no mention of having walked out on him on Monday, and gave no explanation of why she showed up to plead for him at his hearing on Thursday. Listening to her, Richie got the distinct impression that she was exerting tight control to keep her voice uncmotional.

"When are they taking you to the training school?" she asked.

"Monday," Richie told her. "The transfer bus goes down every Monday."

"I want you to know that I'm not just going to leave you down there until you're eighteen, Richie," the caseworker said determindedly.

"It's okay," Richie said, with his customary shrug. "You already done all you could. I'll be okay. Least I'll have three meals a day and a regular place to sleep."

"I want you to promise me that you'll continue to study hard in school, and *please*, whatever else, keep on reading."

"Sure." She reminded him of his mother telling him goodbye the first time he went to a foster home.

"You know, Richie, your love of books is so rare in a boy your age," she emphasized. "It would be a shame if you fell out of the habit of reading and lost your appetite for it."

"I won't," he tried to reassure her. "I'll always read. I love reading."

"I know. I know you do." Her voice softened for the first time and she patted his hand on the table. There were other kids having visits in the big room, but Richie was not embarrassed; he did not care whether they saw her gesture of fondness or not. Even if they did, no one would make any cracks about it. Nobody had fucked with him since the beating he gave Jerry. Several kids had even made friends with him in the hope that he would stick up for them if anyone picked on them. When Richie realized what they were doing, he was struck by the incongruity of life. Just because he could fight now, he could have new friends. They reminded him of the followers the schoolyard bullies always seemed to have: nervous kids who knew how to praise and always laughed at the right time. In the juvenile hall, Richie did not reject his new admirers, but he did not allow himself to develop any close friendships either.

"I 'preciate all you done for me," Richie told Grace Menefee now, looking down at the table. "I'm sorry I was always causing you so much trouble."

Grace Menefee smiled. "I got pretty angry at you sometimes, didn't I?"

"Sure did." He looked up and grinned at her.

"You know, Richie," she said, putting her hand on his and leaving it there this time, "things have been so tough on you so early in life, I have a feeling that somewhere down the line a lot of good things are going to happen to you. All the hard times you've been through, all the bad things you've endured, there's bound to be some reward for it in your future. If life gets difficult for you in reform—I mean, training school—I want you to remember that it's just another obstacle on your way to a better life, and that you'll get past it, just like you've gotten past all the other hardships. Will you remember that for me?"

"Sure," he promised.

When the visit was over, they both stood and Grace Menefee gathered up her purse and briefcase. "Goodbye, Richie," she said.

"So long, Miss Menefee."

Blinking back tears, the caseworker brushed the hair off Richie's forehead and hurried out.

The trip from Cook County Juvenile Hall was made in what looked like an ordinary school bus, except that it had a wire-grille separation between the driver's seat and the passenger section, and a uniformed detention officer rode up front. Richie sat next to a window on a seat by himself and looked out at the countryside along the way. There were a dozen other boys on the bus—white, black, brown—all between the ages of twelve, the legal minimum, and sixteen. Among them, there was little conversation.

The Illinois State Training School was located in St. Charles, Illinois, two counties west of Chicago on the highway to Iowa. It might as well have been in Asia, it was so completely foreign to Richie, who knew only the tenements and the streets of the city. The color and terrain and natural beauty of the countryside stimulated a spark of appreciation deep inside him somewhere, but at the same time his street instincts were never far away. It might be pretty, he thought, but how the hell could anybody survive here? To survive, you needed doorways, alleys, rooftops.

A boy across the aisle moved next to Richie. "You see them black-and-white cows back there?" he asked.

"Yeah," said Richie.

"I never knew there was black-and-white cows. I thought they was all brown."

"Yeah, me too," Richie nodded. His eyes flicked over the boy, sizing him up. The boy was older, perhaps fifteen, bigger than Richie, with a natural confidence. He had red hair and a pug nose. In demeanor, he reminded Richie a little of Stan Klein.

"Hey, where you from?" the kid asked. Richie understood he did not mean from which city, but which neighborhood.

"West Side," said Richie. "Madison and Kedzie." It was the neighborhood he knew best.

"Yeah?" the red-headed boy's eyebrows raised. "I'm South Side. Twenty-second and Sacramento. We wasn't too far apart. Hey, my name's Freddie Walsh. What's yours?" Richie told him. Freddie lowered his voice to a confidential tone. "What they got you on?"

"I'm uncorrigible," Richie said. He did not know if that was exactly the right word, but the juvenile judge had said he was something like that. When he saw a puzzled look on Freddie's face, he added, "I run away a lot."

"Oh," Freddie nodded in understanding. "I'm down for burglary," he said with an odd hint of mixed pride and fear. "Me and three guys stole this here safe from the closet of a guy's house over in one of the fancy neighborhoods. We used a little kid's wagon to haul it away, stole the wagon too. Then we stole some crowbars from the streetcar barns and pried the thing open in this one guy's basement. Took us four days to get it far enough open for me to wiggle a hand inside it. But it was worth it, man. We got two thousand bucks! On'y thing is, when the guy come home and seen the safe gone, he had a fuckin' heart attack and croaked. So my three pals, who was all over sixteen, got sent to Menard and I'm on my way to Charleytown."

"Charleytown?" Richie frowned. "What's that?"

"That's where we're going. This guy I met back at Juvie said that's what everybody calls it. It's near this town of St. Charles, see? St. Charles, Charleytown, get it?"

"Oh, yeah," Richie said, "I get it. Charleytown." Looking back out the window, he said, "I wonder what it'll be like?"

"We'll soon find out," Freddie Walsh said, slumping down in the seat and putting his knees up.

They rode together for the rest of the trip.

The two barrackslike structures set off in one corner of the high barbed-wire rimmed fence had signs above their respective entrances that read RECEPTION and DETENTION. When the transfer bus pulled up in front of the former, the boys were guided single-file into an arrival room where they sat on benches and waited as their court records and commitment papers were delivered and a man from administration checked the face of each arrival against the photograph in his folder. Then the escort officer got back on the bus and it left.

Richie and Freddie Walsh watched it longingly out a window as it pulled away.

The man who had accepted their records turned to two older boys wearing dark-blue denim trousers and light-blue denim shirts, and said, "All right, run 'em through."

The two boys immediately handed out wire baskets, one to each arrival, from a stack in the corner. "Strip," one of them said. "Everything off. Come on, let's go. Everything in the baskets."

Richie and Freddie and the others began taking off their clothes. From his trousers pocket, Richie removed his Buck Jones billfold. It was old and tattered now, its zipper broken, the leather peeled off in places; the picture of Buck had long since worn off completely. But it was still a treasure to Richie, something that had been through everything with him.

"What about stuff like this?" he asked the boy collecting the baskets.

"Everything in the basket, kid."

"We get the stuff back?"

"Sure, kid. Don't worry about it."

Richie watched the baskets get piled on a small dolly which one of the boys pushed out the back door and was gone. Richie had the sick feeling that he would never see his Buck Jones billfold again.

The boy who remained guided them naked into a room that contained a single straight chair and nothing else. Next to it was an electric shaver plugged into an extension cord. "Haircut time," the older kid said, pushing one of them toward the chair.

One by one they took their turn in the chair. To Richie, the electric clippers sounded like an airplane with a bad engine. It took only seven or eight strokes of the clippers on each boy, and his hair was sheared down to a bluish scalp. Some of the boys laughed nervously at what was happening, but none of them liked it.

Next they were herded into a shower room where thick bars of brown laundry soap were stacked on a ledge. Turning all the spigots on at once, their guide ordered, "Get under the water, scrub down all over with the soap! Get all the hair off! Come on, let's go!" The water was hot, and despite the caustic smell of the soap the shower felt good to Richie, reminding him of Midwest Gym. It felt odd to wash his newly bald scalp. Hair-conscious, he noted with relief that most of the boys, like himself, had only light pubic hair; just Freddie and one other boy had a full growth.

Presently the water was turned off and the boy in charge directed them to a pile of unfolded towels on a table. "Dry off and line up against the wall," he directed. As soon as they were in place, he moved along the line with a can powered by a rubber pressure ball, dusting their heads, feet, armpits, and pubic areas with great clouds of yellow powder. Some of the boys began to cough and were cautioned, "Don't breathe the powder! Hold your breath!"

From the shower room they filed into the clothing-issue room where two boys behind a counter took eyeball measurements and gave them their reform school clothing: dark-blue denim trousers and light-blue denim shirts, just like the boy in charge of them and the others were wearing; white briefs and undershirts; heavy gray socks; black, state-manufactured shoes, unfinished on the insides.

"Don't we get no belt?" Freddie Walsh asked.

"No belts in Charleytown, kid," he was told with a grin. "See, a belt with a buckle, wrapped around a guy's fist wit' four or five inches dangling, can be used as a weapon. We had three guys in one year lose eyes in belt fights. Belts has been banned at Charleytown ever since." Richie and Freddie exchanged apprehensive looks.

When they were dressed and carrying their extra clothing under one arm, bedding under the other, the group was led next door to the Detention Building. In an empty barracks of a room on the upper floor, they were told to select cots and a brief lesson was given in how to make one up. "Yez'll be in this here detention cottage for two weeks," they were told. "The onliest places yez can go is here and the fenced rec yard outside. All your meals will be eaten in the dining hall downstairs. During the two weeks, yez'll be called in for examinations by members of the ins'itution staff. If there's nothing wrong wit' you, like if you ain't got the clap and ain't loony in the head, then yez'll be sent to a reg'lar cottage."

When they were left alone in the big, barren room, some of the boys looked around as if they might cry. It struck a few for the first time—with their stiff new clothes and clipped heads—that they were actually in reform school. Freddie Walsh sat down on his unmade bunk and shook his head sadly. "Guess I won't be going to a reg'lar cottage with any of you guys," he announced dejectedly.

"Why not?" Richie asked anxiously, as everyone looked at Freddie.

"I'm loony in the head," Freddie said with a straight face, "and I got the clap."

Freddie looked quickly around to see how many fell for it. When he saw that several had, he grinned widely. Richie and a couple of others saw his grin and began to laugh.

A moment later, they were all doing it. Laughing the tension away.

Physical examinations were given to four boys at a time. When it was their turn, Richie and Freddie stood naked with a kid named Joey Lupo who had a crooked right eye, and another named Phil Phillips who had a speech impediment due to an enlarged tongue. About Lupo the examining physician said to his nurse, for the medical record, "No treatment. Both eyes have to have amblyopia to qualify for corrective surgery." About Phillips: "You'll have to do the best you can; we don't provide speech therapy here."

Richie was found to have scar tissue on both lungs, which was at first suspected to be tuberculosis but turned out not to be. "Multiple healed lung abscesses," the doctor decided after additional X-rays. "Probably a result of untreated staphylococcal pneumonia." He asked Richie, "You sick a lot in the winter? Have a lot of colds?" Richie acknowledged that he had. To his nurse the doctor said, "Beats me how some of these mongrel kids survive."

Freddie Walsh was found to have healed scars also: strap marks on his buttocks and back. "Old man give you these?" the doctor asked. Turning red with embarrassment, Freddie said yes. The doctor grunted. "Guess he didn't give you enough of them or you wouldn't be in here."

After medicals came dental exams. There was one standard for everyone. Trench mouth was treated. Pyorrhea was treated. Ordinary cavities were let alone until they reached the pain threshold, then the tooth was extracted. The Charleytown dentist didn't do fillings. Richie, who had taken care of his teeth when and however he could, had never been to a dentist before. He had five cavities about which he was told, "When they start hurting real bad, come back and we'll yank 'em." Richie silently resolved to brush his teeth as many times a day as he could, thinking that maybe he could brush the cavities away. He swore not to let them pull any of his teeth, no matter how bad they started hurting.

Psychological evaluations followed. All of them seemed to Richie to be sex-related.

"Look at this inkblot," one of the examining psychologists said, "and tell me if it looks like a dirty picture."

Shrugging and shaking his head, Richie said, "Looks like a dynamite 'splosion to me."

"Where did you ever see a dynamite explosion?" The psychologist seemed intrigued.

"Serials," Richie said. "At least one chapter always ended with a dynamite 'splosion."

"Movies, I see, yes. Tell me, how often do you masturbate in dark movie theaters?"

"I don't!" Richie replied, taken aback.

"Have you ever had sex relations with a man in a dark movie theater?"

"No!"

"How about a public restroom?"

"No!"

"Public park?"

"I ain't never done nothing like that nowhere!" Richie protested indignantly.

"How about sex relations with a relative, someone in your family, have you ever done that?"

"No!"

A sheet of paper and a box of eight crayons were in front of him. "I'd like you to draw me a picture of a naked woman. Use as many different crayons as you wish."

Calling upon vivid memories of Frances, Richie used the black crayon to sketch a rough outline of a somewhat voluptuous female figure: narrow-waisted, wide of hip, big bosomed. Selecting other colors, he gave his drawing yellow hair on top, and a triangle of brown public hair. He made the eyes blue, the lips and nipples red.

Before he left the office, Richie heard the psychologist say to a colleague, "Take a look at this. I think this kid must know that little blonde over in administration."

Most of the boys were unnerved by the psychological examinations. The psychologists were all unsmiling, unblinking, soft-spoken, somehow subtly intimidating people whose attitude and demeanor seemed to suggest that there was something terribly, terribly wrong with the boys or they would not be there. "It's like dey t'ink we're warped or something," said Joey Lupo, the kid with the crooked eye.

"Dey dus dank dey bewah dan us," Phil Phillips said in his afflicted speech.

Only Freddie Walsh was not bothered by the examination. He had seen a female psychologist, and been asked to draw a male figure. "I drew her one that had a dick that hung down to his knees," Freddie said, laughing. "You shoulda seen her turn red when she looked at it."

Job counseling was the last interview scheduled before they were released into the general population. The counselor Richie got was a thin pale man with a shirt collar too big for his neck. In front of him was a printed form on which he made checkmarks as he asked questions.

"Ever have any experience doing yard work?" he wanted to know.

Richie felt like laughing. *Yard* work? Around Madison and Kedzie in Chicago? "I hardly ever even *seen* a yard," he said, making no effort to conceal his contempt for the inquiry. It seemed so stupid; they *knew* where he was from.

"Know anything about animals?"

"Sure. In the slums, cats survive and dogs don't. And rats can't resist potato peels."

The counselor's thin lips compressed. "Ever worked as an office boy or messenger?"

Richie shook his head. "No."

"Ever worked as a busboy or kitchen helper?"

"No. You gotta be sixteen and have a work permit for jobs like that, mister."

The lips compressed further. "All these questions are on the form. Just answer them. And," he tapped his desktop with a pencil, "say 'sir' when you speak to me."

"Yessir." Prick, Richie thought.

When the counselor finally got to the bottom of the form, he asked the question Richie thought should have been at the top. "What kind of work, if any, *have* you done?"

"Pinboy in a bowling alley. Sir."

"That's all you've done, set pins?"

"That's all. Sir."

The counselor smiled a humorless smile. "I guess this isn't your lucky day. When they built the recreation center here, they forgot to put in a bowling alley. I'm assigning you to the garbage detail. And you won't need a work permit for it. You're excused."

Real prick, Richie thought as he left. But he realized that his own tough-guy attitude had probably caused it.

"What'd you get," Freddie asked when Richie got back to Detention. Richie told him. "I'm on a field crew," Freddie said. "We hoe weeds and stuff like that ina summer, shovel snow ina winter. What'd you get, Loop?" he asked Joey Lupo.

"Laundry worker," Joey replied, cocking his head for better focus.

"What about you, Philly?"

"Dabentery keen-op," said Philly.

"Dispensary clean-up," Richie interpreted. For some reason, he was able to understand Philly quicker than the other boys. He did not know if it was because his vocabulary was larger due to his reading habits or not.

The four of them went outside and sat on the ground in the R-and-D yard, feeling the hard pattern of the cyclone fence as they leaned back.

"Well, tomorrow's the big day," Freddie said. "Tomorrow we go out there wit' all the rest of the bad boys."

"Wonder what it'll be like?" Richie said, the same question he had asked on the bus.

"Prob'ly like everything else in life," Joey said cynically. "A kick in the balls if you ain't careful." The smallest of the group, Joey added tentatively, "I hope the four of us gets to stick together. My brother was in here coupla years back an' he tol' me you gotta have friends if you wanna get along. Otherwise, there's guys in here'll take advantage of you."

"That's a good idea," Freddie said. Philly nodded eagerly.

"Yeah, good idea," Richie agreed at once. Even though he could fight now, Richie was still scared of what tomorrow would bring. This was another new schoolyard for him, and there would always be bigger, tougher, meaner kids to deal with. Having Freddie, Joey, and Philly for friends was as reassuring to him as it was to each of them. "Shake on it," Richie said, recalling how Buck Jones had once sealed a bargain that way in a movie.

The four boys self-consciously shook hands all the way around. It made them all feel a little better about the uncertainty of tomorrow.

*R*ichie, Freddie, and Joey stood on the porch of the Detention Building and watched as a man with an odd, loose-jointed, rolling-hipped walk came over to them.

"My name is Mr. McKey," he said. He had sharp, edgelike features, none of which moved when he spoke. "I'm the house father of Polk Cottage, where you three are assigned. You will address and refer to me as 'Mister' and you will always say 'sir' when speaking to me. Any time you fail to do so will result in your receiving a demerit. Ten demerits will result in punishment. Form a single line and follow me," he ordered. "No talking."

As they walked away, all three boys looked sadly back at Philly, who stood with some other kids, assigned to a different cottage. Richie felt sorry for Philly, but was glad it was the other boy and not him who had been left behind. He hoped Philly would soon find someone else, like himself, who could understand his impaired speech and interpret for him.

McKey led them along a winding sidewalk across grass-covered grounds, past other cottages and buildings—schools, shops, the administration building, the infirmary—to a long narrow barracks that was called Polk Cottage. In an anteroom just inside the double-doored entrance, the house father directed their attention to a bulletin board. On it was thumbtacked a newspaper clipping with a headline that read: GORDIE MCKEY MAKES ALL-STATE.

There was a photo in the clipping of a handsome, smiling boy of about fourteen, wearing a football helmet.

"My son, Gordon," said McKey. "He made the varsity team his first year in high school. He's the only freshman ever named to an all-state football team. I put news about Gordie on this board to show the boys in my cottage what a decent kid does with his life. Might encourage some of you to change your ways." McKey's eyes narrowed slightly. "It's a requirement of this cottage that you read everything I put on the board about Gordie. I sometimes ask questions about it. Anyone who can't answer correctly is given a demerit."

Each boy was assigned a locker. McKey showed them how their spare clothing and towel were to be placed. "Failure to keep your locker neat gets a demerit." He showed them the shower room. "Wasting soap gets a demerit. Not turning the water all the way off gets a demerit."

At one point, when McKey's back was turned, Freddie Walsh whispered to Richie, "Breathing too much air gets a demerit."

McKey's head snapped around to catch the last movements of Freddie's lips. "Whispering behind a house father's back is disrespect and gets a demerit," he said, taking a small spiral notebook and pencil from the pocket of his khaki shirt. "Walsh, isn't it? That's one down and nine to go, Walsh."

Watching the house father, Richie had a distinct feeling that McKey enjoyed giving demerits.

Probably punishment as well.

Richie, Freddie, and Joey soon learned that life in Charleytown was a never-ending, usually futile effort to avoid demerits. It was practically impossible to do; there were too many pitfalls. An unbuttoned shirt collar got a demerit. Raising your voice got a demerit. Failure to clean your tray in the dining hall got a demerit, as did not being where you were supposed to be when the whistle was blown, looking at the body of a female staff member, walking on the wrong side of a sidewalk, any kind of horseplay, communicating with boys from another cottage except during supervised activities, stepping on the grass, spitting, closing a door too loudly. A shirttail hanging out, slouching posture, even the expression on a boy's face that the house father did not like, resulted in demerits, as did a multitude of other indiscretions, most of them committed innocently, carelessly, thoughtlessly, or playfully. It was a system, Richie and the other newcomers soon learned, that made for a lot of tension. Most of the kids sent to the training school were already old beyond their years. At Charleytown they got much older.

While Freddie went out on the field crew every afternoon to hoe weeds, and Joey reported to the laundry building to operate a hand-cranked wringer,

Richie rode the big garbage truck that came through the gate at one-thirty to make its way around the institution to collect all kitchen waste and shop trash. He hung on to the rear of the truckbed with a black kid, nicknamed Jazz because he was always jiving and shucking. At every stop, they hopped off, hoisted the big metal drums of garbage, and emptied them into the truckbed. The driver, a St. Charles townsman who contracted the work, shouted the same thing to them at every stop.

"Come on, you punks, snap it up! Get the lead out! I ain't got all day for this job!"

Richie, following the example set by Jazz, never varied his speed faster or slower. As Jazz told him the first day, "You work faster on Monday, he gon' want you to work even faster on Tuesday. Don' give the man nothin' you don' *have* to give him. He gonna bitch about yo' work no matter what."

Jazz was right. At the end of every run, when the truck dropped them back at Polk Cottage, Mr. McKey would ask the driver how the two had performed. The driver always gave a variation of the same reply.

"Slow, real slow. I could get outta here a half hour earlier if they was to work faster. They're just too damn lazy to do it. I can see why they're in here."

Every day, McKey would give each of them a demerit.

Just working on the garbage truck got Richie and Jazz enough demerits to qualify for punishment three times a month.

Mornings at Charleytown were given over to school. Based on a boy's age, without regard to prior education, he was placed in a classroom which theoretically was subdivided into three levels of ability, with the teacher, called an "instructor," supposed to impart knowledge according to the capacity of each group. In actuality, the classrooms were not apportioned in any way; the boys sat where they felt like sitting, usually unchallenged. Worn textbooks of one subject or another were distributed to all, with instructions to read any one of three sections. No controls monitored the reading. When a given time was up, the instructor asked questions about the assigned sections, receiving infrequent and almost unanimously incorrect answers. The instructor then told the class what the correct answer was. The class was never retested.

"This school is stupid," Richie said after his third day. "It's a waste of time."

"A kid tol' me these teachers ain't really teachers," Freddie confided. "Tha's why they're called instructors. They're cheaper than real teachers."

Jesus, Richie thought. Longingly he recalled Miss White and how she usually managed to make even the slowest pupil in her class at least a little smarter. She worked at being a teacher, Richie realized. But these Charley-town instructors did not even try; they repeated the same ineffective, unsuc-cessful routine day after day.

Thinking of Miss White made Richie think of Linda. She was on his mind a lot, especially at night when he was trying to go to sleep with an annoying erection demanding attention. He remembered with bittersweet melancholy her warm breath when they kissed, her growing young breasts, the soft inside of her thighs. When Richie gave in to his nighttime urges, his deep craving, and slipped into the bathroom to relieve himself, it was not Linda, however, but Frances that he thought of while doing it. He thought of her body, anyway; he tried not to think of her face, because of the way he had seen it last. Frequently his lustful image as he masturbated in the dark toilet stall was without features. But it was always the body of Frances; the carnal memory when he climaxed was a faceless Frances.

Besides school, another deficiency Richie found at Charleytown was the li-brary. It was, from a point of view stemming from his own reading skills, the most inadequate he had ever seen—worse even than the juvenile section of the Damen Avenue branch library back in Chicago. The vast majority of the books at Charleytown—which were shelved in a small, single room in the educational building—were for the lowest age level sent to the training school, which was twelve. When Richie inquired of one of the instructors, who took turns minding the room in the afternoons, why there were no books for older boys, he was told, "You got me there, kid. I've only been here about a year. But it's probably because they figured that most kids being sent to a place like this probably didn't read books anyhow."

The instructor, a man about thirty named Mr. Simms, had his feet propped up on the desk and was holding a paperback edition of *Babbitt* by Sinclair Lewis. Eyeing the book, Richie asked on impulse, "Mr. Simms, could I have that paperback when you're finished with it?"

Mr. Simms smiled tolerantly. "You wouldn't understand it," he said. "It's an adult book."

"I've read adult books," Richie told him. "I've read John Steinbeck, John Dos Passos, Thornton Wilder, John O'Hara, F. Scott Fitzgerald—"

"Where'd you read books by them?" the instructor asked in amazement.

Richie decided to see whether the truth would get him anywhere. "I used to sneak them out of the adult section of the library, then sneak them back in when I finished reading them."

Simms stared at him for a long moment, then shook his head in wonder. "Well, I'll be damned," he said. "Okay, sure, you can have it. But if you get caught with it, don't say you got it from me. I'll call you a liar if you do."

"I don't rat on people," Richie said in John Garfield style.

A week later he had the copy of *Babbitt*.

Richie, Freddie, and Joey had been approached their first day in Polk Cottage by a strikingly handsome, superbly built black youth of sixteen who was nicknamed "Lightning."

"They call me that because my hands are so fast," he advised them with a dazzling smile. "I'm so fast I can catch flies in the air. I can change hands when I'm jacking off without missing a stroke. I can hit you in the face before you can blink." His smile disappeared. "Let's talk business. Old Man McKey runs this cottage from the outside, but *I* run it from the inside. I settle all arguments, make sure everybody shares in anything that gets smuggled in—candy, smokes, reefers, eight-pagers, fuck pictures—and I assign cleaning jobs on Saturday mornings when we blitz the cottage. For this I get two bits of every dollar allowance you get from home, or half of every food package your folks bring in on visiting day. Now then," he looked at Freddie, the biggest, "how much allowance you expect to get?"

"Not a dime, man," Freddie told him. "The only thing my old man or my old lady ever gave me was a beatin'. I won't be getting no food packages neither."

"Me either," said Richie. "No allowance, no packages, no visitors."

Lightning turned to Joey. "You?"

"Prob'ly salami and stuff when my ma visits," he said. "She always brung stuff to my brother when he was here. But they ain't got the dough to give me none."

Lightning glowered. "If you guys are bullshitting me, I'll whip your asses all over this fucking cottage."

"We ain't bullshitting you," Freddie said evenly. "And we ain't gonna take no ass-kicking, unless you figure you can handle all three of us at once, 'cause we made a deal to stick together."

"You can't stick together *all* the time," Lightning pointed out.

"You can't stay awake all the time either," Freddie countered. "No matter how tough you are, you gotta sleep sometime."

"Look," Richie cut in, "we'd pay you if we could. But we can't. So what the fuck's the sense in fighting about it? When the fight's over, we'll all be right back where we started at."

"Yeah, but the others in the cottage would know I was still in charge," Lightning asserted.

"They can know it anyway," Richie said. "Just *tell* them we're paying you; we'll go along with the story. It'll save trouble all around." He was remembering the confrontation between Vernie and Alonzo on the el platform. Vernie had let Alonzo save face in that dispute and a fight had been avoided. Richie had the distinct feeling that Lightning did not want a fight any more than Alonzo had.

Lightning thought over Richie's proposal and finally agreed to it. Like Alonzo, however, he had to back away with bravado. "Okay, we'll do it that way. But if any of you squeal about it, I'm gonna kick the shit out of *all* of you. Got that?"

"We got it," said Freddie. "Thanks for the welcome." After Lightning left, Freddie looked curiously at Richie. "Would you really pay him if you was getting an allowance?"

"Fuck no," Richie declared. Those days were gone forever. "He'd have to kill me first."

Freddie grinned. "That's what I thought."

"Do I have to share my food package with him?" Joey asked.

"Nope," Freddie said, draping an arm around the smaller boy's shoulders, "only with Richie and me."

Punishment in Polk Cottage was administered every night at seven-thirty. Any boy who had accumulated ten demerits was called into the anteroom by Mr. McKey, who returned from his home in town after supper each evening to supervise personally the punishment period. Later, when punishment was over and all the boys locked in the dormitory, McKey went home again, turning the cottage over to a night orderly until his return the next morning.

There was hardly a boy in Polk Cottage who did not receive demerits for failing to answer questions McKey randomly asked, without warning, about items he had put on the bulletin board regarding his son Gordie. Not only sports items: GORDIE MCKEY THROWS WINNING PASS; GORDIE MCKEY LEADS VARSITY TO BASKETBALL TOURNAMENT, GORDIE MCKEY SETS NEW STATE RECORD FOR 100-YARD DASH, but items from a Boy Scout newsletter: GORDIE MCKEY EARNS 15TH MERIT BADGE; a Presbyterian Church bulletin: GORDIE MCKEY SE-LECTED AS VACATION BIBLE SCHOOL TEACHER FOR YOUNGER CHILDREN; a high school newspaper: GORDIE MCKEY NEW R.O.T.C. LIEUTENANT; GORDIE MCKEY ELECTED SOPHOMORE CLASS PRESIDENT; and a National Honor Society magazine: GORDIE MCKEY EARNS PERFECT SCHOLASTIC RECORD FOR THIRD STRAIGHT YEAR.

It was not that the boys in Polk Cottage failed to read everything that McKey tacked up; it was simply that they were unable to understand most of it, could not individually identify with it, therefore were unable to remember it. Most of them knew nothing of the Boy Scouts, R.O.T.C., or the National Honor Society. The news they read of All-American boy Gordie McKey was just a lot of words that did not register. That was why the house father caught them so often.

"You there, Walsh," he would challenge, "name the softball team that my boy Gordie pitched a shutout against last week."

Freddie would think and then shrug. "I can't remember, Mr. McKey, sir."

Out would come the spiral notebook. "That's a demerit, Walsh."

And: "You, Lupo. When my boy Gordie won the high school debating contest, what subject did he debate?"

Joey's expression would twist into a squinting frown. "What does 'subject' mean, Mr. McKey?"

"It means another demerit for you, Lupo."

Or: "You"—pointing to Richie—"what organization wrote about my boy Gordie's perfect grade average?"

Richie always tried to answer. "The National Grade Society?"

"Close, but not close enough. One demerit. Pay more attention to what you read next time."

Punishment varied. Push-ups were the most common for the younger kids. Those a little older were made to hold their arms straight out in front of them, palms down, with a broomstick laid across the backs of their hands. Within minutes it made them feel as if their arms were being torn out of the sockets and their necks were going to burst.

There was also the Spot, a white circle on the floor, near the wall, on which a boy had to stand perfectly still, looking at a white line on the wall, for several hours at a time.

And there was Old Faithful—Mr. McKey's leather razor strap. Old Faithful was optional. Instead of push-ups, the broomstick, or the Spot, McKey occasionally let a boy choose a predetermined number of licks with the strap. The licks had to be taken in undershorts, without trousers, while leaning over a straight chair. The punishment reminded Richie of the foster home run by the Hubbards.

The worst punishment by far was the fire hose. The big canvas hose hung rolled in a wooden box on the wall of the anteroom, connected to a large spigot next to the box. Long enough to stretch far into the dormitory, it could also stretch down a short flight of stairs to the basement of the cottage. The basement was empty except for an oil furnace that heated the cottage in winter. There was a brick wall near the bottom of the stairs. Mr. McKey had come up with the idea of making the boys with the most demerits each month line up naked in front of that wall, and he would drag the fire hose down the stairs, have the night orderly turn on the faucet, and blast them with the powerful spray. It was like being beaten with wet towels.

Freddie Walsh got the fire hose every month. Richie got it about half the time. Joey only got it once in a while; unlike Freddie and Richie, he rarely received work demerits because the laundry superintendent did not believe in the demerit system. Freddie's field crew supervisor, like Richie's garbage truck driver, routinely reported half a dozen boys a day for demerits. Freddie, because of his attitude, was usually among them.

The first time Richie and Freddie were sent down for fire hose punishment, they had been advised by others who had undergone it to start crying and pleading as soon as the water hit. "The quicker you start bawling and begging," they were told, "the quicker the old bastard'll send you back upstairs."

"Fuck him," Freddie said defiantly, "I ain't gonna crawl for the old son of a bitch."

"Me either," Richie vowed. "I don't beg. Fuck him."

When they got downstairs and stood naked in front of the wall with four other boys, they continued their defiance even as Mr. McKey descended the stairs with the hose. When he had the water turned on and opened it up on them, Richie and Freddie felt themselves driven back against the rough wall by the force of the blast. Immediately they doubled up in protective crouches on the floor. Their faces contorted in pain, they heard the others begin to cry and plead. McKey moved the nozzle back and forth like a tripod-mounted machine gun, lacing them as they slipped, twisted, and turned trying to find a way to escape. But there was only one way—and they knew it.

One by one, as they groveled and appealed, beseeching the house father to let them go, he did, shouting their names as he released them. Richie and Freddie held on until last, but finally Richie could take the brutal stream no longer and yelled, "Lemme—out—please—lemme—out!"

McKey let Richie go, and kept blasting Freddie until he too capitulated.

"Tough guys, eh?" McKey taunted as they stumbled pitifully back upstairs.

They hated McKey even more after that, because he had made them beg for mercy.

Richie's days in Charleytown flowed into weeks, then months. His life on the outside had not been easy, but at least, as he remembered it now, he had never had to endure the terrible malaise that grew out of his existence in the reformatory. The tedium of his everyday routine was numbing. Attending the pathetic excuse for a school was daily torture; even when he *tried* to learn, it was futile: the blatant lack of interest in the other boys, coupled with the incompetence and indifference of the instructors, created an atmosphere in which Richie found learning impossible.

Afternoons on the garbage truck with Jazz were, for a time, a welcome relief, but with the advent of winter even that became trying. The state issued only wool gloves, not leather, and the metal coldness of the truck and the garbage cans penetrated the wool at once, leaving the fingers of the two boys painfully frigid. It took them longer on cold days to empty the icy cans, with their sometimes semi-frozen contents, making the driver complain all the more to McKey, whose pencil was always ready to give extra demerits. Richie and Jazz grew to hate the driver so intensely that they wished he would wreck his truck some day and be trapped inside to burn alive.

"If he be on fire burning, I wouldn't piss on him," Jazz swore.

"Me either," Richie concurred. "I wouldn't spit on the son of a bitch."

"Just let the motherfucker fry."

"To a fucking crisp."

Nights in the dorm weren't much better. Once Richie and Freddie tired of playing checkers or tossing bean bags—which Joey seemed to enjoy without limitation—there was nothing left to do except talk. The subject matter was nearly always the outside: what they did, who they knew, where they went—litanies of life on the street. Compared to what they had both been used to, Charleytown, as far as creature comforts were concerned, was not that bad. The food was adequate and often tasty; Richie had already gained eight pounds. The bunks were better than some he had slept on, and the cottage was well-heated during the bitter Illinois plains winter. And Richie was able to steal a few precious minutes of reading each day from paperbacks Mr. Simms passed to him; for part of that winter he devoured, although slowly, *Random Harvest* by James Hilton.

It was the devastating boredom that Richie could not take. He felt as if his mind were wasting away, his brain decomposing by the ounce. A dreaded thought was that in two or three more years, he would be sitting every night like Joey, contentedly playing checkers, the ultimate mental challenge in his life just to win the next game. The prospect was frightening.

As winter dragged along, Richie began to think privately of something that demanded attention in his suffering mind.

Escape.

*R*ichie was walking out of the infirmary, one side of his mouth bulging with dental wadding, when he heard someone call, "Eh, Ri'ie!" Turning, he saw Philly hurrying toward him, grinning with delight. They had not seen each other since their last day in R and D.

"Hey, Philly," Richie said, bobbing his chin.

"Wha' de do you?" Philly asked, looking at Richie's cheek.

"Pulled a tooth," Richie said, realizing that with the novocaine he was talking almost as thickly as Philly.

The tooth he had lost was the fifth one from the middle on the bottom. It had begun hurting a week earlier and by the previous day had been giving Richie fits, the pain had become so excruciating. He had held out as long as he could, using icicles in his mouth to numb the pain for a while, but when that no longer worked, and despite the vow he had made to himself when he entered Charleytown, he eventually could stand it no longer and reported to sick call. Because the dentist did not start until ten, he had to wait two hours. Finally he was given a shot in the gum and the decayed tooth was extracted.

"How you been, Philly?" Richie asked.

"Ah'm doon otay," Philly replied. "You 'till wih Fweddie and Doey?"

"Yeah, we're all still in Polk Cottage." Richie slung an arm around Philly's shoulders. "You made some new friends, I bet, huh?" he asked hopefully.

"Yah, ba nah like you guyd. Ah wid ah bas wih you guyd."

"You're better off here," Richie assured him, "working inside where it's warm. Me and Freddie are outdoors all afternoon freezing our balls off."

Philly laughed raucously. "Fro'den balts! Dat funny, Ri'ie!"

Richie laughed too, mostly at Philly's amusement. "You wouldn't think it was funny if it was *your* balls, Philly," he told him.

When Philly stopped laughing, he asked, "Dey gib you an'tang por pain?"

"Two aspirin," Richie said. "I'm supposed to take them when the stuff in my gum wears off."

"Dey wan't do no good," Philly said. "Way heah." Richie waited on the cold porch, moving from one foot to the other to keep warm. In a moment Philly was back, slipping him a single white tablet smaller than an aspirin. "Dih id mor-peen," he said. "Fits you aup good."

"Thanks, Philly." They said goodbye, Richie promising to tell Freddie and Joey all about seeing their old friend, and promising to encourage them to pretend to be sick sometime so they could come over and see him too.

Hurrying across the barren winter grounds of the institution, Richie got back to the cottage to find it deserted. His mouth already beginning to hurt, he paused at the drinking fountain and swallowed the pill Philly had given him. At his bunk, he took off his coat, made a pillow out of it, and lay down on the floor where he could not be seen if anyone came in. His anger over losing his tooth was increasing. Goddamned fucking bastards, he silently cursed the Charleytown staff. Rotten pricks, all of them. From the very first day in the place, he felt he had been degraded and demeaned. Beginning with the goddamned haircut down to the scalp, then the goddamned demerit system, being forced to try and remember a lot of shit about McKey's fucking kid, getting the strap and the fire hose, and now having a tooth pulled because the bastards wouldn't fix it. Well, fuck them all! He was now going to make definite plans to escape. Be goddamned if they were going to pull all his teeth. Tonight, Richie decided, he would mention the idea of escape to Freddie. So far, Richie had kept it to himself; now he was going to take action.

As he lay there on the floor, Richie gradually became aware that his mouth did not hurt anymore and that he was beginning to feel rather pleasant, rather mellow, *smooth* inside. He tried to remember what Philly had called the pill he had slipped him: "feen" something, he thought. Whatever it was, sure as hell worked—

A sudden thought exploded in his mind. *Dope.* Philly had given him some kind of dope! That had to be what it was; it was making him feel too good to be anything else. At once he began to worry. Could he become hooked?

On one pill? No, that wasn't possible; with his mother it had always been a gradual buildup measured by his trips to Lake Street for her. One pill couldn't do it, he was certain.

But one pill sure as hell was making him *feel* good. For the first time he had some inkling of why his mother might have used dope. Previous explanations he had heard, from Vernie, Stan, and others, had always been a little cryptic, involving terms like "getting high" and "feeling no pain." He had known it made its user feel good in a way like masturbation, he presumed, but he had no idea *how* good. That one little pill from Philly had him floating in a fine, soft euphoria.

So, Chloe, he thought, this is what it was all about.

Grace Menefee came to visit him in the spring. Sitting at a visitors' table when he walked in, her mouth dropped open at the sight of him.

"Richie, my god!" she exclaimed when he sat down. "Look how you've grown! You must be as tall as I am! And you've gained so much weight! What in the world do they feed you down here?"

"Different stuff," he told her with a shrug. "Lot of the guys call it slop, but I think it's kinda good, most of it."

"Well, how *are* you?" she gushed, patting his hand.

"Okay, I guess." She had not changed much, he thought, her hair still looking as if she had been interrupted in the middle of combing it.

As if reading his thoughts about hair, she said, "I see I don't have to push your hair back off your forehead anymore," referring to his Charleytown crew cut.

"Yeah. We should've thought of this a long time ago."

Still shaking her head in wonder at the size of him and the way he looked, Grace Menefee was ebullient. "I'm so pleased that you've settled in and seem to be doing so well, Richie. I'll have to admit, I was worried about you after you took that John Garfield position and refused to tell the juvenile court where you'd been living all that time. But you've really come through with flying colors!"

Inside Richie, Grace Menefee's joy was tying a knot in his stomach. Why in hell did she have to pick now to come see him, when he and Freddie were making their final plans to escape? He was just going to be another disappointment to her now. Why didn't she just forget about him and leave him alone? He didn't like having to worry about upsetting her and hurting her feelings.

"Are you still reading as much as you used to?" she asked eagerly, smiling.

"Not as much," he admitted. "The library here's not all that hot."

"I'm sorry to hear that."

"But I get paperbacks from one of the staff," he amended. "Right now I'm reading *Kings Row* by Henry Bellamann. Have you read that?"

"Uh, no, I haven't," Grace Menefee replied. "I'm afraid I haven't had as much time to read as I'd like to. Our office has really been swamped." Changing the subject, she tapped his arm with her fingers and said, "I've got a bone to pick with you, young man. Why didn't you tell me you'd been *born* in that little town in Tennessee? The name of the town is Lamont, incidentally."

"I guess I forgot. I even forgot the name of the town. All these years I've been saying I was born in Chicago. I *feel* like I was born in Chicago."

"Nope," Grace Menefee said, shaking her head. "Lamont, Tennessee. I found it listed on the very first school enrollment form your mother filled out for you eight years ago, when you were six." Smiling again, she sat back and added, "We're in touch with the Tennessee state welfare people trying to locate your grandmother. So there's a possibility you might be out of here soon, Richie."

Sooner than you think, he had the urge to say, but did not.

"That's swell," he told the caseworker. She had still been trying to help him, all the time he had been in Charleytown and now he was going to let her down again. God*damn!* Why did things never work out for him? If he stayed where he was and let her get him out her way, then he would be letting down Freddie, his best friend, who had been helping plan their escape for nearly two months. Freddie wanted out of Charleytown as badly as Richie did. Tougher than most other kids in Polk Cottage, Freddie was able to take punishment better, and it was obviously galling McKey; he gave Freddie demerits at the least excuse, bringing him up for punishment as frequently as he could. Richie *had* to go through with his plans with Freddie.

He just hated like hell to make Grace Menefee suffer for it.

Richie was convinced he had found the ideal way to escape from Charleytown: on the transfer bus that brought new kids down every Monday.

"It's perfect," he said the first time he confided his plan to Freddie. "The bus always gets here between twelve and one, when nearly everybody's at lunch except the R-and-D people. While the escort hack takes the new fish inside to get their I.D.s checked and turn 'em over, the driver pulls the bus around to the side so it won't block traffic at the gate. I been skipping lunch for the last six Mondays and hiding behind the trash cans to watch him. He always does the same thing while he's waiting for the escort hack: walks around to the front of R and D and sits in the office to have a smoke. He leaves the bus door open, and the escort hack has already hooked the cage door open for the new fish to get off. All's we gotta do is sneak aboard and hide behind a couple seats in the rear. Then we ride back to Chicago on the return trip. Not only do we get out of this fucking place, but we get back to the city before they even realize we're gone. The reason most runaways get caught is that they never make it out of the St. Charles area. That won't happen to us; we'll be long gone."

"Yeah, but what about when we get back to Chi?" Freddie asked. "The hack'll prob'ly lock the cage door and we'll be trapped on the fucking bus."

Richie smiled. "We'll get Joey to swipe us a hacksaw blade or a file from the plumbing tools in the laundry. Wherever they park the bus, we wait until dark and cut a hole in the grille."

"Joey goin' too?"

"If he wants to," Richie shrugged, "but I don't think he will. His old man's got a bad heart an' he's promised his mother not to get in no more trouble. But he'll get us something to get out of the bus with. Joey won't let us down." Richie paused for a moment, studying Freddie Walsh closely, hoping he had not misjudged his friend, hoping that Freddie, who had taken an enormous amount of punishment from McKey over the past few months, had not lost his heart, his nerve. If he had, Richie was determined to do it alone. "You with me?" he finally asked.

Freddie did not let him down. "I'm in," he answered with a smile.

From that point on they worked on the plan together. Richie let Freddie hide and watch the bus driver for several Mondays, just to confirm that the routine did not vary. In the meantime, Richie made contact with one of the R-and-D orderlies who took care of disposing of the clothes of new transfers. Everything that was put into the wire baskets on arrival, with the exception of watches, rings, and religious medals, was thrown into the main furnace and burned. Talking to the orderly, Richie realized that he would never see his treasured Buck Jones billfold again. And realized too that it had gone the same way Buck himself had, or nearly so. But Richie had no time to feel badly about it; he had to tend to the serious business of escape.

The R-and-D orderly agreed, for some morphine, to steal the best clothes he could find that would fit Richie and Freddie, and at a specified time to hide them in the trash barrels next to the building. That deal made, Richie then sneaked over to the infirmary to see Philly again.

"I need six of those pills like the one you gave me when I had the tooth pulled," he said.

Philly was reluctant. "Dos mor-peen ain' no good to take doo many, Ri'ie. You can ge' 'ooked."

When Richie explained what he wanted them for, Philly still hesitated. He did not want to be responsible for anyone, even a kid he did not know, getting hooked. Richie had to do some fast reasoning. "There's no way the guy'll get hooked, Philly. He'll have a few highs and that'll be that. Sure, he might have a bad time for a couple days when the pills run out, but it'll prob'ly be worth it to him." Richie put on a grieved expression. "You're not gonna let Freddie and me down, are you, Philly?"

Philly gave him the morphine tablets.

Richie and Freddie were set to go.

On Sunday night before the planned escape on Monday, McKey returned to the cottage after supper with an unexpected announcement: he was going to conduct the monthly fire hose punishment a week early, because the following Sunday night his son Gordie was being inducted as a Young Deacon in their church. When the news spread through the dormitory, Richie and Freddie looked at each other in surprise. Both of them were due for fire hose punishment; they had scheduled their escape to avoid it.

"Son of a bitch," Richie said in disgust. "Wouldn't you know it? Jesus, I hate his goddamned kid."

McKey came in and called out the names of those to receive the punishment. Like the others, Richie and Freddie started stripping. Walking over to them, McKey asked, "You going to be the last one to beg again tonight, Walsh?"

"I don't know, Mr. McKey, sir," Freddie answered. He always looked McKey straight in the eyes, and McKey hated it; the house father was more comfortable when kids cowered before him.

"I think you'll beg early tonight, Walsh," McKey said almost clinically. He smiled his cold, humorless smile and walked away.

"Don't let him sucker you," Richie said as they finished stripping. "Let's just get it over with and get back up here. We'll beg right away."

"Not me," Freddie told him. "I ain't gonna let the lousy son of a bitch bluff me. I'm coming up last, just like I always do."

"Fuck him, Freddie. That's just what the cocksucker wants."

"That's what he's gonna get, too," Freddie said grimly. "I don't back down from *no* motherfucker like that."

They marched into the basement with four other boys whose demerit totals were high for the month, and lined up in front of but not touching the wall. McKey dragged the hose down, got a good grip on the big brass nozzle, and yelled up to his night orderly, "Let her go!" The boys tensed fearfully as they watched the flattened hose inflate with the sudden surge of water, and the shiny nozzle bucked in the house father's hands as the blast was released.

The water hit like a mule's kick, knocking the naked boys down as if they were figures in a shooting gallery. As soon as they were all down, curling their bodies into the smallest possible target, McKey turned the spray down, washing them back, rolling them over, causing them to begin their crying and pleading for relief.

Richie and Freddie, on their knees, sitting back on their heels, bent as far forward as possible, kept away from the wall if they could. They knew from experience that bracing against the wall with one part of their body and taking the force of the hose with another part, was like being crushed in a vise. Better to let your body go as limp as possible and keep it moving so that the surging squall of water could not build up its impact in one place. Raised shoulder protecting one ear, arm curved around their faces, hand over the other ear, opposite hand covering their testicles, the two best friends gasped for breath and took the jolt from the hose as McKey slowly released all the other boys to run back upstairs.

With only the two of them remaining, McKey directed the water anyplace that seemed vulnerable to him: heads, necks, shoulders, backs, buttocks—whatever he could hit.

"Hang on, boys!" he taunted gleefully. "You're tough, you can do it!"

Richie and Freddie kept turning and twisting, sliding and slipping, dancing and dashing away from the water, as McKey shifted the nozzle to keep up with them, catching one, then the other, knocking them back down in turn. Finally Richie was hit in the lower back, just above the hipbone, and felt a bolt of pain all the way up to his eyes. "Okay! Please!" he begged. "Lemme—out—please!"

"Upstairs!" McKey ordered.

Staggering, feeling his way along the wall, Richie saw the house father smile the same tight, mean little smile he had shown upstairs before the punishment began. "Okay, Walsh!" McKey yelled. "Let's see how long you can take it!" With the rod of water, he pinned Freddie Walsh's curled-up form to the line where the wall met the floor.

Half crawling up the stairs, a crying Richie looked back and saw through his tears that Freddie was not dodging the water any longer, not moving and maneuvering to make it hard on McKey. Grimacing, wiping his eyes, Richie realized that Freddie was not moving at all. Starting back down the stairs, he shouted, "Cut it out! Let him up!"

McKey kept the hose blast on Freddie, holding it steadily, low on the crouched boy's back.

"Cut it out!" Richie yelled again. "Please, Mr. McKey, let him up! Please, sir!"

Finally Mr. McKey also realized that Freddie had stopped moving, because he yelled up to the night orderly, "Turn it off!" As the water ceased with a long, slow dribble, McKey looked angrily at Richie and ordered, "Get upstairs! Now!" Disobeying, Richie started for Freddie. McKey grabbed his arm and pushed him to the night orderly, who was coming down the stairs. "Take him to his bunk! Lock down the dorm!"

Struggling against the strong grip of the orderly, naked, dripping wet, angry, and frightened, Richie was dragged out of the basement.

Richie did not run away the following day. With Joey and the other boys in Polk Cottage, he had watched out the window on Sunday night and seen Freddie Walsh taken out and carried toward the infirmary on a stretcher. After seeing that, Richie could not go ahead with his escape plan without first finding out how Freddie was.

After supper on Monday, McKey came into the dorm and called the boys to order. "I'm sure some of you," he said, avoiding Richie's stare, "are wondering what happened to Walsh. Well, I want you to know he's all right. He just passed out, that's all. I guess," McKey forced a smile, "he wasn't as tough as he thought he was." There was a smattering of nervous laughter. "Anyhow, he's going to be in the infirmary for a couple of days, then I'm having him transferred to another cottage. I don't like trouble-makers in Polk Cottage," he glanced at Richie now. "The rest of you straighten up and fly right, and maybe we can do away with fire hose punishment altogether. I don't like it any better than you do, you know. All right, that's all."

Richie and Joey were both greatly relieved to hear that Freddie was okay, but disappointed that he was being sent to another cottage. "Check with the guys who drop off bed linen from the other cottages," Richie said to Joey, who still worked in the laundry, "and find out which cottage they send Freddie to."

"Gotcha," Joey said, winking his good eye.

When ten days had passed and there was no word of Freddie Walsh transferring into another cottage, Richie began to worry. "If he's still in the infirmary, maybe he's worse off than McKey said," he brooded.

"Maybe you could get back over there and see Philly again," Joey suggested. "He'd know."

Richie did that, the next afternoon. Philly was in the infirmary ward hallway, sweeping the floor, when Richie found him. Motioning from the door, Richie got his attention and Philly came over, broom in hand, looking nervous.

"Philly, I wanna find out how Freddie's doing," Richie said. "How long's he gonna be in here?"

Philly stared at him sadly, lips parted, enlarged tongue covering his lower teeth. He began to blink back tears. "Freh'ie deah, Ri'ie," he said.

Richie stared in shock. "*What?*"

"Freh'ie deah," Philly repeated. "Hih ki'neys 'topped wor'ing."

Richie knew about kidneys; Myron had taught him how to shift his body to avoid illegal kidney punches during clinches. "The kidneys won't take as much abuse as some parts of the body," the trainer had emphasized. Richie thought of the force of the fire hose stream hitting the still form of Freddie Walsh, low on the crouched boy's back. He remembered McKey's mean little smile as he did it.

The son of a bitch.

"Da dah'ters cudn't figger out why his ki'neys stopped. Dey fi'ny tay it ki'ney fa'wer."

The dirty, rotten son of a bitch.

"Ah'm torry, Ri'ie," said Philly, tears running down his cheeks. Richie put a hand on the back of Philly's neck and squeezed, gently, fondly.

"I'm sorry too, Philly." With his thumb, he wiped away Philly's tears. "Go on, get back to work so you don't get in trouble."

"Otay, Ri'ie."

As Philly resumed pushing his broom down the hall, Richie walked back outside.

He's got to pay for it, Richie found himself thinking. *He's got to be punished.*

All the way back across the grounds toward Polk Cottage, all Richie could think about was McKey.

Somewhere between the infirmary and the cottage, he made up his mind to kill McKey.

Three months later, Richie was summoned to the superintendent's office and found Grace Menefee waiting there for him. With her was a stout, gray-haired woman. Miss Menefee said, "This is Mrs. Clark, Richie. Do you remember her? She's your grandmother."

The woman did not rise from her chair to embrace him or otherwise display any affection. She just nodded, studying him closely.

"Sure, I remember," said Richie, playing their game. "Hi, Grandma," he added, putting on an artificial smile. Whatever it took to get out of this fucking place, he would do it.

There was no place for him to sit, so Richie stood between the chairs of the two women, facing the superintendent's desk. "Richie," the superintendent said gravely, "you are a very lucky boy. Through the efforts of Miss Menefee here, your grandmother was located and has agreed to let you come live with her in Tennessee."

"That's swell, sir," Richie replied, with what he hoped was the right combination of humility and enthusiasm.

"There are certain conditions, of course. Your grandmother is a widow with a pension and cannot assume the obligation of feeding and clothing you, so it will be necessary for you to work and to take on that responsiblity yourself."

"He won't mind that, will you, Richie?" Grace Menefee interjected. Then to Mrs. Clark, "He's always been a very hard worker."

"The welfare department in Tennessee," the superintendent continued, "has verified for us that Lamont High School, which you will attend, has a Distributive Education class in which students are allowed to take their four required classes in the morning, eliminate study periods from their schedule, and leave school at one o'clock every day in order to work. From what we understand, the town merchants cooperate in the program by hiring their part-time help through the school."

"It sounds like a marvelous program," Grace Menefee enthused. She squeezed Richie's hand. "You'll fit right in, Richie."

Sure, sure, Richie thought behind his artificial smile. Just like I've always fit in.

"You have to understand, of course," the superintendent made clear, "that even though you will be out of state, the Illinois juvenile court will still have jurisdiction over you until you are either twenty-one or enter the military service. Any future runaways, any violations of the law, any trouble of *any* kind, will be reported back to the court in Chicago, and you could either be returned here or sent to Menard Reformatory, depending on your age. Do you understand that?"

"Yessir," Richie said firmly. "I've learned my lesson, sir. No more running away for me." Glancing at Grace Menefee, he saw the slightest suggestion of a frown.

"Have you anything you'd like to add, Mrs. Clark?" the superintendent asked.

"No, sir," Mrs. Clark said, speaking for the first time. She had a pronounced Southern accent without the attendant drawl. "So long as he promises not to run off and not to get in no trouble with the law like his daddy done, why, I'll let him live with me. I just can't support him. I barely get along on my pension check and what little I can make working at the tomato-canning factory of a summer. But the house is mine, so there's a place for him to live. If he'll work and buy his clothes and help with the groceries, why, I expect we can get by."

"I'll work, Grandma," Richie promised earnestly. "And I'll be as good as can be, you'll see." Glancing again, he saw that Grace Menefee's eyes had a hint of suspicion in them.

"Fine, fine," the superintendent said, rising. "I'll get release papers prepared and we'll send him over for some discharge clothes."

"While that's being done, may I take Richie outside for a few minutes?" Grace Menefee asked. "I'd like to talk to him in private."

The superintendent gave his permission and Miss Menefee led Richie out to the front porch of the building, where they sat on a bench.

"Richie," she said, sitting half turned toward him, "you're not playing some kind of game with these people, are you? Just to get out?"

"What do you mean?" he asked, trying to appear virtuous.

"You know very well what I mean," she scolded. "All that 'I've learned my lesson' and 'I'll be as good as can be' stuff. You know, if you mess up this time, Richie, you could end up in Menard. They don't have fences there; they've got walls and bars."

Richie shook his head ironically. "You used to threaten me with this place," he reminded her. "Now that I'm here, you threaten me with Menard. You've always got a worst place, don't you?"

"Oh, Richie," she pleaded, "I'm not trying to threaten you, or scare you, or bully you into being good. I'm trying to *warn* you. It's so easy to go off in the wrong direction in life, and even easier to *keep* going in that direction. This is your chance not to let it happen to you. I know you can walk out of this place and in a few hours ditch your grandmother and be on your way back to Chicago—but what'll it get you? Chicago is a mean, hard city; it breaks people very easily. It broke your mother. You *mustn't* go back there and let it break you. Go with your grandmother, Richie, *please*. Go down to that nice little Southern town, go to school, get a job, read all the books you want to read, someday go to college . . . Richie, there's no limit to what you can do if you go in the right direction. Do you understand what I'm telling you?"

Leaning forward, elbows on knees, looking at the weathered wooden planks of the porch, Richie nodded. "I understand."

"Will you try? Please."

Don't let her down again, his mind told him. The one person who always stuck by you. Don't keep being a prick with her.

"Okay, I'll try," he said, with no trace of John Garfield in his words.

"Promise?" she asked.

"Promise," he said. She smiled a smile that for the first time made her look very pretty to him.

That afternoon, Richie and Mrs. Clark boarded a southbound Illinois Central train in a little town to which Grace Menefee drove them. Richie was wearing Charleytown discharge clothes and had an extra set of everything in a cloth zipper bag. Miss Menefee gave his grandmother a welfare draft for thirty dollars to subsidize them until Richie could get enrolled in the Distributive Education program at school and get a job.

As they waited for the train, Richie could hardly believe things were moving so quickly. He had been processed out of Charleytown in less than three hours, and had not even had a chance to say goodbye to Joey or Philly or Jazz or anyone. As they had driven toward the gate, Richie had seen Mr. McKey come out of Administration and pause on the sidewalk to light his pipe. Seeing Richie looking at him out the car window, the house father had raised his pipe in a farewell salute, almost as if he were saying goodbye to a friend. You dirty bastard, Richie thought, glaring at him as the car went on past. I'm not forgetting Freddie Walsh, he promised himself. Wherever I go and whatever I do, I won't forget Freddie. And, he silently swore, he would not forget his promise to kill McKey either. Someday, somehow, Richie vowed to return and do it.

Shortly after the train started rolling along, the conductor came through checking tickets. Mrs. Clark showed him hers and Richie gave him the ticket Miss Menefee had bought for him. After the conductor punched the tickets and moved on, Richie and his grandmother settled down for the eight-hour trip. They sat in facing seats, not talking much except when Mrs. Clark asked him a direct, curious question.

"Was it hard in that reform school?" she asked at one point.

"Not too hard," Richie replied, shrugging. What good would it have done to tell her anything, he thought.

A while later, Mrs. Clark said, "I know that Chloe was on dope; that caseworker lady told me. Did she treat you bad a lot?"

"Not so bad, I guess," Richie replied. Then he asked, "Grandma, do you know where my dad is?"

"Lord have mercy, no!" she exclaimed. "How in the world would I know where Richmond is?"

"I just asked," he defended. "*Somebody's* got to know where he is."

"Well, it's not me," she declared. After a moment's silence, she said, "I don't much like being called 'Grandma' either. Haven't never been called that by nobody."

"What do you want me to call you?" Richie asked.

"Ethel," she said. "My name's Ethel."

"Okay," Richie agreed. Adding, "Ethel."

"*Miss* Ethel," she modified. She pronounced the title 'Miz.'

"Miss Ethel," Richie conformed. He studied her for the first time. She did not, he thought, resemble his mother very much. She was heavier than his mother had ever been, of course, not fat as much as heavyset. Her gray hair was, he guessed, very long, because she had it rolled and twisted into a large bun at the back of her head. She was wearing a plain black dress and black oxfords.

When dusk fell outside and the coach became hazy inside, Richie rested his head back and closed his eyes. He wondered about Lamont, the little town of his birth, and how it was going to be to live there. It's probably a nice enough little town, he thought. Had to be better than Chicago, that was for sure.

Anyplace had to be better than Chicago.

The Lamont town square was just as Richie remembered it from the last sad time he'd seen it with Chloe: an old county courthouse in the middle of a slightly raised square of land, faced on all four sides by a block of small-town businesses with perpendicular parking at their curbs. Just off the town square was the post office. A little farther out, as if serving as a link between the commercial and residential sections, were several churches, all Protestant. Gasoline service stations were out past the churches. At the far north end of town, near Mrs. Clark's home, was the Illinois Central depot; at the far south end was Lamont High School, the students of which were all white. Beyond the town limits in all directions were farms.

His second day there, Richie walked out to the high school to register for classes. It was a two-mile walk: a mile up to the square, a mile past it to the school. Grace Menefee had given Richie the name of a teacher he was supposed to see, Mrs. Reinhart, who was in charge of the Distributive Education program, and whom the local welfare officials had contacted about Richie. She was, Miss Menefee had told him, the only teacher in the school who would know he was transferring in from reformatory.

Lamont High was unlike any school Richie had ever seen. It was all on one floor, laid out in wings around a gymnasium with bleachers on two sides and a raised stage at one end so that, with folding chairs set up, it could be converted to an auditorium. On registration day, the halls were crowded with students coming and going, shouted greetings, hushed discussions about who was teaching what that year, lots of rushing about to get the best lockers, consultations among friends who wanted to have study hall at the same time, and a plethora of other activities with which Richie was totally unfamiliar.

He found Mrs. Reinhart in the Distributive Education classroom, and told her who he was. She looked up at him from her desk, a slightly heavy woman with an ample bustline, a few gray streaks in her dark hair, and eyes that were alive with intelligence behind her glasses. Looking at him quite frankly, she said, "Well, hello. I didn't know if you were coming or not. They never really said for certain. But you're here."

"Yes, ma'am."

"All right," she began shuffling papers and folders about on her desk, "we have to get you signed up for classes *and* get you a job, correct? Correct.

Let's take care of the classes first. Let's see, I don't have your date of birth, but you're fourteen, aren't you—"

"No, ma'am. Sixteen."

"I thought the people who spoke to me about you said fourteen?"

"I don't know about that, ma'am," Richie lied easily and convincingly, "but I'm sixteen."

Pursing her lips slightly, Mrs. Reinhart said, "You wouldn't try to fool me, would you?"

"No, ma'am," Richie professed emphatically.

Mrs. Reinhart opened a desk drawer and handed him a single sheet of paper. "This is the freshman and sophomore English literature reading list. If you're sixteen and ready for the junior class, you will have read at least some of these books. Would you like to select three of them and tell me about them?"

Richie's eyes flicked over the typed list. Smiling, he handed it back to her. "Why don't you pick three, ma'am. I've read them all."

Mrs. Reinhart did pick three, including *Ivanhoe*, and Richie gave her oral reports on each of them, complete with names of characters, descriptions of locales, and his personal evaluation of the story, the writing, and the author. When he finished, Mrs. Reinhart put the list away and said, "You are *definitely* ready for the junior class." Writing his name on a schedule sheet, she said, "All right, you have to take English three and History three; then you have a choice of a math class or a science class. For juniors it's geometry or biology. Which one?"

"Biology, ma'am.

"All right, I can give you that in second period. Now then, you have to take one elective. A lot of the boys take an agriculture class; then there's a health and hygiene class, there's typing—"

"I'd like typing, please," Richie said. He had often watched Miss Cashman type back at the Damen Avenue branch library in Chicago, and had been fascinated by the way her fingers flashed across the typewriter keys without her even looking at them. But a sudden apprehension occurred to him. "Do I have to buy a typewriter?"

"No, of course not," Mrs. Reinhart replied quietly. "The school furnishes the typewriters." She gave him his class schedule, then said, "Now, let's get you a job. Have you worked before, and if so, what have you done?"

Richie shrugged. "I've set pins in a bowling alley, delivered papers, and at Charley— at the place I just came from, I worked on a garbage truck."

Mrs. Reinhart tapped one fingertip against her bottom lip. "We don't have a bowling alley in town, the paper only comes out once a week, except for the Memphis paper which is delivered by a pickup truck, and down here only Negroes work on garbage trucks. But I have a job in mind for you that I think will be perfect," she said, flipping through a card file. "Mr. Rollie Chalk, who owns Chalk's Drug Store up on the square, is looking for a boy to work behind his soda fountain. No experience is necessary; he'll train you. All that's required is that the boy be neat and clean, and you look like you are. Do you think you'd like working in a drugstore?"

"Yes, ma'am!" Richie said eagerly. A job in a drugstore, behind a soda fountain—it sounded too good to be true. Richie had often watched soda jerks in Chicago and admired the way they scooped ice cream and constructed sundaes and sodas. He made up his mind that if he got the job, he would become the best soda jerk in town.

"Here's a note for you to take to Mr. Chalk; you can't miss the drugstore, it's right next to the Corner Café. And," Mrs. Reinhart searched for another form, "speaking of food, we'll fill this out so you can get a free lunch here at school."

Richie's honed logic seized on her words. If lunch was free, why did he have to fill out a form? "Does everybody get lunch free?" he asked.

"No, just the ones who can't afford to pay."

"I don't want it," Richie said without rancor. "I'll pay for my lunch."

"You're entitled to the free lunch," Mrs. Reinhart emphasized. "Your circumstances, living with a pensioner grandmother, certainly qualifies you—"

"No, ma'am, I don't want nothing free," he insisted, shaking his head.

"Very well," Mrs. Reinhart said, putting the form away. She looked at him with an expression of admiration mixed with sadness. "If you change your mind, please let me know."

When Richie left to go uptown, for some reason he turned to look back at the school. Mrs. Reinhart was watching him from the window of her classroom. He waved to her and she waved back. It reminded him of the way he and Frances had once waved to each other.

Rollie Chalk was a short, dapper little man in his forties. He had a cherubic face and a fixed smile with which to greet customers. His drugstore, which was the nicest of three in Lamont, had a pharmacy in the rear—some things were the same everywhere, Richie thought—a soda fountain with several tables and chairs in front, and glass showcases and merchandise counters occupying the center. Everything was shiny and sparkling throughout. Richie fell in love with the place the minute he walked into it.

Reading Mrs. Reinhart's note, Rollie Chalk said with his stationary smile, "Well, you'd like to work behind my soda fountain, eh?"

"Yes, sir!" Richie said with all the buoyant enthusiasm he felt. This place was *wonderful!*

"Are you a fast learner?" Rollie Chalk asked.

"Yes, sir! I learn real quick! And I'll work hard for you too, Mr. Chalk."

Rollie Chalk chuckled at Richie's forthrightness and spunk. "Well, let's see," he said, leading Richie behind the gleaming stainless steel and marble fountain. He gave Richie a spotless white apron and showed him how to put it on. "Let's start with sodas," he said, taking a tall soda glass from a shelf.

During the next half hour, Rollie Chalk taught Richie the basics of making sodas, sundaes, malteds, banana splits, limeades, Coke floats, and several other fountain items. Richie's keen mind locked in each instruction and filed it in his surface memory for immediate recall. When Mr. Chalk tested him on the quantity and order of ingredients for several of the items, Richie repeated them without hesitation or error.

"My, it looks like you are quick," the drugstore owner praised. "All right, tell Mrs. Reinhart you're hired. Two to six every afternoon, nine to nine on Saturdays—we work a long day on Saturday because that's the day everybody comes to town—and noon to five on Sundays. Pay's fifty cents an hour; eighteen-fifty a week. That suit you?"

"Yes, sir! Thanks a lot, Mr. Chalk!"

As they were talking, a boy a couple of years older than Richie came in and approached them. A beefy kid, he walked with his shoulders hunched slightly, bouncing a little on the balls of his feet. "Oh my, here comes Billy Pastor," said Rollie Chalk. "He's been after me to give him the job I just gave you." Chalk enlarged his set smile. "Hello, Billy, how you today?"

"Fine, Mr. Chalk," the boy replied. "I was wondering if you'd made up your mind about the job yet?"

"Matter of fact, I have, Billy. I just hired this young fellow right here. He's part of the Distributive Education program at school and I promised to support it. Sorry, Billy."

After Billy Pastor left, Chalk said, "It's not like he *needs* the job; his family's got more money than I have."

Rollie Chalk showed Richie around the store a little more, explaining who else worked there and what their duties were, then told him to report for work—"always clean and neat, with your hair combed"—at two the next day.

When Richie left the store, Billy Pastor was loitering on the corner, waiting for him. "Hey, you," he said roughly. "Come 'ere." Richie walked over, sizing him up. The boy was taller, heavier, probably stronger than Richie, and probably slower too. "You're not from around here," he said. "Where'd you come from?"

"Chicago."

"Chi-*ca*-go! What are you doing in Lamont?"

"I came here to live with my grandmother."

"Well, you just took a job I wanted," Pastor said, voice becoming angry.

Richie shrugged.

"Sorry."

"Sorry ain't enough," the resentful boy said. He put a stiff finger on Richie's chest. "You better watch your step, hear? You do me any more bad turns and I'll whip your Yankee ass all over this square!"

Richie did not like Billy Pastor's finger poking his chest, but he checked himself against doing anything about it. The Charleytown superintendent's words surfaced on his mind: *The Illinois juvenile court will still have jurisdiction over you . . . trouble of any kind will be reported . . . you could either be returned here or sent to Menard . . .*

"You hear me?" Pastor demanded.

Richie knew he could hit Pastor six times before the hostile boy could even get his fists closed and up. But he did nothing except say, "I hear you."

"Better remember it too!" Pastor concluded his threats, pushing Richie aside and stalking away.

Richie walked on down the street, not even angry at Billy Pastor, so excited was he about his new job. He could not wait to get down to the house and tell Miss Ethel about it. And he could hardly wait until the next day when he would put on an apron and take over that beautiful, gleaming soda fountain. He had promised Grace Menefee that he was going to try—and try he would. She had told him once that she believed there was something good in life waiting for him; maybe this was it: this little Tennessee town where he had been born. Maybe he could *belong* here, be a part of things that were good: a home, a school, a job.

Feeling good, he stopped halfway home at a little combination grocery–filling station called Luckey's and got a cold bottle of Coca-Cola out of the icebox. Standing there drinking it, he felt very pleased with the way his life was going. Maybe, he thought, his dark days were over. No more being hungry, wearing ragged clothes, freezing, running dope, stealing; no more scratching out a day-by-day, sometimes hour-by-hour existence.

Maybe at long last he had finally made it into the sunshine.

School did not turn out to be exactly what Richie had hoped for. His classes were interesting and challenging, and the Lamont High teachers *taught*, rather than merely oversaw, as the Charleytown instructors had, but socially, the school—or Richie himself, he could not decide which—was sorely lacking. He could not seem to make a friend.

He knew he was different: in attitude, personality, even his speech. He was a lone Northern brogue in a sea of Southern drawls. Because of it, he found himself subjected to a new kind of bullying. In the halls between classes, there were "accidental" bumps followed by sly apologies of "Sorry there, Yankee." Disparaging remarks, always somehow incorporating that same term, "Yankee," were a daily challenge, to which he refused to respond. Occasionally one of the acknowledged school ruffians, among whom Billy Pastor was prominent, would go to great lengths to aggravate Richie enough to get him to start a fight: knocking his books out of his hands, trying to trip him, shoving him out of the lunch line. Whenever, wherever it occurred, Richie simply walked away.

When the treatment first started, when Richie realized, to his surprise, that he was not going to be accepted, that a pattern of antagonism and harassment was developing, he imagined that it was going to be very difficult to keep his instincts tethered. It was one thing to exercise restraint on a schoolyard because he could *not* fight, something altogether different to withstand that kind of aggravation when he *could* retaliate—and effectively. But he was mistaken about the degree of difficulty; he found it surprisingly easy to retreat from the insults, the threats, the challenges, even in the wake of derisive laughter that usually followed it. Some things, he concluded, you just couldn't figure.

The thing that amazed Richie about Lamont High was that the girls were almost as bad as the boys. There were two distinct types of girls in his classes: the bright, bouncy cheerleader kind in their tight mohair sweaters, swirling pleated skirts, and bobby sox, and the tall, cool, more ladylike academic set. The former delighted in observing and even participating in Richie's ridicule— they seemed to love the word "Yankee"—while the latter, with whom Richie had much in common intellectually, chose to ignore him. He finally understood his position clearly, and knew his ostracism was complete, when one of the girls gave a party for the biology class and he was the only one not invited. He could only shake his head at the absurdity. He talked different— so he was a Yankee. Never mind that he had been born right there; he had *turned out different.* It would have been funny if he had been able to convince himself that not being invited to the party had not hurt his feelings. But it had.

For every overcast moment in school, however, Mrs. Reinhart generated a bright one for him. "I have been told by your English literature teacher," she said one day, "that you write absolutely marvelous book reports. How would you like to work on the school newspaper staff? The *Hi-Life* could certainly use a little lucid writing. We could change you from early lunch to late lunch and give you an hour for the paper before you have to leave for work."

"Sounds swell," Richie said, "but hasn't the deadline passed for changing schedules?"

"My husband happens to be principal of this school," she said archly, throwing him a wink. "I pretty much get my own way around here. Want to do it?"

"Yes, ma'am!"

So he went to work on the *Hi-Life* staff, writing mostly sports items, which no one else was thrilled about doing. It did not change his status socially—staffers came and went at odd times, so there was not much opportunity to get to know anyone any better—but it opened up an entirely new vista for him as far as *words* were concerned. For the first time, he was writing not about something he had read, but about something that had *happened:* something current, familiar, personal. It was exciting.

Reading again, writing book reports again, and now writing for the school newspaper, Richie eagerly looked forward to school every day in spite of the disagreeable times.

At Chalk's Drug Store, Richie became an expert soda jerk. He mixed perfect sodas, blended exceptional malteds, and constructed flawless sundaes. He prided himself on quick, courteous service to everyone: even Billy Pastor and his friends when they ambled in on Saturday night while looking for trouble around the crowded square; even the taunting cheerleader types and the aloof intellectuals who stopped in for Cokes after school. He let them all take their cuts at him, enduring their malice. And occasionally, as time passed and he became less of an oddity, there would be a cordial greeting from someone, a comment that did not include the word "Yankee," even a neutral remark directed to him by name.

One of the first girls to talk to him decently was a sophomore named Midge, a freckle-faced, round-bodied, outdoorsy fifteen year old who reeked of good health. The daughter of a well-to-do farmer, Richie had seen her in the drugstore numerous times with her clique of friends from school. One evening, just before he got off work, she came in alone. She had driven up in a shiny Dodge pickup, wearing farm jeans and a sweatshirt.

"Can you fix me a nice cold limeade *real* fast?" she asked. "I am about to *die* from this Indian summer heat!"

"Coming up," Richie said, taking a glass off the shelf. In the mirror behind the fountain, as he squeezed the limes, he saw her studying him with furtive glances.

"What's Chicago like?" she asked when he set the drink in front of her.

"Big," he told her.

"I already know *that*." She drew some of the limeade through a straw. "Did you like living there?"

"Sometimes."

"You like it better than here?"

"No."

She gave him an annoyed look. "Can't you say more than one word at a time?"

"Sure, I can. When I want to." He bobbed his chin at her drink. "You want that put on your bill?"

"Of course." She raised her own chin an aloof inch. "I never carry money."

Grunting softly to himself, Richie wrote the limeade in his charge book and then put a CLOSED sign on the fountain. Taking off his apron, he put it in the linen service bag and went to the back of the store to tell Rollie Chalk goodnight. When he got back up front, Midge had finished the limeade so he put the glass under the sink to be washed. As he walked out the front door, she walked out with him.

"Want a ride home?" she asked. Richie stopped and faced her.

"How come you're talking to me and offering me a ride?" he wanted to know. His tone was not so much suspicious as curious.

"Maybe I think you're cute," Midge replied candidly. "Come on, get in. I won't bite."

"I might," he told her. Midge looked frankly at him.

"Get in anyway." When they were both in the truck, she asked, "You want to go right home?"

Looking at the outline of her young breasts under the sweatshirt, Richie was reminded of Linda. "No," he said.

Midge smiled. "Neither do I."

She drove out of town, toward the country roads.

When Richie got home two hours later than usual that night, Mrs. Clark demanded to know where he'd been.

"I went for a ride in the country with a farm girl," he said.

"More likely you've been settin' around some pool hall," she remarked.

"I don't sit around pool halls."

"You take to running around nights, you'll be back in trouble again," she warned. "And don't look for me to help you next time."

"I never look for anybody to help me," he said.

"You'll have to eat cold supper," she told him. "I'm not warming it up."

"Cold supper's fine. I *like* cold supper."

They had a precarious relationship, Richie and his grandmother. Each was wary of the other, neither entirely convinced that their arrangement would work. A severe woman with a tendency to be dour, Mrs. Clark, like her grandson, had taken some bitter licks in life. Marrying early, she soon discovered that her husband was a drinker. A labor foreman for the Illinois Central, he kept his liquor in a tool shed next to the tracks. Every night after supper, he would walk down to the shed for a drink. One night he drank too much and stretched out on the tracks. The City of New Orleans streamliner quartered him.

"I can travel anywhere in the country just by showing it to the conductor." She shook a finger at him. "Don't you ever go to drinking while you're under my roof," she put him on notice, "because I'll not stand for it."

"I won't, Miss Ethel," he promised.

The house her husband had left her, its mortgage paid off by his death, was a very modest little white frame structure at the end of Moreridge Street, just up a hill from the railroad tracks. It was old and weathered now, its paint faded and peeling, one end of the front porch leaning, window screens rusting, a few shingles missing. But to Richie, aside from the apartment where he, his mother, and Johnny Eaton had lived, and which he still remembered fondly, this plain, simple little house was the best home he had known. What made it so, more than anything else, was its permanence; there was no landlord knocking at the door, no moving out in the middle of the night to avoid back rent, no constant threat of eviction. And it was clean: no roaches, rats, bedbugs. Richie liked it so well, felt so at home sleeping in the very same room in which he had been born, that when he could he gave Mrs. Clark a dollar or two more than the agreed upon half of what he earned.

After his first ride with Midge, when she began to come uptown to see him nearly every night, and when Richie began going out to meet her after supper, he finally told Mrs. Clark that he had a girlfriend and who she was. Mrs. Clark knew the family.

"Her daddy owns one of the biggest farms in the county, and she's an only child," his grandmother said. "You could do lots worse."

"I'm not marrying her, Miss Ethel, just going for rides and to movies," Richie pointed out.

"Girls pick their husbands early down here," she warned. "Sometimes their daddies help them with a shotgun."

From their first encounter, Midge was crazy about Richie. On a lonely dirt road, their petting had become impossibly passionate and within minutes they were both undressed, doing things on the cool leather seat of the truck, both doors open, cab light off, only the moon to see each other by. Midge was not a virgin, but neither was she knowledgeable about the kind of foreplay that Frances had taught Richie. When he spread her legs and stood outside the truck burying his face in her soft lower hair, and worked his tongue under the cap of her clitoris, she thought she would die.

"Where in the world did you learn *that?*" she asked in a velvety, sated voice when they were finished.

"They teach it in eighth grade up north."

She let him come inside her, wetly and deliciously, that first night, but warned, "We can't take a chance like that again. Steal some rubbers from the drugstore tomorrow."

Richie thought he had given up stealing. But for what he was getting from Midge, he knew he would readily go back to it.

One afternoon as the weather was beginning to turn cold, a stooped, scowling farmer in moleskin hunting clothes and muddy boots, came into the drugstore and stood looking curiously at Richie long enough to make him uncomfortable. "Help you, sir?" Richie asked.

Just then Rollie Chalk came out of the back, smile in place, and said, "Well, Mr. Lester, long time no see. How are you?"

"Like to have a word with you in private," the farmer named Lester said. He walked to the back of the store, Rollie Chalk following.

The two men stood talking at the pharmacy counter. As they conversed, they seemed to take turns glancing up at Richie behind the fountain. Richie had the peculiar impression that they were talking about him; he tried not to look back at them, and was relieved when Midge drove up and came in.

"Hey, sugar," she said.

"Hey," Richie replied. He did not like Midge calling him "sugar." Every time she did it, he was reminded of his mother. But he did not ask her to stop because he did not want to have to explain why.

"Are you about ready to close up?" she asked.

"Yeah." Richie gave the marble countertop one last wipe and set the CLOSED sign on it, as the man named Lester left.

When Richie went to the back of the store to get his coat and say goodnight to Rollie Chalk, the druggist asked, "Was your daddy Richmond Howard, the bootlegger who disappeared after he was let out of the penitentiary?"

"Yessir." Richie felt like ice water had been poured down his spine. "Why?"

"Oh, no particular reason," Rollie Chalk said through his set smile. "Somebody just happened to mention that you were, and I wondered if they were right." He resumed what he had been doing. "Goodnight, now."

Richie left the store that night with a swelling sense of foreboding.

The following Saturday night, when Rollie Chalk closed the store and called Richie into the back to be paid, he said, "I'm letting you go tonight, Richie. I've decided to cut back on overhead by eliminating my fountain help. I'm going to have the other clerks cover the fountain. Tell Mrs. Reinhart I'll be glad to give a recommendation if you need one."

Richie walked out on the still crowded town square in a half daze, stunned by his firing in spite of the ominous feelings nagging him since the farmer Lester's visit to the store. Midge was parked in front of the courthouse with the pickup engine running to keep the cab warm. Turning up his collar against the cold wind, Richie trotted over to the truck and got in.

"Hey, sugar. What's the matter? You look downright ill."

"I just got fired," he said. The words almost caught in his throat. His wonderful job, his beautiful soda fountain, the earnings he needed to pay his own way—all suddenly gone. He felt sick.

"What in the world happened?" Midge asked in surprise. Richie told her what Rollie Chalk had said about reducing overhead. "Oh, sugar, I'm so sorry," she commiserated, putting a warm palm on his cheek. "Listen, as soon as school's over, I'll get daddy to give you a job on the farm."

"I'll need a job lots sooner than that," Richie said. "I have to pay my own way, you know. My grandmother's only got a small pension."

"Well, you can find another job in the meantime," Midge said optimistically. "Mrs. Reinhart can probably help you."

Mrs. Reinhart could not. When Richie saw her on Monday and reported what had happened, she was immediately disheartened. "Oh, no! That man. He promised to support the D.E. program for the full school year. Well, business is business, I suppose." As always, Mrs. Reinhart rallied her usual high spirits and perked up. "Well, we'll just have to find something else for you. There's nothing available right now, but I'll make a few telephone calls and see what I can do. In the meantime, you'll have to attend study hall the last two periods in the afternoon. It'll give you a chance to do some extra reading; I'll see about letting you use the *Hi-Life* room one of those periods to do some extra work on the paper."

When Richie told Mrs. Clark that he had been fired, she immediately asked, "Was it for stealing?"

"No, it wasn't for stealing," Richie replied irritably. "How come you always think the worst of me right away?"

"I only asked. What was it for?"

"Mr. Chalk's just cutting back on help, is all."

"You're fixing to find another job right away, I hope," she said. Richie nodded.

"Mrs. Reinhart's going to help me look."

"That's good," Mrs. Clark said, "because *I* can't support you, you know that. It's all I can do to take care of myself."

"Don't worry, Miss Ethel, you won't have to support me." Putting on his coat, he started for the door.

"Where are you going this time of night?" Mrs. Clark wanted to know.

"For a walk."

"It's cold out," she warned.

"I like the cold," he said, leaving.

Walking down the hill to the depot, Richie started along the cinder path next to the tracks. The air was thin and crisp, the night very clear and light with a glowing full moon. As he walked, Richie wished he had someone to talk to: Linda or Stan Klein, or Myron or Mack, or Vernie. It was impossible to talk to his grandmother; she had too many defenses. Aside from her there was only Midge, and all she had on her mind was sex: having it, planning it, talking about it, getting ready for it. She did not read, except for movie magazines, so they had nothing in common there. She professed to love him, and insisted that he say he loved her, which he accommodated her by saying, but he doubted that it was love he felt; it was not nearly as compelling and pleasant as the feelings he had experienced with Linda. What he *did* love was what they did together in the cab of her pickup. To that extent, where it involved her body, he was definitely in love. But aside from the physical there was nothing.

Walking along the moonlit tracks, the cold cinders crunching under each step, Richie wondered why he always ended up alone.

And wondered if it would always be that way in his life.

A week later he was walking by Chalk's Drug Store and saw a new soda jerk behind the fountain. At first incredulous, then coldly angry, he turned his head to glare at Rollie Chalk, who was standing in the front door, looking out, smiling at the world. Chalk refused to meet Richie's eyes, his gaze going right past Richie as if he were not there. Richie stalked home infuriated.

"He hired somebody new for my job!" he announced lividly to his grandmother. She was sitting in front of their oil stove, hand sewing a quilt which she would later try to sell.

"There must have been some other reason he fired you, then," she remarked with her usual candid logic. Staring at her, Richie's mind churned and fitted together pieces of knowledge.

"Do you know a farmer named Lester?" he asked. Mrs. Clark stopped sewing.

"I know of him. Why?"

Richie told her about the scowling man's visit to the drugstore and his feeling that the conversation had been about him. "Right after that was when Mr. Chalk asked me if I was Richmond Howard's son and I told him I was."

Mrs. Clark avoided his eyes. "Maybe that was it, then. Maybe Rollie Chalk don't want a bootlegger's son working in his store."

"But I was a good worker!" Richie protested the inequity. "He told me himself that I was one of the best soda jerks he ever had."

"It's his store," Mrs. Clark said flatly.

"Well, it's not fair!" Richie stormed. Inside, he was seething. "I'd like to take Rollie Chalk by the throat and make him admit why he fired me."

"Go on and do it, if you want to go back to that reform school," his grandmother said.

"It might be worth it!"

"Do it, then. Nobody's stopping you. You'll only have to stay there three more years."

The thought of three more years in Charleytown tempered Richie's outrage a little, but he was still bristling. "It's not fair, it's just *not* fair," he stewed.

"Life's not fair," Mrs. Clark observed calmly.

Richie shook his head in utter frustration. It was just like the goddamned Off-the-Street Club; the rules had been changed on him again. Only this time, he suddenly decided, he wasn't going to tear up his book report and quit. This time he was going to fight back, he was going to *make* it. He wasn't going to be made to give up—not again.

Richie swore he was going to get through the school year no matter what.

Even if he had to start stealing again.

For the month before Christmas, Mrs. Reinhart got Richie a temporary job as stock boy for Family Shoe Store. Because of the volume of holiday business in shoe sales, particularly house slippers for gifts, the store wanted its sales clerks to be able to wait on several customers at a time without having to leave them to get shoes from stock. After being shown how the stock numbers were sequenced, Richie ran back and forth bringing out the styles and sizes the clerks needed.

"I'm sorry it's only a Christmas job," Mrs. Reinhart said when she told him about it, "but maybe after the first of the year we can do better."

"Any kind of job's okay with me," Richie assured her. "I just need to work."

"I know," the teacher said quietly. "I know you do."

Christmas day for Richie was more an annoyance than anything else. Midge's parents took her with them to Arkansas to spend the holidays with her father's brother and his family. "It is such a *pain!*" she complained. "But there's no way I can get out of it. We rotate—Christmas at our house one year, theirs the next. I just *hate* not being with you at Christmas."

"It's okay," Richie said. "My grandmother and I are having a big dinner at home."

That was a lie. Mrs. Clark had been invited to spend Christmas day with a friend of hers, a spinster named Miss Bessie, who also lived on Moreridge

Street. "I'll ask Miss Bessie if you can come too, if you want to," Mrs. Clark offered.

"Thanks anyway, but I'm having Christmas dinner out at Midge's farm," Richie lied again.

On Christmas day he stayed home alone, eating bologna sandwiches and reading *The Valley of Decision* by Marcia Davenport.

The shoe store kept him on for a week after Christmas to help put the stock back in order, then let him go. Although she had been looking, Mrs. Reinhart had not been able to find anything else for him. "I'm sure something will turn up," she said with her usual optimism. "In the meantime, why don't you let me help you apply to county relief for some temporary help—"

"No, ma'am," Richie refused to even entertain the idea. "I don't want any welfare help. Anyway, I can get along all right for a few months; I've got some money saved up." That was only half a lie; he had enough savings to last a few weeks, not months.

In February, he stopped eating lunch at school, going to the study hall instead. He began stealing candy bars, paying for one while slipping two or three others into his coat pocket. Instead of giving Mrs. Clark the full amount of his weekly board, he asked if he could supply some of the groceries instead.

"The manager up at Kroger's said I could do some odd jobs for him— sweeping up, that kind of thing. He'll either pay me or let me take it out in merchandise at wholesale prices."

Richie had devised the scheme after discovering that Kroger's was a shoplifter's paradise: narrow aisles arranged in such a fashion that the clerk at the cash register counter could not see most of the store while checking out a customer. By leaving his coat hanging open and slipping what he wanted inside his shirt, Richie was able to steal three or four items at a time: small canned goods, packaged lunchmeat, sticks of butter, wedges of cheese, boxes of salt and pepper, and other staples that Mrs. Clark told him they needed. He would always pay for at least one item, usually bread, milk, or eggs, and get a paper bag to put the stolen food in before he got home.

Midge, suspecting that he was not getting enough to eat, started "just happening" to have a little food in the truck when she picked him up.

"I want you to try this cake," she would say. "I made it with my own little hands." Or she might have a bag of pretzels and a couple of Dr Peppers, " 'cause I was hungry and I thought you might be too."

Richie was not fooled. "I'm not a charity case, Midge," he finally told her. "You don't have to feed me like some hobo."

She played it as lightly as she could. "I assure you my reasons are strictly dishonorable. Afer all, we *do* burn up energy out on these country roads."

Now and then, Midge broached the subject of a future together. Unaware that Richie was actually a year younger—she thought he was a year older—she clearly had ideas that included marriage. "You know, sugar, whoever marries me will eventually become a partner in my daddy's farm. Do you think," she asked coyly, "that we could make a cotton farmer out of a city boy like you?"

"I doubt it," Richie replied with an edge. It was because of a goddamned farmer that he was out of a job.

In March, Richie's money ran out and he was completely broke. He did not have the price of a haircut, did not have money to buy a loaf of bread as an excuse to go into the Kroger store to steal food, had no money at all to give to Mrs. Clark for his board. He had already asked at every store around the square if there were any odd jobs he could do, any work at all, just as Mrs. Reinhart kept periodically trying for him. But there was nothing. The cold winter months in a rural farming area were slow; businesses, like the farmers themselves, just dug in and tried to get by. Even on Saturday, the traditional day to go to town, many people opted to stay home. It was easier—and cost less.

Richie knew he had to begin some serious stealing if he was to get by. There was, as he saw it, no alternative; he would *not* ask for, or take, charity. He had drawn a line at that, and he would not step over it. Looking around town, he decided at once against shoplifting merchandise to sell, as he had been so successful doing in Chicago; stores in Lamont were much smaller and carried less expensive items, and even if he were able to snag something good—a watch or some costume jewelry—he had no place to sell it; there was no Midwest A.C. here where people open to the purchase of hot merchandise gathered. There were no newsstands either, from which to filch coins, no liquor store loading docks where deposit bottles might be swiped—but there were, Richie had already noted, several vending machines around the square.

The first one he took was a nickel peanut machine the Chamber of Commerce had in an arcade of small stores next to one of the banks. The stores closed at six, but the arcade itself was open all night so that people could window-shop. After estimating the size of the machine, and surreptitiously checking to make certain it would unscrew from its stand, Richie found the proper size empty cardboard box behind one of the stores, and late that night boldly walked into the arcade and made off with the machine. Using a screwdriver shoplifted from the hardware store, he pried off the bottom plate and retrieved more than six dollars in nickels. Putting the machine back into the box, he tossed it into the coal car of a passing freight train. The next day, with the nickels tied securely in a sock, the sock wrapped in a shirt, all of it in a paper bag, he hitchhiked to the town of Overland, sixteen miles away, and cashed the coins in at a bank for currency. On his way out of Overland, Richie saw a gumball machine outside a gas station next to the highway. Getting a Coca-Cola, he loitered at the side of the station drinking it until the attendant got busy helping two customers. Then he carried the machine into the men's room, pried it open on the floor, and left it there after filling his sock with pennies and wrapping it up again. He was out on the highway and had hitchhiked a ride back toward Lamont while the attendant was still cleaning windshields.

For the rest of that month, Richie spent Saturdays and Sundays scouring the little towns within a thirty-mile radius of Lamont, stealing any kind of vending machine he could find. It turned out to be surprisingly simple to do. Setting his empty box on the sidewalk, he would loiter next to the machine as if waiting for someone. Two or three times he would put money in the machine, each time turning it as much as he could. When he was certain it was loosened on its stand, he would wait for the right moment, slip the box over it, and walk away holding the bottom closed with the machine inside. Although easy, it was nevertheless gut-wrenching work that tied his stomach in knots every time he did it. He never looked back as he walked away; it was only when he was half a block down the street or up the highway that he began to relax. At the first convenient place he found—an alley, some bushes, a restroom—he pried open the machine, got the money, and with his empty box headed for another town. As soon as he got there, he would cash the coins in for currency before stealing a machine there. His routine of theft did not earn him the eighteen-fifty a week he had been making as a soda jerk, but at least he was able to pay his board most weeks, and even have enough left over occasionally to eat lunch.

In April, Richie was asked if he wanted to work at Family Shoe Store again during the two weeks before Easter. He jumped at the chance and was once again running shoe stock after school. During that period he had lunch money again and was able to buy, at a discount in the store, some badly needed socks. But the two weeks went by quickly and he was faced again with no income and a long six weeks remaining until school was out. It was then that he began thinking about going back to Chicago for the summer. When he talked to Midge about it, she naturally opposed the idea.

"What in the world will I do all summer long without a boyfriend?" she asked. "And what about the job I was going to have my daddy give you on the farm?"

"Midge, I don't know anything about farm work," he told her. "And even if I did, I wouldn't fit in with your daddy's other help any more than I fit in at school."

"Things are getting better for you at school," she said. "I see people talking to you in the halls now and I never did before."

"Sure, there are a few people who talk to me," Richie admitted, "but that's as far as it goes. I'm still not accepted by most of them; I'm never invited to any social activities, never invited to join anything; hell, I wouldn't even be working on the school paper if it wasn't for Mrs. Reinhart. Don't get me wrong, I'm not complaining about it; I'm pretty much used to it now, just like I'm used to the fact that Billy Pastor is never going to let up on me. But I don't want to stay here all summer and put up with the same thing. If I'm not doing it in order to go to school, it just wouldn't be worth it."

"Which means, I suppose, that *I'm* not worth it," Midge said stiffly.

"I didn't say that—"

"You might as well have." She looked away, teary-eyed. "After all we've been to each other, I just can't believe you're going to go off and *leave* me like that. I mean, what in the world am I supposed to do all summer, sit and twiddle my thumbs while you're up there in Chicago having a good time?"

"I won't be having a good time; I'll be working," he said patiently.

"All right, suit yourself," Midge said finally, "go on and go. But," she warned, "don't expect me to sit around and wait for you to come back."

"If that's the way you feel about it, maybe I won't even come back," Richie retorted, his own anger rising. What the hell, he thought, he had made it on his own in Chicago once before without getting caught. There was no reason he couldn't do it again. Fuck this little town with all its petty-minded people. Maybe, by god, he just *wouldn't* come back.

"Have you made up your mind about this?" Midge asked when she dropped him off that night. "You're definitely going?"

"Yes, I am."

"I guess that's that, then," she said coldly.

When she drove off, Richie knew she would not be back.

There was a pool hall in one of the little towns near Lamont that Richie had noticed when he was looking for vending machines to steal. It had an old-fashioned skylight in the roof that was opened and closed with a long pole to let air in. The only lock was a simple slide bolt that was pushed back and forth with the pole. There were two pinball machines and a big red Coca-Cola machine in the place. Richie figured that with a little luck he could get ten dollars worth of nickels out of each one. A train ticket to Chicago was twenty-one dollars.

When the last day of school was over, instead of going home, Richie went up to the Blue Star Café where the buses stopped, and caught a local Greyhound bus. Arriving in the town where the pool hall was, he checked the schedule back to Lamont; the last bus was at a quarter past twelve. The pool hall would have to close no later than eleven o'clock for his plan to work. Crossing the square, Richie entered the pool hall and, using the best Southern accent he could manage, said to the counterman, "I want to meet my brother here later on tonight. What time do y'all close?"

The counterman said eleven o'clock. It would work, Richie decided. On his way out, he glanced up at the skylight; the bolt wasn't even closed. Going up to the corner, Richie went around to the alley and walked back past the rear of the pool hall. There were iron bars covering both windows. Perfect for climbing, he thought.

In a drugstore, Richie bought a candy bar and stole two others, then walked up the street to the movie house.

Several hours later, sitting on the curb across the street, concealed by the shadow of a big tree, Richie watched through the front window as the counterman started getting ready to close, counting money from the register and putting it into a bank bag. Promptly at eleven, the man hustled two remaining customers out and went around turning off the lights. Leaving, he locked the front door and Richie saw him walk down to a bank on the corner, put the bag in a night depository, then get in his car and drive off.

Richie walked briskly to the corner and ducked around into the alley. Flattening himself against a building, he waited in deep shadows, counting to three hundred to see if anyone was following him. When he was sure he had not been seen, he hurried down to the rear of the pool hall. Just in case, he carefully tried the back door. It was locked. At the window, he gripped the bars, swung his feet up, and climbed them to the top. Gingerly he stood up on the top cross-bar and gripped the edge of the roof parapet. Straining, he pulled himself up as quietly as he could and hooked one knee over the side. When he got all the way up, he lay flat near the edge and once more counted to three hundred. Again there was no indication that he had been seen.

Creeping across the roof, remembering earlier that the skylight had been unlocked, Richie tried to lift it open. It was now locked. Son of a bitch, he silently cursed. Removing the screwdriver from his pocket, he wrapped its metal handle in his handkerchief and firmly rapped the pane of glass over the latch. Breaking, the glass fell into the pool hall below. As soon as he had done it, Richie ran in a crouch to the front of the roof and peered out at the dark town square. He saw no movement, heard no sound.

Back at the skylight, Richie opened it and put the bar in place to hold it. Then he lowered himself over the edge, hung by his hands and dropped onto a pool table below. Vaulting off, he kept in a crouched position and looked out the window, checking the street again. All was quiet. Moving to the front counter, he slowly depressed one of the cash register keys. As the drawer opened, a bell inside the machine sounded briefly, causing Richie to freeze and look anxiously out the front window again. Still no one, nothing. In the register drawer he found twenty dollars in currency and coins, change to start the next day's business.

From the register, Richie moved to the two pinball machines. Each of them had a hasp and padlock on the front panel covering the coin box. With his screwdriver, he had both of them pried open in three minutes, working quietly and carefully without noisily splitting the wood. He emptied both change boxes, pouring the nickels into a pair of socks he had brought along. Knotting one of them, he left the other open and moved to the Coca-Cola machine. For ten minutes he worked and pried and jimmied on the built-in lock that held the machine's door closed, but it remained firm; Richie's screwdriver was not strong enough to force the mechanism.

Sweating, breathing heavily, Richie put a nickel into the machine and got a bottle of Coke. He drank it all down in three long swallows, and stuck the empty in a wooden case next to the machine. Looking quickly around, seeing nothing else worth bothering with, he put a straight wooden chair on top of a pool table, carefully balanced himself on it, and climbed back out through the skylight.

It was five before midnight when Richie walked into the bus station, cash register money in his pocket, knotted socks full of nickels in a paper bag under his arm. There were three other people in the waiting room. No one paid more than cursory attention to him. Richie sat down to wait the twenty minutes for his bus.

The next morning, Mrs. Clark found Richie packing his belongings in a zipper bag. "What are you fixing to do?" she asked.

"I'm going to Chicago," he told her. "I'm going to find me a job up there." He folded a pair of trousers over the socks of nickels.

"If you go," his grandmother said, "you won't come back."

"Maybe I won't," Richie allowed.

"Just remember what that welfare lady told you about Chicago being a hard city. Remember what she said about it breaking you."

"I'd rather be broken by Chicago than starved to death by Lamont," he countered.

"Well, it's your life," Mrs. Clark said, trying to sound indifferent.

"At least up there I'm not an outcast. Up there nobody cares how I talk or who my father was."

"You're making a mistake," his grandmother warned.

"Won't be the first time," Richie replied, zipping the bag closed. At the front door, he said, "Thanks for letting me live here. Thanks for trying to help me. So long," he said, and added wryly, "Miss Ethel."

Bag in hand, Richie walked down the hill to the train depot.

*G*etting off the streetcar, Richie walked up Madison Street toward Cascade Bowling Lanes. He had a little more than sixteen dollars left, all of it in nickels, most of it still in the zipper bag he carried. Feeling good, he walked with a bounce and energy that had been missing for several months. Being back in Chicago again, feeling the throb and beat of the city, he didn't give a goddamn whether he ever saw Lamont, Tennessee, and its spiteful, small-minded inhabitants again. Striding up to Cascade's entrance, he felt as if he were coming home after a long absence. Tonight, he figured, he would be back in the bowling alley pits and sleeping in the ladies' lounge, just like old times.

At the counter, Richie found an overweight man in an open collar sport shirt, sweat rings under each arm, a half-smoked cigar clenched between his teeth. "Red around?" Richie asked.

"Red ain't worked here for over a year," the man said. "What'd you want him for?"

"I was hoping to get a job spotting," Richie said, surprised. What a difference between the cool, dapper Red and this fat slob. "I used to work here, but I been gone a couple of years. Been living in Tennessee where my dad was working."

"Well, I got a reg'lar crew of pinboys," the man said. "You want me to,

I can put your name on my extra list to fill in if somebody gets sick or don't show. You can check back with me about five-thirty."

"Sure, thanks."

Before leaving, Richie went upstairs to the locker room. It looked pretty much the same, but the combination locks he had on three of the lockers were gone, and there was now a name stenciled on each locker door. Looks like I'll be sleeping without a blanket or pillow tonight, he thought. He was relieved to see that the ladies' lounge was still in the same place, and through the door as a woman was entering he caught a glimpse of the divan. It looked like an old friend.

When he left the bowling alley, Richie walked down to Hamlin Avenue and into the Midwest Athletic Club. The sight and smell of the gym flooded his mind with memories; he stood for several minutes just looking around fondly, not only at the gym floor but also the balcony bleachers where he once peddled his stolen merchandise. For some weird reason, thinking back on those hard times, they did not seem all that terrible. It was strange, he thought, how life changed with the perspective of time.

Walking the length of the gym to the corner where the club fighters used to train, Richie encountered no one he recognized or remembered. All the fighters working out seemed to be older, adults, probably pros. After hanging around for a while, he finally went to the gym office and stuck his head in the door, asking for Myron. A man with his hat on looked up from a cluttered desk. "Myron? Myron who?"

"The guy who trains the club fighters," Richie told him.

"Oh, the old Jewish guy. He passed away."

"Passed away?" Richie was stunned. "He died?"

"Yep. Died right up there in one of the bleachers seats, sitting up. We thought he was asleep until we got ready to close and tried to wake him up."

"Jesus," Richie muttered, feeling sad and sick.

"Yeah, when the state banned club fights, the old guy didn't have nothing to do with his time. Used to come in here every day and just sit and watch. All day long. Finally just closed his eyes and conked out."

Richie left the gym in a daze. Feeling desperate to see someone he knew and who knew him, he decided to ride a streetcar down to Mack's garage. All the way he kept thinking about Myron just sitting there in the gym until he died. Several times during the streetcar ride, Richie felt like crying. Then, when he got where he was going, he suffered his third disappointment of the day. The garage had been turned into a motorcycle shop. "Mack moved down to Florida somewheres," the proprietor told Richie. " 'Bout two years ago. I ain't got his address."

Riding back up to the West Side, Richie could hardly believe the incredible run of bad luck he was encountering. No longer was he feeling buoyant about his return to Chicago; now he was beginning to feel like a stranger in a foreign land.

Back at Cascade, the counterman told Richie that all his regular pinsetters had shown up, but he could try again tomorrow if he wanted to. Thanking him, Richie left again and wandered up Madison. For a few minutes he stood aimlessly on the corner of Pulaski Road, not knowing which way to go next. When a newsstand operator began to look at him suspiciously, Richie moved on.

At Cascade again, later that night, hanging around watching the second league finish, Richie noticed a uniformed security guard go behind the counter and punch a timeclock. What the hell? he thought, frowning. As soon as the guard left, Richie went over and spoke to the counterman. "Excuse me, sir, I just wanted to find out how early I can get my name on that extra list tomorrow?"

"I start taking names about four," the counterman said.

"Swell, thanks. Say, who's the guy in the uniform? I don't remember him being here."

"Night watchman," the heavy man said. "Been here about six months. The joint was burglarized a couple times. Guys was getting in at night and prying open all the vending machines. Now the watchman sits in here all night with a pistol; we don't have no more trouble."

And I don't have a bed anymore, Richie thought.

Leaving the bowling alley, shaking his head ironically, Richie hopped a streetcar down to lower Madison Street and was pleased to see that the old all-night Haymarket Theater was still there. At least he had *someplace* to sleep.

The next day, stiff and sore from spending the night in the theater seat, sniffing a little from a slight head cold caused by the air conditioning, Richie was back out on the West Side wandering around again. He had spent the morning trying to find Estelle, his mother's old friend, to see if she had a couch he could bunk on for a few nights. Or maybe, Richie secretly fantasized, even share her bed; he vividly remembered Estelle's voluptuous body, the way her buoyant breasts swayed and shifted when she moved, and the things he had seen her do with men when he spied on her through the keyhole. In his imagination, he had decided that a sexual encounter with Estelle would be spectacular.

Starting with the last place he had known her to be living, Richie traced Estelle through three other apartment buildings and two jobs, but eventually lost track of her completely. At her most recent address, the landlady was still holding mail for her; at her most recent job, no one had ever called for an employment reference. Estelle seemed to have fallen out of the city entirely.

Back on Madison Street, Richie was thinking that if he did not get to work at the bowling alley that night, he would go over to Lake Street and see if he could find Vernie. Maybe she could figure out someplace for him to stay. Walking past a pool hall on the corner of Springfield, Richie suddenly heard someone say, "Hey, kid, wanna go rat-killing?"

Head snapping around, Richie saw that it was Stan Klein. "Hey, Stan!" he said loudly, grinning. Stan was in the doorway of the pool hall, holding a cue stick, wearing nice slacks and a stylish polo shirt. Just behind him stood Bobby Casey.

"Where the hell you been for so long, man?" Stan asked, punching him lightly on the muscle.

"Charleytown," Richie said, omitting his nine months in Lamont; that was too involved to explain just then.

"Charleytown, no shit?" Stan said, impressed. "Well, welcome home!" Stan was obviously glad to see him.

"Where'd you get them clothes?" Bobby Casey asked derisively. "The Salvation Army?"

"I bought 'em," Richie said, looking down at his cardigan sweater and corduroy trousers. "Why, what's the matter with them?"

"They're hick clothes, man. You look like you just got off the boat."

"Leave him alone, Case," said Stan. He put an arm around Richie's shoulders. "Come on inside."

The pool hall was deep and narrow, five old tables with drop pockets, all of them set horizontally in the room like big green stepping stones. Only one table had its light on: the rear one, where Stan and Bobby had a game in progress.

"How 'bout shooting a game for five bucks?" Bobby immediately challenged Richie.

"Hey, didn't I just say leave him alone?" Stan reminded. "What do you wanna try and take his dough for?" Stan got a bottle of Pabst Blue Ribbon from a cooler, flipped a quarter to the counterman, opened the bottle, and handed it to Richie, all in one smooth, unbroken motion, as if it had been choreographed. "Here, have a beer."

"Thanks, I could use one," Richie said. He had never tasted beer in his life, but he was not about to let Bobby Casey know that. Taking a good swallow, he felt its bitter taste spread through his mouth.

"So, you living with your old lady or what?" Stan asked.

Richie shook his head. "She's dead. I don't have a place to stay yet."

"You'll come home with me," Stan declared at once. "There's just my old lady and me now; my sister got married. I got my own room. You can stay long as you want."

"Thanks, Stan." Richie saw Bobby Casey glowering at him from across the table. Ignoring him, he said to Stan, "This is the second time you've found me a place to sleep. First time was that cave in the newspaper bundles, remember?"

"Yeah, I remember."

"Come on," Bobby Casey said impatiently, "we shooting pool or what?"

"Drink your beer," Stan said to Richie. "Soon's I beat this guy's ass at rotation, I'll take you to my place."

Richie just sipped at the beer, except when Bobby Casey was looking; then he took bigger swallows. It began to make him feel light-headed, and by the time the pool game was over and Stan was ready to go, Richie was a little tight. Putting up his stick, Stan said to Bobby, "We'll see you later, at the candy store."

"Yeah, we'll see you later," Richie chimed in. "If we can't make it, we'll write."

Looking askance at him as they left, Stan asked, "You drink much beer?"

Richie cupped a hand over his mouth and said confidentially, "Counting the one I just drank, I've had one."

"I thought so. Come on, let's take a shortcut through the streetcar barns; I don't want no cop seeing you and getting Solly in trouble for selling beer to minors."

Stan and his mother were living at the Parkside Residential Hotel on Hamlin Boulevard. "I'll be damned," Richie said. "My mother and I used to live here. After she came back from having her kid."

"No shit. You ought to feel right at home then."

In Stan's postage-stamp room, which had a double bed and a bureau, nothing else, Stan cleaned out a drawer for him. "You can wear some of my clothes too," he said, opening a tiny closet. "Case was right, those things you got on gotta go. And that haircut, Jesus! This is what you gotta have, man," he modeled his long, slicked-back ducktail style. "You gotta let your hair grow, you know?" Stan's older, experienced eyes studied Richie for a moment, then asked, "So what are you gonna be doing now?"

Richie locked eyes with his friend. "Whatever you're doing, Stan."

"Solid!' Stan smiled widely. "Hey, it'll be like old times! Like when we was kids!"

They were both barely sixteen.

That evening, in the Daylight-Savings-Time grayness between sunshine and darkness, Stan took Richie over to Maypole Avenue to Jo-Jo's Candy Store where they found Bobby Casey lounging outside with several other teenaged boys all dressed in the same fashion: lapelless Cugat jackets, pegged trousers, keychains running from belt to pocket, square-toed Hardy Brothers bulldog shoes.

"Well, well," Bobby Casey cracked at the sight of Richie, "look who got all dressed up."

Richie was wearing a set of Stan's clothes. He made an incongruous picture, with his plain-toed Lamont shoes and short, small-town haircut. But at least, he knew, he did not look as much a hick as in his own clothes. "Innerduce him around," Stan instructed Bobby. Holding out his hand to Richie, he said, "Gimme that sack of nickels." Richie handed him the nickels from the poolroom burglary and Stan took them into the candy store.

Bobby Casey introduced Richie to the others, saying pointedly, "He's a friend of Stan's," without including himself.

"Just move to the neighborhood?" one of them asked.

"I lived at the Parkside a few years ago," Richie told them. "I just got back from Charleytown."

"I was in Charleytown," another said. "Buchanan Cottage. Where was you?"

"Polk."

Stan returned and handed Richie some currency. "Jo-Jo handles any money changes we need," Stan said, bobbing his chin at a dwarfish man of about fifty who sat on a high stool next to his cash register. "He lets us use his storeroom to play cards, shoot craps, hide things, that kind of stuff. In return, we keep the neighborhood clean; we don't allow no punks to bother him, no street fights that could get his windows broke, shit like that. And if somebody runs up a bill and don't pay it, we go have a talk with them. We got everything nice and peaceful an' we keep it that way."

"Sounds good," Richie said. The thought of being part of this band of boys excited him and made him feel vital and strong.

The boys loitered around the little store, waiting for darkness. They smoked cigarettes, drank Cokes, sat around on upturned wooden boxes, lagged coins at a sidewalk line, talked about things that amused or annoyed them—there was not much in between—and in general passed time to finish out the daylight hours so that they could come alive as their nighttime selves. The nearer it came to darkness, the more impatient they became.

"Hey, Stan, we're gonna go looking for rubber machines," one of them finally said, indicating himself and another. "You wanna come?"

"I'm waiting for the broads," Stan said, shaking his head.

"How 'bout you, Richie? Wanna come?"

"I'll stick with Stan," Richie replied. "Thanks anyhow." How quickly acceptance came with some, he thought, how slowly—or not at all—with others. With Stan's friends, Richie already felt like he belonged. Except for Bobby Casey, of course. That, Richie was sure, was a lost cause. Bobby could not accept the fact that when Richie was around, Bobby was not Stan's best friend. Hanging out on the street that first night, Richie wondered how long it would be until he and Bobby fought. That they *would* fight some day went without saying.

Shortly after dark, the teenage girls of Maypole Avenue came out of their homes and congregated near where the boys were. They all wore bobby sox and loafers, pleated skirts and scooped-neck blouses, and makeup applied in hallways out of sight of their parents. They talked loudly about records and movies and other girls, and in whispers about the boys and the park at night and things sexual and exciting. On this night they talked about the new boy with the short hair and funny shoes.

"Hey, Richie, this is Marcella," Stan said, going over and slipping his arm around a pert Italian girl. "She's crazy about me." Marcella aimed a slap at him, but Stan easily ducked it. "C'mon, Richie, meet the girls," Stan urged, and Richie went over. After introducing Richie, Stan took Marcella's hand and started pulling her away, toward the corner. "I'm giving you one more chance to take a walk in the park with me without getting fresh," he warned, "but I don't want no monkey business. I'm saving myself for the girl I marry."

"You got nothing left to save, you jerk," Marcella said. She turned to another girl, olive-skinned with a Roman nose, and said. "Toni, come on, you and Richie come for a walk with us."

Toni looked at Richie. "Want to?" she asked.

"Sure."

They walked behind Stan and Marcella, who held hands and laughingly kidded around, until they had crossed the boulevard and entered the shadowy park, then Stan and Marcella stopped at a bench and Stan said, "You guys walk on around the lagoon and get acquainted. We'll wait for you here." In the dark, before he walked away, Richie felt Stan press a rubber into his hand. Glad it was dark, Richie knew he had blushed.

Following the asphalt path around the Garfield Park lagoon, the park lamplights casting shadows all around them, Richie asked, "Is Toni short for something?"

"Antoinette," she said.

"That's pretty."

"Did you just move here?" she asked.

"I lived here before, at the Parkside where Stan lives, but I just came back."

"Were you really in reform school?"

"Yeah."

"What'd you do?"

"Just ran away a lot."

"That's not so bad," Toni slipped her hand into his. "Do you mind? This part of the park is a little scary."

"I don't mind," Richie said holding her hand firmly. "I like it."

The park got very dark for a short distance, overhanging willows blocking out light from both behind and in front of them. "They call this part the kissing lane," Toni said. Stopping, she turned to him and Richie put his arms around her and they kissed, briefly, drily, without using their tongues. As soon as their lips parted, they decided to do it again, and this time it was longer, it was moist, and Toni flicked her tongue against his. Richie felt himself harden, and knew she could feel it too. "Come on," she whispered, "I know a good place."

Taking his hand again, Toni led him past the park boathouse, where people were renting boats to row around the lighted part of the lagoon. They turned into a dirt path that led up a thickly treed low hill. Behind a wild, untrimmed hedge, Toni found a broken-down cardboard box that unfolded to the size of a bed.

"You've been here before, I guess," Richie said.

"Sure," she replied matter-of-factly. "This isn't your first time, is it?"

"No, I didn't mean it like that."

"How did you mean it?" Her face looked like dark marble in the moonlight.

"I just meant you seem to know your way around."

"I do," Toni confirmed. "All the way around."

Presently they were kissing again and Richie was trying to collate in his mind the fact that he had only known this girl for a few minutes, and now she had made them a bed of cardboard and was pressing herself against him greedily. Pulling her lips back from his, she turned in his arms and said, "Undo me." Richie undid the buttons up the back of her blouse, and looked for her bra hook. "It's in front," she whispered, turning again. He found and unhooked it, and cupped her breasts in his hands. Her nipples were like bee stings: swollen, lumpy, hard. As he bent to kiss them, Richie felt her hands unbuttoning Stan's Cugat jacket, pulling up Stan's polo shirt, unzipping Stan's trousers.

"Have you got something?" she asked, bending to slip off her panties.

"Huh?"

"You know. To put on it."

"Oh. Yeah. I've got something," he said, searching frantically for the rubber.

Toni lay down on the cardboard and when Richie knelt to kiss and lick her between the legs, she stiffened and said, "No, I don't do dirty things like that. Tomorrow night you can do that with one of the other girls. Just fuck me."

While she made herself moist, Richie put the rubber on, thinking: *Tomorrow night*? *The other girls*? Lying on top of her, he felt her hand check to make sure the rubber was on, then she guided his erection into her and said, "Tell me you love me."

"I love you," Richie obliged, and began to thrust.

The little town of Lamont was fading farther into memory.

ichie stood in shadows at the edge of a movie theater parking lot, serving as lookout in one direction, Bobby Casey next to him watching the opposite way, as Stan used a wire coat hanger to fish inside a car window for the door handle. After several nervous minutes, they finally heard the unmistakable *click* that told them the door was open. Seconds later, Stan hurried over to them and slapped Bobby on the shoulder. "Okay, go get it." As Bobby hurried over to the car, Stan said to Richie, "Case always does the hot-wiring; his fingers is lots smaller than mine and he can handle them skinny little wires better."

"Where'd you guys learn to do this stuff?" Richie asked, whispering.

"Around," Stan shrugged. "From other guys. A guy who used to work for Solly at the poolroom learned us to drive. He was a wheel man on some stickups; he's in the joint now."

Presently they heard the car engine start and watched as Bobby Casey backed out of a parking place and drove over to get them. When the car stopped, Bobby slid over and let Stan get behind the wheel. "You get in the back," Bobby said to Richie, jerking a thumb over the seat.

As Stan guided the car down the alley and into street traffic, he said, "I usually do the driving 'cause I look older. We never been stopped once, right, Case?"

"Not once," Bobby Casey confirmed. "So far," he added, with a surly glance back at Richie.

Staying off the main boulevards, Stan drove side streets and uncrowded avenues to get to several of the many railroad yards that were sprinkled throughout the city. Each time he came to one, he would slowly cruise the street adjacent to the yard siding, as he and Bobby scrutinized any railroad car that might be parked there. When they found tankers, cattle cars, grain carriers, or empties, they drove on to another yard. "We never try nothing that don't look good," Stan emphasized. "We don't have to; there are dozens of these yards, from the Loop all the way out to the suburbs."

When they found a siding that suited them, one reasonably close to the street, with a good selection of closed boxcars, Stan parked and the three of them sat in the dark car and waited, watching. "This is where you gotta have patience," Stan told Richie.

When they had been sitting there an hour, they saw a beam of light bobbing up and down along the line of boxcars. "Yard cop," Stan said quietly. As they watched, the light moved from car to car, flashing up at each door as the watchman checked the seals. The eyes of the three boys followed the bobbing light for half an hour as it went the length of the siding and then circled back in the direction from which it came. They waited another fifteen minutes after it was gone, then Stan said, "Okay."

Out of the car, they scurried down the street embankment, up the cinder-covered siding rise, crossing the tracks to the fifth pair, where the boxcars were parked. Bobby went in one direction, Stan in the other, taking Richie with him. With a lipstick-sized penlight, cupping his hands around the beam, Stan started checking the bill of lading on each door. "This tells us what's in the car," he whispered. "It don't do us no good to bust open a load of refrigerators or furniture."

They had checked half a dozen cars when Bobby Casey came hurrying up to them in the darkness. "Typewriters," he whispered urgently.

"Good deal," said Stan. Nudging Richie to follow, he started back with Bobby.

At the door of the selected boxcar, Stan double-checked the bill of lading, then took a pair of wire cutters from his pocket. "This here is the seal," he said, showing Richie a shiny aluminum band running through the locking lever and a hasp on the side of the car. "We snip it in the back, like so," he demonstrated, "and put it on the track right under the door so's we can find it later."

Stan quietly, slowly raised the locking lever and slid the door open several feet. Inside, stacked almost to the door, were cartons marked ROYAL TYPE-

WRITER CO. Climbing into the car, Stan handed a carton out to Richie, another to Bobby, and set one down for himself. Seconds later, they were lumbering back to the car with them. When the cartons were on the back seat, the boys hurried back across the embankment and the tracks and put three more cartons on the ground.

"This is all we can fit in the car," Stan said. They closed the boxcar door and Stan retrieved the seal. As Richie watched, Stan looped it back in place, twisted it together where it was cut, and put the twisted part inside the hasp where it was not immediately noticeable. "This way," Stan whispered, "the stuff might not even be missed until it gets where it's going. Keeps the heat off these yards."

With the six cartons in the back seat, and again driving on side streets, Stan took them to a pawnshop on Roosevelt Road. Parking in the alley, he rang the night bell. A short man in a colorful Greek vest opened the door and Stan carried one of the cartons inside. Several minutes later, he hurried back out and said, "Okay, unload 'em." Richie and Bobby carried the others into a back room where the first carton, sitting on a table, was now open to reveal a shiny new black Royal office model. "Okay, wait in the car," Stan then ordered.

In five minutes, Stan was back and driving away to ditch the car somewhere. In half an hour, they were on a streetcar heading for the West Side. They sat in the rear of the car by themselves.

"We got two bits apiece for them," Stan reported. He slipped Richie and Bobby each five ten-dollar bills.

Richie stared incredulously at his share. It represented nearly three weeks work in Lamont, when he'd had a job; a small fortune when he hadn't.

Feeling very prosperous, he folded the currency and buttoned it into his shirt pocket as he had seen Stan and Bobby do.

In a doorway across the street from the Pulaski Road branch library, Richie shook a Lucky Strike out of his pack and lit it with a new flip-top lighter he had recently bought. He had been smoking three of the four weeks he had been back, starting for no better reason than the fact that everyone else who hung out at Jo-Jo's smoked. Richie fit in perfectly now. The Cugat jacket, pegged trousers, fancy polo shirt, and Bulldog shoes were part of a wardrobe he was building up with his new resources. His hair, longer now, was being trained into a glossy ducktail. In one trousers pocket was the unfamiliar weight of a switchblade. Stan had given it to him, saying, "Here, better carry this. Everybody else does." At night, in the room they shared, Stan helped Richie practice flicking the blade open.

□□ 414 □□

From the doorway, Richie watched the library. It was early, not yet nine, and he had sneaked out, leaving Stan asleep. For a frustrating month Richie had been randomly walking through Linda's neighborhood at odd times without once encountering her. Finally, the previous night, he had asked two younger boys on the street if they ever saw Linda around.

"Naw, she's never around," he was told. "She's got a summer job, ina library over by the Crawford Te'ater."

I'll be goddamned, Richie thought, mentally kicking himself. He had been past that library half a dozen times since he'd returned, almost going into it once. And all the time Linda had probably been right inside.

From the doorway he saw her get off a streetcar, carrying a purse and two thick books. She was taller, and he thought her hair was longer, but he could not really be sure. She had grown into one of those young girls, he saw, who had naturally perfect posture: ruler-straight spine, evenly squared shoulders, finely curved chin held without effort at a precisely ideal angle; the kind of girl who made other girls look like they were slouching.

Crossing the street to intercept her, Richie fell in beside her and said, "Can I carry your books?"

Giving him only a cursory glance, Linda said coolly, "No, thanks," and walked a little faster.

"Hey, wait a minute," Richie said, taking her arm. Linda immediately jerked away.

"I'll yell for a policeman," she threatened.

"Linda, it's me, Richie!" he declared urgently. "Don't you remember me?"

Eyes sweeping over him in astonishment, Linda's lips parted in mute confusion. Hugging her books and purse protectively to her bosom, continuing to look him up and down, she finally found enough composure to say, "Oh, my god. Richie? It's really you?"

"It's been a long time, huh?" he said, grinning.

"My god, yes. I can't believe this. Where have you *been?*"

"I was in reform school for a couple of years—"

"Looks like they let you out too soon," she interjected lightly.

"What do you mean?"

"You look like you just stepped out of a teenage hoodlum movie."

Turning red, Richie said defensively, "Hey, I paid good money for these threads. What's the matter with them?"

"They make you look like you're carrying a switchblade," she chided. Richie could feel himself turning redder. "I'm sorry, I didn't mean to embarrass you," Linda said then. "Golly, you sure got tall," she changed the subject.

"Yeah, you too," Richie replied quietly. He felt like a freak now, as if people on the street were staring at him.

"Miss White told me you were in trouble after some social worker came to see her," Linda said. "I asked her to try and find out where you were, but she wouldn't; she said she thought it would be best if I just forgot you. I tried to find out myself, over the telephone, but no one would give me any information; I guess they could tell by my voice that I was too young to be inquiring."

"The reason I didn't write to you," Richie started with his own explanation, "was because I was afraid they'd check my mail and maybe get you in trouble. They were on me to tell them who all knew where I was that last year." He decided then and there not to tell her about Lamont, because he had no excuse for not writing her from there.

"So," she said after an uncomfortable pause, "what are you doing with yourself these days? Besides dressing like a tough guy, I mean." Immediately biting her lip, she added, "There I go again. I'm *sorry*. It's just that I'm so surprised to see you like this. Anyway, are you working or what?"

"Yeah, I'm working for the Illinois Central railroad, typing up bills of lading."

"Typing! You know how to type?" Linda was clearly impressed.

"Yeah, I learned how in St. Charles. I worked as an office boy my whole time there."

"Why, Richie, that's wonderful! I do a little typing at the library, but it's the hunt-and-peck method, you know?" When he looked confused, she explained, "Hunt for the right key and peck it." Looking at her watch, she said, "Golly, I'm almost late. I've got to go."

"I'll walk you," Richie said,

"No, that's okay." Linda glanced nervously at the library. She's afraid somebody'll see her with me, Richie thought.

"I was going to ask you to a movie sometime," he said, "but I guess you wouldn't want to be seen in public with me."

"Oh, Richie, I said I was sorry. You just really caught me by surprise, that's all."

"Sure." He bobbed his chin at the library. "Better hurry, you don't want to be late."

Starting to walk away, Linda suddenly turned back. "Listen, let's meet somewhere and have a talk, you want to?"

Shrugging, Richie said, "Okay."

"You know where they have the band concerts in Garfield Park, on Wednesday nights? Let's meet there. One of the benches back by the drinking fountain. We'll be able to hear the music and can talk without disturbing anyone. That okay?"

"Yeah, sure."

"See you then," Linda said, and winked.

When she winked, Richie fell in love with her all over again. Standing on the corner, watching her walk away, her young body splendidly erect, carriage almost regal, he felt like a ragged peasant who had just been spoken to by a princess. Not certain whether he was looking forward to Wednesday night or not, he headed back toward Maypole Avenue, where everyone was the same.

Stan, Bobby, and Richie roamed the alleys behind Rush Street and other near North Side avenues known for the number of bars and lounges on their blocks.

"It's like in the old days when you and me used to prowl the loading docks," Stan said to Richie, "looking for deposit bottles to steal. 'Member?"

"Yeah." Richie nudged him with an elbow. " 'Member the cases of soup we stole?"

Stan laughed. "Yeah! Soup, for Christ's sake!" Stan in turn nudged Bobby. "You shoulda seen us, Case. We'd steal any fucking thing."

"Sure, sure," Bobby Casey replied drily. "The good old days."

Bobby Casey sounded peculiarly like John Garfield and Richie resented it. He resented most things Bobby Casey said and did, and it occurred to him that he now felt about Bobby the same way Bobby had always felt about him. Everybody, Richie knew, was waiting for him and Bobby to duke it out. Richie was doing nothing any longer to prevent it; Bobby still did not know Richie had fought in club fights, and Richie was almost eager to surprise him with his skills. On several occasions already he and Bobby had come close to throwing punches, but something had interfered each time. The one important thing that kept them at arm's length, they both knew, was the success the three of them had stealing together.

"There's one," Stan said now, indicating a rectangle of light that was the open back door of a bar. On warm summer evenings it was common for bartenders to open the back door for a few minutes to let some of the smoke and beer odor out. "You do the front," Stan said to Bobby, handing him a package of firecrackers. "We'll meet you at the car." As Bobby trotted away, Stan and Richie stood across the dark alley from the open door. Stan slipped a chisel from under his belt. "When we get inside, you stand between the men's room door and the front of the joint. If anybody heads back toward us, warn me. Keep your blade handy."

"Right," Richie said, wetting his suddenly dry lips, wiping his palms on his slacks. He would never understand why his lips got dry and his palms got wet.

About five minutes after Bobby left, Stan and Richie heard, all the way through the bar, the pack of firecrackers going off at the front door.

"Let's go," Stan said urgently.

Through the back door they went. Up the hall they could see the bartender and several patrons hurrying to the front exit. Stan ducked quickly into the men's room, leaving the door open. Richie planted himself in front of the door, eyes flicking from the bar to the men's room and back, one hand around the closed switchblade in his coat pocket. Even as his stomach churned acid in the tension of the moment, he could not help wondering whether he would actually use the knife or not, if anyone ran back to challenge them. He *thought* he would, to protect Stan, who after all was the best friend he'd ever had, but he was not totally, completely certain.

Standing tensely outside the men's room, Richie's darting glances inside caught Stan as he expertly used the chisel to pry the rubber machine off the wall. In less than a minute, Stan was back out and they were going through the rear door and hurrying down the alley; not even running because it was not necessary, they had not been seen. At the car they had stolen for the night, Bobby was waiting. As they drove away, Stan behind the wheel, Bobby used the chisel to pry off the back of the machine. He passed handfuls of quarters to Richie in the back seat, who put them in a shoebox, and handfuls of Trojan prophylactics, which he put in a second shoebox.

"Just like in the old days with the gumball machines," Stan said with a happy smile as he drove, "on'y now we get quarters instead of pennies. And"—he glanced in the rearview mirror at Richie—"we get free rubbers for ourselves and the rest we sell to Jo-Jo."

"We sure owe a debt of gratitude to Max," Richie said seriously.

"Max? Max who?" Bobby asked, looking over his shoulder.

"Max Prophylactic," Richie said. "He's the guy who invented rubbers."

"No shit?" said Bobby, amazed. "Is that why they're called prophylactics? 'Cause they was named after . . . ?" He saw Stan unable to suppress his laughter then, saw Richie grinning at Stan in the rearview mirror, and knew he had been tricked. "You're asking for it, asshole!" he said angrily to Richie. "Just keep it up and you're gonna get it!"

"Sure, sure," Richie said, in a *real* John Garfield voice.

He wondered how it was going to feel to smash his fist into Bobby Casey's obnoxious face.

□

Dressing to meet Linda at the band concert, Richie left his Cugat jacket at home and wore his sport shirt with the collar unbuttoned, the way the squares wore them. He still had to wear his pegs and his Bulldogs, because he had thrown away the Lamont corduroys and shoes, but he modified the look by leaving his shirt out to cover the high waistband, and not draping his keychain into his pocket. There was nothing he could do about his hair, short of getting it cut, which he would not do.

Linda was waiting for him when he got there, a purse and two books on her lap. She was wearing one of the "new look" long skirts and flat ballet shoes, and had on a little beret. "Ili," she said, getting up as he approached. "Want to get some ice cream before the music starts?"

"Hi. Sure."

"The ice cream man just went that way. If we go around, we can meet him."

As they walked, Richie took the two books out of her hands and looked at them. "*Gentleman's Agreement*. Good book. *The Snake Pit*. That's good too."

"You've read them?" Linda asked, surprised.

"Sure. When they first came out."

"I'm so glad you're still reading," she said. Putting her arm through his, she leaned her head briefly on his shoulder, a kind of in-motion half hug.

When they found the ice cream vendor, Richie bought them both Creamsicles, fishing one bill out of his pocket to pay for them so he would not have to take out his entire roll. He seldom carried less than a hundred dollars now, and he knew Linda would never believe he had earned that much honestly. With their ice cream, they walked back toward the band shell.

"So what school do you go to now?" Richie asked.

"Austin High. I got a permit to go there because my grades were so good. I'm not really in that district."

"I hear it's a nice school."

"Oh, it is! It's in a real great neighborhood and the nicest kids go there."

"Now that you're in high school, does your old man still watch out the window for you to come home?" he asked lightly.

Linda immediately looked away; there was still enough light for Richie to see that she was blushing.

"There's just my mom and me now. She divorced my dad."

"Oh."

They got back to one of the park benches farthest from the bandshell just as the lights came on and the music began. It was a pop concert and the first selection was "I'm Looking Over a Four-Leaf Clover."

Sitting shoulder to shoulder with him, Linda said, "I have a confession to make. I should have told you the other day, but you surprised me so, just popping up like that. Anyway, I have to tell you now—I have a steady boyfriend."

"Oh." Richie could not think of anything else to say.

"His name is Glenn and we've been going steady for over a year. We met in this church group that my mom and I started going to after she divorced my dad. Glenn's a real nice boy, very clean-cut and honest; my mom really likes him."

"That's nice," Richie said, managing to keep the rancor out of his voice. Forcing a smile, he said, "I guess he probably dresses more to your taste, huh?"

"Oh, now, Richie, don't be mad about that," she pleaded. "I said I was sorry. Anyway, that doesn't have anything to do with it. At least, it doesn't have a *lot* to do with it—"

"Look, if you've got a steady, why'd you even offer to meet me tonight? Why'd you give me that little hug a while ago? What the hell are we doing sitting in the park in the dark?"

"I want us to be friends, Richie, that's why. I used to help you, remember, when you were all alone? You told me I helped you stop stealing once. I can help you again if you'll let me."

"Help me how?" he asked. "I don't need any help—"

"Oh, Richie, you must. The kind of clothes you wear, the way you comb your hair, you've got to be hanging out with a gang of some kind. You couldn't have very nice friends. Nice boys just don't go around looking like that."

"Linda, you don't know my friends," he said impatiently, "you don't know anything about them, so what the hell are you talking about them for?"

"You don't have to use vulgar language," she chastised. "You never used to say 'hell' when I knew you before." Linda put a hand on his arm. "If you'll just listen to me, Richie, you'll see that what I'm trying to tell you is for your own good. I think what you should do is come with me to one of our church group youth meetings. You can meet some nice people, maybe join in some of the activities—"

"No!" he said, shaking her hand off. "I don't want to go to your church group." She had made him feel like a freak again. "Look, I'm not interested in meeting your friends any more than you're interested in meeting mine. Maybe I shouldn't even have tried to see you, I don't know. But we used to like each other so much, we used to have so much fun togehter, and we never did anything with your friends or my friends; there was just you and me—"

"We were kids then, Richie," she insisted. "We're almost grown now. If we're going to be friends—"

"What do you mean, *if*? Aren't we friends now?"

"Well, sure, I guess we are, only—"

"Only it can't be like it used to be, is that it? Can't be just the two of us liking each other, enjoying being together, talking, having fun. You've made up a few new rules for us, haven't you?"

"You can really be nasty when you want to, can't you?" Linda was looking at him with the same severe expression Mrs. Hubbard always had. Like he was scum. "Maybe this wasn't a good idea," she said coldly. "Maybe you and I have grown too far apart to even be friends."

"Maybe you're right," he said in quick, clipped words. Linda's expression became knowing.

"Still playing John Garfield?"

"Not anymore," he said. Inside his blood was boiling. "I'm not *playing* anything anymore."

Rising, he handed her the two books. "So long, Linda."

Walking away, leaving the park, he headed once again for Maypole Avenue.

Where he belonged.

*R*ichie, Stan, and Bobby were slouched down in seats at the Savoy Theater far out on West Madison Street, watching the last showing of *Key Largo*, with Bogart and Robinson. The picture was almost over when Richie noticed an usher walk down the side aisle nearest them, step into a little alcove near the screen, and check the emergency exit to make sure it was locked. Nudging Stan, Richie bobbed his chin at the usher, and both boys then watched him as he crossed the front of the first row and did the same with the door in the other side aisle.

Five minutes later, the picture ended, the house lights went up, and the sparse late-night audience moved out of their seats and up the aisles.

"Wait until we're the last ones out, then cover the two aisle doors for me," Richie whispered urgently to Stan and Bobby. They each took an aisle and sauntered along behind everyone else. When everyone was out except them, Richie dashed to the nearest exit alcove, pushed down the opening bar, and covered the locking slot with a half-empty pack of cigarettes he had. The door still closed all the way, but the bolt did not go into its slot, leaving it unlocked.

Hurrying up the aisle, Richie caught up with Bobby and they walked on out, joined by Stan in the lobby.

"It's open," Richie said when they were walking down Madison Street.

"Think it might be wired?" Stan asked. Richie shrugged.

"No telling."

"If it's a silent alarm, the heat could be on us before we knew it."

"What could we get out of the place?" Bobby Casey wanted to know.

"There's probably twenty bucks change for the ticket booth and the candy counter, to start tomorrow with," Richie appraised. "Could be money in the manager's office from tonight; might be in a safe, might not. Two pay phones in the lobby we could rip open, and probably a dime Kotex machine in the ladies' room. Toni told me they usually have one in every theater. Must be cartons of candy under the candy counter, that we could sell to Jo-Jo. We might make a bill, a bill-and-a-quarter."

They found an all-night coffee shop and had something to eat while they evaluated the plan further. It was something new and therefore to be approached with caution and consideration, but it was also exciting and energizing, already igniting in them a spark of the thrilling fear they knew would be experienced if they actually did it. To Richie, it was a feeling, that fear, unlike any other in the world, second only to ejaculation in its utter effect on every nerve-end in his body. Stealing, especially at night, in darkness, stealthily, gave one, like sex, a totally unique sensation. From the expressions Richie had seen on the faces of Stan and Bobby, he knew they felt it also. None of them ever discussed it. They *did* discuss how sex had been with this girl or that, what kind of blow job she gave, how she tasted when they ate her, but how they felt in the throes of robbery was too intimate, too personal.

After an hour, they decided to hit the Savoy. Returning to their neighborhood, they retrieved several chisels and screwdrivers, wrapped in a towel under the coal chute in Bobby Casey's basement. From a dark residential block a mile from the theater, they unlocked a parked car with a coat hanger, hot-wired it, and drove along side streets to park around the corner from the Savoy. It was nearly three A.M. when they slipped down the alley and found the exit door Richie had fixed.

It took them a total of twenty minutes inside the dark theater. While Bobby pried the Kotex machine off the wall, Stan forced open all the drawers in the manager's desk, and Richie jimmied the lock on the storage compartment under the candy counter and stacked all the unopened cartons of candy and chewing gum next to the exit door. Ten minutes after they were inside, they knew there was no alarm system or there would already have been a response. Bobby broke open the Kotex machine right in the ladies' room and left it there, empty of dimes, and Stan emptied the contents of two change boxes, and with his switchblade slit open a locked bank bag containing the night's receipts. The last thing they did, because they were certain it relayed some kind of signal, was pry both pay phones off the wall and empty their coin boxes. Then, each with an armload of candy and gum cartons, they hurried back down the alley to the car.

The robbery netted them sixty-eight dollars from the bank bag, twenty each from the change boxes, eight from the two phones, three from the sanitary napkin machine, and thirty dollars from the candy and gum they sold to Jo-Jo: a total of one hundred forty-nine dollars, or nearly fifty dollars each.

"Not bad," said Stan Klein the next day. "I just read in the paper the other day that the average working stiff only makes forty-nine dollars and seventy-five cents in a whole week. We made that much in one night. I'd say we're doing pretty fucking good."

"We sure as hell are," Bobby agreed. "This is a hard fucking city; lots of people ain't making it at all."

Richie stared at Bobby for a moment. The boy's words triggered a memory; from somewhere in Richie's mind a thought surfaced: *It's a hard city, and it can break you.*

Shaking his head, Richie tried not to pay any attention to it.

Richie, Stan, and their friends lived on the underbelly of life. Most days they slept until noon, after staying up until three or four in the morning. Their daylight hours started with midday breakfast at some coffee shop in the area of Solly's Pool Hall, and from there they went at once to the rear pool table, which was seldom in use. For half the afternoon they shot pool, drank beer, smoked cigarettes, and kept Solly's jukebox fed with a continuous supply of quarters. The music was cut off only when some of the Italian or Jewish mobsters came in to shoot some high-stakes games on one of the front tables, at which time Solly walked back and unplugged the Wurlitzer and no one said anything to him about it, even if it was in the middle of Peggy Lee singing "Mañana," which was their favorite and which, on an average day, Richie and Stan played twenty times or more. When the mobsters shot pool, the boys all sat around and watched them in awe: the Italians in their pork-pie hats and silk sport shirts buttoned at the neck; the Jews in their flowered neckties with diamond tie tacks, and perfectly creased snap-brims. They were quiet men who spoke with their eyes or with gestures, or by not speaking at all. Sometimes when a game ended, fifties and hundreds changed hands.

When the smoke and beer of Solly's became oppressive, they left and sought other amusement. Sometimes they rode a streetcar downtown to one of the big first-run houses to see a new movie just out; sometimes they bowled a few lines—in the very bowling alley where Richie had once worked and slept; sometimes they used Jo-Jo's back room to play cards or shoot dice;

sometimes they simply stretched out on the grass in Garfield Park and talked about things that intrigued them.

"You seen a picture of that new swim suit they call the 'bikini'? Jesus Christ, a broad is practically naked in that thing!"

"I heard on the radio that this guy Eben whatever-his-name is, that wrote "Nature Boy", lives in a vacant lot and don't eat nothing but nuts and berries."

"They're finally giving Jake LaMotta a shot at the middleweight title. He's gonna fight that French guy Cerdan. That jack-off will be lucky he don't get killed by LaMotta."

"What is it with these fucking German cars they're bringing over here, this Volkswagen thing? We just barely got through kicking those cocksuckers in the ass during the war, now we're gonna let 'em sell us *cars?*"

"Wonder what they're gonna do about that spade Jackie Robinson playing ball for the Dodgers? Those fucking people in Brooklyn must have shit for brains."

And so it went until at last the summer sun began to go down and the boys returned to their rooms and took showers and, some of them, shaved, and carefully recombed their ducktails until they were perfect: shiny, glossy, every hair in place. They changed into pressed pegged trousers, their fanciest shirts, snappiest Cugats, highly polished Bulldogs, and went back out to loiter again, first around the drugstore where they ate supper, then around Jo-Jo's to wait for the girls.

Richie's and Stan's favorites were Marcella and Toni, and they traded them back and forth like chattel, deciding between themselves, without consulting the girls, who would go with whom for the evening. Marcella and Toni did not seem to mind; Richie and Stan were the best looking of the gang, and the girls were happy to be with either. Bobby Casey got whoever he could, which a lot of the time was no one because of his acne. The couples had sex when and where they wanted to: on the cardboard behind the hedge in the park, in the back seat of some car they hot-wired and took joyriding; in Stan's apartment when his mother went away for the weekend; sometimes just standing up in the hallway of one of the buildings where the girls lived. When they did it standing up, Richie and Stan were able to get away with not using a rubber, because Stan had convinced both Marcella and Toni that a girl could not get pregnant if she did it standing up.

A lot of the time when Richie was with one of the gang girls, he would find himself thinking about Linda. As earnestly as he tried not to, the thoughts simply came to mind, and he became aware that they were there, that he *was* thinking about her, much as thoughts of his father had surfaced when he was younger. Particularly in movie theaters, when he was in a back row petting heavily with Toni or one of the others, he would find himself thinking that he had his hand inside *Linda's* blouse, up *Linda's* skirt, feeling *Linda's* breast or thigh. It bothered him, frequently making him moody or quiet, causing the girl he was with to need reassurance several times that she had done nothing wrong. Occasionally, before his disposition returned to normal, the vexation erupted into anger. Once, in the Paradise Theater, when Richie, Stan, and Bobby Casey had girls in the back row, an usher shone his flashlight on Richie and told him if he wanted to undress the girl, to take her to a hotel. Richie was out of his seat and after him in an instant as the usher walked back into the lobby. Grabbing him by the shoulder, Richie jerked the bigger, older usher around.

"You trying to be a fucking wiseguy?" he challenged.

"Don't start any trouble," the usher warned, pointing his flashlight at Richie.

"You're the one starting trouble, jack-off!" Richie told him loudly. "We weren't bothering anybody in there!" Stan and Bobby edged out the door to back him up as another usher and the manager started toward them. The girls, as they had been told to do, came out a different door and were already walking toward the street exit.

"You bought a ticket to watch a movie in here, not get laid," the usher said.

Richie knocked the flashlight out of his hand, feinted a left, and drove his right fist into the usher's face. The usher stumbled back and Richie stepped in quickly with a left and a right to the stomach. As the usher doubled over, Richie winged a right cross to the side of his face, then converted his next punch to an uppercut that straightened him back up. Seeing a splotch of blood in the middle of his face, Richie used it as a target and drilled two right crosses directly to it. The usher dropped to a heap on the floor, his gold Balaban-and-Katz coat splattered with his own blood.

"I'm calling the police about this!" the tuxedoed manager threatened.

"You do, you motherfucker," Richie snapped, "when you come to work tomorrow you'll find a pile of ashes where this fucking theater used to be!"

Still seething at the arrogant audacity of the usher, he stalked away, Stan and Bobby backing up after him.

They never went back to the Paradise that summer.

And Bobby Casey, after what he had witnessed, became considerably softer in his attitude toward Richie.

One thing that Richie did not do that summer was resume looking for his father. It was not a conscious omission, more like a headache that one suddenly realizes has passed. With everything else that was going on in his life, the longtime, frustrating search simply had not surfaced. Richie might not have even thought about it if Stan had not mentioned it one day.

"You ever find out what happened to your old man?" Stan asked.

"No, never did," Richie replied. They were sitting on the Garfield Park lagoon pier, idly tossing pea-sized pebbles into the water and watching the ripples.

"Man, that sure used to piss you, not knowing where he was. Remember?"

"Yeah." Richie grunted softly. "Twelve years old, looking for one guy in a city the size of Chicago. Real bright."

"I used to wonder which one of us was the worse off," Stan confided. "You, not knowing where your old man was, or me, knowing he was just a few hundred miles away but only getting in touch with me on my birthday and Christmas."

Richie looked at his friend, surprised. He had never known Stan was bothered by that. "Did you ever decide?" he asked. "Which one of us was worse off?"

"Neither," Stan declared. "We were both better off. If a kid's old man don't care enough about him to stick with him, then he's no fucking good as far as the kid's concerned anyway. He may be a great guy as far as other people are concerned, but he'll never be nothing but a drag to the kid. You're smart not to be looking for your old man any more. Whatever happened to him happened years ago; it don't have nothing to do with today. Who the fuck cares about yesterday, man; it's over, right?"

"Yeah, right."

At that moment, Richie believed it. Stan was right. Richie realized that he no longer needed to know what had happened to his father, any more than he any longer needed his father. What was past, was past. What had happened, happened. Fuck it.

The one person from the past that Richie did go look for that summer was, on an impulse one night, Vernie. He told Stan he was going to see an old friend of his mother whom he had promised to visit when he got out of Charleytown. There was nothing planned for that night anyway; they were laying low after burglarizing five movie houses in four nights.

When Richie got to Lake Street, he made his way along the once-feared avenue with one hand in his Cugat jacket pocket, thumb on the release button of his switchblade. Because it was summer, there was evening activity on the street: people sitting in doorways talking, smoking, drinking beer, the men in their undershirts, women in loose cotton dresses obviously with nothing on underneath; other men in zoot suits, loitering in twos and threes, passing around a pint bottle with a brown bag wrapped around it; an occasional younger woman with one breast out, nursing a baby; smaller kids running and playing under the el tracks; older teenagers jiving and shucking, trying to be bad. The eyes of all of them followed Richie as he ambled along, purposely with a swagger, never keeping his own eyes on anyone's face long enough for it to be considered a challenge, his outward attitude one of disinterest and confidence, the one hand in the pocket clearly a caution.

He found Vernie near the corner of Washtenaw, standing in a group of other girls, just as she had been the last time he saw her. The girls looked him up and down as he approached, curious because white johns came to Lake Street only in cars, never on foot. Vernie glanced at him, also apparently without recognizing him, so Richie had to walk all the way up to them.

"Hey, Vernie," he said, and then her eyes got wide and her full, pink-colored lips parted in surprise.

"God*damn!*" she exclaimed. "Hey, baby, you looking *good!*"

"Yeah, you too," Richie said with a grin as Vernie gave him a full body hug and kissed him on the cheek.

"What you doing down here?" she asked. "You carrying for yo' mamma again?"

"No," Richie replied, blushing. "I just came down to see you."

Taking his arm, Vernie drew him away, saying, "Le's go over where we can have some privacy. You don't want to be seen wif' girls like these; you wouldn't *believe* the things they do for money!"

Amid a chorus of jeering and scoffing, Vernie led Richie to a yellow Cadillac parked at the curb and eased her tightly bound buttocks down on the front fender. "Oooh-eee, you sure do look sharp, Richie," she praised. "And you so tall!" Her large brown eyes became knowing as she said, "You can take that hand out your pocket, honey; you with Vernie again. Now— I want you to tell me all about where you been and what you been doing wif' yo'self."

Richie reviewed the last few years for her, beginning with his mother's death, which seemed to make Vernie sad, to his time in Charleytown, which made her mad, to the school year he had just spent in Lamont, which impressed her. "Richie, that is so *fine!* You always been good in school," she said, winking. "I knows 'cause I be the one that signed mos' of your report cards, 'member?"

"I sure do remember," he said. "I remember *every*thing you did for me. That's another reason I came to see you. I wanted to give you this—" He slipped her a folded hundred-dollar bill, one of several he now had saved in a money clip in his buttoned shirt pocket.

"Where you get this kind of money, boy?" she asked critically.

"I saved it. I been working all summer."

"Doing what?"

"I'm an usher at the Paradise Theater."

"And you want to *give* me this? A *hundred* dollars?"

"Yeah." He glanced down. "For always being so nice to me."

Vernie looked as if she might cry. "You are the sweetest white boy," she said, putting a palm on his cheek. Suddenly her eyes danced with mischief. Sliding off the fender, she hooked her arm in his and said, "Come on. I got a little surprise for you."

As they walked past the other girls, there were several gibes made, cracks about Vernie robbing some po' white mamma's cradle, and giving up the street to become a wet nurse.

"You bitches jus' jealous," Vernie retorted. "This here happens to be my fiancé. We gon' get married and I be living out in the white suburbs while you 'hoes still down here in the ghetto. " 'Bye, y'all."

Vernie took Richie half a block down the street and up a flight of dark stairs to a hallway dimly lighted with yellow bulbs. Knocking on an unmarked door, she called softly, "Ella Mae? You busy?"

"Come in," a quiet voice answered. To Richie, Vernie said, "Wait here a minute."

Vernie opened the door just wide enough to slip inside. As Richie waited in eerie lighting, he put his hand back on the switchblade. A door down the hall opened and a black woman with a hairnet on her head looked out at him for a moment, then went back inside. Suddenly feeling like he had to go to the bathroom, Richie began shifting from foot to foot. He was getting ready to knock on the door when Vernie came out.

"I gots to get back downstairs now," she said. Lifting her face, she kissed Richie full on the lips. "This is a little present for you," she told him, opening the door and pushing him inside.

The door closed behind him and Richie stood in a sparse little bedroom lighted by a single small lamp in one corner. Sitting on the side of the bed, nude, was a brown girl of perhaps fourteen, placidly painting her fingernails. She had a compact young body with tight, coned breasts and rigid, very light nipples.

"Hi, Richie," she said, smiling up at him. "Go ahead and get undressed. I'll be finished in a minute."

An erection starting, Richie locked the door and began taking off his clothes.

It was shortly after his visit to see Vernie that Richie's depression set in. It had nothing to do with his experience with Ella Mae; that had been a memorable encounter leaving him pleasantly drained for two days. Rather it was, several days later, an annoying thought, which would not go away, of Vernie selling herself night after night on the street corner like she did. It was nothing new to him; he had known for a long time what she was doing. But for some reason it had never bothered him before. Incongruously, he kept remembering her beautiful cursive handwriting, and his irrational, rambling young mind persisted in telling him that someone with that kind of penmanship should not have to be a whore.

Then Stan got maudlin on him that same week, talking about his father in Ohio, his father's new family, new life: respectable, pretty wife, two little girls, ranch-style home with a fenced backyard. Stan had lived there for a year when his father was trying to straighten him out. But it had not worked. Like Richie in Lamont, Stan did not fit in the little Ohio town, and eventually he ran away back to Chicago. But he had liked it in Ohio; despite his tough, cynical exterior, he would have liked to fit.

"It was quite a place," he reminisced to Richie. "American Legion baseball games, Fourth of July parade and fireworks, town picnics, flags out on holidays. I wouldn't have minded staying. But people would take one look at me and decide what I was. I never got invited nowhere the other kids did. Some parents even told their kids not to have nothing to do with me. So finally I just said fuck it and took off back here."

It was Stan's disclosure about Ohio that compounded Richie's distress about Vernie. The way he looked at it, Stan should have been welcomed in Ohio by the same righteous set of rules that should have kept Vernie off the street corner. The goddamned world, he brooded, was uneven, unjust, and unfair. As his despair over it deepened, something happened that he did not expect: he became angry—angry as he had been in Lamont at the inequities there. Now he felt the same bitter resentment in Chicago, where he never expected it. Chicago, which had now made him prosperous, in a way; independent, in a way; free, in a way. Chicago, which had paid him back for all the hard times. Given him a place to be again.

But, he eventually realized, at a *very* high price.

He finally became aware that the city *was* breaking him. He was not reading anymore, not feeding his mind. With Stan and the other guys, he survived on instinct, like an animal; with Toni and the girls, he *performed* the same way. Intelligence played less of a part in his life every day. Just as he had once dreaded he would end up like Joey Lupo, endlessly playing checkers in Charleytown night after interminable night, so now he began to fear that he would end up like Vernie or Stan: nothing to sell but oneself, nothing to act on but raw nerve.

Richie's original plan had been to come to Chicago just for the summer. After falling back in with Stan again, he had changed his mind, not caring if he ever saw Lamont again. Now, when it should have been easier for him to make the decision to stay, when life was softer for him than it had ever been, he found that he could not do it. He *wanted* to go back. He was afraid not to. The only thing he hated about it was walking out on Stan . . . again.

One day when they were lounging on a park bench, with no one else around, Richie finally told Stan the truth about being out of Charleytown for nearly a year, and living in Lamont. When he was finished, Stan looked at him astutely and said, "So why are you telling me now?" Richie shrugged and did not answer. "You're going back, right?" Stan asked.

Richie looked away. "I been thinking about it."

Stan grunted quietly. "Bobby said you wouldn't stick for long."

"Fuck him," Richie said irritably. "He don't know shit."

"Yeah, well he was right about this, wasn't he?" Stan retorted, an edge creeping into his own voice. "And I'll tell you something else, Richie. Case might not have your looks or your style or your smarts, but there's one thing he's got that you never had—when I need him, he's *there!* Seems like every time I cut you into a deal, you find something more important to do and walk out. It's getting old, man."

"Stan, it's not you I'm walking out on," Richie tried to explain. "It's this fucking life. I don't want to go on stealing all my life. There's got to be something better—"

"For you, maybe!" Stan snapped. "But not for me! Not for Bobby!" He was suddenly angry. "Stealing's all there is for us, unless we want to be pick-and-shovel slaves all our fucking lives! And we don't! We don't!" As quickly as he had become angry, he seemed to calm, his voice quieted. "We don't," he said one last time, not as loudly but just as firmly.

They sat in awkward silence on the green wooden bench as two young mothers walked past pushing their toddlers in strollers. The late August day was getting hot and there were a lot of flies in the air. Stan brushed one away from his face.

"Fucking flies, I hate 'em," he said. "The goddamn scientists can make a camera that'll develop a picture in one goddamn minute, but they can't do anything about the goddamn flies." After a moment, he reached over and slapped Richie on the muscle. "Go ahead, find a better life for yourself. Shit, I hope you make it. Just, if you ever come back, make sure it's to stay next time." Shaking his head woefully, he added, to himself, "Case'll be saying 'I told you so' for five fucking years." Then to Richie, with another slap on the arm, "Go on, beat it."

"Thanks, Stan." Richie stood and looked around the familiar park. "Well, so long."

"Look after yourself."

"You too."

Leaving the park to go get his things from Stan's room, Richie could not help feeling that he had let somebody down yet again.

*G*etting off the train, Richie walked up the hill and turned down Moreridge Street. He was wearing jeans and a tee-shirt, and his hair was trimmed short again. In his zipper bag was a second set of clothes and several hundred dollars. All of his sharp Chicago clothes he had left for Stan.

As he walked down the gravel street, he saw his grandmother sitting in her rocker on the sturdy end of the front porch, shelling peas into a pan. When he reached the porch, she said by way of greeting, "Never expected to see you again." She looked apprehensive for a moment. "Are you in trouble?"

"No, Miss Ethel, I'm okay," Richie said. He had not set his bag down. "Uh, can I stay here while I finish high school?"

"Don't see why not," Mrs. Clark said. "Long as we have the same arrangement as before. And if you can manage to keep a job."

"I've got money saved that'll take me through part of the year if I can't," he told her. "I had a good job all summer working for a vending machine company." Studying his grandmother, Richie thought she looked a lot older than he remembered. And she looked very tired. "How was your summer?" he asked.

"Long," she replied. "Every year that I work at the canning factory, it seems that the days get longer, the weather gets hotter, and my back hurts worse. But I have to do it if I want to keep the taxes on the house from going delinquent. That happens, there's a penalty." She nodded her head toward the screen door. "There's iced tea if you're thirsty."

Richie went into the house and put his things away and fixed himself a glass of iced tea. Returning to the porch, he handed his grandmother two hundred dollars. "To help with the taxes," he said. Mrs. Clark frowned.

"You don't have to do that; it's not part of our arrangement."

"Yeah, I know." he said. "This is good iced tea," he added, taking a swallow. He quickly went back inside in case his grandmother decided to thank him. *That* he could not have handled.

In the little room that was his, he thought about what he had left behind in Chicago: friends, girls, quick money, good times, being part of something. And he thought about what he had taken in exchange: no friends, probably no girl any longer—if he knew Midge; maybe no income at all, and certainly not being accepted as part of anything. But he was nevertheless glad to be back, to be sitting in the little room where he had been born, to know that it was his as long as he wanted it. The rigid, severe little town of Lamont might not be his home, but this little house *was*.

It felt good to be home.

When Mrs. Reinhart saw him, she smiled delightedly and patted him on the arm. "I wasn't sure you'd come back for another year," she told him.

"I wasn't either," he admitted.

"Well, I'm glad you're here. I've got the perfect job for you. Sam Levy's Department Store needs a part-time stockboy. They want someone neat and presentable, as well as reliable. I'll fill out a form and send you right up to see them. Oh, and I think you should go back on the *Hi-Life* staff too, if you can fit it in." She got a teasing twinkle in her eyes. "I presume you'll be paying for your own lunch again this year."

"Yes, ma'am." Richie could not help smiling.

After he had signed up for all his classes, Richie walked back uptown and took the Distributive Education form to Sam Levy's. He was directed to Sam Levy, the owner, a cocky, self-assured little man who at once reminded Richie of James Cagney. He wore a bright green shirt and a dark green tie. The cuffs of the shirt were turned up and buttoned backwards because the sleeves were too long for his arms.

"Two to six on weekdays," Mr. Levy told him, "and nine to nine on Saturdays. Sixteen dollars a week and twenty percent discount on purchases."

That was it; he got the job. As a "department store," Levy's was nothing like Richie was used to—Marshall Field's and the Boston Store in Chicago— but it was nevertheless as wondrous a place to him as had been the soda fountain at Chalk's Drug Store. Herbie showed him the shoe and soft goods stockrooms, and taught him how the stocked merchandise was arranged. He instructed him in how to check the displayed merchandise every day to see what needed restocking, how to price tag the various items, how to clean the display counters and shelves. One half of the store was set aside for menswear, the other half for ladies' and children's goods. Both shoe departments were in the rear, as was the wrapping counter and the cash register counter. Just as Chalk's had been the nicest drugstore in Lamont, Levy's was the nicest, most modern, and best-stocked department store. Richie could not believe his good fortune in getting a job there. He just hoped to god nothing went wrong on this job as it had on the last one.

As Richie was leaving Levy's after getting the job, Midge drove up in her pickup and blew the horn at him. Richie went over to her. "I see you came back after all," she said without preliminaries. "Did you have a good time in *Chicago?*" She elaborately emphasized the city's name.

"I was too busy working to have a good time," he lied, then wondered why he had.

"I guess you've heard that I have a new boyfriend?"

"I haven't heard anything."

"Well, for your information, I am now going steady with Leroy Sadler. He's a senior this year, like you. His daddy owns the place two farms down from ours. We got to talking at the cotton gin one day and hit it off right from the very start. After he graduates, instead of going to college, Leroy's going to help his daddy run the farm. So he'll always be around." Pausing a beat, Midge then said, "I suppose you're going to be upset because I didn't wait for you. But you know I told you before you left that I simply was not going to *waste* my whole summer just sitting around, while you were up north doing Lord knows what with those Yankee girls."

"I'm not upset, Midge," he told her simply. "I didn't expect you to waste your summer."

"Well, I felt I had to tell you about Leroy myself," she said, "so there wouldn't be any misunderstanding. I have to go now. Leroy's daddy has a house down on Reelfoot Lake and Leroy and me meet down there of an evening." She lowered her voice. "We go swimming in the buff."

"Sounds like fun," Richie said. He could not help envying Leroy a little. As shallow as Midge was in other respects, when it came to sex she was sensational. He imagined Leroy went around with a smug look on his face most of the time.

"All right then, no hard feelings, okay?"

"Okay," Richie agreed.

Midge drove off, leaving Richie standing in the street. Before he could get back to the sidewalk, a car came by, missing him by inches. It stopped and backed up. Billy Pastor smiled at him from behind the wheel. There were three other boys in the car with him.

"You better not be standing around in the street like a fool, Yankee," he said. "Somebody's liable to run over you."

"Thanks for the advice," Richie said, trying to control his voice. Billy's car had scared the hell out of him.

"You going to school down here again?" Billy asked.

"That's right."

Billy grinned at his friends. "Good. I was scared it was going to be a boring year."

"What the hell have you got against me anyway?" Richie asked sharply. "Don't tell me you're still sore about the soda jerk job?"

"I'm not *sore* about nothing," Billy said, his grin disappearing. "I just don't like Yankees."

"That's stupid," Richie snapped. Billy put his car in neutral and got out. "You calling me stupid?"

Richie saw Mr. Levy standing in front of the store. A fight on the town square could not possibly escape attention. "I didn't call you anything," Richie backed down.

"If you called me stupid, I'll whip your ass right here, Yankee."

"I didn't call you anything," Richie repeated. "I just meant it was stupid to stay mad about something like that soda jerk job. But since you're not mad about it, you can't be stupid."

Grunting derisively, Billy got back into the car. "Chickenshit," he said as he drove off.

Humiliation searing his whole being, Richie started home. He had been excited about telling his grandmother about his new job. Now, swallowing his shame, he was too deflated to care.

School, as usual, went well for Richie. He was still not socially acceptable to the vast majority of his peers, still found himself referred to as "Yankee" instead of by his name, and was still subject to occasional, though less frequent, "accidental" bumps, shoves, and trippings. Now that Midge was treating him with studied indifference, he had no one at school to talk to, and rarely spoke except to a teacher or when called on in class. The one exception was the other members of the *Hi-Life* staff. Because they all worked on the same project, and were in and out of the *Hi-Life* room at odd times, Richie was at least included in their conversations about the school paper. He was not embraced as one of them, but it was about as close as Richie expected to get.

His work on the paper became his most rewarding activity at school.

Where once his greatest challenge, and thus his greatest enjoyment, had been the crafting of a book report, now he was caught up in the work of understanding a factual happening and committing it to the written word. The entire process fascinated him: to see something with his eyes, take that thing into his mind, translate it from *seeing* to *telling*, and then, most challenging of all, write about it for others to read. Unlike book reports, what he wrote for the paper was read by many people. *His* words—read by many people. Ironic too, he realized, that the very same students who did not like the words he spoke, read the words he wrote.

Even though he was not as much a pariah among the *Hi-Life* staff, it did not endear him to them that the work was easy for him, that he always finished his assignments far ahead of them, and seemed to find it all so enjoyable. Some of the members of the staff labored over their stories. One senior, Jennie, was prone to temper tantrums when there was no teacher present.

"I *hate* this!" she frequently announced, jerking paper from her typewriter and tearing it to shreds. "Everything I write sounds stupid!"

"Why do you do it if you don't like it?" Richie asked one day when they were in the room alone. The school newspaper was an extra-curricular activity, not a required class.

"Not that it's any of your business," she replied icily, "but I'm doing it for extra credit in English. The reason I need extra credit in English is because none of my book reports make sense. Mrs. Reinhart thought this experience might help me. Does that satisfy your curiosity?"

"Sure," Richie said, shrugging. "Sorry I asked."

As Jennie rolled another sheet in and resumed her toil, Richie surreptitiously studied her. She was a tall girl with a long face and waist-length, tobacco-colored hair. The way she dressed reminded him of Linda: full swirling skirt, neat, starched blouses, ballet slippers. She wore little makeup and was paler than most of the other girls. The daughter of an attorney, she drove her own convertible, smoked, and occasionally muttered a "goddamn it" in the *Hi-Life* room. Richie had read in Lamont's weekly newspaper that she was engaged to marry a previous year's graduate who was going through naval officer training school.

"Do you want me to help you with your article?" Richie finally asked impulsively when Jennie jerked the next sheet of paper out.

"Just how," she inquired in the same glacial tone, "could you do that?"

"Give me all your notes and any drafts you've written so far," Richie said. "I'll take the stuff home and rewrite it for you tonight."

"You're the best writer in the class," she said, frowning. "They'd know you did it."

Richie shook his head. "I can use your drafts as a guide and make it read like you wrote it."

Jennie's pale face became suspicious. "I suppose you'd brag to the rest of the staff about doing it." It was not a question, it was an accusation. Richie shook his head again.

"I don't brag."

Studying him in the wake of that, Jennie's frown and the suspicion in her expression disappeared. "I guess I should have known that," she rationalized. "Nobody's ever heard you mention Midge." Caught off guard by the remark, Richie could not conceal his astonishment. Jennie suppressed an amused smile. "Midge *does* brag," she said, to alleviate his surprise. Embarrassed now, Richie felt himself turn warm with color. "Well, my goodness," Jennie said at that, "aren't you the modest one!" Again, it was not a question, but her way of evaluating him.

"Look," Richie said, irritated, "don't do me any favors by letting me help you." He went back to his own work, which was writing an extra credit book report on *Hi-Life* time.

Several minutes later, Jennie came over and put her draft and notes on his desk. "All right," she said. "Thanks." She kissed her finger and touched his cheek with it.

At the store Mr. Levy began teaching Richie about the men's clothing and shoe business. Without being overbearing, but sensing that Richie had a genuine desire to learn, Herbie, as he taught him how to unpack, invoice, tag, and stock new merchandise, managed to include in his conversation bits of knowledge that he knew Richie would pick up.

"These broadcloth shirts are $3.95," he would say, "and these oxford cloths are $4.50. The broadcloth is the smooth, flat fabric, and oxford has the texture to it."

Or: "These wingtips, the ones with a curved design on the toe, I think we'll stock over here on the side."

Or: "The garbardine suits will be $45. I like the way gabardine feels. Here, run your fingers over this sleeve. No other cloth in the world has the feel of gabardine."

He could just as easily have said the shirts in these boxes are one price, the shirts in those boxes another. Or, all the shoes on those shelves are a certain price, all the suits on that rack. It was not necessary to explain to a stockboy *why*. But Sam Levy did.

Richie loved the store. The shining glass and chrome counters and display cases, with their multicolored stacks of shirts, socks, neckties, pajamas, belts, were an endless source of delight to him. His orderly, logical mind liked everything in neat, precise order, spotless. As quickly as anyone opened a case or touched a counter, he was there wiping off the fingerprints, straightening the merchandise a quarter of an inch. He segregated merchandise by color as well as size, although no one told him to. On Sundays, when Levy sometimes changed the outside window displays, Richie went up to the store and helped him without being asked. Watching Levy select outfits to dress mannequins, Richie began to develop a sense of style and an appreciation of how colors mixed and changed when put next to one another. Seeing the fashions coming into favor in the little Southern town—khaki trousers, plaid shirts, saddle shoes—Richie realized how accurate Linda had been about the way he dressed in Chicago. The zoot suit fad was ludicrous here.

Gradually, with his store discount, Richie began to build up a decent wardrobe for himself. Sometimes in class, or to and from school, he would notice someone admiring how he looked. Most of the students drove or had regular rides to Lamont High; Richie was one of a very few who walked—and the *only* one who walked from one end of the town to the other. Often during the first half of his senior year, when cars passed him, he would see a girl turn for a better look as she went by. But—still—no one stopped to offer him a ride. The only acknowledgment he got from a car was when Billy Pastor cut close to the curb trying to splash him on rainy days.

At home, the relationship between Richie and his grandmother had settled into a mold that was comfortable for both of them. He gave her at least ten dollars a week for his room and board, occasionally a little more—tapping his savings if necessary when there were extra expenses of some kind: a broken water pipe, or when she had to go see the doctor about something. She no longer questioned his coming and goings, seeming to be satisfied that he was not going to get falling-down drunk, engage in brawling, try to rob the Bank of Lamont, or otherwise scandalize her good name.

Occasionally they even had a pleasant moment together, sharing hot chocolate in front of a wood fire on a cold winter night just before bedtime. Sometimes she talked about her own youth as a girl in Kentucky, her stories of turn-of-the-century rural America fascinating Richie. Other times she discussed more mundane subjects, such as the burial insurance on which she had been paying twenty-five cents a week for years, and which would see that she was properly buried next to her husband in the Lamont cemetery.

Now and again they talked about when her daughter was a little girl: how she looked, what she wore, the games she played. Richie had never thought of his mother as being that young. She had always been a happy little girl, Mrs. Clark said, loved and protected, especially by her father, as long as he lived. "I reckon we spoiled her," she concluded during one of their talks. "Gave her too much. Got her used to not doing for herself. Maybe that's what made her so weak."

Whenever they talked about Chloe, it made Richie acutely aware of his grandmother's advancing years. She seemed to be aging so fast. He wanted to do something especially nice for her, so as the holidays approached, he picked out a pretty new linoleum to replace the worn one in her kitchen and put it on layaway for Christmas, paying for it by the week.

It was as close as he could come to telling her he cared for her.

After Richie rewrote Jennie's article for the *Hi-Life*, they settled into an unspoken agreement that he would continue to do so. At first, she did not take it for granted, asking him pointedly the next day. "What do you expect to get out of this?"

"What have you got?" Richie asked back. Then he grinned. "Just fooling. I don't want anything." He shrugged. "I like to write. It's good practice."

"You're a funny one," she said quietly.

"I'm a Yankee, remember? We're all funny." Noticing on her desk a copy of *So Big* by Edna Ferber, he asked, "That your assignment in English? Want me to do the book report for you?"

"God, *would* you?" she asked, as if he had just offered to pardon her from the guillotine. She started to hand him the book. Richie shook his head.

"I don't need it. I read it when I was a kid."

The next day he gave her a neatly hand-printed three-page report to copy over. She was amazed.

"How in the world can you remember a book you read so long ago?"

"When I read a book," he said, shrugging, "it becomes sort of like an old friend. You can't forget an old friend."

"You are strange, Richie," she said. It was the first time she had ever addressed him by name.

"Yeah, I know," he replied. "Just pretend you don't know me."

Within two months, Jennie's grade average in English went up from a C-minus to a B-plus. Richie did three more book reports for her, carefully incorporating into them her own rather bland writing style and projecting himself into her attitude as best he could for a female point of view. Jennie was euphoric over the results; she had never received higher than a C in English in her life.

"My mother and daddy are positively *thrilled*," she told Richie. "Daddy even raised my allowance to twenty-five dollars a week."

Richie stared at her. She got more for allowance than he *earned* in a week. And he was doing *her* schoolwork. You're not too bright, Richie my lad, he told himself.

"You want part of my allowance every week?" she offered.

"No, thanks. I've got more money now than I know what to do with."

He noticed from time to time, when he and Jennie were not alone in the *Hi-Life* room, that she would look at him as if she wanted to talk to him in front of the others—really *talk* rather than just say something—but for some reason could not bring herself to. Richie shrugged it off; if she had conflicting notions concerning him, that was her problem. He wasn't trying to get invited to any senior class parties; just doing a little extra writing to help her out. But more and more he became mindful that a deeper awareness was growing between them.

Their relationship crested one Saturday night when he left Levy's after work and found Jennie parked in front of the drugstore next door, her convertible top up, smoking a cigarette behind the wheel. He was on his way with a casual wave when she rolled down the window and asked, "Where are you going?"

"Over to the City Café to get something to eat."

"Want to come out to my house?" she asked. "I'll fix you something to eat."

"*Your* house?" Richie winced in disbelief. "Very funny."

"I'm not fooling," she said evenly. Their eyes held. "My parents went to Memphis for the weekend."

Standing next to the car, Richie looked down through the window at the contour of her breasts under a green turtleneck sweater where her coat was open. She seemed paler than usual, but he decided it might be the artificial light of the street. Her long hair, with its shiny tobacco color, glistened in the neon. There were still a number of people on the square as Saturday night wound down.

"Where do you want to pick me up?" he asked, remembering that she was engaged.

"Over by the post office. There won't be anybody around there."

Richie nodded and walked away. Five minutes later she pulled up next to the dark post office and he got in.

Her house was on the nicest street in Lamont, built up off the sidewalk with cement steps leading up to a columned front porch. Richie had seen it many times in the daylight; it was big and formidable, like a fort.

Jennie drove up the inclined driveway and pulled into an already open garage. "Wait here five minutes and then sneak in the back door. I'll have the shades down by then."

When he let himself in and went into the kitchen he saw that Jennie had taken off the turtleneck and put on a man's wool shirt, leaving the tail out. "It's Daddy's," she said. "I know it's too big, but it's comfortable. Sit down at the table."

As he watched, she fried a hamburger patty and melted cheese on it while toasting a bun and putting mustard and pickles on the table. When it was ready, she served it to him with potato chips and a bottle of Coke, opening one for herself as well. Richie, as usual, wolfed down his food as if there might be someone around who might take it away from him.

"Where in the world did you learn to eat so fast?" she asked.

"Reform school," he replied.

"Oh, of course," she said skeptically. "In for murder, I suppose."

Richie smiled as he ate. It amazed him how often the truth was disbelieved, a lie accepted as fact.

When he finished, Jenny got him a second Coke and said, "I've got a hi-fi in my room. Want to listen to some records?"

"Sure."

She led him through the elegantly furnished and decorated house to a wide, angled staircase and up to the second floor. On the way, Richie took in as much as he could of the place without being too obvious and gawking. It was easily the most beautiful home he had ever seen, like something in a movie about wealthy people. Jennie's room was done in peach and pale blue. She had a four-poster bed, her own easy chair, a desk, a bookcase filled with books—what a waste, Richie could not help thinking—a hi-fi in one corner, and her own bathroom. What must it be like, Richie wondered, to be *born* into this kind of life?

"Do you like Vic Damone?" she asked.

"Sure." He stepped over to her desk and looked at a photograph of a serious young man in a white navy uniform. "This your fiancé?"

"Yes. Jerry Lyle. He graduated last year."

The sound of Vic Damone singing "You're Breaking My Heart" softly filled the room and Jennie came over and put her arms around his neck. "Dance with me," she said. It was almost an order.

"I don't know how to dance."

"Just put your body up close to mine and move when I move."

Richie tried it for a minute, awkwardly, and Jennie backed them up to the bed and stopped.

"You ever been lonely?" she asked quietly, in a different voice than he ever heard her use before.

"I'm lonely all the time," he said, just as quietly, and immediately wondered why he had been so frank.

"I thought you were. Only a very lonely person would offer to do someone else's assignments just to make a friend."

"That wasn't why I did it," Richie told her. The reason he had helped Jennie was because he felt sorry for her, but he knew he could never tell her that.

"You don't have to be ashamed of it," Jennie said. "It's all right. I understand. I'm lonely too." She pulled him down onto the bed. "Come on . . ."

As Richie took her in his arms and they began to kiss, he could not help wondering if her pubic hair was going to be that same strange tobacco color.

One Saturday morning in March, Richie's stomach felt as if it were going into a knot as he looked up over the shirt counter and saw the farmer Lester stride into the store. Because Richie was kneeling behind the counter checking stock, Lester did not notice him as he passed. A sick feeling rising in his throat, Richie watched the farmer walk back and say something to Sam Levy. The store owner shook hands with Lester and escorted him up to a small open mezzanine office that looked out over the sales floor. There the two men began to talk. It was, Richie thought, the same goddamned thing that happened at Chalk's Drug Store.

Rising, Richie picked up several empty shirt boxes and walked back into the rear stockroom. A heavy, almost physical depression came over him. Why couldn't that son of a bitch Lester leave him alone? What the hell did the bastard get out of finding him on a job and telling his employer who his goddamn father had been? God*damn* it, Richie thought dismally.

Glumly, Richie thought about how much he admired Sam Levy. The little dynamo of a man, in his brightly colored shirts and ties, always had a cheerful word for everyone, white and black alike. He extended credit more liberally than any store owner in town, and never dunned a man when he was having hard times. Universally well-liked throughout the county, he had a rich repertoire of marvelous stories with which he frequently entertained customers as well as employees. It hurt more than angered Richie to think that this fine gentleman might now be reduced in his esteem to the same low level as Rollie Chalk.

After he had been standing in the stockroom for a few gloomy minutes, Richie heard the sound of footsteps coming down from the mezzanine. Stepping over to the door, he saw Lester stride through the store and leave. Then he heard Levy's voice.

"Richie, are you down there?"

"Yessir," Richie said, walking out of the storeroom.

"Come up here a minute, please."

"Yessir."

Climbing the half flight of stairs, Richie felt like he imagined a condemned man must feel walking up to the gallows. There was not even any anger at Lester now, although Richie knew without thinking that it would come back later. But at that moment there was only an impotent misery.

When Richie reached the mezzanine, the store owner, sitting back in a swivel chair, asked, "How long have you been working here, Richie?"

"Nearly six months, Mr. Sam."

"Like your job?"

"Yessir. I like it a lot."

"You doing well in school, getting good grades?"

"Yessir."

"That's good. School's very important for a young man." Levy pursed his lips in thought for a moment, then said, "Starting next week you've got a five-dollar-a-week raise." Richie's mouth fell open and he stared incredulously at Sam Levy as the little man got up from his chair. He patted Richie on the arm, said, "Go on with your work now," and started down the stairs.

Richie finally mustered the composure to say, "Thanks, Levy!"

Sam Levy waved over his shoulder without looking back.

Richie's relationship with Jennie escalated into a total, compelling affair that quickly began to dominate both of them.

Their first physical encounter lasted most of the night, with Richie slipping out the back door and walking the deserted streets home at four in the morning. Before he left, he had satisfied Jennie and she had satisfied him every way either of them knew how. Like Midge, Jennie seemed to thrive on uninhibited sex, giving her tall, lean, pale body to him any way he wanted it, and responding with abandon to everything he did, including pressing his lips far into her thick, curly pubic hair—which, to Richie's delight, *was* tobacco-colored.

"Sweet Jesus, that feels good!" she exclaimed as he alternately worked her clitoris with his tongue, then entered her with his erection, switching

□□ 445 □□

each time she climaxed, as she did time after time. At one point when they were resting, she said, "God, I thought it was good with Jerry, but he didn't know hardly any of the things you know how to do. I think I'm falling in love with you."

"With me or with this," Richie asked curling his fingers around a new erection.

"With both of you," she said, quickly sitting up and leaning over to kiss the head of his erection, then moving her lips up the length of his body to his mouth. "And with your tongue too," she added, parting her lips on his, working her own tongue into his mouth. Without leaving his mouth, she swung a leg over and put him back inside her. Grinding her hips as she moved up and down him, she whispered into his mouth, "What do they call what we're doing, Richie?"

"Fucking," he whispered back.

"Say it some more."

"Fucking, fucking, fucking . . ." The word brought on a spectacular climax for both of them.

In the weeks that followed, Richie and Jennie saw each other every Saturday night and every Sunday night, and whenever they could manage it during the week. On the weekend nights, Jennie picked him up after work or at some other predetermined time and place, and they drove to one of the surrounding towns—Covington, Dyersburg, Halls, Brownsville—where they could move about more freely without as much fear of being seen together. There they would go into a café and have something to eat, go to a movie, or just walk around town as if their relationship were not clandestine.

Their weekend nights always ended with them parking in some isolated place, next to the railroad tracks or a cemetery, and getting into the back seat to make love. As confining as it was, their eagerness helped them find a variety of positions that were enjoyable. Their favorite, which because of Jennie's height they would not have been able to indulge in had she not had a convertible, was for Richie to sit upright and Jennie straddle him with her clothes open and breasts in his face for him to suck. The convertible's cloth-top flexibility gave them the couple of extra inches they needed.

Occasionally they were able to use Jennie's room, and sometimes during the week they would manage a brief interlude somewhere, down next to the closed train depot, behind the box factory outside town, at the deserted football field. Whenever, wherever they met, parting became increasingly more difficult for them each time they were together.

"I don't know what's the matter with me," Jennie would say sometimes. "I have to *make* myself say goodbye to you."

□□ 446 □□

"I do too," Richie said. "I hate to leave you."

"Are we in love, do you reckon? I mean really in love—you know, besides the sex part."

"We must be," Richie allowed. "I've never felt this way before, I know that."

"Me either," she admitted.

Being apart from each other at night became agony for them. Being together in school and having to control their feelings was even worse.

In April, Mrs. Reinhart called him into her office and handed him a list of colleges that offered English literature scholarships.

"I think you might be able to get into one of these," she said. "We'll have to write to that state school you were in up in Illinois—what was its name, St. Charles?—and get a transcript or letter or something showing what your grades were in your first two years of high school . . . what's the matter?"

Richie had looked down in embarrassment. He had known this moment was coming, and had dreaded it. For several weeks Mrs. Reinhart had been talking to him about scholarship material she was receiving from various colleges and how she was going to have to get his academic records in order so he could apply for them. Because of his great love of books and writing, she assumed without even asking that he would try to pursue a higher education in literature or journalism.

"I asked what's the matter?" she said now, sitting back in her chair, her expression turning from efficient-serious to trouble-serious.

"I don't have any high school grades at St. Charles," he quietly admitted. "I only attended seventh and eighth grade classes there."

"Oh, no." All of her optimism, all her confidence, all her natural cheerfulness, faded without reserve. She looked as if her best friend had just died. Removing her glasses, she pinched the space between her eyes and sighed. "It's my fault," she said. "I should have checked when you first came here. I suspected, you know. But I went against my better judgment. You were so convincing; all those books you'd read! And even when my conscience bothered me, I convinced myself that I was doing what was best for you."

"You were," Richie assured her. "Listen, if it hadn't been for you, I would never have stayed here. I wouldn't have been able to stand it in the freshman class, trying to get interested in things I already knew. The only reason I stayed was because you took an interest in me. And if I hadn't stayed, there's no telling where I'd have ended up."

"Yes, but what are you going to do now that it's over? Where do you go from here?"

He shrugged. "I don't know."

"You have such a fine mind; it'll be dreadful if you don't continue your education, if you waste your life."

"I won't waste my life," Richie said. "I guarantee you that." He hesitated a beat, then asked, "What about graduation?"

"Oh, you can graduate," she replied, her voice sounding irked. "I can't very well *not* let you graduate, now can I?"

Richie could not suppress a slight grin. "I don't think so."

"I should only give you half a diploma." Shaking her head in irritable resignation, the teacher leaned forward on her desk and pointed a pencil at him. "I want you to promise me something," she said. "I want you to promise me that someday I will be able to tell myself that I did the right thing."

"I promise," Richie said.

On the night of the senior prom, Richie put on his new graduation suit. It was medium blue, double-breasted; Sam Levy had helped him pick it out and seen to it that it was altered properly. It was Richie's first suit and he felt like he was donning the robes of a king.

"You look all grown up," his grandmother said.

"I was *born* grown up," Richie cracked.

It was just turning dark outside. Jennie was going to pick him up next to the post office. It had been her idea that they attend the prom together, and she had been adamant about it. "I don't *care* what anybody says and I don't *care* what anybody thinks," she had proclaimed. "We are *going* to the prom together."

Richie tried to dissuade her, for her own good. "Just how are you going to explain it to your parents?"

"I'll simply tell them that it's just an informal date, a convenience date so I won't have to miss out on my own senior prom just because my fiancé is becoming a naval officer. I'll tell them it's strictly platonic."

"I think it's a mistake," Richie said. "You're asking for trouble."

"I was asking for trouble when I took you home that first time. We *deserve* this, Richie—one night together, out in the open."

"It's not smart," he said, shaking his head.

"I don't *care!*"

That had been that. He had agreed to go because he could not say no to anything she wanted, he loved her too much. And the fact that she was so insistent about going, so emphatic about not caring what the consequences were, so unrelenting in her decision, made him finally believe, without reservation, that she loved him too. Encouraged by that, he turned his mind loose and let forth a deluge of ideas that he had previously dared not consider.

They could get married, he and Jennie. They'd have to leave Lamont, of course; he could not ask her to come and live in his grandmother's dilapidated house, nor would he feel comfortable moving into her parents' big home. But if she would come to Chicago with him, he was certain they could make it. With a high school diploma, no one would bother to check his age; he could get a job, they could find a little housekeeping apartment, be together every night, their own bed—god!

It could work, he convinced himself, as he reknotted his necktie. It was so outrageous, so unexpected, that it definitely could work. And he felt in the deepest, warmest part of him that Jennie would do it.

"Don't forget the flowers," Mrs. Clark said as he buttoned his coat.

Richie got a florist's box containing a white corsage out of his grandmother's rickety old refrigerator.

"Have a good time," she yelled, waving to him as he walked briskly up the street. If he had not known better, he would have sworn she was close to being teary-eyed. But that was silly. Not Miss Ethel.

It was ten past eight by the post office clock when he got there. He was five minutes early. With the clean handkerchief he always carried—good old Miss Menefee; he wondered how she was—he blotted his forehead and upper lip of the light perspiration he had worked up walking to town. Able to see his reflection in the post office window, he checked his necktie to make sure the knot was still centered. Then he stood off to the side in the shadow of a big tree, and waited for Jennie's headlight to swing around the corner.

At eight-thirty, when she was fifteen minutes late, Richie began pacing. She was always on time within a couple of minutes. But then, he rationalized, she didn't always have to put on a formal gown and do her hair up fancy, either. God, how he loved her hair—*all* of it.

Eight-thirty-five.

Eight forty.

Eight forty-five.

Jennie was half an hour late. He thought about walking over to City Drug and calling her. But if her mother or father answered, he did not know what he would say. Jennie *said* she had told her parents about their date, but Richie was not too sure; she may have just said that so he would relent and agree to go. Besides, what if she was already on her way? He decided to wait a few more minutes.

At nine o'clock he started walking. Her house was ten minutes from the other side of the square. From across the street he could look up the incline and see through the open garage door that her car was not there. He shook his head, completely at a loss. Could he have misunderstood their plans? After all the times she had picked him up at the post office, had he simply gone there out of habit, when perhaps she meant for him to meet her at school? Now he shook his head in irritation: no, that was ridiculous. The meeting place was the post office; he would not have gotten that wrong.

From Jennie's house, Richie walked briskly on until, another ten minutes later, he arrived at the high school. The parking lot was full, as well as the wide drive and the street along one side. Walking back and forth, Richie scrutinized the cars. He knew Jennie could not have been in an accident; he had walked the entire route she would have driven. If her car was not at the school, he made up his mind that he would call her home.

But it was there. He located it in the middle of the lot, with the top down. What in the hell, he wondered, is going on?

He paused inside to get a drink of water at the fountain, and again blotted away the perspiration, from his neck as well this time. Then he walked into the gym. Bedecked with crepe paper and balloons, its usual glaring lights lowered to a subdued level, tables scattered around the outside of the basketball court, and a five-piece band playing on the stage at the auditorium end, the big room had been transformed into a magical, romantic place. A long table with punchbowl and party sandwiches stood near the bleachers, where there was also a chaperone table for the senior class counselors to sit. As Richie entered, Mrs. Reinhart saw him and smiled and waved. He waved back. The band was playing "My Foolish Heart" as couples, in their stocking feet so as not to mar the basketball court, danced slowly and lazily under the low lights. Scanning the crowd, Richie found Jennie almost at once. She was dancing with a man in Navy dress whites.

"So the rumors were true," said a voice next to him. Richie's head snapped around and he found Midge standing there. "I thought they might be, but I wasn't sure." She bobbed her pert chin at Jennie and the sailor. "Jerry came home unexpectedly to surprise her and take her to the prom. Wasn't that sweet of him? I just love a considerate man."

Richie said nothing. There was nothing *to* say. Jennie and her fiancé were dancing together as if they were on a goddamned honeymoon, and he was standing on the sidelines with a goddamned wilting corsage in his hand.

"If you'd stayed home last summer," Midge vexed, "you wouldn't find yourself left out. You'd have a steady girl."

Richie's eyes narrowed. "And half a farm?" he asked.

She glared at him. "I suppose you'd rather be left out?"

"I wouldn't know how to act if I wasn't left out," he said flatly.

Leroy Sadler, Midge's boyfriend, walked up to them. "You want to dance some more, sugar?" he asked Midge.

"I'd love to," Midge said. "Slow and close, so we can rub bodies like

Jennie and Jerry are doing." As they walked away, Midge looked over her shoulder and said, " 'Bye, Yankee."

Leaving the gym, Richie tossed the corsage into a wastebasket and left the school.

Walking back uptown, Richie realized once and for all that he was never going to become a part of this little town where he had been born. Simply too much was against him. Too much had been taken away by his time in the hard city of Chicago—and what he got in return, his experiences on the streets, was not understood in Lamont. His credits in life were not transferable.

The one place he could make himself fit in was the one place he did not want to go: Chicago. Earlier, he had been excited by the prospect of asking Jennie to run off to Chicago with him, but that was a different proposition entirely. With Jennie he would have *had* someone; without her, he would be alone again. And he would, he knew, unless he had some other purpose, gravitate back to Stan Klein and Bobby Casey. If he fell into that snare again, he might never get out. *If you ever come back*, Stan had said, *make sure it's to stay*. Richie could not, would not, do that.

He needed time, he decided. Time to figure things out, decide what he should do, what he could make of himself. He needed to get away from everything old, everyone familiar.

As he walked around the quiet little town square, necktie now pulled down, coat slung over one shoulder, he was drawn to a poster in a metal frame next to the courthouse steps—a poster he passed every day on his way to school. Walking over, he stood looking at it. The graphics were bold, the message unequivocal. THE MARINE CORPS BUILDS MEN.

He studied the poster for several moments, before walking away, his expression still somber but a little more purpose to his step. Why not? he thought.

*R*ichie came out of a bunker dug in the side of a hill and stepped over the body of a dead Marine named Elizondo. Setting his submachine gun on an empty ammunition box, he began searching his pockets for a match to light the cigarette that hung loosely from his dry, cracked lips. Shivering once in the thin, high Korean air, and finding that he had no matches, he knelt and rummaged through Elizondo's pockets until he found a lighter. As he lighted his cigarette, he noticed that Elizondo's face had frozen and turned purple during the night, making the eyelids, lips, and nostrils look as if some grotesque makeup had been applied. Starting to put Elizondo's lighter in his own pocket, Richie hesitated, then put it back in the dead man's pocket.

Picking up his submachine gun again, cradling it naturally in one arm as if it were part of him, Richie walked across pinto-patches of snow to an outpost trench a hundred yards away where two other members of his squad, Haven and Dobcik, lay ripped open and dead from a mortar hit. Taking a pair of field binoculars from around what was left of Haven's neck, Richie uncoupled the dried frozen blood-encrusted strap and tossed it away. Holding the lenses close to his mouth, he breathed on each of them until a coating of ice melted away and wiped them with one of his wool trigger-finger mittens. Then he lay forward against the front of the trench and focused the glasses on a valley several thousand yards below him. He shivered again, not from the cold this time, as he looked.

The fucking Chinese were still there.

Like a swarm of little bugs in their puffy, quilted coats and bloomer pants that ballooned out at the knees, they were sloshing about in the mud where the snow had already melted, cooking breakfast on camp stoves, drinking from steaming bowls, squatting off on the sides to defecate. There were still a few women with them, Richie noticed. They made him think of Reynolds, a sergeant from California whose wife had Dear-Johned him, and who, during the attacks of the previous three days, had taken particular delight in singling out and shooting the gook women. Even though Reynolds was a good shot, Richie saw now that there were at least half a dozen or so of the little fighter-whore-cooks left. Reynolds would never have the opportunity to shoot them because Reynolds himself had been shot—perhaps appropriately, in the groin—and was now dead.

Forgetting about the women, Richie moved the glasses slowly along the edge of the enemy camp, mentally counting heads to see what the odds in the next fire fight were going to be. When he got to a hundred, he thought, fuck it, and quit. Shoving the binoculars as far as they would go into a pocket of his field jacket, he tossed the butt of his cigarette away and trudged back up the hill. In the bunker, Vinnie Casino, the only other Marine left alive, was transmitting the map coordinates of their location on the field radio. An intense little Italian, he looked around apprehensively when Richie entered. "They coming?" he asked nervously.

Richie shook his head. "Eating breakfast."

Sighing relief, Vinnie resumed transmitting. They did not know whether their signal was being picked up or not because the radio's receiver was not functioning. So Vinnie just kept on sending, hoping some other unit was getting it.

The area they were in was called the Punchbowl, and they were on the high ground on the north rim. It lay fifty or so miles above the thirty-eighth parallel, the boundary between North and South Korea. To the west were two perfectly formed peaks called Jane Russell Hill. To the east was Sok-cho-ri, a fishing village on the sea of Japan. It was there that they had made an amphibious landing six months earlier, in November. The navy was presently off the coast of that same fishing village, evacuating the western sector in the face of an early spring offensive by a combined North Korean–Chinese army. The outfit Richie and Vinnie were in had no way to get to the fishing village for evacuation because Sorak-san, a five-thousand-foot mountain, lay in their way, and all roads around Sorak-san were now held by the Chinese. So the outfit had dug in and radioed for evacuation assistance while being decimated by daily Chinese attacks.

"Shit, maybe we should just surrender," Vinnie suggested wearily, leaning his head against the damaged radio. "It's better than dying."

Taking off his helmet, Richie shook his head. "Remember Jake," he said.

Jake Jacobs had been captured in an earlier action when the First Marines had been driven back several miles. A month later, when they retook the same ground, they had found him submerged head-down in a frozen honey pot. A honey pot was a well in which human excrement was saved to fertilize rice paddies. The captain let them execute six prisoners as payback for Jake, but it had not done any good. Nobody who ever saw Jake's feet sticking out, dogtags hanging from one toe to identify him, would ever forget it.

In the bunker, Richie smoked another Lucky, then said, "The bodies have to be propped up."

"Will you do it?" Vinnie asked. "I'll stay on the radio."

"Sure."

"You don't mind doing it, do you?"

"I don't mind." Richie was a corporal and Vinnie only a PFC, but he knew that Vinnie did not like to leave the bunker now that they were the only two left.

Outside again, Richie walked to the MLR—the Main Line of Resistance—which lay halfway between the bunker and the perimeter outpost trench. The MLR was a long dugout in which many Marines lay dead. Hopping down into it, Richie began to drag the dead men up and prop them partly over the outside lip of the dugout. He made sure each one had a helmet on, and worked a weapon into each corpse's stiff arms. By doing that, it would look from the enemy camp as if there were many Marines still alive waiting to resist the next assault. The gooks that were left would then send more troops up the hill, and the Marines that *were* left—Richie and Vinnie—would be able to kill more of them before being overrun.

When he finished propping up bodies, Richie went back down to the perimeter outpost and scanned the Chinese camp with the binoculars again. The gooks were sitting around in groups now, filling ammo clips, oiling machine-gun mechanisms, sharpening bayonets. But where were the women, he wondered; he did not see any of the women. Then one came out of a small pyramidal tent, her bulky coat unbuttoned in front, and a Chinese officer came out after her, buckling his belt, smiling. You dirty bastard, Richie thought, wetting his cracked lips. I'm waiting up here to die and you're down there fucking. Irritably, he focused the glasses sharply on the officer, studying him. He was taller than most of them and had a Mandarin moustache. Richie concentrated on his features, memorizing them. If you come up this hill today, motherfucker, he silently swore, you are dead.

Looking at his watch, seeing that it was nearly nine o'clock, knowing that the gooks usually launched their first attack of the day around ten, Richie went back up the hill and into the supply bunker. Randomly ripping open C-rations until he found a can of spaghetti-and-meatballs, his favorite, he took it, along with some instant coffee, a portable cookstove, and a new set of mess gear, and returned to the bunker where Vinnie was.

"It's time to get down there, Vin," he said.

Picking up a bandolier of six submachine-gun magazines, Richie returned to the MLR, to a space he had left near the middle of the long line of dead Marines he had propped up. Setting up the stove, he got the spaghetti and coffee ready to heat. Opening a tin of hard biscuits, he spread grape jelly on them for an appetizer. As he ate, Richie glanced back several times at the bunker. Finally he sighed quietly and walked back there again. Vinnie was staring dully at the radio.

"Come on, Vin," Richie said. He pushed a submachine gun and a bandolier of magazines into Vinnie's hands, and put a helmet on his head. "Come on," he said again.

With an arm around Vinnie's shoulders, Richie walked him out to the MLR. In the dugout, Vinnie sat on the ground and stared at his thermal boots. Richie put on the spaghetti and coffee. "Want some chow?" he asked. Vinnie shook his head.

Before he ate, Richie scanned the Chinese camp again. There was more activity now: packs were being folded, leggings wrapped, helmets held over fires to be blackened so they would not reflect the sun. They were getting ready, Richie knew. He played the glasses around until he located the tall officer with the Mandarin moustache. Hope you enjoyed it, Gook, he thought with jealousy.

When the coffee boiled and the spaghetti bubbled, Richie took them off and sat down on a dry patch of ground to eat. He tried to concentrate on the food, but for some reason his mind kept going back to the Chinese officer and the woman, and the things they had probably done in the tent. Richie had not been close to a woman in six months, since the battle of the Punchbowl began. Before that, there had been plenty of them: Korean girls in Seoul, Japanese girls in Kobe, Mexican girls in Tijuana, golden girls in Oceanside, California, pale girls in Beaufort, South Carolina. His experiences of the past two years had all but eclipsed the bitterness he had felt when Jennie dropped him so abruptly. His recent memories, half of them of prostitutes, including two fifteen-year-old Japanese girls in a threesome in Kobe, were all warm, fond recollections. For that reason it irritated him that the gooks had women in their ranks; women who not only fucked but fought—they charged up the goddamn hills right along with the men. A Marine Corps morale officer had told Richie's outfit that the women were volunteers who *wanted* to be there; Marines, he emphasized, need have no reservations about killing them in combat. Everyone knew the gooks had kids in their ranks too: thirteen, fourteen years old. Richie tried not to think about that. He tried to keep the primary rule of combat uppermost in his mind: kill everybody that moved, and let God sort them out. But this was difficult for him at times. Women and young kids; it did not digest easily—

A sudden single rifle shot punctured Richie's thoughts and he leaped up, spaghetti thrown aside, machine gun in his hands. Vinnie leaped up beside him and they peered over the edge of the dugout down the hill. A white flag was being waved back and forth. The figure carrying it stepped out of the ranks of quilted-coated soldiers lined up just out of firing range and, keeping the flag high, moved precariously up the slope.

"Maybe the war's over," Vinnie said.

"This fucking war won't ever be over," Richie said. "It's probably somebody coming up to ask us to surrender."

"I think we ought to," Vinnie proposed again.

"Remember Jake," Richie said.

"Fuck Jake! There's no guarantee they'll do the same thing to us. Look," he tried to reason, "we got the short end of the fucking stick here. You, me, all these guys, the whole outfit. 'Member all the bullshit they taught us about Marines never leaving their dead behind? Well, that's just what it was, bullshit! They've left the fucking dead *and* the living behind, man. I say we give up."

"Give up if you want to," Richie said. "Me, I'll take one in the gut before I'll let the cocksuckers stick my head in a pile of gook shit."

The white flag bobbed and weaved and the lone figure made its way along a rough path toward where they were. Lighting another cigarette, Richie studied Vinnie as the little Italian chewed nervously on his chapped bottom lip. Presently it started to bleed a little.

"Listen, Vinnie, why don't you go back to the bunker and start sending those coordinates again," Richie said. "I'll see what this gook has to say. If I think they'll give us fair treatment, I'll come and get you and we'll surrender."

"You're not bullshitting me?"

"No, I mean it." Richie nodded toward the bunker. "Go on."

"Okay, yeah, okay!" Vinnie looked like Jennie had looked the day Richie offered to write her book report the first time. "You'll come get me now, right? Promise?"

"Word of honor," Richie said.

Vinnie scurried out of the MLR and ran back to the bunker. After he was gone, Richie took all of the magazines out of the bandolier and laid them in a row on the lip of the dugout. He had already made up his mind to kill the gook with the white flag; he would have to because the gook was going to see that all the Marines in the MLR were dead. As soon as Richie did it, he knew they would attack. But he decided he might as well get it over with; then Vinnie could do whatever he wanted.

When the figure with the white flag got almost up to him, Richie saw that it was one of the women. Frowning deeply, staring at her face, he realized with revulsion that she looked like an Oriental version of his mother. It was Chloe at twenty-five, except that her eyes were slanted and her cheeks were slightly rounder. Approaching closer, she smiled slightly, and it was his mother's smile. Richie's eyes widened, his sore lips parted, and his left hand, with the cigarette between his fingers, began to tremble. Only the weight of the submachine gun kept his other hand steady. The nearer to him the woman came, the more she looked like Chloe: the young, vibrant, determined Chloe before drugs ravaged her. Stunned, Richie climbed out of the dugout to meet her. When the Chinese woman stopped in front of him, he half expected her to speak his name.

"What do you want?" he asked thickly. He knew she must speak English or they would not have sent her.

"Marine give up," she said. It was his mother's voice. "Marine cannot win. Give up, go to nice camp, war over for you." As she spoke, she looked curiously at the line of men on both sides of Richie. Expression turning incredulous, she said, "All dead?"

"Yeah," Richie replied, almost in a whisper. "All dead." *I can't kill her,* he thought.

Suddenly, from behind Richie, came a sound he almost did not believe: the chopping-blade sound of helicopter rotors. Head snapping around, he saw half a dozen evacuation helicopters flying in formation over the crest of the hill above the bunkers. At once the horror of the Chinese woman's presence vanished and Richie's mind raced urgently: *Jesus Christ, they were coming to get them!* Vinnie came half running, half stumbling, out of the bunker, no helmet, no weapon, waving his arms frantically. Richie and the Chinese woman watched almost hypnotically as the first craft landed and half a dozen evacuation personnel leaped out and began pulling the bodies of the dead Marines from one end of the dugout. A second helicopter set down and more men disembarked, pulling stretchers after them. Vinnie was going crazy, running around screaming, patting men on the back, trying to shake hands, until a Navy corpsman took him aboard one of the helicopters. The other three craft set down and evac Marines fanned out all over the area.

Richie looked back at the Chinese woman. He knew he should take her prisoner but on impulse he decided not to. She was pretty, like his mother had once been, and if he turned her over to the military police, there was no telling what the fucking apes would do to her. "Go back down," he said, bobbing his chin toward the valley.

Her face took on a vile mask then and she looked at him with anger and growing rage. Now she was the Chloe desperate for a fix, infuriated because something or somebody prevented her having it. Fiercely she threw the white flag on the ground and spat on Richie's field jacket, snarling something at him in Chinese. Richie reached out and shoved her toward the path.

"Go on back down!" he snapped.

Instead, she pulled open her coat and reached for a pistol in her belt.

"No!" Richie yelled.

She drew the pistol anyway.

Richie stroked the trigger of the submachine gun and riddled her body, plunging her thirty feet back down the hill.

In the valley, the Chinese saw it and started their screaming uphill attack.

Jumping across the dugout, now teeming with evac personnel removing bodies, Richie trotted toward the nearest helicopter. He had done it all now, he supposed. First he had fucked his mother when he was with Frances, and now he had killed his mother in Korea. He felt tears stream down his raw cheeks, whether from happiness at being rescued or remorse over what he had just done, he did not know. Maybe, he thought, there was no way to separate them.

He climbed aboard the helicopter.

In the rest camp at Inchon, behind the lines, Richie sat on his cot and looked at a stack of Red Cross stationery that was lying on the footlocker that went with the cot. Every day a Red Cross worker visited every tent and left writing material on all the footlockers. Every afternoon, when the Marines in the rest camp returned from showering after calisthenics, most of them sat or lay on their cots and passed the hour before evening chow writing letters home. Richie did not write letters. The only person he had written to was his grandmother, and he had received a letter just before Christmas the previous year, from a funeral home, telling him that Mrs. Clark had died. After that, there was no one to write letters to.

The stack of Red Cross stationery was becoming embarrassingly high; they left a certain amount every day whether it was used or not. Richie did not know what to do with it. Somehow, it did not seem right to throw the stuff away. As he looked around the tent, it appeared that everyone was writing letters. Occasionally one or another of them would pause and look up—always, it seemed, directly at him. It was as if they were silently asking, "*Well?*"

I'll write a book report, he decided. There's no way anyone will know; it'll look like I'm writing a letter. Removing his boots, he sat on the cot with his knees propped up and opened one of the Red Cross tablets. Pausing in thought, he tried to decide which book to write about. He had had no difficulty getting interesting books to read in Korea; just since being in the rest camp he had read paperbacks by John O'Hara, James M. Cain, Horace McCoy, and W. R. Burnett. And for months, up on the lines, he had carried around a ragged paperback of *An American Tragedy* by Theodore Dreiser, reading random parts of it over and over, always moved.

At the moment, however, he could not make up his mind which book he wanted to report on. Actually, the thought of doing it at all was no longer challenging. Richie knew, the moment he decided to do it, that it would not —be fun now. Writing book reports seemed somehow ridiculous, superfluous, illogical. It was like masturbating when there was a naked woman on the bed waiting for you. Maybe, he thought, if he wrote something he had not read. Something he just made up. Something original . . .

On the tablet of Red Cross stationery, Richie wrote a title: "Hit and Run". Thinking about his fight with Willie Wakefield, he began composing a story about boxing.

*R*ichie knelt to brush some dead leaves from his grandmother's grave, then placed a bouquet of flowers at the base of her headstone. Standing up, he dusted off the knee of his khaki uniform trousers and stood looking at the grave.

He had only been in town an hour. After getting off the morning train from Memphis, he had left his seabag at the depot and walked uptown to the florist. With the flowers he bought, he had walked all the way out to Lamont Cemetery, which was past the high school, and roamed back and forth among the tombstones until he found Mrs. Clark's grave. Now, after putting the flowers on it, he was standing there thinking that he should say something but not knowing what. Across the cemetery, a funeral for someone had just ended and people were walking back to their cars while two black cemetery employees waited nearby to start filling the fresh grave.

Finally, with a restless sigh, Richie said, "Well, Miss Ethel, I'm sorry we didn't have a little more time together." But it was clearly time to go now, to put this place and everything in it behind him: his grandmother, the town, the past . . .

As he turned to leave, Richie saw a man walking toward him from the funeral group that was departing. A tall man with blondish-silver hair, he wore a seersucker suit and carried a leather-bound Bible that zipped closed on three sides. Smiling, he waved for Richie to wait. Approaching, he asked, "Are you Mrs. Clark's grandson?"

"Yes, sir."

"Then you're Tennessee Slim's son?"

"That's right," Richie said, dropping the "Yes, sir."

"I'm Brother Cecil of the Latter Jehovah Church. Would you be interested in some information about your father?"

Richie felt his stomach knot up. His *father!* After all this time? Across all those hard years?

"What kind of information?" he asked quietly, his mouth drying with the words.

"One of the members of my flock is in the hospital dying of throat cancer. If you'll come see him with me, you might be very glad you did."

"Who is it?" Richie asked. Could it *be* his father? Jesus Christ!

"I'd rather you came and saw for yourself," Brother Cecil said.

It actually crossed Richie's mind to decline, to walk away from it. Even if it was his father, what was to be gained now from seeing him? Richie was even a little afraid inside, not certain he wanted to dredge up any of the past again, unsure about how it would affect him. He had put so many things behind him now: he had a whole new life planned for himself, a future to which he was eagerly looking forward. Did he want to take a chance of upsetting that by learning something new that might interfere with the peace of mind he had worked so hard to achieve?

The answer, he quickly decided, was yes.

There was no way he could have refused. Whatever it turned out to be, was *part* of him. Part of what he was. He could not walk away from that.

"Okay," he said. "Let's go."

Brother Cecil drove Richie to the hospital in a big shiny Packard that had a gold cross for a hood ornament. "My loyal flock gave me this car," he said. "They had that hood ornament made special for it. Praise Jesus." He glanced at Richie. "Are you saved, son?"

"Not that I know of," Richie said.

"Today," Brother Cecil speculated, "may turn out to be the most glorious day of your life!"

Or the most fucked up, Richie thought.

At the hospital, Brother Cecil led Richie along an antiseptic-smelling hallway, past doorways through which he got glimpses of patients, to an end room that had a screen around the door. Following Brother Cecil in, Richie saw that the blinds were closed and only a small nightlight was on, leaving the room very dim. Several women sat around the bed on metal hospital chairs, while one of them prayed quietly out loud.

"Ladies," Brother Cecil said, "I'm going to ask y'all to take a break for a little bit. The Lord has sent a special visitor today."

The ladies filed out, looking curiously at Richie, as he and Brother Cecil stepped closer to the bed. When Richie got up close, he saw that the man in the bed was not his father at all. It was the old farmer, Lester, who had got him fired from Chalk's Drug Store.

"What the hell is this all about?" Richie demanded of Brother Cecil.

"It's about an opportunity!" Brother Cecil exhorted, clutching the zippered Bible to his chest for emphasis. "An opportunity for two souls to meet in the name of Jesus!" He pronounced the name "Ja-hay-us."

Richie turned to leave.

"Wait!" he heard a horribly strained voice say. Looking back, he saw Lester raise a weak, pleading hand. "Wait . . . your daddy . . . I know . . ."

Richie stepped over to the bed. "You know what?"

Lester turned his hollow, dark-circled eyes to Brother Cecil. "Leave us alone . . ." Brother Cecil bowed slightly and backed out of the room. "Come closer . . ." Lester rasped hideously to Richie. "I'll . . . tell you . . ."

After sending Chloe and the boy down Moreridge Street to wait for him, Slim went over to the highway and started hiking toward his daddy's farm. He had been hoofing it for about half an hour when a farmer in a pickup truck pulled over and gave him a lift.

"You're Solon Howard's boy, ain't you?" the driver asked.

"Yessir. I been away for a spell. On my way back home now."

The driver, an older man, spat tobacco juice out his window. "Good time to show up," he allowed. "Cotton's about ready. Some places," he bobbed his chin at a mile-long field they were passing, "are already picking."

Slim gazed out at the field hands in their straw hats, bent to the cloud-puffy cotton bursting out of its sharp bolls to draw in the morning sunshine. "Been a long time since I picked cotton," he said quietly. "I reckon the bolls still slice a man's hand up right smart."

"Cotton picking don't change," the farmer said. "The bolls tears up your hands, the bending wrecks your back, and the cotton dust clogs your lungs. God didn't mean for us to get cotton cheap."

"Or anything else," Slim muttered. He turned to stare at the farmer, his expression solemn, even a little frightened.

"Somethin' the matter?" the farmer asked.

"Just looking at your bib overalls," Slim said. "I once told somebody I'd never go back to wearing bib overalls."

The pickup continued on past the blanket-white cotton fields and fol-lowed the highway as it cut down into lower, more thickly wooded bottom-land along the Mississippi River. The air changed from morning fresh to muggy wet. The river along the road was brown with mud.

Suddenly Slim said, "Let me out along here, will you? I need to walk a little and do some thinking—"

"I was about to pull over anyway," the farmer said as he eased the pickup to a stop. "Take a look-see at that right rear wheel for me, will you? I thought I felt a shimmy."

"Be glad to," Slim said as he got out. He walked back, knelt at the wheel, and ran his hand over the tire for a bubble. Then he gripped each side of the tire and tried to shake it. "I sure don't see nothing wrong with it, mister," he hollered, rising. As he turned, he found the farmer with a shotgun pointed at him.

"My name's Lester," the man said. "Back just before you was sent to the penitentiary, a boy of mine drank some of your bootleg hooch at a high school dance. Tried to drive home drunk and got in a car wreck. Killed him. Now I'm fixin' to kill you."

Extending his hands in a plea, Slim said, "Wait a minute, mister—"

"I been waitin', you son of a bitch, all these years. Now my waitin's over."

Lester shot him point blank, blowing Slim's chest open and hurling his body a dozen feet along the muddy bank. It landed silently in the wake of the shotgun echo.

Lester walked over to the body and, with the toe of one work shoe, eased it into the river where it immediately sank.

Richie stared at the old man in the hospital bed. The story he had told reverberated in Richie's head like a shrapnel grenade, all the exploded pieces rebounding off the inside of his skull. *His father . . . dead all these years, shot-gunned and dumped in the river like garbage.*

Putting a hand over his eyes, as if to block a blinding light, Richie gave a deep, hollow sigh. God, how he wished his mother were still alive, so he could tell her, so she would know that her husband had not just walked away from her like she wasn't worth staying with. Jesus Christ, how one little bit of knowledge could so totally reshape the picture of the past . . .

Richie let himself look again at the old man in the bed. As Lester had told the story, a thin line of green sputum had run slowly out of one corner of his mouth and dried grossly on his chin. His voice had become so rasping that his words were now little more than grunts. But Richie understood him.

"Way I knew . . . he was back," Lester strained to tell, "was . . . a friend of mine . . . got off . . . that same train. He called me . . . from the depot . . . "

Richie's mind was still racing. He had known all along that Lester had got him fired from the drugstore job, and had tried to get Sam Levy to fire him too. Lester's kid got drunk on bootleg whiskey and was killed in a car wreck, and the bootlegger's kid was still alive. Richie wondered if his grandmother had known all that; if she suspected that Lester might have also been responsible for Slim's disappearance. And not told him to prevent trouble.

Richie found himself wishing Miss Ethel was still alive too, so he could tell her that he knew at last. Everybody that he wanted to share this new revelation with was dead. The last piece of the tormenting jigsaw puzzle was now in place—and he was the only one left to look at it.

"Why are you telling me this after all these years?" he asked the old man. "Because you're dying?"

"I want . . . forgiveness," Lester whispered. "Don't want to . . . go to my maker . . . with this on . . . my soul . . ."

Forgiveness? Staring coldly at Lester, Richie felt his jaw clench. Glancing over his shoulder, he saw that the door to the room was still closed. Stepping closer to the bed, he slowly moved his right hand toward Lester's emaciated neck. Dread fear surfaced in Lester's eyes. Richie stopped his hand just before it touched the old farmer's throat.

No, he thought, that was too easy. That would be a favor.

Drawing his hand back, he sighed quietly. "Jesus, the thousands of times I looked for my father on the streets of Chicago," he said aloud, but to himself, remembering the endless questions he had asked Mack and Estelle, thinking of all the time and effort, the young hopes, the dreams—all for a man already dead. "You want forgiveness?" he said to Lester. "All right, I forgive you. *I* forgive you—for what you did to *me*." Lester tried to smile. "But how do you get forgiveness for what you did to *him?*" Richie asked. "And to my mother?" The old man's attempt at a smile faded.

"You . . ." he said weakly. "Forgive me . . . for them . . ."

"No," Richie said, shaking his head emphatically. "Only they can forgive you for themselves. And they can't because you killed them. You killed both of them."

"No . . . no, only him . . ."

"Both of them," Richie repeated firmly. "Because when you killed him, you took away her last hope—and that's what finally killed her too. You're going to your grave with *two* murders on your soul. You're going to burn in hell, old man."

"No, please . . . no . . ."

Ignoring the pleas, Richie left the hospital room. Brother Cecil was in the hall with the women who had been praying around Lester's bed. He stepped up to Richie at once.

"Did you forgive him, son?"

"Yes, I forgave him."

"Praise Jesus!" Brother Cecil and the women said in chorus. Clutching the Bible to his seersucker-clad chest again, the preacher asked, "Will you come back in and pray with us, son?"

"I can't," Richie said. "I have to catch a train. I was just passing through."

Leaving the hospital, Richie walked back through town and down to the depot again. The platform was deserted, the northbound train not due for two hours. Sitting on one of the wooden benches, Richie lighted a cigarette and leaned forward with his elbows on his knees, smoking.

The dying old man's story still swirled in his head. Lester told him that Slim had asked him to stop that day down by the river. Slim had wanted to get out, "to walk a little and do some thinking . . ."

All that talk about cotton bolls and bib overalls, Richie thought. Was Slim about to back out? Had he figured that he couldn't do it, after all? *Had Chloe been right?*

And did it make any difference?

In spite of himself, Richie felt his eyes well up with tears. In his mind was the memory of a ragged kid prowling a hard city looking for a man he thought had abandoned him, feeling deep inside himself that somehow he must have *deserved* to be abandoned. When all the time he might not have been abandoned at all. If Slim had lived, whether he had gone straight or not, Richie was certain his father would have taken care of him.

But that really didn't matter either, he realized. What had happened, happened.

Tossing the half unsmoked cigarette on the tracks, Richie let himself cry over those days one last time.

*I*n the Veteran's Administration office in Chicago, Richie sat next to a desk where a man in a necktie and cardigan sweater looked over a variety of forms Richie had given him.

"Everything seems to be in order," he said. "I should be able to get your first tuition check and your first living allowance processed by the end of the week. You can stop in Friday afternoon and pick them up. Have you registered at Northwestern yet?"

"I'm doing that this afternoon," Richie said.

"Okay, bring me a copy of your class schedule when you come in on Friday." He smiled at Richie. "How's it feel to be home?"

"Real good," Richie replied. "A little odd once in a while. I mean, here I am a discharged Marine, a veteran of Korea, with three combat decorations, and I can't legally order a glass of beer in a bar because I'm not twenty-one yet."

"Hey, just because you're old enough to die for your country doesn't mean you have any rights," the V.A. man joked. "Next thing you know, you'll be wanting to vote."

When Richie left the V.A., he caught a bus over to the Far North Side, where Northwestern University was located, to keep an appointment with a counselor to register. As a veteran, all he had to show was his high school diploma; there was no minimum grade-level requirement. When Richie had read that in the G. I. Bill information packet given to him in San Diego, where he received his discharge, he had decided at once to take Mrs. Reinhart's advice and go to college. He had three full years of tuition coming and was sure he could work his way through the fourth year. When he had to decide where to go, he had without hesitation chosen a school in Chicago instead of one in the south. With his luck, if he had elected to go to the University of Tennessee, Billy Pastor would have been there. No, he belonged up north. And it did not bother him, going back to the hard city. After what he had been through, no city could break him now.

Richie felt good about life. The terrible knowledge of what had happened to his father had not, as he had briefly feared, upset his plans for the future or dampened his spirits in any way. On the contrary, it had seemed to make him, at last, a whole person. There were now no gaps in his past, no loose ends dangling. It was as if he had finally been paid in full for managing to get through all those bad times. His father had *wanted* to come back to him; that fact had not helped him then, but it made him feel very good now.

The terrible knowledge would, he was certain, help and not hinder him in making something of his life.

The freshman counselor at Northwestern was a pleasant woman of forty who welcomed him back from the Korean War and helped him organize classes that would accommodate his interests and also fulfill requirements for certain degrees.

"If we keep you in English, journalism, and creative writing classes," she said, "you'll be within the parameters necessary to decide later whether you want your degree in journalism or English lit. You'll have until the beginning of your junior year to make your final choice." When she completed processing his registration, she asked, "Do you have lodgings yet?"

"No, not yet."

"Here's a form that you can take to the housing office to get a dorm room. They're reasonably priced and meals are included."

As he was leaving the administration building, Richie saw a girl who looked familiar crossing a hall in front of him. She was carrying several books along with her purse. Frowning, he followed her. As he watched the way she walked, he realized that it was Linda. Surprised, he hurried to catch up with her.

"Can I carry your books?" he asked.

"Thanks, but I'm okay," she said with a brief smile. Then she stopped and stared. "Oh, my god."

"You say that every time," he reminded her. "Who writes your material?"

"Richie, how *are* you?" she said, smiling in surprise. "What are you doing here?"

"Registering."

"You mean you *go* here?"

"I'm just starting. On the G. I. Bill. I just got out of the service."

"How marvelous! What are you taking?"

"Writing, journalism, English."

"Me too! Maybe we'll have some classes together."

"You're probably a couple years ahead of me, aren't you?"

"No," Linda said, coloring a little, "I'm just starting too."

"Oh." Richie glanced at a gold wedding band on her finger. "You married that guy you were going with, huh?"

"Yes. Yes, I did." She blushed a deeper red. "You sure look different from the last time I saw you," she said, changing the subject.

"I guess I dress a little better now," he said, looking down at himself.

"You know, I thought about you when I read that John Garfield had died. I wondered where you were."

"I was in a rest camp in Korea. I read about it in *Stars and Stripes*."

Looking at her watch, Linda said, "Listen, I have to run; I have an appointment about a campus job. We'll be seeing each other again, I'm sure."

"Maybe we can have a cup of coffee or something," Richie suggested eagerly. He hated to let her go so quickly. "We could talk about the old days."

She did not say yes or no, just " 'Bye now."

He watched her all the way down the hall, her model-perfect posture seeming to make her taller than girls who passed her. Inside him was an old familiar feathery feeling. Christ, is it happening again with her? he wondered.

On his way to the housing office, Richie gave a hand to two other freshmen who were moving a bulky television set into one of the dorms. When Richie saw the room—the dearth of personal space, the lack of privacy because rooms were shared—and when he heard the noise up and down the halls, he decided to see if he could find someplace else to live. He had spent too many years in communal living—foster homes, the Charleytown cottage, Marine Corps barracks; the only place he'd had any peace and quiet was in the tiny room in his grandmother's poor little house. But he remembered being happy there, and he wanted someplace like that to live now.

Leaving the campus, Richie started walking, away from the university and its older but solidly upper-middle-class neighborhood. He walked toward the inner city, observing block by block as the houses and buildings became less impressive, less cared for, and their apartments more attainable. Then he began inquiring wherever he saw a FOR RENT sign. The first few places he checked, he was asked for identification because he looked too young to be renting a place himself; some buildings would not rent to anyone under twenty-one. Just like buying beer, Richie thought, irked. Finally he went back to the Y.M.C.A. in the Loop, where he was staying, and put on his uniform with the corporal stripes and his ribbons, and started looking again. He found a place he liked and was allowed to rent it at once. The uniform makes the man, he thought wryly. He moved in that night.

Richie's new home was a second-floor housekeeping apartment: a large room with a small Pullman kitchen, a bed that folded into the wall, and a tiny bath with a shower stall. It rented for less than a dorm room, but he had to cook his own meals. He did not mind. When he set down his seabag and stood, doorkey in hand, he looked around with a sense of wonder. This was *his*. There was a pretty good chest of drawers with a mirror over it; a little table with two chairs—that matched—and an overstuffed armchair with a reading lamp next to it. It was perfect, he thought, as he went around touching everything, opening drawers, trying light switches and faucets. *Perfect. And his*. Humming happily, he set about unpacking his clothes.

It was good to have a place to live.

When Richie started school the following week, he was pleased to see that Linda was in his creative writing class. They did not sit together; Richie had been the first one to arrive in class and had taken the end chair in the first row, because he did not want to miss anything. By the time Linda got there the front chairs were filled and she had to find one in the rear. But she saw Richie and waved as she sat down.

The creative writing teacher was Mr. Crane, a tall, intellectual-looking man with a mop of prematurely gray hair who wore bright-colored vests— red, green, sometimes plaid—under his tweed sport coats. At the first meeting of the class, he went through each student's class card to familiarize himself with his new group, and made a comment to each.

"I see you're on the yearbook staff, Miss Phelps; you won't expend much creative writing there. About all you'll write is photo captions."

And: "A political science major, I see, Mr. Jenkins. I hope you learn well in here; most political speeches are pure fiction, you know." Laughter.

And, to Linda: "A graduate of Austin High, I see. Excellent school. I'll expect good things from you."

Then, when he got to Richie: "What's this—a Korean War veteran? Well, well. Going on the G. I. Bill, are you?"

"Yes, sir," Richie replied.

"How nice. I understand it pays your living expenses also, is that correct?"

"There's a living allowance, yessir."

"A free ride. Lucky you."

Richie felt himself blush. What the hell was this guy's problem? he wondered.

After class that day, Richie waited for Linda in the hall. It was mid-morning and they had twenty minutes between classes. "Want to have that cup of coffee?" he asked.

"Sure, okay." She was wearing a tight, sleeveless dress, over which she slipped on a loose, belted jacket while Richie held her books. They went outside, where Richie got them containers of coffee from a catering wagon, and sat on the steps of the building to drink it.

"What brought on that crack Mr. Crane made about the G. I. Bill?" she asked.

"Beats me," Richie said. "Maybe he's one of those taxpayers who don't think vets should get educational benefits."

"I thought he was downright snide."

Richie shrugged. "I'm not going to let it bother me. I'm in his class to learn how to improve my short story writing, and that's what I intend to do."

"What short story writing?" Linda asked, surprised.

"I've been kind of playing around writing short stories," Richie admitted, a little sheepishly. "I started it while I was in a rest camp in Korea with nothing else to do. I found out I liked it."

"Richie, that is marvelous!" she exclaimed. "Are you going to try and get them published?"

"Someday, I guess. If I ever get good enough."

"Oh, you will! I know you will. I keep saying I'm going to do something like that, but so far I haven't."

They fell silent for a moment, both sipping their coffee. It was only mid-September, but the leaves on the many campus trees were already yellowing, and the air had lost its summer mugginess. Richie was sitting close enough to Linda to detect the fragrance of her.

"Does your husband go to school here too?" he asked.

"Richie, I don't have a husband," she admitted. "Glenn and I got a divorce a few months ago. We were married for about two years, right out of high school, but it just didn't work out."

"Why do you still wear that?" he asked, indicating her wedding band.

"Do you really want to know?" Her tone was almost belligerent. "Because I got tired of every cheap Casanova I know making a pass at me. The minute word gets around that a girl is divorced, every guy she ever said hello to comes running to get the leftovers. They seem to think that if you're divorced, you're suddenly sex-starved and ready to jump into bed with anybody in pants. When I decided to start school, I put the ring back on. I thought that way I'd have an excuse not to date, and I wouldn't be bothered. All I want to do is study."

"Why are you telling me the truth, then?" Richie asked.

"Because we've known each other for so long. Besides," she raised one eyebrow disarmingly, "I know I can handle you, Richie. You've never been as tough as you like to think."

"In that case, can we start seeing each other? I've always wanted to date a divorced woman. I hear they're sex-starved."

"That's cute, but the answer is no." Linda's voice was stoical. "It has nothing to do with you, Richie. I just don't want to go out with *anybody*. I had a very unpleasant marriage; maybe it soured me on men in general, I don't know. All I want is to be left alone. Do you understand what I'm saying?"

"Sure," Richie said. "I won't bother you."

"Thanks."

They finished their coffee and went back inside.

Richie began a solitary life of study. Not solitary during the day, for at school he made many acquaintances and was seldom without someone with whom to discuss a class, visit the library, eat lunch. Often even Linda was part of a group that got together informally. But when the school day ended, Richie, like many others who lived off campus, Linda included, went his own way and thus did not become a part of the non-academic, social life of the university. It did not bother him; he rather liked being alone. In his little apartment he began making improvements, adding touches to personalize the place. He bought an unfinished bookcase, painted it, and began to fill it with books as soon as it was dry. He bought a portable typewriter, a couple of old movie posters for the walls, and a little radio to listen to while he fixed meals.

In addition to throwing himself into his studies with vigor, Richie also got out the short stories he had written in longhand in Korea, and typed them up to see how they would look. He also began to buy *The Writer* and *Writer's Digest* to study market requirements for freelance short stories. He bought every magazine on the newsstand that contained short fiction, and read them all voraciously, studying each story to see what he could learn from it. It did not matter to him who wrote the story, whether the author was well-known or *un*known; the story was *published*, and that, to Richie, was the primary gauge.

Sometimes, on a weekend when there was no school, Richie would find himself becoming restless for something to do besides study, read, or type. He was tempted several times to call Linda and invite her to a movie, but reminded himself that he had promised not to bother her. Once, during the week, he tried to call Grace Menefee to see if she would like to meet him on the weekend for lunch, but he was told she no longer worked for the welfare department; she had gotten married and moved to California.

Inevitably, when he needed to get out and do something different, Richie would find himself drawn back to the West Side neighborhoods where so much of his life had been lived. Taking a bus out to Madison and Kedzie, he strolled up Walnut Street, down Carroll Avenue, stood looking at Biedler or Calhoun or Grant elementary school and the schoolyards he had so dreaded. Once in a while he would sit in the Senate or Kedzie Annex theater for a couple of hours, or wander through some of the stores where he once shop-lifted, remembering. The thing that amazed him more than anything else in his rovings was how small everything seemed to have become. Streets and alleys where he had once run and hid were incredibly narrow; schoolyards were like postage stamps; the great, cavernous movie houses were small and claustrophobic, their seats inadequate and uncomfortable.

How the world shrinks, he thought, as a person expands.

One Saturday afternoon, Richie went out to Cascade Bowling Lanes and watched some people bowl for a while, then walked over to Midwest gym and watched a few fighters working out. He walked through Garfield Park, tossed some pebbles into the lagoon, and poked around behind the wild hedge where Toni had shown him the broken-down cardboard box that they used to make love on. It was hard for him to believe that the two of them had actually stripped naked and had passionate, lengthy intercourse right there in a public park. But then, it was becoming increasingly difficult for Richie to believe a *lot* of the things he had done.

On impulse, he decided to walk over to Maypole Avenue and see who might be hanging around Jo-Jo's these days, thinking that maybe if Toni were still around, or Marcella, he might invite one of them to spend the weekend with him in his apartment. When he got there, however, no one was around. The dwarfish little Jo-Jo was still on his high stool near the cash register, but he did not recognize Richie.

Richie bought a Coke and leaned against the counter drinking it. "What happened to all the kids who used to hang out in front?" he asked.

"Who knows?" Jo-Jo said, hunching his sloped little shoulders. "Kids come, kids go. Who can keep track?"

Finishing his Coke, Richie walked up Maypole and cut down Pulaski Road. He was very close to Linda's block now and wondered if he should just stroll by and maybe run into her. But he decided against it. He was yearning to spend more time with her, to try to make up to her for some of the bad experiences of her marriage, show her how to have fun again, but he respected her need for privacy and was determined not to intrude in her life. Walking past the Paradise Theater, he forgot about Linda and recalled the usher he had so brutally beaten up summers earlier. Thinking about it now made him feel ashamed.

When he got to Madison Street, Richie turned down toward Cascade again, having made a complete circle from where he started. Before he realized it, he was outside Solly's Poolroom and a voice was saying, "Well, well, look who's back."

Richie saw Bobby Casey standing there, leaning against the doorframe, smoking a cigarette. He had the same tightly curled hair and unfriendly eyes. Wearing a one-button-roll suit and dark sport shirt buttoned at the neck, he looked older, smarter, more confident. When Richie stopped, Bobby did not offer to shake hands.

"Where you been this time, bigshot?" he asked snidely. "Alcatraz or Harvard?"

"Korea," Richie said. "I've been in the Marines." Bobbing his chin at the door, he asked, "Stan inside?"

Bobby fixed him in a flat stare. "Stan's on Death Row, man. Waiting to go to the electric chair."

Richie felt the color leave his face.

*A*t the main branch of the public library, the massive building in which he had once spent so many hours of refuge from truant officers, welfare investigators, and just plain cops, Richie sat at a microfilm viewer scanning old editions of the *Sun-Times*. Turning the handle of the machine, he kept going to front page after front page until he found the headline he was looking for. It read: COP KILLED IN HOLDUP. A sub-head said: *Killer Wounded, Captured; One Other Escapes.*

The story that followed was what Bobby Casey had told Richie at the pool hall. Two armed men had abducted a currency exchange owner on his way to work and accompanied him to his business on the Northwest Side. As they were cleaning out the safe of some six thousand dollars in currency and rolled coins, an off-duty policeman, who lived in the neighborhood and was on his way to work, became suspicious because the exchange was late in opening. Driving around the block, he returned just as the two holdup men were leaving, each of them carrying a large briefcase. Pulling over, the officer identified himself and attempted to stop them for questioning. Both men dropped their briefcases and drew guns; the officer drew his own weapon. In the ensuing gunfight, the officer was killed, one holdup man wounded in the right shoulder and side, and the second holdup man escaped down an alley, leaving the money behind. The wounded holdup man, identified as twenty-one-year-old Stanley Klein, was in serious condition in Cook County Hospital jail, but was expected to recover.

Subsequent editions of the newpaper told the rest of the story in head-lines: KLEIN RECOVERED, READY FOR TRIAL; KLEIN REFUSES DEAL WITH DISTRICT ATTORNEY; KLEIN ON TRIAL FOR MURDER, D.A. SEEKS CHAIR; KLEIN WILL NOT TAKE STAND; KLEIN GUILTY; KLEIN SENTENCED TO DEATH.

The deal Stan had been offered was a life sentence in exchange for a guilty plea and identification of his accomplice, who had not been caught. Bobby, Richie thought. It had to be Bobby.

Going back to the West Side, Richie found Bobby Casey in Solly's again. Bobby was sitting on a raised spectator bench in the back, smoking a cigarette, drinking a beer, studying a racing form. There was no one nearby when Richie sat down next to him.

"It was you, wasn't it?" he said quietly, a statement as much as a question. "You were the other guy."

"What's it to you?" Bobby replied. "You a cop now?"

"I thought you were Stan's friend."

Bobby grunted. "Better friend than you ever were."

"Then why are you letting him go to the chair when you can save him by turning yourself in?"

Bobby looked at Richie as if he were an idiot. "You are so fucking stupid I can't believe it sometimes." Glancing around to make certain no one was near enough to hear, he lowered his voice anyway and said, "If I *was* the other guy, and I *did* turn myself in, all's they'd do would be put me on trial and I'd end up right where Stan is. Then we'd both fry. What the fuck would that accomplish—except maybe make you happy."

"The paper said the district attorney offered him a deal—"

"That was *before* the trial, you asshole. Jesus, you're dumb. Look, he's been tried and sentenced; the only way he can beat the chair is with an appeal or if he gets commuted to life."

"There must be *some* way to help him," Richie said fretfully.

Bobby Casey took a deep drag on his cigarette and studied Richie through the smoke he exhaled. He seemed to be weighing a sudden thought against some long-held premise that conflicted with it. After several moments, as Richie leaned forward and began to restlessly chew on a thumbnail, Bobby said quietly, "There's a way we can *try* to help him."

"How?" Richie asked, turning toward him eagerly.

"If we could raise the dough, we could pay this lawyer named Ned Fields to handle Stan's appeal. Right now, the fucking public defender is handling it, but they ain't gonna do no more than they have to. But this Ned Fields is a top criminal lawyer. I already had Solly call him and feel him out. He said he'd do it, but he wants his dough up front. Seventy-five hundred.''

"Jesus," said Richie. He had a little over a thousand saved from Korea, and from the retroactive combat pay he'd recently received. But a thousand was a long way from seventy-five hundred.

"There's a way to get it," Bobby said quietly, continuing to study Richie closely.

"How?" Richie asked again, suspiciously now, already knowing what was coming. Bobby Casey only knew one way to get money.

"Before the currency exchange job," Bobby confided, "Stan had figured out a new heist that he told me all about. Sticking up the spade drug dealers in the projects. It's a snap; they operate out of apartments where nobody can spot what's going on, and they can't call the cops after it's over. Stan figured we could get a grand or fifteen hundred off each one." Bobby took another long drag and shrugged his shoulders. "You and me ain't never been friends, but I'll hand you one thing—you always had balls and you never chickened out on nothing we ever did. If you and me was to throw in and knock off these niggers—"

"Forget it," Richie said emphatically. "That kind of shit is behind me, man. I'm in college, for Christ's sake. I'm trying to make something of my life."

Bobby drew away, his eyes and expression turning cold and contemptuous. "Forget I asked," he said scornfully. "I should of knowed better."

Rising, Bobby walked out of the poolroom.

The maximum security visiting room at Cook County Jail had two-inch plate-glass windows in each booth, with a speaker system activated by buttons on each side. Because of its size and criminal population, Cook County had its own electric chair and death row. Annually it put to death more men than the chair at Joliet Prison, which served the rest of the state. When Stan Klein was brought to the other side of the window, in handcuffs and a waist chain, wearing bright yellow condemned-man coveralls, he smiled at Richie in pure delight. Pressing the button, he said, "I couldn't believe it when they told me who my visitor was! Where the hell did you come from this time?"

Smiling back, Richie said, "Korea. I was in the Marines. Been back a few months now. I'm going to college out at Northwestern."

Stan shook his head in amazement. "I'll be goddamned. Well, it shouldn't surprise me." For a moment his expression turned serious, his thick eyebrows meeting above his nose. "While we're talking," he said evenly, "you don't mention no names unless I mention them first, understand? None of us in here know if the screws can listen in on visits or not, but we don't take no chances." Sitting back, smiling again, resting his cuffed hands on the ledge of the window, Stan said, "So tell me all about what you been doing since you left. The Marines, huh?"

Richie went over his last year in Lamont, his job at Sam Levy's, his involvement with Jennie, his enlistment in the Marine Corps, boot camp at Parris Island, South Carolina, infantry training at Camp Pendleton, California, weekends on the beach or in Tijuana, Mexico, and finally being shipped out to Korea, making the landing at Sok-cho-ri, and ending up trapped in the Punchbowl.

"Jesus," Stan said, "you sure manage to do a lot of living, kid. And now you're in college?"

"Yeah." Richie explained about the G. I. Bill and how he hoped to get a degree either in English literature or journalism. Stan made a sour face at the latter.

"Stay away from that," he advised. "One thing I learned in here— newspaper reporters are the scum of the fucking earth. The biggest fucking liars in the world."

Finally, quietly, Richie asked, "How does it look for you, Stan?"

"Just a matter of time. The public defender will go through the motions, lose the appeal, the fucking governor will turn down my request to be commuted to life, and one fine morning they'll strap me down to Old Sparky and my worries will be over. Just a matter of time."

"Suppose you had another lawyer? A *good* lawyer?"

Stan shrugged. "Takes a lot of dough. Anyway, even if I had the *best*, my chances of beating the chair, even for a life sentence, are very slim. I'm a cop killer, Richie. In Chicago, cop killers go to the chair."

When Richie's time was up, he promised to come back in two weeks, when non-family visitors were allowed, and on his way out left twenty dollars in Stan's account at the jail commissary. As he was getting his receipt at the commissary window, he found himself surrounded by four men in suits. Three of them had their hands under their coats.

"We're police officers," one of them said. "Will you come with us, please?"

Taking him into a nearby office, Richie was asked to identify himself, then questioned about his relationship with Stan Klein. "I've known him since we were kids," Richie said. "We went to grade school together, lived in the same building. I put all that on my application for a visit. What's this all about?"

"Klein's stickup partner has never been caught," said the detective, who was older and seemed to be in charge. They all stared somberly at Richie, who finally nodded in understanding.

"Sorry to disappoint you," he said, taking out his wallet, "but I've been in the service. I was in Korea when the holdup took place." He showed them a photostat of his discharge.

"We're going to have to check with the Marine Corps to make sure you weren't on leave or anything like that," the detective advised. "Nothing personal."

"Sure." They took his address and wrote down that he was attending Northwestern.

"You seem like a nice young man," the older detective said. "Marine veteran, college. What are you doing visiting a killer like this?"

"He wasn't always a killer," Richie replied evenly. "There was a time when he was just a kid, and the only place he fit in was on the street. That's who I'm visiting—that street kid." Unflinchingly meeting the detective's gaze, he asked, "Can I go now?"

They let him go, but he knew they were watching him all the way down the hall.

In the creative writing period, Mr. Crane reviewed the papers and grades of an assignment that had been turned in several days earlier.

"The assignment, as you know," he said, "was to rewrite a number of sentences in order to make them stronger. Overall, you did very well; a few of you did excellently; one or two did not do well at all. Our veteran, for instance," he handed Richie his papers, with a large red D on the front, "did nothing more than take each sentence and simplify it. You did understand that the object was to *strengthen* the sentences, did you not?"

"Yes, sir," Richie said. "But I thought that simplifying them, making them easier to read and understand, did strengthen them."

"Sorry, but I don't agree," said Crane. "I think that often by simplifying sentences, we make them weaker. If a reader is not challenged by a sentence, it can easily float right past that person's mind. But when a reader has to work at a sentence, when the mind has to digest it, then it, or at least its thought, remains permanently."

"I can see where that might apply to sentences written to teach," Richie argued. "Textbook writing and such. But this is 'creative' writing, which I thought was to entertain, possibly enlighten, but not actually to educate, as in a math or science book, for instance. If we're writing to entertain, shouldn't we keep it as simple as possible?"

"For what purpose?" Crane asked.

"So that a greater number of people can enjoy it."

"My, my, that sounds almost communistic," Crane commented. He smiled at the class. "I thought our veteran fought against Communism in Korea."

The class laughed as Richie felt himself turn red. No matter what he said in class, Crane always made him look not only mistaken but foolish. Richie had yet to receive a grade higher than a D. And Crane never addressed him by name, referring to him only as "our veteran." Had it not been for the fact that he was getting an A or B in every other class, he might have begun to harbor serious doubts that he was college material. As it was, he only wondered why he wasn't learning anything in Crane's class.

After classes that day, with his D paper in his canvas book bag, and with troubled thoughts of Stan Klein on his mind, Richie stood just outside one of the doors watching rain come down in torrents. He had a two-block walk to the streetcar and did not want to get his books and papers wet. As he was standing there, Linda came up beside him with her own book bag and an umbrella.

"Hi," she said. She was opening the umbrella.

"Oh, hi."

"Wouldn't you be closer to the dorm going out the other end of the building?" she asked.

"I don't live in the dorm. I've got a little apartment a couple of miles from here."

"I didn't know that," Linda said, surprised.

Shrugging, Richie said, "How could you? We never talk about anything personal."

She colored slightly. "That's right, we don't." Looking around at the pouring rain, she said, "Would you like a lift home? I have a car."

Now it was Richie who was surprised. "I didn't know you had a car."

"How could you? We never talk about anything personal. Listen, you hold my books, I'll take the umbrella, go get my car, and pick you up." Without waiting for his concurrence, she handed him her book bag, put the umbrella over her head, and dashed away through puddles toward the student parking lot.

While she was gone, Richie thought of Stan again, sitting in a cell wearing yellow coveralls, waiting to go to the electric chair. He knew Stan was guilty, knew he should be punished for killing the policeman. But in Richie's mind there was mitigation: the policeman was also trying to kill Stan. Granted, that was his job, but Richie knew how it felt to kill under the pressure of fear; he remembered the Chinese woman with the white flag.

Linda pulled up beside him. Her car was an old Studebaker with a body that had seen better days, but as she said when he got in, "It gets me to and from school and it's cheaper than living in the dorm, and more convenient than taking the streetcar." When they got off campus and stopped for a red light, she said, "Sorry about your D from Crane. What's his problem with you anyway?"

"Beats me," Richie replied. "Maybe he doesn't like vets."

"He's really on you. Several people in class have commented about it. I hope he doesn't fail you."

"Doesn't worry me," Richie told her. "What bothers me is that I'm not *learning* anything. I took the class to learn how to write better. That's not happening." He looked at her. "Are you learning anything from him?"

"I'm not sure," Linda said. "It's very interesting, the theory and all—"

"But is your writing improving?"

"I don't know—"

"Then it isn't," Richie stated emphatically. "If your writing was improving, you'd know it. I can *feel* the writing I do outside of class assignments getting better, but as far as what he's having us do in class is concerned, I'm getting nothing. Hey," he suddenly expanded the subject, "I finally sent a story to a magazine."

"You did? Richie, that's wonderful! When? Where?"

"Well, there's this magazine called *The Writer*—"

"Yes, I've seen it in the library."

"It has freelance market news in it every month, telling which magazines are looking for stories, what kind, how much they pay, that kind of stuff. I dug out a story I wrote longhand on Red Cross stationery while I was in the rest camp in Korea. It was only 917 words long, but I rewrote it and made it three thousand words, and I sent it to one of the magazines on the market list."

"Aren't you excited?" Linda enthused. "Actually having your own story at a magazine?"

"I'd be more excited if they bought it," he said. "They probably won't, but I think it's good experience anyway, actually submitting something. I think it's a sign of commitment."

Studying him, Linda said, "God, you're getting deep, you know that?"

"Stop at the next corner," Richie said. "Just drop me off at that pizza parlor; that's where I'm having supper."

"Want some company?" Linda asked suddenly.

"Yeah, sure, if you're serious," he said, surprised.

"I'm serious."

Linda parked and they hurried into the little neighborhood pizzeria, shaking the rain off when they got inside. Richie took Linda's coat and hung it with his own on a rack inside the door.

Waiting for their Italian sausage and meatball pizza, Linda wanted to know all about the short story he had submitted for publication. Richie told her how he had remembered Willie Wakefield and written "Hit and Run" about a young fighter losing for the first time. Explaining how he had plotted the story, he got excited, telling her exactly how he had lengthened it, how easy it had been. No research at all had been involved; everything he needed to know was already in his mind from his own days in the gym and the club fights he had fought.

"I think it's marvelous," she said when he finished. "I just know it's going to sell!"

"Wish you were an editor," he told her.

Linda excused herself to go call her mother and tell her she would not be home for supper. While she was gone, Richie's mind went back to Stan. It seemed that whenever he had an idle moment, when he was reading or studying or working on a story, he thought of his friend. A compelling particular of his thoughts was always how many times Stan had helped him when he needed it, and how he was helpless when Stan needed help.

When Linda returned to the booth, the pizza was there, thick with cheese, piled with meat. "I'm glad to see you're eating stuff like this," Linda commented. "It'll put some weight on you. You're too skinny."

"You've been telling me that ever since we've known each other," Richie said.

"Yes, I know."

They became awkwardly quiet as a mutual memory of the past swept over them. Linda colored slightly again and they both smiled self-consciously when their eyes met. They ate the pizza and talked about school and Linda told him how uncertain she was about what she wanted to do in life.

"One minute I want to teach and be like Miss White, really make a difference with kids, you know? But the next minute I hear about you actually submitting a story you wrote, and I get goosebumps thinking maybe I can become a writer. Does that happen to you?"

"Never," Richie said unequivocally. "I don't want to be anything but a writer."

"You are *really* getting deep," she said again.

It was just becoming dark when they left the pizzeria. The rain had stopped and the air was cool with a hint of winter. "I love the way the city smells after it rains," Richie said. "It's the only time I consciously enjoy breathing. Hey, I've got to get my books out of your car."

"I can drive you home," Linda said.

"I just live right here, the fourth building," Richie said. He paused a beat, indecisively, then asked, "You want to come up and see my place? It's nothing fancy, but I've kind of fixed it up."

Linda's expression became softly solemn. "All right, Richie," she said.

He got his books and took her up to the little efficiency that he had settled into so comfortably with his books and movie posters and radio and a small study desk he had bought. Everything was in its place and in order, as he had been taught in the Marine Corps, and Linda was immediately impressed. "What a nice place, Richie. And how neat you are. I'd be embarrassed to show you *my* room."

Richie put his hands on her shoulders from behind. "You should never be embarrassed about anything with me," he said. "We go back too far for that."

She twisted away from his hands. "Don't, please. I didn't come up here for that." Facing him, her eyes became accusing. "I hope you're not going to be like all the rest, Richie."

"What do you mean?"

"I told you the day of our first class why I put my wedding ring back on—so I wouldn't have to fight off the guys who think divorced women are pushovers."

"You know me better than that, Linda," he said quietly. "I'm the guy you used to sit in the back row of the Paradise with, remember? I always stopped when you wanted me to."

She turned away and he barely heard the sob that she choked back. Richie went to her again, put his hands on her shoulders again.

"What changed you, Linda? Was it Glenn?"

She did not answer at once, but he sensed that she was trying to, looking for the words, so he waited. Finally she said it.

"There are some . . . things . . . that I didn't think I should have to do. Some things that I didn't want to do. But he made me. He was very ugly about it . . ."

Richie put his lips close to her ear. "It's okay. You don't have to talk about it."

Turning again, she came into his arms. "I haven't been very fair to you, have I?"

Don't look for life to be fair. Stan had told him that years ago.

"You haven't been fair to yourself," he said. "You can't cut yourself off from someone who cares for you, because of someone else." He lifted her chin and made her look at him. "I'm not Glenn, Linda. I won't ever make you do anything you don't want to do."

"Promise," she said, swallowing nervously.

"Promise," he assured her.

Helping her out of her coat, Richie hung it with his own in the closet. Flicking off the overhead light so that only a small reading lamp was on, he turned back and unbuttoned her cardigan sweater all the way down, exposing a white bra and part of her breasts. They put their arms around each other and kissed softly, gently, and then Richie pulled his own sweater over his head. As Linda took off her skirt and sat in his reading chair to remove her shoes and stockings, Richie turned on the radio and found some music and pulled the bed out of the wall. Undressing, he saw Linda turn her back and slip her panties from under the half slip she wore. Dropping the straps of her bra, she twisted it around and unclasped it in front.

When he was naked, Richie sat on the side of the bed and drew her to him. He started to pull the half slip down but she stopped him. "I want to leave it on for now," she said. "I'm self-conscious about my thighs; they're heavy."

Drawing her onto the bed, Richie lay partly over her and they began to kiss in earnest, sucking each other's lips and tongue wetly. Moving his face down, he kissed and licked and sucked her nipples, while with one hand he stroked between her legs through the slip. He ran his tongue along the underside of each breast as he held them up, then drew a line of wet down to her navel and spiraled the tip of his tongue into it. Gradually he moved his mouth to the soft mound under the slip and kissed it through the thin material, alternately blowing his warm breath between her legs. When finally he pressed his tongue to her and began licking her with the slip still between them, he heard Linda moan softly and felt her relax. Spreading her legs, he felt the slip becoming wet as he pressed his open mouth onto her and started to suck.

After a while, the half slip became so soggy that she allowed him to take it off. By that time she was holding on to his head.

*B*obby Casey parked the stolen car at the curb across the street from one of the housing project buildings. Next to him, Richie looked out at the long line of uninspired and uninspiring ten-story low-rent buildings that stretched, run-down and overcrowded, for blocks in all directions. Bobby had parked the car deliberately under a streetlight so that it could be seen from the windows of the nearest project building.

"You ready?" he asked quietly.

"Yeah," Richie replied, just as quietly, "let's go."

Getting out, they tried to act casual as they crossed the street and started along the sidewalk leading to the building. It wasn't easy to do; each of them had a gun stuck in the top of the army surplus combat boots they wore. As Richie walked, the trouser leg covering the boot with the gun seemed to drag uncomfortably; he nervously wondered if it could be detected by anyone looking at him.

Richie had waited two weeks after visiting Stan Klein before going back to Solly's to see Bobby. "Do you think Stan might have a chance at a life sentence if we get that lawyer you told me about?" he asked.

"There's always a *chance*," Bobby replied. "Not much of one, I don't think. But even one in a million is worth having when a guy's looking at the fucking chair."

Sitting on a rear spectator bench again, Richie buried his face in his hands for a moment, as if girding himself for what came next. Then he looked up, sighed resignedly, and said, "Okay, tell me about the dope peddler heists."

He and Bobby took a walk in the park. "The way Stan had the thing figured," Bobby explained, "was that individual dealers had to be hit hard and fast, before they could get together and work out any protection. Stan had six apartments picked out, all in different buildings; he located them through a little Filipino junkie that lived at the Parkside Hotel for a while; he used to pay Stan to go with him to make buys 'cause he was scared of getting jumped and rolled by the spades in the projects. Anyways, Stan's idea was to hit two of these places early Monday night, after the heavy weekend trade; then hit two more late Tuesday night when business was just about over and they was starting to relax. Then lay off for a couple nights, see, like it's all over, but come back for the last two early Friday evening when the dealers have cash on hand to make wholesale buys." Bobby paused to light a cigarette. "It's been a while since this was planned, so I'll have to case the places. But if everything's okay, and if we can average twelve-fifty each hit, that'd give us what we need for the lawyer."

"You're sure he'll take the case?" Richie asked.

"Solly checked with him over the phone, without giving no name. The guy said if seventy-five hundred was left at his office with Stan's name on it, he would figure it was a retainer and go see Stan right away."

Richie took the final step quickly, before having a moment to evaluate the senselessness of what he was committing to.

"Okay, let's do it," he said. "Set it up."

"Solid!" Bobby Casey said. He came close to smiling at Richie for the first time ever. "I've got a rod stashed for myself, but I'll have to get one for you—"

"No, you won't," Richie said. "I've got a forty-five automatic. I brought it back from Korea."

"No kidding?" A cynical expression settled on Bobby's face. "What for? An ace in the hole in case you didn't make it in college?"

"A souvenir," Richie told him.

"Sure, sure," Bobby Casey said mockingly. "Naturally you never intended to do nothing illegal with it, right?" He grunted derisively. "You know something, Richie, underneath you ain't no different from Stan and me. Never have been, never will be. No matter how much you pretend."

Glaring at him, Richie had said coldly, "Just set up the jobs, Bobby. I'll check back with you in a few days."

Richie had been nagged by Bobby's words. Why *had* he stolen that pistol from the Marine Corps and brought it home hidden at the bottom of his seabag? Was it because somewhere deep in his subconscious he knew he would someone revert to his former self and have need of it? Was Bobby Casey right: was he really no different from them?

That thought continued to plague him even now as he walked side by side with Bobby Casey into the project building. Then, as they got into the self-service elevator, as all else left his mind except that they were about to *do* it, he felt his stomach knot up and his hands begin to tremble. Glancing at Bobby, he saw him wet his lips, and saw that his hands were trembling also. Bobby caught his eye.

"You okay?" he asked quietly.

"Yeah," Richie said. "You?"

"Yeah. Be glad when this first one's over."

On four, they left the elevator and found the apartment where Stan's Filipino friend had once gone. Bobby knocked softly. A voice on the other side said, "Who is it?"

"Junior sent us," Bobby replied. That had been Stan's original idea. "There ain't a nigger alive who don't know somebody named Junior," he had told Bobby.

The door opened not on one chain but three. An unsmiling black face peered out and asked, "Junior who?"

"Junior from over to the other building, man. Come on." Bobby flashed a roll of bills and shifted from foot to foot as if he might be on edge for a fix. "Come on, man," he said again, half whining. Jesus, he's got balls, Richie thought with grudging admiration.

The door opened and they stepped inside to face three black men, one of whom held a small chromed revolver on them. "Got to search you, boys," he said. "No offense."

"Okay man, just don't take all night," Bobby said irritably. He and Richie raised their hands and one of the other men quickly felt around their waists and under their arms. If whoever patted them down found their guns, Richie and Bobby were agreed that they would not try to score, merely say the weapons were for their own protection, then make a buy and leave. But as Stan had predicted, the search was cursory; if no guns were found above the knees, they would pass inspection. And they did.

"They clean," the man who searched them announced. The one with the pistol smiled and put it away.

"What you need, boys?" he asked.

"Five dime bags," Bobby said, peeling off fifty dollars, tossing it on a table. "Okay if I sit down?"

"Make yourself comfortable." One of them took the money and went into the bedroom. Bobby sat at the table. Richie, leaning against the wall, knew Bobby had pulled his trouser leg up as he sat down, uncovering his gun. The man with the chrome pistol in his pocket stood near the windows, watching them closely.

Presently the first black man returned to the room with five glassine envelopes which he put on the table. Bobby started to reach for them, then looked across the room and said, "Hey, man, somebody's looking in the fucking window!"

The man with the pistol whirled around and the other two snapped their faces open-mouthed toward the windows. Then they heard Bobby say, "One move, just one, motherfuckers, and you are gone!" He had them covered in an instant, and Richie was pulling his automatic out of his boot-top to back him up. Disarming the man with the gun, Bobby had two of them lie on the floor with Richie covering them, while he took the boss dealer into the bedroom.

In five minutes, the drug money had been found, the men's wallets and pockets cleaned out, and all the glassine envelopes of heroin collected in a paper bag.

"Okay, get up and stand by the window, all of you," Bobby ordered. "Look out the window. See that blue car under the streetlight? That's our car. Now listen carefully 'cause I'm gonna make you a deal. My partner's gonna take your dough and your dope down to the car while I stay here with you guys. When he gets down there and signals me, I'm gonna go down the fire stairs and you guys are all gonna stand in front of the window where he can see you. If nobody follows me, when I get out to the car, we'll leave your junk on the curb and drive off. That way, you'll only be out the dough. But if anybody tries to follow me, I'll shoot the motherfucker and we'll take the fucking shit with us; then you'll be out everything. It's up to you." While they were digesting the deal, Bobby nodded brusquely to Richie. "Go."

Sticking the automatic in his belt, leaving his coat unbuttoned so he could get to it quickly, Richie left the apartment and started down the enclosed fire stairs. He walked briskly, passing two young black boys reading comic books on one landing, a teenage boy feeling up a girl in the dark corner of another. When he reached ground level, he pushed open the fire door and cut across the bare, grassless front yard of the building to their car. Looking up, he saw Bobby's face at the window and waved; then he saw Bobby move away and the three black men kneel side by side, looking out.

Getting into the car, Richie turned the ignition that Bobby had hot-wired earlier and started the car, leaving it in neutral, letting the engine idle. He kept glancing up to make sure the three faces were still in the window.

Removing the money from the bag, he stuffed it into his shirt. Sweating profusely, he got back out, letting the chilly night air cool him. He checked the faces again; they were still there. Leaving the driver's door open for Bobby, he went around the car and opened the passenger door for himself. Then he saw Bobby trotting across the street to the car, looking back over his shoulder at the window.

"Leave 'em their dope," Bobby said as he hurried up.

Richie stepped over to the streetlight and set the paper bag on the curb. As he straightened, he looked at the men in the window again. They were still there, watching, doing nothing to jeopardize getting back their stock in trade. Suddenly Richie thought of his mother. In his mind he saw her young and pretty as she had once been, and watched in horror as the image slowly changed to drug-ravaged and degenerated. Grimly he snatched back the bag and began removing the glassine envelopes. There was a sewer grate just in front of the streetlight and Richie methodically began dropping the shiny envelopes into the dark sewer.

"What the fuck are you doing?" Bobby demanded from the car. He had the headlights on, ready to leave. Ignoring him, Richie continued to cram the heroin through the sewer grating. When he had disposed of it all, he looked up and saw that there was only one face left in the window. Grabbing his muscle with one hand, he rotated his fist at the black man: Fuck you. Then he hurried to the car and Bobby screeched away from the curb. Two of the black men were running out of the building as they sped away.

"What the fuck did you do that for?" Bobby demanded as he guided the car into boulevard traffic.

"Because I felt like it," Richie said coldly.

"Why? 'Cause your old lady was a junkie?"

"Mind your own fucking business!" Richie snapped.

"Hey, my old man was a juicer, but I don't go around breaking bottles of booze—"

"Good for you. Now drop it!"

"Okay, I will!" Bobby snapped back. "But on the next one, it's *my* turn to leave with the bag and *your* turn to stay behind. And I'm leaving the dope, see? That was part of Stan's plan—leave the junk and they prob'ly wouldn't come after us. You're gonna fuck things up and put too much heat on us!"

"Okay, okay!" Richie conceded. "We'll leave the shit from now on!" Snatching out a handkerchief, he wiped a sheet of sweat from his face.

Bobby was right, he knew. It was a little late to try getting even for his mother. The main thing right now was to try and help Stan.

As they drove, Richie kept one hand under his coat, on the grip of the automatic. His souvenir.

Linda was coming home with Richie two or three nights a week. They usually stopped at a market to pick something up for supper, then went to the apartment, put the groceries away, and got undressed immediately to make love. From a frightened, almost frigid girl, Linda had quickly become an eager, sensual young woman who lusted for Richie's body and ministrations as much as he did for hers. Sexually they were highly attuned, compatible in attitude, smooth in intercourse, pliant in experimentation. Like Frances Rozinski had been nearly a decade earlier, Linda was fascinated by Richie's ejaculate; she could not get enough of watching him come, so much so that half of their lovemaking was done with hand or mouth.

"I love it when you spurt," she said often, delighting in masturbating him into her mouth or onto her breasts.

They made love, one way or another, twice each night that she was over. Because Richie had later classes on some days, he gave her a key so that she could do the shopping and take care of putting supper on, then be ready for him when he got home. Neither of them wanted to waste a minute; their time together was precious to them.

The compulsion for each other took a toll in other areas. Richie's work on his short stories slackened, and his study time, particularly for Mr. Crane's creative writing class, where he was striving so diligently to grasp what he was missing, was reduced significantly. Linda was having problems at home. "My mother knows something's up," she told Richie. "I keep telling her I'm going to the library or to a special tutoring class or something, but I don't think I'm fooling her. I've been so relaxed lately, I'm sure she's noticed a difference in me. The other day I saw her rummaging through my laundry basket, looking at my underwear. Probably checking for stains."

When Richie began the drug-dealer stickups, he had to have an excuse for the nights he would be out. He hated lying to Linda and tried to stay as close to the truth as possible. Telling her about Stan Klein's situation, he said, "A few of us are trying to raise money to help him get a better lawyer. We're soliciting donations from people who might want to help him. It'll only be for a few nights now and then."

Linda's face had registered disappointment. "Oh, Richie," she said unhappily. "You're not going to get mixed up with hoodlums again, are you?"

"Stan was a close friend of mine, honey; at one time he was the *only* close friend I had. I can't let him down when he's in trouble."

Nodding her head knowingly, Linda said, "Some friend. I remember reading about his case in the papers. That officer he murdered had a wife and three children."

"Look, I know he did a terrible thing; I'm not saying he shouldn't be punished. I just want him to have a fair chance at a life sentence instead of the electric chair."

"I wish you'd just stay away from the whole thing and everybody involved in it," Linda said stoically.

"I owe Stan, honey," he said resolvedly. "It'll only be for a few nights, then I'll drop it."

When Richie and Bobby Casey pulled their second stickup the first night, in a building far across the projects, they had, as agreed beforehand, reversed roles, with Bobby leaving first with the loot and Richie holding the drug dealers at bay. Without telling Bobby, Richie had pinned his Sharpshooter pistol medal from the Marine Corps on his shirt, and after Bobby hurried out of the apartment, he had pulled his coat back to show it to the men he was covering.

"See this?" he said coldly. "Take a good look at it! It means I know how to use this fucking gun I'm holding! Any of you fuck with me and I'll shoot you right in the fucking balls!"

At that moment, he had felt ready to kill. Not only for what people like them helped do to his mother, but also to preserve the new life he now had, and his future with Linda. He did not *want* to kill, but he wanted them to know he could, and would, if necessary. The men believed him; nobody did anything foolish. On that holdup, Bobby Casey left the heroin on the curb, as he had agreed.

From the two stickups on Monday, Richie and Bobby netted thirty-one hundred dollars. After they ditched the stolen car, Bobby insisted that Richie take care of the money. "You're clean," he said. "Aside from that bullshit at the jail when you visited Stan, the cops don't even know you no more. Juvenile records in Illinois are destroyed when you're eighteen, so you're practically a cherry, man. The dough'll be safer with you."

Richie wrapped the money in an undershirt and put it at the bottom of his old seabag in the back of his closet.

On the second night of holdups, carried out in still other far-flung areas of the vast housing project, Richie and Bobby varied their routine a little. In case word had spread about *two* white stickup men, one of them now hid on the stairs and waited while the other one went in alone. After the one going in got control, he let the other in. The third and fourth holdups went as smoothly as the previous pair, and each time the heroin was left behind as balm to mollify the dealers who had lost their money. The second night, they grabbed twenty-three hundred dollars which increased their legal fund to five thousand four hundred. "One more night should do it," Bobby Casey said. "Friday night, the way Stan planned. Okay with you?"

"Yeah, sure," Richie said. When he got back to his apartment after the second night of holdups, he felt thrashed, drained, lifeless. He slept for twelve hours, missing his morning classes the next day. When he finally went to school at noon, he encountered a very concerned Linda.

"Richie, my god, you look terrible. Are you sick?"

"I think I've got stomach flu or something," he said, not too convincingly. Linda felt his forehead to see if he had a fever.

"How late were you out last night?" she asked peevishly.

"I got home around midnight," he said, and instantly regretted not lying. There was no way she could check on him; he had no telephone. But he had told the truth without thinking, and he could tell by the look on her face that she was upset.

"Why you are running around until all hours trying to help that lowlife is something I simply cannot understand," she said crossly. "And where in the world do you solicit money that late at night? Are you sure you're not involved in something you're not telling me about?"

"Yes, I'm sure, Linda," he replied evenly. "Anyway, Friday night is my last night to help, then I'll be through with it. Okay?"

"Well, I hope so, " she said adamantly. "I've made up my mind to tell my mother about us. That means I'll be taking you out to meet her. I wouldn't want to have to conceal anything from her that I was ashamed of. After what she went through with my father, and what I went through with Glenn, we are both very choosy about men, very discriminating."

"I'll try to come up to everyone's standards," Richie remarked.

Linda's lips compressed as she readied a retort, but at that moment a buzzer signaled the call to class. "We'll discuss this after creative writing," she said instead.

Richie shook his head. "I've changed my mind about going to class; I don't think I could take Crane today. I'm going back home. Come on over later," he said walking away. Over his shoulder he added, "If you want to."

Walking off the campus, for the first time Richie felt about the university as he remembered feeling about Lamont. Once again he was not sure that he belonged where he was.

On Friday night, Richie and Bobby hit it lucky on their first holdup. In the car as Bobby sped into boulevard traffic to drive to still another part of the projects, Richie quickly counted their loot. "Jesus Christ, we got twenty-seven hundred bucks off those guys," he said elatedly. "That gives us over eight grand. Skip the other one, let's ditch the car."

"Let's hit the other one for ourselves," Bobby said. "I could use a little quick bread."

"No deal," Richie said. "I was in for seventy-five hundred; we've made that and more. Now let's ditch the car."

"Sure, what the fuck do you care?" Bobby grumbled. "The fucking government's giving you a free ride."

The remark made Richie think of Mr. Crane. "Hey, fuck you, Casey! I've never had a free ride in my life. And I'm not going to pull a stickup to give you one. You can have whatever's left after you hire the lawyer. When that runs out, get a fucking job. Wise up and get off the street before you end up where Stan is."

Bobby gave him the surliest look he could muster and fell silent. Guiding the car off the boulevard he kept to side streets back across town to the edge of the Loop, then cut up Lake Street, driving under the el tracks, as he headed toward the fringes of the black neighborhood where they would ditch the car. Bobby always left the car in a black area, so blacks would be blamed for the theft and keep the heat off the white neighborhoods where he circulated.

As they cruised up Lake Street, Richie suddenly said, "Stop the car."

"What for?"

"Stop the fucking car!" he ordered, grabbing the wheel and swerving them to the curb, narrowly missing one of the steel pillars of the el tracks.

"Jesus Christ, are you crazy!" Bobby yelled. "What the fuck's wrong with you? You almost wrecked us!"

Richie ignored him. He was staring out the window at a circle of light under a streetlight at the corner of one of the dark little alleys that punctured Lake Street. In the circle of light, a snappily-dressed black man was slapping a black woman's face as she tried futilely to ward off his blows.

Expression stone-set with anger, Richie got out of the car as Bobby Casey said urgently after him, "What the fuck are you doing, man? That ain't your business!" Continuing to ignore him, Richie stalked across the street. By the time he got to the circle of light, the black man had his fingers entwined in the woman's short, kinky hair and was butting her forehead against the streetlight. The woman was Vernie, and she was bleeding from a cut above one eye.

"Leave her alone," Richie said, walking up. The black turned on him indignantly.

"You ofay motherfucker, who the fuck you think you talking to?"

Richie's hand came out from under his coat with the automatic. As if feinting a right jab, he clipped the black man across the cheekbone with the barrel. Stunned, the black man dropped to his knees. Slapping a pearl-gray hat off his head, Richie took hold of the man's hair just as the man had done to Vernie. "Open your mouth!" he ordered. When the man did not immediately obey, Richie viciously pushed the muzzle of the gun against his lips, forcing them apart. When the man's mouth came open, Richie shoved the barrel three inches into it and cocked the hammer. "Taste it, you mother-fucker!" he snarled. "That's what death tastes like."

"Don't hurt him, mister," Vernie said, holding on to the streetlight for balance. "Please don't hurt him . . ."

Her voice had an odd, injured tone to it, like the last words of a con-demned person begging forgiveness for the executioner. Richie stared at her. "Vernie, don't you remember me?"

She squinted suspiciously at him. "I know you?"

"I'm Richie, remember? You used to walk with me to keep the colored kids from taking my money when I came down here to buy paregoric for my mother."

Wiping the blood out of one eye, Vernie smiled almost lazily at him. "Oh, yeah. Po' skinny little white boy, had a junkie for a mamma." She grunted softly. "Now we all junkies. I be's a junkie, he be's a junkie," she pointed to the terrified man with the pistol barrel in his mouth. "Please don't hurt him," she begged again.

"You, Vernie?" Richie said incredulously. "You're a junkie?" He thought about her beautiful handwriting, her confident strut, the way she had always moved through life like she owned it.

"Take the gun out his mouf', Richie," she begged. "He scared."

"But look what he did to you, Vernie," Richie protested. "He was smash-ing your face; you're bleeding. He's a fucking animal!"

"He all I got, Richie," she said.

The enormity of her simple statement impacted on Richie like a rifle butt to the chest. *He all I got . . .* Suddenly feeling ill, Richie took the gun out of the black man's mouth and stepped away from him. Vernie dropped to her knees next to the trembling man and put her arms around him. Rocking him gently she cooed, "You okay, baby. Vernie take care of you now." Looking up at Richie, she said just as gently, "Go on, Richie. I ain't your business."

"Sure," Richie said, barely a whisper. *He all I got.*

Richie walked listlessly back toward the car. In the middle of the street he encountered Bobby Casey, gun in hand, ready to back up whatever Richie was doing—whether he himself approved of it or not. And Bobby clearly did not; he was intensely agitated as they got back into the car and he angrily drove them away.

"You're crazy, you know that," Bobby lambasted him. "I'm glad we're finished tonight. I don't want nothin' else to do with you. College, shit! You oughta be in a fucking nut ward. You're dangerous, man."

Richie did not respond. *He all I got.* He was too haunted by Vernie's words to digest what Bobby was saying. All he could think was: It got Vernie. The fucking hard city got Vernie.

They left the car near an el station and waited on the platform for their respective trains. "Bring the dough up to Solly's tomorrow and I'll see it gets to the lawyer," Bobby said. When his train came, he simply added, "See you," and got on.

Richie took a train the other way, to the Loop, and transferred to a North Side train. All the way home, he sat staring at his reflection in the window as Vernie's pathetic words echoed in his mind. *He all I got.*

What a rotten fucking goddamn world it is, he thought as he entered his little apartment. Turning on the reading lamp, he stood next to the table and tossed the money onto it and put his gun on top of the money. Only then did he see Linda sitting in his big chair where she had been waiting in the dark. She shook her head in disgust.

"I thought it was something like this," she said sanctimoniously. She was looking at him as if he were slime. "You'll always be a hoodlum. I know that now."

"You don't know a goddamned thing about anything," he said quietly.

"I know one thing," she retorted, gathering up her coat, purse, and books. "I know how to say goodbye."

Richie did not even look at her as she walked out.

*R*ichie was hanging his coat on the back of the visiting cage chair when they brought Stan in on the other side of the window. With a strained grin, Richie pressed the speaker button and said, "Hey, Stan. Happy New Year."

"Happy New Year, kid," Stan replied, adjusting his wrist cuffs and waist chain as he sat down. "You look like hell. Too much celebrating?"

"Not really celebrating. Just too much wine last night. How was Christmas in here?"

"Wonderful. Big, beautiful tree with lots of decorations. Presents for everyone. Lots of singing and gaiety. And as a special treat we got to fuck the guards up the ass. How was yours?"

"Exactly the same except for the guards."

"You spend it alone?"

"Yeah. New Year's Eve too."

"That's what happens when you're an asshole and lose your girlfriend."

Richie had told him about breaking up with Linda, but had not told him why. Similarly, Stan had told Richie that a well-known criminal attorney, Ned Fields, was now handling the appeal of his death sentence, but Stan had never mentioned how Fields was being paid. Richie assumed that Stan figured Bobby Casey had something to do with it, but had no idea whether Stan even suspected that he himself had also been involved. Bobby's name had never been mentioned during any of their dozen visits.

"How's your mother?" Richie asked, to direct the conversation away from himself.

"Fine, fine. Yeah, the old lady's finally doing all right for herself. After she married that guy with the little neighborhood bar, she really settled down. Helps him run the place and everything. She keeps thinking I'm gonna beat this rap and get out someday; got it all planned that I'll go to bartender school and then work in the place. She never gives up."

"You sound like you have," Richie observed.

Stan shrugged. "I always expect the worst; that way I'm never disappointed. Anyway, I ain't complaining. I took my chances and I lost. That's the breaks."

"You ever feel sorry about the cop?" Richie asked quietly. Stan shook his head emphatically.

"Nope. No more than he would have felt sorry for me. He took his chances too. We both lost. He just lost quicker." Stan paused to light a cigarette, then changed the subject. "You really look like hell, Richie. You drinking too much?"

"What's too much?" Richie asked. His words had the edge of a challenge. "I drink a little wine at night to relax. Anything wrong with that?"

Ignoring the question, Stan asked another of his own. "How's school? You think that guy Crane will fail you?"

Grunting, Richie said, "No, he'll give me a D and let me pass just so he'll have me in the second semester of the class. I think I'm half the guy's fun in life."

Stan called Crane a few filthy names, then sat forward eagerly for the part of Richie's visits that he liked best. "Okay, so tell me all about what you been writing the last two weeks."

Richie leaned forward also; it was his favorite part of the visits too. The make-believe world was so much easier to talk about, and think about.

For both of them.

Richie was correct about his final grade in creative writing; he received a D-minus, the lowest possible passing grade, and went into the second semester of the class. In all his other subjects he received either A or B.

Life in the new class was no better for him than it had been in the previous one. When they were in the area of plotting, Crane judged Richie's work to be uninventive. "Our veteran has used too many ordinary ploys in an attempt to keep the reader interested. That is what I refer to as 'common' writing. A really polished writer holds on to his reader with smooth, interesting prose that stimulates the mind, original phrasing that lures the reader ever onward. Our veteran's writing is at best crude.''

Richie fared no better when they turned to characterization. "I'm afraid our veteran's characters are much like his narrative prose—totally lacking in style. Characters in a story ideally should be on a higher plane than the reader, so that the reader can mentally reach up to them and, grasping those characters, raise himself to their level. Reading for pleasure is, after all, supposed to be an uplifting experience.''

Whatever phase of creative writing the class undertook, Richie's work, in Mr. Crane's estimation, always fell far short of even the most modest plane. Not that Crane criticized Richie exclusively; he did not. Several others in the class endured unfavorable review of their work on a more or less regular basis. But it was Richie who seemed to get it the most relentlessly.

Dedicating himself diligently to improving his understanding of what Crane was teaching, Richie borrowed other students' essays that had been graded highly, and studied them at night for style and content. Most of them beautifully reflected the themes and topics that Richie recalled Crane emphasizing in class—but to him their sum total did not make a *story*. A vignette perhaps; a story, no. Richie's concept of a story, born in dark movie theaters, nursed on comic books, fed by the *Saturday Evening Post* and *Collier's*, maturing through the ''best plays'' of each year as far back as the 1930s, and finally buffed to a deep, shining belief by hundreds of paperback editions over the years—Richie's concept was that a *story* had a beginning, a middle, and an end. So many of the papers that Crane praised had only a middle; they left Richie hungry to know what came before, what happened afterward. Richie did not believe in leaving a reader hungry.

Eventually Richie found that he could not contain his feelings; he began to argue openly with Crane. "I don't see how," he would challenge, "you can call that piece of writing good. It uses archaic language that ninety percent of the population today wouldn't understand, and even though it's supposed to be a modern setting, all of its characters exhibit outmoded values. People don't think or talk that way anymore.''

"Well now, is our veteran presuming to speak for the world at large?'' Crane asked.

"No,'' Richie replied patiently, "just for myself. In my opinion, that kind of writing would not sell today.''

"It is also your opinion that the purpose of writing *is* to sell?'' Crane asked.

"The end purpose is to be published,'' Richie declared.

"One can be published without being paid," Crane declared back.

"I would consider my work to have more value if I were paid by someone to publish it."

"Have you ever *been* published?" Crane asked, looking down his nose at Richie.

"No, I haven't," Richie replied. "Have you?"

Crane put on his smuggest expression. "That is an impertinent question which I do not intend to address."

After class, Linda fell in beside him for a few steps. "Why do you argue with him like that?" she criticized. "Challenging him isn't going to get you anywhere."

Richie stared incredulously at her. She had not spoken to him in more than three months, and now, without preliminaries, she was reproaching him. "I argue with him because I don't think he's right. What do you care anyway?"

"I don't," she snapped, and stalked away.

In the midst of this cheerless time, waiting for news on Stan's appeal, estranged from Linda, alienated from his teacher in the one class in which he had hoped to learn so much, and now nightly overindulging in wine to try and forget all of it—in the midst of all this bleakness, came a small miracle. In his mailbox one evening he found an envelope with the return address of a magazine. Ripping it open without even closing his mailbox, he quickly unfolded a letter from an editor: an offer to buy "Hit and Run" for two hundred dollars. Richie's eyes widened, his mouth dropped open.

I'm a writer, he thought.

In a daze, he closed the mailbox and went upstairs. Turning on the lamp, he sat in his overstuffed chair, schoolbooks on his lap, and reread the letter, over and over again. Across the top of the stationery was the name of the magazine in which *his* story, with *his* name on it, would actually appear. Something inside Richie's chest was glowing; he felt like running into the seedy little street and shouting the wonderful news to everyone within earshot; or running through *all* the streets, telling *all* of Chicago, that goddamned hard city that was going to break him.

Suddenly he realized that he had no one to tell. No one with whom to share this incredibly magic moment. Not Linda. And certainly not Mr. Crane or anyone in the writing class. The only person Richie knew who would be really happy for him, probably as excited as he himself, was Stan—and Richie could not visit him again for eight more days.

But there was a better way, he thought, to celebrate. And he did not need anyone else to do it with. Tomorrow morning before leaving for school, he would write a letter accepting the offer of two hundred dollars for "Hit and Run". But tonight, he would revel in his success and exalt his magnificent accomplishment by sitting down and doing it again.

His celebration would be to write another short story.

The following week, Mr. Crane gave his creative writing class its next major assignment.

"I want from each of you a short story of no less than twenty-five hundred words," he said. "I want it to incorporate everything you have learned in this class to date. Choose any subject, period, and locale you wish, but give me your very best work. The grade on this assignment will constitute one-third of your semester grade. And please be advised that this is a critique assignment; each story will be mimeographed and handed out to the class for group analysis, commentary, and criticism. So don't fictionalize any personal or family secrets unless you're prepared to discuss them with the rest of the class. That's it. I expect good things from you—most of you, that is." Looking at Richie, he added, "From our veteran, my minimum requirement is correct punctuation." There was the usual laughter from the class sycophants.

When the class was dismissed, Richie did not move from his seat in the first row. Making no effort to get his study materials together, he remained absolutely still, his eyes fixed unblinkingly on Crane. Linda looked back apprehensively as she left with the other students. At one point she paused, as if intending to say or do something, but finally she continued on out the door.

When the room was empty except for Richie and the teacher, Crane glanced up from his desk and asked, "Something I can do for you?"

"Do you know my name, Mr. Crane?" Richie asked.

"Why do you ask?"

"You never use it, either in addressing me or referring to me. Why is that?"

"A little idiosyncrasy of mine, perhaps." Crane smiled slightly. "Does it bother you?"

"Yes, it does."

"How unfortunate."

"Do you have something personal against veterans in general, or is it just me in particular?"

Crane drummed his fingertips soundlessly on the desktop. "Do you know how *I* got through college?" he asked rhetorically. "By washing dishes, mopping floors, emptying wastebaskets, shoveling snow, stoking the dorm furnace. It was during the Depression. From lack of sleep and lack of food, my weight, which was normally one-hundred sixty pounds, dropped to one-hundred twenty-five. I'm sure you don't know what it is to go hungry—"

"Of course not," Richie interjected.

"At any rate, it rather galls me, after all I went through, to see someone like you get a free ride. Oh, I can see educational benefits for *handicapped* veterans, and in moments of generosity I even extend my blessing to World War Two vets. But *Korea?* For god's sake," he belittled, "it wasn't even a *real* war."

"It seemed like one," Richie said evenly. "Anyway, it was the only war I had. I'm sorry it didn't meet your standards." Gathering his study materials, he rose to leave.

"No plea for understanding?" Crane asked, eyebrows raised. "No entreaty to address you by name in the future?"

Richie shook his head. "I knew a kid once who died because he wouldn't beg for mercy. I was remembering him just now. I don't think he'd want me to ask you for anything, Mr. Crane."

"A kid who died because he wouldn't beg for mercy. That's quite interesting," Crane commented, ignoring Richie's aspersion. "Perhaps you should write your short story about him."

"I'll write a story about him someday," Richie said. "But it won't be for any class you teach."

Crane's eyes narrowed, the first sign that anything Richie said had affected him. "You are becoming a very insolent and disrespectful student. Do us both a favor and don't sign up for any more classes that I teach."

Richie turned to leave, but Crane had one more thing to say.

"If I were you," he advised, "I'd change my major too. You're too shallow and crude a person to ever become a writer. I'd think about finding something else to do in life."

Richie walked out, aware that Crane was glaring coldly after him. Just outside the door, he found Linda waiting. "You just never learn, do you?" she said tensely. "That man is going to *fail* you."

"I don't give a goddamn if he does," Richie told her flatly. He kept walking and she fell in beside him.

"You think you're so tough! Sometimes you make me sick."

"I thought you said goodbye to me," he reminded, stopping and facing her.

"Just because we're not seeing each other, doesn't mean I wouldn't still like to see you make something of yourself."

"I *am* going to make something of myself," he declared. "I'm going to make a *writer* of myself. Remember that story I told you about? 'Hit and

Run'? Well, I sold it. Last week. I celebrated all by myself. Which is how I intend to do *everything* from here on out. I know how to say goodbye too."

He walked away from her.

Richie never told Stan Klein about selling his first story. Before their next visit, Richie read in the newspaper that Stan's appeal had been denied and that his death sentence was affirmed. Stan had immediately been taken back to the court that sentenced him and a new execution date was set. When Richie went to see him, Stan had thirty-one days left to live.

"Well, that high-priced lawyer tried like hell, I'll give him that," he said resignedly to Richie. "My on'y chance now is for the governor to commute me to life, which is like no chance at all. Never been a cop-killer commuted in the history of the state."

"Maybe you'll be the first," Richie said without much conviction.

"I don't think so," Stan said. He was quieter, moodier, more contemplative than Richie could ever recall seeing him. "No, I think this is it for me, kid." Sitting back in his chair, waist chain stark against the yellow coveralls, he lighted a cigarette and took a long, deep drag. "I been giving things a lot of thought since I heard the appeal was turned down," he said reflectively. "You know why I think I ended up in here? I think I ended up this way because I never really tried *not* to end up this way. I just lived from day to day without ever thinking about where I was going."

"That's easy to do," Richie told him. "It's probably the easiest thing in the world."

"You didn't do it," Stan said. It was almost an accusation.

"No, I didn't do it."

"Why? What made you different?" There was a plea in Stan's voice, as if the question were critical to him.

"I honestly don't know," Richie replied.

"Was it the books?" Stan asked keenly. "Was it all them books you read?"

"Maybe," Richie said. "I know they opened up a lot of new worlds for me. But I don't think the answer is that simple. I think the books were just part of it."

"Then what was the rest?" This was clearly something Stan had to know.

"Something in the blood maybe," Richie said, shrugging, "in the genes, the past; maybe I had an ancestor who passed something on to me that I'm not even aware of. Or maybe it wasn't even that far back; maybe I got something from my father, some of that quiet strength I remember in him; or my mother's sensitivity—before the junk ruined her; or even some of my grandmother's pragmatic good sense. Listen to me—I sound like a goddamn psychology major. But I honestly don't have the answer, Stan. Hell, maybe it's simply the difference in the people I came into contact with. The people *and* the books. I know that a lot of people—mostly women, now that I think about it—treated me extra well because they seemed to know or just sense that I had a . . . a *hunger* for something, and I was trying to feed that hunger through reading. Miss White, a teacher I had, and Miss Menefee, the welfare lady, and a librarian named Paula Hovey, and another teacher down south, Mrs. Reinhart, all gave me a little extra something—attention, encouragement, friendship, a gentle nudge in the right direction.'' Sitting back in his chair, Richie shook his head. ''Or it might just have been plain old blind luck, Stan. Y'know, a random thing. Who can say?''

''No, man, it was more than luck,'' Stan asserted. ''I like what you said about having a hunger for something. You did have that. You always seemed to be going forward, moving, reaching. I never done that. All's I was interested in doing was staying where I was at, not sinking down to a lower level. But I never tried to get no higher. You took *steps*; I stood still. An' pretty soon,'' he concluded resignedly, ''life caught up with me.'' Stan suddenly sat forward urgently. ''I want you to do me a favor, Richie.''

''Sure.''

''I want you to see if you can help Bobby out.''

Richie was taken aback. It was the first time in any of their visits that Stan had mentioned Bobby Casey by name, or in any way alluded to him. Even now, he was careful not to use his last name. ''I want you to see if you can make him take steps like you done; if you can steer him in another direction. Toward something better.''

''I don't know,'' Richie hedged. ''I've never been Bobby's favorite person, Stan.''

''Not when we was kids, I know. But we ain't kids no more. Maybe if you and him started thinking of each other as men, you might be able to talk to one another. He ain't a bad guy, really he ain't. He's worth helping, honest to god. You might save him,'' Stan indicated his chains, ''from this. Try, will you, Richie? Do me one last favor.''

There was no way Richie could say no. Not to this kid who helped him make a place to sleep in a pile of newspaper bundles. ''I'll try,'' he promised.

When it was time for the visit to end, and two escort guards unlocked Stan's cage to take him back to Death Row, he said quietly to Richie, ''I'd just as soon you didn't come see me no more this last month, kid. It's gonna be hard enough to walk in there and sit down in that fucking chair without having a fresh memory of you going back out into the sunshine. Understand?''

"Sure," Richie said, "I understand." He felt his throat constrict, and fought back the urge to cry. Jesus, he hoped Stan could not tell.

Stan winked. "Take care of yourself, kid."

"So long, Stan."

Walking out of the big county jail, Richie found it hard to believe that he had seen Stan for the last time.

57

_T_oday," Mr. Crane said to the class, with a note of satisfaction in his voice, "we will critique the short story of our veteran. As you know, if you've read the mimeographed copies I distributed at the end of our last meeting, he has written a sports story for us. Its title, which sounds somewhat like an automobile accident, is 'Hit and Run,' and it is about the sport, if one can call it that, of boxing. I daresay that this will probably be the only work of this particular genre that we will have to critique, so for that reason alone we must admit that it smacks of originality. Unfortunately, as I'm sure you've already found out for yourselves, it has no other redeeming qualities . . ."

Richie had in his pocket at that moment the uncashed check from the magazine for two hundred dollars; the endorsement side of the check stated that it was full payment for a short story entitled "Hit and Run." Richie had been carrying the check for days, waiting for the class in which his story, the same story word-for-word that had already been sold for publication, would be critiqued. He was not sure exactly what he planned to do with the check; humiliate Crane in some way, he knew that. But now, when the moment was at hand, he was not even thinking about it. His session in which to be critiqued had come on the wrong day.

Stan Klein was due to go to the electric chair at ten o'clock that morning.

Glancing up at the wall clock, Richie saw that it was nine-thirty. Maybe, he thought, the governor would still come through. Ned Fields, the lawyer, was at the state capitol in Springfield to make a personal plea. Maybe Stan would get a commutation.

That was what Richie hoped. But he did not really believe it.

Forcing his mind to focus on the class, Richie learned without surprise that Crane's evaluation of "Hit and Run" was merciless, almost brutal. He had absolutely nothing good to say about the story. His comments, stretched over a fifteen-minute period, attacked every element of the piece.

"The characterization, if we can call it that," he intoned, "is hollow. I, for one, did not care in the least whether this young prizefighter named Ralphie won or lost. I'll admit to being mildly surprised that he did lose, because I expected the typical twist ending—for him to score a knockout in the final round, or something equally as trite. But when that did not happen, when this young thug actually did lose—well, I merely shrugged and thought, so what?

"The story's narrative I found to be totally flat, totally dull. The dialogue, well, can we really call this gym slang type of communication dialogue? I got the impression, in the conversations between Ralphie and Max, his trainer, of two Neanderthals grunting at each other. And the boy fantasizing that Max is his father, because his real father has abandoned him, is simply soap opera nonsense.

"The sentence structure of the story is atrocious, of course; there is nothing lyrical or rhythmic to carry the reader forward, only an endless line of stale words laid one after the other through which the reader has to wade. And, of course, without proper sentence structure, where does that leave our poor paragraph construction? In dire straits, I'm afraid. Story pace? There is none; the story drags like a small boat with a large anchor. The evocation of feeling? As I said earlier, the sum total of the emotion generated in me was, so what? Who cares? Forget it."

As Crane strolled back and forth across the front of the classroom, Richie glanced at the clock again. Nine-fifty.

"Why," Crane asked rhetorically, "does this boxing story have no style? Is there one shortcoming we can pinpoint, one defective element that we can say, 'Improve this and the story will work'? Unfortunately, no. This piece of writing is like a malignancy; it is shot through with such inferiority that no amount of doctoring could save it."

Crane halted in front of Richie, never more narcissistic than he was at that moment; tweed jacket pulled back, one thumb hooked in the pocket of his cardinal red vest, a protector of literature about to pour lime over one who would infect it with plague.

"I find it most distasteful to have to fail a student," Crane said solemnly, "but there are circumstances that dictate that an academician hold true to his profession for the good of others who will follow him. I have no choice but to give our veteran an F. I can only hope, as I've already counseled him in private, that my grade might persuade him to direct his energies elsewhere than a writing career."

Richie accepted the F-graded story that Crane handed him, and looked past the teacher at the clock. It was two minutes after ten. Stan was dying; Richie could feel it. The hard city, he thought. The hard city had broken another one.

But not me, he reminded himself. It will never—*ever*—break me. I am fucking alive! And in my pocket is a check for two hundred goddamn dollars that says *I am a writer.*

Looking back at the supercilious teacher, Richie's mind urged: Do it! Flaunt that check in the son of a bitch's smug face! Make him eat every goddamn word he just said about your story! Castrate the motherfucker—if he's got anything down there to castrate! Do it!

Instead, Richie merely shook his head, briefly, causing Crane to frown. What for? he asked himself. He gathered up his notebook and papers, and rose to leave.

"Well, I must say," Crane remarked in astonished delight, "I didn't expect you to take my advice quite so quickly."

Richie suddenly remembered some words he had heard many years before, from the stage of the Senate Theater on the West Side. *There's nothing you can't do if you try hard enough. Don't ever let anybody tell you different.*

"I'm not taking your advice, Mr. Crane," Richie said as he crossed the room. "I'm taking some advice that Buck Jones once gave me."

"Buck Jones?" said Crane. "Who's that?"

At the door, Richie looked back with a slight smile. "Somehow, Mr. Crane, I didn't think you'd know."

Glancing at Linda, he saw that she was looking at him incredulously. He pushed on out the door and walked down the hall. On his way to the exit, he dropped his books and study material into a trash can.

When Richie got home, there was another letter in his mailbox from the magazine. The editor wanted to buy the second story Richie had submitted. Called "The Last One To Cry," it was about a boy in reform school who was killed by fire hose punishment. A great sense of accomplishment swept through Richie as he read and reread the letter. And he thought: *McKey, you son of a bitch, I've told the truth about you! And it's going to be published!* This one, he told himself, was for Freddie Walsh.

He *would* be a writer now, he thought, no matter what. And he harbored no illusions that it was going to be easy; he had written, rewritten, and rewritten again the two stories he had sold. There was much for him to learn, a lifetime of it, and his love of the written word told him that he would probably still be learning when that lifetime was over, but he could, and would, learn how to write. It did not matter to him if he ever achieved fame and fortune from it; just to be able to *do* it was reward enough. All he wanted as a writer was for each thing he wrote to be a little better than the last thing.

Folding the letter and putting it in his pocket, Richie thought of Stan Klein and made up his mind about something else also. Without even going to his apartment, he went back outside and started down the street. Before he had gone a block, Linda pulled up at the curb in her old Studebaker. Leaning across the front seat, she rolled the passenger window down to speak to him. Ignoring her, Richie kept walking.

"Goddamn it, Richie," he heard her say. Without turning off the engine, she opened the driver's door and stood up out of the car. "Richie! Don't walk past me like that!"

Richie turned back and stood on the other side of the car from her. "What do you want, Linda?" There was no animosity, no hostility in the question. His voice was detached, impersonal.

"Where are you going?" she asked.

"Out to the West Side." These words had a hint of resolve in them.

"I'll drive you," she said. "Get in."

Richie did not move. He was suddenly in a quandary. He still wanted to be with Linda; that feeling had never died. But every instinct he had warned against it. Especially now, at this moment. If he got into the car with her, he knew it would be like lighting a fuse.

"It's on my way home," Linda insisted. "There's no sense in you taking a streetcar. Come on."

He got into the car with her and they drove off.

"Drop me at Madison and Hamlin," Richie said.

For several minutes they said nothing. Richie stared solemnly out the window as if he were riding a bus. Linda glanced at him several times, then finally broke the silence.

"Your story that Crane critiqued was already sold. You could have totally humiliated him, gotten even for every nasty thing he ever said. Why didn't you?"

"You can't get even with a person like Crane that way," Richie replied. "Humiliation doesn't change people like him." He sighed quietly. "It seems like all my life there's been somebody I wanted to get even with, somebody I wanted to hurt." In his mind flashed images of George Zangara, Mr. McKey, the Hubbards, Rollie Chalk, Billy Pastor. "There's always been a Crane in one form or another; there probably always will be." He looked steadily at

Linda. "But I think I've finally learned that you don't get even with people by hitting them or humiliating them; you get even by *overcoming* what they're trying to do to you. That's the worst punishment you can give them: don't let their influence have any effect on you. There was a man in reform school, a house father, that I swore I'd go back and kill someday, because of something he did to a friend of mine. I was a kid when I made that promise to myself; I didn't know what the hell it meant to kill someone. Now I do. I could go back and kill McKey without batting an eyelid—only now I don't have to. I wrote a story about him and about what he did; I've sold that story too, and it's going to be published. I got even through my work, my writing. It's the same with Crane; I got even with him by selling the story he said was worthless. I succeeded and he failed—because I didn't let him influence me or change me. Crane's a perfect example of someone who isn't worth getting even with any other way." Richie looked back out the car window. "He doesn't matter anymore, anyway. I'm through with school."

"Oh, Richie, no—" Linda bit her lower lip. "Books and reading have always meant so much to you."

"I didn't say I was through with books and reading; I said I was through with school." He turned slightly in the seat to face her again. "Look, let's be honest. I didn't fit in that class any more than I fit in the little Southern high school I told you about. I've seen too much, *done* too much, to try to learn anything with a bunch of eighteen year olds who've never gone hungry, never stolen, never fucked, never *killed*. Everything I've learned, including how to survive, I learned out in the world, not sitting in a classroom. Crane's creative writing class was completely worthless to me—and the other classes I've been taking were just requirements—I *had* to take them to take the writing class. I want to write; I am determined to be a writer. But what happened today convinced me that I can do it better without going to school."

"I think you're making a mistake," Linda said stoically.

"That doesn't surprise me," he quickly retorted. The fuse had been lit. "According to you, everything I do is a mistake—unless it includes you or you approve of it. Especially if it has anything to do with my friends. Well, I'm through turning my back on people just because they don't measure up to your standards."

"I have never tried to do anything but help you, Richie, and you know it!" she snapped.

"Yeah, you've tried to help me, all right," he accused. "You've tried to *change* me, that's what you've done. You've tried to make me over into one of those nice young men types that you and your mother think are so wonderful. You have never—*never*—been able to accept the fact that I don't fit that part. I am *not*, never *have* been, never *will* be, a fucking nice young man,

Linda. I am a fucking street kid still trying to grow up. That's probably all I'll *ever* be. Even if I make it as a writer, which I intend to do, I'll still be a fucking street kid inside!''

"You don't have to be," she pleaded. "If you'd break away from those hoodlum friends of yours—"

"Those hoodlum friends of mine," he interrupted, "are people that I grew up with, went hungry with, depended on, and *survived* with. The guys I ran with on the streets of this city are part of me, just like the people down in Lamont are, just like the people I knew in Charleytown, in the Marine Corps, even the people in that class of Crane's . . . and even Crane himself. *Everybody* who touches your life becomes part of it, Linda. You don't have to like the person, you don't have to know them long, they don't even have to be *good* for you, but one thing they've got in common—they're indelible. They leave their mark, whether it's a scratch or a gash. The guys I grew up with on the streets are as much a part of what I am right now as anyone else who's ever touched my life—including you. If I reject them, disclaim them, I'd be rejecting and disclaiming part of myself. I can't do that, Linda. This may come as a big surprise to you, but I *like* myself. I like what I am and I like what I'm going to be. I won't throw any of myself away."

"I see," she said stiffly. "You're quitting school, you're on your way out to the West Side where your friends hang out, and you don't think that's throwing part of yourself away? What do you call it?"

"I call it being myself. I'm on my way to see a guy named Bobby Casey. He's a guy I don't even like, and he doesn't like me. But I'm going to offer to be his friend and I'm going to try to help him turn his life around. One of the reasons I'm doing it is because I promised Stan Klein I would. But the main reason, Linda, is because I've finally realized that I *should* do it."

"Would he help you if you needed help?" Linda challenged.

Richie thought of Bobby with a gun in his hand, standing in the middle of Lake Street, ready to oppose anyone who interfered with Richie when he was trying to help poor, pathetic Vernie.

"Yes, he would," he answered Linda.

"And you think this Bobby Casey is as much a part of your life as I am? As important to you as I am?" There was a tremor in her voice.

"I didn't say he was as important as you are. There's a difference."

"If I said you had to choose between helping him and having me, what would you do?" They stopped for a red light and Linda turned to face him.

"I'd still try to help him, Linda," Richie said quietly. "Because it's something I have to do. And because it wouldn't be right for you to make me choose."

When the light changed, Linda drove through the intersection and pulled to the curb. "Maybe you'd better take a streetcar after all," she said. The tremor was not in her voice anymore.

"Sure," Richie said. He got out of the car and leaned down to look in the window. "Go back to your church group, Linda. Find another nice young man . . . like Glenn."

Lips compressed in anger, she drove away, leaving him standing there.

On the streetcar, watching West Madison's familiar blocks go by, Richie wondered for what seemed like the millionth time whether he would ever have anyone permanent in his life, or whether he was destined to be a loner into whose existence people came and went. Slowly shaking his head, he reviewed his losses. A demented farmer—or maybe Prohibition—took his father. Heroin took his mother. Old age took his grandmother. The class system took Jennie. The ghetto took Vernie. The electric chair took Stan.

Now he had lost Linda because he would not compromise. It was a good thing, he thought, that he was going to be a writer. He had read a description of writers as lonely people in quiet rooms. If ever anyone was born to be alone, it seemed like it must be him.

As the streetcar churned through the lower West Side, Richie's eyes took in life along the sidewalk. Winos, hookers, hustlers, panhandlers, junkies— the silt at the bottom of the vat. The hard city's leftovers. He had been part of that bleakness for so long that the sight of it should have been too familiar to disturb him. Instead, it turned his spine cold and his mouth dry. The wino could be him twenty years in the future, just like the ragged kid delivering papers *was* him ten years in the past. The kids he had to get away from; the wino he had to keep away from. You could never let the hard city catch you off guard.

It won't, Richie grimly promised himself. I've made it this far, I'll keep on making it. Alone or not, it made no difference. All that mattered was making it.

At Hamlin Avenue, Richie alighted from the streetcar and started up the block. Before he got to the poolhall, he saw Linda's car again, parked. She was standing in a doorway across the sidewalk, waiting for him. Richie saw that she was crying. He wanted to turn back, cross the street, go around her— but he could not. It was not in him to leave her standing alone, crying over something he was a part of.

Stepping into the doorway, he took her into his arms. She sobbed against his chest.

"Richie, I'm sorry, I'm so sorry . . . I don't know what's right or wrong anymore . . . I just know that I want us to be together . . ." She turned her tear-streaked face up to him. "I guess I either love you or I don't. And if I do, then I can't go on criticizing the things, the people, the life that went into the person you are . . ." She used the heel of one hand to wipe away her tears. "I just know that I love you and I want to be with you. Can't we try? Please . . ."

Richie stared at her. He wanted to say yes. More than anything in the world at that moment, he wanted to say yes. Yes, let's try.

But he could not.

"It won't work for us, Linda. I wish it would—but it won't."

"I'll change, Richie. I'll try to understand you better—"

"No," he shook his head. "If *either* of us has to change for the other, then it's no good—and it'll never be any good." Some strands of hair were stuck on her cheek by the tears; Richie brushed them back with his thumb. "I can't let you do for me what I won't do for you. Letting you change would be as wrong as making myself change. We've got to be true to ourselves, Linda—both of us."

"But if we lose each other, Richie," she pleaded, "what will be left for us?"

"We'll have what we are," he said. "What we are inside. If we compromise that, either of us, we'll always regret it. We've got to stay who we are and what we are; we can't lose ourselves."

Suddenly she knew he would not relent, not on this: it was too important to him. "Can we . . . be friends?" she asked, groping for something.

"Sure we can."

Linda smiled a tentative smile. "Maybe if we stay friends, someday we might, well . . ."

"Someday we might," Richie said, knowing exactly what she meant.

But he knew they never would.

"Sometimes people just need time," she said solemnly.

"Come on . . ." He led her across the sidewalk and held the car door for her.

"Maybe we'll run into each other," she hoped.

Richie smiled. "Sure. In some library."

That made her laugh. He laughed too. They kept their faces happy as she drove away.

Presently Richie started down Madison Street toward the pool hall. He suddenly felt very good. He was still himself, the way he was meant to be.

He hurried on his way, to keep his promise to the kid who taught him how to kill rats.

AUTHOR'S NOTE

Hard City is based in large part on my life, but it is a work of fiction. Names and descriptions of most persons and places have been changed, and the characters are either fictional or composites of several people. My parents, James Richmond "Tennessee Slim" Howard and Chloe Clark Howard are real people, and the city of Chicago, at least as I knew it, is also obviously real. All the rest is not meant to be an historically accurate portrayal of any person or place and should be read as fiction.